West into Ruin

Book One of

Out of Ruin

The Seventh Series

of the Chronicles of Nightstar

By Eric John Loc[illegible]ood

ISBN: 9781709204012

For Cindy, without whom none of this would be possible

ACKNOWLEDGMENTS

There are many people I would thank, for making this possible. First, my mother, Janet, who instilled in me at the earliest age the love of language and the Queen's English. My friends of very old: Dave, Chris, Todd and Scott (Chewy), who were integral in my finding a creative voice, through our endless weekend journeys into worlds of imagination. Chief among those friends is Jay, to whom I owe special thanks. His voice is found in this book and in books yet written.

I would also thank my latter-day fellows who helped me create this new world, providing much of the inspiration of the characters herein: Gary, Nick, EK, Jordan and Rob. A muse is a difficult thing to find, and they were all invaluable in this.

Finally, I would thank my team of editors, who were indispensable in the creation of this novel: Don Bisdorf, Lexi Mahoney, Jay, Jenny, and, of course, my lovely wife, Cindy. Without their input, critical assessments, and keen eyes, this final product would have been far less.

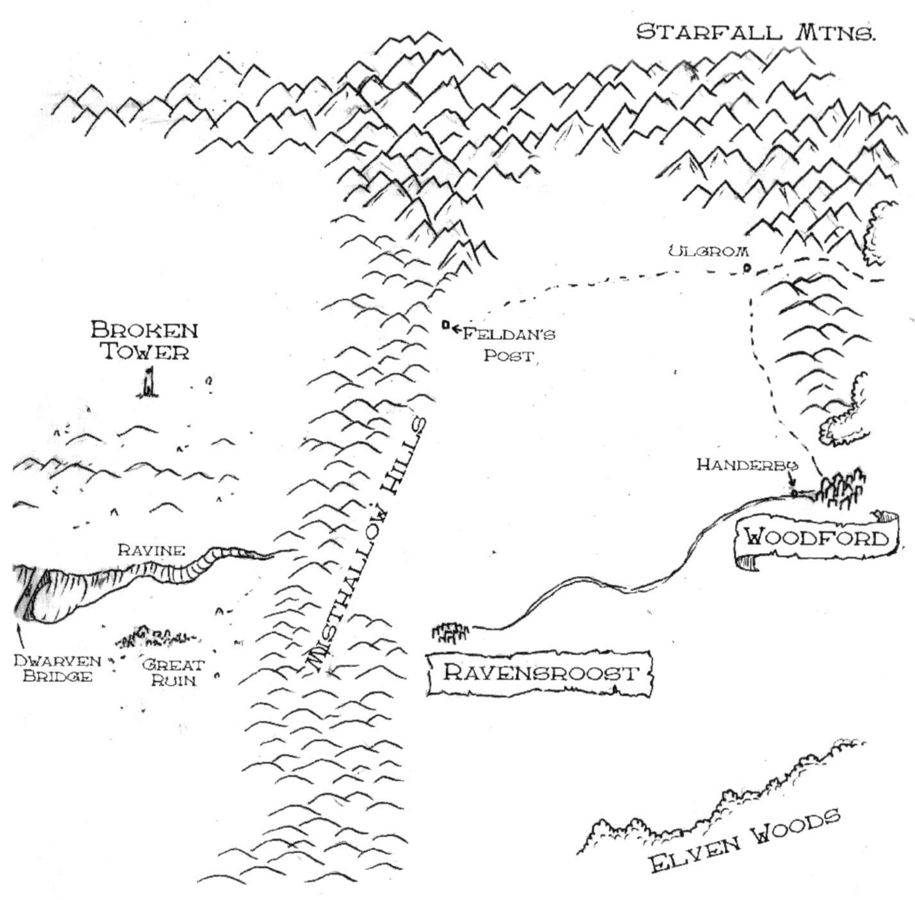

WESTERN REACHES
OF THE
KINGDOM OF EASTVALE

THE FIRE

A Prologue to the Series *Out of Ruin*

A Very Long Time Ago

Ella woke to the sound of the crackling fire. It was still dark. And so very cold. The pile of furs and blankets her Grandpa had buried her in kept her comfortable. Her face was the only cold part.

Mostly her nose, she thought, as she blinked sleepily.

Her grandfather was a large man, reminding her of a big bear as he put more wood on the fire. He must have just started it, since the smaller pieces of wood were burning brightly but the big logs hadn't caught fire yet.

He had shown her how to build a fire and even how to make the sparks from the stones. She didn't know if she could do it herself. He hummed something as he built the small, pointy mountain of wood, around three larger pieces. He called it a tripod, she remembered.

It was snowing a little, but she could see the stars already. They were so bright this time of night. It wasn't deep night, it was closer to dawn, she knew. He had his cooking pans out, near his sleeping furs.

His boots crunched loudly on the snowpack as he moved around the fire, making sure it lit evenly. She snaked one hand out from under the warmth of her blankets, to wipe her nose. He must have seen her move.

"Ella! Did I wake you? I'm so sorry," he said in his deep, rumbling voice. "You were sleeping so nicely."

"It's all right, Grandpa. It will be dawn soon, won't it?" she piped cheerily.

Her Grandpa looked about, peering through the nearby barren branches. "Well, I think you're right, Ella bell," he said, scratching his beard. "Who taught you so well in the ways of reading the stars and the skies?"

She giggled. "You did!"

"Oh, yes, I suppose I did. But I've never taught such a smart little girl before," he said, raising one bushy eyebrow. "You just stay warm there, while I try to coax the flames from this wood, my dear."

Ella frowned at that. "What do you mean *coax*? Does that mean the fire is hidden in the wood and you make it come out?"

The old man stopped his stacking of wood for a moment, and stared at her, his mouth slightly agape. "Ella, sometimes you really do astonish me."

"What do you mean, Grandpa?"

Shaking his head, making some final adjustments to the stack of firewood, he let out a low chuckle. "Yes, Ella, the fire is hidden in the wood, as it hides in many things. It just takes a little, well, nudging I guess you could say, with something else that is hot."

"Like the sparks, or other fire, right?"

"Yes, exactly. See how the small sticks are burning bright? Their flame is hot, and it's heating the bigger, colder pieces of wood. After a time, the logs will catch fire from the smaller sticks, just like the dry leaves I lit with the sparks caught the small sticks afire."

"So, you can make a big fire, from a tiny one, right?"

"Yes, my little Ella, you can. From the smallest spark you can light big fires, bigger than this," the old man said.

She watched him a bit longer, studying how he prodded and nudged the sticks, growing the flames a little as he went.

"Is fire magic?"

He didn't seem to hear her question at first. There was no wind, and her Grandpa had assured her there were no animals around, like wolves or bears. The sound of the crackling fire was the only thing that broke the silence of the deep, dark starlit winter sky. She was about to ask him again, when he finally spoke. It almost made her jump. It was so quiet here. Their camp was off a quiet road, far from the big towns and cities. But she knew they were on their way to a big city. The biggest and grandest city in all the world.

"Some wise folk say fire is a kind of magic, a deep magic that anyone can summon," he said. "Just strike flint and stone, and the sparks will make the fire, yes?"

Ella nodded, but she wasn't sure she really understood what he meant.

"Grandpa, what is magic?"

He laughed a little. "That's a big question for such a little girl."

She furrowed her brow. "I'm five, Grandpa! I'm not a baby."

"I'm not saying you are a baby, Ella, my dear. I'm saying, it's a *very* big question," he replied, lowering his voice. He saw the intended response in her eyes.

"Is it a bad question?"

"No, not at all. And I'll try to answer it for you," he said, stepping away from the fire. He sat on his pile of furs and looked across at her tiny face, nestled within the vast heap of bear and wolf skins. He smiled at her, and she felt the warmth of his love in that expression. She grinned back at him.

"Magic," he said, "is nothing."

She scowled at him, thinking he was having fun with her.

"And everything," he added, his hand describing an arc over the fire. She looked at him with a quizzical expression. "There was a time when there was no magic, so they say."

"Really? Was it a long time ago?"

He chuckled. "Yes. Longer than any dragon could ever remember, I think."

"But then it came to the world?"

"Yes, and now all manner of folk, and creatures, live and die by it," he said.

"But...what *is* it?"

Grandpa looked at Ella, almost as if he was studying her. He sighed loudly.

"Magic is the power to change something," he said.

Ella was entirely unhappy with his simple answer. She had expected something more amazing, especially from her Grandpa. He had no end of amazing stories.

"Change something? What does that mean?"

"Well, like changing a broken plate into a whole plate. Or, moving a stone from the ground into the air. Or making the lightning in the clouds come down to the ground where you want it," he said, gesturing a little with a stick. *That* sounded more interesting to her.

Ella thought about his answer, as she watched him poke the fire. The larger logs were beginning to burn now.

"Can you do anything with magic?" she asked him.

He seemed to think about his answer before speaking, his thick gray brows furrowing. "Almost anything. Yes."

She looked at the growing flames, fascinated by the colors, the brightness of them in the darkness of the night.

"Grandpa, if fire is a sort of magic, can you make fire using magic?" she asked. Sometimes thoughts like this just popped into her head, almost like whispers in her ear.

He looked at her from across the fire, his eyes almost angry looking. For a moment, Ella thought she had done something wrong. Then he blinked, and she knew he was not angry.

"Oh, yes, you can make fire using magic. But one must be careful," he said, his concerned eyes reflecting the orange glint of the flames. "Fire can burn down a whole house. Or even an entire forest. Or…"

"The whole world?" Ella said, interrupting.

Grandpa poked the fire a little more, causing sparks to fly upwards into the darkness. The bright orange motes danced in the night air, fading to red before winking out.

"Yes. I suppose it could," he said. She thought his voice sounded a little sad.

"I would never do that, Grandpa, if I could use magic," Ella declared.

He smiled at her, his eyes sad. "I know, Ella. Because you're a good girl."

"But why are you sad?"

"Not everyone is good, like you. There was a time when the world was very nearly destroyed by the fires of magic," he said.

"Really?" Ella said, sitting up a little. She could sense it. He was going to tell her a *story*!

"Yes. It was a dark, terrible time. The world was broken."

Ella wasn't sure she wanted to hear this story now. But she was *so* curious.

"Couldn't anyone fix it?"

"Well," Grandpa said, his voice suddenly heavy with sorrow. "There were those who tried. They came together to fix the world. Though, at the time, they did not know it."

Ella felt the sadness in her Grandpa's heart. "You don't have to tell me the story if you don't want to, Grandpa."

He smiled at her, and in his smile, she knew it was all right. "I will tell you the story, my little Ella."

"About how the fires of magic almost destroyed the world?" she said, barely able to contain her excitement.

"Well, I'll start at the end of that story," he said.

"The *end?* That's silly!" she said.

"Oh, but no, Ella. For the end of one story is always the beginning of another," he said, sitting up a little now. "Remember that. *Always*."

She nodded, her eyes widening. "Yes, Grandpa."

"All right. Now, let's see," he said. He poked the fire with a stick. More embers rose into the sky, swirling brightly, dancing, forming shapes. Each glowing mote was a voice, a thought, a place in the story…

Grandpa spoke, and Ella listened.

PROLOGUE

She watched the sky rage. Energies terrible and magnificent played across the seething cloudscape, as titanic battles waged above and below. She knew the outcome of the battles, at last, and she had surrendered herself to that final fate.

Drawing her cloak about her shoulders, she felt the magic within the fabric falter, some of the cold of the wind cutting through. Its once-lustrous white was faded and worn. She did not care. The wind blew strands of her brown hair about her face, the tips nearly silver now.

"Is there nothing to be done to prevent so much death?" she murmured.

The figure beside her surveyed the ruined city that lay many miles away and well below them. They stood together at the highest point of a towering ridge that overlooked a broad, wooded valley. There was once a broad plaza here of polished blue stone, but it had been blasted away in a battle days ago. Their view was unobstructed in every direction.

Though the sun was high overhead, it was choked off by the endless clouds of the raging storms. On a cloudless day, sunlight would reveal the valley's once glorious colors – gold and burgundy great-trees, the glittering architecture that once adorned the gentle hills and shores of the lake, and greens of the foliage, bright and deep.

There were no green now. All was ash and dust, rage and fire. Except for the vast, yawning pit beyond the edge of the city. An immense lake of serene water had filled that space not long ago. Now it roiled and hissed with energies beyond comprehension. Even from here, it was almost painful to stare directly at the flashing, coruscating lights within the yawning abyss.

"I am sorry, Ori," the man said. She almost smiled at hearing him call her by that name. She had many titles and a few names, but this one was reserved for him alone. He continued. "What death occurred is the folly of the races of man. There will be little more of it, I think. At least, I will do what I can to prevent suffering."

"And you still care for us, Ved? Simple mortals, living so briefly?" Her words were tinged with anger, and perhaps, resentment.

"I am not immortal, despite what you may think. I will do what I deem is necessary to end the conflicts, the pain. I will not supplant the will of anyone, however, not a single person."

"No, you simply seek to end their life as they know it, to take all they have learned, all they have accomplished!" Ori said, her voice breaking.

Ved sighed, his shoulders slumping. "And all their pain, all their mistakes. You learned that which you should not have learned. It cannot stand. This is the...best solution."

"And for me? Death? Oblivion? Am I not the guiltiest of them all?" she asked, a tear now running down her unlined face.

He shook his head slowly. "You are as anyone else, I will make sure you are safe," he said. A fleeting smile played across his lips. "Perhaps you will find a husband and bear children. You wanted that, once."

She laughed, a wretched utterance at best. He would know *that*, of course.

Across the valley, far above the ruined city, the chaotic clouds shifted. They parted slowly as a mass of stone miles long plunged groundward. It filled the sky before them, it was so large. Ori had seen so much in her relatively short life, wonders that would defy the imaginings of saints and archmages alike.

Yet this sight still amazed her, and for a moment even distracted her from the catastrophe unfolding around them. The 'hold was fully fifteen miles long, if not more, and five wide, a nearly perfect rectangle when viewed from above. Other 'holds were smaller, or different in form. This was one of the first 'holds, and one of the last still intact.

The further-most features were obscured by the wind and storms and all the dust and debris it carried. But she could see the depth of the monolithic edifice, at least a thousand yards top to bottom.

Turning slowly as it fell, it appeared to right itself as the moments passed. They both watched, transfixed by the descent. Towers and domes atop the gargantuan length of stone were burning, along with tall forests. Flying figures could be seen over the descending mass, some in pitched battle.

They remained silent as it descended more slowly. It seemed to drift in the wind as it settled over the seething pit of chaos and light. Slowing almost to the point of hovering, it moved as though some guiding force positioned it with precision over the raging chasm. Plumes of vapor and bolts of energy erupted from the edges as the bulk of stone settled closer and closer to ground.

When it at last made landfall, it seemed an almost gentle event, but the result left no doubt of the force of impact.

Billowing clouds of dust burst forth and swelled, enveloping what remained of the city. Tall towers and domes disappeared under the expanding ring of gray. Several seconds later, they could both hear the dull roar of the impact, joining with the cacophony of the storms and battles on all sides of them. The ground shook beneath her feet, and her knees threatened to give way.

He grasped her by one elbow. The dark blue robes he wore seemed almost untouched by the winds.

The vast cloud of dust rushed outward from the stone mass and soon obscured the entire city. The energies lancing through the clouds increased in their tempo and ferocity. The wall of choking dust rushed across the wooded valley, toward them.

Ori turned to look behind them. A wall of blue and green energy, like living lightning, filled the horizon, racing toward them, sweeping across the lands. Her heart quickened. She could not tear her gaze from the impending doom.

"It is done, then?" she said, tears flowing freely now.

"It is. You have nothing to fear, Ori. You will feel nothing. I cannot save everyone, but I have saved many. You among them," he said with a voice heavy with sorrow. Ved raised one hand and touched her cheek, wiping a tear. "You will awaken free from this madness, far away…"

"So much lost! So much." She wept. Turning to him, she asked, almost pleading, "Will it ever be remembered? Will anyone ever know, or discover even some of what is lost today?"

The raging wall of energy crackled all around them. The chaos above seemed to rush downward, a roiling mass of malevolent blackness. The spreading wall of dust began to sting her eyes as she lost sight of Ved. She felt his hands lock onto her arms. Despite this, she struggled to keep her footing.

She could not see him when he spoke. She could only hear the words, the last words of a life soon to be forgotten, as her body was buffeted on all sides by light, wind, force, and noise.

"I do not know for certain, but…I hope they will not."

She felt a moment of panic, then...nothing.

CHAPTER ONE - CANDISSA

24 Pluvius, Year 192, Eastvale Calendar

Candissa stared at the man through the torrents of rain and wind. She had just run from the west gate of Ravensroost. The storm had worsened on her run out to the square of gray stone they called the Wardenstone.

He stood upon the stone surface unsteadily, staring blankly, as rain and wind buffeted him. She noticed his clothes were burned at spots. She could even smell the smoke, but that made no sense to her. They were strange clothes, black leather and dark canvas, with a lot of pockets. He had a cut on his head. Blood ran down one side of his face.

Lightning cracked overhead. He blinked and started, but Candissa was unafraid. Storms never frightened her.

"Deesa!" came a faint voice.

She turned to see two figures running across the field. They had come from the wide, open gates behind them, east and just a little south of the Wardenstone. She could tell it was the ranger Delvin and Master Penston. They had seen her dash out of the gate, just as the Watch was trying to close it.

Candissa's mother would be very cross with her. She was only twelve years of age, and it was entirely improper to be running out into a storm. But Candissa knew she had to get out here. She had felt it, all the way from home. It was one of those strange sensations she had been feeling of late. Someone needed help, she knew it. She *had* to come.

And here he was, standing in the rain, on the very corner of the enormous span of gray stone. The man was handsome, having a short beard and dark hair tinged with gold. Despite the low storm clouds and slashing rain, it was still bright out. His eyes were an unusually dark blue, she thought.

"Sir?" Candissa called to him. Her white dress was plastered against her now, as the wind drove against them both. Her hair, blonder than his, was matted and dirty-looking in the rain. "You are hurt? Do you need help getting down?"

She leaned closer, putting both hands on the gray block. It was a little more than four feet in height, so she stood well over a foot above the edge. Candissa was tall for her age.

"Deesa! Careful!"

That was Master Penston shouting to her. The scholar's voice was usually calm, soothing. She always thought his voice was older than his face. He had warned her in the past to never touch the Wardenstone. No one knew what it was for or why it was there. If she asked anyone about it, they would just say "Best to leave it alone!" and nothing else.

This was not the first time she had dashed out to the broad, square platform of stone. She had been gathering flowers with her sisters and others, during a spring ritual last year. Her mother had been there too, but everyone was picking flowers from the long banks between here and the gate. Candissa decided to see what the Wardenstone was all about. It stretched more than one hundred paces on each side. The surface was perfectly flat and all four sides had decorative inscriptions. She had touched the long, low walls of the Wardenstone, finding the texture of the gently carved stone interesting. It was then that her mother's shriek cut short her little adventure.

After that, she had promised to never visit the stone again. She didn't keep the promise, and visited it twice more, out of sheer curiosity, before today. Today was different.

Glancing over her shoulder, wiping rain from her eyes, she saw Master Penston's cloak looked sodden and silly. He was the one who should not be out in the rain. Delvin was closer than Penston, and like the other Rangers of Ravensroost, he was quick on his feet.

Something caught her eye to the south. It was another ranger, like Delvin, wearing the traditional brown leather tunic and high boots. He was also trotting toward her and was much closer than Penston or Delvin. She thought it was Vink, but she couldn't be sure through the storm.

She turned back to the stranger, looking up at him. He said something to her, but she couldn't hear him clearly. He was staring at her now. She now saw that his eyes were almost purple in color, but somehow dark and hidden.

"What did you say, sir?" she called, hoping he would repeat himself. The stranger mumbled something once more. She shook her head. She saw he bore a sheathed weapon, a knife of some sort. It looked quite large for a dagger. His right hand touched the handle of black leather.

Candissa gasped. It was like when a hammer struck an anvil, but the sparks were flying inside her head. She had told almost no one about these moments; her mother merely dismissed them whenever Candissa had mentioned them.

In that instant, she knew something was wrong, terribly wrong. Someone was in pain, but it wasn't the man standing before her. She was confused. Staring up at the stranger, a bolt of lightning tore across the sky above him, intensely bright. It should have left a searing mark in her vision, as when she stared at the sun. But it didn't. Something happened in her eyes; she could feel it.

Purple light skittered across the vast gray surface of the Wardenstone and danced up along the stranger, tiny dots and streaks. It played across the black leather handle of his dagger.

Thunder shook the ground, rolling over the block, filling her ears with its roaring.

Move!

She jumped to her right, acting purely on instinct. She lost her footing, falling on the muddy ground. A sword cut through the air where her head had been an instant before.

Vink's shortsword struck the gray stone, sparks showering. Looking up at Vink, Candissa saw his eyes were as black as pitch, staring down at her. In that instant, he did not seem human to her. He raised his shortsword, preparing to strike at her once more.

She scrambled backwards, kicking with her feet against the wet ground. One foot found the solid surface of the gray stone block. She pushed hard and skittered backwards.

Vink lunged forward, his shortsword high over his head.

Candissa knew she could not move quickly enough to avoid his next strike. She screamed.

Vink's eyes, black and empty, went wide. His mouth opened, as if trying to speak. The sword fell to the ground behind him.

The stout ranger collapsed in a heap, falling across her legs, pinning her to the wet ground. She tried to pull her legs free from the muddy grass, but he was too heavy. In desperation, she pushed against his balding pate, trying to escape.

Then she saw the black leather handle of the stranger's blade protruding from Vink's back.

She looked up. The stranger's eyes were fixed on hers, his right arm lowering now. His stare was still vacant, but his expression was one of confusion.

"I…am…" Vink spoke, his voice barely a whisper. Candissa looked at the dying ranger. His head was resting on one of her legs, still trapping her.

His eyes looked up at her. They were no longer black and empty. Instead, for a moment, they were full of fear, and something else. Sadness. Then they were vacant. His body slumped. She knew he was dead.

Suddenly, Delvin was lifting her, pulling her free of the slain ranger. He turned her around, so she would not see the body. Master Penston grasped her by the shoulders. Her feet were unsteady.

"Are you all right, Deesa? Did he hurt you at all?" Penston said, his voice loud over the howling wind. He wiped some of the rain from her face. His looked concerned, his brows knitted together. He led her slowly away from the Wardenstone.

She tried to speak but her voice began to quake and hitch. Her legs were too weak, and she slumped to the ground. Master Penston stayed with her, trying to shield her from the rain with his dark cloak. "It's all right, Deesa. You'll be fine."

Candissa found comfort in his words. He was always kind and trusting and even a little funny. Not like the other tutors and teachers in Ravensroost, most of whom were older and had gray in their hair. He was young for a scholar, or so her mother had told her. She looked at him, and he managed a little smile, despite what had just happened.

Someone else was suddenly with them. Candissa shook for a moment, fearing another attacker. It was a pair of the town guardsmen. The lead guard was a young man with a familiar face. He had helped father sometimes.

"Thendarick, bring the captain here at once," Penston said.

Thendarick looked down to see Candissa there. His amber eyes went a little wide, apparently shocked at her state. "Is the young miss all right, sir?"

"She's fine, Thendarick. Oh, send word for Mother Meshana as well, if you please," Penston said, smiling at the guard's concern. The young guardsman nodded to Penston then looked at Candissa. "I'll be right back, miss." With that, he turned and ran at full speed back toward the western gate.

Candissa heard something and turned to see what was happening behind them.

The stranger was still standing atop the corner of the Wardenstone. Delvin bent to examine the body of Vink. His eyes were open and lifeless.

"He...he died," was all Candissa could say, her voice to hitching.

"Don't look at him, Candissa," Penston said. He took her chin by his thumb and forefinger, directing her gaze to his brown eyes. "You need not look."

She could not help it. Vink had died in front of her, after trying to kill her. But why? Part of her wanted desperately to know, at once. The other part wanted to run, to find her mother, to cry, to hide. She felt tears running down her face, mixing with the rain.

Penston put an arm around her, and she cried into his damp cloak. Her crying turned to sobbing, as she began to shake as she clutched him tightly. He patted her shoulder, his bright silver scholar's pin pressing into her cheek.

"No one will hurt you now. Don't worry," Penston said. She had always liked Master Penston. He was Ravenroost's resident Scholar and taught many classes to children of various ages. Candissa had known him since she was just able to read. She had always had a voracious appetite for books and tomes on any subject.

He was also a close friend to her family and had always had a fondness for Candissa. She had learned much from him, during both her regular schooling and from impromptu sessions, when she would pose a question to him. They had been engaged in one such session when the storm had struck the town, prompting her to race out of the western gate.

"Careful, watch him!" Delvin called out suddenly to the other guard. Penston instinctively rose, ready to whisk Candissa away. But the stranger only appeared to be collapsing now, as Delvin and the guardsman eased him off the edge of the Wardenstone and onto the ground.

The wind slackened suddenly, and the sky looked to be brightening. While it was still raining a bit, the rain clouds had moved further east. Thunder still rolled and echoed across the open plains surrounding Ravensroost.

Candissa heard horses approaching now. She looked to see several riders. The hooves were kicking up bits of mud as they rode toward the gray block.

Captain Conmerren was first off his horse. He was a tall man, and a powerful warrior, according to Candissa's sisters.

"Is she well?" the captain asked Penston, his piercing gaze on Candissa. The scholar simply nodded. The captain looked briefly at the stranger, then at the fallen ranger lying face down, the knife still in his back.

"This ranger, isn't he Steeg?"

"Yes, sir," Delvin answered him. "Vink Steeg."

"This one killed him?" Conmerren said, pointing to the stranger.

"Aye. But he saved Candissa," Delvin said, winking at Candissa as he spoke. "Vink was about to kill her."

"That's preposterous," the captain said, scowling, shaking his head. Dark brows furrowed over his steely blue eyes. "I knew Steeg. He wouldn't do such a thing."

"It's true, Captain. We both witnessed the attack," Penston said. "She barely escaped his first swing. If the stranger hadn't thrown the knife, Vink would have killed her."

"What by the six and seven would have possessed Vink to act in such a way?" Conmerren said, scowling over the corpse of the dead ranger. He looked to Delvin. "Was he behaving strangely at all?"

"No, sir, he was his usual self," Delvin said. "I even spoke to him this morning. He was joking about something that happened last night."

The stranger was still standing, though he needed Delvin's assistance to avoid collapsing. Candissa was glad he was not hurt. Captain Conmerren inspected him from head to boots.

"Strange looking fellow," the captain commented.

"I found him," Candissa said, her high-pitched voice sounding a little silly amid all this serious talk. The captain glanced at her only briefly, then turned back to the stranger.

"What is your name, sir? We owe you thanks," Captain Conmerren said firmly, stepping up to the stranger.

The stranger blinked, trying to focus on the captain, or so Candissa thought. He tried speaking, but it sounded more like croaking. The stranger managed to clear his throat.

"What was that?" Conmerren said.

The man reached into a pocket of his vest, his hands fumbling and weak.

"My...orders…" he said, his words strangely accented. He drew forth a handful of powdery bits. They blew away in the wind, which was still coming in hard from the west.

He looked at his hand, as the last fragments of dust and debris vanished. His eyes rolled upwards as he collapsed, this time completely. Delvin and the captain lowered him down to the ground.

"Is he hurt?" Candissa said, suddenly very concerned about his well-being.

"He's fine, Deesa. He's fainted is all," Delvin said, winking at her.

"Penston, take her to the Bonerest. I'll have questions," the captain said to the scholar.

"Of course," Penston said. "Candissa, let's head to the tavern, and we will send for your mother."

"Do we have to?"

"Yes, come along, get up now," the scholar said, helping her up.

As Candissa rose to her feet, a wave of exhaustion swept through her and she nearly collapsed again.

"Here, put her on my horse," a voice called. Candissa looked up to see Mother Meshana approaching on her gray mare. "I will see to her at the Bonerest."

"Yes, Meshana," Penston said, as the older woman slid off the saddle.

Meshana was there. That made Candissa happy. She would help the stranger. A great exhaustion seemed to wash over her as she stared at Mother Meshana. The woman had graying hair, bound back tightly. Her skin was darker than most of the townsfolk, with wrinkles about her eyes and lips. Her eyes were wise and gray. She was old but she moved as a younger woman would.

As Penston helped her up onto the gentle horse, Candissa saw a wagon being drawn toward the Wardenstone, and others on horseback. She slumped in the saddle, utterly tired.

"Can you make the ride back to the tavern?" Penston asked her.

"Yes, sir, I can," she said, her voice weak. It was a short ride, after all.

As Penston guided the mare back toward the gate, Candissa tried to stay upright. The horse was walking slowly, but it was still difficult for her. He looked up at her.

"Deesa, whatever possessed you to run out into a storm, out here?" the scholar said, his voice reproving. "You've heard the stories. The Wardenstone is not to be trifled with. Your mother will be very upset with you."

"I know! It's just that…I just had to, I had to try to help," she said, not sure exactly why she said it.

"Help? Help who?"

"That man...I think." Even as she said the words, she doubted them.

The scholar only frowned, shaking his head. She slumped in the saddle. She closed her eyes, letting the thumping rhythm of the ride lull her. She remembered little after the ride was over.

She did remember being laid down on one of the long benches in the Bonerest Tavern. People were fussing over her, and that bothered her. She was so tired but didn't understand why.

She heard her mother's voice. She was nearly shrieking, but Candissa didn't know if she was angry with her or other people. Her head was lifted, and a pillow was placed beneath it.

Her eyes fluttered open briefly. She saw the kind eyes of Master Evan, the master of the Bonerest tavern. She thought about him for a moment. He was half-Elven, and she liked him. His hair was long, bound in the back. It was a dark brown with strands of blonde and gray and gold mixed in. His eyes always smiled and now was no exception. He nodded at her as she tried to focus on his face.

She seemed to sleep again, but not for long. Someone was putting a cup to her lips, and she drank something mildly sweet and bitter. She felt immediately refreshed. A hand, cool and comforting, pressed against her forehead. Candissa knew it was Mother Meshana.

"She's awake," was all the elder priestess said. Candissa had known Mother Meshana all her life. She served on the council of the temple in town, where Candissa had been studying and training for more than two years. Candissa had displayed aptitudes in the healing arts among other areas of study, according to Meshana. That pleased Candissa a great deal, although her mother did not seem to share her enthusiasm.

"Candissa, my sweet, wake up now," her mother said, all too insistent.

"Mother, I'm fine," she said, her voice still weak. Blinking, and taking a deep breath, Candissa shifted, lifting herself up on her elbows.

She was surrounded by several people, most of whom she knew. Penston was still there, as was Delvin. Captain Conmerren was speaking to one of his junior officers, the one named Thendarick. Candissa had always liked that soldier. He was not that many years older than her and was always very kind.

Her father, a tall mug of ale in one hand, was talking to Master Evan, and seemed unconcerned with Candissa's situation. Mother Meshana was putting away something in a satchel. She smiled at Candissa, lines forming at both ends of her mouth.

"She is fine, Lady Demarrae, just give her a moment," Meshana said. She looked pointedly at Candissa. "Young lady, I will see you tomorrow at temple. Eight bells sharp!"

"Yes, Mother Meshana," Candissa said, nodding. She sat up, assisted by her mother, though she didn't need any help. She looked around the Bonerest Tavern. She had only been here a few times, as taverns were not the sort of place young girls frequented in Ravensroost.

But this was one of the nicer taverns. Not like the ones on the south side of town, or so she had overheard. She liked this place. Tall beams of dark wood rose and curved, to meet even wider beams crossing the ceiling. The walls were split by tall windows with narrow glass panes in a lattice of dark metal. They were cracked open, allowing in a fresh breeze, while the outer shutters were thrown open, providing more than sufficient light. The tables were of thick wood, lacquered and dark, grained deeply. Suspended from coppery-colored brackets set high in the ceiling beams were great wheels of wood, sheathed in strips of copper, set with cressets. Some of the cressets were lit, despite the daylight. It lent a warmth to the tavern that pleased Candissa.

She glanced around but could not see the stranger she had found. Aside from the guards and those involved in the event at the gray block, there were only a few midday patrons, talking about the stranger and the storm.

"Where is he?" she said quietly, looking up at Penston.

"Mother Meshana sent him to the temple. She will look after him," the scholar said.

"Young lady, I would like a word with you about what happened," Captain Conmerren suddenly said, his deep voice startling her. Penston stepped away. "If you would allow it, Lady Demarrae."

Her mother smiled at the captain's courtesy. She nodded gracefully, stepping back. As she did so, she cast a stern gaze at her daughter. A silent be-on-your-best-behavior glance passed from mother to daughter.

"Yes, sir?" Candissa said, scratching her hair. It was still damp, which irritated her.

"I was talking with Master Penston and the ranger Delvin, about the incident out there, and I wanted to get your account of it. All right?"

Candissa nodded.

"As I understand it, you decided to run out into the storm because, if I understand correctly, you *like* storms," he said. With that, he looked at Candissa expectantly. She nodded vigorously.

"Very much so, sir."

"All right. Given that, you felt compelled to dash out of the western gate, even though the rangers were closing it," he said. At this point, his gaze became a little more serious. "You know that's unwise. Why did you do that, Candissa?"

She thought about it. He wouldn't like her answer. "I don't know, sir. I felt I needed to."

"Did you hear someone out there?"

"No, it was too loud to hear anyone, with all the lightning and thunder," she said.

"Which could have killed you!" her mother blurted. The captain looked at her mother sidelong but said nothing.

"But then I saw him, standing on the corner of the gray block," Candissa said. "I thought perhaps he was hurt."

"And that's when you ran out to him, despite Penston and Delvin calling after you," the captain said.

She only nodded, trying to look a little ashamed.

"Did you know the ranger named Vink Steeg?" he asked her in a gentler tone.

Candissa grew still at the question, remembering the man falling on her, dying, his last words. He was trying to say something. He never had the chance to finish.

"I knew of him, sir, but I didn't know him really," she said, shaking her head a little. "I said hello to him a few times."

"He never took an unusual interest in you?" Conmerren asked her.

She shook her head.

The captain looked at her, compassion in his eyes, and nodded. "Very well. Thank you, Candissa."

He turned and spoke to others, including Penston, Evan, and Thendarick. Her mother spoke to him briefly and came over, a long cloak in hand.

"Come along, young lady. Wear this to ward the chill, that wind is still blowing," she said, draping the cloak over Candissa's shoulders.

She didn't argue, as she felt very tired. It had been a strange day so far. It was still light out, but a warm bed at home sounded wonderful right now.

Her mother guided her out of the front entrance of the tavern. Penston followed, as others slowly filed out to return to their duties and tasks.

Looking west, the two wide gate doors were still open. Through the opening, Candissa could see the setting sun now, lowering over a vague horizon. Clouds were still moving overhead, some roiling, some breaking up. The red and golden rays of the setting sun caught the undersides of the clouds, creating fantastic shapes, billowing like a fire slowly consuming the sky.

"Deesa, come along now!" Her mother was insistent, but at the moment her words were unwelcome.

She fixed her eyes on the horizon, resisting her mother's tugging.

"What is it, Candissa?" Penston said. His voice was low, sounding almost like the wind that was blowing back her flaxen hair, strands of it golden in the setting sun's rays.

"What is out there, Master Penston?" As she asked, she didn't really expect an answer from him.

The scholar looked out of the gate, toward the horizon.

"Out there?"

She nodded, still staring.

"Nothing, Candissa. Well, the hills of course," the scholar said. "But you never go out there. It's much too dangerous. Even the Rangers don't venture out very far. Everyone knows that."

She resisted rolling her eyes. *Everyone knows that.* It was a phrase drummed into the head of every child raised in Ravensroost. Everyone knows you don't leave the safety of home and community. You don't venture into the deep woods, the high mountains, and you certainly do not go west into the hills draped in mist.

"But what lays past them?"

The scholar studied her face, but her eyes remained fixed on the setting sun.

"Only ruins."

The moment seemed to pass. She turned as her mother pulled her sleeve even more forcefully. She looked up at the scholar.

"I will go there one day," she said to him.

CHAPTER TWO - KORAYMIS

4 Tempestus, Year 195, Eastvale Calendar

Koraymis wept.

He didn't know why exactly. He was alone, in his small room, with his books. No one could see him. That's when he cried. Coughing a little, he wiped his cheeks. He didn't mean to start crying. He suspected it was because he had remembered something about his mother. Maybe something he smelled. He was quite young when his parents died, and he had no clear, vivid recollections of them. Only vague feelings, memories of memories.

The only inheritance he could claim from them was his name. And it was not a very good name at that. *Sleeth.* He did not use it often. It was a name he knew, even when he was so very young. But he recalled nothing else about them, not even the day they had died.

Killed. *They were killed.* He had to remember that.

Koraymis had read tales of heroes avenging their parents' death or exacting revenge on barbarian chieftains who ravaged their village. These tales were in the printbooks so favored by well-read younger people. Koraymis had dozens of printbooks piled in his room, half of them tales, the others concerning lore and history. He also had a few books, of which he was proud. His house-family had provided well for him, especially given the misfortunes of his younger years.

Koraymis had seen children on the streets of Woodford, those without parents or a home. The Watch tried to get them into workhouses, or temples, or the homes of those willing to devote time and gold to the training of urchins. Most were likely fledgling members of a Takers guild, or so he imagined, training under cruel masters as petty thieves and pilferers.

He knew he had come close to that state, that grim lot. If not for…

"Koraymis!" a woman's voice called from downstairs. "Sausage and fry cakes!"

The young man composed himself. His stomach growled at the thought of eating.

Heading down a narrow, steep flight of stairs, he joined the woman and her husband at the long table of stained oak, along with their son, and two other house brothers. Koraymis sat between the woman and the younger house brother. To sit next to the son or the bigger house brother would likely invite a stubbed toe or elbow to the cheek.

The house brothers, like Koraymis, were without parents. They were raised here in this house by the kindness of Tebbrick and Nylora, as Nylora was often wont to point out. *Kindness - and a moderate stipend from the crown*, Koraymis reminded himself. She never mentioned that point.

They all wore fairly plain and simple tunics and breeches, sewn from the rougher fabrics typically reserved for the lower classes. Evun had the nicest tunic, a brighter green, while Tebbrick and Ben had drab grays. Koraymis's was almost black, which he favored.

The room was narrow and tall, with soot-stained rafters, and masonry walls cracked with age and patched over too many times. Higher on the walls were hung framed pictures, family heirlooms or pieces of art Nylora had found at one of the many odd little shops in Woodford. The lower portions of the walls were mottled and blemished from too many years of too many boys throwing food and scraping chairs against them.

Tebbrick sat at the head of the table, wearing the heavy woolen shirt he always favored on work-days. His expression was dour and disapproving as always. Opposite him sat Nylora, her narrow face and slender frame in stark contrast to her husband's round head and stout body. She wore a house dress and apron, as she did every day. They were usually worn at the edges or patched here and there. She had finer clothing when she needed to browse the shops. Her expression was usually a sort of reserved kindness, never too warm, and often quite harsh. Koraymis could never tell what she really thought, behind her arched eyebrows and long nose.

The boys made motions to grab the larger cakes or sausages, but Tebbrick thumped the table forcefully with his clasped hands. "Bow your heads," he intoned.

The boys and the woman obeyed dutifully.

"O gentle mother, thank you for leading us out of the wilds and setting our feet on the path of the good, and for granting us this bounty. By your wisdom and kindness, we are fed. And so it is."

"So it is," the boys murmured in response. Then hands flew as the larger boys tried to capture the largest fry cake and sausage. Koraymis didn't mind having one of the smaller, since Nylora always made them nearly the same size. He was glad to see a steaming pot of bitterblack brew being passed down the table. The younger boys didn't like it, but Koraymis had been enjoying the drink for the last two years. It was especially invigorating in the morning.

"How are your studies coming along, Ben?" Nylora asked the smaller boy.

Ben nodded, replying around a mouthful of cake. He was a markedly diminutive boy, with a face that was always dirty under a mop of unruly black hair. His eyes were merry, however, and Koraymis enjoyed his company. "Very good, I've learned all my letters. Master Yarrowton is teaching us how to write."

"Very good. Flendas, how are your studies?" she asked the older house brother. Koraymis knew the boy was not especially bright. He was destined for a future involving working with wood or stone, or perhaps a free farmer. With large hands, shoulders already broad for his age and no lack of muscles, he would do well in the more physically challenging trades.

Flendas shrugged. "Good enough. Long as a I can do numbers, that's all I'll need."

"You should make sure you learn the basics of letters, young man," Nylora chided him.

"Let the boy be, Ny, he's doing fine. I'm having him work with Garruld the mason," Tebbrick said. "With his hands he'll be a fine builder."

Flendas nodded and smiled, always happy to hear approvals from them. He glanced at the shorter, slighter form of Koraymis. "Why don' you ask about Kor's letters?" the boy asked, sarcasm clear in his voice.

Tebbrick's son Evun, older—and larger—than any of them, answered him. "Oh, Koraymis is smarter than all of us put together, plus half the folk on the street!"

The other boys laughed at the jest. Tebbrick suppressed a grin. Nylora frowned.

"There's nothing wrong with that! The Kingdom needs smart boys as much as strong backs," she said, turning a baleful glare on the older boys.

Koraymis had been teased far too much in his life to be affected by this trivial banter. Besides, he wasn't entirely sure if Evun was goading him or complimenting him. Koraymis had helped them all with their letters and worked with Tebbrick on his books. In either case, he appreciated Nylora standing up for him, as she was sometimes wont to do.

"You're learning a lot at the library after school then, Koraymis?" she inquired.

The young man attended Woodford's School of Letters for Boys in the mornings and then helped at the town library in the afternoons. His collection of printbooks and books had been improved with his work at the library. The librarians had given him some of the more worn and common copies, while a handful of the more intriguing printbooks and a few books had simply gone missing. No one was the wiser.

"Yes, mum, I am. Master Donnen has been letting me copy the simpler scrolls," he said. "And I have access to a lot of books."

"Books, pfft!" Flendas blurted, picking at his last sausage. "What good are they?"

The other boys grinned at his comment. Koraymis sighed, looking at Flendas with an almost tired expression. Flendas just grinned, grease from the sausage running down his chin. He half-winked at the smaller boy.

Flendas was tall for a boy of sixteen, being more than a year older than Koraymis. With a strong build, a good eye for crafting, and a fairly handsome face, Koraymis knew he was bound for success in the stone trade. He wasn't especially mean or cruel to Koraymis, but he did make sure every boy at the table understood who was in charge. Koraymis could respect that, though he never admitted that to the older boy.

Koraymis would typically let Flendas' remark pass unchallenged and unanswered. But something inside compelled him to do otherwise.

"Don't you want to be remembered?" Koraymis asked Flendas. The question caught the older boy by surprise, which was Koraymis' intent.

"Wha' ya mean by that?" he said, his expression wary. Koraymis sometimes mocked him in careful, quiet ways, and he likely suspected this now.

"In a hundred years, there will be a book on the history of Woodford. Don't you want your name to be in it, as one of the finest masons ever known to the town? Maybe it will even say you went off to Eastvale to cut stone and build facades for the King himself," Koraymis said.

"Ya think..." Flendas' eyes lit up. Then he glared at Koraymis. "Yer making fun, aren't ya?"

Nylora became alarmed, seeing there could be an incident in the making. "Boys..."

"No!" Koraymis declared firmly, silencing everyone with the conviction in his voice. He seemed ready to stand. "I will never have your skill of your hands nor your strength of back nor your eye for what is good stone and how best to cut it. But I will always need a well-made building to shelter from the storms. And what you can do with your hands can last a thousand years!"

Flendas seemed taken aback. His expression relaxed visibly, disarmed by Koraymis' words. "Well, I s'pose. But I bet ya read some books older than that in your library."

Koraymis returned to eating his fry cake. "No, not even close."

"Well, I'm sure they'll let you read the very old books someday," Nylora said, clearly grateful the table was at peace again.

He shook his head. "No, they allow me access to any of their books. None are especially prized, this far from the City. I've read the oldest of them, and it was written barely two hundred years ago."

"Enough of this book talk. We have work and studies to attend to," the master of the house declared. "Off with us all."

That ended all conversation, as his word was always obeyed. Koraymis learned soon after arriving at the house to heed his declarations or risk a broad strip of leather across his backside. Nylora always interceded, however, and made sure he was never punished unduly.

After washing, changing into his school robes and making sure his dark, stiff hair was presentable, he slung his bag over his shoulder and headed out onto the street. It was cold, as the snowy winds from the mountains chose this time of year to come down into the valley lands. There had been an early snowfall last week and a few patches yet remained in the shadowed alleys of Woodford.

Woodford was a large town, or so it was said. Koraymis had explored most of Woodford, as it had been his home since he was very young. There were many large avenues, lined with two or three-story buildings, and innumerable alleyways, narrow and shadowed. The temples were truly inspiring, Helmir's silvered dome shining so brightly on high summer days, Arushana's round towers a brilliant blue-green, and Landrom's spires reaching forty paces into the sky, topped with golden caps.

The streets were paved with round riverstones of many colors, and the carts made a tremendous clatter as scores of them trundled to and from markets twice a day. Koraymis knew well the streets and paths and shortcuts throughout Woodford, the hawkers corners, merchant's square, the districts and estates, and the garrisons and watch towers. He often enjoyed the wandering minstrels of the brightly-colored theater row during summer, and the savory smells that would waft down Bakers Way in autumn.

It was late autumn today, and one day soon the streets would slick with snow and ice.

His boots were in poor shape, but it was a short walk to the Woodford school. He enjoyed school for the most part. He was learned enough that the teachers who appreciated his brightness utilized him in assisting with test preparations, distributing paper and the like. He had learned all he would from the School of Letters. His teachers probably agreed, as they excused his occasional absences without comment.

Except for Master Stonefall, the Quillmaster. For some reason he simply did not like Koraymis, and he made sure the boy knew that as often as possible. His lessons were required for every student at the school. They would have to do well in the Quillmaster's class if they hoped to post a favorable grade. Stonefall was keenly aware of this and held it over any pupil he saw as an upstart. And he certainly saw Koraymis as an upstart.

The tall, shrill-voiced, nearly bald man had long, talon-like fingers, every one of them stained with ink. As master of the quill, it was his duty to instruct every boy in the use of the quill and ink in the shaping of letters. Koraymis found the instruction invaluable and, despite having what he considered one of the best turns of hand in the entire school, he always sought to improve it. He wanted to master not only the written word used by Humans, but also that of the Elves and Dwarves.

Unfortunately, Stonefall was the only person in his life he would call an expert in languages. There was little he could do to improve his chances of finding another tutor in this subject. While there were a number of Elves and Dwarves that frequented the streets, markets, and establishments of the town, there were no scholars or teachers among them.

Woodford was the most remote of the baronial capitals in the Kingdom of Eastvale. He had read that nobles in the East called it the *raving edge* of civilization. While that was not true, it was true Woodford was as far as it could be from the centers of learning.

Koraymis intended one day to journey to the city of Eastvale, for which the Kingdom was named. He was only fifteen summers old, not yet old enough to leave his home and fend for himself. Until that day, Koraymis intended to squeeze every ounce of learning and knowledge he could out of everything and everyone in his life. That included the taciturn and reproachful Master of Quills, Stonefall.

He was soon at the school. Glancing up against the bright sky, Koraymis was always impressed by the structure, the dense, dark stone that comprised the walls, narrow windows set deep, shuttered by heavy oak, the squared and hard-cornered character that spoke to anyone passing by, *I will remain.* The edifice was among the oldest in Woodford, or so some scholars claimed.

Taking the dark stone steps leading up to the wide entryway two at a time, he soon joined the crowd of other students as they jammed the narrow corridors of lacquered pine, poorly lit by chandeliers of iron hanging high in the rafters. The students whispered to one another in hushed tones, careful not to catch the ire of the older students tasked with herding them to their respective classrooms. Soon, the babbling murmurs faded from the corridors as doors latched shut and the echoes of scraping chairs resounded through the school.

Koraymis took his seat in Master Stonefall's room, careful not to make too much noise as he adjusted his creaking chair.

A chill wind blew through Woodford, rattling the nearby window, as Koraymis was dutifully penning out the prescribed series of letters and words Stonefall had written on the slate at the head of the classroom. While most of the boys were struggling through the whole series, to finish them before this segment of instruction was complete, Koraymis was on his third set. He relished the opportunity to exercise this skill and hoped every day that Master Stonefall would give them something new and different.

As they scratched their quills on the coarse parchment provided for practice, their teacher would instruct them in various bits of technique and lore regarding the written word. Despite his intractable personality, Koraymis found his tutelage fascinating.

"Can anyone tell me what this ink that you are all using is made from?" he said. Stonefall would pose questions such as this every morning. Koraymis knew from experience not to offer his answer first, as he'd received more than one bruising at the hands of jealous classmates for displaying his intellectual superiority.

"My pa says ink is made from the blood of dragons since they gave men the gift of writing," one particularly dull student offered. His fellows snickered at him and Koraymis hid his own grin. He hoped the boy was just repeating the old tale for comedic purposes.

"Really, Donnerby, surely you know he was saying that only in jest," Stonefall said with derision in his voice, sighing heavily. "Blood of any sort is a poor ink, as it lacks indelibility. And everyone knows there are no such things as dragons."

Donnerby lowered his head as he continued to slowly work his quill.

"Anyone else? Any ideas at all?" the quill master said, casting about the room with an expression of mild disappointment.

Koraymis was about to say something when one of the boys he actually respected spoke up.

"I heard lampblack is sometimes used in making ink," the boy said. He was named Illiam and was the son of a potter.

"Very good, Illiam, yes. Lampblack, or soot as it is better known, is a common ingredient," Stonefall commended him. "But there are at least one or two more ingredients required to make any ink."

He was slowly walking down the aisle as he spoke, toward Koraymis's seat. Koraymis tried not to look up at the instructor.

"Surely our redoubtable classmate, Koraymis, can tell us what is required to manufacture a proper ink, other than the primary pigment, in this case lampblack."

He looked up at Stonefall, placing his quill down carefully. "Yes, sir. One requires a binder such as pine resin, and usually an oil, such as walnut."

"Correct as usual, Master Koraymis," Stonefall said. He stood over the slight boy for a moment, perhaps considering more challenging questions that might put the boy in his place. Or so Koraymis imagined. Instead, he turned and kept slowly walking down the aisle, continuing his lecture.

Ignoring the whispers and snickers of his fellows, Koraymis continued exercising his writing skills, working through the series of letters and words as Stonefall went on about the variety of materials one could use in creating inks.

Near the end of the lesson period, he finished a fourth sheet of paper, setting it atop the others to dry. He looked at the blank sheet now in front of him and blinked in curiosity. It was entirely unlike the other sheets of paper.

Every student received a daily allotment of sheets to use for writing, ciphering, or any school-related activity that may require it. Koraymis always took a thicker stack than his fellow students, as he used more than anyone else.

There was no shortage of paper, apparently. The school never put a limit on how many sheets students could use, with the only restriction being one would have to use it on school grounds or at home for schoolwork. He had once heard of an ambitious student stealing off with a hundred sheets and trying to sell them at market, only to be expelled by the masters and fined by the Watch.

The stacks of paper used in the school, which Koraymis had seen many times in dusty storerooms, were typically the common fibrous sheets. He had read they were made from used paper or linen, finely shredded somehow and turned into a slurry that was then dried on screens. He had read of it and had seen the process once when a maker of papers visited the library.

This piece now before him, seen by the watery light of the glazed window and overhead lamps, was clearly different. He picked it up and examined it more closely. It was far smoother, almost translucent, with a slight amber color to it. His eyes picked out what appeared to be tiny lines criss-crossing the sheet, almost like rivers on a map, or creases of worn leather. There was a pattern to it, but it was hard to pick out. And it had a sheen to it as daylight caught it just so, a purplish glimmer, or at least that's what Koraymis saw.

He realized it must be a sheet of fine vellum, something that was unusual to find loose in a stack of common paper. He had seen vellum before, the sort made from calf or sheep skin. This was different. He put the sheet down before Stonefall turned around again.

The writing lesson ended, and students filed out after gathering their things. Koraymis packed away his small stack of paper but kept the one sheet on his desk. As the others left the room, he approached Master Stonefall, who was just returning to his desk. An older student serving as his assistant was about the task of gathering everyone's lesson sheets and putting them in the correct slots in a large cabinet behind the instructor's desk.

"Yes, Koraymis, what is it today? Another fascinating question I assume?" Stonefall said, a mild sneer in his tone. Koraymis couldn't help but give that a half-smile. He had thoroughly vexed every instructor in the school with his endless stream of questions and observations.

"Sir, it's this sheet I found in my stack. It's vellum, isn't it?" he said, handing him the sheet. He knew full well it was vellum, but he had learned to avoid being presumptuous. The instructor took the sheet and glanced at it, holding it up.

"Yes, it is. This was in your stack?"

"Yes, sir. I picked up a stack this morning from the materials table, this was in it," Koraymis said.

"Curious, Barthelm usually separates the vellum from paper. But," he said, handing it back. "There's no harm in you having a sheet of vellum to practice on."

"Thank you, sir," the boy said. "But is this normal vellum? It seems...different somehow. From what I've seen in the library."

"It's of no concern, Koraymis. Off with you," Stonefall said, waving his hand toward the door as he turned his attention to his grading ledger.

Koraymis simply nodded and left the room, carefully tucking the sheet of vellum away. The rest of his classwork proceeded uneventfully. The classes ended two bells after midday. He then headed off to the library, his pack slung over his shoulder.

He was looking forward to his studies there. While the School of Letters had given him the basics in writing, numbers, and history, what he was learning at the library represented his true education.

The lessons were getting more interesting with each passing week and thinking about what he may learn today was always exciting. Unfortunately, this distracted thinking prevented him from seeing Roddam in time to avoid him. He was with his usual brace of three schoolboys, all four of them irrepressible bullies.

Roddam was three years his senior and highly intelligent. Koraymis, however, was quickly gaining notoriety as the smartest pupil in the forty-year history of the Woodford School of Letters for Boys. This did not sit well with Roddam. He and his gang must have followed the smaller boy from the school and taken another route to intercept him. They were just across the street from the columned arch that was the entrance to the library, blocking it nicely.

"Well, look who's off to the library. Woodford's brightest boy," Roddam mocked him. "How are you today, little 'Mis?"

Koraymis only glared at him with his dark eyes. "What do you want, Roddam?"

"Your pack," he smiled brightly. He did have fairly dazzling teeth and a handsome face. He was smart and popular with the girls. His voice lowered as he spoke. "Hand it over."

"No," the smaller boy said.

Roddam laughed, and his three friends joined in his laughter. "Oh, look at the little orphan prince, he is so defiant."

Koraymis only stared back at him, showing no signs of fear despite his heart beating faster. This angered the bigger boy.

Roddam nodded to his friend on his right. "Ban, take his pack."

The boy named Ban nodded and stepped forward aggressively. Koraymis stepped back, saying "You shouldn't, Ban."

This elicited more laughter. The taller boy jumped forward and grasped the bag by the strap over Koraymis' shoulder. The smaller boy yelled, "No!" and pushed his open right hand against the taller boy's chest, trying to force him back.

Ban instantly jumped back with a short scream of shock, tripping and falling against Roddam. The other boys were surprised by the unexpected turn of events, trying to get out of the way of the flailing lad or attempting to catch him. This allowed Koraymis to dash around the lot of them and reach the door to the library before they could react. He turned to see the boys glaring at him with alternating expressions of shock and anger.

Ban had his shirt open and, even across the street, Koraymis could see the red mark in the shape of a hand. Ban was staring down at it, touching it tenderly.

"He burned me!" he said, his face betraying the growing pain. "It's blistering!"

Koraymis fled into the safety of the library's dim and cloistered halls. The attendant librarian looked at him with mild alarm, given his swift entrance and unnecessary slamming of the tall, oaken doors.

There were three patrons sitting at the long tables today, but the boy paid them no heed. He hurried to the chambers in the back of the old building and found his work waiting for him. He was left almost entirely alone some days and he enjoyed that. But not today. While he had work to do, he had lessons that would follow, lessons that could not wait.

After an hour spent copying, inspecting and sorting books, he made his way to the back stairwell of the library, used only by those who worked there. Climbing the dimly-lit, steep and narrow length of stairs, he walked a short, shadowed hallway and entered one of the less utilized rooms. It was one of the old archive rooms, used to store records and works not suitable for public access, for one reason or another. There were several archive chambers, but this one was the least used. It was therefore an ideal place to meet with someone privately.

The room had a pair of long, clearly older tables, with rickety chairs arrayed on either side. The chamber was tall, with cobwebs adorning the corners and hidden shadows above the shelves. It smelled of old, worn leather, cracked parchment, and dust. It was smell Koraymis had learned to cherish.

Along the walls stood more than a dozen tall bookshelves. They were stacked with some of the library's oldest archives, many in poor condition, along with hundreds of damaged books and tattered printbooks.

The man was sitting at the end of one of the tables, near one of the two tall windows, reading a large tome.

"Good day, Master Telmik," Koraymis said, trying not to sound too cheerful. He had once asked the man his first name but was told it did not matter. For as long as Koraymis could remember, he had called him by the one name.

Telmik did not look up as he spoke.

"You were most unwise today, Koraymis."

The boy's exuberance at seeing his teacher soured immediately.

"I didn't want him to take my pack," he said.

"Do you really think those boys are common thieves?" he looked up at Koraymis.

Telmik was perhaps in his early forties, though Koraymis had never been good at guessing ages. He was handsome, but not notably so. He had the look of most in Woodford, though his complexion was bit darker. His hair was neatly trimmed, dark red, laying in tight waves against his scalp. His eyes were a very neutral gray, deep set, with steeply arched brows, especially when he was assessing Koraymis' answers or performance. He wore clothing that seemed scholarly in appearance yet lacked any trim or insignia that would usually indicate one's scholarly profession or specialty. His face was neutral but behind his shadowed eyes, Koraymis felt his mood. He was clearly disappointed.

"No, sir, I suppose they are not."

"Does your pack contain riches and irreplaceable works?"

"No, sir, but it's-"

"They would have teased you and toyed with you but then you would have gotten your bag back," Telmik said patiently.

"How do you know? Roddam is-"

"Not a cruel boy. He and his friends are simple bullies. They were just having a little sport with you. You should have let them assert their dominance and be done with it. *No harm done.*" The last three words were spoken with a particular emphasis.

Koraymis sat down at a high-backed wooden chair in the middle of the table and put his pack on the table. His eyes were downcast. "Yes, sir. I am sorry for that, sir."

"We've worked hard to get you where you are today, and that escapade today could have led to a lot of questions that we don't need asked," Telmik said, turning a page slowly.

The young man frowned and looked up. "Sir, what do you mean, *could have*?"

"There won't be any questions asked, that is all you need to know. And be certain not to mention that incident to anyone tomorrow. And don't talk to Roddam and his friends."

Koraymis drew a breath to ask something else, but a sharp glance from Telmik ended any further questions on the matter.

"Now, I have some reading for you today, and you can feel free to ask me any questions when you are done," Telmik said, slowly sliding the book over toward the boy.

Koraymis positioned the remarkably heavy book in front of him, admiring the brilliantly illumined pages. "How many pages?"

"Seven," the man said. "Do you have another question for me?"

The young man noted to himself once more how his tutor always knew when he had a question on his mind. "Yes, Master Telmik, I do."

He drew the piece of vellum out of his pack, then stood and walked over to the end of the table. "This was in my stack of lesson paper today, in among the normal paper. It's vellum, isn't it."

Master Telmik took the sheet from Koraymis, holding it up. He smiled a little. "Yes, it is."

"But it's not normal vellum, from sheep or calfskin, is it?"

"No, it is not," he said, almost amused in his expression. "What do you think it is?"

"I don't know but it has a strange sort of gleam, if you hold it just right. Do you see it? Sort of purple?" the young man said, indicating he should hold it up against the light of the window.

"Oh, yes, I see that," Telmik replied, without holding it against the light. "You can see that, then. Interesting."

"Why?" Koraymis asked. He couldn't guess why that would be interesting.

"This vellum is rare beyond knowing, Koraymis. It isn't made from the hide of a calf, or a sheep, or even a griffon, as some of the finest vellum is," Telmik said, turning the sheet in his hand. "No, it is made from the hide of a dragon."

Koraymis' mouth fell open, his eyes widening.

"Yes, a dragon. And yes, of course, they are real," Telmik said. His brow furrowed a moment, thinking on that. "Well, they *were* real, and *are* real. Both I suppose you could say."

"I... don't understand what you mean," the young man managed. "You're certain? This is from the skin of a *real dragon*?" Koraymis found this almost incomprehensible.

His reading and studies had granted him a vast amount of knowledge, some of it quite rare, known by only those with access to the old tomes. Yet in all the works he had read, any mention of dragons was in the context of fanciful myths and discounted imaginings. To realize they had actually existed was difficult to imagine.

"Oh, yes. I am certain," Telmik said. He peered at the vellum more closely now. "And it is no easy task to make vellum from dragon skin. It takes a great deal of preparation, by the hand of a master, no doubt. Their hide is much thicker than ordinary leather, you see, and requires many hours of treating with chemicals and magic and working it flat."

Koraymis was still dumbstruck, unsure what to say.

"Of course, the hardest part is killing the dragon. They are loath to part with their skin, you see," Telmik said, his face alight with a strange grin. He winked at Koraymis as he handed him back the piece of vellum. "It is from a blue, I think."

"Blue?" Koraymis said, finding his voice at last. Questions sprang to mind, but he knew there was no reason to ask them. Telmik was always guarded with his lore.

"Yes, a blue dragon."

"Is that why it gleams so?"

"It gleams like that because it's draconic vellum, not because it's from a blue," Telmik clarified. "But the gleam you see, it's something...very few people in Woodford, could see."

"What do you mean?"

"What you see, that purple gleam you describe, is magic," his tutor said, without inflection or solemnity.

Koraymis just blinked. After a moment, he said, "I can...see magic?"

Telmik smiled. "Don't worry about that right now, we don't have all day. Read, and when you're finished, ask me questions regarding the reading."

The young man nodded, his head almost ready to burst from all the questions raging in his mind. He took a few deep breaths, using the concentration techniques he had learned from Master Telmik, and began reading.

The reading went on as expected, and the contents of the pages did not disappoint Koraymis. He asked his tutor questions afterwards but made a point of avoiding any questions about dragons, or why he could somehow *see* magic.

It was dark when he returned home. Supper was one of his favorite meals, but he barely noticed, his mind was so consumed with all he had learned and read that day.

The following day, Roddam and his friends passed him in the corridors of the school. Koraymis readied himself for a confrontation. But they only looked at him briefly as they passed, with typical expressions of amusement or disdain. Ban only snickered as he passed Koraymis. The tall boy's shirt was open enough for Koraymis to see his chest where he had burned him.

There was no mark upon it.

CHAPTER THREE - ERROL

8 Auctus, Year 197, Eastvale Calendar

Errol Blackmar sat on the edge of the Wardenstone, one leg hanging off the short drop. He studied the walls of Ravensroost. The fine autumn morning was clear and bright, a cloudless blue sky overhead. Even the mist of the hills to the west was barely visible, if he cared to turn around and look. The perfect square of stone lay on a slight rise, allowing him an excellent view of the surrounding countryside.

He idly twirled a long dagger in his left hand, a habit of his that made almost everyone around him nervous. Not because he appeared to be carelessly flipping a remarkably sharp blade, but because he was so good at it. His breathing was stilled once more, after an invigorating run around the perimeter of the town.

His keen eyes could make out several carts and wagons coming into town from the east. Three were coming up the south road to enter through the west gate. There were a few brave and hardy homesteaders that settled to the south of town, though they defied common wisdom and custom in doing so. No one settled to the west of Ravensroost.

He didn't know them by name, but he admired them. Errol had no love of strict rules and laws that made no sense. Those homesteaders made their homes where they chose, despite the warnings. You don't settle west of Ravensroost, you don't leave the Kingdom, you never, ever think about venturing west into the Misthallow Hills. *Everyone knows that.*

That was a phrase Errol would be happy to never hear again. He had heard it far too often over the past five years. He understood it was the common view of those who had dwelt here all their lives. Errol couldn't say he agreed with it. But he was not in a position to judge them, as he knew almost nothing of their lore, their history.

Errol grinned. He knew scarcely more about himself. He did not know what he knew or did not know. His memories began only five years ago. All he could recall began the day he was found here, on the corner of the square of stone they called the Wardenstone. He bore nothing save his outlandish clothing, burned and torn, with pockets full of dust, a few lumps of what appeared to be melted gold, and the finely crafted dagger dancing between his fingers.

And his name. Errol Blackmar.

More intriguing - and more important - than the scant possessions he had on his person when he was found, were the skills he possessed. He was clearly highly skilled in the use of his blade. Out of curiosity, he had sought training in other weapons. That was two years ago, when he engaged the services of the sergeant of the militia at the town garrison.

He had demonstrated competence in a wide range of weapons, and expertise in several shorter, bladed weapons. His eye was as keen as their best archer and his instincts in practice melees were frightening. His training sessions ended quickly, given that he would embarrass anyone attempting to train him. He found it amusing at first, but he left unspoken his concern, and his alarm.

Who was he? Where did he learn all that he knew? He had asked himself these questions many times, and no answer was yet forthcoming. He had spoken to many of the learned men of Ravensroost: scholars, teachers and even a wizard. Yet none could answer his questions. They offered a variety of ideas and suggestions, ranging from the unlikely to the outlandish to the laughable.

It had become clear to him over the past several months that to solve the mystery that was Errol Blackmar would require him to journey east. He had arrived at the westernmost point of the Kingdom of Eastvale and the farthest from the grand City of Eastvale. There, some said, he would find the oldest books, the wisest sages and scholars. He simply needed to decide when he would be leaving. He thought he had made the decision several times this year. Yet every time he thought he was ready to depart something would prevent him from doing so. It was as if something was keeping him here.

Perhaps it was the gray stone upon which he now sat. It was where he was found. Perhaps he was bound to it by some unseen force. The thought made him smile. It sounded not unlike one of the farcical theories on why he was found here. *You incurred the wrath of a powerful wizard somewhere in the mountains, who robbed you of your memory and dropped you there in a storm as punishment for some unknown crime,* one mildly ancient traveling wizard had told him.

A silly idea, and Errol dismissed it as he had the others. Still, he could come up with no suitable explanation for why he was here, how he had arrived, or anything about what had transpired in his previous life.

"Errol!" a voice called from near the western gate. The lanky figure of Taldrephus was approaching at a decent pace. His ridiculously long legs served him well in covering ground. Errol jumped down and sheathed his blade, awaiting the arrival of his friend.

"Dreff, what do you need?" he called loudly, mildly annoyed but smiling. The younger man had taken to Errol two years ago, and in some respects behaved like his serving man, though they had never formalized any such relationship. He was much taller than Errol, though clearly didn't weigh as much. The lad's hair was a mop of unruly dark brown curls he had to keep under a cap at all times. His pale skin, common to those of this region, was still marked with the blemishes of youth, and his beard had yet to start growing in properly. His clothing never seemed to fit his unwieldy frame, despite Errol having given him coin in the past to find a tailor. Perhaps the oddest part of his young friend was his voice. It was absurdly low for the youthful face.

"Sir, I was asked by Delvin to kindly request you stay off the Wardenstone," Taldrephus said, a bit winded from his walk across the hundred yards or so that separated the west wall of Ravensroost from the enigmatic gray square.

"Delvin needs to drink a tonic," Errol quipped. "I've been coming out here since I arrived, and as you can see, I'm still here!"

"I understand, sir. It's just the local ordinances are very clear on this, and they make no exceptions," Dreff said, shrugging his broad shoulders.

Errol knew the ordinances, top to bottom. He had made it a priority to learn all the local laws, rules and customs, as soon as he had mastered the written language. The Wardenstone, as it was commonly termed, was a source of suspicious activity and folklore. Some claimed to have seen strange lights emanating from it, and there were cases of people disappearing while walking across it.

Errol had walked across the square uncounted times, and nothing ominous had ever occurred. There were some strange events he had witnessed. He was playing dice one day, throwing down eight carved cubes at a time, when one disappeared as it rolled. Errol had been near the center of the Wardenstone, so there was no nook or cranny or edge it could have slipped off. It was simply gone. Another time, he caught the powerful smell of acrid smoke in a sudden gust of wind. For reasons he could not understand, the smell struck fear in his heart. But it passed, and he could not discern the source. He also could sometimes hear things he knew were not there, when sitting on the edge of the square or walking across the perfectly flat surface: distant chimes, a dull roar, drums, even laughter.

But Errol did not mention these to anyone. They would either be dismissed as evidence of some afflicted madness, or they would be attributed to the general lore of the place, with no further thought or investigation to follow.

He was sure the block of stone was somehow tied to him or to his past. Some townsfolk supposed outsiders had simply deposited him there, for reasons outlandish or unknown, but that made no sense.

There were three witnesses on hand, and all of them had the same account - he was found simply standing there on the corner of the stone, during a thunderstorm. There was no opportunity for anyone to *deposit* him there. He had spoken to Candissa on several occasions over the past several months, just to see if her memory would perhaps yield another clue. But her account remained unchanged, along with the ranger's and the scholar's.

There was a fourth witness to his arrival, but Errol had killed the man, as he attempted to kill the young Candissa. He remembered none of that, however. His memory only began after he had been moved to the temple in town and awoke late that evening.

So, his life continued here in this western border town of Ravensroost, with no answers and only questions. He was grateful to the folk here, however. They had shown kindness and generosity in taking him in, allowing him to recuperate from whatever had happened.

When he first arrived, he spoke a different language, as many attested. Those first few days were a fugue. As he recovered, he began speaking a strange and heavily accented dialect of their language, as it was a secondary language, at least in respect to Errol. It didn't take him long to adapt, and after several months of work, his accent was nearly gone.

Still, he wondered about that other language. He remembered vaguely speaking to them in the curious tongue, and they could not comprehend it in the least. To his frustration, he was unable to simply call it up. There was so much he could not recall. But he could *feel it.* So much was there, just out of his reach. Sometimes he found it intensely aggravating.

On a few occasions, such as when he had been errantly wounded in practice, or hot water had splashed on his leg, he recalled uttering a phrase in anger. He was certain it was a curse, but it was nothing anyone had ever heard before. No doubt it was in that elusive, *first* language of his. That was the only word from that language he used regularly, if under his breath. *Sard.*

He picked up a stone from the ground next to the edge of the gray block and lofted it into the air, high over the surface of the square.

"Sir! That's bad luck!" Taldrephus cried, staring wide eyed at the rock as it fell. Errol only chuckled.

"I've thrown dozens of stones onto it, Dreff. My luck doesn't seem to change," he said, walking toward the town.

"You have?" Dreff said, looking out onto the smooth, featureless and perfectly flat surface. "Do you ever collect them?"

"No."

"Well, then, who does?" the long-limbed boy said, following after Errol now. He looked back at the Wardenstone with concern on his long face.

Errol turned on his heel quickly, forcing Taldrephus to nearly collide with him.

"Creatures crawling out of the hills at night!" Errol said, eyes wide, mimicking claws with his hands. The youth only frowned, which looked almost comical.

"You are having fun at me, sir!"

Errol clapped him on one shoulder. "Yes, Dreff, I am," he said, before turning and heading back to the western gate.

What he didn't tell Taldrephus was that was something that puzzled Errol about the Wardenstone, and always had. No matter how many stones or pebbles he cast onto the surface, within days, even hours, they would vanish. Sometimes, they would reappear days later. There was no pattern though, no discernible span of time before they would disappear or reappear. At one time, Errol had so determined to solve this mystery, he even spent the night sleeping on the stone, thinking perhaps it would whisk him away as he slept. But alas, on the two attempts, he awoke with only a neck ache for his trouble.

Taldrephus caught up with him easily. "Master Evan has need of your services at the Bonerest," he reported.

"Of course he does, it's accounts day and I'm the best keeper of books he's ever seen," Errol proclaimed. "Which really isn't saying much since his accounts consist of the purchasing of ales and meat and breads and the paying out to barmaids."

"He does appreciate you, sir," the lanky youth said. "I once overhead Master Temdrel, the counting house clark, talking about your skill with accounts and such."

"Oh? And what did the spotty Master Temdrel have to say?" Errol asked, referring unkindly to the clark's skin condition.

"Well, he'd had an ale or two and he was complaining that you were not keeping in your place, or something like that, as he had passed those tests they have for accounts clarks, and you were just an unknown pretending to do book," Taldrephus recounted. "But really I don't recall exactly what he said. And bear in mind he was a bit in his tankard."

Errol chuckled. "Common men grouse about those who do better, it's always been that way."

"It is odd though, sir, if you don't mind my saying," Dreff added, looking at the patchy grasses as they moved closer to the western gate of Ravensroost.

"What's that?"

"Well, you're very skilled with the quill and ink and keeping accounts," he said, scratching his face. "But...well, who trained you? Where did you get so book-learned?"

The young man left the question hanging in the air.

"A fair question, Dreff," Errol said. "One I intend to answer someday."

"Can't see how you can do that," his friend said. "Unless you travel east to the City. Mayhap a wizard or priest could figure it out for you."

"Perhaps. But from what I've read, they may not be of much help," Errol mused. "But then again I don't really know if I can trust my own judgment, since I have no idea what I do or do not know."

Taldrephus shook his head at that. "Now you're gettin' me all puzzled, sir."

They passed through the western gate, nodding at the watch. Errol was well-known throughout Ravensroost, despite - or perhaps because of - his origins. At first viewed with suspicion owing to his mysterious arrival and strange accent, he quickly enamored himself to the townsfolk.

Even in the face of being a true stranger, his witty banter, natural gregariousness, and remarkably handsome features turned those wary of him to feeling at ease with him, almost immediately. He had a true gift of affability and could read a stranger quickly, and engage them in disarming conversation, dispelling any apprehensions.

His accent was as mysterious as his appearance, but after many weeks, it faded almost entirely. In fact, Errol could easily speak without an accent, and could even mimic the particular speech patterns of Dwarves and Elves, and the eastern folk of the Kingdom. He chose to keep a hint of his accent, wherever he had acquired it. It added to the bit of mystery that shrouded him, and which he had always fostered.

It was a curious exoticness that did not alarm but rather added to his persona and likeability. He also found the young ladies were especially drawn to that part of his alluring character.

So, Errol had many friends in Ravensroost, from the shopkeepers and market vendors, to the town watch and rangers, and the common folk and homesteaders. He made a point of treating everyone equally and with equal geniality. He had made a special point of befriending those in the town he deemed of utility. They included the town wizard, Emphry, the chief priests of the two major churches, Penston the scholar, and the captain of the watch, one Knight-Sergeant Eskus Conmerren. While Conmerren's town watch rank was merely Captain, he sometimes enjoyed being called by his royally-granted title. Errol had shared a few tankards of ale with the man and learned he had a small swath of land some distance to the south. Conmerren hoped one day to build a keep upon that land as a minor noble.

There were others of note as well, who called Errol friend. Errol spent no small amount of his time engendering and growing those relationships. At times, in the dark of his room, in the twilight hours, as he twirled and flipped and practiced clever tricks with his blade, he wondered why. He felt a natural compulsion to befriend people, as many as may be. Yet in his heart, he was unsure if he truly felt friendship.

There was something about his own mind, his motivations, that he did not understand. He liked the people he befriended, all of them. Yet too often he would look at someone and assess what use they were to him, instead of thinking first of how they may be feeling, or if he could help them.

It was frustrating, but only a little. He could never shake the feeling, however. This is what drove him, slowly, inexorably, on his quest to uncover who he was and where he came from. He would not rest until he did. He knew he had to leave Ravensroost one day, and probably soon.

The town was getting busy, and quickly. The hour was approaching midday and the markets were filling with buyers and sellers. He made his way slowly, Taldrephus in tow, across the square toward the tavern.

The Bonerest Tavern was not the busiest in Ravensroost. That honor belonged to the Silver Shield, favored by more of the locals and boasting a larger common room. The Bonerest was favored by the travelers, few though they were, that visited Ravensroost, as well as the rangers and some of the more colorful sorts in town. That, certainly, was a group to which Errol belonged.

He also liked the Bonerest for another reason. It was one of the oldest structures in the town. The town scholar had even suggested it was *the* oldest, possibly having been an initial fortified keep, before the larger central keep was erected. Its foundation and the interior square tower that housed the rooms were built of the same unusual stone from which some parts of the town walls were constructed, including the wide, square structures on either side of the western gate.

They called it Waystone, though no one could ever tell him why it was so named. The material was unique, in that it resisted plant growth, could not be cut or carven, or had no signs of cracks or erosion exhibited by other stone materials.

Errol wasn't sure why he was drawn to this aspect of the place, but he could not deny it. He had spoken of this affinity with no one.

Inside, the tall, oaken beams, stout chairs and tables all gleamed in the generous amount of sunlight the tall windows afforded when unshuttered. The tavern master, Evan, enjoyed having the place well-lit and ventilated on days such as this. Come evening, he would shutter the windows and let the inevitable smoke fill the rafters, as cook fires, hearths, and pipes were lit.

Evan was at the bar, as he was usually, with the midday fare simmering in a cookpot behind him. He had his large, leather-bound accounts book out, surveying it by the light of a low-hanging lantern over the bar of dark, varnished wood.

"Don't strain your eyes, Evan," Errol quipped. "Or that which lies behind them."

Evan Devenuar looked up at the roguish figure with disapproval. "Clever. Are you sure you're not one of those quick-witted bards?"

"Ha! You haven't heard me sing," he said quickly, leaning on the bar and putting one foot on the rail. A serving woman walked by with an empty tray, having just served stew to a table of patrons. "Beshi, be a dear and fetch me a tankard. You know what I want."

Without pausing, the young woman replied, "Aye, I know what you want. But what will you have to drink?"

Errol looked at Evan with feigned astonishment, pointing at her. "She's the wit! Not I."

"Drink what you will. But keep *your* wits about you. I need these numbers resolved. I think Master Eldrim is overcharging, and my account at the Counters House seems to be off," he said, frowning. He slid the heavy book toward Errol. "Feel free to work in my study, or here."

"I'll have it resolved in no time, or at least tell you how much trouble you're in."

"Thanks. I believe you have some work waiting for you with your other two clients. They were asking after you earlier," Evan said, returning to tending the stew and pouring a tall tankard of ale.

The young woman returned with a slender glass of yellow wine.

"Your wine, good sir," she said with a smirk, curtseying in mocking fashion.

"I'll pay you properly later, my sweet Beshanu," Errol said, using her full and proper name as he winked at her.

"Promises! I prefer the silver in my palm to your silver tongue," she replied. Errol had always appreciated how quick she was with her replies, and how clever. He had always suspected she was much smarter than anyone knew.

He drew out a few silver coins and placed them on the counter. The bar was comprised of a long span of deep brown wood. Errol thought it might be hickory or something more unusual. It was marked with scratches and scrawlings from generations of patrons. A few of the scratched characters had been cut by his own blade.

Inlaid at intervals were large diamonds of an even darker, clearly more unusual wood. This wood was black as pitch. He slid the silver maples to the four corners of the inlaid diamond of black wood before him.

"Here is your silver, two for the wine and two more if you can answer me this," Errol said. Beshanu was intrigued and stepped over to play along with whatever game he had in mind. He had seen other, typically inebriated patrons, entreat Beshanu to join them only to pat her behind or take even less appropriate actions.

But no one would suspect Errol of such behavior. He was considered many things by many people in Ravensroost, but his honor was intact, and he would never allow himself to be accused of any impropriety.

"What's the question?"

"What is this wood here, that makes these inlaid diamonds of black?"

His question had caught the attention of Evan, who smiled a little.

She frowned. "I never asked anyone that question, so I have no answer."

"Then you may have the other two for the honor of educating you. It is called ebony, a remarkably dense, utterly black wood, pitch black, dark as a moonless night," he said, sliding all four silvers toward her. She scooped them up without blinking.

"Never heard of ebony," she said, winking at him as she slipped the coins into a concealed pocket. "Thanks for the lesson!"

Evan stepped over to examine his bar. He frowned. "I was told that was black oak."

Errol shook his head. "No, I'm certain that's ebony. The grain is too fine for any oak. It's used for some very exquisite carving, it is so dense. It actually sinks in water."

"Who uses it for carving?" Evan asked.

Errol regarded the innkeeper for a moment. "I think I read it somewhere?" he suggested, with a half grin.

"I've never heard of a wood called ebony, Errol. And I've known many Elven woodcrafters along the forest," he added. Evan Devenuar was of half-Elven blood himself, his mother being Elven, his father a ranger from the Kingdom. His home was originally along the southern border of Eastvale, along the long and unknowably deep Stoneroot Forest. Evan had slightly tapered ears and eyes that turned a bit upwards on the ends. His eyes were a blue not typical among Humans.

"Are you calling me a liar or just delusional?" Errol grinned back at him. He sensed someone approach from behind but was in no way alarmed.

"You're neither, Errol," came a gentle voice from over his right shoulder. He knew who it was before she had spoken.

"How do you know I'm neither, Candissa?" he asked, turning. "Frankly, I think I'm a little of one and a great deal the other."

Candissa seemed a little out of place in the Bonerest, Errol commented to himself silently. Then again, he thought she was out of place in most settings. She favored clothing that always seemed too white, and for that reason she stood out wherever she went. Aside from her garb, her appearance was always remarkable. Her beauty had grown over the past few years. During her schooling and training in the ways of the healers, she had matured and was now possessed of a beauty unrivaled in Ravensroost.

Sometimes Errol found her presence slightly unsettling, but today was not one of those times. He smiled at her radiant face framed by flowing blond hair. Her sparkling, sky blue eyes were both knowing and alluring. Her pale-rose lips had dared many men to earn the right to kiss them, yet as many men had failed.

"Because I know you well enough," she said, a small smile on those lips. "You are not suffering delusions and while you can lie if need be, you are not doing so now."

"Lady Candissa, how are you doing today?" Evan said, nodding his head. While Candissa was the daughter of the town's most successful baker, and a student of the healing arts, she had gained a stature in the border town beyond that of the minor nobility to which her family belonged. At the age of eighteen, Errol was surprised the townsfolk would address her as a lady. Anyone else in her situation would be addressed as Miss, until they were married. When Errol asked around carefully about this unusual consideration, he could never get a satisfactory answer from anyone.

"Very well, thank you, Master Evan," she said, her face almost glowing as she smiled.

"You're an exceptionally well-read student, Candissa," Errol gestured with one open hand. "Have you read of the dark hardwood called ebony?" He indicated the inlaid wood pattern.

Candissa stepped over to examine the bar. She placed one long-fingered hand on the smooth, clean surface. Errol suppressed a grin as he thought to himself, *she smells like wildflowers.* Her habit of reading and her overall intellectual acumen was well known in town. She went well beyond the requirements of her training under the healers in this. She devoured any book she could have long enough to read, and she was on an unending quest to gather more.

"I don't recall a dark wood by that name in anything I've read, no," she said, after several seconds of thought. "This is not a surprise to me."

"What is not a surprise?" Errol asked.

"Your remembering this *ebony* from your previous training or schooling. A memory from your forgotten past," Candissa said. She waited for a response.

Errol shrugged with characteristic nonchalance. "Yes, I suppose so."

"Why is it of any importance to you?" she asked him.

"It's just one of those small clues. Things I know but cannot explain. I'm hoping one day I'll find something out that could lead me further along," Errol said, drumming his nail on the ebony.

"Along the way to finding out who you are?"

Errol nodded. Sometimes Candissa made him feel uncomfortable. Her questions often cut to the root of a matter, without the courtesy of social niceties.

"Has anything else stirred your memories?" she asked.

"No, but if something does, I'll be certain to send a messenger," Errol quipped. It was one of his lightning-quick ripostes, usually reserved for more adversarial encounters. He immediately regretted his tone.

Candissa studied him with narrowing eyes. He had seen her do that quite often, as had others. Her stare caught the attention of the tavernkeep.

"You know, Deesa, he's not really the marrying sort," Evan chuckled, as he sorted pewter utensils. They both knew the comment was meant in jest. Errol suspected it was merely to ease the momentary tension.

"As my mother and father can attest, nor am I," Candissa countered. She didn't address Evan, but his chuckle died away instantly.

"Not for lack of being asked," came a plaintive remark from across the tavern. Errol looked over to see the wainwright's son, Garvin, finishing a meal. He was a solid, dependable young man, who had tried to woo the young Candissa into marriage. Their fathers were both prosperous and respected. She had rejected the notion of marrying him, along with a half-dozen other smitten young men over the past several months. As the age of seventeen was generally considered the age at which a father could marry off a daughter, the suitors had started springing up like weeds more than a year ago.

To the disappointment of Candissa's mother, those offers were already drying up, or so Errol had heard. He imagined she simply needed more time to figure things out for herself. There were plenty of girls who waited until nineteen or twenty to marry. Not many, however, if they wished to marry well.

Garvin stood, straightening his tunic, and nodded curtly to Errol and Evan. He was taller than Errol, and already gaining the girth of a man of middle years, with strong hands. His reddish beard was beginning to fill in. He looked at Candissa steadily. "Deesa, you're looking well." Errol muffled a laugh, owing to the almost stiff formality of the compliment. Candissa shot him a stern glare.

"Thank you, Garvin, and congratulations on your recent marriage. I can see you are both very happy," Candissa said, smiling in a fashion that could only be construed as genuine.

It almost seemed to put off the journeyman wainwright. He smiled briefly. "Thank ye," was all he managed in reply before heading out of the Bonerest, likely to his father's shop.

"Forgive me if my questions are intrusive, Errol," Candissa said, turning back to face him. "It's just that I feel strongly that you should take steps to try and recover your memory."

Errol didn't disagree with her, but he wasn't going to be that open. He countered, "Why?"

She drew a breath to answer at once and then stopped. She considered his question, blinking and looking down. He seemed to have caught her in a conundrum. The more he dealt with the young woman, the more he respected her.

She looked at him, drawing a little closer. Her gaze was intense and somewhat unnerving, even for Errol. For a moment, her eyes seemed not quite blue, but somehow lighter. *A trick of the light*, he thought.

"It's important to me. And I think it will be important to...well, perhaps everything," Candissa said in a hushed tone, spoken when Evan was not in earshot.

Errol had no idea what to make of that. "What do you mean, *everything*?"

"It's...not something we should discuss here, now," she said, her expression momentarily flustered. She flashed a convenient smile. "Another time, soon. We will talk of it."

Tempted though he was to press her on the curious exchange, he relented. "I'm certain you didn't come here to comment on my knowledge of exotic wood."

"No, of course. I'm here to collect Master Evan's bread order," she spoke louder now, nodding to the innkeeper.

"Oh, of course," Evan blurted, realizing he had forgotten about it. He disappeared into the kitchen, returning a moment later with a note. "Here it is, m'lady. Tell your father his black bread is the most popular, has he changed the recipe?"

"He's always nudging it this way or that. I think this month he's been using more of the Dwarven *dorchaseegle*, it's a darker form of rye they grow in the higher mountain valleys I understand," Candissa explained.

"Well, be sure to let him know we like it that way," Evan said, returning to his duties.

"I will let him know, certainly. Well, I have more errands to run. I bid you both a good day," she said, nodding to the innkeeper and Errol as she turned.

"Be sure to drop by sometime soon," Errol said as she neared the door. "And we can talk about...everything."

She didn't turn, only paused and tilted her head before exiting. Errol picked up the quill the innkeeper had provided and began reviewing the notes and numbers.

Evan returned to the bar momentarily, as Errol was scratching out some figures with the quill.

"I'm not sure if I understand that girl," he said, rubbing the vague stubble that grew but slowly on his jaw. "She likes you, but not in the marrying sense."

"She's intrigued by me," Errol said without looking up from his work. "And in all honesty, she intrigues me. Besides, I'm too old for her I think."

"Oh, I think not. How old do you think you are?" he said flippantly. Errol glanced at him with a sharp expression. "Sorry, I didn't mean to ask you that."

The innkeeper knew Errol was sensitive about his origins, as he had confided more of his thoughts to Evan than to most other folk in Ravensroost.

"Pay it no mind. It's a fair question. But I judge myself perhaps seven years her elder, maybe one less than that."

"That seems about right," Evan shrugged. "Then again, I'm not what most would call a fair judge of age, given my roots."

He was referring to being raised in a mixed Human and Elven community, himself a mixture of both bloodlines. Errol had always meant to ask Evan how long those of mixed heritage lived, but it seemed a rude question. Elves were said to live for well over three hundred years, though no Human was really sure. Given the lack of any real history in the Kingdom, it was impossible to tell. Kingdom records reached back two centuries at best. Rumors had it that some Elves living deep inside the Stoneroot were much older than recorded Human history. That nugget of lore intrigued Errol more than he would admit.

"I'm not a matchmaker, Errol. Please don't think I'm trying to-" Evan began.

Errol laughed, waving his hand a little. Clearly, the tavernmaster had mistaken his thoughtful silence for displeasure. "No, no, nothing of the sort. You're right. I'm not too old for her. But I could never think of her those terms, as a wife. Sard, I can't imagine her a wife to *anyone*!"

Evan laughed at that. "I must agree with you. She would be a formidable mate for any man."

"Still, I cannot help but think…" Errol began, his thoughts getting the better of his tongue.

The tavernmaster glanced up at him from putting away something under the counter. "What's that?"

Errol shook his head, deflecting the Evan's gaze. He had not meant to give voice to his thoughts, and he certainly did not wish to finish saying what he was now thinking.

The utterly certain realization that somehow, for reasons he could not fathom, Candissa would become one of the most important people in his life.

CHAPTER FOUR - CAM

17 Laborus, Year 197, Eastvale Calendar

Cam Bronwyer slung the pack over his shoulder, comforted by its familiar weight.

Today was a good day for hunting. The morning air was crisp and bright, and his hunting leathers felt particularly comfortable. The wood he chose to hunt today was between two tracts of farmed land, well north of Woodford. He would be surprised to hear or see anyone else this morning.

He didn't especially need to hunt, but most of the venison would go to the tavern where he would get a free meal and ale, while some would go to the butcher to turn to jerky, which he loved dearly.

Of course, the pelt was his to tan and turn to fine leather. From that, he could create any number of articles to sell. So, with any luck this morning, he would be able to add to his store of pelts and tanned leather.

The leaves were all turning magnificent colors of autumn, and his umber-colored leather jerkin and leggings blended in well. He made his way to a patch of woods where he had enjoyed success in the past. Longbow in one hand, he adjusted the straps holding his pack and quiver in place. He reveled in the solitude and gentle noises of the wilds. He had spent too much time in Woodford of late, working with his leather, tanning and dyeing. It had made him a fair amount of coin though, which allowed him some freedom.

He truly loved exploring the wilderness, seeing sights he had not before, and finding ancient trails leading to unknown destinations. While he enjoyed hunting, it was not the object of his travels. Immersing himself in the natural world, finding paths, seeking the unknown. These were his true passions.

Perhaps this was not surprising, given his heritage and upbringing. Like his mother and father before him, he was half-Elven. The Elves were a mysterious race, at least to the Humans. His inclinations may have derived from the innate mystery of this race. Though to look at him, Cam knew he was not immediately identifiable as being half Elven. He had coarse brown hair that covered the slightly pointed tips of his ears, and he sported a short but thick beard, something few Elves in his experience could grow. His mother had told him once, when he was very young, that her father was a thick-bearded man, and he probably inherited the trait from him.

Settling onto his favorite perch, an immense stump surrounded by several saplings providing excellent cover, Cam got comfortable and had a sip of water from his skin. He strung his bow, readied his arrows, and situated the first arrow so that it could be nocked easily.

Letting the arrow rest on his hand, he recalled his father's instructions for the bow. Cam remembered forays into the woods with his father, often to hunt game when Cam was old enough, but more often just to teach.

As the sun rose higher over the wooded meadows, he let himself be surrounded by the hum of insects, the call of birds and the quiet passage of wind through the golden and red leaves of the oak, maple, and hawthorn trees. These times let him recall more clearly those lessons his father taught, how to read signs in the woods and meadows, how to track, how to cover your own tracks and conceal yourself. How to listen, to watch, to smell, to sense all the things the natural world offered.

His father had taught him many skills that served him in the woods and hills, as well as skills focusing on other areas. It seemed his younger years with his mother and father were an endless course of instruction, all of which he absorbed greedily, his thirst for knowledge and lore never slaked. The tranquility of the wilderness also helped instill a serenity within Cam, something he often needed. For his years with his mother and father ended far too soon and far too abruptly.

It often kept him awake at night, wondering why they had to leave.

A crack interrupted his reverie. Motionless, he studied the surrounding thicket. After three long breaths, he saw a shadow move. A buck was advancing slowly through the tall grass, not twenty yards away. Cam was safely downwind, and the buck showed no sign of detecting his presence.

He sighted a gap through which his quarry would pass momentarily. He slowly eased the bow up, arrow in place, and began to draw back. All was as it should be. The buck moved into his line of sight. He tensed and relaxed, as his father had taught him, bearing all his focus on the quarry. In the back of his mind, something struck him as odd about the buck, but he brushed it aside as a trick of the light.

He released. Something alerted the buck, perhaps his arm brushing against a branch. The shot found its mark, but it was not a clean hit. The arrow struck but the buck burst from the thicket and vaulted off into the woods.

Cam sprang from his perch. One thing his father taught him was not to let an animal suffer needlessly. If it was an especially bad hit, the deer could linger in pain for days. Quickly reaching the spot he had struck the deer, Cam saw spots of blood.

Good, easier to track, he thought. He was off, running, no longer in need of stealth. His quarry had a good lead and Cam was concerned he could lose the trail. But the creature slowed in its flight, and the spots of blood grew more frequent. He tracked the buck for more than an hour, as he wended his way northward through the thickening woods and rising hills.

Cam knew he would have to exercise caution. The woods grew more perilous as one moved further north. The Shadowfall Mountains were home to clans of wildmen, and a few Dwarves. They were also home to more monstrous creatures, including the Chom, a few Ur'chom, dire wolves, and even giants. These more dangerous types had been driven far from the safe and settled valleys of the Kingdom of Eastvale many generations ago, but it was not unheard of that a few might venture down the mountain valleys and slip past the camps of the clansmen.

By the time the sun had reached its zenith, he had closed in on his wounded prey. The trail had become easier to follow as the wounded creature slowed. The stag had chosen to seek shelter along the rocky base of a rising hillside. Cam knew there were some overhangs here that wildlife sometimes sheltered under.

He spotted the stag standing unsteadily near a rising wall of rock covered in vines, his eyes wide with pain and fear. Cam was keen to end the hunt, as the creature had suffered so much. He moved in through the underbrush, arrow nocked and ready to grant a quick and merciful end. To his surprise, the creature used the last of his energy and darted, seemingly impossibly, into the wall of tumbled rock.

Approaching warily, Cam saw the vines obscured a gap in the stone surface. Nearing it, the opening into the rock face was clear. Hearing nothing untoward, he brushed the vines aside and slipped into the shadowy gap.

It was an entrance into a cavern beneath the rocky hillside. The deer had not gone far. It lay on its side, a few paces inside the vine-choked entrance, breathing his last ragged breaths. Before Cam could draw his knife to end its suffering, it released a final, wheezing exhalation. It was dead. Cam drew out the arrow and cleaned it off, silently cursing his poor marksmanship.

Laying a hand on the flank of the fallen creature, he murmured a simple Elven phrase particular to this situation. "Enu beluthae khami'eu." *I am sorry for the pain I have inflicted.*

Inspecting his fresh kill, Cam realized what it was that had bothered him when he had first sighted it. The buck's rack, which was an impressive ten points, was not typical. Instead of being one of the usual light brown or woodish colors he had seen all his life, these antlers started brown but then ranged to a deep blue. At the tips, the antlers were almost blue as the sky. He would have to ask Gondrim about that.

Looking up and around, he inspected the narrow passage into the hill. His first impression was that it was a shallow alcove. Now that his eyes had adjusted to the darkness, he saw it stretched further back. He could not see how far by the dim light filtering through the vines.

Putting his bow and quiver down next to the carcass, Cam unslung his pack. Unfastening a pocket, he drew out his firestarter and a torcstick. The stick was especially made for illuminating dark chambers, consisting of a core of hardwood around which were twisted tight strands of fibrous material soaked with oils and some sort of alchemical mixture. It allowed the torcstick to burn slow and bright.

The firestarter took only two flicks before it lit the torcstick. Cam fastened his heavy pack onto his back again and proceeded deeper into the shadowy passage.

The light allowed him to examine the passage more closely. He saw evidence it was not entirely a natural crevasse but bore signs of walls being chopped out of the rock. It stretched several paces into the hillside before ending in a chamber, perhaps thirty feet around. The chamber was clearly man-made, being far smoother than the passage and almost perfectly circular. Some cracks could be seen in the domed ceiling, with evidence of seeping water and tree roots. The stone was lighter in color than the native rock. Cam didn't know if this was just the nature of the stone, or some form of masonry. Regardless, the torcstick provided excellent light owing to the stone.

The floor bore signs of previous animal habitation but was bare otherwise. What drew his attention was that which dominated the center of the chamber's floor. Bringing the torcstick closer, he crouched to examine it. He scratched his short beard.

Perhaps ten feet across, a perfectly circular stone disc rose from the center of the chamber, standing just a few inches off the floor. The disc was of an unfamiliar stone, reddish in hue, looking something like sandstone. Cam had never seen anything like it. He had seen ritual circles before, made by the shamans of the clans, or by druids. But this was devoid of any markings, symbols or remnants that would indicate a ritual or ceremonial use.

He touched it cautiously, finding the surface flat and even, if slightly rough. Standing, he stepped onto the circle and walked across it. Aside from a few bits of debris and dust, it was unremarkable.

No clues could be gathered regarding its nature or purpose. He spent a minute more looking for something along the edge, hoping to find tiny runes perhaps. He found nothing more. Shrugging, he left the chamber and returned to the slain stag and his bow.

Dousing the torcstick and replacing it once it cooled, Cam muscled the heavy carcass onto his back and hauled it out of the hidden cavern. He noted the hillside and other markers, in case he ever needed to find the place again.

A hundred yards south, he had seen a clearing with a large tree. He slung rope over a stout branch and strung the carcass up. He had dressed plenty of larger animals in his day and, being a skilled tanner and leather crafter, he knew how to expertly divest a carcass of its hide. For the sake of an easier walk home, he chose to dress it now.

As he started his long trek back to Woodford, he was glad for the cooler day. It was not a light load, but Cam was stronger than most men his age, whether Human or Elven. He had trained with broadsword and shield, as any good youth would in case the militia was called up. He had also worked with one of the smiths in town for a time, hammering and hauling coal, wood and metals. His stature was remarkable, given his Elven blood. The Elves were known to be a tall folk, but slender of limb, graceful and lithe. No one would think he had any Elven blood if they saw him from a distance, until they were close enough to see his slightly upturned and tapered ears and eyes that were perhaps just a little larger than most Humans.

His work under Gondrim the Dwarve, learning the trade and craft of tanning and leather working as his apprentice, was not always easy work, and that too helped keep him in good condition. Gondrim was an old Dwarve, so Cam did all the heavy work their business required.

Cam was proud when he graduated from apprentice to journeyman. This allowed him to purchase and operate his own shop in Woodford, while still under the authority of Gondrim. As a master leather crafter, Gondrim was a ranking member of the Guild. Cam imagined he too would one day ascend to the rank of master, but that would be years away,

Cam only wished his father could be there that day, whenever it may come, when he did finally earn the rank of Master. While he was now apprenticed under Gondrim, it was his father who had taught him all the basics of leather craft. For his father had been a master leatherworker himself, better than the Dwarve by a good measure, according to Gondrim.

He was back in Woodford soon enough, with plenty of daylight left. He and Gondrim operated the tannery at the edge of the town, a long and well-built beamhouse, well away from any homes and downwind as well. While he had grown accustomed to the odors of the tanning facility, it was still a shock to his nostrils every time he came in from the outside. It was here that Cam took the time to carefully remove the hide from the carcass. Afterwards, he salted the lengths of hide and placed them in curing drawers to prepare them for the next step in tanning.

Heading out again to the hanging carcass, he was greeted by two monstrous mastiffs, standing attentively a few paces from the dressed remains of the stag. Cam smiled.

"Wallach, Bearbane," he greeted them both. Laying out a length of linen he had obtained inside, he set to trimming off the pieces of the carcass the butcher had no interest in. This included the lower portions of the legs, and most of the neck and head, plus a few other bits.

Cam let these portions fall beneath the carcass, all the while the two guardians sat licking their chops. The head he left hanging high, out of reach. The blue antlers were certainly worth preserving, as he would be making inquiries about the strange color. Perhaps it was a variety of deer with which he was not familiar.

The dressed carcass ready for the butcher's shop, Cam placed it on the rough linen and wrapped it with line, for easy hauling back to town. Hefting the much lighter quarry over one shoulder, he looked at the two dogs Gondrim had raised from pups, and then to the sloppy pile of sumptuous deer remains.

"Have at it!" he said loudly, waving an arm sharply. The barking, snarling, chomping and tearing that ensued as the massive dogs tore into the remains could be heard all the way to the eastern wall of Woodford. Being a well-known citizen of Woodford, Cam just nodded to the guards as he strolled through the impressive eastern gatehouse.

Woodford was the capital of the barony of the same name. Both were named for the first Baron of Woodford, Jantrick, who died more than a century ago. It boasted remarkable walls, most of the enclosure measuring fully twenty feet tall and half as thick. As Cam understood the history of the city, it was a western bastion against the threats of the wild clansmen and the monstrous ogres and their kin, the Ur'chom and lesser Chom, more than a century ago. It was the largest fortified town, or city depending on who one spoke to on this matter, in the western region of the Kingdom. The only other town of any appreciable size was Ravensroost, which lay several days ride to the west.

Making his way to the market district with the carcass, Cam found the butcher Glegnar arguing with his friend the miller, named - for better or worse - Miller. They found reasons to argue about anything and everything, even the color of clouds.

Glegnar broke from his red-faced tirade upon seeing Cam enter his shop. "Cam, m'boy! Ya got a nice deer for me?"

"Yes, I do. Could you make sure to get some of the back to Chander for jerky? You can put this on my account, we'll settle up later," Cam said.

"What a good lad!" Glegnar said, hoisting the carcass with one immense arm. He looked at Miller. "Isn't he a good lad, Miller? Wouldn't you say he's a good lad?"

Miller looked at the butcher with a shrewd expression, one eyebrow raised. "I suppose I can't argue that point wit ye."

"You suppose?" Glegnar said, wide-eyed.

"The lad chased after m'gurl Dallia when they was both too young!" the miller exclaimed. "So don't be sayin he's all swathed in white robes!"

This, of course, led onto a fresh round of acrimonious bellowing between the two friends. Cam just sighed and left the shop to the sound of their bickering and Glegnar's cleaver chopping away at the carcass.

He was back at Gondrim's shop in short order, navigating the bustling streets of Woodford easily. It was later in the afternoon, with the low sun casting long shadows along the cobbled streets. Plumes of smoke were rising all over town now, as the temperature dropped, and evening approached.

The shop was one of the older structures along the broad avenue called Crafthome. It was paved, as were most roads in Woodford, and well-maintained. Gondrim's home, and attached workshop, were built from thick, dark oak beams, cut by hand more than a hundred years past, held together by unmatched Dwarven skill and - according to Gondrim - a wee bit of Elven magic. The shingles were broad planks of yew and maple, lacquered and colored, and faded a little by the passing of time. Everything about the place was solid, somehow permanent, as though the place was grown from the ground.

Cam found the old Dwarve relaxing in his great-chair by the fireplace. The late sun was still streaming into the room through two tall, glazed windows. The beams of yellow cut through the gentle billows of his pipe smoke, stirred by Cam's entrance into the sitting room.

Gondrim was a typical Dwarve, standing just under Cam's shoulder in height, with limbs heavier and a girth far greater than most Humans. He was old. His face was deeply grooved and lined, his beard and moustache more white than steely-gray. His eyes, light gray like many of his clan, were still sharp. Dressed in his leather and canvas day clothes, bearing numerous buckles and pockets, Gondrim reclined comfortably, reading a heavy book he had propped on a pillow.

"Hullo, Cam," he mumbled, not taking his eyes from the tome. "How was the hunt?"

"Good, I brought in a younger buck, good hide and meat though. I set the skin to curing," Cam reported. "I'm finishing up a saddle today. Is there anything else you need me to work on?"

The old Dwarve let the book relax in his gnarled hand. "Hmmm...no, I think not. Attend to yer customers, we're good today," he said, his voice a sonorous grumble. He lifted the book again to continue his reading.

Cam paused, thinking on the notable events of the morning. "Sir, I found something strange today, on the hunt."

"Did ye? Tell me." It was a common response from the Dwarve that Cam had heard for many years, typically when he was younger, with something exciting and new to share.

"The deer led me into a hillside cave, I had never known it was there. It's on the south face of the hill up at the head of the low ravine off the Gutterwash, you know?" Cam said, using the local points the Dwarve would recognize.

Gondrim put the book down again. "Aye, I know the hill. A cave ye say? Good shelter?"

"Yes, actually. A fine refuge. But that wasn't the odd thing. It was what was *in* the cave that was odd. Well, there's two odd things, really," Cam said, his story wandering.

The old Dwarve reached toward the fire and drew out a smoking taper, relighting the ember in his pipe and puffing out a few thick clouds of smoke. "Take yer time, Cam. What did ye find in the cave?"

"Well, the cave wasn't deep, but it led to a strange chamber, shaped like a dome. It was clearly made by someone, probably long ago," he said, growing excited in his recounting.

"Hmm, the land has old, forgotten places like that in plenty," the Dwarve said, nodding. "Go on."

"In the middle of this room was…a platform, I guess you'd call it. It's round, and just a hand high maybe, but made of some strange red stone, stone I've never seen before."

The Dwarve drew another puff from his pipe, nodding. "Alright, sounds unusual enough, aye."

"Have you ever heard of such a thing? I can't guess what it may have been used for."

Gondrim shook his head. "Can't say I have, lad," he replied. "What's the other *odd* thing?"

"Right. Ah, the deer. I left its head outside the beamhouse. It is very strange," Cam said.

Gondrim seemed to sit up at this, turning to face the young man. "What d'ye mean, strange?" he said, concern clear in his voice. His gray, stony eyes were unblinking.

Cam was mildly taken aback at the Dwarve's reaction. "Ah, the rack. The deer's antlers are blue. Have you ever heard of deer with blue antlers?"

The Dwarve's wizened eyes bore into Cam with an intensity he had rarely seen before. He stared for several beats of Cam's heart, before suddenly swinging his stout legs off the cushioned stool and onto the wooden floor of his sitting room. His thick leather boots thumped soundly as he did so. He closed the book, placing it on a table and plugged his pipe with a bit of wadding.

"Aye, lad, once before," was all he said, before he was suddenly about his shop, buckling his vest, fetching a few things from his nearby desk and grabbing his overcoat.

"What...what's the matter? What are you doing?" Cam asked his master.

"Where's Ulgred? D'ye know?" Gondrim asked Cam.

"Likely home now, his studies are done by this hour, and we don't need him until tomorrow," Cam said. The Dwarve was referring to his other assistant, a young boy who would apprentice under Gondrim one day. "Why?"

"Fetch him for me, would ye? And bring his father along, too. I need to talk to them."

"Very well, sir. Anything else I can do? Are you going to tell me what this is about?"

"Yes, Cam, I will, tonight. But for now, get the boy and then put together anything you'd need for a long trip," the Dwarve said in a low voice.

"But -" he began in reply. He was cut off.

"Do it now, Cam. I insist. Fetch the boy and his pa, then go to your shop and put together whatever you want for a trip by horseback. And you may not be back for a long time."

"Wait, you're not going with me?"

"No! I'll go along 'til we're out of town, but I'm not to go wi' ye all the way. Now move along!"

Cam was bursting with questions and he was beginning to feel a little indignant. He knew he had to trust in his master's intuition and counsel. He simply nodded firmly and headed out the door, leaving the Dwarve to his own hurried tasks, whatever they were.

He quite surprised the young boy, Ulgred, at his family's flat over a potter's shop. They were as surprised as Cam was. But if the Master crafter, to whom their twelve-year old son was apprenticed, wanted him at his shop, they wouldn't question him. They assured Cam they would be there promptly, as soon as they finished their supper and dressed appropriately.

Cam headed over to his shop and residence, not a block from Gondrim's shop. He felt he had only just settled into the place. He found a canvas saddlebag that would suffice, and he began packing clothing and personal items needed for the extended journey.

Half-way through his packing, he stopped, staring at his belongings. To no one, he shouted, "But *why?*"

Despite his exasperation, he pressed on, implicitly trusting Gondrim. It was the old Dwarve who had brought him here, at the express wish of his parents. His mother and father had trusted Gondrim with their only son, so

Cam would have to extend that same trust now. The large canvas bag contained his better clothing, a few personal items, his tradecraft tools, and a bedroll. He would take his rucksack, of course, but it would not be in the canvas bag.

His pack was the only thing that remained from his young life with his parents, before Gondrim brought him to Woodford. He treasured it, and it never was out of his reach. He took it with him when he was working, hunting or in town.

His father, being a master leatherworker, had made it before he was born. It was given to him not long before he had to leave his home. It was a masterwork piece, made of leather that Cam did not recognize and stitched and seamed using techniques he had yet to master. It typically contained an assortment of useful tools, supplies and miscellany, and sometimes things Cam had forgotten he had packed away long ago in one of the numerous pockets or compartments.

Gondrim often chuckled at how Cam could produce just the right blade, bit of string, or utensil for whatever situation he was in. It was the only thing that Cam would need when traveling, in his opinion, but he nonetheless packed the larger bag at the old Dwarve's urging. Perhaps they were moving to another town, but that made little sense. In any case, he would need the larger sack for clothing and blankets.

This turn of events reminded him of the day his life turned upside-down, when Gondrim brought him to Woodford. He felt much the same way as that day – the frustration at not knowing why things were happening, feeling forced to leave when he had no wish to. The Dwarve had never done wrong by him before, so Cam had no reason to think otherwise now.

With his pack firmly strapped over both shoulders, his bow across his back, his broadsword at his belt and the large canvas bag over one shoulder, Cam made his way back to Gondrim's place. It was nearly twilight, and the markets were emptying. He had to dodge quite a few carts and wagons on his short trek.

Arriving back at the Dwarve's establishment, he saw young Ulgred and his pa heading back down the narrow street, having just left from their meeting with the Dwarve. Inside, Gondrim was relieved to see Cam.

"I was wonderin' what might ha kept ya," he said. "I just told Ulgred and his father that his boy would be taking over as my apprentice. Don't worry about your obligations, I'll make sure any contracts you have outstanding are completed."

"You still haven't told me why!" Cam said, frustration evident in his voice as he dropped the large bag, throwing his bow on top of it.

"I will...just as soon as we're on the road. Give me just a little while to get some things together, and we'll take my cart."

"You said something about horseback?" Cam pointed out.

"Aye, but I'll hitch up my old Barri and your horse, and when we reach Handerby, you'll continue on horseback from there," Gondrim explained. He saw more questions arising in Cam's expression but only put up one broad hand. "Save the questions, boy."

He darted back into his private chambers and returned a moment later, holding a slender tube of pewter.

"This is for you to read," he said, handing Cam the container. "There's a scroll in this. You just need to break the seal."

"I don't understand, where did you get this?"

"It...it was given to me with instructions to give it to you, on…*this day*. The damn blue antlers...I'll tell you more soon," he said, sounding uncertain of the account even as he offered it. Then he was away in his chambers, packing his own things. What the Dwarve said sounded more than improbable, if not ludicrous.

Cam looked at the cylinder of polished metal. He sat down at a table and twisted the end firmly, breaking the wax-bound paper seal stretched across the cap. Tipping it, a small, tightly-wound parchment roll popped out into his hand. It too had a wax seal on it, green with a tiny shape pressed into it. Turning it in the fading sunlight, he saw it was an oak leaf.

"Gondrim, who gave this to you?" Cam asked aloud.

The Dwarve appeared in the doorway, a half-filled pack in one hand. When he spoke, it was almost with reluctance. "It was...given me by Adreassa, the druid. Do ye remember her?"

Cam was about to say that he did not, but the words died on his lips. A sudden remembrance seized his mind. It was as though a hundred fragments of memories came flooding back into his head.

Adreassa, why do you have to go with my mother and father? Can't you stay here with me and Gondrim? He remembered asking her this, that evening he had to leave his home. Tears were running down his cheeks as he slung the heavy rucksack his father had given him, over his narrow shoulders. It was so much larger then.

Cam closed his eyes, remembering.

"No, Cam, I must see to the safety of your parents. We will see each other again someday," the tall, elegant druid said, tousling his hair. "The Dwarve will take you to Woodford. He will take care of you."

She was as tall as his father. Her narrow face was beautiful, slender, with arching eyebrows, and long, deep brown hair. Her skin was bronze, and her eyes were a pale green. She always wore robes of green and brown. It was made of some finely embroidered linen with a lightweight leather sewn in at the collar, cuffs and hem. Sometimes it appeared light in tone, when it was in full sun. But in the shadowy depths of the woods, it blended in with the deep browns and grays.

He remembered her ears now. They were upswept, tapering gently...he blinked.

"She was an Elf..." he whispered. "I'd forgotten that."

"Aye, she was," Gondrim nodded. "A moment more Cam, then we're off."

He remembered her parting words to him. She had knelt down before the trembling boy and embraced him.

"You will be a bold hunter one day and a master crafter of leather, just like your father. Keep this pack your father made by you always. Remember this. One day, before you know it, you'll have to leave Woodford. Gondrim will know when. But remember that day, for you will find something, something hidden away that you won't understand, but that will be very important," she told him. He recalled the words but also recalled that he did not understand any of it. He only understood he was leaving his home and parents and that made him sad.

"Now take a deep breath, still yourself. You'll have to grow up a little faster now, Cam. Your mother and father must go, so that you will be safe. Always remember that," she said, placing a hand on his cheek.

He cleared his throat, wiping one eye. "I will, Adreassa. I'll be strong."

She smiled at that. "That's my Cam. Now, I need you to close your eyes. I'm going to help you through this by letting you forget some of it, all right? You'll go with Gondrim and you won't have to worry about all this."

"Will I forget my parents?" the young Cam had said.

"No, no. But this will make it easier for you. You will forget some of what we talked about, some of what you've learned, and perhaps me," she said, grinning. "But you'll remember again one day, I promise."

He remembered only glimpses of more conversation with her, before she placed both hands on his head. After that, he could remember nothing.

"Cam, you all right?" Gondrim was there again, a pack over his shoulder.

"Yes...I'm fine, just...remembering her now," he said. The Dwarve nodded, understanding his expression. He looked at the still-sealed scroll.

"Did you want to read that now?" he asked. "I want to head out before full dark. We'll be stopping at Handerby for the night."

Gondrim referred to a small but prosperous village on the road to Ravensroost, that lay perhaps two hours by wagon. "I'll read it there," Cam replied. He slung his pack around, found a suitable pocket and tucked the tube away.

"All right then, I already sent for the wagon with both horses. They should be here soon," he said. "If anyone asks, we're heading west on business, that's all."

Cam nodded and re-fastened his pack by both straps and his belt strap. The wagon arrived momentarily, heralded by the uneven clops of the two horses. Gondrim's horse was a light-colored roan named Barri, bred for pulling a cart. Cam's horse, a dark chestnut, was not. Darbo was far too restless to tolerate being bound to a wagon for too long. Once the bags were loaded in the back, along with a bundle of leather goods, they were off.

The trip out of Woodford was uneventful, and they spoke little as Gondrim drove the wagon though the tall western gate, not long before it would be closed for the night. Cam noticed he was pushing the horses faster than he would normally, with Darbo pulling harder than Gondrim's horse. The sun was a great orange orb nestled into the autumn forest by the time they saw the rising plumes of smoke from the village of Handerby.

They found rooms at a small inn called the Hangman. Cam thought it a strange name for a place to sleep. Their cart and horses were safely attended to and Gondrim took care of their charges. After a filling meal of ham and potatoes, he treated them both to a cool mug of ale. Returning to their rooms, Gondrim spoke quietly to Cam, ensuring no one was in the narrow corridor outside.

"Cam, why don't you read that scroll now. It should answer a lot of questions you have, and I'll try to answer any it cannot," the old Dwarve said. "I am truly sorry for uprooting you like this. Again. You must think me a terrible fellow for it."

"I don't think anything of the sort, Gondrim, you must know that," Cam assured him. "I'll read it and maybe in the morning I'll have a question."

Gondrim nodded and closed the door as he left Cam to read the scroll. A taper was already lit in the room, but Cam lit another. He sat on the narrow bed, and hefted his weighty pack onto the pillow, to retrieve the scroll tube.

In a flash, he recalled another memory, from his last minutes of his conversation with Adreassa. *Someday, I will send you a message. It will be written on a small piece of paper I put in the hidden pocket. Check the paper now and then. You will find a message from me. It will be the first of many*, she had said.

Cam quickly opened the pack and inspected it.

She had shown him the pocket, so many years ago. It was well-concealed, the lip of it hiding beneath a heavy line of stitching inside the main compartment of the pack. He had to run his thumbnail along the tiny seam. Cam thought it almost bizarre he hadn't found it in all these years. He supposed when she had somehow caused him to forget what she had told him that night, he also forgot about the hidden pocket.

Carefully running his thumbnail along the edge to break the seal of the long-unused pocket, he slipped his fingers in and found the piece of paper. His heart almost stopped. Retrieving it delicately, he held his breath as he turned it over. He was disappointed to find it blank on both sides. He remembered she didn't say when she may leave a message, so clearly it was not yet. He replaced it.

Pulling out the scroll tube, he popped it open and retrieved the sealed parchment. The wax seal cracked easily, and he carefully unrolled the tightly wound parchment. Sitting close to the rickety table bearing the two lit tapers, he began reading. The characters were fine and small but perfectly legible. The writing was classic Elven script, penned in a deep green ink.

Dear Cam,

Now that you are reading this, something has happened. I suppose our friend Gondrim has made it clear that you must leave Woodford, heading you know not where. Do not judge him ill, for I asked him to do this, as I knew this day would come.

You pursued a deer today, one with antlers of the color of sky. I foresaw this day in a vision. I told Gondrim to take certain steps when you told him of this. You found the cavern, with the red stone disc. Remember well that disc, for you shall find others like it, and this is important. I cannot tell you all right now, for I know not all of what you must know. But I have seen events yet to take place, and some of these events involve you. Please believe me, it is vitally important you keep traveling down the road that Gondrim has set you upon.

He will turn back soon, but you must keep forging ahead. Do you recall the slip of paper in your pack? Check the pocket and you will find it. I will leave you messages on that slip of paper. And you will be able to write messages back to me. Always keep a piece in that pocket, even if it is not the one you find there today.

One day, if disaster does not visit you or I, we will meet again, and I will tell you more about your parents and their fate. Know that they love you dearly, as does Gondrim. As do I.

Seek to learn, to follow clues, and keep yourself safe in your travels. When I know more, I will write.

Blessing to thee,

Adreassa.

Cam fought back tears. It was more than he could have hoped for, at least for now.

He put out one taper, and undressed, preparing for sleep. He was exhausted from the days' events and revelations. He couldn't stop thinking of what she had said in the scroll. *They love you*, not *loved*. He felt hope at that phrasing, and he did not think it accidental.

He poured water from a pitcher in the provided basin and washed his hands and face. He relieved his bladder in the common water closet in the corridor. The inn was quiet, save for the sonorous snoring emanating from Gondrim's room.

Returning to his bed, he was about to put out the second taper when he started. He thought for a moment someone had said something, perhaps his name, but he had heard nothing. It was more an awareness. He looked at his pack.

Opening it, he reached into that hidden pocket and drew out the parchment. He nearly gasped when he saw writing on it. It was Elven script, written in the same green ink.

Destiny has awoken, Cam. It calls you. Your journey will take you many places. But you must remember this - Destiny will call you into the hills and beyond the hills, to the West - Adreassa.

He ran a thumb over her name. The tail end of the last character smudged.

The ink was still wet.

CHAPTER FIVE - KORAYMIS

17 Laborus, Year 197, Eastvale Calendar

Koraymis examined all the items he had laid out on his bed. He corrected himself mentally, *the* bed, not *my* bed. His black leather satchel was large enough for it all, but he wanted to make sure he had everything he needed for the journey to Ravensroost. While the journey would take a week by carriage, to reach the border town, he would not be returning to Woodford. His belongings were minimal. The hardest part of his preparations were his books. He had spent a great deal of time condensing his collection of printbooks down to only those he would be taking, as he started this new chapter in his life.

Tebbrick and Nylora had been generous in providing him with the coin necessary to purchase other necessities - a new pair of sturdy walking boots, a few traveling items, and a voucher for the carriage. He had overheard them a week before, discussing the boy they would be taking in to replace him. That was expected. The city was generous to those households who brought up children off the street.

Koraymis had passed his final examinations at the scholia with exceptional marks. He was a bit young to have done so well, but there was no rule against a youth passing through with high marks. Those same high marks, along with his work at the library, led to a letter of recommendation to a scholar in the border town.

He would be working with a local scholar in cataloging and maintaining the local library. Koraymis had learned all he could from his work at the Woodford library and had earned a small pile of coin from it, as well. He didn't know if he would be needing much gold where he was going, as room and board were always part of such an apprenticeship. Regardless, it would be useful. At least in the short term.

The thought of enrolling formally in the scholia as an apprentice Scholar had crossed his mind more than once. It would be the next logical step in his career as a young man of letters. The scholia was a far more challenging - and rewarding - institution of learning. But it was not meant for him. Such a course would take him eastward, ultimately, to Eastvale.

He felt the need to move, a compulsion he could not deny. But why west? As a scholar, he should be following a path toward the largest city in the Kingdom. It was there he would find all the known records and writings on any subject he cared to study, as well as the society that appreciates the learned. But no.

Koraymis was not sure why he was attracted to the prospect of going to Ravensroost, but he did not wish to go where there were certainly *more* people. So west it was.

He picked up a small hand mirror he would be packing. The mirror was silvered on the one side, and otherwise unremarkable. He regarded the face reflected in the small, polished surface. He remembered his tutor's words, some of the first he had spoken to Koraymis, when he was still a young boy.

I give you this mask, that you may live among and move about the Humans. But know, you are more than just a Human...

At that moment, so long ago, Telmik's face was burned into Koraymis' memory. Beyond those words, it was difficult for him to recall much else of their initial meeting. He could, he knew, but preferred not to. Still, Telmik had saved his life, without a doubt.

Looking closely at the mirror in his hand, Koraymis could see a subtle glint of blue and purple along the polished metal edges of the frame and handle. For the longest time, he thought that blue-purple glint he could see was a trick of the light, perhaps the color of the metal. Only after Telmik told him he could see the magic in things did he realize the mirror has some magical quality.

He slowly turned it over and stared at the smooth metal surface of the back of the mirror. It took a moment, but the lusterless dark metallic surface changed, becoming as silvered and clear as a noblewoman's looking glass.

He frowned a little as he regarded the visage reflected on this side of the mirror. One coppery-red hand, with black claws in place of nails, moved up to touch the deep red, bony growth protruding from the temple.

"Koraymis! Are you up there, dear?" the mildly shrill voice of Nylora sounded from the stairwell. He quickly packed the mirror.

"Yes, ma'am, I'm here," he answered dutifully. He had been trying to improve things between himself and his fosters, having no wish to depart their house on a sour note.

"I have some food for your journey, don't forget," she called.

"Thank you, I'll be down soon!"

They weren't sad to see him go, he was certain of that. Perhaps Nylora was feeling a little remorse that they had never truly connected with him. He had never made a concerted effort to do the same, so it was not surprising – or upsetting.

He quickly finished stowing all the items for the road. The carriage was leaving in less than two hours and he had to get over to the library.

Downstairs, he was relieved to find it was just Nylora. Tebbrick and his sons were busy at work, thankfully. He didn't know how his house-brothers would treat him if they knew it was their last opportunity.

"Be sure to stay in the carriage, Koraymis, or wherever you stop. There could be brigands or ogres or who knows what in the wood between here and Ravensroost," Nylora said, sounding genuinely concerned. That both surprised and amused Koraymis.

"I think I'll be fine," he said, seeing a few bundles of food neatly wrapped in canvas and bound with twine. "Thank you for the food."

"It's not much, some cheese, bread, meat, a little dried fruit," she said. She seemed to want to say something more, perhaps more meaningful. He thought he could see tears threatening to form in her eyes. "Take care of yourself, Koraymis. And be sure to visit if you're ever in Woodford again, all right?"

"Yes, I will," Koraymis said, more as a courtesy. He couldn't imagine what circumstances would compel him to visit this house, given the mildly malevolent treatment he'd received at her son's hands and those of the other boys. They weren't exactly cruel, but they did nothing to engender friendship. He tucked the rations away in his robe pockets.

"All right, I'll say your farewells to the boys when they're home," she said. She nodded quickly, seeming to want to extract herself from the situation. He was fine with that.

He departed, happy to do so, but feeling a little trepidation as he took his first steps onto the streets of Woodford, truly on his own now. He pulled the hood of his traveling cloak over his head against the light mist that was falling. He was in the library within a few short minutes.

Koraymis first made his way to the Head Librarian's wing. Master Tentrovis was predictably occupied with sorting out a number of unwieldy tomes on the long oak table. He was quietly arguing with Philena, the ranking woman on the library's staff. It seemed to be a discussion about how to categorize one of the tomes.

Upon seeing Koraymis, he held an imperious hand up to Philena's face, evoking a scowl from the woman. "Koraymis, good to see you, join me in my study," he said. After a few sharp words with his peer, he led the young man to the dusty, high-ceilinged chamber. All four walls were shelves of books, printbooks and scrolls. It almost made Koraymis envious, to see such accumulated knowledge.

"Sit, please," he motioned to a chair. The stout archivist seemed in a good mood. "I must say, I am not pleased you are leaving. I do not wish to say farewell to such a rising scholar as yourself! But I am glad to see you are making your way out into the wider world."

"You are very kind, sir," Koraymis replied. "I have enjoyed my work here a great deal."

"Of course," he rummaged around on his desk, a miscellany of scattered curios, paper, ink, quills, lenses, tapers and other oddments Koraymis could not identify. "Ah here. I wanted you to have these."

He handed Koraymis a weighty pouch of velvet. Pulling the drawstring loose, he saw several gold oaks within.

"Sir, I think you're too generous-"

The librarian cut him off. "Now, I know it will be challenging to start your life abroad, I insist on this small gift. Please accept it. But there's more there, look."

Moving the coins aside, he found a small silver badge, with a pin on it. It was a circle, with a depiction of a scroll and quill crossed over it. Koraymis knew what it was. For the first time in a long time, he felt genuinely touched. Given Koraymis' nature, he was immediately suspect of the older man. He pushed his instincts aside, knowing they were entirely misplaced.

"I know you haven't *formally* pursued the scholarly path, but I am well aware of your capabilities and your remarkable acumen," he explained. "I spoke to other scholars regarding this and, based on your accomplishments, it is more than merited."

The young man turned the small pin over in his fingers. He knew how significant this was. It indicated that he had reached the lower rank of scholarly achievement, commonly called a Master of Quills. It meant he had credibility within the learned circles of the Kingdom and could legally pursue a career as a teacher or a scholar to a lower house.

"Be sure to wear that in town. You'll be accorded the respect due you, I'm sure," Tentrovis said. "You have that letter of recommendation to present to the librarian Efflewhist, yes?"

Tentrovis referred to a small scroll he had given Koraymis a week ago. It was tucked securely in a vest pocket. Koraymis nodded, patting the pocket.

"Good! He's rather on in years, and I suspect he's weary of his role. I'm very excited that you're so bold as to head to Ravensroost, Koraymis. Not many young scholars would be so courageous. It is on the frontier of the Kingdom after all. Do be mindful."

"I will, sir, and I will write you when I can and let you know how my studies are going," he said. That appeared to please the librarian.

"Very well, off with you then," he said as he smiled warmly and patted Koraymis on the shoulder. He saw the young scholar to his study door before returning to his argument with Philena. Koraymis kept the gift in his palm, intent on showing it to his master, and headed for the back stairwell.

He was soon upstairs. It was always quiet up here, as very few people ever used these chambers. Entering the archives room, he saw the long, dim hall in which he had studied under Master Telmik for the past five years wasn't as he remembered it just a few days ago.

The long tables were moved off to one side, the windows thrown open. The many bookshelves were empty, and some removed entirely. There was a servant in the far end of the hall, sweeping the wide-planked floor with a besom of highland straw.

"Hello, what's this?" Koraymis called to the man. As a student, he outranked the commoner and could expect an answer. The man looked at him with dull, rheumy eyes.

"Sirrah?"

"What are you doing here? Why have they changed this hall?"

"I... was told they be turning this to a classroom," he said.

"What sort of classroom?" he asked, becoming annoyed. He needed to find his tutor.

"The sort a' classroom where ye learn how to survive, *boy!*" the man's words turned to malice in an instant, his bleary eyes turning to angry red slits. He drew a long, dark dagger from behind him and advanced on the stunned young scholar.

"Hold! What are you doing?" Koraymis was shocked and took two or three defensive steps backwards. It was fortunate the tables were off to one side, giving him room to retreat.

"I'm gonna plant my knife in yer gut, ya stupid whelp!" the man growled, moving faster.

There was no time to consider the situation, no opportunity for Koraymis to engage his gifts of language and intellect. He was being attacked, and he knew it. A voice inside him awoke, one he hadn't heard in many years.

He threw his hands up in front of him, his cloak flying back. Both hands erupted in flame, his fingers now blackened claws. One was held before his attacker, almost as a shield, while the other he held back, close to his face. He could feel the heat from the flames on his face. They should have been searing hot at such close range, but to Koraymis, they were soothing.

"Stop," he commanded, his voice low and menacing, but pervasive. It didn't sound like his own voice.

The man stumbled, pausing in his advance, eyes wider now.

"Come closer and die," Koraymis said, thinking it sounded a little silly. The man opened his mouth, unsure what to do. Then his eyes turned dark and

determined, and he shouted gutturally, charging forward, dagger held over his head.

With almost no thought, Koraymis snapped his right hand forward. The flames enwreathing it flew forth like a fiery dart, blazing a short trail through the air. It struck the man square in his face. He screamed and dropped the dagger, falling to his knees, his face and hair afire. He collapsed, shuddering and choking.

Oddly, Koraymis' first thought at the sight was how to best prevent the spread of flames. The idea of being responsible for starting a fire amid so much accumulated knowledge filled him with dread.

Then he smelled the burning flesh. A sickening feeling settled in his stomach. His hands were suddenly normal again, but shaking. The man was still, curled up in a feral ball. The flames had thankfully been doused, but smoke still curled above his ruined head.

For a moment, Koraymis thought he might piss his robes. He didn't know what to do. Then the man let out a low, warm laugh. He stood, as Koraymis almost fell back onto a table.

"Well done, Kor," Telmik said. The visage of the short man with a scorched face and hair dissolved, replaced by his tutor. He stood tall in long gray robes, untouched by any fire.

"You...that...was a test," Koraymis said, breathing hard, trying his best to keep his composure.

"Yes, and I am impressed. You could have screamed and fled, or let the man kill you with the dagger. But you stood your ground and did what needed to be done," Telmik said, pulling out a nearby chair and sitting. He motioned for his pupil to sit in the chair behind him. Koraymis nearly collapsed into it.

He clutched his stomach. "I think I may be sick."

"That's not unusual, you thought you had killed someone," his master said. "And the truth of it is, that would have killed an ordinary man. Remember that feeling. You will need to do it again, I think."

"Again? Why do you say that?" he almost shouted, suddenly angry at the manipulation his master had executed. "Is that why you trained me? To kill?"

"I trained you to do what must be done, when the time comes," the older man countered, his voice calm.

"You've talked about 'when the time comes' before, yet offered no further explanation," Koraymis said, his exasperation evident. "I'm about to leave Woodford, for a long time. You aren't coming with me. So why won't you tell me about this 'when the time comes'?"

"I know you've sacrificed a great deal on this path," Telmik said, with a steady voice. "You've never told a soul about our...training and teaching. You have foregone friends and any sort of family bonds, to do as I instructed. I am not forgetting that."

"Yes, I know you aren't. And you know I did what I did because of everything you did for me, and for showing me all that I could do," Koraymis said, feelings conflicting within him. "But why? If you're staying here, and I'm moving on, why did you ever take me as a pupil?"

"Still your emotions, Koraymis," Telmik said, a slight edge on his voice. It was an edge the young man had learned to sense, knowing how sharp it could become in the blink of an eye. "My reasons are my own, today. But you *will* know the reasons one day, I can promise you that. As for your training, your...gifts, they will be of use to you soon."

"The other day, Evun made light of the fact that I'm heading off on my own, with no skill at arms," Koraymis said, looking at his folded hands. His stomach was feeling a little better now. "Why didn't you ever suggest I should train with a dagger or bow or sword?"

"It is important your mind and spirit lead the way in your training, Kor," Telmik said. "You will find that this training, instilled so deeply, will help in any physical or martial training you choose to undertake in the future. And I would suggest that you do so. It will be useful. But understand your other skills will be vastly more important."

"My other skills...I still don't understand what that means," Koraymis was having trouble finding the words. "I feel as though I'm half taught, as if you've shown me a half, *quarter*, of the book and there's so many more pages to be turned."

Telmik chuckled in appreciation at this analogy. "An astute observation and quite a pertinent analogy. There is more, Koraymis. *Much more.* And some of it will come to you as time goes by, and in times of need."

"What do you mean by times of need?"

Telmik narrowed his eyes, looking away, as if into some distant future. "Situations when the need arises, when there is a conflict, a crisis, you - or your friends - are threatened. You will find a way to take what you have only *read* about and turn it to action."

"That sounds improbable. No, it sounds ridiculous! How can you see me venture out into this world lacking such vital experience?" Koraymis asked. He didn't even bring up the dubious point about having *friends.*

"There will always be knowledge you lack. But you will come to know what you must, in time," his master said. "It was you who expressed the desire to journey west to Ravensroost. I have only supported you in this decision, despite whatever lack in training you perceive."

"Then why will you not join me there?" he nearly shouted, anger clear in his voice. "If there's so much more to learn, who will teach it? You won't be there! And for that matter, who's going to ensure my...I..." he trailed off, gesturing vaguely to his face.

"Your appearance won't change, because I'm far from you. It is part of you now. I am not concerned, so *you* should not be concerned," he replied. "As for other matters, I have a gift for you. One that I hope will provide you with some reassurance."

Telmik reached into the folds of his robes and placed an object on the table. It was a ring, made of some dark gray metal, mounted with a single round stone. Koraymis picked it up. The stone was nearly black in color, smooth and finely polished. It was otherwise unremarkable. It took only a moment before he saw the gleam of purple in the polished surface. Then it flared intensely from within the stone. It was like the strange glow he sometimes perceived upon magical objects, but much brighter than any he had seen before.

"This has an especially powerful enchantment placed on it," he said, turning the ring over in his fingers.

He had learned how to identify strong or weak emanations of magical energy over the past year. Telmik had provided many small objects imbued with a variety of enchantments for Koraymis to study and decipher, and he had proven adept.

Still, for Koraymis, magic remained a mystery. Despite his readings, Telmik's tutelage and his own demonstrated skills, the arcane was as elusive to him as it was to the vast bulk of the populace. While he did not fully understand magic, Koraymis was not fearful of it, as so many were. Wizards and spellcasters of all varieties could be found in most towns and cities, or even traveling the road, providing simple services. A hundred years ago, they would not have been well received and may have even found themselves lashed to a stake atop a burning heap of branches.

That all changed ninety-five years ago, when King Deldriam declared magic to be a legitimate practice. Court wizards had been common ever since, from the royal court on down through the lowest barony. Despite the passage of time and the royal decree, magic and wizardry remained something of which most villagers were highly suspicious.

Despite the fear and suspicions of the common folk, Koraymis knew better. All of Telmik's tutelage and the extensive reading he had done regarding magic revealed to him that it was not so impressive. Wizards could provide simple predictions, mend broken objects, and sometimes even convince someone to act against their nature, for woe or weal. Yet, there were few historical examples of a wizard performing a truly powerful feat.

Koraymis was not a wizard. His magic was something else entirely. It had a name, though it was one people were unwilling to speak. He had read it in more than one dusty tome, many years ago.

Sorcery. At least that's what he suspected, based on how his abilities manifested and the common descriptions of what people called spells. Koraymis had never asked Telmik directly.

"What does this ring do?" Koraymis said, after studying it carefully. He could see no markings or inscriptions.

"It's made to be worn on your middle finger, your right hand is best. It will...assist you," Telmik said, in his typically enigmatic style.

Koraymis sighed. "Must I beg for more?"

Telmik frowned. "You never need to *beg*. I resent the implication. What I've done for you, for all these years, will serve both of us. I've never told you otherwise. But I've never asked anything from you, save your continued devotion to your studies. And given that I *saved your life*, I think it fair that you continue to heed my advice and suggestions."

There was that pressing edge to his voice again. He could deny nothing his tutor said.

He nodded and slipped the cold ring onto the middle finger of his right hand. There was the instant sensation of heat, light, darkness, a roaring? It was too quick. He didn't jump, or even register the sensations outwardly.

"Good," Telmik said, nodding in reply. "Now, you will learn more of what the ring does as time goes by. But I will tell you this much. It will aid you in the use of your abilities, enhancing them in some ways. It will allow you to better sense someone's emotions, intents, possibly even their thoughts. There will be times when you can use the ring to aid you in seeing something from afar."

"Scrying?" Koraymis asked, having read of the ability in several tomes.

"Something like it. While it *may* help you foresee a possible future, it can also aid you in seeing distant locations in the present. It may also help you understand situations or offer you glimpses of insight."

"Will it speak to my mind?"

"Not exactly. But by wearing it, your mind may see things it may not otherwise. Imagine it is listening to you. By doing so, thoughts or solutions may become apparent. These solutions may even sound like a voice in your mind, though it may not directly speak to you."

"Will it ever speak to me directly?" Koraymis asked.

"Possibly. I must confess something to you," his master said, turning to look out the tall window. "I do not know the extent of the ring's powers, nor precisely how it will manifest itself to you. But I do know – or more precisely – I have come to know that you must have it."

Koraymis was not satisfied with this, but he was not satisfied with many of Telmik's revelations. He chose not to ask his master any more on that point. He was confident Telmik would reveal little more or nothing at all.

"Do you know how old it is?"

Telmik looked at his pupil with a curious, raised eyebrow. "How old do you *think* it is?"

"Well, common wisdom would say it's no more than two hundred or two hundred and fifty years old, since that's as far back as records go within the Kingdom of Eastvale. No one would ever say it was made *before* that time," Koraymis said slowly, still studying the ring. Then he looked up at his master with a detached expression. "But it is much older than that, isn't it?"

"Koraymis, I'm shocked. You dare speak of the time *before*? Have you not heeded the wisdom of your elders? No one should ever ask such things or ponder what may have occurred before the rise of the Kingdom!" he said, grinning, sarcasm almost visible upon his lips.

"Yes, I know, and we can never pass through the woods to the south, nor the wild mountains north, nor enter the Dwarven realms of the east, or..." Koraymis said with a practiced lassitude. Then he looked at his master. "Or cross the Misthallow Hills to the west?"

Koraymis had felt the desire to journey westward for a very long time. At first, he thought it was simply to experience something new, the frontier town of Ravensroost, perhaps. But over the past several months, he had come to realize it was far more than that. He had slowly come to the unspoken realization that his journey westward would not end with Ravensroost.

Telmik chuckled, a dark, hollow noise, nodding. "Or cross the Misthallows."

The young man grinned a little, wondering for a moment what his future held. He looked at the ring on his finger, making a fist. It felt substantial, weighty. He wondered what it might reveal. He wondered why his master would not head to Ravensroost with him, to continue his training, as Koraymis had hoped. He had even pleaded with Telmik once, insisting he would stay in Woodford to continue his training. But Telmik had refused, telling the student he would have to go to Ravensroost without him.

It is not that he chooses against going west, the truth is he cannot *go any further west than this city.* Koraymis slowly realized this thought was not of his own making. *You must go west because he cannot. He needs you.* The ring, he knew, looking at it again. The ring was already speaking to him. He could sense the words forming in his mind, far more directly than Telmik had implied. Then it said something else to him.

Looking up at his master, Koraymis wondered if Telmik could read his thoughts. His master's eyes looked at him with an expression of guarded curiosity.

"I will trust in what you say, Master," he said. He rarely called Telmik by that designation. The older man did not like formality in custom for unknown reasons. "Aside from taking on this position with the library in Ravensroost, what else would you suggest I do? There's no one there to train me any further, at least not anyone you've mentioned."

"No, there is no one else, to my knowledge. As for that position, it will serve for a time, but you must look for your path westward."

"I imagine by *path* you don't mean an actual road," Koraymis mused.

"You are correct. There will be signs, perhaps. Follow them as you see fit. Remember the ring, it may be able to guide you in your decisions," his master said. "But don't become over-reliant on it, of course. It may offer occasional suggestions or encouragement, but not with all things."

"I understand," the young man replied, nodding. "Is there anything else you can share with me, about this path westward?'

"I can tell you this, though I wasn't planning on revealing it today," Telmik began, looking uncharacteristically unsettled. He breathed in deeply, pausing, perhaps phrasing his following words. "You are not alone."

Koraymis had been expecting more than that. "What?"

"What I'm saying is that...you are not alone in how you appear, in *what* you are," his master said. He let the words and implications hang there. Koraymis took a moment to comprehend what he had said.

"There are...others that look the way I actually look?" he said quietly.

"Yes. Out there," Telmik said, one hand gesturing in a westerly direction.

His pupil's eyes narrowed. "Are you simply lying to me? To help assure me in my decision to journey west?"

His master smiled. "Shrewd caution and skepticism will help keep you alive. But no, it is the truth. I don't know if it is bane or boon, to find one of your kin. They may be…"

Telmik paused, considering his next words, Koraymis guessed.

"What?" Koraymis asked.

"They may not be especially friendly. You had me to help temper your abilities. By helping you fit in with others, you are wiser, more thoughtful, perhaps even a bit kinder, than you might have been otherwise."

"And others like me, they could have had harsher lives?" Koraymis posited.

"Precisely. And for that reason, they may not take kindly to strangers, or those who claim to be like them. I want you to be forewarned," Telmik said. "But be assured, there are others like you in the world without."

"And you're certain I'll encounter some of these...people?"

His master sighed. "Yes. You will encounter them."

"Thank you for a direct answer," Koraymis said, smiling. "I will be careful. There is something else though, I wish to ask you."

"What is it?" Telmik asked.

"I was wondering if you might allow me to take...the book…" Koraymis said, clearing his throat a bit at the end. It seemed unlikely his master would acquiesce to the request. The book was unique, but it was also quite cumbersome given its size.

A half-smile appeared on his tutor's lips. From the folds of his robe, he produced what Koraymis at first assumed was a leather satchel. He quickly realized it was a compact tome bound in leather and attached to a leather casing that stretched around the book. It was formed and attached to an iron ring.

"A girdle tome? I don't understand," Koraymis said as Telmik placed it on the table next to his pupil.

"It is the tome you've been reading. Just a smaller version to ease your burden when traveling. Take a look."

The older man pushed the leather-bound book toward Koraymis. The exterior leather sleeve was bound by several sturdy buckles and had a watertight seal to prevent damage by rain He unbuckled them and pried the casing open. Within, the tome was attached by its spine to the leather. Sturdy, leather-clad wooden planks that formed the book's covers, bound and cornered by brass fittings and ornamentation. It also had a latch Koraymis had to use both hands to activate.

"Be careful when opening this. If you do so too hastily, it may sting you a little," Telmik said, a small smirk on his lips.

Koraymis looked closely at the latch mechanism. *There*, he could see it. A tiny gleam of a certain color and – he was not sure how to describe it in his mind – a *flavor*. It was a trap of some sort. He pressed the latches slowly. The tome opened easily. Within were the hundreds of pages of vellum with a great deal of lore he had already read, and at least as much he had yet to study. It also bore many intricate illustrations and illuminated pages.

Koraymis breathed a sigh of relief. It was his fervent wish he would be able to continue his studies. This tome, while it was not the larger version, would serve him well in this.

"Is there anything I need to know regarding my studies? Will simply reading this aid me in growing my knowledge and understanding? Can it do more?" Koraymis asked.

Telmik seemed to concentrate for a moment before answering. "Read well the passages that describe actions and spells that seem almost beyond the realm of possibility. These may serve you one day."

"But magic is not an especially powerful force, is it?"

His master smiled. "It doesn't appear to be, if you look at what your typical *wizard* is capable of. But know this, magic is not what it *should* be."

Koraymis' expression conveyed his confusion. His master continued. "What I mean is this...magic, true magic, is hidden. Buried if you will, or perhaps suppressed is a better term."

"What does that mean?"

"I am not entirely certain, but it *should* be far more than it is now. And while what you know, what you are capable of, is not exactly what most would call magic, you will find that you are capable of exceptional things."

"Sir?" Koraymis asked, feeling quite lost at this point.

"Trust in this, you will do things that will amaze," was all Telmik offered. He waved a hand. "I'll say no more of it. Read your girdle tome and heed the lessons therein."

Koraymis simply nodded, dismissing the hundred questions that crowded his mind. He looked at the book, patting it.

"I can't thank you enough for this," he said. "I will certainly endeavor to continue my education to the best of my abilities."

"I am certain of that, Kor," Telmik nodded. "But you must away, so we must now say our goodbyes."

The young man stood. He was ready for this. While he felt close to his master, there was a definite distance between them. No warm embrace awaited them at their parting.

"Will I see you again?" Koraymis asked.

Telmik chuckled. "Oh, you can be sure of that. We will again meet, but I could not guess when."

"If I happen to head back to Woodford again, should I seek you out here?"

"No. I will be leaving this town today, soon. It will be a long time before we meet again."

Standing now himself, Telmik extended his hands in the traditional double hand-clasp that marked a meeting after a long time, or a parting expected to be of a lengthy duration.

Koraymis sighed, feeling the sure strength in his master's grip. Telmik's hands were strangely warm.

"Thank you for everything you've done," he said, thinking that would suffice.

"It has been my honor," Telmik said. He released the younger man's hands. "And thanks to you."

"For what?'

"For everything that you *will* do," he said. Koraymis didn't know how to take that. He simply nodded.

Gathering his pack and placing the girdle tome within it, he tightened the strap as he slung it over his shoulder. He looked at Telmik and nodded once more before leaving the room. Shutting the door quietly, he walked down the dim corridor. Checking his belongings one last time, he realized with a start that he must have dropped the silvered badge the librarian had bestowed upon him.

Turning around, he was back in the long hall only a few breaths after he had closed the door.

"Sir, I-" he began as he entered the hall.

He was alone. Telmik was nowhere to be seen in the long hall. "Master?"

It was to no avail. He was gone. Koraymis walked over to the table where they had been sitting. There was his silver pin, placed next to the long, dark dagger his master had used in his feigned attack on the pupil. He picked up the dagger. It was almost paper thin, so finely worked was the blade. The edge curved to and fro as it worked to a point, adding to its menacing appearance. The metal was a deep, dark, almost indiscernible reddish-black hue. The surface seemed smooth, but Koryamis' eye caught faint, subtle shapes worked into the metal.

He put both of them in his pack before leaving the hall. Taking the back exit out of the library to avoid further goodbyes, Koraymis walked the streets of Woodford lost in thought. Soon enough, he arrived at the station.

The carriage was ready to depart by the time Koraymis reached it. Presenting his voucher, he found a seat in the third of four cramped rows. He was next to a heavy-set merchant wearing a badge indicating he was an agent of some house, likely working the route between Woodford and Ravensroost. There were a few other likely merchants on the carriage, along with some ladies of higher station than himself. They were accompanied by a rough-looking manservant. The ladies did not deign to meet Koraymis' eyes; the manservant only glared at him with a challenge in his eyes until the young scholar grinned a little and turned away.

He reflected on what he had learned at the library, and from Telmik, and his learning at the school. A knot formed in his stomach as the carriage lurched forward. They were through the gates within a minute and on the road to Ravensroost. The carriage was well-built and, while there was a brisk autumn chill in the air, Koraymis was warm enough inside.

After a few hours of riding, it was getting dark and they stopped at a village called Handerby. Exiting the carriage, he found himself in front of a tavern. The sign bore the image of a hooded man bearing a noose.

"Pleasant," Koraymis remarked. The merchant who had made the trip with him from Woodford, stepped out of the carriage, clapping a meaty hand on the young man's shoulder.

"The Hangman is a fine little tavern. I saw your voucher didn't grant you your own room. I'd spend a few silvers to get one, if you can. The common room can be noisy on crowded nights like this," he advised. Koraymis followed his advice and spoke to the innkeeper, and for those few silvers, he was given his own room key.

The eight carriage passengers were soon about their own business, eating, drinking, or gaming in the common room. Koraymis didn't feel especially social tonight so he kept to his room after he had a small meal of bread, ale and cheese. There was a taper sufficient to read by and he nodded off after studying his girdle tome for a few hours.

In the morning, he was up early, as was his habit. After his morning ablutions, he went downstairs and had a bowl of brose and cream. The morning was cold, the sky was clear. The sun had not risen yet and the false dawn was brightening the east through thinning trees. His breath hung before his face as his boots crunched over newly fallen leaves.

After relieving himself behind the stable, he came around a corner of the tavern. There was a small wagon, with a Dwarve at the reins, a single horse hitched to it. The Dwarve was talking to a young man standing next to the wagon. He gave the young man something and they shook hands. The young man wore brown leathers that told Koraymis he was perhaps a hunter or ranger.

He also had a curious-looking backpack slung over his shoulder, with a variety of buckles, pockets and straps. Without meaning to, Koraymis stepped forward as the young man waved at the departing wagon, though the Dwarve was looking eastward as he slowly rounded a bend in the road. The scholar felt compelled to examine the pack more closely, despite the rudeness of advancing on someone from behind unawares.

His footfalls did not go unnoticed. The young man in leather threw back his hood, which had been partially covering his head, revealing a head of brown hair and slightly upswept ears. He was clearly of Elven descent, at least in part. He did not turn to look at Koraymis.

"May I help you?" he said, turning his head a little at this point.

"My apologies, that was rude," Koraymis said, standing upright and nodding his head respectfully.

The young man turned and smiled, an easy and pleasant expression. Koraymis was almost envious of his ability to look so disarming. "I am not offended. You move quietly, I'll give you that."

Koraymis was just a few steps from him now. He looked at him head to foot. He appeared far more prepared for travel on the road, or the wilds for that matter, than he was.

"I hope you don't think me forward, but are you a ranger?"

"No, but I would be pleased to aspire to that noble profession," the young man said. His eloquence struck Koraymis as atypical. He appeared to inspect him in return. His eyes fixed on the small silver pin attached to the black tunic. "And you are a scholar, I think?"

Koraymis nodded slowly. "You are learned, friend. I am a student still, in truth, but with some scholarly achievements."

"My name is Cam Bronwyer," the young man said, extending a gloved hand.

The scholar considered it for a moment, then took it, clasping. In the dim morning light, Koraymis realized there was something odd about the man's eyes, but he didn't ask, as it would be inappropriate.

"I am Koraymis Sleeth, it is an honor to meet you, Master Bronwyer," he said, with appropriate respect. Until he could determine otherwise, Koraymis would assume they were equals.

Cam shook his head. "Just Cam is fine. Are you bound for Woodford?"

"No, Ravensroost. Yourself?"

"The same. Do you have family in Ravensroost?" Cam asked.

"No," was all Koraymis offered in reply. For a moment, he said nothing more, then spoke. "I have a scholar's post awaiting me there."

"They have a library there, don't they? And a school?"

"Yes, both. I'll be at the library," Koraymis said. "You seem like an educated fellow. Have you been to the library in Woodford?"

"A few times, when I was younger. My parents provided me a thorough education at home. They placed a high value on knowledge," Cam said, almost wistfully.

"Are you going to continue your education in Ravensroost?"

"No, my reasons for going to Ravensroost…"

"Are your own, of course," Koraymis interrupted him, bowing his head slightly.

Cam smiled. "No, that's all right. I'm heading to Ravensroost because...it's to the west."

Koraymis stared at the young man. He suddenly felt the weight of his ring on his right hand. His eyes darted to Cam's pack again.

"You have an interesting backpack there," he said. "Did you have a hand in crafting it?"

"Yes, but how did you know that?" Cam asked, clearly surprised at the assumption.

Koraymis could see clearly now, by the light of the sun just now piercing the trees behind Cam. The pack *gleamed.* Without meaning to, he found he was fiddling with his ring.

"Just a guess," Koraymis smiled. "Well, we're both heading west. I'm heading off this morning by carriage. And you?"

"I have a horse, in the stable," he said, nodding toward the outbuilding.

"Where are you staying when you get there?"

"I was told the Bonerest is a good place, I think there," Cam said, scratching his stubble. "Should we meet, share an ale?"

Koraymis considered this. He looked down to see his left hand turning the ponderous ring on his right. There was a warmth to it, and he had to resist the urge to nod.

"Yes, I've heard good accounts of the place. Master Evan is the innkeeper, and the food is highly recommended. So, we shall meet there, perhaps in a week's time," the young scholar said.

"I look forward to it," Cam said, nodding curtly and turning to attend to his mount in the stable. The sun finally caught the hunter's eyes, allowing Koraymis to see them more clearly. He had read of people with different-colored eyes, though he had never met one until this morning. Tebbrick had even told the boys of an iron monger who had one brown eye and one blue. But Cam's eyes were oddly different. It appeared the upper portions of his irises were blue, while the lower half of the ring were green. Perhaps it was something to do with his mixed heritage.

"Safe journey, Cam Bronwyer."

"May it be dry and even," Cam responded with an older but still traditional well-wish for traveling.

Back inside the inn, Koraymis had but a few of his belongings to pack before taking his seat on the carriage. They were underway before the sun had topped the tree line. Not too long after leaving Handerby, Koraymis saw Cam on his mount. The brown-clad rider nodded to Koraymis as he passed.

He nodded in reply, then settled in for a long ride. He spun the ring on his right middle finger.

Koraymis had never heard of the Bonerest Tavern in Ravensroost, or Master Evan, who he now knew was of half-Elven blood. He even knew their stew was the most popular dish there. He didn't know any of this until this morning, when Cam mentioned the place.

Now, as he caught a glimpse of the rider's silhouette through the trees ahead of them, Koraymis felt the familiar warmth of his ring. He was suddenly and completely certain that Cam would accompany him west, into and beyond the hills they called the Misthallows.

CHAPTER SIX - CANDISSA

19 Laborus, Year 197, Eastvale Calendar

Candissa was up early again, practicing her drills in the small, walled area that was part of her family's considerable estate. Her father had done quite well, as had his predecessors, in the family business of baking. Four generations ago, they were simple bakers and merchants. Since then, their enterprises had grown steadily. Candissa's father, Dalton Demarrae, was heavily invested in the buying and trading of grains, which also served to provide the flour for his bakeries. The noble title their family enjoyed was earned by her Dalton's grandfather, Brandic Demarrae, who had served the Crown in the Second Mountain War. That war had taken place more than eighty years ago, somewhere far to the east. Since then, House Demarrae had become the most successful bakery in the west, with shops in Ravensroost, Woodford and a few of the nearby smaller towns.

Being a young woman of House Demarrae, everyone in Ravensroost assumed she would be a highly skilled baker, simply by virtue of blood. It also meant she would be a highly-prized catch, at least in the limited social structure of the frontier town.

She wasn't thinking of her skill in baking or cooking or her prospects of marriage this morning. She was focused solely on her drills using the stout staff of polished white oak she had found in one of the estate's attics. She suspected it was some sort of old ceremonial accessory, as it had a curiously carven head and faint decorative runes. It was just collecting dust, so she took it for her own and put it to good use.

She learned over the past few years that training with the staff was best done in a setting where no one would see her, the back half-acre of the grounds being ideal. Only the somewhat dubious eyes of the groundskeeping staff or her governess would spy her here, engaged in her highly unusual activity. They would typically stare for a moment before turning away, heads shaking in disappointment or disbelief. Fortunately, they were wise enough to keep word of her practices to themselves. So far, her parents and sisters had no idea.

She wore a close-fitting tunic and leggings of her own devising, having taught herself a good deal of sewing and stitching. Sewing was one of the few pursuits of which her mother approved. Candissa had been up since before dawn, first going through the ritual prayers and studies of her faith, then moving on to training with her staff. She sometimes questioned why the martial training was so important to her, but she had learned not to think too deeply on the impulses and motivations that compelled her to do what she did. Rather, she had learned to simply trust them. She could only hope it would be for the better.

She knew she was more than simply disappointing her parents. She feared her actions and choices could be damaging her relationship with them. Candissa was closest with her youngest sister, Elena, who she counted as a true ally. Elena tried to understand her older sister's behavior, but merely managed to accept it without grasping her reasons.

Candissa had first learned how to use the staff from a member of the town watch, a young man named Thendarick, whom she had known for some years. He was enraptured by Candissa, as was nearly every young man who came into close contact with her. She tolerated the attempts at courtship from various nobles. With Thendarick, she made it clear from the outset that the only thing he would be providing her was martial training. She judged him a respectable fellow and that had been borne out by his actions.

She swore him to secrecy, as she knew her parents would put an end to her training the moment they were made aware. The young guardsman had agreed, and her training began, and not only in the staff. He showed her the rudiments of the bow and how to use a shield, broadsword, and the spear. She also received training in basic hand-to-hand combat and defensive techniques. Of all the weapons training she received, however, she favored the staff.

They trained three or four times a week for several weeks, until it became too challenging to sneak off on a regular basis. Thendarick was well-compensated with pastries and breads that Candissa spirited away from her father's stores.

Since that time, she had been keeping up her training and drills on a regular basis, always in the early morning. Her days were filled with activity, from her studies at the library, her devotions and training at the temple house and helping out with the family business. Her father had three bakeries operating in Ravensroost, and two in Woodford, where he had been spending an increasing amount of time.

While Candissa was a blessing to her father, given her penchant for numbers and records keeping, as well as her ability to draw customers in whenever she worked, she was anything but a blessing in her mother's eyes.

Young women of her station and age were usually busy being courted, if they were not committed to a profession. Given Candissa's unusual maturity for a young woman eighteen years of age, she could easily be married off by now. Yet she ignored every attempt by her mother to put her in social situations. Various attempts to entreat the attention of well-to-do young men and even minor nobles had fallen by the wayside, and word had gradually spread.

It was not as though her behavior was entirely novel. Candissa's mother followed the cultural norms established by the first kings, more than two hundred years ago. Things *had* changed. Candissa had seen young women in roles once thought restricted to men. There were women serving as rangers patrolling the outskirts of the wilds, as archers on the town walls, and as smiths and stonemasons in the working quarters. She had even seen a few taller women in soldiers' livery and chain, bearing spear and shield. These were the exception, far from the rule. Her mother would not like to have her eldest daughter joining their ranks.

Candissa's saving grace was her three younger sisters, who would inevitably consume her mother's attentions. They were all attractive, and good prospects, and likely more than willing to jump into the games of courtship. With the possible exception of Elena, a fact that brought a grin to Candissa's lips.

"Deesa!" a shrill voice cut into her spinning kick and strike routine.

It was Lendra, the matronly senior upstairs maid kept by House Demarrae. She was in charge of Lady Demarrae's daughters, which meant she spent most of her efforts and time on Candissa. The others were not nearly as difficult or headstrong.

"Have you forgotten about your lessons with Master Rathbyrn? You must be prepared for the reception! It is nearly upon us," she yelled over the gathering wind through the turning trees of the modest estate.

Candissa sighed loudly, her breath steaming in the brisk morning air. "No! I haven't forgotten, just wishing everyone else had!" She wouldn't speak that way to her mother, but Lendra was more her friend.

"Such impudence! M'lady, you are positively dreadful sometimes, do you know that?" the heavy-set woman nearly shouted as she bustled up to the perspiring young woman, staff still firmly - and perhaps defiantly- in hand.

"What is that you are wearing? Entirely indecent for a proper young woman, and not nearly warm enough against this chill!"

"I'm not at all chilled, Lendra," Candissa said, leaning on her staff playfully.

"Put that silly stick away and get to your chambers this instant. We must get you washed and your hair set. I will not have my charge wilding about in such-"

Candissa cut off the woman's exhortation by whirling the seven-foot long staff over her head in a complex spinning maneuver, whistling just over Lendra's steely gray heap of hair.

"Oh! Awful girl!" she shrieked, turning and running back toward the manor. "Hellion! Contumacious hellion!"

Candissa stifled a laugh. She did love the dear woman. Lendra had served as her nanny when she was a babe and knew her better than most people in her life.

She put her staff away in the tool shed, where her parents would never look for it, and returned to the house. Later, when the house was quiet, she would retrieve the staff, and take it up to her chambers using the servants' stairwell. She didn't like leaving it in the shed, as they had several gardeners and groundskeepers in their employ who could find it, but it was too late in the morning to secret it upstairs.

Walking along the pebbled paths leading to the manor, Candissa looked at the buildings by the light of the rising sun. House Demarrae was almost the finest house in all of Ravensroost. She knew that meant something, but she also knew where Ravensroost was in relation to the whole of the Kingdom of Eastvale. The house had two floors throughout, with a third floor in two of the square towers. There were also two round towers rising above it all, one being an unused chapel tower over what was once a temple generations past. The other tower was the library. All was clad in a fine but aged plaster, over stout beams of oak, everwood, and ironpine.

The house had glass windows throughout, finely made doors, fixtures, tiles, and other decorative features that spoke of their station. While Candissa's mother would like to call their family noble, they were - Candissa knew from her reading - low nobility, at best. As a younger girl, she had joined her parents on more than one trip east to the city of Woodford, and even beyond, to the city of Callcove. Their family had guested with several fine houses, and while House Demarrae had tall ceilings, colorful tapestries and fine, hand-worked archways, they compared poorly to the houses she had seen further to the east.

Returning to her rooms, she found the red-faced and puffing Lendra there, laying out appropriate clothing for her lessons. She was muttering to herself, "I really don't know why I put up with that insolent, obstinate...oh, there you are, Deesa."

Lendra shuffled over to her dressing table, quickly selecting complementary jewelry for the gown. She whirled about and shook her fist at the girl. "You will be the death of me, girl!"

"I am sorry, Lendra. I didn't mean to startle you," Candissa said in a soothing voice. "I'll be good now."

The governess merely harrumphed in reply. "I'm drawing a bath. You will get in and scrub off that dirt and sweat from all that...whatever you were doing!"

She marched into the bath chamber and checked the temperature while laying out a tin of bath salts and a wooden brush.

Candissa had exerted herself during her training, she knew that. But she also knew herself. She disrobed dutifully and entered the bath chamber. "Lendra, do I really need a bath? Here look."

The maid turned and inspected the disrobed young woman. Candissa took both hands and ran them through her blonde locks, shaking her head. Lowering her hands, it was as if she had just bathed and had her hair pressed and scented. Lendra scowled at her.

"None of that, girl!" she said, wagging a finger at the broad copper basin filling with warm water. "I don't care for your little tricks, in you go!"

"Fine," she relented with a huff, stepping into the bath.

She had been able to do that for several years at least. No matter how disheveled she appeared — whether smudged, soiled or sweaty — she had to just concentrate a moment, shake her head, and it was as though she had spent an hour cleaning up. It was not something she understood, but she did enjoy her 'little trick', as Lendra called it. She was the only one who knew of it; Candissa had never mentioned it to her mother. It often saved a great deal of time in preparations for the many social events her parents insisted she attend.

She let Lendra go about her task of ensuring the young lady in her charge was cleaned and scrubbed, despite the needlessness. Bubbles frothed about her as she idly scrubbed her arms.

"Now, I trust you're schooled in all the necessary customs of greeting Eastlanders? The noble Lords favor that sort of thing. Master Rathbyrn covered that in his last lesson, didn't he?" Lendra said as she rinsed the long, blonde curls straight, pouring water from a copper ewer.

"Yes, yes, I'm familiar with all that," she replied. She sensed a curious lilt in the older woman's voice. "I'm sure my father is planning something. He'll probably try to throw me at the *young* Lord Allenfar!"

"Oh, now, I don't know anything about that," the governess began, but to no avail. She had lost the ability to deceive Candissa long ago. The younger woman turned and stood slowly in the bath, her feet firmly rooted on the textured copper floor of the tub, hands on hips, towering over Lendra.

"You know how I feel about that!" she said, almost imperiously.

"You just sit back down now, girl, and rinse off," Lendra countered after recovering from her momentary shock at the girl's countenance.

"Your father has every right to introduce you if he so wishes, and you know it!"

"Ugh!" was all Candissa said in reply, as she dropped back down into the water, causing no small amount of it to splash out of the copper basin. She hurried through the rest of her bath and dried off quickly.

Back in her bedchamber, she sat in front of a mirror, wearing a simple white robe, and considered her face, as Lendra rummaged through her assortment of cosmetics.

"I'm hungry. Could you have something brought up here if you're going to take all morning?" Candissa said, making sure it was apparent she was annoyed. "Is all this really necessary? It's just a lesson!"

"Yes, it is! I'll get something, and you just you sit right there and don't think I'll let you out of my sight for a moment!" the maid said, having too many experiences with the young woman escaping her to avoid a social commitment. Lendra called for a maidservant, who fetched a plate of fruit and sweets.

Candissa let Lendra go about her tasks, even as her mind turned to a dozen things she would rather be doing. She decided to make use of the older, wiser, and more knowledgeable woman in the meantime.

"Lendra, what would you say if I told you I wanted to journey beyond the Kingdom?"

"Beyond? You mean outside of the Kingdom of Eastvale?" the woman asked, sounding astonished as she selected the dress Candissa would wear for the day. Candissa had learned long ago to avoid arguing with the governess on matters of fashion.

"Yes, if I wanted to get on a horse and just ride, say, west of the hills?" Candissa suggested, with an almost playful tone to her voice. She slipped into the undergarments Lendra handed her.

"I'd say you'd lost your wits! *No one* goes into the Misthallows," she shook her head. "And if they did, they never come back!"

"Well, how would anyone know that if no one ever goes?"

"Child, put my heart at ease and tell me you're just vexing an old woman," Lendra said, her concern genuine. "You cannot seriously consider that. Only the rangers wander the lands north and south of here. I've heard tell of a few fierce homesteaders settling along the hills, or the plains. But none, *no one*, ever tries to go *past* those accursed hills. *Ever!*"

"I know, I've heard the tales. *Everyone knows* you don't venture past the hills," Candissa sighed, slipping the dress over her head, shaking her head briskly as she did so. "What tales have you heard about what lies beyond the hills? I've read things, but the best sources are people."

"Well, I don't know about that. I've never thought about it, but I have heard a few things," Lendra said, musing, as she helped fasten the long gown about the young woman's torso and waist. "It was, oh twenty-five years ago, a young ranger named...oh, what was his name? Thengood, that's it. He got it in his head that his destiny, or some such nonsense, was to go beyond the Misthallow Hills and explore what lay there."

Lendra continued to tuck and fasten, tighten and tweak the dress.

"I suppose he was never heard from again?" Candissa offered.

"That's right! Never a trace or sign of him, and some rangers went as far the edge of the hills, but no further," she said, shaking her head. "And he wasn't the only one. There were others over the years. They disappear, hoping to return with riches. *None* return."

"And I suppose you've never heard if anyone was ever allowed through the Elven woods to return?" she asked, speaking of the long, unknown southern frontier of the Kingdom.

"No, they don't. Good folk, the Elves, gracious, decent folk," Lendra said. "But they don't take to Humans in their woods. Never heard of anyone making any sort of long trip through those woods to return."

Candissa sighed. She knew too well the other options. To the north lay the intractable Shadowfall Mountains, where dwelt wild clansmen, barbarians by most descriptions. Beyond them, the creatures called Chom and their larger, more dangerous cousins, the Ur'chom. If tales were to be believed, there were also giants and other monstrous creatures. Then to the distant east, past even the capital of the Kingdom of Eastvale, the City of Eastvale, were the mighty Dwarven mountain holds. Finding any passage into these mountains was said to be even more difficult.

"So, you see, my dear," Lendra sighed. "It's just not done. You can't think any more of it. Decent folk simply don't! The Kingdom of Eastvale is your home and it is safe from the dangers and perils that lie beyond. Let the Dwarves have their mountain ranges and their lost caverns, and the Elves their dark woods. We have so much here in the Kingdom, you'll never want for more."

"If you say so, Len," Candissa said, wincing as she fastened a silver clasp to her hair.

"You haven't even seen the grand city of Eastvale! Oh, it's a wonder. I was lucky enough to journey there when I was a younger woman," she said. "I can't imagine how it looks now. I've heard they've built even taller towers than I remember."

"I would like to see the city one day," the younger woman mused. "I've heard so much of it and read some fantastic accounts."

"You'll see it. I'm certain your father will take the family on a trip there, or at least some of you," Lendra assured her, as she helped Candissa slip on her street boots. Even though she did not anticipate leaving the house, she preferred footwear for the street, rather than the soft-soled slippers typically worn within a home. The boots required some lacing and tying, much to Lendra's chagrin. Regardless, Candissa had always preferred this.

Candissa knew the city lay hundreds of miles east of Ravensroost. It was many weeks travel, by horseback or wagon. Yet somehow, it didn't seem like an impossible distance. She actually liked the idea of a long trip by horseback.

Such a suggestion would give her mother fits, and worse if she knew her eldest daughter had actually been training and practicing with Delvin, one of the rangers. She trusted Delvin not to divulge her crimes to her family. Candissa had been training on horseback at least once a week since spring. Some weeks, she managed two sessions, but these were difficult to arrange without arousing suspicion.

She had few real friends she could trust, to help her in her machinations. The only trusted allies within her own household were sister, Elena, and the old steward, Quence. Elena would keep her secrets unto her grave, or so Candissa imagined. Her other sisters, Brenissa and Nalliath, were far more concerned with their society schemes, appearances and climbing the decidedly short social ladder of Ravensroost.

They would be far more interested and engaged in the reception a few days hence, than Candissa or Elena, and so they should be, as they were likely to be the first daughters of House Demarrae to be wed. Lendra was nearly done with the limited cosmetics and final touches she needed to apply.

Candissa regarded the portly woman as she departed the chamber. Lendra held the title of head maidservant, but everyone called her governess, as she was such in every way. Candissa felt there was more to the woman than she would let be known. Lendra was in all ways in her station, and dutifully so. The woman had never let anyone think otherwise, despite Candissa's suspicions.

She turned her attention, or at least part of it, to the victuals that had been left. She had a few pieces of cheese and fruit, and a sip of light wine. She glanced at her collection of books and scrolls. She would not be surprised if it was the largest collection held privately by any noble's daughter in the entire western region. There were just over forty bound books, two dozen scrolls, and a collection of printbooks exceeding a hundred, neatly stacked in four piles. Still, she wanted more.

She pulled down one book in particular, an accounting of the houses, holds, knights and provinces of the Kingdom of Eastvale.

She quickly scanned through the list of names and flipped to a crude map the author had scrawled on one page. This was one of the older books, copied by hand, and more valuable for it. She preferred the printed books, though she had few. They were said to be in abundance in the City, where some claimed an ancient printing press was in working order.

Frowning at the crude map, she closed the book firmly. Replacing it, she carefully reached behind the row of books, ensuring first that no one was coming down the corridor to interrupt her. She drew forth a long scroll of patchy parchment and paper, bound by a cord.

Moving to her spacious bed, she drew the curtains aside to provide more light. Untying and unrolling the parchment, she gazed over it with a mixture of delight and pride. The study of maps was not something expected of a young woman in her station, though it was not in any way forbidden. It was just not *normal.* In truth, if you weren't an official of the government, having any map was something to be concerned about. Those who had maps were more likely to be curious about what lay beyond the borders. That was something one simply did not think about. *Everyone knows that.*

She had assembled the map from pieces and fragments she had been collecting for more than two years. Some were purchased from vendors traveling from Woodford or from a passing tinker. Others were copied from sources she had found in dusty old books, while others came from Master Penston's collection. She had a passing hand in copying the shapes, lines and figures, at least for someone who was not a professional artist or limner.

There were portions done by a skilled, practiced hand. These were done by her enigmatic friend, Errol, at her instruction. She thought briefly on him, but shooed the thought away. She did not need to dwell on that conundrum right now. She studied the map, pieces held together by narrow strips of fine vellum adhered with the use of bone glue. The map was as complete a depiction of the Kingdom of Eastvale as she could manage.

More accurately, she noted mentally, it was the entire *known world.* Along the northern edge, the mountains called the Starfires wended along the entire border. They were called the Shadowfall Mountains closer to the Kingdom. At the far eastern edge, they joined to what was called the Dwarven Mountains, though the term "Drakindry Peaks" was found in more than one old text. Along the southern border were the endless woodlands of Elves. They were as imposing as the mountains above, though they wandered a great deal more. A vast lake cut through them, called the Silverim. The northern shore of this lake was settled by Humans, who fished it. It was the only source of the large lake trout she sometimes enjoyed. The Human fisherfolk could not cross to the shore beyond, where the Elves lived, as they lived throughout the entire length of the Stoneroot Woods.

A vast swamp in the southwest prevented these woods from stretching off her map. The Dim Vapors Marsh was noted in many texts, but almost no details were available. A few older accounts by rangers told of a vast ruin, others told of the same ruin peopled by unspeakable monsters.

That left the western border. The town closest to this edge was Ravensroost, and it lay only thirty miles or so from the edge of the

Misthallow Hills. She sighed heavily. She had spent no small amount of time comparing the limited texts available on the Kingdom and her dimensions. As far as she could ascertain, it was barely nine hundred miles across and half that deep, north to south.

For reasons she could not grasp, she found this notion not just unacceptable, but laughable. The world was much, *much bigger*. She knew this to be true. Since she was a little girl and had first conceived the notion and put it into a question, she had been rebuked.

At first, she thought it was because she was thought to be presumptuous. Yet, as she grew older and asked teachers the same question, it was deflected or dismissed out of hand. Every time.

She remembered one instance when an elderly and kind scholar had promised to look into it. Yet, two days later, when she asked him if he had found anything about the world beyond, he claimed to recall no such conversation. She would have dismissed it as a failure of his memory, if he wasn't known as one of the sharpest intellects in the western half of the Kingdom.

Similarly, people had a penchant for forgetting such questions or topics. It was frustrating to her as she grew older and more learned. She eventually realized she could not ask questions like this directly. Regardless, there was no real information, records, documents or even stories about what happened beyond two centuries ago. It was as if all the Humans and Elves and Dwarves had just sprung to life around the time the Kingdom was established.

She scanned her aggregate map again, noting the regional capital cities and towns, wondering when, or even if, she would ever see them. She looked at the Misthallows again, wondering, wishing she knew what lay just beyond the ragged edge of her map.

A voice called her from below. Frowning, she quickly rolled up the map and replaced it in the hidden gap. Making final tweaks to her hair and dress, she headed downstairs to meet with Master Rathbyrn. Glancing in a full-length mirror before she left her chambers, Candissa was pleased with the dress Lendra had chosen. It was a light blue, which was Candissa's favorite color, if white was not an option. It had a laced bodice and long sleeves with floral symbols woven into hem.

Her street boots made soft thumping noises as she stepped swiftly down the main staircase. The main entrance hall had high ceilings, usually illuminated by a half-dozen chandeliers of brass. But now, during full day, the tall windows facing east were unshuttered, allowing daylight to fill the area.

The broad floor of the hall was tiled in squares of ivory and burgundy. She knew the ivory was some variety of marble recovered from ancient ruins to the east, but no one had ever told her what the burgundy tiles were.

The scholar Penston suggested they were a rare mineral found deep in the Elven forest, though he admitted this was mere speculation.

She was shortly in an antechamber off the main hall, accessed by a short corridor that split off to a richly-furnished lounge and a small gallery. The antechamber had once been the war room of the fabled general of old, Garruld, or so Quence had told her when she was young and thirsting for stories. Quence was ever want to indulge her yearning for stories, tales and fables.

Master Rathbyrn was seated on one end of a short, thickly lacquered table inlaid with mother-of-pearl and intricately carven pieces of fine wood. The antechamber had one wall lined with tall shelves filled with books. It was lit by daylight, with a tall, glazed window thrown open against the morning sky. The window faced west but high clouds reflected the light of the sun.

Rathbyrn was a tutor in the employ of House Demarrae, though she knew he was more than a simple teacher. He was a scholar and historian in his own right, but had never pursued a career as a scholar. That would involve dealing with too many people. Candissa knew Rathbyrn did not do well in social situations. He preferred the quiet corners of comfortable quarters, the known and familiar.

As Candissa approached him, he did not acknowledge her. He appeared consumed by reading a heavy tome laid open on the long table, while taking spidery notes using a very small quill.

Of middling age, Rathbyrn had dark, almost greasy hair swept over his enormous cranium. His dark, flinty eyes were aided by one of his sets of spectacles, as he read the book. The lenses of glass were set in a delicate frame of brass, perched on his short nose. The thin arms of the spectacles, called temples, wrapped behind and around his ears. The eyepieces were not common, at least in Ravensroost, though Candissa had seen many older scholars and teachers wearing them.

When her lessons started with the tutor, more than a year ago, she was warned that he was *odd*, somehow. Lendra said he had some sort of dreadful thing happen when he was a child, but she wasn't sure and didn't think it appropriate to spread gossip. But he was sometimes prone to mumbling to himself or staring out at nothing when sitting alone. Some of the servants had even accused him of arguing with the shadows, or engaging in shouting matches with the trees in the garden.

Candissa knew he was different, but she had grown to enjoy his peculiarities.

"Good morning, Candissa," her tutor said in a surprisingly forceful voice. She had never thought it matched his short, decidedly hunched stature.

"Good morning, Master Rathbyrn. I hope the day finds you well and the sun shines over your House," Candissa replied, grinning a little as she sat.

"Good, good. You've completed your assigned studies, then?" Rathbyrn said, still not looking up from his notes.

"Yes, it's all a bit boring. The various greetings and responses, what you can talk about, all that," she sighed.

Rathbyrn put his quill down neatly next to his tome, finally lifting his prodigious head to not quite look at her. Since she had known the man, he rarely if ever stared directly at someone when addressing them, preferring to look just above and to one side of their face. It was strange, but she had grown accustomed to it.

"Lady Candissa, I have been charged with preparing you to interact with the Eastern families on a social basis. You must conform to their ways of society, if you wish to be accepted, or even taken seriously," he said.

"Of course, sir. I will do my best to represent my House and my town," she said, nodding. "What is today's lesson about?"

While she found some of the social lessons droning and dull, there was a great deal of underlying information about the East she readily absorbed. Candissa loved learning new things, and never felt an end to her thirst for knowledge.

Rathbyrn slid a stack of papers toward her. "These are descriptions and notes of all the major Houses. I want you to study them. I will test you tomorrow. You have demonstrated proficiency in all the social lessons we've reviewed over the past weeks, so I'm sure you'll do fine with the reception in a few days."

"Truly? I rather thought you were disappointed with my *social graces*," she said, recalling their last session when she had to demonstrate behavior in various social settings.

"Don't be ridiculous. You are more than capable of the appropriate behaviors," he chided her. "You simply must *choose* to engage those behaviors. And I have no doubt you will choose to do so, when the situation demands."

She looked at the tutor with mild surprise. "You really think so? I've never thought I was very well suited to social engagements, banquets, and so on. I just hope I don't disappoint my parents."

"Your pa- Candissa, to say you astonish me is an understatement. You really have no idea what you are, do you?" the tutor said.

Rathbyrn's words took Candissa by surprise. "What do you mean, *what* I am?"

Instantly, the tutor's expression turned from one of familiar warmth to a downcast gaze of shame. "I...I didn't mean to say that *exactly*."

"I wasn't offended, Master Rathbyrn!" she said, fearful she had given him the wrong impression. "It's just a strange thing to say."

"Of course, I am not offended. Let's just…" his words trailed off, as he began to mumble silently, seeming to look into at the corner of the table. Candissa was about to speak when he jerked, turning suddenly in his seat. "No! I won't tell her that!"

Candissa's eyes went wide as she slowly backed up against her chair. He was having one of his spells, or so it seemed. He was staring at nothing, in the middle of the air over the table.

"Master Rath-" she began. He cut her off.

"Candissa, perhaps we should reschedule our lesson," he said, seeming to recover from his momentary derangement. His dark eyes seemed to actually meet hers for a moment, which was unsettling in itself. "Why don't you just study these summaries and tomorrow you can go west into the hills."

The older man seemed to freeze, his face appearing mildly horrified at what he had just said. Candissa's mouth fell open, for a moment. "*What?*" she said, incredulous.

Master Rathbyrn's reaction was instant and almost violent. He jumped upwards from his seat, attempting to stand, pushing the table in the process, his chair falling backwards against the wall. His hands flailed, knocking the heavy book he had been reading to the floor.

"My lady! Please, forgive me!" he said in a quavering voice his eyes studying a point against a far wall. "I must go, please…"

"Master Rathbyrn, please, it's all right," Candissa began. She stood as well, raising her hands in an attempt to calm his apparent agitation.

He struck the table with his fists. "No! I'm not ready!" he said, his eyes shut hard, grimacing. His voice was quavering, unsure.

Candissa acted without thinking. Her tutor was upset, in a state of disarray, *hurting*. She reached out instinctively. She meant to touch his shoulder, but her hand went to his face instead, her palm cupping his jaw.

Her eyes felt strange as she stared at him in that moment, as if she could suddenly see more. His eyes, dark, darting, always looking away, met hers. In that instant, he was different, changed.

"Destiny," he said. Just that word, in a voice that did not seem to belong to him.

"What?" she whispered in reply, still touching his face. There was something there, something deep, distant.

"Destiny is moving across the land, trying to find a home," the tutor said, his eyes suddenly wide, wonder playing across his face. Then those piercing eyes riveted onto hers. "She cannot walk the land as a person. She must find other ways."

"I...I don't understand," Candissa murmured. She drew her hand back, but he grasped her wrist, preventing her from breaking contact.

"Candissa, listen to me. All my life, the voices have spoken to me, plagued me, tormented me! I never knew why, until now," Rathbyrn said. "I am only a messenger. Destiny is reaching out to *you,* and those closest to you, those yet to come. You must seek the signs, listen to the whispers, feel destiny moving through you all!"

"I think you should-" she began, still confused, bewildered by what he was saying. She attempted to move backwards, but he maintained his hold on her wrist.

"Candissa, time is running out!" he leaned in, his grip almost painful now. His eyes were unlike she had ever seen, so intense, so utterly direct. "Your staff, keep it close. It will reveal much."

She was confused by her tutor's words and actions, and a little frightened. But then she realized in a flash: *enough.* Candissa lowered her gaze at Rathbyrn and felt the strange sensation she recalled only a handful of times in her life. The first time had been when she had first seen Errol.

In that instant, Master Rathbyrn's eyes went wide, and he released her, nearly stumbling backwards into his chair.

Candissa was aware of someone behind her, entering the antechamber.

"Is everything all right, Master Rathbyrn?"

It was the sonorous voice of old Quence, the chamberlain. Her tutor seemed to revert to his familiar countenance. Rathbyrn rubbed his nose in an agitated fashion, not looking directly at the tall man behind Candissa.

"Of...of course, Master Quence," Rathbyrn said, his voice almost stuttering. "It was a momentary...nothing to be concerned about."

The tutor moved his chair back, sitting quickly. Candissa blinked, feeling her eyes change somehow.

"Lady?" Quence said quietly.

She turned to look at him and smiled. "It's quite all right. We were just finishing some lessons."

The old man regarded her from under heavy black brows that offset his silvery hair. He raised one eyebrow. He did not believe her entirely, she knew.

"As you say," was all he said before withdrawing from the chamber.

Candissa turned and sat again, facing Rathbyrn. Her mind was still reeling from everything he had said.

The tutor had regained his composure, apparently, and was adjusting himself as he sat. He picked up the book from the floor and began to neatly tuck away his quills in a leather case. He appeared to completely ignore Candissa.

"Master Rathbyrn?"

Still, he did not respond, as he concentrated on stacking note papers in preparation for leaving. Candissa remembered his first name, though she had never used so familiar a term with him.

"Danul?" she said, more softly.

He stopped in his putting away of things, his hands coming to rest on a heavy tome. He stared into a blank wall, blinking.

"Stormshine," he said, his voice as quiet as hers.

"What did you say?" Candissa said, her voice catching a little. The word rang so familiar to her.

"That's what I called you, when you were a little girl," he said, turning to look at her. There was a faint warmth of remembrance in his face. "Even before that incident with Errol, at the Wardenstone."

Candissa blinked, recalling now. Rathbyrn had been in the employ of House Demarrae for many years, arriving here only a few years after her birth. She remembered seeing the tutor even before she began her studies with him.

"Why did you call me that?" she whispered, trying to remember.

"You loved playing outside whenever it stormed, drove your poor mother mad. That's when I noticed your eyes."

"My eyes?"

"They always shined, when you were laughing and playing in the storm, the rain," he said, his own eyes misting over. "It was almost unearthly. I thought to ask your mother about it, but no one else seemed to notice. And I had forgotten about it entirely. Until today."

Candissa knew what he meant. When she forced him to break contact with her.

"They...shined?" she asked.

"Brighter than I ever recall. Little Stormshine, laughing at the wind," he said, smiling at her again. His smile faded. "I think our lessons are done for the day."

"But...what about everything you said? I have so many questions!" she said, sensing his quick retreat.

"Please, I will say nothing more of it. I must go, Candissa," the tutor said, not quite looking at her, as he picked up his books and satchel.

"Perhaps next week, after the reception, we will talk more," she said, trying not to sound too pleading.

Rathbyrn stopped at the open door of the antechamber. He sighed heavily as he turned back to her once more.

"I think not. I feel my task is done, Lady. I have only one request. *Remember* all that I said. Please," he said, his voice strained on the last word.

"Why is it so important I remember?" she asked.

Turning to depart, he paused only long enough to reply, not turning his head as he did so.

"Because, as sure as Destiny walks the land, tomorrow I will have forgotten all of this."

The tutor marched down the adjoining hall, his hunched, martial gait making a thumping noise as it faded, echoing on the polished tiles.

Candissa realized she was breathing faster than she should be. Questions and confusion whirled about her mind.

The next morning, she trained with her staff, finding it in no way remarkable, despite what Master Rathbyrn had said. After the session, she sought out the small but comfortable room Rathbyrn kept, in the forward hall of the servant wing. She found the door open, and only a neatly made bed within. All his personal belongings were gone.

She raced to find Quence, nearly colliding with two servants in the process. The old steward was finishing up a meeting with Arbon, the chief cook.

"My lady, you seem upset," Quence said, rising as Arbon excused himself. In truth, Candissa was still a little sweaty from her exertions and had taken no care to make herself presentable.

"Forgive me, but I am upset! Where is Master Rathbyrn?" she said, realizing her voice sounded a little too demanding.

Quence raised an eyebrow, tucking his ever-present ledger under one arm, as he nodded "Join me in my study, won't you?"

Candissa only nodded in reply. They were soon in his private chamber, a broad desk of polished yew dominating the center of the compact room. She always enjoyed the room, with the tall shelves, filled with curios and tattered books.

"He asked I extend his apologies for his abrupt departure. As far as I could gather, he had pressing family matters in the East. He said you would understand," Quence said, settling in and opening a thin printbook filled with tiny notations.

"Did he say anything else?" she asked, hoping her insistence wouldn't arouse any undue suspicion.

"Well, there was something strange. I asked him if he had any other tutors in town to recommend, to continue your training," Quence said, gesturing to her. Candissa nodded, as that seemed reasonable.

"He said only this in reply, *she will need no more tutors. She is ready.*"

"Truly?" Candissa said, making no attempt to mask her astonishment. "Ready for what?"

The steward only shook his head. "I didn't have the chance to ask him. He told me just one more thing, before he left."

Candissa leaned forward. "What?"

"He told me to tell you just one thing, that *you must remember*," Quence said. He held out one open long-fingered hand. "I asked him, remember what?"

"What did he say?" Candissa said, hoping perhaps some clue to his words had been left with the steward.

Quence shook his head. "He just looked away, you know how he is when he just stares off at nothing. Then he said, *I've already forgotten.*"

CHAPTER SEVEN - ERROL

20 Laborus, Year 197, Eastvale Calendar

Errol's work for Evan took up the balance of the day. Between sorting out orders and making trips to two vendors and the counting house to reconcile balances, it was late afternoon before he finished. He would attend to his other customers on the morrow.

After reviewing the books with Evan, who was always satisfied with his work, he helped the innkeeper with a few of his tasks prior to the evening traffic. Part of his work for the Bonerest tavern was reorganizing their stocks and stores, including all the dry goods and items in the extensive cellars.

He fetched a few small items for the kitchen, including vinegar and spirits, but in doing so found the shelves were in considerable disarray. Returning to the lower level of the tavern after completing his duties, a bright lantern in hand, Errol set to reorganizing the collection of jars, cases, small tuns, bottles and boxes. If there was a foible in his character to which he would admit, it was his intolerance of disorder.

After an hour, he had completed his task to his satisfaction. There were, however, several items having nothing to do with larders or kitchens. These things, including hooks, a hand-broom, and sanding stones, belonged in another storeroom.

The basement consisted of a labyrinthine collection of chambers, all lined in neat masonry that was likely a hundred years old or more. He knew the purpose of nearly every room, having worked at the Bonerest for more than a year. The items he had culled from the kitchen storage chamber belonged in a room with which he was not familiar. It was in the oldest part of the lower levels, in the base of the square tower that formed the center of the Bonerest.

Taking his torch into the chamber, he carefully burned away the few webs that blocked the doorway. It was an unusually thick wall that seemed almost fortified. The chamber was larger than he thought it would have been and filled with what could easily be described as junk. Chairs that needed mending, a cracked table, older pots and other kitchen devices and utensils in dusty crates, and many shelves with a variety of odd objects.

Errol sighed deeply, then muttered to himself, "This is going to take a while."

He knew he could not abide the chaos and complete disarray of this storeroom, and with that his evening was charted out. Propping the torch in an empty pot well away from anything flammable, he headed back upstairs to tell Evan of his intention to organize and clean up the old storeroom. Evan just shook his head and assured him if anyone came inquiring for him, he would direct them to the handsome chambermaid in the cellar.

He found a second torch, as the chamber was too large to be adequately lit by only one torch. Settling into the disorganized room, Errol set about categorizing objects, determining if they were of any use, and stacking or arranging them. He found this sort of work immensely satisfying. He was the first person to admit he was not fond of simple hard labor. The thought of lugging barrels like a common dockworker all day made him shudder from the sheer boredom.

That made him stop. He sighed aloud. He had no idea what a dock worker was. Shaking his head, he continued in his labors.

Spending hours turning disorder into order was something he could sink his teeth into. And so, he did. The sun set over the misty hills to the west, and Errol continued his work. He ordered food and ale at one point and Besh delivered it, along with a lingering kiss.

After more than four hours, the torches had been replaced by two lanterns and several old candles he had found in the room. They burned remarkably bright and emitted no odor whatsoever, which pleased him.

Working his way to the far corner, the room was almost entirely explored, boxes and shelves moved or cleared, and items neatly stacked and classified, awaiting a long-overdue re-shelving. Finding an archaic-looking hanger of metal attached to the crumbling masonry in the far corner, Errol hung one of the lanterns on it, to shed more light on this last area he had to get through.

He had just started to look through a box of dried ink jars and cracked leather bindings full of dust, when the bracket creaked noisily. The lantern broke free from the wall.

"Sard!" Errol blurted, moving like a cat in catching it. Hs reflexes were exceptional, and it did not strike the floor. Righting it and placing it on a table, he realized the metal bracket had given way, along with a large section of the masonry.

Examining it, he was perplexed. Typically, masonry - bricks and mortar - were placed over rough stone walls in cellars like this, to dress it up. This was not the case. The bricks were shallower than typical bricks, and the mortar was likely more than a hundred years old and failing. They had fallen away from a perfectly smooth wall of stone.

Errol thought perhaps there was a defect in the hidden walls. The area he could see, which was not much, appeared solid and unmarred by cracks or pits.

"Wait a moment…" he murmured to himself, retrieving the lantern. Holding it up, he realized the wall here, behind the old masonry, was that same odd gray stone from which the old tower of the Bonerest was formed.

He found it strange that whoever operated the Bonerest a hundred years ago chose to wall over a surface that appeared smooth and sound. Testing the surrounding masonry, it crumbled away easily at the merest touch. The bricks were sound, but the mortar had weakened with the passing of decades. With just his hands, he cleared a two-yard wide area of bricks easily, leaving a tumbled heap on the floor.

"This will not do," he said to himself. One section of the wall was broken and exposed while all the rest of the chamber was not. "Not at all."

He would have to explain to Evan later why he had done this, but it was a minor mystery he had to solve. So, with more work ahead of him, he enlisted the assistance of Rebnar, the stable boy, in hauling the bricks to the alley behind the Bonerest.

After the masonry was brought down, he used a stiff brush to clean the remnants of the mortar off the wall. As he did so, he made another discovery. Engraved in the wall, along the line of the ceiling, was a symbol of some sort. It was etched into the stone with thin lines and set in a square not quite a yard on each edge. The symbol was not familiar to him, consisting in part of what appeared to be an anvil, with a sword over it, and a circle over the sword.

Errol had to don a linen kerchief to avoid breathing too much dust. As he brought down pieces of the masonry, he also piled and moved things closer to the center, to allow for room to create the piles of brick and give Rebnar enough room to get a large basket into the room for the bricks. As the room was taller than the typical cellar, nearly eight feet, he used an iron rod and spade to bring down the highest pieces of masonry.

He was not surprised when he found another inscribed symbol enclosed in a square. This one appeared to be a depiction of a tree over water, perhaps. While he had discovered the pictograms on the wall, beneath the aged masonry, he found absolutely nothing wrong with the smooth, otherwise featureless gray stone. The evening moved on, with Errol bringing down the old bricks as gently as possible, and Rebnar complaining he would be sore the next day. Errol gave the boy several silvers to ensure both his silence and continued effort.

While it was a great deal of work, Errol did mention to his sweating young friend that their labor was creating a larger storeroom. He estimated at least twenty-five additional square feet of floor space. This revelation did little to improve Rebnar's mood.

Errol decided to stop work before midnight, when they were perhaps done with half their work. He promised more work tomorrow. Before the lad left, he gave him five more silvers, which helped both lift the lad's spirits and ensured he would be back to assist him in the morning.

Heading back to the rooms he rented, situated over a few shops along the main avenue in town, Errol fell into a quick and deep sleep, well-worn from his exertions. The following morning, he insisted Evan inspect his work, both to ensure the innkeeper was all right with him continuing, and to show his progress.

The innkeeper was visibly shocked at the change in the storeroom.

"I suppose it gives me a bit more space, and I think this wall is an improvement over the bricks…" he began, looking at the piles of neat but tumbled brick with mild dismay. "How long will this take?"

"I'm sure Reb and I can have it done today," Errol assured him. "And it will be nice and neat when we're finished, you can be sure of that."

"I have no doubt in your ability in that regard. Goodlady Baraben tells me you keep your living quarters in impeccable order," Evan said, referring to the elderly woman from whom Errol rented his chambers.

"After we've cleared it all out, I'll make sure the room is as orderly as the others. Aside from all this mess, I have to say you've accumulated a lot of things you just don't need. You'll find it all piled in the back. I'll have a refuse man collect it," Errol said.

"Yes, be sure to," the innkeeper said. "Otherwise, I see no problem with this. It is odd though, this old chamber in the base of the tower. Any idea about those inscriptions?"

Errol shook his head. "I may draw them out and show them to Penston. Perhaps he'll have a book that can help."

Evan grunted and headed back upstairs, having much to do to prepare for the day. Errol returned to his work, along with Rebnar. By midday, they had three of the four walls cleared off, with only the wall opposite the entrance remaining. Taldrephus sought out Errol at that time, surprised at how much they had done.

The tall youth had to lower his head slightly as he entered the dusty but well-lit chamber, now bearing three lanterns. "This is...a lot of work you've made for yourself, sir."

"You don't sound impressed, Dreff," Errol said. "I'm a little disappointed."

"Right, sir. Don't forget you need to look at the books for those other two shops yet," he reminded him. Errol sighed.

"Yes, I do need to do that. Very well then. It shouldn't take long. Tell you what, you stay here, oversee Reb, maybe take down some of this yourself and yes, I'll make sure you're compensated for it," Errol said, slipping off the workman's gloves he was wearing and handing them to his open-mouthed friend.

"But...well, all right then, sir," Taldrephus said with a resigned expression on his long face.

Errol appreciated the break from his project. He was able to wash up, change, get a quick meal and do his book work, all in less than three hours. Upon his return to the cellars of the Bonerest tavern, he was impressed.

Taldrephus and Rebnar had finished the last wall and were in the process of clearing out the bricks and sweeping up the dust of the mortar. "Lads, well done!" he exclaimed.

"Wasn't too hard, sir, the brick comes down so easily," Dreff said, leaning on a broom. "Looks like fifteen of those carvings, all told."

Errol examined the walls by the lantern light. Fifteen it was, four on a side except for the side opposite the entrance; that side bore only three of the framed inscriptions. It wasn't spaced evenly either, with a large gap remaining on the northern corner.

"You think they were going to put up a final one on that wall?" Dreff asked.

"Perhaps," was all Errol offered as reply.

"Well, I'll get about sweeping and dusting off all these items in the middle, if that's all right."

"Yes, thanks Dreff, that would be wonderful," Errol replied, his eyes moving from one inscription to the next. He walked along the space along the perimeter of the storeroom, that had been cleared over the course of the project.

Most were a mystery to him. Even if some of the inscribed shapes were clear to him, they didn't make sense together. He studied each of them, committing them to memory. He knew drawing each of them out carefully would make a more lasting impression in his memory.

He was on nearly the last symbol, which was inscribed on the last of the walls to be cleared of the cracked brick work.

"What do you think they could mean, sir? Do you have any thoughts?" Taldrephus asked, more to make conversation while he swept slowly, trying not to send too much dust into the still air.

"None at all, but I'm hoping the scholar…" Errol said, his words trailing off. His mouth hung a little open, his eyes unblinking.

Taldrephus stopped sweeping, turning to look at his master. "Sir? Is everything all right?" Errol stood mute and transfixed on one of the inscribed symbols.

Within the square was a large circle, and within the circle was what appeared to be a ship, facing toward the viewer. There were three sails, the prow of the ship below, and what were likely stylized depictions of waves breaking at the bow. Behind was a horizon of ocean. On the main sail was a five-pointed star.

Errol slowly drew forth his dagger from his sheath. The sound it made reminded him of a memory. The room seemed to disappear around him. Holding the dagger up in the light of the lanterns, he turned it point down and looked at the broadest part of the blade.

On the flat of the blade, near the guard, was a small inscription, just an inch wide or so. It was simpler than the pictogram on the wall, but there was no mistake. It was the same symbol. A ship breaking the water, with a star on the larger sail.

He couldn't shake the memory it dredged up. He was standing on the Wardenstone, burned, dazed, lost...and a young woman, just a girl, was standing there, her blond hair wet with rain, her white robes dingier, but still unmistakable. But her eyes weren't right. Still, he drew forth the blade, the grip wet from the rain. The weight of it in his hand was reassuring, a tenuous link to *before*. The memory faded, almost snapping shut in his mind.

He nearly stumbled, but Taldrephus caught him.

"Sir! Are you ill?" he said, concern clear in his voice.

Errol shook his head, still clutching the deadly sharp blade. "No, of course not, I was just...I must be overworking myself with this," he said by way of an excuse.

The taller man looked at the inscription on the wall. "You were looking at this one. Is there something about it? If you need a tool, I can find something. I wouldn't wreck that fine dagger of yours on picking at a wall."

Errol was already sheathing his dagger. "Thanks, Dreff, please just finish your fine work here. I need to get some parchment and ink."

Upstairs, he found a quiet booth and signaled Beshanu to bring some wine. She brought him a glass and was going to engage in her typical flirting but sensed at once he was in no mood.

"Are you alright?" she asked. He grinned and sighed. Clearly, he was not doing his usual job of masking his feelings.

"I am just fine, my dear. Merely thinking," he assured her. She nodded and left him alone.

Sipping the wine, he drew out his dagger again.

He had heard the account from the three who had been there. When he had been found on that immense block of gray stone more than five years ago, he had almost nothing.

His singed, torn articles of clothing were still bundled away in a sack under his bed. They bore no insignia nor indication of where they were made. They were a source of surprise to the town's tailors. Apparently, the stitching was quite beyond their level of mastery. Errol eventually had his clothing made to resemble the ruined vest, tunic and pants. But he could not bring himself to throw away the original set of clothing.

His pockets had had a quantity of dust and debris, or so he was told, which was strange. Stranger still, in one pouch they found lumps of featureless gold, each about the weight of a typical gold oak. After a time, when he had recovered and began building his life in Ravensroost, he took the lumps of gold to the counting house. The master of weights was astonished at the apparent purity of the precious metal. Those lumps helped fund the start to his life here. Why they were lumps and not properly minted coins remained a mystery.

The only other item on his person was his blade. He could not recall the details of that day when he was found, until today. The image of the inscription somehow awoken the memory of when he had first seen Candissa, and how he had drawn his dagger as he stood there in the rain.

Why would I draw my dagger, he thought. The obvious answer was that the ranger Vink was attacking the girl. Everyone assumed he killed him defending her. He just could not recall any image of the ill-fated Vink.

He stared at the smooth, shining surface of the dagger, placing it on the table in front of him. The town wizard, a stout and older fellow named Emphry, had once examined the blade, during his first few weeks when many people in Ravensroost were trying to figure out where he had come from.

I feel a definite enchantment about this blade, young man. Keep it close to you. If others know of it, they may try to steal it. Such blades can fetch a high price in the darker markets, Emphry had told him. *If you ever travel to Eastvale, you may want to have someone at the Scholaria examine it.*

The wizard's revelation explained why the dagger seemed to sometimes catch the light of the setting sun and almost glimmer with an otherworldly sheen. There were also times when Errol could see the blade, even though the room was almost pitch black.

Another point he never mentioned to anyone, was the blade never seemed to dull. He rarely used it in a utilitarian fashion, only occasionally to cut leather or a small tree limb. There were a few occasions when he had hunted with a party from the town, and once had to use it against a charging boar. It cleaved through the boar's hide and ribs as though they were soft leather. When he shook the blade, the blood just slid off.

Errol had taken it to the smith, Grumber, a few years ago, to see if he had any insights. After examining the metal and the making of the blade, he only shook his head, saying it was well beyond his talents to either guess on how it was made or even what the metal was.

Then there were the tricks he used to amuse himself and others with. He could twirl and flip the blade easily, with the skill of a well-trained acrobat. He practiced with it almost every day, enjoying how far into a tree's bark he could bury the tip.

At times like those, he felt the blade was very much a part of him. He had shown the symbol on the flat to the scholar and others long ago, to no avail. Now, he found the symbol in the storeroom, next to other symbols. There was a chance he could find some clue to who he was or whence he had come.

He had never doubted the wizard's claim of it being enchanted. Errol had even played a game on many occasions, using the blade to guide his actions. He was once lost on the footpaths of the moors to the south on a cloudy afternoon, on an errand for Evan. It was approaching evening and he did not wish to be out alone in the desolate tracts where he might be food for wolves or worse. He had jokingly twirled the dagger in the air and asked aloud which direction he should travel. All three times he asked, letting the dagger spin and fall on its own accord, the blade had pointed in the same direction, and not the way he was inclined to go.

Still, he followed the direction the blade had indicated, and after less than an hour, he had sighted a road marker that led him home. Sometimes he would spin the blade on a table, asking where someone was or where he could find something he had lost. The perfect balance of the remarkably crafted blade allowed it to spin easily. It rarely gave him an inaccurate answer.

He had asked questions in the past it clearly could not answer. The one he had asked most often was simply, *where did I come from?* The blade would never point in the same direction. Clearly, it had limits.

He had to ink the sketches of all the symbols he had found in the storeroom. That was his next step now. Once that was done, he wondered who would be able to answer his questions or provide any more insight into his origins. He grinned to himself, drawing out two coins, a copper pine and a silver maple.

He placed them on the table, away from the blade.

"All right, the silver means Penston will have an answer and the copper means I travel to Eastvale," he murmured quietly, so as not to attract the attention of any midday patrons. "So, good blade, tell me. Where must I go for my answers?"

Placing the coins above and below the blade, he spun it with a sharp twist of his wrist. The first attempt was inconclusive, as the blade was pointing well away from either coin. This was not typical.

He spun it again, with the same result. Again, he spun it. Again, it pointed in the same direction, nowhere near either coin. He picked up the coins and pocketed them. He spun it again, and again. *And again.*

Every spin, the same result to his question of where he must go to seek his answers.

He looked out the door of the Bonerest, in the direction indicated by his blade, to the darkening skies over the misted hills.

West.

CHAPTER EIGHT - CAM

23 Laborus, Year 197, Eastvale Calendar

Cam guided his mount through the eastern gate of Ravensroost sometime around midday. Darbo had weathered the journey well. Cam was glad it was not too warm this time of year. The sky was clear but chilly. He wouldn't be surprised to see an early squall of snow roll out of the north within the week. The Starfire Mountains never disappointed in the months of Tempestus and Procellus.

The guards asked his name, where he came from and his business. Cam told them he was a leatherworker and had business here. A lie really, as he had no actual engagements. Still, perhaps he could find his way here as a tanner and hunter. He shook his head.

West. He couldn't shake the message he had received, *somehow*, six nights past. He had checked his mysterious slip of parchment many times since. Nothing but that simple message.

Gondrim had told him to stay at the Bonerest but gave him no more advice. He would not tell him why he had to leave Woodford so hastily. Only the message left behind by Adreassa offered any clue. He had no direction, no idea what he was to do here, if anything at all. Would he start a new life in Ravensroost, or would he forge a path into the trackless wilds beyond the Misthallows? He felt lost.

The Bonerest Tavern was easy to find. It was the largest building nearest the western gate of the town, facing the open square. Most shops and markets were on the eastern side, where the busier roads offered more traffic every day. The center of town was dominated by a tall, fortified structure, built of gray stone, with a thick wall of darker stone pressing into it. The edifice aroused his curiosity.

He pressed his mount through a bustling market, catching the eye of a merchant. The round, happy-looking fellow was a hawker of metal ware. He saw Cam looking at him and smiled broadly, clearly hoping to secure his custom.

"Good day to you, sir!" the merchant called. "Are you looking for something of iron or steel? Perchance a trap, or length of chain? Cook pots or mayhap a knot of fish-hooks?"

Cam smiled at the man's endearing if excessive expressions. He swung his leg over the saddle, dropping to the ground. His mother had always told once, *It's rude to start a conversation on horseback with someone on foot, unless you mean to establish a superior position.*

He looked about at the iron-monger's stall. It had no end of curios as well as every sort of iron or steel device he could recall - metal loops, flat cook-pans and round, tall pots, stakes, hinges, hooks, prods, plates, pins, screws, and bundles of wire, thick and thin.

Cam saw a collection of clearly disused oddments in a wooden box near the back of the stall. Clearly, it was a catch-all of items least likely to sell. Something caught his eye, an inscrutable device of polished metal, cubic and heavy, with oddly spaced holes on three sides. He hefted it in his palm.

"How much for this?" he asked the man, entirely uninterested in the object. It was simply a means to an end. The metals merchant raised one eyebrow.

"That, sir?" he said, scratching his head. "There a funny story behind that little trinket, it comes from-"

"I've no doubt," Cam said, fishing out three maples from his pocket. "Will this do?"

The merchant extended his hand, smiling obsequiously, accepting the three silver coins. "I can see you have a discriminating eye, sir."

Cam grinned, reaching back and depositing the metal cube in his pack. "Thanks. My name is Cam, and you are…"

The man bowed abruptly, a little too deeply in Cam's opinion. "Ferrick is my name, Master Cam. At your service!"

"Could I ask, what is this immense building here?" Cam said, gesturing to the towering construct of dark and light stone sprawled across the center of Ravensroost.

"Oh, that is the Kings Garrison and Justice, as it's called," Ferrick said. "The magistrates are in there, and on the other side of the wall is the garrison house, and the council halls."

Cam nodded. It made sense. "Does the King have a strong hold here, so far from Eastvale?" he asked.

"Oh, may the gods bless him and his line. But you know, as they say, only spoken, merely token," Ferrick said, winking. It was a reference to the

King having never visited the town.

Cam nodded, grinning. It was as he suspected. Ravensroost was a very independent town, being so utterly removed from the center of civilization.

"Is there anything else I can interest you in, Master Cam?" Ferrick said, gesturing broadly across his stall of goods.

"Just directions to the Bonerest Tavern," Cam said, planting one foot in a stirrup. He felt Darbo brace himself. Cam was not a light rider.

"Oh, hardly necessary, sir. You just keep on this main way that way and it will put you in the west gate square. The Bonerest is there," Ferrick said. "Master Evan is the tavernmaster, you tell 'im Ferrick sent you. He knows me!"

Cam seated himself on Darbo.

"I thank you, Master Ferrick," he said, nodding. He looked across the market square. "That way, then?"

"Yes, just keep heading…" Ferrick began, motioning across the market. His merry eyes seemed to widen and fix on Cam's. The hunter grew instantly alarmed.

"What is it?" he asked the ironmonger.

"Just keep moving...west…" the man's words seemed to diminish. He blinked, his gaze moving from Cam as he lowered his hand. His wits appeared to recover as another customer moved between Darbo and the ironmonger.

Cam stared at the man, but Ferrick was entirely caught up in an animated conversation regarding the quality and consistency of his iron. Cam moved off, guiding Darbo through the press as he glanced back at Ferrick, wondering if the merchant would meet his eyes again. He did not.

As he moved down the main avenue, Cam found the western end of Ravensroost consisted of poorer houses, rangers, stables, craftsmen who needed larger lots and a few odd shops.

He had stopped at a handful of street vendors on his way through town. He purchased some small things to eat but was more interested in talking with the locals. The Bonerest had a reputation for welcoming travelers, scant though they were. No one traveled west from here, just north or south to the steadings held by the more courageous or foolhardy.

After stabling his horse for a few silver maples, he entered the greatroom of the tavern. It was well lit, with windows thrown open, allow the lowering rays of the late autumn sun to warm the room through glazing the color of Elven wine. There were a dozen patrons scattered about the place, seated at well-made chairs and benches of gnollpine and blue oak.

A long, wooden bar with a foot-rail lined the eastern wall of the room and a few men were perched at one end of it, enjoying a midday ale. With his saddlebag over his back, Cam approached, drawing out a gold oak in case it was needed to show. Ofttimes, barkeeps would refuse strangers unless coin was in evidence.

A tall man dressed in a green tunic and gray apron stepped out from the kitchen, a tray of mugs in hand. His hair was light brown, his eyes green, and at once Cam realized he was of mixed Human and Elven blood. His realization must have been revealed in his stare. The man grinned and nodded, saying quietly, in Elven, "Greetings, brother." It was a common phrase exchanged by those of mixed descent upon meeting one another. It put Cam at ease immediately.

"Greetings," Cam replied in the same tongue.

"May I help you? A room, I expect?" the tavern master spoke now in the common Human language.

"Forgive my stare, but you must be Master Evan. My friend, Gondrim, recommended I find room and board here," Cam said. He extended his hand as an afterthought. "My name is Cam Bronwyer."

The tall half-Elven man shook it, after putting his tray down. "Glad to know you. Gondrim is a good fellow. Will he be joining you here?"

"Sadly no, he has business in the east," Cam said. It was a minor deception, but he was not about to go into any detail on why Gondrim could not join him here. "How much do you charge for room and board? I'm not really sure how long I'll be staying, to be quite honest."

"Nine silver maples a day should suffice. I can give you nicer quarters if you want to spend more," Evan said.

"I'm sure the room will be fine for me. When are meals served?"

"Morning meal is available just before sunrise, dinner halfway between midday and evening, privy's outside next to the stable. Use the piss pots if you please and keep it clean," Evan recited what was likely a well-practiced litany. "Here's your key. Your room is up the stairs, fourth on the left, room nine. Do you read and write? I mean no offense by the question."

"I would take none. Yes, I do," Cam said. He knew there were some who had no skill in reading or writing their letters. The innkeeper slid the ledger around to face Cam.

"You can put your name, or mark, if you please," Evan said. "I'll need three days in advance."

Cam took a moment to scratch his name neatly on the line the tavern master indicated. He fished around in his pockets before producing two oaks and three maples.

"There you are. So, the day's meal is ready soon?"

"Yes, would you like a plate and bowl brought to your room or will you be eating here?"

"Down here. I'm expecting a friend on the next carriage from Woodford. Do you happen to know when it would be arriving?" Cam asked.

"If the weather didn't delay them, and if the driver pushed the horses, perhaps this evening, around four or five. But it's far more likely they will arrive tomorrow, midday or later, perhaps three," Evan said, glancing at the wall over the archway leading into a common room.

Cam turned and followed the tavernmaster's gaze. Over the arch, affixed to the wall, was a device of metal and glass, mounted in a frame of wood. It featured a large disc of metal, silvery in color, divided into thirds, each section decorated with inscribed shapes and images. The perimeter of the circle had marks visible across the room. He recognized the device at once.

"A clock," Cam said, wonder clear in his voice.

"Just that, yes," Evan replied. "You know about timepieces?"

"Only from what I've read, and what my parents told me. I've seen one, at the library at Woodford, but it doesn't work. Where did you find it?"

"It was found in the underchambers in this building, many years ago. An elderly Dwarve repaired it. He was a master with the gears and springs and that sort of thing. Apparently, it only needed a few adjustments and a good winding."

Cam studied it, fascinated, for a moment. He recalled how clocks typically worked by winding a spring housed within. He also recalled that the craft of making clocks was lost. Some said the Dwarves kept the secrets deep within their mountains, far to the east. From his limited experience in towns, there were no Human artisans or metalworkers who could make a clock. Perhaps there was one in Eastvale.

"I would like to know more about it, perhaps we could talk later?"

"You know where to find me," Evan said, a faint smile on his lips. The young man nodded, hoisting the heavy bags on his shoulder again, then looked at his key.

"Stairs on the right, fourth room on the left. Number nine," the tavern master reminded him again. Cam thanked him and was upstairs quickly. Opening the door, he realized the lock mechanism was far nicer than the simple latches and locks he had seen on other inn doors. The room was simple but nicely appointed. For a tavern said to be of a middling character in town, the furnishings and mattress were very much to Cam's liking.

There was a tall shelf for him to store his belongings, a small table, a padded chair, tapers, towels, a basin and pitcher full of water, and even a broad trunk. There was no padlock, but he could get one if needed. Sorting out his belongings and where to put them, Cam wondered how long he would call this room home. Once he had distributed his possessions to his satisfaction, he considered his pack. He had not heard that Ravensroost was especially prone to thievery, particularly by day. He checked the windows and shutters and found them to be secure.

Leaving his pack on the bed, as there was little point in trying to conceal such a bulky item, he buckled his belt pouch, ensuring his coins were safely within. Locking the door behind him, he went downstairs to enjoy some food and await the arrival of his new acquaintance. Finding a table easily at this time of day, he was soon served a bowl of savory stew comprised of beef, barley, potato and onion, along with a slab of a dark rye bread with honey. A flagon of cold ale completed the meal. Cam found it immensely satisfying.

A serving woman came over to remove his plate and bowl. She was a pretty, young woman with long blond hair and remarkably smooth skin. "Did you find the stew to your liking, love?" she said with a sweet lilt to her voice.

"Yes, very much. Please let Evan know it was probably the best stew I've ever had in my life," Cam said, trying to sound as sincere as he truly was.

She laughed lightly. "He does get a few compliments on the stew," she said, winking at him as she removed the plate and spoon. "I'm Beshanu. Let me know if you need anything else."

Cam liked the way she looked. He puzzled a moment over his reluctance to let a woman be part of his life. He had had a few opportunities, young women in Woodford who were clearly open to his advances. Aside from a few tumbles in the stables with willing women after a cup of wine or two, he had never wanted to let anyone in. The mere thought of sharing his life with a woman right now was inconceivable.

However, looking at the retreating form of the serving woman, he realized he wouldn't mind sharing his bed.

"Later," he growled to himself, quietly. He had to first figure out why he was here at all. It certainly wasn't to bed down serving girls. Instead, he chose to divert his attention somehow. Looking about the room, he surveyed the other patrons.

They appeared to the lower classes of townsfolk, but not the dregs he sometimes saw in Woodford. There were a few middle merchants as well, evidenced from the cut of their clothing or the language of their conversations. One fellow appeared to be one of the rangers of Ravensroost, assuming they dressed the same as they did in Woodford. Cam made a note of the fellow with the intent of introducing himself at some convenient time.

He suspected the innkeeper would be an excellent source of information, if he had any questions about Ravensroost. If he couldn't answer a question, he would likely be able to point Cam in the right direction.

Sipping his ale, he glanced further about the room. Then he noticed the clock on the wall again. It intrigued him. He walked over to inspect it more closely, ale in hand. The face of the clock, as he remembered the name of the circle of metal, had a hole in the middle of it, through which a spindle protruded. Attached to the slowly turning spindle was a long, pointed piece of metal, the name of which Cam could not recall.

"The arrow?" he murmured to himself. That didn't sound right, but it was shaped vaguely so. It pointed toward the hour of the day. The face of the clock was divided into three segments, each representing an approximate period during any day. Walking closer, he could make out the small drawings inscribed and illuminated on the face.

He had seen pictures of clocks, aside from the broken one in Woodford. A memory nagged at him, of a clock that wasn't broken. Something from long ago. He could recall the pictures he had seen in his mother's books easily. Illustrations of the mechanical workings behind the faces of clocks like this one.

Looking underneath the box of dark, almost black wood, Cam could see two holes. The clock was mounted out of reach, over a seven-foot tall archway leading into a common dining hall. He suspected if he had a ladder, he would find a metal tool lying atop the box, hidden from view, for the purpose of winding the spring using one of the two holes.

"Wondering what that is, are you?" someone said to him from a table close to his left. Looking over, Cam saw a man dressed in a fine tunic and trousers of dark green with light gray trimming. His boots were fine leather with brass buckles. He knew at once he was of a distinctly higher social station.

"No, good sir, just examining it more closely," Cam said, nodding. "It appears to be a clock of fine craftsmanship."

"That it is. Not too many know they're called clocks," the man said, rising to his feet, a glass of wine in one hand. He extended the other. "My name is Orrendar, of House Allenfar. I hope you don't think my question offensive."

Cam shook the young man's hand. He judged him to be from the east, by his accent. He appeared not especially young or old, with brown hair common among most Humans. "Not at all. I am Cam Bronwyer, just arrived in Ravensroost, from Woodford."

"Would you join me?" Orrendar asked, motioning to the chair opposite his. Cam nodded and sat.

"You are too kind, my lord," Cam said. The young man chuckled, shaking his head.

"No *my lord* for me, good sir. I am a distant cousin of the noble Lord Allenfar. Perhaps someday I will earn my own holding, but not yet," he corrected Cam. He pointed up at the clock. "Do mechanical things interest you?"

"Yes, certainly, they do. I've read quite a bit on them, since I was younger. Remarkable what a few bits of well-tooled metal can do."

"Well-said. We have a working clock at my home estate, in the east. Dwarven-made as they are all, I suspect. It has a simpler face than this one.

Remarkable inscriptions in the three sections of this one, don't you think?"

Cam looked back up at the face. "Yes, it is quite elaborate. There's a broken one in Woodford, but it is far simpler in its inscriptions. So, you suspect all clocks are made by the Dwarves?"

"I can't say for certain, but that is what I've been told by others," Orrendar said. "Where did they acquire this one? It seems a little extravagant for a tavern on the selvage of civilization."

Cam noted a hint of condescension in the man's voice but that was not a surprise. "The tavernmaster, Evan, told me they found it in one of their cellars, years ago. Must have been there from some time in the past."

"And how long will you be visiting Ravensroost, if I may ask?" Orrendar said, sipping his wine.

"I'm not sure yet," Cam replied. He looked over his shoulder, up at the clock to check the time. Looking back at his new friend, Orrendar had an expression of expectant curiosity on his face. The courteous way of asking why Cam was looking at the time.

"I'm expecting an acquaintance on the carriage from Woodford. It should be in town around four or five setting," Cam said, though he didn't know if Koraymis would arrive today or tomorrow.

"I'm sorry, four or five *setting*? I'm not familiar with that term," Orrendar said.

"The three trinals on the face of the clock, the old names for them are rising, setting, and dark," he explained, pointing at the clock's face. "With eight hours in each, you have one through eight rising, setting, or dark."

"Fascinating," Orrendar said quietly. "I've never heard that before. So right now, it's between...three and four setting?"

"Correct. The high mark is midday, and that separates the rising hours on the left and the setting hours on the right. The dark is the trinal on the bottom of the face, see how it's illuminations are tinted blue?"

"Of course, to signify the darkest hours. Fascinating."

They drank for a few more minutes, while Orrendar spoke of his estate and the fruits they grew there. While he was a distant relation of House Allenfar, Orrendar was more accurately in their employ. Cam was growing somewhat disinterested in the accounts. He thought his expression may have betrayed that, as the noble suddenly rose to his feet. He finished his second glass of wine and rapped the table. "Master Bronwyer, it has been my honor, but I must away. Perhaps your friend will be along soon."

With that, they exchanged the appropriately courteous goodbyes, and the noble made his way out of the Bonerest, after paying Beshanu at least three gold oaks more than was due.

She came over to clean up the table and looked at the departing young man clad in green.

"Now who was that exactly? I'd like to make sure and serve him if he ever shows up again," she said, pocketing the excess coins with a wink.

"That would be Orrendar of House Allenfar. He'll be in town for several days perhaps, or so he says," Cam said. "I, however, will be in town for much longer."

"Well, as I've always said, longer is better," she said, winking. "I hope to see you again soon."

He found himself momentarily taken by her figure, as well as her flirtatiousness, as she walked away. Shaking his head after a momentary reverie, he stood and made his way out the door to the stables, to make use of the privy. Returning to his room, he checked his appearance in the tarnished mirror hanging on the wall. He retrieved a comb from his backpack, where he kept it with other morning ritual necessities. He pulled it through his somewhat disheveled hair.

After it was somewhat more presentable, he checked his teeth. They were in generally good condition, but felt almost caked, as he had neglected to brush them over the course of his journey to Ravensroost. After a search through his belongings, he was dismayed to find he had forgotten his boar-bristle toothbrush. He recalled now, in his rush to leave Handerby, he had left it behind the wash basin. He would have put it in his pack, in one of the side pockets. He checked and re-checked each of them, to no avail.

Cam sighed. His teeth felt awful. He upended his nearly-empty pack onto the bed. Nothing.

Something tugged at his thoughts, a remembrance, perhaps. No, a realization. He had felt this before.

His hand slipped into the hidden pocket, easing it open, drawing out the small piece of parchment. Since he had left Handerby, it had born only that one message, in green ink.

With a certain expectation, he saw the writing had changed. The previous message was gone, replaced by the new one.

Be mindful not to abuse this, Cam. Once, perhaps twice with each rising sun. It will respond to your needs, and the needs of those around you. Envision the need, and reach into it.

The message made little sense, at first. Then Cam knew.

Without intending to, he held his breath, then reached into the large compartment of his pack. The contents yet lay spilled across the bed. His fingers found the bottom of the pack. They touched rough bristles, the sharp, thick hairs slipping under a fingernail.

Cam drew forth the toothbrush, *his* toothbrush. He blinked, his mind refusing to accept what he held in his hand. Yet, there it was. He had left it a hundred miles to the east, and here it was.

He looked at the note, and remembered what the letter had said. Picking up a quill and stoppered ink bottle, Cam penned a hasty message on the other side of the parchment square. *"Does it recover things I lost, or that others have lost?"*

He slipped it back into the hidden pocket, only half-believing it would actually reach the intended recipient. He shook his head. *I'm a fool!* he chided himself.

Retrieving the parchment, his mouth fell open as he saw it was in fact a *different square* of parchment, as if torn from the same sheet. Wet, black ink formed a freshly-penned reply.

Not simply that. It can produce objects you need yet have never possessed. It can even yield things you only imagine. The only price is that sometimes you must place things in the pack with the understanding they will vanish.

Cam was dumbfounded. It took him a moment to realize what had just happened. He clapped both hands on his head. *That* was his first message to Adreassa.

He quickly penned another message. *"Is that truly you Adreassa?"* He had to know.

Stuffing the parchment into the pocket, he felt immediately stupid for it.

He almost started, feeling the strange sensation he knew to be the signal that something had changed in his pack. Retrieving the note, it was the same piece of parchment. Under his hastily scrawled question was a short message.

Yes, darling boy. But these chances are always brief - we cannot waste them idly. Write again when you must!

Cam's breath hitched. Darling boy. That was what she had always called him. Tears threatened as he was suddenly eight years old again, as he sat looking up into the gentle eyes of Adreassa as she instructed him in some bit of wilderness lore.

Cam sat up, dropping the note in his lap. He felt ashamed. What had he been thinking? His father's pack, his *gift*, was not to be squandered. He would not act so foolishly again. He yearned to reconnect with Adreassa - he could not deny that. But this was something much more important than mere boyish infatuation.

He began collecting the items he had scattered on the bed, placing them back in the pack. For a moment, he hesitated. Something nagged his mind. It was an itch he could not put a source to, but he felt compelled to act, *somehow*. He took a deep breath, closing his eyes. She had written, *with the understanding they will vanish.* Eyes snapping open, he quickly replaced everything into its proper compartment.

Bundling the pack and slinging it over his shoulder, he headed downstairs. Evan was at the near of the bar, collecting mugs on a tray.

"Master Evan, do you sell bottles of wine?"

"Yes, I have a few I'm willing to part with. Are you looking for something in particular?"

Cam thought for but a moment. "A red. Could I see what you have to offer?"

Evan nodded, disappearing into the kitchen. A minute later, he returned with a rough-tacked crate containing several bottles, clanking as he placed them on the bar.

"A few Eastern reds, always popular, a Dwarven berry wine, far too sweet if you ask my opinion," the tavernmaster said, drawing forth the bottles and placing them in front of Cam. "A rare Elven *zalforren*, that I could not part with for less than a full three gold oaks."

Cam surveyed the selection, but one bottle remained in the crate.

"What's that?"

"It's spoiled. An old vintage from Longhart. You don't want that one," Even said, pulling out the bottle and examining the stopper. It was blackened with rot.

Cam noted the bottle was different from the others. The surface was not smooth like most glass bottles, but had strange, serpentine ridges wandering around and up the length of the container.

He reached for the bottle, taking it from Evan's hands. "Curious, the bottle."

"Master Penston says it's something that was left behind," the tavernmaster said. He looked at Cam with a sort of expectant expression. Cam understood.

When Cam was a boy, his father had told him about some objects people would find. They would find them in old buildings, forgotten cellars, caves or even ruins. They were often simple items, yet their origin was not understood. They could be crafted from porcelain, metal, or glass, like this bottle. Yet the secrets of their creation remained elusive, and some could never be replicated, even by the most skilled craftsmen. People called such objects *left behind*. Cam once asked his father who left them behind. His father said only that no one ever speaks of that.

The bottle, despite the soured contents, intrigued Cam. The asymmetry of the wandering, decorous ridges held his fascination.

"How much for it?"

Evan seemed ready to protest Cam's apparent intent. Perhaps it was politeness, or perhaps it was a tavernmaster's practical nature, but in any case, he did not object to Cam's inquiry.

"Five silver, and I'm a thief at that price," Evan said.

Cam pinched a stack of silver maple from his belt pouch and counted out five of the discs of silver, each bearing a maple leaf, the symbol of the first King of Eastvale, Marvachus. Evan took the coins with a nod and half-smile. Slinging his pack under one arm, Cam slipped the bottle into the larger compartment. As he did so, he recalled the words of Adreassa in the note she had penned.

He did not give the wine and the note much more thought, as he laid down more coin and called for a tall mug of cool, Dwarven ale. He let go his concerns, enjoying the music of the evening and engaging in friendly, idle banter with other patrons. A bard by the name of Surjore was keeping the place lively with popular tunes played on his many-stringed instrument. He spoke with many patrons, making a handful of friends, or so he hoped. He also obtained the names of two prominent leatherworkers in town. He would seek them out, on the morrow, and get the lay of the land, so to speak. Evan had some excellent suggestions for places that Cam should visit, including the Ranger's Lodge, where the rangers of the town gathered and trained.

The hour was late when he finally climbed the stairs to his room. Looking back, he saw Evan gently rousing a pair of snoring patrons, as Beshanu filled her tray with empty mugs and dirtied plates. She winked at him as he surveyed the room. The clock read nearly an hour past low dark, or midnight as it was more commonly called. His pack over one shoulder, Cam headed upstairs.

Back in his room, he lit one of the slow-burning tapers and changed into night-clothing. He was of a mind to read one of the several books he had brought with him from Woodford, despite the late hour. Looking at the table next to his bed, it had a second taper. But even two of them would provide poor light for reading.

He wished he had one of Gondrim's oil lamps, heavy, angular works of glass, with a squat brass base for the oil. One of those would light a room this large as though the setting sun was streaming through a window

Cam glanced sharply at the door to his room, expecting a knock. His instincts had alerted him to something, but it was not a visitor. He had felt this particular sensation before.

With a small smile, he looked down at his pack, on the floor next to his bed.

Lifting it, he felt the increased weight.

Reaching in, he felt something. The bottle of wine was gone. He drew forth the Dwarven-crafted table lamp and grinned. The brass base was even full of oil.

CHAPTER NINE - CANDISSA

24 Laborus, Year 197, Eastvale Calendar

The hall was well-appointed today. Her mother ensured the finest flatware and serving ware were out and the tables were all covered in their best linens. The servants were in their best and the windows were all thrown wide open to provide ample illumination in the hall.

The foods — snacks really at this point — were already being brought out. Her father, being the preeminent baker in Ravensroost if not better than most in Woodford, considered the offerings on his table a source of pride. He was hovering over the spare but exceedingly well-crafted baked goods.

At the far end of the hall, near the more comfortable chairs, her mother was standing amid a few other figures. She waved Candissa over toward her with a forced air of indifference, trying not to betray her inner tension. These sorts of affairs always frayed her poor mother's nerves, Candissa knew.

Candissa walked smoothly over toward her mother and the guests.

"Candissa, my dear, I want you to meet Lord Urenson Ythanford, his house owns and operates several very important mines to the north. Lord Ythanford, my daughter, Candissa," her mother said with practiced ease. The minor noble took Candissa's hand in the appropriate fashion, not quite bringing it to his lips. His eyes flashed momentarily as he studied her face, and she thought for a moment he might have been speechless. She sometimes had that effect on men. Urenson Ythanford was of middle age, with a middle figure and clearly powerful hands. His nails showed evidence of a working life, so Candissa suspected he had earned his title and wealth honestly, instead of having it bestowed by right of inheritance.

"I am honored, and entirely smitten by your beauty, Lady Candissa," Ythanford said.

"My lord, it is my honor, and may I say I have heard much of your eminent mining facilities," she replied. "You are to be congratulated. I understand your iron mines and smelting facilities are yielding some of the highest grades of iron in all the Kingdom."

The minor lord seemed genuinely impressed and taken aback, unaccustomed to hearing such praise from a beautiful young daughter of a noble house.

"Why...yes, that's right, thank you very much. I had no idea House Demarrae had such educated daughters," Lord Ythanford said.

Sidelong, Candissa saw her mother's eyes flash and narrow. She was not amused by her eldest daughter's demonstration of her education.

"Your reputation for quality is known by many, my lord," she said.

"Let me introduce you to my son, Treluren, he's working on his mastery of the business, so I'm sure you'll be hearing more of him as time goes by," Lord Ythanford said with a note of pride. The young man he had to almost push forward was a bit pudgy and far shorter than Candissa, with a somewhat blotchy complexion and squinting eyes.

"Hello, my...lady," he almost stuttered. His eyes bulged on getting close enough to see her clearly. "Oh, my you are pretty!" His father rolled his eyes at his son's blurting of the clumsy compliment. Candissa only smiled kindly.

"My thanks, good sir," she said, curtseying gently. "Tell me, what aspect of your father's trade do you find most interesting?"

The lad was still staring at her with unblinking eyes. "What? Oh, I don't know. Counting the profits, I suppose," he said, adding an unpleasant laugh at the end.

"Aha, of course, m'lord," she replied, a shallow smile on her lips. She was about to extract herself from the inane conversation when Lord Ythanford prodded his son from behind.

"Ask what she likes to do, you idiot," his hoarse whisper was too loud.

"Oh, um, so my Lady Can..dissa, what do you like, to do?" the boy lord asked, nearly tripping over the words.

"My lord is too kind to inquire," Candissa said with the same wan smile. "My father would have me learn more of the family business, which I confess I do enjoy. Baking, after all, must be in my blood."

"Ah, you must be able to make some very delicious treats in the kitchen, then? I've had a few of your father's wares here, they are excellent," Treluren said, his eyes darting to the spread of treats on a nearby table.

"But for myself, I also enjoy other areas of study," Candissa said. She heard a sharp hiss from her mother, somewhere behind her.

Treluren's eyes moved from the food back to the beautiful young woman before him. She could see the conflict in his eyes, between conversation and appetite, and it amused her. "What's that? Study? Oh, yes, I'm quite accomplished in reading and writing myself."

"Most astute, my lord. What languages have you studied? I have a passing understanding of Elven script and some Dwarven runes, and I even speak some Elven, though I have little opportunity to practice," she said, looking away as if in thought, one finger on her lips. "I've begun lessons in Dwarven, I rather enjoy that tongue. What do you favor in your studies?"

The young lord Treluren blinked at her for a moment, his mouth slightly agape. "Um, we have a dwarfish smith at our keep, he's shown me some of his words," he said, clearly unsure what to say to the learned young woman.

"Dwarfish? Surely my lord is aware that term is an insult to the Dwarves. The proper term is Dwarven, in all ways relating to their race. Dwarfish is a word meaning small and stunted," Candissa corrected him, bringing to bear on him a stern countenance.

"My dear Lord Treluren, I must insist you meet my other daughters," Candissa's mother cut in loudly, grabbing the confused young lord by an elbow and directing him toward the stairs. As they turned, her mother seethed quietly at her eldest daughter, "We will *have words later!*"

Candissa only grinned as her mother directed the dull boy toward Brenissa, Nalliath and Elena, who were now descending the narrow stairs into the hall. The elder Lord Ythanford was still at hand, speaking to other local guests. He cleared his throat by way of getting Candissa's attention.

"My Lady Candissa, I would also like to introduce you to our Master Factor and my new business agent," the Lord said. Candissa sighed silently and turned, putting on a pleasing smile. Her expression turned to one of mild surprise. "My Lady Candissa, this is Errol Blackmar."

Dressed in a black tunic, dark gray cape, black trousers hemmed in silver, and black leather boots, he had his typically ragged dark blond hair tamed in a short ponytail. His rakish smile was broad, as he cocked his head. "The pleasure is all mine, my dear lady." He took her hand pressed it against his lips. Lord Ythanford looked at the exchange with a little concern.

Candissa raised one eyebrow at him. He did not wear a beard, but he was not clean-shaven.

"Don't you ever scrape that face of yours, Errol?" she said with a note of familiarity.

"I don't enjoy using a blade on myself," he said, winking.

"You...two know each other?" Lord Ythanford interrupted.

"My apologies, my Lord. Yes, we are well acquainted," Errol replied. "The young lady was present when I arrived in Ravensroost."

"Ah, well, that is interesting," the noble leaned closer to Candissa.

"You'll have to favor me sometime with that story. I cannot seem to get a scrap of it out of this rogue."

She laughed lightly. "Of course, my Lord."

Ythanford was drawn away by another guest and Candissa accepted the arm offered by Errol as they strode slowly toward the far end of the tables of foods.

"Did you have a hand in making any of this?" he asked, seeming to be genuine for the moment.

"I kneaded some of the dough, I expect. I try to help out an hour or two a day in one of my father's shops," she replied. "But I favor cooking other things besides breads and pastries."

They were well away from earshot of others, as Errol glanced around. He looked at Candissa with a shrewd expression. "This doesn't seem to be your sort of...fete. How do you manage?"

"My parents' demands on me have never been too terrible. In all honesty, I have not been very cooperative with many of them," she replied. "And this one is proving to be why I have that attitude."

Errol looked back at the young lord Treluren laughing too loudly at one of Brenissa's witticisms. "Yes, that one in particular is not quite up to your standards, I imagine."

"*My* standards? That's rather presumptuous of you, my dear Errol," Candissa chided him. "I'd like to hear what you know of my standards."

"More than you would admit, my lady, if I may be so bold," he replied quickly.

She did not deny his assertion, she merely thought on it a moment. Looking over the selection of sweets, she chose one, and nibbled on it.

"I suppose I should offer my congratulations on your new position," Candissa changed the topic. "Master factor and business agent for Lord Ythanford, that's a nice cut above doing the books for a number of shops."

"Yes, thank you, I'm enjoying it," he nodded. "It is a... stepping stone, I suppose you could say."

"I don't see you settling into it for too long," she smiled at him. "What are your plans after this?"

"You never did follow up with me," Errol redirected their conversation, choosing a small tart topped with anise and sugared apple.

"Follow up?"

"You remember. Back at the Bonerest in Auctus."

"Auctus?" Candissa said, frowning. It was a term she hadn't heard before.

"I'm sorry, I mean Highsal, the month of Highsal. It's called Auctus…" he said, letting the statement trail off. His usual expression of amusement dissolved into one that was far more serious.

Candissa paused, framing her reply. "You meant to say, it's called

Auctus *where I come from*, didn't you?"

He corrected his expression. "That doesn't really matter, does it? Since no one, most of all me, knows whence I come. Unless it has to do with that conversation you promised."

"Back at the Bonerest," she said, nodding.

"Well? You said something about *everything*," Errol reminded her.

She hadn't thought on that for some time. *It could be important to everything*, she had said to him. Candissa wasn't truly certain why she had blurted such a thing. It didn't make sense, even now. It was said in one of the moments she sometimes had, when her daily life seemed to fade away to something small, as if something greater beckoned. The hammer striking the anvil, the lightning across the clouds.

"I owe you that conversation, don't I?" she said, more to herself than him.

"When you feel ready, yes. I want to hear what you have to say."

"It was just being silly, it was nothing-" she began, perhaps attempting to dissuade him from taking her remark seriously. He cut her off, his gaze deliberate in its lack of levity.

"Silly? That is the *last* word I would ever use to describe you. You're trying to change the subject, and it will not work." His words cut into her somehow. "I do not know where I came from, but if I didn't know better, I would say you came from the same place."

"What do you mean by that?" she asked, genuinely puzzled by such a statement.

"We are not like others...like," he waved his hand around to indicate the house, the hall, her family and guests. "All of this. This is not *our* world, Candissa. You are not meant for this. I am not meant for this."

Hearing his thoughts - and perhaps fears - stated with such naked candor shocked Candissa. She could put on any face she wished to family and friends, but she could not deny the truth in Errol's claim. She had begun to feel outside of the world of her family and Ravensroost many years ago, when she was a little girl.

Errol appeared to see the confusion in her face and took her silence as a reluctance to speak her feelings on it. He shrugged.

"But as you said at the Bonerest, we'll have that conversation another time. I will leave it to you."

"That's not fair to you," she murmured. "But we can't have this discussion here and now, my father's expecting that...noble or such from the east," Candissa said, thinking now, looking at the table absently. "This evening perhaps. I will make an attempt to get to the Bonerest."

"Fair enough, I do appreciate it," he nodded. "How's that map of yours coming? Completed?"

"Completed? Are you joking?" she found herself saying, almost to her own surprise.

"But you have all the regions and baronies of the vast Kingdom of Eastvale stitched together, don't you?"

"Yes, but…" she hesitated to say what was on her mind. Then she realized he was possibly the only person she could possibly share it with. "You know there's more beyond."

He cocked his head. "Know? I cannot say with any certainty I know anything. But yes...I feel as though the world is much - *much,*" he emphasized the word, "larger than what is accepted as known here."

Others were approaching, looking at the fare on this end of the table, slowly encroaching on their space. One of her father's business associates was looking at her, as he assessed the table's offerings. He nodded at her, attempting a pleasant smile. He was an older, balding man who always appeared to cast a mildly repellent stare at the young woman. Today's social event was an exception. She feared she would have to engage in feigned pleasantries with many of her father's associates today.

Candissa took Errol by the arm and they walked around the end of the table.

"Well, what do you *know* about this younger Lord Allenfar? I suspect my father will attempt to throw me into his path today."

"From what I've heard, your father is wise to do so," Errol said, raising his eyebrows. "The young Lord Allenfar is a rising star in the King's court, I understand, and looking for a pretty young wife. He's not so much in need of an advantageous marriage with an eastern noble's daughter and may look at you as a fine catch."

"Delightful. Now I have *this* with which to contend," Candissa sighed. "There's too much to learn and study to be forced into dealing with this foolishness."

"Your studies are going well, I understand. There are those at the temple who say your gifts for the healing arts border on the, well, remarkable is one of the less alarming terms, I think," Errol said, with a small grin.

"I cannot help that. I don't understand why I have such *gifts*, only that they come to me unbidden," she said. She stopped and turned to him, clearly vexed. "How do you know so much in any case? Do you make a habit of spying on me?"

"Don't think of yourself as unique or special in that regard, my lady. I make a habit of knowing as much as possible about everyone around me. You should know that by now," he replied smoothly. "Besides, I'm not the one you have to worry about. It's this young Lord Allenfar."

"Why do you say that?"

"I'm still puzzled as to why he would come to Ravensroost instead of simply staying in Woodford, to the east. That's the baronial capital and the Baron of Woodford has three very eligible daughters. Though none of them are half as beautiful as you," he said, seeming to mull over the matter as he spoke to her in hushed tones. There were more people closer to them now. "There is a chance he has heard of your beauty and perhaps your accomplishments and has set his mark upon you. Just a warning, my Lady."

"You really do not need to call me *lady*," Candissa said. "I was that twelve-year old girl who found you shivering and wet on the gray square those years ago."

"I remember that fact every time I see you," he said, bringing her hand to a respectable distance from his lips. "My Lady."

He bowed and blended smoothly into the growing crowd of guests and family. Candissa was quickly escorted to her mother's side by a mildly frantic Lendra.

After what seemed like an interminable flurry of small talk and introductions to local persons of note, she and her family were seated at one of the head tables, in preparation of the arrival of their honored guests. No sooner were they seated than the chamberlain announced the long-expected arrival of the party from Woodford. Standing along with her parents, siblings and guests, Candissa watched as the elder Lord Allenfar, baron of a small but wealthy patch of land far to the east, entered her father's hall. While her family's estate was nearly the grandest in Ravensroost, by comparison to what Lord Allenfar was accustomed, it probably appeared modest.

Candissa remembered her lessons and readings at once. The fifth Baron of Longhart, Ellias Allenfar was part of a lineage closely allied with the King for several generations. His son, Enthessar, was only a few years older than Candissa. He was known to be skilled with the bow and sword, and enjoyed reading poetry to courtiers, to the heady delight of many a young lady.

The elder Lord Allenfar was dressed in a long cape of deep blue, under which he wore exquisitely embroidered clothing befitting his station, hemmed with silvery threads and festooned with a few choice insignias of rank and achievement. He had been part of a force that responded to the Silverdell rebellion twenty years past and was involved in a few military campaigns into the mountain foothills to the north of his holdings. He had a full head of iron-gray hair, somewhat craggy features, but was still an undeniably handsome man.

The younger Lord Allenfar followed his father. Candissa had to admit to herself, he was worth staring at. Extraordinarily handsome, he had deep brown hair verging on black and eyes so piercing green, she could see them across the length of the hall. His face had a darker countenance than his father's, probably from his mother's side. He wore a cape of light blue, with the insignia of his house emblazoned on the breast of his green tunic. Despite the finery, she could see he had a fine physique, with broad shoulders and a powerful chest. Taller than his father, his eyes scanned the crowd of onlookers, guests, social climbers and family.

His eyes found hers quickly, and she detected a sort of smile in his dark, deep-set eyes. Her breath caught a little in her throat and she had to concentrate a moment to regain her composure. Her sisters were all a-titter at the sight of him. Their murmuring squeals were distracting and unseemly.

Candissa let her gaze wander about, so as not to seem taken by him. Her eyes found Errol's quickly, behind Lord Allenfar's party. He threw a mock scowl at her, and grinned. She narrowed her eyes at him, then quickly darted her eyes to the younger Lord Allenfar and back to Errol. She hoped he could read her mind. Apparently, he did. He nodded and seemed to dissolve into shadow before her eyes.

The noble guests were making their way past the other attendees, arriving at the head of the hall relatively quickly. Lord Demarrae stood at the fore, as Lord Allenfar approached, flanked by his wife and eldest son.

"Lord Allenfar, it is truly an honor to have our humble home graced by your august presence," Lord Demarrae intoned formally, although a bit on the overflowing side in Candissa's consideration. He bowed, as the rest of his family curtseyed.

"Lord Demarrae, I am most pleased to call upon you, and offer you my most heartfelt greetings and affections from the east," Lord Allenfar responded in a surprisingly deep voice. He bowed as well, though not quite as deeply, and was likewise followed by his small court of attendees.

Introductions followed in a formal manner, with her father presenting his wife, followed by Candissa and her three sisters, Elena being the last. The Lord from the east followed suit, presenting his wife, Enthessar and his younger son Broderam. He included apologies for being unable to present his two daughters. It was a traditional apology, as young women did not typically make long journeys.

The two families mingled and made small conversation as the afternoon's meal was readied. Candissa listened patiently to the somewhat rigid conversations, eager to slip away at the first opportunity after the meal. Her plans to engage in the bare minimum of discourse were soon thwarted by the handsome young Lord of Allenfar, Enthessar.

He appeared with unexpected suddenness before Candissa, causing her to jump.

"Lady Candissa, my apologies if I startled you," he said in a pleasingly deep voice, smooth and practiced in his eastern accent. "I saw an opportunity and wished to speak with you."

"My Lord Allenfar, not at all. I am more than happy to make your acquaintance," she replied. They exchanged a formal bow and curtsey. He offered an arm and she laid her hand on it as he led her along one wall. She realized he had a finer physique than she had suspected, if his arm was any indication. She knew they were being followed by many eyes. She also knew they were inarguably the fairest couple in the hall.

"My lady, I don't know if you were aware, but this is my first trip to the borderlands of the west. I've never visited Ravensroost before," Enthessar said.

"I hope you find our modest town to your liking," she nodded. "I can only imagine what it lacks in comparison to the greater towns and cities of the east."

"Oh, I must risk your displeasure, my lady, for I wholeheartedly disagree with you on that point," he replied, a smile playing on his remarkably well-formed lips.

"My lord, you are too kind, and you could never incur my displeasure, rest assured," she chimed in. "I am glad to hear you approve of it."

"What your town may lack in the height of buildings or the number of streets, is more than compensated for by the open cordiality of her folk and the natural warmth they offer," the young lord said. "And, I am as taken aback by another most unexpected surprise."

"And what may that be, my lord?"

"You, my lady," he said, looking at her with a careful but undeniably captivating gaze. Candissa could hear more than one gasp from onlookers some yards away, likely younger ladies seeing him stare at her.

"I'm quite sure I do not know what you mean, my lord," she replied, in a customary fashion.

"I've seen many courtiers, daughters of noble houses," he said, looking about and leading them a step away from others. He leaned in closer to her, almost conspiratorially. "And even princesses. Yet it is here, on the edge of civilization, that I find someone of such sublime beauty, that her face would at once put to shame any others in the royal court."

Candissa, despite her training, her ability to concentrate and control her wits, could not prevent a blush from creeping over her face.

"My lord is far too kind," she murmured in as demure a fashion as she could find. "Your reputation for the language of the bards is most well-earned."

"Oh, this is not simply poetry, my lady," he shook his head gently. "You are the most beautiful young woman I have ever seen."

His last reply was spoken as he stared directly and openly into her eyes, his spring green piercing the silver blue of hers. She felt something melt inside of her, and for a moment feared getting somehow drawn into something beyond her control.

A glass shattered on the floor, a few paces behind. She jumped, and the young eastern lord turned, his gaze suddenly terse. "Is all well?" he asked. The young woman who had the misfortune of dropping her glass fled in tears.

Candissa's eyes narrowed as she saw a familiar shadow meld into the crowd behind where she had stood.

"My apologies, my lord. I think your presence is causing quite a stir among the young ladies," Candissa said, recovering her wits.

"I am not interested in causing a stir in any of *them*," he said pointedly. A bell sounded over the murmur of the crowd in the hall. "Ah, the meal is ready. Shall I escort you?"

She nodded her assent, and they were soon seated at the long table, along with their two families. The meal was superb, by the standards of Ravensroost at the least, and the conversation mildly engaging. At least until the two elder lords began talking of contracts and output of mines and harvests of wheats.

Candissa was seated, not surprisingly, next to Lord Enthessar. He was charming in all ways as the meal progressed, and she found herself actually enjoying her time there. A round of red wine was served to all, accompanied by a meat and bread course.

Quite suddenly, the table was in a mild uproar. Several seats away, toward the head of the table, a servant lifted a silvered clocca and there was absolutely nothing underneath it. This led to the lord and lady of the house expressing their severe displeasure, along with some kindly stifled but still obvious giggles and grins from their noble guests. Servants flew out from the kitchen, and each tray was checked.

Even Enthessar joined in the mildly amusing incident, suggesting — almost diplomatically — that it was an intended omission to break up the meal and lighten the mood. In all the commotion, he was looking toward his father.

A servant brushed Candissa's arm as he was checking trays. She noted the difference, however, in this servant, and the action being taken.

Given her years of training at the temple and with those who had been training her in matters martial, she had developed certain senses and skills which were likely lacking in most young ladies of her age and station. It was these senses that made her suddenly aware of something amiss.

She glanced to her left and noted this servant bore a dagger on his belt under his serving garb. It was Errol's blade. She realized the servant *was* Errol.

Amid the commotion, he deftly moved in and replaced her glass of wine with another, secreting the first glass under his arm as he drew away, having checked the tray closest to her.

No one noticed anything amiss, as everyone's attention was on the humorous incident and reactions. Candissa thought quickly and turned in such a way as to brush a silver spoon off the table. It clattered noisily on the floor next to her. This allowed her to turn to retrieve the spoon. It also gave her the opportunity to glance back toward the kitchen.

There, moving fluidly into the kitchen was the unmistakable form of

Errol, wearing a servant's tunic. He chanced a glance at her and caught her gaze. She couldn't afford to look for but a moment, and he simply nodded.

She returned at once to the light-hearted banter that followed. There was an immediate call for a toast, led by the elder Lord Allenfar, to the effect of thanking his host and reassuring him he was well pleased.

She drank along with everyone else, having no reason not to trust Errol. As she drank the wine, she wondered if there were eyes on her, eyes perhaps hiding an intent not entirely in her best interest.

CHAPTER TEN - KORAYMIS

24 Laborus, Year 197, Eastvale Calendar

The afternoon sun was lowering in the sky, as the carriage approached the low walls of the border town of Ravensroost. Koraymis leaned out the open window of his seat, to the dissatisfaction of his fellow carriage passengers. It was a chilly day, after a frosty morning. But he would not be deterred.

He wanted to see the walled town on the approach. It was the only other town he had ever seen. Koraymis had spent the entirety of his life in Woodford, and while he had visited small villages surrounding Woodford on several occasions, none were so large as this.

The road leading toward Ravensroost had flattened out almost entirely as they neared the town. Trees had vanished a few miles back. Koraymis had no idea why there were no copses or stands near the walls, but looking north and south, he assumed it was something to do with the nature of the land and not intentional logging. There were farms and patches of cultivated land just east of the town, but they dwindled away along with the scattered trees.

Even from a distance, Koraymis could see the town lacked the taller buildings and temples that formed the center of Woodford. There were a handful of taller structures, near the center. Otherwise, it was comprised of two or three level buildings of wood and stone, with sloped roofs on most. As the carriage slowed to navigate outgoing market traffic, another feature caught his eye.

The walls, while a modest height of perhaps fifteen feet, seemed oddly disparate. The blockish structures that formed the gatehouse and a length of wall extending some yards north and south from them were made of a darker, featureless stone, while the remaining walls stretching further north and south were of a more traditional stone and mortar design. Then at corners nearly out of sight from the eastern gate, Koraymis could make out squarish, narrow towers of the same dark stone.

His brows knitted as he studied them. He would not have noticed but for the strange symmetry of the darker works. They were clearly from another period of construction.

After the carriage eased between the monolithic gatehouse, it turned and stopped in the large market square that greeted those newly arrived in the town. He was glad the journey was over. It had been a long seven days, and he was tired of sleeping in a different bed or pallet each night, usually at the cheapest inn available. He had been fortunate to get a room of his own three of those nights, but the other evenings were miserable, as he did have a terrible time trying to sleep amid a cacophony of snores and wheezings.

As Koraymis disembarked, sliding his pack over one shoulder, he saw there were some few hawkers still plying their trades on those walking near enough to their stalls and carts.

The young scholar avoided them. He had a vague idea of where he was going, and if he struck a purposeful stride, he was far less likely to be targeted by the more aggressive merchants. As he wound his way through the crowds, he noted the people were not unlike those in Woodford, just not as many in finer dress. He also noticed a few of them glanced at his silver pin, nodding in respect as they let him pass before them. Koraymis was not accustomed to such treatment. It unnerved him.

He knew the scholar's quarter was just south of an intersection with the main avenue where he would find a large round raised kiosk. Bundling his cloak about himself, he was soon in sight of just such a structure. Nearing it, he saw it had steps leading up to it on two sides, columns ringing it supporting a domed roof.

But the base was different stone. It was the same dark stone he had noted the gate structures were formed from. He frowned, more at his having noticed it than the unremarkable mystery of differing stonework.

Telmik once told him something during his studies, when he had been gazing out a tall window one spring afternoon instead of concentrating on his studies. Koryamis had noticed a single blue-winged butterfly among a gathering of red, all of them clustered on a branch festooned with blossoms. He remarked on the curiosity. It earned him a mild fright when his master rapped the table with his knuckles, though it sounded like a metal rod striking the wood.

"Koraymis, do not be so easily distracted. You will see things in passing, throughout life. Note them, but do not become fixated on them. They may be important one day, so just put the memory away. But be on your task.

Focus."

The scholar simply nodded, turning south. He was soon in sight of the library, a structure notable in its construction, the tall, glazed windows, and of course, the carven image of a scroll over the main entrance. Climbing the steps, he gathered himself, making sure his scholar's pin was clearly visible, and knocked on the tall, oak doors.

The wait was long, but that was not unusual. Libraries were always by appointment and his arrival, while expected, had not been confirmed for this day. He was nearly ready to knock again when he heard the clanking of a lock.

A tallow-faced young man with red-splotchy skin answered. He wore simple but neatly made clothing. The expression he wore was an attempt to project perhaps authority, certainly disdain. But his comportment could not disguise his youth, likely not yet nineteen years of age.

"Do you have an appointment?" the youth said, his voice oddly high-pitched.

"I am expected by Master Efflewhist," Koraymis said, reaching up to touch the pin. "I am Koraymis Sleeth, from Woodford."

The young man's eyes darted to the silver scholar's pin, and Koraymis could almost see a mask of resentment move over his young face.

"The Librarian is seeing no one today!" the young man slammed the door firmly, latching it as well.

Koraymis took a step back. He had dealt with doors being slammed in his face throughout his life, for various reasons, but this one was unexpected. He frowned, turning toward the stone steps. He really didn't know what recourse he had, if the elder librarian was indeed refusing to see anyone.

His right hand seemed to itch. Examining it, he spun the ring with his left thumb and forefinger.

He will see you.

Koraymis looked back at the tall doors. There were very narrow, thickly glazed windows set within, barely three fingers wide. For a moment, he thought he could see a shadow against one of the panes. But no. It was more than that. He sensed - he knew - the pimpled youth stood there, watching the shape of Koraymis through the thick glass, waiting for him to depart. The rude, young man would receive no such satisfaction.

Koraymis knocked again, this time more forcefully. The young man did not respond.

"I must insist you allow me to see Master Efflewhist," he called through the door, knowing the young man was there.

Koraymis scratched his temple. On the six full days he had to endure on the carriage to Ravensroost, the road was blessedly smooth for long stretches. This allowed him to study his girdle tome at length. He also studied it every night, regardless of where he ended up sleeping.

Master Telmik was certainly correct in saying the book would reveal more as time went by. Koraymis had already read about several very useful disciplines. Some would call them charms, or even spells, though Telmik detested that term. One of the charms, called a glamour in the oldest of Telmik's works, involved influencing someone in making a particular choice. Koraymis didn't understand it entirely, of course, but he knew enough to make an attempt. The result, he knew, depended as much on the mental fortitude of the target as Koraymis' abilities.

Breathing deeply, Koraymis recalled the phrases within his mind, focusing. Raising his right hand, he placed it flat on the door.

"Let me in, *please*," he said in a low voice, the last word sounding strange to his own ears. The ring on his right hand tingled as he spoke the words.

A bumping noise could be heard behind the door. Without seeing past the portal, Koraymis knew the young man had just stepped backwards into a small table against the wall, nearly knocking over a delicate lamp.

Koraymis had no way of knowing if his effort had any effect, but after thirty seconds or so, the door latch could be heard.

The young man still attempted to maintain his imperious gaze as the door swung open before Koraymis.

"Very well, if you must be so insistent," his voice seemed a little less confident. "Please wait in the first chamber while I consult the Librarian."

"Thank you very much," Koraymis said, nodding respectfully as he entered the dim hall. The young man vanished up a flight of stairs.

A small, comfortable parlor was just off one side, and he took a seat on a small but well-covered chair. The room was tastefully decorated, with tapestries depicting wilderness scenery, a woven rug of various colors, two tall, tinted windows, and shelves lined with as many books and curios. The room was all gentle shadows, dark, polished wood, the faint smell of rosewater and leather. It was comforting and strange to him.

As with many smaller, more rustic libraries, this was both Master Efflewhist's home and the library. Scholars, or commoners with sufficient need, would always have an appointment to peruse the library. There was probably a large room at the far end of this building containing the many shelves and hopefully hundreds of books and scrolls, which Koraymis would one day oversee.

But no, he thought to himself, looking down at the ring. It was not a certainty at all. He sighed.

On one shelf, his eye was caught by a large, squat stoppered jar. He stood to inspect it. It was a strange thing, as large as it was. The clear glass revealed the contents: coarse dust of some strange sort, more broken bits than dust. He could just make out a tattered fragment of a book binding within it. The seal on the jar was old, very old. The wax was aged, discolored and cracked. A faint symbol was worked into the glass of the jar, etched very slightly into the surface. It was a rune from one of the several old tongues Telmik had schooled Koraymis in.

The rune meant *preserve*, or *keep*, or *protect*, depending on the context.

The young man appeared at the parlor entrance. "Master Efflewhist will see you now."

He simply turned, expecting Koraymis to follow him, which the young scholar did.

"My name is Lornan. I am Master Efflewhist's assistant, in all matters," he said as they climbed the steps. They reached a landing on the stairs. Lornan turned to Koraymis before they continued, speaking in a low voice. "Please understand that my master is not entirely himself some days. He has...maladies of the mind. You may find your conversation with him difficult."

Koraymis nodded. "Thank you for informing me."

Lornan seemed to look up and down at Koraymis for a moment before continuing. At the top of the flight, he led the scholar into a brightly lit bedroom. All was comfort, gentle colors, waxed woods, cushions and finely worked ornaments of brass and dark metal. A broad desk dominated one wall.

The hunched figure of Efflewhist sat at the desk, wearing a robe that hung too loosely.

"Master? The visitor is here," Lornan said, his tone quiet, soothing, Koraymis thought perhaps a little patronizing. "Koraymis Sleeth of Woodford. Do you remember our-"

"Of course, I remember! I'm not entirely daft, boy!" the elder barked. He turned, a quill in one bony, shrunken hand. His appearance was almost haggard, with loose, unkempt hair of silver and a ragged beard on his hollowed face. Koraymis kept his composure. At least the old man's eyes seemed to have a spark of intellect in them.

He wobbled unsteadily to his feet, clutching the back of the embroidered chair for balance.

"Sir!" Lornan almost leapt forward, as his master waved him off.

"I'm fine, Lornan! Master Sleeth, let us sit by the window, I can see you better there," the old man said, motioning toward two very comfortable-looking chairs placed at angles next to a broad window of clear glazing. "Lornan, why don't you change the bedsheets, I'm certain I soiled them last night."

Koraymis heard the loud sigh from the young man, quite intended to be heard he was certain, as he began pulling off sheets and blankets, bundling them.

Efflewhist sat carefully, gathering his loose robes about, as Koraymis sat opposite him.

"Please, call me Koraymis. I've never liked my surname," he said quietly to the elder scholar.

"As you wish, Master Koraymis. Now, as I'm certain Lornan told you, I'm a bit addled. But I have my good days, and this is one of them."

"Of course, Master Eff-"

The librarian cut him off. "But I don't know how long my *good day* will last, so let us be to the point, and brief."

Koraymis nodded.

"I know you came here to apprentice under me as a Librarian, and I have every confidence you would make a wise and capable master over my collections," Efflewhist said. His eyes moved to the figure of the young man by the bedframe, as he struggled to roll the heaps of blankets. "Lornan there wanted the job, but he's simply not schooled appropriately, and lacks any true scholarly experience."

At that, Koraymis could see Lornan's eyes turn to daggers, as the blotch-faced youth stared with undisguised loathing at Koraymis.

"But I am sorry to tell you, Koraymis, that for the time being, Lornan will have to do."

Koraymis and Lornan both said, "What?" at the same time, as the youth dropped the blankets.

"Oh, do pay attention, Lornan! Get those to the laundress at once!" Efflewhist snapped.

"Yes...yes sir!" the boy said, stuttering, as he gathered them again.

"I don't understand, sir," Koraymis said. He was confused. His first thought was the old man was slipping again. Efflewhist appeared to address his unspoken concern.

"This is not a decision I make lightly. Nor is it evidence of my failing intellect. It is something I've come to realize over these past few months," the old man said, his eyes almost kind as he spoke to Koraymis.

"My position here seemed assured. I have a letter…"

"Yes, your scholarly accomplishments are known. Master Tentrovis is an old friend and he speaks very highly of you. But this decision has nothing to do with libraries or books, or old men with fading memories."

"Then what, sir?"

"Very soon, far too soon, my mind will slip away into the dim caverns of decrepitude. After today, we may never again have a meaningful conversation. That is why I must hasten, Master Koraymis," the elderly scholar said, leaning in closer. He glanced at the departing form of Lornan, as the youth clomped down the stairs with his burden. "Something is happening that I do not fully comprehend."

"Sir?" Koraymis said, doubts about Efflewhist's mind still nagging him.

"You cannot stay here, not now in any case. Your path must lead you further away from Ravensroost. I think you know that, don't you?"

Koraymis just stared at the old man, his mouth hanging open slightly.

Efflewhist nodded. "I think that is answer enough. You may be a fine scholar one day, and who knows, perhaps Librarian over this house, but not in the foreseeable future."

"How do you know this?" Koraymis asked.

"I have been given visions, perhaps you would call them, a glimpse into things to come, mayhap, I'm not certain!" the elder waved his bony hand irritable. "I did not ask for this gift, it is something that has arisen very lately. And not just with me alone. Many in Ravensroost have spoken quietly, of signs, visions, whispers of something approaching."

"And you think I'm involved in this?"

"Involved? Of course, you are! You are a man of books, of letters. Well, instead of tending a small library at the end of the word, your task is far greater. You must go out into the greater unknown and seek the lore, the writings that were lost!"

"I don't understand," Koraymis began, raising his hands.

"Silence! From what I have been given to know, you will be here only a short time, then you must leave. But before you do, you must visit Master Penston!" Efflewhist said, his eyes growing a bit wider. He snapped his bony fingers. "Yes! Penston!"

"Penston? I don't know that name."

"He's the town Scholar. You hadn't heard of him? He's really quite brilliant, especially given his age," Efflewhist said, his eyes wandering suddenly. "Now, what was I... oh, yes, you must visit Master Penston, tell him I sent you. He will give you things that you must take on your journey."

"My...journey?" Koraymis said. He wondered how the old man knew about what Koraymis had told no one save his master.

"Don't be insolent!" Efflewhist shouted, jumping to his feet, nearly falling in the process. "Do as I say, stupid boy!"

Koraymis rose to his feet, alarmed at the outburst. "Sir, I'm very sorry, I didn't-"

The old man snaked a bony hand out to clutch Koraymis' right arm, pulling him close with a shocking strength. "You will not be unopposed in this," the old man's voice was almost a growl.

"What are you doing there?" the high-pitched voice of Lornan shouted from the door. "Leave him be!"

"I was doing nothing to him," Koraymis said, as Efflewhist collapsed into the chair.

Lornan's face was a brighter shade of red as his blotches reddened further with anger. "Leave at once! He cannot tolerate this any longer!"

Koraymis could see Efflewhist was nearly gone, his eyes unfocused and wandering, a bit of drool escaping his lips. "Very well. I am sorry if I caused this...outburst."

"Go!" was all Lornan said as he struggled to move the shaking, almost-delirious old man back to the bed.

Downstairs, Koraymis waited a moment, but it was evident Lornan was having some difficulty with his master. With a sigh, Koraymis left the Library, hoping it was not for the last time.

Long shadows were striping the streets of Ravensroost now, as the sun settled. It would be evening soon. Traffic was much diminished at this late hour, making his walk far easier.

It was easy to find the Bonerest Tavern, as the main avenue through town ended at the western square. There, he met Evan Devenuar, the tavernmaster, although Koraymis had the uneasy feeling he already knew the man. After putting his belongings in his newly rented room, he asked Master Evan about the scholar Penston. The tavernmaster seemed surprised Koraymis did not know of the scholar, who was apparently a well-known figure in town. He directed the young scholar to the office of Master Penston.

As shadows slowly painted the town deeper shades of blue, Koraymis found his way to the Penston's office. To his disappointment, it was locked, with no reply to his knocking.

Heading back to the Bonerest, the cobbled streets of Ravensroost were occasionally lit by sprays of yellow lamplight spilling out open windows of taverns or homes, as the evening deepened.

CHAPTER ELEVEN - RENTHER

24 Laborus, Year 197, Eastvale Calendar

Renther Drepp shook his head, then cried out in pain. He had a splitting headache. Blinking, he realized he was in the dark. Light from under a door led him to his feet. His hands fumbled for the latch.

The door flew open before he could find the latch. A serving girl stepped in as light flooded the closet. She shrieked, startled by his sudden appearance there. Renther fell backward onto a pile of linen.

"Renther! What by six and seven are you doing here?" the young woman screeched after recovering her wits.

"I - Prina, I don't know, I -" he stuttered, trying to remember.

"You're drunk, aren't you? Get out of here and straighten up before Krebbs sees you!" she said, grabbing him as he stumbled to his feet. "Lor' I don't know what's to be done with you! Go, go!"

Renther could only nod and try to thank the serving girl as he recovered his bearings. He tucked in his shirt and neatened his tunic. His aching head was getting better now, but he was having trouble remembering how he found himself in that supply closet.

He had duties to attend. The kitchen boss, Arbon, would likely have his head for any absence. Renther was back in the kitchen in moments.

"I don't even want to hear it, Drepp!" the head cook bellowed, amid the frenzied activity of the post-dinner kitchen. "Just get scrubbing pots!"

He just nodded and did as he was told. Renther was sure that Arbon would extract some price later, likely involving privy duty. As he set to gathering the soiled pots and pans and baking stones and getting them into the hot water, he tried to piece together his afternoon. Clearly the dinner was over, and the guests were either leaving the premises or had retreated to one parlor or another, perhaps the gardens.

It was all still foggy. He scrambled to catch up with his work, with the unrelenting demands of three different superiors, so he had little time to puzzle it out. More water was needed but he couldn't get to the well inside the keep, so he headed out to the corner of the gardens.

An ancient Dwarven well-wheel was there. It was old, some said more than a hundred years, yet it never seemed to rust or break down. Two stout wooden buckets in hand, he placed one under the spout and started turning the heavy wheels. He could feel the resistance as his muscles strained against the rising water. Moments later water came gushing out of the spout, splashing noisily in the buckets.

The gardens were impressive, if compact. Renther looked around, needing to take a piss. Moving into the safe seclusion of high evergreens, he went to it. Through the shrubs, he caught sight of someone wearing white. Finishing up, he peered around the shrubs.

It was Lady Candissa.

Lady Candissa, the name shot through his mind.

He remembered now. It was late last night, he was enjoying a cheap and potent mug of spirits in the commoners' tavern called The Gnolders Rest. His friend, Tremmy, had convinced him to do something. Something he didn't want to do at first. In fact, Renther remembered he had resisted for a while.

"They're a rich family, and our families are poor. We'll never get what's ours, but they will always have everything they need!" Tremmy had pointed. "I just want to give 'em a little of what we got. My poor girls suffer from briar flux somethin' awful. But with their fine, well-paid healers, they never have to worry about that."

It was then that the stableboy produced the tiny pewter vial. He put it on the table. "I don't want nobody dead or serious hurt, just a good month-long sick will show 'em they can suffer along with the rest of us!"

"What is it?" Renther had asked, picking up the small but heavy vial. The stableboy, still reeking of dung, leaned in.

"It's a bit a' tainted water. Just slip that in our lovely's wine and she'll be dog-sick for weeks!" he grinned, his breath smelling of rot.

"How do I know you're not wanting to poison the lass?" Renther had asked. He had no love for Candissa, but she had always seemed sweet and never talked down to him on the few occasions they spoke.

"Look, it's not her, it's the old man, and how he's climbed over the back of lacks like you and me! See, it wasn't that long ago his family was simple folk, but now they're all silk and cloth-a-gold, by talking to 'em," the stableboy said, spite clear in his expression. "This'll just show 'em they ain't no better."

He also placed a neat stack of five gold oaks on the table. *Gold.*

"Where'd you get that? That must be two months wages for you!" Renther had suspected something foul from that alone.

"It's from a *benefactor* who wants 'em put in their place just like the rest of us. He collected it from certain parties, never you mind who," Tremmy said. "Just remember, drip this vial in her cup, *just her cup*, of wine. She'll be on her back with the sweats before the meal is over. If we're lucky, she'll put her fine supper right back on the table in front of all her family!"

"I don't like it, Tremmy, and just so ya know, I don't really like you," Renther had said, trying to add a little menace to his tone. Tremmy chuckled darkly.

"Ya don't have to like me, Ren, just help us give back a little a what they got coming," he said, nudging the coins forward.

Renther struggled. He knew it was wrong. But...something urged him on. He felt the heat of resentment build up, a sense he had been wronged all this time. He shouldn't do this, *he knew it.* But the dark feelings continued to well up within his gut. Looking at the unhealthy, unblinking gaze of Tremmy only reinforced the hatred he felt surging.

He remembered his mother's dying words to him, *You have to choose what's right, Ren.*

She had died of some foul sickness, coughing up blood. They were too poor to warrant a visit by the temple priests. *The same temple that welcomed Candissa with open arms*, a voice whispered.

Renther told himself the gold tipped his decision, though that was a silent lie. "Fine! But if she ends up bad hurt from this," he began. The stableboy waved his hand.

"It won't come to that, everyone gets a good flux now and again. Helps clear out the bowels, I say. An' this stuff, I'm told, can't be cured by a healer's arts!" he assured his nervous co-conspirator. "But if something goes awry, the dinner is put off, or they take you off the kitchen, meet me at the stable after dark, all right?"

Renther just nodded and slowly palmed the oaks and the vial. Tremmy grinned, his mouth wide with yellowed and cracked teeth. He clapped Renther's shoulder as he got up and slipped away. Leaving the tavern, nearly stumbling drunk at that point, Renther could feel it. A darkness that seemed to latch onto his heart. He had made his choice. He knew he wasn't strong enough to turn away now.

The following day - today - had gone well enough. He was kept on the serving staff and dinner went off as planned. With the vial palmed, he had determined *for certain* which glass was Lady Candissa's, thanks to Prina. She liked him, or so he thought, and she saw no harm in telling him whose glass was whose. Then, with the kitchen staff distracted, he dripped the foul bit of water into the dark wine. He made sure to keep the vial at a distance from his own mouth and had resealed it quickly, pocketing it.

He had even watched to make sure the table girl had put them down in the right order, and she had. The right glass was in front of the Lady Candissa.

Yet now, there she was, walking and talking with guests, the upstairs maid Lendra in tow. No sweats or shakes or any sort of disease he could see. He wondered if it had worked or if maybe someone else had her wine after all.

He blinked. He couldn't remember much after the wine was out. He had something to do back in the storeroom, someone needed help. After that, he couldn't recall anything. He wanted to watch Candissa longer, to see if she was showing any signs, but he couldn't spare the time. Returning to his duties, he put off his curiosity. In one sense, he was relieved she wasn't sickened. *Worthless fool,* the voice whispered, *you failed!* Renther shook his aching head. If she wasn't sick, though, he knew he would have to give up the gold coins. He was glad he hadn't spent them.

That evening, after the house was quiet and his duties were done, he hurried off to the stables, just as the sun was setting. He needed to figure out what happened, or didn't happen, with Tremmy.

He found Tremmy in the far end of the stablehouse, in the small workshop there. He was leaning back on some hay, drinking out of a large bottle.

"Ren! How are you my fine sir?" he said with a heavy slur in his voice.

"Tremmy, I'm sorry, I don't think that vial worked," he began, but Tremmy held an unsteady hand up.

"Not to worry, dear fellow, we'll get it right next time!"

"Next time?"

"This...is...meet our new friend, he's the one what gave me them gold oaks for ya," Tremmy said, pointing vaguely behind Renther.

Renther turned. A man in dark riding leathers and a hooded cloak was standing behind him. He yelped in shock.

"Sir, I'm sorry, I didn't hear you," Renther stammered. The man had a bottle in one hand.

"I'm the one who is sorry, I didn't mean to startle you," he said in a smooth, almost relaxed voice.

"No, sir, I must have botched it, sir, I'm sorry," Renther said. He pulled out his coins. "You can have these back, sir."

The man shook his head. "Keep them on account, we may not have sickened the young lady, but we have made friends of one another, and that is more important to me."

"Of course, sir," Renther said, unsure of what to say.

"I insist we share a drink with Tremmy here," the man said, handing the bottle to Renther. "Drink up and enjoy yourselves."

Renther considered the bottle. It seemed odd, if generous. "Well, yes sir, of course."

Instinct told Renther not to trust the man, but then he felt the dark feelings within him stir once more. He had failed, but it was *her* fault. Somehow, she would pay. Renther frowned. He didn't understand why he would think such things.

That strange darkness clutched at his heart again. He knew then it was too late to turn back. Too late.

The man sat down on a bench, and Renther slowly sat on a bundle of hay next to Tremmy, who was busy gulping down another mouthful from his bottle.

"Arr, this is good stuff!" he spluttered, giggling as he did.

The man produced his own flask and tipped in toward Renther. "To our new alliance."

He sipped from it and Renther unstoppered his bottle. He felt obligated to drink the wine. An echo of apprehension vanished. He did not want to risk an insult to the fellow. Drinking the wine, he found it to be tasty, if a bit spicy.

"This is good, sir!" Renther said. "Seems not quite right to waste it on the likes of us."

"No, I enjoy sharing good wine with new friends, Renther," the stranger said.

"Oh, begging your pardon, sir, I didn't catch your name," Renther said with as much courtesy as he could manage, while swigging greedily from the bottle.

"How rude of me. You may call me William," he said. He smiled and nodded and sipped again. Renther nodded and drank more of the enticing wine. He noticed he had trouble forming his next question.

"Sir, you're not from Rave...Ravens...from town, are you? I mean, I don't seem to recall seeing you before," Renther managed after some effort. The wine was powerful indeed.

"No, I'm not. Actually, I'm from the city of Eastvale, though I've been in the employ of a house not too far from Woodford," the man replied. "Ah, I see your friend Tremmy has had a little too much to drink."

Renther looked at his friend. The stableboy was lying on the hay, his mouth agape, the bottle having rolled out of his hand. His eyes were fixed, staring at the cobwebbed beams of the ceiling, barely visible in the fading light of day.

"Tremmy? Tremmy?" Renther said, trying to shake his friend. Panic rose in his gut. His legs were suddenly numb.

"Now, don't get excited, that may make it worse, you see," the man called William said in a patronizing voice.

"What d'ya...what's this wine...I'm feelin'..." was all Renther could manage, as he stared in sheer terror at the man. The stranger was standing now.

"Pity about that wine you two shared, they will find it's quite spoiled, a mold of some sort they will determine," he said casually. "It kills those who drink it too quickly, such a shame."

"Sir...plea…" Renther said feebly, his breath failing him. The last thing he saw was the shape of the man, looming close.

"You won't need these where you're going," the man said, as he fished the gold coins from Renther's pocket.

The bottle slipped from Renther's hand, as panic seized him. Unable to move, his eyes frozen open, he could only stare at the webbed shadows above. He had failed. He had chosen, and he had failed. The dark knot within laughed at him before fleeing his failing heart.

The last thought within his mind, before slipping into unending darkness, was of his mother, weeping.

CHAPTER TWELVE - ERROL

24 Laborus, Year 197, Eastvale Calendar

Errol waited outside the gates to House Demarrae's small but well-kept estate. The entourage from House Allenfar had departed the grounds an hour ago, the last few trailing out not long ago. It was late in the day, and the sun was casting long shadows between the one and two-level homes, estates and shops of this quarter of Ravensroost. The sky was clear and promised a chill evening. Perhaps snow would fall, a prospect Errol did not relish. Warmer weather always made him happier.

The walls of the estate were well-maintained, consisting of smooth-cut ashlar masonry, with a fine mortar in the seams. Walking to a corner, Errol examined a cracked area behind a shrub along the curb of the avenue. The stone appeared to be a form of granite, but Errol couldn't be sure. He dismissed his musings. Sometimes, when he would recognize something from his past experiences, a dull pain would result. He had learned to avoid doing this too much.

He heard a large party exiting the manor house, making their way toward the open gate. He quickly resituated himself across the avenue, sitting at a corner bench, and retrieved a small printbook from his vest. As they exited the estate, he appeared to be lost in his reading.

Out of the corner of his eye, he saw the broad-shouldered Lord Enthessar Allenfar escorting Candissa out of the compound, followed by a small retinue. The group included two of Candissa's sisters and paired young nobles who were likely of a mind to court them. There were also a pair of guardsmen, for propriety's sake.

As they walked casually down the avenue, no doubt toward the central district of Ravensroost which featured the finer dining establishments and a few shops still open at this late hour, Errol watched them without staring at them, as he feigned reading.

He heard a quiet peal of laughter from Candissa, in response to some witticism of Enthessar's. She turned her head toward Errol as the young lord looked in the other direction. She nodded her head in a quick, sharp fashion. Errol nodded without looking directly at her. As their party passed, he followed, on the opposing side.

Instincts which he did not understand compelled him to twice, on the way to the central district, turn off on side alleys and observe the street behind them, to ensure no one was following them, or him. On the second occasion, he took a minute to observe a pair of low merchants he didn't entirely trust, having met them once or twice in the past. They ended up turning down an alley leading to a tavern more suited to their tastes.

To catch up to the party, he took a narrow alley behind some shops, moving at an easy lope. The buildings and shops here were generally two stories, with residences above or behind, and shops facing the avenue. The lower sun made for deeper shadows here, but Errol felt entirely in his element under these conditions. Darting between stacks of crates, barrels empty or full, and leaping over puddles of water collected from recent rains, he somehow felt a little more alive than when he was doing the accounts for a shopkeeper or house.

A figure stepped out from a small gap between two shops, not so close as to throw Errol off his stride, but close enough to make his intent clear. That intent was to stop Errol's broad strides down the alley.

"Errol, where ye off to 'n such a hurry?" he said.

Errol nearly skidded to a halt on the ancient, broken flagstones of the alley. "Bursley, up to no good, are you?"

"Query by query, this isn't off to a happy start, is it?" Bursley said, rolling his eyes as he leaned heavily against the corner of a smithy's shop. Next to him was a pile of badly rusted iron scraps, and a barrel half-full of rainwater.

Bursley was not an old man but could pass for one. He was not a young man but could appear to be if he affected the proper gait. Of an unremarkable height, stature and comportment, Errol admired the man for his ability to blend into a crowd, a garden, or even a dull stone wall.

"I'm off to the Bonerest. Join me there for an ale?" Errol admitted.

Bursley's odd eyes went wide. "You know what Evan would do to me if I showed my face there!"

"All the more reason for you to join me," Errol grinned evilly. "I must needs be off, friend. I'll see you later."

With that, Errol was off again, his stride quicker now to catch up to Candissa's party.

"Sometimes I think you enjoy paying me no mind!" Bursley shouted as Errol ducked around a corner in the dim alleyway.

Errol spotted Candissa's party and quickly surmised they were heading for Barrowman's Tavern. This was an establishment that catered more toward the upper echelons of Ravensroost's decidedly limited social strata. This was not a surprise.

He thought briefly about slipping into the place, to confirm with Candissa that she would be meeting him later at the Bonerest. He chose not to, trusting her to follow through with their intent. Without the need to hurry, he took a more leisurely route along the avenues of Ravensroost.

He was soon at the Bonerest tavern. Entering, he was momentarily concerned about a stranger seated nearby, facing the door. He looked to be a hunter or ranger, with dark brown hair and a short beard. There seemed to be some sort of recognition, but Errol saw no malice or danger in the younger man's eyes. They were strange eyes, but he couldn't exactly figure out why. The fellow was eating a bowl of Evan's stew, and had a tall mug of something.

Nodding slightly, Errol made his way to his favorite table. It was small, shadowed from the hanging light sources and near the kitchen entrance. He took the seat facing the door.

Beshanu was at his booth momentarily. "What's it today, sweet?" she said with a musical lilt in her voice.

"Do you have any of that Dwarven bitterblack?" he said, his eyes still on the door. He realized it was silly to watch the door. It would be a short while at least before Candissa could convince her party to make their way here.

"Of course. I'll get you a mug. Anything else?" she asked, seeing he was somehow distracted, particularly since he offered no witty or lascivious remarks.

"Who's that fellow sitting at the table over there, near the clock? I don't know him."

Besh looked over and smiled. "You wouldn't, he just arrived in town yesterday. From Woodford, staying here I understand. Goes by Cam Bronwyer, I saw it in the ledger."

"What would I do without you?" Errol said, looking up at her with mock sincerity in his green eyes.

Besh leaned down and tweaked his unshaven chin. "Find another girl to answer your silly questions of course!"

"Oh yes, you're right again," he countered, grinning. She turned to serve another patron. He called after her. "And some walnuts!"

He had a few minutes to sit quietly and reflect on the events earlier in the day, particularly the serving man swapping Candissa's wine. Someone entered the Bonerest, though it was not Candissa or any of her party.

For the second time since arriving at the Bonerest, Errol found himself momentarily distracted by a complete stranger. The young man entered the Bonerest with an almost uncomfortable gait. He was clearly not from Ravensroost. His hands appeared unmarred by labors. He wore all black, which Errol appreciated, yet his clothing bore no indication to the observer as to what the man's vocation might be. It was common, if not expected, that one would dress in such a way to let a stranger know one's station in life. This younger fellow garb offered no clues. That bothered Errol's sensibilities.

His face was unusual, unlike anyone he had seen in Ravensroost. His nose and eyes had a unique character and his skin was a shade darker. His hair was short, black and stiff. His decidedly unusual appearance was clearly out of place here. That wasn't the only thing about him that bothered Errol. He didn't *belong* here. He belonged somewhere else. His appearance was not strange to Errol, just misplaced. The familiar dull pain threatened Errol once more.

The man looked at Errol briefly, before seeing the other newcomer, Cam Bronwyer. The two exchanged nods, clearly familiar with one another. The black-clad man approached the bar tentatively, ordering something from Evan, before joining the ranger-sort at the table near the clock. They spoke briefly, before the young man in black turned and went upstairs.

Besh brought Errol his dark, bitter beer and a small pewter tray with his walnuts. Errol looked at Beshanu then glanced sharply at the newcomer in black. She knew Errol well enough to know he was inquiring. Barely turning her head, she looked sidelong across the tavern. Leaning in a little, she spoke in almost a whisper. "Name's Koraymis, just checked in today. That's all I know," she said, winking at him. Errol slid two maples across the table, which she quickly palmed.

Never terribly comfortable with waiting, Errol scattered the walnuts on the table before him and drew out his blade. Using the deadly sharp weapon deftly, he sliced the chunky walnut halves into smaller sections prior to eating them. He had them diced in seconds.

Sipping the extremely flavorful and roundly bitter ale, he glanced about the room, observing everyone, as well as the newcomers.

The ranger-sort-of fellow across the room looked at him for a while, as he chopped the walnuts and idled, though the man certainly did not know Errol could sense his watching. He didn't know what to make of that one yet.

The pewter dish was slightly concave, and it lay flipped on the table. Errol took his blade and carefully balanced it on the center of the metal plate. It bobbed a little on the spot just below the guard that protruded enough to act as the perfect center point. Testing the flatness of the dish, he was satisfied. He gave the blade a practiced twist. It began spinning smoothly.

Errol continued eating the walnut pieces and sipping his ale, as the blade spun silently. He knew the stranger, Cam, was watching him from across the room. He glanced up sharply at the young man, catching him off guard. The brown-clad man looked away with a mildly sheepish look on his face. Errol grinned in satisfaction.

Amid the relative quiet of the tavern, Errol saw the young man, Koraymis, appear at the base of the stairs. He joined Cam at his table, as Cam rose and clasped the young man's hand. From where Errol sat, he could see faint smudges of ink on the young man's fingers. He was clearly a scholar or student. As the black-haired spoke to Cam, Candissa entered, accompanied by the young Lord Enthessar. They were followed by one of Candissa's sisters and her escort, and a house guard. The young Lord Allenfar was saying something supposedly witty or amusing. Candissa laughed lightly in response, though Errol suspected she was forcing her reaction to the young Lord's remark.

There was a table free in the center of the room, and Lord Allenfar motioned they sit there. As they came into the middle of the room, the black-haired scholar looked at Candissa and she at him. Then her gaze went to Cam Bronwyer. She opened her mouth as if to say something, hesitating in her advance toward the table.

Errol stood, suddenly feeling something akin to alarm. Sometimes his awareness surprised even himself, warning him of events about to occur. This was something like that, yet different. A tingling skittered down his back.

Cam looked at Errol, as did the young scholar. Then Candissa.

"My lady, is there something amiss?" Enthessar said with a voice louder than necessary. He glanced at the guardsman, concerned. He did not notice Errol standing near the kitchen entrance, but he did look at the two men standing close to their table. The room seemed to grow quieter. "Are one of these gentlemen a cause for alarm?"

Candissa looked at each of them again. She did not turn her head to look at Errol, yet he saw her glance sidelong in his direction. There was something about her gaze, a meaning or a connection. It was entirely unsettling.

She shook her head, smiling a little. "Don't be silly, not at all," she said to her escort.

"Then let us sit and enjoy a glass of wine perhaps," Allenfar said, as the others sat around the table. The young lord sat with his back toward Errol. "You bade we visit this fine establishment to sample their, what was it, Elven wine?"

"Yes, they have an unusual vintage," she said. Errol supposed she could be referring to Evan's Amberfield wine. She likely needed some reason to include the Bonerest on her party's excursion, in order to contact Errol.

As the group sat and resumed easy banter, the Bonerest returned to a normal level of conversation. Errol watched sidelong as the young scholar and Cam sat down across from one another. They spoke quietly, their expressions guarded.

He had naught to do now but wait. He wondered if Candissa had some idea of how to extract herself from her escort. Perhaps he would have to help her in that. Regardless, he had no intention of whiling away his evening waiting for the handsome Enthessar to run out of witticisms to delight his audience and impress the locals.

He sipped his ale and spun his dagger idly, rebalancing it on the overturned dish. It spun evenly with a simple flick of one finger. Errol occasionally amused himself by spinning it and seeing how often it would end up pointing west. It was rare when it didn't, defying any sort of probability.

This evening was one of those times. When the dagger stopped turning, it was pointing in a certain direction, but that was not west. He spun it again, with the same result. He spun it in the other direction, again yielding the same. Removing the dish, he spun it on the rough wooden surface of the table. It wobbled and spun somewhat less predictably. Yet, when it lurched to a stop, the tip was once again pointing in the same direction. At Candissa.

The symbol on his blade seemed to glow a faint red, but he wasn't sure, as it was so subtle. He stared at it, transfixed.

Something outside the main door caught his attention, a noise perhaps, or a disturbance. Sheathing the blade lightning-quick, he was on his feet and at the door in a breath. He moved with a fluid smoothness most could not duplicate, but his sudden departure was noted by at least three individuals in the Bonerest.

His eyes brushed over Candissa's suddenly worried gaze, before turning to glance at the two sitting at the small table under the clock. Concern was evident in their glances. But then he was out the main door, in the deepening dark of the young night. He faced the west gate, staring at it. He realized his breath had quickened. His pupils widened as his gaze took in more of the dark of the night. The stars seemed intensely bright, illuminating a great deal. The clear sky murmured something he could not understand.

Everything, Candissa had said. Why did she think his memory had to do with everything?

His ears could pick out conversations in the tavern. He could hear the young Lord Enthessar retelling some scandal from the East, involving a local lord, two prize warhorses and the twin daughters of a rival. He gritted his teeth. *Enough, lordling, time for you to go back to your chambers.*

Looking about, Errol spied the figure of Penston, the town scholar, making his way to the entrance of the Bonerest. *Perfect*, he thought to himself. Errol intercepted him in front of one of the windows, the light revealing his identity. As he suspected, he startled the robed man.

"Ah, Errol. How goes it this fine night?" Penston asked amiably.

"Sir, I must ask a favor of you. Might you have a quill and paper on hand?" Errol asked, knowing full well the scholar was never without.

"Certainly, let's go inside and you can use them," he said, motioning through the window.

"That...would work against my objectives, I must confess. Would it be possible to slip off to your apartment?" he implored, knowing the scholar kept his rooms just across the street and up some steps.

"Well, that seems a little unnecessary," he began, looking inside the Bonerest. He glanced around the room, appearing to want to go in. Then he seemed to change his mind. "But you seem to have a need. I can certainly delay my evening ale. Come."

"Thank you! I will be once more in your debt," Errol assured him.

"Think nothing of it," Penston replied.

They were in his rooms after a brief and brisk walk. Penston adjusted a lamp and brightened the small, comfortable room. "Here, you sit at this table," he said, neatly arranging a quill, ink pot and parchment before Errol.

"Again, I cannot thank you enough," he said, quickly putting quill to parchment.

Penston glanced at him writing briefly. "I don't imagine I need to know what you're writing," he said with a wry smile.

"It's nothing objectionable, just...mildly devious," Errol replied, grinning back. "Worry not, it involves you not in the least."

He was done with his note in another moment, quickly ensuring it was dry enough before folding it. He was up and at the door. "Remember Penston, I am your man, if you need anything at all," he said with a wink.

"Quite all right. Perhaps I'll see you at the Bonerest in a bit," the scholar said, occupying himself with some sort of busy work now.

Errol made his way back to the tavern, checking through a window to ensure Candissa was still at the mercy of Enthessar. Heading back to the kitchen entrance, he found Beshanu and gave her simple instructions, handing off the note. With that, he made his way through the kitchen and eased himself back to his seat at the booth. Being one of the less-illuminated tables, he was able to utilize his innate finesse to affect an entrance unnoticed.

His ale was still there, and he took a careful sip. Candissa happened to glance in his direction and was momentarily shocked to see him. She recovered quickly, a hidden smile behind a hand as she enjoyed a bit of cheese. Not a minute later, he watched as Beshanu moved over to the entrance of the tavern, near where the house guard were standing. She approached one of them, murmuring something as she handed him the note.

Walking over to Lord Allenfar, guard handed him the note. "A message for you, my Lord."

"Thank you," Enthessar said nodding. He opened the folded piece of parchment, his brow furrowing. "It seems our evening is at an end my friends. I've been called back to our quarters for some reason."

"Must we?" cried Nalliath. "We were having such fun!"

"I'm afraid so. I'm happy to escort you both back to your own House before returning to where we are staying," Enthessar said. He looked expectantly at Candissa. "My lady?" He extended an elbow for her to take.

"My lord, if it please you, I have some small bit of business to attend to here," Candissa began. "On behalf of my father. I missed an earlier opportunity to discuss the matter with the tavern master. Once that is done, I will find an escort home, rest assured."

"My lady," the young Lord of Allenfar said, one eyebrow raised. "I am doubly surprised, if not amused. Your father would ask you to conduct business here, at this hour? This seems unlikely. And your suggestion I would leave you here unattended is just as unlikely."

Candissa managed to keep a graceful smile on her fine face, despite what Errol suspected was a slight to the young lady, though Enthessar may not have even realized it. Errol was quite amused and saw his opening.

"My Lord Allenfar, if I could intercede," Errol said smoothly, stepping up to the finely-dressed young man, whose expression clearly connoted what he thought of the interruption. "Please forgive my eavesdropping. I would be more than honored to ensure the Lady Candissa has a safe and quick journey home after her business is conducted." Errol glanced meaningfully at Candissa at this point. She understood.

"Enthessar, may I present Errol Blackmar, Master Factor for House Ythanford. He is a friend of the family. As well, he keeps the books here, and I will need to speak with him regarding my father's business," she said by way of introduction. Errol could see the initial expression of disdain and annoyance fade to one of comprehension and acceptance. He nodded slightly as Errol bowed stiffly.

"I see. Well, my lady, if you are determined, and you trust this gentleman," he said with some trepidation.

"My good Lord of Allenfar, I'm confident he will be able to conduct me back to House Demarrae without incident," she smiled lightly, putting a hand on his arm. "I would appreciate you doing so for my sisters, of course."

"My lady," he said, taking her hand and kissing it gently. "I hope we will have occasion to spend some time together again while I am in town."

"I have no doubt of that," Candissa said, smiling. It was a genuine response. Her mother would not allow her to spend but one evening out with the man, not someone of his stature.

"Good sir, I leave the lady in your care," Enthessar said to Errol. He extended a hand, to Errol's surprise. He shook it appropriately, allowing the man of higher station to clasp his hand more firmly than Errol did his.

"I am honored, Lord Allenfar," he replied. With that, Candissa's sisters and their escorts followed Lord Allenfar out of the front door, tailed by the house guard. Candissa turned and nodded carefully to Errol.

"Errol, why don't you get that larger book of Evan's," she said, for the benefit of others. She then slipped to the end of the bar closest to where Errol had his table and asked Beshanu to summon Evan.

The tavern master did not seem taken aback by the unusual request for the two of them to review an accounts ledger and produced it momentarily.

She perused the ledger for a few minutes, before turning to Errol. As they both sat, he took a moment to appreciate her winsome appearance. She wore a pleated white skirt of an appropriate length for walking in the street, a v-waisted bodice of a stiff linen trimmed in white leather and bound along the front with hooks, a shirt of modest neckline and only slightly puffed sleeves. All was white, or a light shade of gray. Her hair was a sort of pale gold by the light of the tavern.

Only her eyes of palest blue offered any contrast in color. Those, and her lips of red, of course. Errol frowned a bit, wondering about his feelings at the moment.

"Thank you for arranging that," Candissa said, taking her seat after Errol rose respectfully. "I assume the note was your doing."

He nodded. "Yes. I need to explain what happened today."

"Regarding your replacing my wine?" she said.

"Precisely."

"Are you here by yourself in this regard?" she asked.

The question seemed out of place. He was intrigued. "Of course. Why?"

"I thought perhaps those two young men over there were with you, the way they seem familiar," Candissa said, looking over at the two of them. "I know that doesn't make much sense, does it?"

"No, they're not with me. But I agree with you. There is something about them that caught my eye, as well," Errol said. "I will have to introduce myself, I fear."

"Be courteous, they may simply be travelers," she said, amused by his declaration. She looked over at them again to find they were staring back at the two of them. "Ah, well, an introduction does seem in order now."

"A bit later, but yes," Errol said. He leaned in. "Someone at the feast, back in the kitchen, slipped some liquid into your wine. I switched glasses to prevent you from drinking it."

Candissa was shocked. "Who would do that? What was in it?"

"I don't know what was in the glass. It was dumped before I could investigate, after I had switched it with a proper one. But I know who was behind it. I was asking about among the kitchen staff, and apparently a servant named Renther was at hand during the pouring of the wine, including yours. That was whom I spied slipping a vial of something into it. One of the kitchen staff recalled him asking which glass was yours, by name."

"Renther? Yes, I seem to recall who that is. What did he have to say?"

"I lost him. Right after his little trick, he disappeared into the crowd in the kitchen. I looked for him as best as I could after I switched the glasses, but without any outstanding reason to stay, I had to return to the hall. I wanted to get back there to interview the staff, or perhaps the head servant. Do you have any idea what he may have against you?"

Candissa looked perplexed as she thought on the matter. "No, I've always treated the staff with consideration. This is a bit hurtful, to think one of them would want to act against me. Whatever do think may have been in the wine?"

He shook his head slowly. "I need to speak with this Renther. Perhaps you could introduce me to the head servant tomorrow. No, perhaps even tonight. If it's not too late."

"Of course. I don't want any delay in figuring this out. But bear in mind, if you were the only witness and the wine is gone, there's no proof of wrongdoing," Candissa pointed out.

"I am aware. However, if I have a chance to speak with him alone, I may be able to learn something," Errol said with a slight but menacing smile on his lips. It seemed to make Candissa a little uneasy.

"I want your assurance you won't let him come to any serious harm. We don't know if he was trying to poison me," she said.

"Candissa, really, isn't that a bit naive?" Errol chided her. "What would he put in your drink if it wasn't a poison of some sort? Although, it could have just been something to render you unable to resist when he visited your chambers later tonight."

Candissa's eyes went wide for a moment, and Errol thought perhaps he had said too much. "Forgive me if I shock you, my lady, but these are things that do happen."

"Yes, it's all right. I'm not shocked. I'm just disappointed someone, *anyone*, would have ill intent against me. We should go. I need to find out why Renther would do this," she said.

"Wait, I must know something. No, that's not fair, I would *like* to know," Errol said, seeming to change the subject. "You said those months ago, here, that *it may affect everything*. My memory. Why did you say that?" Having asked the question, Errol thought it ill-timed. He had to know.

She seemed taken aback, as he would have expected, by the sudden shift in conversation. She looked away, clearly in thought.

"My first question should be...why do you ask me this now? How is it important compared to someone perhaps attempting to poison me?" Candissa said, looking down at her hands. "But I confess, I think it's perhaps the most sensible question you could ask at this moment."

Errol looked at her with a thoughtful expression, not replying.

"That sounds a little off, doesn't it?" she said, almost laughing.

"No, it doesn't sound off, Candissa, not at all," he said, with an earnestness he couldn't hide.

"But as I said, I owe you this, an explanation," she said, taking a deep breath. "I have my map, as you know, I've been adding onto it for a long time, longer than anyone knows. After you...were found, outside there on the Wardenstone, I came to realize, as I grew older, that the world was much larger than anyone knows, than anyone cares to admit."

"Larger than anyone wants to say, yes. I've encountered the same attitude, from many people. Almost anyone who I try to discuss it with, really," Errol agreed. "No one wants to even think about what lies beyond the mountains or the forest, or the…" He made a motion toward the exit.

"The hills," Candissa said. "As my awareness of this grew, it was as if my own world here shrank, and I knew that you, your very existence, was proof there was something greater beyond all of this."

"West. We need to go west," Errol said, almost as an aside, as though speaking his thoughts without realizing it. Candissa's eyes lit up.

"Why did you say that?" she asked, seeming almost excited. Her quick demand caught Errol off guard. His lips parted to speak, but he just blinked, staring at her.

"I cannot say for certain, but...it's something I think I've known for some time," Errol replied. "It sounds mad as moons, but my destiny lies to the west."

"No, you said *we*! *We need to go west*," Candissa implored. She was speaking too loudly, Errol thought. He looked across the room and Candissa followed his gaze.

The two newcomers to the Bonerest were staring at them. Upon being noticed, they did not look away. They continued to study Candissa and Errol for a long moment, before turning back to a whispered discussion. Their eyes continued to glance over to Errol and Candissa.

He felt instincts aroused he did not understand. Errol knew without a doubt that if he so wished, he could bound across the room in a heartbeat and have his blade at a throat before they could draw a weapon.

"Why do they stare at us so?" Errol whispered, his eyes narrowing. His right hand moved across his belt to his blade, his fingertips touching the grip lightly. He felt an almost living quickness within the weapon. It was part of him, part of what he was. Staring at the two, he felt Candissa's hand on his, and a sure calm supplanted the agitation threatening to engulf him.

He diverted his gaze from the two and looked at her, into her eyes as they locked onto his.

Since the first moment he had seen her, years ago, the first moment he could recall in this new life, her eyes were as blue as the sky, often reflecting a sunny day or a cloudy pall. But always a fair, bright blue.

Time seemed to slow down as her hand rested on his.

Her eyes were turning from blue to a light gray, and *then silver, a radiant, glowing silver.*

Errol could not speak, his mind paralyzed. She turned slowly, bringing her silvern gaze upon the other two. To Errol's eyes, everyone within the Bonerest was still, motionless. Her eyes met the gaze of the two across the room.

Errol managed to turn his head, although it was as though he was underwater, his head moved so sluggishly. Cam and Koraymis were both rising from their seats, moving too slowly. Errol could not understand what was happening. Stranger still was his own lack of apprehension. Two strangers, standing as they stared at Candissa, should have triggered an instant alarm in Errol. They did not. For reasons as mysterious as the slowing of their apparent motion, he knew they were friends.

In a blink, the four of them were on their feet. Candissa was still staring at them.

We are arrived, Errol heard Candissa's voice, though her lips did not move. The black-haired scholar pressed two fingers to one temple, as if to soothe a headache.

Not all of us, the group is not complete, the scholar spoke as Candissa had, without voice. His eyes betrayed deep concern, and alarm. Cam glanced at his friend, then at Errol and Candissa, whose eyes still shimmered brightly silver.

Yes, there is one more, Candissa said. Her hand suddenly gripped the table as her knees seemed to buckle a little. Errol reached out quickly to steady her. She closed her eyes, gasping.

Time snapped back to what Errol would expect. The inexplicable exchange seemed to take place outside of the normal flow of things, and for those few brief moments, he did not even notice or hear the crowd of patrons within the Bonerest. Now, he realized nearly everyone was staring at the four of them.

A hush descended on the tavern. The tavernmaster stood attentively behind the bar, studying the mood of the room. He quickly made his way out from behind the length of black oak, to stand in front of the large round table in the center of the Bonerest. No one had taken a seat there since Candissa's previous party had departed.

Evan Devenuar studied the four, glancing back and forth. His gaze settled on Errol and Candissa. "Lady Candissa, Master Errol, is everything all right?"

"Of course, Master Evan," Candissa reassured him after a momentary pause.

"Then, please permit me to introduce our most recent guests," the tavernmaster offered, looking to the other pair. They both nodded their assent. "Master Koraymis Sleeth, a scholar, and Master Cam Bronwyer, lately both arrived from Woodford. Gentlemen, Lady Candissa of House Demarrae, and Master Errol Blackmar, of Ravensroost."

They all nodded to one another. The large round table beckoned to them all, and as one, they each moved slowly to one of the five chairs around it. A low level of murmurs and chatter returned to the common room, as they each sat. Errol noted how many eyes were on Candissa. Clearly, her display was not as subtle as he had hoped; others had seen her eyes. His ears picked out a few hushed whispers postulating on what had happened, and how her eyes could shine like molten silver. Evan Devenuar nodded and returned to his post behind the bar.

"Hello, I am Cam Bronwyer. Can either of you tell me what just happened?" Cam asked by way of introduction.

"So, you both saw her...eyes?" Errol asked. Candissa glared at him suddenly.

"What's wrong with my eyes?"

"Nothing," Errol said. "But a moment ago, they...shined, I suppose is the best word. You didn't realize, did you?"

"Shined? No, I didn't," Candissa was clearly annoyed or perhaps alarmed.

"A silvery gleaming, lady," the scholar named Koraymis said. His voice was a surprise to Errol, for some reason. He spoke in an almost hushed tone, but they could hear him easily.

She blinked in confusion, uncertainty evident in her expression.

"I am not sure if we should continue this conversation here," Errol said, leaning in. Candissa shook her head.

"No, we should stay here. I have nothing to hide."

"Lady, people don't understand what just happened and that includes the four of us. Unless either of you two gentlemen can explain how we all just heard her, and you, if I'm not mistaken Master Koraymis, speaking without the benefit of our voice?" Errol posed. No one challenged him on his claim, and no one offered an answer.

"I heard our voices as well," Cam said. "Though no one actually spoke aloud."

The four looked at one another, with expressions ranging from doubt to incredulity.

Candissa seemed to draw herself up, sitting a little taller, looking almost regal in Errol's eyes. She looked at each of them, then furrowed her brows, frowning.

"What's wrong?" Errol asked, seeing concern etched on her face.

"Something, I'm not sure," she replied, looking at the table. Her eyes fell on the single empty chair between Errol and Cam. She cocked her head a little.

Errol noted the scholar, Koraymis, turning the ring on his right hand. He was looking at the chair now, his eyes narrowing. It looked like a nervous habit. Still, Errol wasn't sure he liked this one.

"We're missing someone," Koraymis announced.

"That was my thought," Candissa said quickly, looking at the scholar. "As I...*said* a moment ago. There is one more, we are not complete."

"We?" Cam asked.

Errol felt it, too. It was the same feeling he had earlier, when he had to rush outside, a nagging, an urging, a calling. He wanted to resist it, but he knew it was something he had to follow.

"Yes," he growled to the group. "We. The sorcerer is right. *We* are a group. We all heard it a moment ago." He nearly didn't hear his own words. There was a quiet gasp from Candissa, while Cam's mouth just opened, as he glanced sidelong at Koraymis.

"Sorcerer?" Cam said, nearly whispering.

Errol looked at the dark-haired scholar. He had no idea why he just called Koraymis a sorcerer. The black-haired man's expression was as stone. "Forgive me, I meant to say scholar. No slander was intended." He understood the term to be a brand no one would want upon their character. Errol had no qualms about someone calling themselves a sorcerer, but in this culture, it was associated with the calling of dark powers, demons and that sort of thing. He leaned in closer around the table, and the others followed suit.

"My first question is this...why are we here? What drew the four of us together, if we are indeed a group, as it seems we are?" Errol asked them.

"I would defer to the lady here, and what she said a short while ago," Cam replied.

"And that was?"

"West. We must go west. Perhaps, we will find our fifth there."

Errol suddenly felt uncomfortable. Their conversation had become too loud again. Several patrons were staring at them openly, drinks down, looking at them with suspicion, perhaps even a hint of malice in some of their eyes.

"I must insist we go elsewhere to speak of these things," Errol said in a low voice.

Taldrephus spun into the tavern, nearly tripping in his haste. His eyes wide, he rushed over to Errol. "Sir...you should probably come outside," he panted. Then he spoke to Candissa. "You as well, my lady."

Errol knew better than to ask his tall friend what the matter was; he trusted him that something was amiss. He stood at once and exited the Bonerest, followed by Candissa. Koraymis and Cam followed her almost immediately.

"Can you give me any warning on whatever this is about?" Errol asked his friend in a low voice as his eyes quickly adjusted to the dark twilight. He instantly saw a group heading toward the inn, comprised in part of town guards, and led by the young Lord Enthessar.

"Them, sir," was all Taldrephus managed.

"There he is, sergeant," Enthessar said loudly, with almost theatrical bravado. "Lady Candissa, you should step away from that fellow at once."

"Whoever are you talking about?" Candissa said, her voice almost demanding.

"Errol Blackmar, of course," Enthessar said, slowing as the guards approached, forming a semicircle around the group. "Sergeant?"

The ranking member of the guard, the sergeant cleared his throat. Errol knew the man, his name was Carreck. He raised an eyebrow at the sergeant as he spoke. "Errol, we need you to accompany us back to House Demarrae."

"Why is that, Carreck?"

"There's been, ah...a murder you see," he said, clearly uncomfortable in his duty. "Two, actually."

"Murders? At our estate? Who?" Candissa demanded, stepping toward the sergeant. Errol was impressed with her comportment. She could be quite commanding when necessary.

"Servants, nothing more," Enthessar cut off the halting reply the sergeant was trying to make. "No one you would know, I'm certain."

Candissa only glared at the young noble, her eyes narrow.

"And I'm a suspect?" Errol said, raising an eyebrow.

"You were looking for one of them earlier today, by more than one account. The question is, did you find him? Lady Candissa, I really must insist," Enthessar said, extending his hand toward her in a clearly patronizing gesture.

"Errol is my friend, Lord Enthessar. I will accompany him to my home, where this matter will be resolved to our mutual satisfaction," Candissa said in her commanding tone. "Is that understood?"

The eastern noble raised both eyebrows in surprise and disdain, apparently at her display of attitude. Errol knew at once he did not like this one.

"My dear lady, you needn't get so upset, the situation will be handled, rest assured," Enthessar's voice was thick with pretentiousness.

Errol could sense she was on the edge of taking action. He smiled calmly, putting a hand gently on Candissa's shoulder.

"It's entirely understandable, noble sir. I would have the exact same reaction in your position," he assured the young man. "Let us make haste and see what can be found out regarding this matter." His smooth tone and comportment put the noble and attending guards immediately at ease.

He leaned close to Taldrephus as he moved forward, whispering something to him briefly. Then he was passing Enthessar. He touched his elbow.

"You were entirely appropriate in your concern for the lady, and I will certainly note your kindness when I speak to her father," Errol murmured, close to the noble, as he nodded to him.

Enthessar's reaction was one of hesitation, but he returned a courteous nod. As Errol led the group east along the street, followed closely by Candissa, he noted his new friends Koraymis and Cam stood near the entrance of the Bonerest.

"Don't concern yourselves, gentlemen. We will talk again tomorrow morning and conclude our business then."

As Errol strode briskly through the night air, his mind raced to recall all the events of the day. He doubted the interview with Renther would take place, as he was almost certain the poor fellow was one of the dead servants.

CHAPTER THIRTEEN - KORAYMIS

24 Laborus, Year 197, Eastvale Calendar

"Should we follow them?"

They had returned to their seats inside the Bonerest. Koraymis resisted the irrational urge to bolt out the door after Errol and Candissa. He had known Cam Bronwyer only a short time, yet he trusted the hunter for reasons he could not grasp. He knew that trust was due to their strange shared experience. In those brief exchanges, when they had all heard one another's voices in their heads, Koraymis had the feeling he was peering into each of their minds - at least in a small way. He was strangely confident the trust he felt for them was not misplaced. It was easy to ascribe such a bizarre incident to matters of profound meaning; otherwise, he - they - would be suffering from some form of insanity.

Touched by the gods, as his house mother had often quipped. Gods or no, Koraymis had enough understanding of magic to know this was not something that *just happened.*

"Yes," was Cam's reply. Koraymis felt an inexplicable relief at Cam's straightforward utterance, though he could not understand why. "He...they, may need us. There's no telling if there will be trouble."

"Then, what to do?"

"Get whatever you need. I need to get a few things from my room. Perhaps you could wheedle out the location of this House Demarrae from someone here? I don't think they would appreciate us openly following them. I'll meet you outside shortly. I've already paid for our food."

With that, Cam was off, heading up the stairs with broad, loping strides. Koraymis needed nothing that was in his room; he always strove to be self-sufficient, keeping whatever he needed on his person.

Looking about the common room, he noted there was a steady buzz of hushed conversation about what had just happened - both before and after the noble and the guards had arrived. He realized he was likely part of that conversation. Anyone who met his eyes turned their gaze elsewhere quickly.

He saw the barmaid staring at him with a little apprehension, as she gathered their cups.

"Pardon me, young lady, those people are heading to the estate of House Demarrae. Is that far from here?"

Beshanu, as he had heard her named, eyed him momentarily. For a moment, he wondered if she would help him at all. "Not far, no sir. Just take the main avenue east, past four corners, and it's a nice walled estate just two streets north of the green temple. You won't have trouble finding it."

"Thank you," Koraymis replied. He looked to the stairwell. With no sign of Cam yet, he felt uncomfortable standing there. He made his way to the entrance, avoiding the gaze of a couple of locals. His heart beat faster in his chest.

Outside, the air was cool, the stars bright. He heard two dogs barking down an alley. Koraymis had only one thought at the moment: *why was he here, waiting for Cam?* He had known his "friend" Cam for a but a few hours. Now, it appeared he was allying himself with not one new acquaintance, but three. If that wasn't strange enough, there was this matter of their communication, which was undeniably beyond the norm. The farmers and townsfolk here would call it supernatural, or the work of evil spirits perhaps.

He knew it was a form of magic the four of them shared, something he had read about in his tome. It was called telepathy, though he had no idea what it meant.

His ring was suddenly warm. Touching it with his left hand, Koraymis became aware of something happening.

Glancing around, he saw no one approaching him. A pair of men were talking quietly while walking casually toward the Bonerest, appearing to be merchants, by the girdles about their waists. The gate to the western hills was closed, but the wall was low enough that he could make out the hills by the light of the stars, and the two moons.

There was a glow just above the line of the hills to the northwest - a pale, faint light. He frowned. It had to be something intensely bright for him to see it from the town. The light was purple, barely within his ability to perceive it in the dark of night.

His breath froze. He realized it wasn't light at all. A moment later, he blinked, and it was gone.

"You ready?" Cam's question caused Koraymis to jump, having

approached the scholar almost silently. "Sorry, didn't mean to startle you."

"It's quite alright, yes ready. The estate is up the main way then north, easy to find," he reported.

"Let's go."

They set off east along the main avenue through Ravensroost. Koraymis struggled a little to keep pace with the hunter's strides. He noted Cam now carried his pack, slung over his chest and back.

His *enchanted* pack, Koraymis noted to himself. Even now, if he concentrated, he could perceive the faint purplish gleaming.

"Cam, why are we going after them?"

"As I said, there could be trouble."

"But, what can we do? We're new to the town, I doubt anyone would trust us. And we barely know them."

Cam Bronwyer looked sidelong at the scholar. "I have more trust in people, perhaps. But these two are different. You must feel the same way."

"Certainly, given what just happened. I just don't know if this is the wisest course of action. If they're in this estate, we have no way of getting in. Are you to just loiter around the gate?"

Cam stopped suddenly, catching Koraymis off balance. "Fair enough. What would you do? We are *connected* to these two. You can't deny it. I came here for reasons I don't understand. All I know is that I - *we* - must go west. If you think I'm suffering from a sickness of the mind, then fine! I will understand if you turn back and wait at the Bonerest."

Koraymis considered his words. "No, I'm not turning back now. You're right, the four of us are connected, somehow. I just want to know more. I don't like going into a situation without a plan."

Cam nodded and continued down the avenue. "I wish I had one to offer you, Kor."

In the dark of the streets, Koraymis grinned. He had had only a few friends in his life. A few fellow students, a couple people at the library. They were the only ones who ever called him Kor, until today.

They passed by several shops, all shuttered now, with lights burning in upper windows. The streets of Ravensroost were lit by occasional lamp posts topped by brightly burning oil lamps. The lamps were brighter than Koraymis would expect, and he could not smell the singular odor of burning oil. He wondered what was burning, to produce such a bright, yellow-white flame. They were unlike the streetlamps in Woodford. He shook his head, trying to banish such strange questions like this. They arose far too often for his liking.

"Where now?" Cam asked, looking for guidance from his friend.

"That corner there, north two blocks," Koraymis said.

They were soon at an intersection with a walled estate on the northeast. The small gate, lit by a nearby lamp post, had the name Demarrae clearly above it, in worked metal. Two guardsmen stood outside the gate. They noticed the pair as they entered the intersection.

Cam stopped only a moment before continuing north.

"What now?" Koraymis asked him in a hushed voice as they moved along the high wall bounding Candissa's estate on the west.

"We walk and wait. I don't know. Do you have any thoughts on the matter?" he said, looking over his shoulder in case the guards followed.

"If he's arrested, they'll take him out the front gate I suspect, and to whatever sort of gaol they have in this town. But this is a large estate. There is certainly a servant's entrance we could investigate. It may have fewer guards, if any."

Cam stopped. "Not a bad idea. We may even be able to bribe a servant to get us in or, at least, get us information on what's happening."

They walked faster, forcing Koraymis to nearly break into a run, as they turned the corner and followed the northern wall. Koraymis found Cam's account to be true - It was not a small estate.

Around the next corner, they found the wall meandered as it followed the corners of streets. They were soon at the servant's gate, a much-smaller, gated entrance than the main. Through the gate, they could see what appeared to be a storehouse or shack. A trio of servants stood just inside the gate, not far from the storehouse, and were in an animated discussion.

There was a corner with a tree tucked along tight residences, Cam pointed at it. It faced the servant's gate, from across the narrow street.

"Let's wait there, see if we can overhear anything," Cam said. They crept across the street and sat in the shadows, avoiding the glare of the streetlamps. They each cupped their ears as they attempted to hear the conversation.

"Can't make out what they're saying," Cam whispered.

Koraymis frowned. There was something he could try, something he had read, something he had been taught, at least in part. He raised his right hand, almost experimentally. Cam raised an eyebrow.

"What are you doing?"

"Just a moment," Kor murmured. He closed his eyes. The ring was warmer now. He could feel it flow through him, the magic. His awareness extended in ways his friend could not perceive. In a moment, it was as though he was close enough to the servants to be standing with them.

"*The lord of the house is up there right now. Lady C. is really upset, they're makin' all manner of accusations agin' this Arrow fella,*" one said.

"*Errol, not arrow. He's the factor for that lord who was at the banquet. Looks like a fine fellow to me,*" another said.

"*Fine indeed. Too fine! Tongue slick as a butcher's table!*"

Koraymis opened his eyes. "I can hear them. They're talking about Errol."

Cam looked at him with undisguised skepticism. "How can *you* hear them and I can't?"

"Wait, something's happening…" Koraymis cut him off, closing his eyes and focusing.

"*I said there's trouble! The guards have their weapons out!*" a servant interrupted the trio, rushing over from the house.

"*Is that Errol fellow attacking them? I knew he was a murderer!*" a maid said, her voice rising.

Koraymis turned to Cam. "Now there's trouble. They're talking about guards drawing weapons!"

As he reported this, the trio of servants near the gate fled, heading into the manor house.

"Now's our chance!" Cam said, moving quickly across the narrow street. The gate was locked, but it was a poor gate. It was secured using a simple latch, easily opened from within to allow for the servant traffic during working hours, which extended well into the dark. A larger iron bar attached to one side of the gate was raised, no doubt lowered only during night when no one was about.

"It doesn't look that easy to open," Koraymis said, trying to spy the latching mechanism. While simple, it was designed to prevent simply reaching through and flipping it.

"Hang on, I think I have a tool for this," Cam said, unslinging his pack. He flipped open a pouch, then another. "This should work."

He used a long, narrow piece of metal with a bent end. Fishing it between two bars under the latching plate, he felt around for something.

"You seem to know what you're doing," Koraymis noted.

The latch clicked, and the gate creaked slightly as it opened an inch.

"My parents made sure I had a... diverse education," he said, grinning. "And it's not that difficult, you just have to be a little familiar with locking mechanisms. Come on!"

They slipped quickly into the compound. There was an open door across the short yard, clearly the kitchen, as they could see untended pots by the light of bright lamps.

A scream sounded from within. It was distant, but they knew it wasn't Candissa. Without thinking, or speaking, Cam rushed in. Koraymis followed, if reluctantly.

A servant girl nearly collided with Cam as she rushed into the kitchen. He grasped her by her wrists, evoking a scream.

"What's happening in there, girl?" he demanded.

She shook free of his grasp, her knees giving way. She sank onto a sack of grain, quivering and panting, fear clearly taking control of her senses.

Koraymis elbowed past his friend. Kneeling, he reached out and placed a hand on one side of her head.

"We are Candissa's friends, and we are here to help her," he said in a calm but forceful voice. Her eyes seemed to flutter, and her breathing stilled. "What's happening? Where is Candissa?"

"She's up the stairs, to the right. Some of the guards are trying to attack her and that Errol fellow, I think. Hurry!"

CHAPTER FOURTEEN - CANDISSA

24 Laborus, Year 197, Eastvale Calendar

"Lord Enthessar, while I appreciate your concern for my safety, I simply want to make it clear that Errol is my friend," Candissa was trying to take a civil tone as they strode quickly down the avenue. "I can vouch for his character. He is guilty of no crime."

"Your loyalty to your friend is admirable, my dear, but we must let the authorities determine his innocence or guilt in this matter."

His reply did nothing to diminish her ire. Just ahead of them, Errol set the pace of their walk to House Demarrae. She caught a faint smile on his lips and a subtle turn of his head, as Enthessar spoke. In the light of the streetlamp they were passing, she had to admit he sometimes appeared a bit rakish, if not outright devious. He was likely suspect simply because he was considered suspicious by many in town, despite having made many friends over the past few years. His strange arrival on the Wardenstone was still something he could overhear people discussing when they thought him out of earshot

"I am in no way worried, Lord Enthessar," Errol said loudly. "Interviewing me makes sense, and I'm confident what I'll have to say will aid the authorities in apprehending the killer."

"Bold words from the only suspect we have," the young lord retorted. Errol only smiled a little more.

Candissa gritted her teeth. Grabbing Enthessar by the shoulder, she spun him around forcefully, catching him entirely off guard, as the entire group halted suddenly.

"I find your words not only ill-thought but offensive and arrogant!" she growled. "Your behavior makes it clear to me you have a great deal to learn about people, *Lord Enthessar*!" Her last words were bitten off in sarcasm.

Left momentarily speechless and slack-jawed, Enthessar struggled to regain his composure. Candissa turned and redoubled her pace, in lockstep with Errol. Enthessar and the guards had to scurry to catch up to the pair.

"Lady Candissa, if I offended you, allow me to offer my most sincere apologies. However, I have had experience in dealing with ruffians and tricksters. I am not saying Master Errol is anything like that, it is simply something I must consider."

They were already turning the corner up the avenue toward her estate. She did not relent in her pace. Some of the guards were already panting with exertion.

"My Lord, I have no doubt you are behaving in a manner you consider correct in every way," she said, without slowing or looking back.

Errol couldn't resist casting a taunting grin back at the flustered noble.

They were at the main gate of House Demarrae a minute later.

One of the attending guards managed a hasty "M'lady!" as Candissa stormed through the open portcullis. The great hall was in a mild state of uproar, as several officials from the town guard interviewed various members of the household, many of which were mortified at the prospect. Most assumed a simple inquiry meant they would be facing the gallows or the headsman's axe.

Lendra came huffing down the wide, curving marble staircase, making straight for Candissa.

"My lady! My lady! Your father is upstairs. You must attend him at once!"

She was nearly hysterical, grasping Candissa by the elbow and directing her to the stairs in a rush.

"He's with the Captain, that's where we have to take this one," one of the guards said to Enthessar.

The noble nodded, gesturing to Errol to head upstairs. No one had yet laid a hand on him, something for which Candissa was silently grateful.

Before they reached the entrance to the hall, Carreck stopped them, turning to Errol.

"I'll have to take that dagger of yours for the time being, Errol," the sergeant said in an almost apologetic tone. "Rules and all. I'll return it as soon as we're out of the hall."

"That is acceptable," Errol said. Candissa could see some hesitation in his eyes as he deftly drew the long knife from the sheath and handed it hilt first to the guard.

The hall was not unimpressive. The floor was comprised of highly polished stone tiles, darker than most, with ribbons of a greenish stone worked between them. The walls were covered in decorative and functional tapestries, some nearly twelve feet tall, and an assortment of portraits and painted scenes. There were four statues of marble, ancient carvings according to the house tutor that schooled Candissa in many of her early subjects. The hall was lit by several chandeliers of brass, each bearing dozens of candles.

There were several people in her father's private receiving hall. Captain Conmerren was the most prominent, being a tall, powerfully built figure. He was speaking with Candissa's father and the elder Lord Allenfar. Her mother sat on a cushioned chair on the far wall, along with Brenissa, the eldest daughter after Candissa. There were also two other officers of the watch, the ranking officer of the House guard, a few members of House Allenfar's retinue, and two kitchen girls.

"Here is Errol Blackmar, Father," Enthessar boomed over the hum of various conversations in the hall. Candissa didn't know how much more of the insufferable man she could take.

"Ah, Enthessar, I was beginning to wonder if you had to give chase to the rascal!"

The guards and guests chuckled at the pot-bellied noble's slight on Errol. Candissa once more gritted her teeth. It didn't help that Errol seemed to favor black in what he wore every day. She always thought it made him appear menacing in some way.

"He is not armed, is he?" Lord Allenfar asked his son.

"No, he handed his weapon over to the guard here," Enthessar said, motioning Carreck to step forward. "Why don't you put his little knife on the desk over there."

The sergeant nodded and quickly placed the dagger on Lord Demarrae's wide, marble desk.

The Captain of Ravensroost's guard approached Errol, who stood with a casual ease, almost seeming to lean on something that wasn't there.

"You there, Errol Blackmar, we have some questions for you," he began.

"I am entirely at your disposal, good Captain."

"There were two murders, apparently. A servant man and a stabler. Are you familiar with either of them?"

"Renther, yes. I was about to head back here with Lady Candissa in order to find the fellow. I had some pressing questions for him myself."

"Now...wait, why would you have questions for him?" the captain asked, clearly thrown off by Errol's declaration.

"At the banquet, I witnessed Renther slip a small vial of something, a dark liquid, into Lady Candissa's wine," he said, motioning to Candissa. A gasp went up from several of those present.

"Oh, come now, clearly he's inventing a fiction to distract us from the matter at hand," Enthessar said, once more too loudly.

"Let him speak, Enthessar. He is the one who stands accused," Candissa said in a low voice, sounding almost menacing. Eyes widened and heads turned at her tone.

"My daughter, I think you owe our noble guest more courtesy than that!" Lord Demarrae said, clearly displeased with her display.

Candissa glared at her father. She loved him as much as any daughter could love a father. But, at that moment, she realized he didn't see much of what she saw. The world in which he moved - where her sisters, her mother, the nobles from Eastvale lived - it was their world, not hers. She saw now how small it was. Their concerns, their priorities, their aspirations – she shared none of these.

As she had this moment of insight, her shoulders moved back, her chin rose slightly. Somehow, she felt taller in that moment.

She turned and stared at her father, drawing in a breath. No, she realized, she was staring *down* her father, without meaning to. "My apologies, Father." Her voice was low, commanding, without a hint of humility. There were no open windows nearby, but she felt a breeze on her face.

Behind Lord Demarrae, Candissa's mother gasped, slowly standing. Candissa's father opened his mouth, and his face seemed to drain of color, as he stared at his eldest daughter.

"Mother!" she cried, seeing her mother almost fall into her sister's arms. Attendants rushed to her side, as Candissa pushed past Captain Conmerren.

"I'm all right. Stop fussing," her mother said, moaning a little. She seemed to have nearly fainted. Candissa knew of her predilection for fainting spells and similar displays of drama. This episode was not like those, however. She was pale, like her father, and clearly upset.

"Mother, I'm sorry, I didn't mean to shock you with my discourtesy," she said, forgetting for a moment the murders and Errol.

Her mother clutched at Candissa's hand. Her eyes seemed instantly riveted on hers. "It was nothing to do with that, daughter. I must rest. Come to me later. We must speak." With the last word, she looked at her husband. Lord Demarrae had risen and moved to stand beside Candissa. His expression betrayed conflicting feelings, but it didn't make any sense to her. He simply nodded to his wife.

Lady Demarrae waved away everyone else and their wishes for her speedy recovery. She was assisted out of the hall by Brenissa and the headmistress of the staff. Brenissa cast a baleful glare at Candissa before they exited the room.

"Father, I -" Candissa began.

Her father put a reassuring hand on her shoulder. "Think nothing of it, my dear, your mother is just fine. Let us continue in this matter now. My lords, Captain, ladies and gentlemen, forgive us for this delay."

He resumed his seat and motioned to the Captain of the guard to proceed. Errol had stood silently and attentively through the commotion. He cast a concerned glance at Candissa, but she just nodded, her expression dismissing his concerns.

"I do hope your good wife is well, and soon, my Lord," the captain said to Lord Demarrae, observing appropriate courtesy. Murmurs and nods of assent followed from everyone there. "Now, Errol Blackmar, there are some questions regarding you and your interactions this afternoon, during the banquet."

"Yes, sir," Errol nodded.

"After the bodies of Renther and Tremmy were discovered in the stables, it was determined that the last person to make inquiries regarding poor Renther was you. These two serving girls can attest to this." He motioned to the two girls who had been trying to hide from everyone else along edge of the hall, behind one of the few marble statues that adorned the well-appointed hall.

One of the guards brought the girls forth, and they immediately started quaking, wide-eyed at the prospect of speaking before such a company of their betters.

"Tella is your name, correct?" the captain addressed one of them.

She nodded her head, not speaking.

"Did Errol make inquiries to you regarding Renther today?"

"Yes...sir, he did," she stammered. The captain nodded to her to continue.

"He...he asked me where he was and what he was doing at the banquet, and... such questions as that."

"Thank you, my dear. Now you, girl, you are Prina, correct?"

"Yes sir, I am. Errol asked me if I had seen Renther, during the banquet service," she said, having calmed herself a bit more than her friend. "I told him I hadn't seen him."

"Thank you, dear girl. Now," the captain said, turning from the girls and addressing the assembly. "We determined, aside from a few inquiries regarding his absence, that no one else had asked after the victim, save Errol. His body was found some hours later, when a search had begun for him, as he had been missed by that time."

He turned to a nearby table and sipped from tankard of ale, being known as a bit of a drinker.

"So, Errol, you claim you saw Renther slipping a vial of something in Lady Candissa's wine. What did you do after you saw this?"

"Well, I made my inquiries as the girls here can attest. I was concerned that Renther had some ill intent regarding Lady Candissa, and I needed to speak to him. So, I donned a house jacket and assumed the role of a servant, for a short time."

The assembly gasped at his admission.

"Really?" Enthessar nearly laughed. "So, we are to add subterfuge to your list of crimes?"

"Lord Enthessar!" the captain boomed. Enthessar shook at the command in his voice. "I am not accustomed to how the law operates in the east, but in Ravensroost, we do not interrupt a Captain of the Guard during an official interview."

Candissa and Errol both smirked visibly.

"My...please forgive me, my lord captain," Enthessar said unevenly. His father's face reddened.

"Once I was in the guise of a servant, admittedly a brief subterfuge," Errol said, nodding patronizingly to Enthessar, whose eyes narrowed darkly at him. "I then obtained a glass of wine that was untainted and replaced Lady Candissa's glass to prevent her from touching her lips to it."

"Can anyone corroborate this claim?" Captain Conmerren asked.

"I can," Candissa cut in. "I saw him when he replaced my glass, I was going to ask him why he was there, but he made it clear that would be unwise."

"Candissa...why didn't you tell your mother or me?" her father said.

"I needed to talk to him first," she replied. "It seemed too strange a thing to bring to your attention without knowing why."

"Fair enough," Conmerren said. "Go on, Errol."

"Once I had replaced the glass, I set it aside back in the kitchen. Unfortunately, after I had asked after Renther, someone must have knocked it over or dumped it, for it was gone when I returned for it. I was hoping to have it examined by someone learned in such matters, to determine if it was for a fact poisoned."

There were murmurs of curiosity and agreement in the crowd. Candissa thought he was doing quite well in his account.

"What then? You had made some inquiries?"

"Yes, I spoke to Tella and Prina. Could I ask the girls for some clarification on my inquiries?"

The captain nodded his assent. Errol turned to Tella.

"Tella, could you relate to the Captain exactly what I asked regarding Renther and what you told me?"

The girl took a few hesitant steps forward, looking again like a frightened animal.

"It's fine, Tella, just go ahead and tell them what we discussed," Errol said in a remarkably soothing voice. Candissa was impressed at how he could evince certain feelings in people with just the tone of his voice and cadence of his speech. She nodded a little and faced the captain.

"Well, sir, Errol asked what Renther was doing there, and I told Errol that Renther was serving wine. Then Errol asked who Ren was serving to, and I said no one really, except that Ren did ask me special which glass was Lady Candissa's. And I told Ren which one it was, it had a nice silver edging along the base. Renther just nodded and thanked me. I saw he put it right in front of him on the serving tray. And I told all this to Errol."

The girl's testimony caused a bit of animated murmuring among those gathered, and the captain raised his eyebrows.

"Go on, girl," the captain told her.

"Well, sir, it was quite busy for a bit after that, and I didn't pay any attention to Ren and I didn't see Errol again until a bit after the meal was done," she said. "Errol found me again and asked if I had seen Renther, but I hadn't. And that's all of it, I swear, sir!" She seemed entirely sincere.

"Thank you Tella. Prina, what did I ask you?" Errol directed his next question to the other girl.

"You just asked me if I had seen Renther, sir," she answered.

"And had you?"

"I'd seen him here and there, but I couldn't say where he was when you asked me. Then you went on about your way."

"But you saw Renther later." Errol said.

"Why...yes, sir…"

She seemed to hesitate. The captain raised an eyebrow. "Go on, Prina."

"Well, it didn't seem to matter before, but it was well after the banquet, I went into one of the storerooms, and there he was, passed out on a pile of linens."

"Prina, why didn't you tell us this before?" the captain asked her gently.

"Well, sir, it didn't seem to matter, and he was just drunk, or I thought so," Prina said. Her face was quickly reddening, and she drew her small, clenched fists up to her mouth. "Please, sir, I meant no harm! I just, I forgot to mention it!"

The captain raised a hand, a gentle smile on his face. "It is quite all right, Prina. Rest easy."

"By then, I had quit the place, having other responsibilities. Candissa was unharmed, but I was intent on finding Renther again today to interrogate him regarding the wine," Errol said.

Amid the quiet murmurings, it was evident at least some of what he claimed made sense. Still, Candissa noticed Enthessar's gaze was venomous and unyielding, as he stared at the back of Errol's head.

"And what about Tremmy? Is there anything you can tell us about him?"

"No, I've had no dealings with the stabler, never so much as said a word to him," Errol said.

The captain nodded and turned to speak to one of his officers. They then stepped over to the two noble lords and discussed the matter with them.

"We'll figure this out, Errol," Candissa assured him, turning to speak to him quietly. Enthessar approached Errol from behind.

"Your little show may delay justice, but have no fear, you will pay for your misdeeds," he sneered quietly.

Candissa wheeled on him. "You are an insolent fool!" she declared, this time in a hushed tone, so as to avoid a complete scene. "After this day, you are no longer welcome in my presence."

"There will be no need for you to apologize once this matter is resolved, dear Candissa," the young noble said, his voice both condescending and ingratiating.

"Tell me Lord Enthessar," Errol said, turning to face his accuser. "How were these unfortunate men murdered?"

"They were found in the stable, apparently poisoned. They both smelt of wine."

"Who made the determination they were poisoned?" Errol said.

"The house priest had the bodies taken to the temple. They found evidence of poison," Enthessar said, clearly agitated by having to explain anything to Errol.

"So, I see Renther slip something into Lady Candissa's drink, and he is later victim of what could have been that same poison. I would say events lend credence to my account."

"And I say you tried to poison the girl yourself, Renther found you out, and perhaps you used that same poison to render him unconscious. Then when he threatened to expose you, you poisoned them both!" Enthessar's words were loud enough for all to hear, as he intended.

Candissa felt something stir within her, something she did not understand. It did not feel good.

Errol smiled broadly to the young noble. Candissa didn't like the smile. He turned his back to Enthessar.

"You were entirely correct, Candissa. The man's an utter fool."

"Swine!" the young noble shouted, enraged at Errol's insolence. With his left hand, he tried grasping and turning Errol about as he drew his rapier with his right.

Errol was far too quick for him. Whirling faster than Candissa could see, he grasped the noble's left wrist, jerking it violently as he twisted around behind the young man. His other hand wrenched the rapier free of Enthessar's grip and flung it across the flagstones.

He pushed the young noble forcefully to the floor, well away from the clattering rapier, as guards dodged aside, drawing weapons in the process. It happened more quickly than Candissa could fathom. Suddenly, the younger Lord Allenfar was on the floor, gasping and spluttering, as Errol stood calmly.

Guards pushed the guests and courtiers toward the doors. Candissa felt the surprisingly powerful grip of Lendra on her upper arm.

"My lady, to your chambers at once!" the matronly governess insisted.

She shook off the older woman's grip. "No, I'm staying, Lendra. Be still."

"Enthessar, what is the meaning of you drawing your weapon in this hall?" Captain Conmerren bellowed, the floor clearing as he strode forward.

"This dog dared insult me, Captain. I demand honor!" Enthessar seethed, rising slowly. "My station as an Eastern Lord clearly gives me that right. If you are in any way unclear on the laws of the land, our chamberlain will be happy to instruct you!"

His cutting derision did not escape the captain's notice. "My *Lord*, I am more than familiar with your rights and *customs*. Dueling is an *Eastern* custom! There will be no needless duels of honor in this hall. Is that clear?"

Just outside the entrance to the hall, guests were gathered, some running down the stairs, some up, to get a glimpse of the scene. Every manner of rumor and wild claim was flying back and forth.

The dozen or so members of the guard, along with the house guards, had short swords drawn, after the rapier had been flung onto the floor. Captain Conmerren had not drawn his weapon, however. Errol was effectively ringed by armed men.

"May I ask why everyone has weapons drawn when there is no threat? I am not even armed," he noted more than protested.

"Perhaps more for your protection than otherwise," the captain said, staring at Enthessar as he stepped between the noble and Errol.

Enthessar had regained his composure, smoothing and straightening his tunic and belt. He cleared his throat and turned to face his father, who stood next to the wide marble desk. Lord Demarrae had risen from his seat to stand beside Allenfar.

"Father, does House Allenfar yield to this outland version of law and stain our honor in doing so?" Enthessar said, scorn dripping in his voice.

"Enthessar, please, I think you overreacted to this...miscreant's slight," Lord Allenfar said, waving at Errol in a vague fashion.

"Father!" the younger noble blurted, clearly vexed his father was not backing his position unwaveringly.

"Pick up your rapier and behave. Follow the example of your cousin, Lanthred," his father said, nodding slowly to his son. Enthessar looked at him for a moment, then seemed to relax his posture.

"Of course, Father. Forgive me." With that, he straightened himself and turned away from Errol.

"All right, no more of that today. Stand down, all of you," the captain said to his guards. They all slowly sheathed their weapons.

Something bothered Candissa as she watched the young noble relent so easily. She whispered to Lendra, who was still standing at her side. "What was the name Lord Allenfar just mentioned?"

"I believe he said Lanthred, a cousin," she said. "Now that it seems to have settled down, don't you think we should get back to your chambers and let them sort the rest of it out?"

"Of course not," Candissa replied. She looked at Lendra with a sharp gaze. "Did you just say something under your breath?"

The governess returned a confused gaze. "No, m'lady, did you hear something?"

Candissa stared at the open door to the hall, and the dozen or so spectators outside. Their attention seemed partially diverted. She glanced at the situation inside the hall; her father was talking with the Captain and Errol about his whereabouts after the banquet. Enthessar seemed to be distracted, discussing something quietly with one of the house guards belonging to Lord Allenfar's company.

Candissa darted from the side corridor leading off from the hall toward the main entrance.

"M'lady!" Lendra called after her, clearly put out.

From the top of the stairs, she could see the source of the commotion. Several servants were either accompanying or trying to intercept Cam and Koraymis, as they made their way resolutely up the marble steps. An under-steward named Chanderby was loudly protesting their presence.

"I must insist you return to the foyer, or I shall call the house guard!" he nearly shouted at the pair.

"We were told the house guard are all up here, so is it not sensible we join them?" Cam replied with a clearly mocking sincerity. The under-steward was on the edge of a fit when Koraymis motioned up the stairs toward Candissa.

"Chanderby, everyone, it's all right, these are my guests," she said in a clear, commanding voice. "I invited them here. Forgive me for not observing the appropriate protocols, I was distracted by events in the hall."

The pair slowed their pace, seeing that Candissa was there now. Chanderby rushed up to her.

"My lady, I beg your forgiveness. These two seem to think they have the run of House Demarrae!"

"Thank you, Chanderby. I appreciate your service and I will mention it to my father. You've done well in your conduct," she said, smiling to him. Her commendations brought an expression of immense relief to his lined face.

The other servants slowly dispersed as they saw Candissa greeting the two intruders with an easy familiarity. Lendra was once more at her elbow. She looked at the dark, unfamiliar features of Koraymis, in his dark robes, and the hunter in his wilderness garb. She blanched, clutching Candissa's arm fiercely.

"My lady! Who are these strangers?"

"They are my friends. Lendra, this is Koraymis, he is a scholar," she said. The scholar took the cue and bowed formally from his point two steps below them. "And this is Cam Bronwyer, a hunter from Woodford."

"At your service, dear lady," he offered a less formal bow to Lendra.

"Well, if they are your friends, m'lady," she acceded. She stepped back.

Candissa motioned for them to join her off to one side of the entrance to the great hall, to prevent her father or the Captain from seeing them there.

"I would ask what you two are doing here and how you managed to get in, but somehow it doesn't surprise me," she said, grinning a little.

"We felt it was prudent to make our way here. Then we heard there were weapons drawn. Clearly there was no need, and I apologize. Koraymis took my lead, I will confess."

The scholar raised his eyebrows at the hunter's assertion, a small smile on his lips, but he did not contradict him.

"Well, it was nearly necessary. Enthessar seems strangely determined to jail Errol or worse."

"Should we leave?" Cam asked.

"No, I want you to stay," she said quickly. Then she thought about it for a moment. "That's strange, isn't it?"

"No," Koraymis surprised them both by answering. "It feels like the right thing to do."

She looked at them both, relieved they would be staying.

"How long will they be with Errol?" Cam said.

"I don't know, they're still asking questions. I'm glad you're here. I want to make sure there are no…problems arising from this interrogation," she said.

Candissa had a thought. "Do either of you know the name Lanthred? A noble name from the east?"

"That's a strange question," the scholar mused. "Why do you ask?"

"He's a somewhat notorious fellow from House Ganterwell," Cam shocked them with the quick, clear answer. He saw their expressions. "I was well-versed in local politics, back in Woodford, although the family hails from the distant east."

"Why is he notorious?" Candissa asked, her apprehension rising.

"Some few years back, he was known for a rather shocking incident involving the killing of a lesser - a manservant who was accused of slighting him at a dance or something. The next day, he found the manservant and killed him. All of this occurred in a neighboring barony. His family made the legal case that he had the right to kill him based on the honor-based laws of his barony. The case was likely resolved in his favor with the help of a generous donation from his estate to someone's bench."

Candissa's eyes narrowed. "That makes sense."

"Should we be concerned?" Koraymis asked.

She looked back into the hall, leaning around the doorway. They were all still talking in reasonable tones, and Enthessar was sitting down across the chamber now, paying no attention to Errol, apparently.

"Perhaps," she said. She quickly explained the exchange that took place moments before, between the elder and younger Lords of Allenfar and Errol.

"And you suspect his father may be telling his son to take certain actions, based on the crimes of this Lanthred fellow?" Koraymis asked. Candissa nodded.

"Cam, do you recall from your local politics under what circumstances this Lanthred murdered the commoner? It was in another barony but was it in a host's home, such as this?"

"No," the hunter said, thinking for a moment. "It was at a tavern if I remember correctly, outside of anyone's estate. That made it easier. He had pretended to befriend the poor fellow before murdering him. Then he fled the barony. After a lengthy legal proceeding and a well-paid magistrate, the matter was dropped. I think there was a payment to the man's family, as well."

"Well, he wouldn't have that concern with Errol," Candissa said, leaning in to check the room again.

"Why is that?" Cam said.

She looked back at them. "Of course. You really don't know him, do you?"

Koraymis smirked at them both, shrugging. "I suspect that will change."

Errol suddenly appeared around the frame of the tall, lacquered doors.

"What by the six and seven are you two doing here?" he blurted. Cam was about to speak when Errol held up a hand. "No matter, I can imagine. Let's meet back at the Bonerest. My lady."

He walked past them all abruptly, nodding courteously to Candissa as he did so. She had the wherewithal to shepherd her two friends into a side corridor as Captain Conmerren and others began walking out of the hall.

"This way, you can leave by the servant's stairs," Candissa guided them through narrower halls. The appearance of two unfamiliar if not common figures behind Candissa caused more than a few whispered remarks from the servants. She didn't mind. They may relate the tale, but they generally had a good opinion of her. At least, she thought so until today, given the behavior of the slain serving man, Renther.

They were down an almost rickety flight of steps quickly. The servant's gate was not far from the exit she guided them to. "Try to keep an eye on Errol and see if one of Lord Enthessar's men is following him. I'll join you as soon as I can."

"Will you have an escort to the Bonerest? It's getting quite late," Cam pointed out.

She tapped her chin with one finger, thinking quickly. "Go to the town garrison bunkhouse, it's the building with the obelisk towering over it," she said, pointing south. Even through the darkness of the night, they could make out the strange pointed structure. "Ask the guard at the gate to send for Thendarick. He's a younger officer, a Lieutenant in the watch, and a friend. Tell him I require his escort, and to wait at the corner, in view of both gates"

"Understood," Cam answered.

Seeing them off, Candissa dashed quickly through the gardens to the tool shed. There, she easily found her gleaming white staff. She didn't know what to expect, but she felt better having her staff in her room with her.

Making her way back up the servant's stairs, she was nearly to her chambers when Lendra intercepted her. With the nearly seven-foot long staff in hand, Candissa no doubt looked more than a bit alarming to the matronly maid.

"Lady Candissa! What are you doing with that dreadful stick?"

"Never mind, Lendra, I'm just going to get this to my room. I'll see my mother in just a moment."

"Yes, you had better do just that, young lady!" Lendra chided her, following in a huff as Candissa strode to her bedchamber door. In her chamber, Candissa stood the staff behind the taller of her two wardrobes.

She sat at her dressing table, running her hands through her hair and rolling her shoulders slightly. She watched as her hair settled perfectly and any stray creases or wrinkles in her dress faded away. Lendra made fretful noises not unlike a growl, wringing her hands and looking down the corridor.

"All right, I'm going there now!" Candissa exclaimed, rising and rushing past the exasperated matron. Despite this, Lendra trailed after Candissa as she walked to her mother's drawing room.

The door was open, and the chamber was well-lit. Unlike the receiving hall, it had a low ceiling, and was more colorfully enameled and decorated. Her mother enjoyed lighter colors and better illumination than was found in most chambers in the keep. A small fireplace burned brightly.

Her mother was in her favorite seat, a high-backed, thickly cushioned armchair. It was ridiculously high for her height and worn with age. It was where she sat to relax and enjoy her reading. Tonight, she didn't appear comfortable.

To Candissa's surprise, her father was sitting across the small chamber on a simple bench. His deep blue robes stood out against the lighter, more playful colors of her mother's chamber. She could not recall seeing him in this chamber before.

"Mother, Father, what ever is the matter?" Candissa said. She glanced back at Lendra, who only nodded to her with a small smile on her lips as she closed the door.

"Sit down, my dear," her mother said, indicating the cushioned footstool closer to the fireplace.

She did as she was told and sat. But she was uncomfortable. She needed to get out and join her friends at the Bonerest, particularly Errol. His life could be in danger, and this had every indication of being a long talk with her parents.

"If this is about my behavior tonight-" she began. Her mother cut her off with a wave.

"No, my dear, not tonight's behavior."

"Not *tonight's?*" Candissa replied, sensing her mother's inference.

"No, my dear, we are more concerned with the pattern of behavior you've exhibited over the past year," her father joined in. He didn't sound angry, and that put her at ease a little.

He sighed deeply, shaking his head slightly, then looked at his wife. Candissa's mother reached out to her daughter, patting her hand.

"Pattern?" Candissa said, trying to put together why they insisted on speaking to her now.

"Your training," her father began. For a moment Candissa froze, thinking he had found out her martial training with staff and sword and shield. "At the temple, with Mother Meshana, for one. She's been keeping us apprised, as she should."

"But, is there something wrong? Have I not been satisfactory in my training for the healing arts?"

"Satisfactory?" her mother smiled, the lines at the corner of her eyes making her face look a little merry. "My dear, you are beyond satisfactory, beyond any expectation."

"And for a young woman of eighteen you've exhibited a manner of bearing, the way in which you conduct yourself, it's, well," her father struggled to finish. "It's just beyond your years!"

"Are you ashamed of me?" Candissa asked, feeling tears threatening. She had always feared being judged different, owing to her unusual maturity. It was undeniable she did not appear to be a mere eighteen years of age.

Her mother clutched her hand. "My dear, no! Not in the least. In fact, we wanted to speak to you about something that has nothing to do with tonight's events."

"My lamb, it may," her father said, addressing her mother by one of his terms of endearment. Candissa was a bit lost.

"Deesa, we could not be more proud of you. You are growing into your womanhood with a grace and presence we could not have hoped for," her mother said. Her words were like a balm on Candissa's heart.

"Then...why..."

Her mother patted her hand again. She looked at her husband, tears brimming in her eyes. Lord Demarrae nodded slowly.

"My sweet, how old is your father?"

The question seemed entirely out of place, catching Candissa off guard.

"Mother, I don't understand."

"Surely you know his age?"

"Yes, he's sixty-three years of age. I know, he is an older father by some measures," she said, grasping for why her mother was asking such a strange question.

"Yes, sixty-three. And I am much younger than he is, but that is not unusual, is it?" her mother said.

"No, it isn't."

"And how old am I?"

Candissa had to think a moment. She realized she didn't know her mother's age, having only a vague idea. "I think you're perhaps thirty-eight?"

Having never considered the question, as asking a lady's age was generally frowned upon and the subject had never been raised to Candissa's recollection, she realized it may not be correct. Her mother had the bearing and appearance of someone in that range, but her wisdom, her comportment, lent her the air someone much older and wiser.

"You are appropriately courteous, daughter," her mother remanded her gently. Looking at her husband, she smiled. "Before we came to Ravensroost, we lived in Woodford. Did you know that?"

Candissa shook her head. The revelation was surprising, as it had never come up in any of their many discussions.

"My love, what did they call you when you were courting me?" her mother asked of him.

Her father sighed, smiling as he recalled. His eyes seemed to look to a far place.

"The bone man, I think, wasn't that it?" he asked his wife, his eyes twinkling. "At least, to me in private, certainly never in public. That would have been a scandal, eh?"

Candissa was bewildered at this point.

"But...a bone man is another name for a gravedigger, isn't it?"

Her mother laughed, an almost musical sound. "Yes, my dear, it is. How amusing."

"Why?"

Her father cleared his throat, looking almost sheepish now. "Because, daughter, my friends and peers made light of me, calling me that, because...I had romantic designs on a woman more than thirty years my senior."

"Oh!" Candissa said. She had no idea there was another woman in her father's early life. "Who was this...older woman?"

He just shook his head. Her mother tapped her hand.

"Candissa, that *older woman* is me."

She blinked. All she could do at that moment was blink. Her mind was having a great deal of trouble comprehending what she had just heard.

"Mother?" was all she could manage.

"Candissa, I profess to my friends to be forty and one years of age. But that is a lie. I am one hundred and two years old."

Candissa just stared. Her senses seemed to stray. She could hear servants downstairs. Someone had dropped a pan, judging by the commotion. She blinked again, trying to focus.

"No, you are not."

"This is going as well as I expected it to go," her father cut in. He stood abruptly. "With your leave, my good wife, I am going to fetch some brandy."

"That would be most welcome, my dear Dalton. We'll be in the study," her mother said, nodding. Her father left the room in some haste.

Candissa was still struggling. "Mother...that's not possible."

Her mother stood. "Come, I must show you something."

The older woman - how old was a matter yet to be determined in Candissa's opinion - surprised her with how quickly she moved. She led her daughter down the hall outside her drawing room, to her father's study. Candissa was only rarely permitted there, as it was her father's one refuge from all else. He sequestered himself there when he wished to have no contact with anyone else. She realized she had been in the room only a few times in her life.

It was dim and warm, with a high ceiling, lined with portraits, hunting trophies, and other dust-clad oddments Candissa could not outright identify. Her father's desk was enormous, made of stout, dark wood. It was festooned with candles in varied states of depletion, beside stacks of papers, ink pots and used quills. Her mother led her to the end of the study opposite his desk, where tall shelves stood, lined with perhaps hundreds of books, clad in dark leather covers.

The shelves were built of thick maple and oak and contained more than books. There were assorted objects, sculptures and ragged tomes she had never seen before. She wondered why he kept as much of this clutter as he did.

"Dear, pull on that cord gently, if you please," her mother said, motioning to a single cord hanging from a dim, dusty lamp affixed high above their heads. She couldn't imagine why. She reached up, straining to do so. Candissa was a tall young woman, much taller than her mother.

She pulled the cord gently. It offered a bit of resistance, then gave way.

A warm light bloomed from within the hanging lamp, growing quickly into a bright radiance. It was not candlelight, nor the light of burning gas, as Candissa had seen before. It was not lamp oil or anything else in her experience. Then she realized.

Her eyes were wide with wonder as she spoke, "Magic."

"Yes, my dear. It's a magic lantern. It's called an everlamp," her mother informed her.

"Where did it come from?"

"Master Penston says it likely comes from a prior age."

Candissa turned to face her mother. "Prior age?"

"My dear, you must surely know by now – what with your maps and your studies," her mother said with kind eyes. She knew so much more than Candissa could have possibly surmised.

"I... don't know what to say, mother," was all she could manage. All her life, she had been instructed by her betters that one never talked about, even *thought* about what lay beyond their home, their kingdom. It was an affront to the sensibilities and an insult to all those who had strived - and died - to give rise to Eastvale.

"Come here, daughter, look here," the older, much older, woman said. She led Candissa to a tall shelf, standing a few feet from the wall. The space behind it would have been completely in shadow, if not for the lantern's light. There was a portrait there, an especially large one.

Candissa stepped over to her mother, looking up. For the second time that evening, she was speechless.

The portrait was clearly old. The frame was intricately embellished, but the gold paint was flaking badly. The dust was thick within the carved features of the floral reliefs. The artwork itself was oil, so it maintained its quality, despite being possibly more than a hundred years old.

It was a portrait of a young woman. She had sky-blue eyes, long, straw-blond hair, a commanding comportment and eyes resolute and compelling. She was dressed in an unusual outfit of white, close-fitting, and in the crook of her arm was a staff. Candissa's staff.

"No." Candissa denied what she saw. Her mind refused to accept it. "Is that…"

It was her. It was a portrait of Candissa.

"It is not you, my dear," her mother said gently, reaching up and touching the cracked edges of the canvas. "It is Galissa, my mother."

"Your mother?" Candissa said. It was all too much. Her mother declaring she was more than a century old. A picture of her grandmother, who was apparently a twin to Candissa. "Please, tell me more before I burst with questions."

"She died just five years before you were born," her mother said. "After a life of more than three centuries, she told me."

Candissa's mind raced, her mouth trying to form words. "Are...are we Elven?"

Her mother smiled at the suggestion. "No, we are not. We haven't a trace of Elven blood. We...no, not we. I am but a caretaker generation, as she put it."

"What do you mean?"

Her mother sighed deeply.

"I am one hundred and two years of age, and I will live another fifty or sixty years, gods willing. You shall live much longer, I suspect."

"Why would I live longer than you? What am I? *What are we*?"

Candissa's mother sat and gestured to Candissa to do the same.

She looked at Candissa with a resolved expression, her eyes set like stone. Candissa felt the hairs rise on the nape of her neck.

"Please understand, what I tell you was given to me by your grandmother. While it may seem unbelievable, I know every word is truth."

"I understand, Mother," Candissa said, nodding.

"You, like your grandmother, are Aevaru," her mother said, her voice measured and resolute. "Your sisters, and I, are Seludecians."

Candissa drew breath to ask another question, but her mother cut her off with a curt wave.

"Save your questions. Aevaru and Seludecians are both entirely Human in appearance. Outwardly, we are indistinguishable. But we are not Human. She told me we are descended from an ancient people who wielded fantastic powers in a lost age. Our ancestors were almost as Gods among Humans.

"From them, came the Seludecians. They were...are a very long-lived folk, at least twice the lifespan of a Human. She also told me Seludecians once had magical powers, though it varied from person to person."

Candissa raised her eyebrows, not voicing the obvious question. Her mother smiled a little and shook her head.

"No, I have never shown any ability with magic. Nor have your sisters. Now, as I was told, Seludecians existed for a very long time, though their origins are lost to history. From what your grandmother said, the ancient Seludecians joined with another people and from that union the Aevaru arose.

"Now, Aevaru differ from them in many ways," her mother said. The older woman seemed to gather herself for a moment, apparently in thought.

"Go on, Mother, please," Candissa said, laying a hand on her mother's. She did her best to maintain an outward calm, but within she felt ready to explode.

Her mother regarded her eldest daughter, with an almost scrutinizing gaze, her eyes narrowing. Then she turned and looked up at the portrait of her mother.

"She told me this was your fate, and she prepared me as best as she could. But I had nearly forgotten. Until tonight. All her talks, her teachings, they're coming back to me only now," she said, looking at Candissa. "It's as if…"

Candissa nodded. "As if a veil is lifting?"

Her mother looked almost quizzically at Candissa. "Yes, that's a perfect description of how it feels."

"Tell me more about Aevaru, Mother, about what I am."

Her mother sighed heavily again, looking down.

"As Aevaru, you will live to be three hundred years of age, or thereabouts, as did your grandmother. You are a warden of lore, an agent of good, a healer, a comforter, a warrior…"

Candissa heard the words but was having trouble truly understanding the implications. It was as if she was in a waking dream. Her mother said things that simply *could not be.* For a moment, she considered the possibility that her mother was somehow wrong, her grandmother delusional. Yet, she knew. No. All her mother said was truth.

"And Father? He knows all of this? Is he Human?"

"Yes, he is Human and he knows all of this. When I knew he was set on marrying me, I told him everything. Even though he knew I would outlive him by decades, he insisted," her mother said, her eyes suddenly distant and brimful.

Candissa began to feel a little dizzy. She put her hands to her temple, pressing in with her fingers. "Mother, I know this is not some grand jest on your part. Yet, this is so much. I'm not Human? You say I'm not Human, along with you and my sisters. I ask you, what am I to do with this?"

"Calm yourself, daughter. Breathe."

She followed her mother's advice, and used a meditative technique learned at the temple, to still her mind. The spinning she felt within slowed, until it stopped. She had to stand, if only to pace in the confined space of the study. She found herself staring up at the centuries-old portrait.

Candissa had felt something earlier that evening, when Lord Enthessar was insulting Errol, something stirring deep within. That same awareness stirred within her once more. Somehow, it was changing her. When common sense dictated she should simply laugh at the insane utterances of her confused mother, she knew she could not. It was truth, and Candissa saw that now.

An otherworldly calm settled upon her as she stood up straighter. She breathed deeply and turned to face her mother.

"Is there more she told you?"

Her mother almost slumped as she looked at her daughter, her eyes wide. "You see? That's it. It is as if my mother is once more alive in you. I saw her today in the receiving hall and now she stands before me again."

Candissa looked up at the portrait again. Her eyes were not quite Candissa's color, but she was tall and regal, a powerful figure. That is how Candissa felt at this moment.

"To answer you, yes, she did tell me more. It's coming back to me slowly, but I tell you all that I can," her mother said.

"Is this why...I've felt all that I've felt over the past five years?"

Her mother nodded.

"But, why did you not tell me sooner?" she let the question trail off.

"Your grandmother told me things she gained from a lifetime of visions, of coming to know things without understanding how she came to know them. I'm only remembering some of it now, but I do remember this. She said I would know to tell you this when you revealed yourself as Aevaru. You did that tonight, in the hall."

"Why are you Seludecian and not Aevaru?" Candissa asked. "And why are not any of my sisters Aevaru?"

"It is a choice we can make," her mother said. "When we conceive a child, we choose if the child will be Aevaru or Seludecian."

Even before her mother explained it, Candissa understood. But that did not make it any easier. "You mean, you chose…"

"My mother told me – no, she *charged* me – with a very important task. She told me I was to have my first born, a daughter, be an Aevaru. But only the first. She had visions, she said, that made it clear. The first would be Aevaru, the rest, as I am."

"Seludecian," Candissa breathed. "Yet, I do not *know* what that means, being either Aevaru or Seludecian!"

She put her face in her hands, forcing back tears that threatened. Her mother stood and put her arms around her shoulders.

"I know...I knew it would be so much, so much to take at once. But know this, my daughter, it is not *too much*. You have a resilience, a strength, a fortitude within that you have not begun to understand."

She leaned her head against her daughter's, as she hugged her, running her fingers through her long, honey-blonde hair. She turned her mouth to Candissa's ear.

"You are more than you could possibly imagine," she whispered.

She hugged her mother fiercely, feeling a strength flow into her body from her mother's. It was more than just a fleeting thought or feeling. It was palpable. In that moment, she realized her mother was beyond anything Candissa had assumed or suspected.

The two released from their embrace, tears on their faces, but smiling.

Her father entered the study, a bottle of brandy in hand, along with three small crystal cups. He spied them at the far end of his room.

"Ah, you've seen the portrait, then," he said to Candissa.

"Yes, Father."

"Good. I had forgotten about all of this. I'm glad you finally know," he said, with an uncharacteristic warmth. He set the three cups down and poured the brandy, then looked up at the portrait. "I knew her for nearly twenty years, an amazing woman. And you promise to be every bit as amazing, Deesa."

Her mind was still reeling from these revelations. She shook her head.

"I must know more, everything you can tell me, but I fear for my friend's life," she told them.

"Whatever do you mean, my dear?" Her mother sounded shocked.

"Lord Allenfar told Enthessar to follow his cousin Lanthred's example when he wanted to duel Errol."

"Oh, by six and seven I should have realized what he meant!" her father exclaimed, standing suddenly. He quickly threw back his cup of brandy.

"You'll tell me what all this means, I'm sure," her mother said, intent on knowing. Candissa stood now as well. She related the tale of the treacherous cousin quickly.

"I sent my friends after him to see if one of his men were following him already," Candissa said. "When are they due to leave Ravensroost?"

"In two days," her father said. "So, if he follows his cousin's example, then his attack would come in two evenings, but we can't trust him to be so predictable."

"I must join them at the Bonerest," she said. She looked up at the tall portrait of her grandmother. What her grandmother wore in the portrait was not a proper dress, nor any sort of clothing she had seen before. Without knowing, she had pieced together an outfit for training that was reminiscent of the unusual clothing. "Was this what she wore?"

"Sometimes, but it was more her garb for what you might call her *adventures*, in her youth," her mother said, smiling in a remembered amusement. Her eyes fell on the staff. "There is something more I should tell you, it's about what she holds in her arm."

"The staff."

"Yes. When she spoke to me about what she was, and who my firstborn would be, she told me of that staff."

"I don't understand."

"Simply put, when the time came for you to, well, go on your own journeys, you would need the staff, to familiarize yourself with it. She told me it was special, a '*staff of the Aevaru*', she called it," her mother said, seeming almost reluctant to reveal this to her daughter. "Dalton dear, where did you store the staff? It was so long ago."

Her father scratched his beard. "Well, I... hmm…"

"The attic above the servants' quarters, in the back, near the round, slatted window. Some old furs were draped over it," Candissa recalled with a wry grin, picturing when she had first found it when she was playing dress-up. "That's where it *was*."

"Was?" her father said.

She looked at them both, seeing an expression of dread in her mother's eyes. "I found it. I've been training with it secretly for more than a year. It's in my room."

Her mother just clapped her hands to her mouth, eyes wide. Her father encircled her in his great arms, patting her.

"We knew this day would come. It's just a little sooner than we thought," he said, trying his best to comfort her.

"I must go," Candissa said, feeling more urgency in joining her friends.

"Yes, go, Deesa. We will talk more later, after you return," her father nodded. "Look after your friend. Though from my own impressions, he doesn't seem like the kind of person who needs looking after."

Candissa managed a small smile, then she was off. Passing the door to her chamber, she hesitated. She felt a strange urge to get her staff, now that she knew there was a real connection with it. She couldn't imagine she would need it.

And what a sight I would make, striding down the street with that white staff, she amused herself with the image. Almost without thinking, almost unwillingly, she found herself opening her door and moving to the wardrobe. She reached out hesitantly.

It's all right.

She jumped. "Who's there?" She blurted aloud. There was no response. She blinked, realizing it was just something she had said to herself, in her mind.

"This is silly," she muttered. Grasping the staff, she imagined it felt different, somehow heavier, yet much more graceful in her grip. She studied the runes for a moment, then recalled Errol.

She dashed out of her room, slamming the door, and taking the steps three at a time. When she reached the foot of the marble stairs, a voice shrieked from above.

"Lady Candissa! Where are you going at this hour? And whatever are you doing with *that*?" Lendra's shrill voice pierced the air, and she looked on the edge of a fit. No decent young lady would be seen carrying such a weapon, she had told Candissa many times.

"I'm sorry, Lendra. I'll be back before too long, I hope," was all she could spare. Passing gawking servants, she made straight for the main door, which was opened by a startled maid.

Outside, she motioned to an attendant house guard. "Open!" She spoke in a commanding tone, and the main gate was open before she reached it. Remembering her escort, she looked east down the darkened street, and saw young Thendarick at the corner. She called loudly to him. "To the Bonerest!"

She turned and started down the lamp-lit avenue, not waiting for the young guard, but hearing his hurried boots as he strove to catch up to her.

CHAPTER FIFTEEN - CAM

24 Laborus, Year 197, Eastvale Calendar

"Do you think Errol is in danger?" Koraymis asked him.

Cam was not certain, but he could not stand by and take no action.

"We'll see once we're at the Bonerest. Is he even armed?"

"I saw him bearing a dagger in a sheath. Not a small dagger, either," Koraymis said.

"Still, if this Enthessar attacks him with a brace of men, he would be hard pressed to escape unscathed."

"He isn't too far ahead of us, assuming he went straight for the tavern," the scholar said. "He *did* say he was going to meet us there."

"Then we go there, and see what comes of it," Cam said firmly. He didn't mean to sound as if he was in charge, and he hoped his new friend did not resent his behavior. Koraymis certainly appeared to be willing to accept him in this role, as far as he could tell.

It was not long before they were back in the Bonerest. They entered the tavern with an unintended suddenness. Scanning the room, they were greeted with the mildly curious gazes of a score of evening patrons. The lot gave the pair only a fleeting glance before returning to their drinks and victuals. They saw no sign of Errol or any guards from House Allenfar. Cam frowned, feeling the fool.

Master Evan saw them and gestured to two open seats at the bar. Koraymis looked at Cam, who nodded in agreement at the unspoken offer.

Wending their way through the common room, around the large, round table at which they sat previously, they settled onto the stools before the tavern master.

Evan nodded to them. "Can I get you gentlemen a drink, or...do you have a question perhaps?"

Cam leaned in a little. "Just wondering if you've seen Master Errol since he was escorted out earlier."

The tavern master shook his head. "Haven't seen him in the common room since that commotion. In fact, it's been very quiet since."

"I hope you don't think of us poorly for that. We didn't mean to be part of anything disruptive," Cam said. Evan shook his head, smiling.

"Think nothing of it. I only hope the matter was resolved to everyone's satisfaction," the tavern master said.

Koraymis cocked his head. "Forgive me, sir, but you have Elven blood, don't you?"

Evan nodded, brushing back his hair slightly. "You noticed the ears, I imagine."

"From your mother, I think. She was Elven, yes?"

The tavern master did not mask his surprise and smiled a little. "A fortunate guess, master scholar?"

"No. Those with Elven mothers make poor liars." The scholar spoke in a hushed voice, that others might not hear him. There was a small grin on his lips.

Cam was shocked, turning instantly to his friend. "Koraymis, I think you owe Master Evan an apology!"

Evan simply looked at him with a neutral expression, then retrieved a bottle of wine and two glasses from under the counter. He poured them, placing them in front of the two.

"On the house."

Cam was confused. "Why? I mean, many thanks, but...why?"

"Because of your friend's perceptiveness. I cannot be slighted when he speaks the truth, while I was not."

Cam looked at the scholar, who only grinned, and once more shrugged. Cam was beginning to think he did not like that shrug so much. His gaze went to the tavernkeep.

"So... our friend…" was all he said.

"In the back and make no sign that you know this."

Cam just nodded, picking up his wine, and nodding to Koraymis to do the same. He did, and they toasted. "To...Candissa," the hunter said.

"To her health and long life," Koraymis returned.

"If you'll excuse me," Evan nodded to them both, moving off to attend to another patron.

"Hmm, Elven white," Koraymis said, considering his glass. "I think I prefer the red."

"Well, I think we can say Lady Candissa's concerns were without merit," Cam said. "At least for now."

"Then why is Errol hiding in the kitchen?"

Cam frowned at his friend's sagacity. Relaxing for the moment, he glanced around at the various patrons, trying not to appear obvious in the process. Someone caught his eye. The man was sitting in the smaller dining room adjacent to the main room.

The man saw Cam staring. He smiled and waved at Cam.

"Oh, hello," Cam said quietly to the scholar. "Someone I met today, he's coming over here."

Koraymis turned his head slightly to observe the fellow.

"Cam Bronwyer, good to see you again," Orrendar greeted him warmly, clasping his outstretched hand. "May I join you and your friend?"

"Of course. Koraymis, this is Orrendar, a friend I met here earlier," Cam said. The scholar shook Orrendar's offered hand.

"Most pleased to meet you, Master Koraymis," he said, taking the seat next to Cam. "I hope I'm not interrupting you."

"No, we are just awaiting a friend, passing the time," the hunter said, trying not to sound as though he was equivocating.

"Well, if it's acceptable to both of you, I'll enjoy a glass of wine while you await your friend," Orrendar said, smiling and signaling Evan.

They did not object, and the nobleman ordered a glass of wine from the tavernmaster, quietly mentioning to Evan that he would cover their next drink.

With his glass of wine in hand, he raised it to both of them. "To new-found friends."

The scholar sipped it, and nodded, smiling. He seemed pleased. He appeared ready to thank the noble, when Cam realized his eyes were drawn to the door. He, too, felt compelled to turn, feeling something more than seeing or hearing it.

Several patrons stared, wide-eyed, as Candissa strode into the Bonerest. She didn't look so different from her previous appearance. Yet, there were marked changes. Cam thought she looked taller, but perhaps she simply carried herself in a more regal manner. Perceptions aside, it was the tall, slender white staff she bore in one hand as she walked directly toward them that gave her such a changed bearing.

"Candissa!" was all Cam could manage. To his right, Orrendar hurried to put his wine glass down and compose himself, intent on greeting her with the appropriate courtesy. Behind Candissa came a member of the town guard, shadowing her.

"Cam, Koraymis," she began. Then, seeing the noble seated next to Cam, she turned to him. "You are with Lord Allenfar's company, aren't you?"

"My dear Lady Candissa, yes, you likely noticed me at the banquet today. My name is Orrendar. I did not have the honor of meeting you formally on that occasion, so I am most humbled to now have that honor," he almost recited in the standard cadence of noble greetings, bowing slightly at the waist.

She nodded sharply, almost ignoring him as she turned to her friends. "Have either of you seen Errol?"

Cam was quick to reply, in case Koraymis said something. "No, we were just waiting for him."

In a flash of remembrance, he tried speaking without his voice, staring at Candissa intently. It was like opening a different mouth and speaking with a voice never used before.

He's in the back, Evan told us so. Shocked by his apparent success, as Candissa's eyes lit up, he pressed on, saying more. *I don't know what he's doing, perhaps waiting.*

"Good sir, please forgive me, I wish to speak to my friends. I pray you will excuse us. A good night to you," she said to the mildly surprised Orrendar.

"Of course, my lady. Farewell, and I hope to see you all on the morrow," Orrendar said dutifully. He stood and found a small table against the wall.

Standing a little closer to them now, she whispered. "Well done, Cam. I wonder, can we all do that?"

I think we can, came Errol's voice. None of the three made any sudden moves. Cam turned and picked up his glass of wine, sipping from it. This allowed a casual glance into the kitchen and back rooms of the Bonerest, through the wide entrance behind Evan's bar. He did not see Errol.

Go around to the right, to that private room Evan keeps for guests. Candissa knows it. Through there, close the doors, I'll meet you at the stairwell behind the kitchen, Errol's voice told them.

"Let us speak elsewhere," Cam said to his friends. "I believe there's private chamber?"

They nodded, and the three of them moved at an unhurried pace through the tavern. Candissa motioned to the guard who had escorted her, and they spoke briefly, and the guard nodded. She then joined Cam and Koraymis at the door leading into the smaller room.

Careful glances told Cam no one seemed to be bothered with their departure, save for a few stares at Candissa and her staff. Cam saw Orrendar was already jovially engaged in chatter with another patron, appearing to take no heed of their departure.

They were through the small meeting room quickly and found their way to the back stairs in moments. Errol was standing there with the door open. "This way, we can talk in a storeroom below."

Errol led them down two short flights of steps, through a crowded storeroom, and finally into a square room that had only a few boxes and tables within. It was lit by a bright lantern. A tall, young man Cam did not know was there, waiting expectantly. One of the tables had bread, cheese, and stew, along with a flagon of beer. Cam thought perhaps the young man head read his mind.

"I took the liberty of victuals, sir. I hope you don't mind," the young man said.

"That's perfect, Dreff, please keep an eye out upstairs," Errol said. "Oh, but first, Masters Koraymis Sleeth and Cam Bronwyer, this is Taldrephus, a friend of mine and an invaluable assistant."

"Pleased to make your acquaintance, good sirs," Dreff said, before departing for the narrow steps.

"First," Errol began, looking a little desperately at Candissa. "*Why* do you have that staff?"

"I - it's the staff I've been training with for the past year," Candissa replied, taken aback by his question and tone. "Is there a problem with me having a staff?"

He looked at her for a long moment, with a pained expression in his eyes, then sat at the table laden with food and drink.

"No, it's just – you just seem to go to efforts to get yourself noticed," Errol said. He shook his head. "Forgive me, I'm not even sure why I asked. But more importantly, I don't trust that fellow…Orrendar, is it?"

"Yes, that's his name, but why?" Cam asked, sitting and breaking off a hunk of dark bread. "I met him this afternoon here, before Koraymis arrived. We talked for some time. He seems a nice enough chap."

"He's with the Allenfar lot, and his manner and words don't sit well with me. I arrived early and was observing everyone who came into the Bonerest. He was here already. I don't trust him."

"Can you offer any reasons why you don't trust him?" Candissa asked. "I'm only curious, not arguing on his behalf. He seems as oily and fawning as any petty noble."

"It's difficult to say, exactly," Errol said, struggling uncharacteristically with his words. "The best I can guess is my training tells me not to trust him."

He looked at Candissa meaningfully. She seemed mildly surprised. "That is...curious."

Cam was perplexed. "Sorry, how is that curious? Errol seems a capable person though I hesitate to ask exactly what his *training* entailed."

"Ha, well put, my friend," Errol said, clapping Cam on the shoulder. "It's a long story which I will share in full with you both one day. Suffice to say, I arrived in Ravensroost five years ago with not a shred of memory. I do not know where I was trained, or by whom, or even exactly what I was trained in. What I can say, based perhaps on that training or simple instinct, is that I do not trust Orrendar."

Cam grunted, finding the wedge of cheese Taldrephus had provided to be too hard to simply break off neatly. Errol saw his dilemma and slid his blade across the table. Cam raised his eyebrows, looking at Errol, who simply grinned and nodded. Cam shrugged, picked up the heavy blade, and proceeded to trim off perfectly clean squares of the fragrant cheese.

"You need not rely on your instincts or training, Errol," Koraymis entered the conversation, as he reached over to pluck one of the squares of cheese from Cam's stack. The hunter cast an annoyed glance at the young scholar.

"Why's that?"

"I'm certain he's the one who murdered Renther and Tremmy," the scholar said.

The three of them looked at him with confounded expressions. Cam broke their moment of silence.

"Go on."

"I cannot say just why," Koraymis began, busying his hands with ladling a small clay bowl of steaming stew. "But I can sense...evil, or at least what I believe is evil. More than that, Orrendar has a stain that I can sense. My insight tells me he has taken a life, and recently. I know that sounds a little unlikely, but I'm quite certain."

There was another uncomfortable silence as his friends considered his words, broken only by Cam sliding the blade back across the table to Errol, who simply spun it in place.

"Well, this is...curious," Candissa said, almost under her breath.

"Curious?" Errol almost laughed aloud. "My lady, we are all of us *curious* and *unlikely* by turns! We speak with one another without the benefit of voices, I'm relying on training in I know not what, we have fallen in fast with two persons, and no insult intended mind you, of whom we know nothing. And one of them professes to sense evil!" He nearly collapsed into one of the chairs around the table and commenced to pour himself a mug of ale.

I think we must be near one another, came Koraymis' voice, apparently ignoring Errol's outburst. *It doesn't work from a distance. I tried earlier.*

I thought I heard something, Cam joined in. *I wonder if we all need to be together for it to work.*

Errol thought of something, then he laughed aloud, looking at them all merrily while stuffing his mouth with a chunk of dark bread. *I just realized, we can have conversations while eating!*

That brought a moment of levity as they all sat slowly, smiling at one another.

"Just a moment," Candissa said aloud. She was looking around the room, specifically at the walls. "What is this place?"

Cam saw she was staring at the symbols inscribed into the wall at intervals along all four sides. They had been cleaned away recently, it appeared. The inscriptions were clear but not deep.

"Another mystery? I cannot say what this place is, but these symbols mean something. I know not what," Errol said, his voice betraying a touch of disappointment or frustration.

"By the gods…" Candissa whispered.

Cam was alarmed. "What is it?"

She pointed at one of the symbols, a largely iconographic inscription, with perhaps some mountains or trees in the background. Then she held up her staff of nearly ivory-white wood. At the top, near the carved head, was inscribed a symbol identical to that on the wall.

They all took turns peering at the inscriptions, on the wall and staff.

"I've never seen that symbol," Koraymis said.

The others shook their heads.

"As with most of these symbols, it does seem vaguely familiar to me, but I can't say what it is," Errol said, shrugging. "With one exception."

Errol stilled his still slowly-spinning blade with one finger. He pointed to the faint rune inscribed on the flat of the blade. The others leaned closer.

Chewing on a piece of bread, Koraymis spoke silently. *That symbol is that one, no?* He pointed at the similar inscription on the wall. Errol nodded, looking up at the symbol: a ship cutting through water, three sails, the largest bearing a star. He gripped his blade with three fingers, as it lay on the table. With a forceful and deft motion, he set it spinning. For a moment, it was nothing but a hazy dark blur.

Candissa watched the spinning blade as she slowly chewed on a pairing of bread and cheese Cam had offered her.

There is much here we do not understand, yet, she told them.

"Where did you get that staff, if I may ask?" Cam said.

"It was in my house, hidden away in an attic. I found it many months ago, and I've been training with it ever since," she replied to Cam, as she picked at a piece of cheese. "I learned today that it was my grandmother's staff."

"I made drawings of these symbols for Master Penston to review, but he couldn't say what they meant. He did say a few can be found on the older monuments or buildings," Errol said.

"Master Penston, did you say? The scholar?" Koraymis asked. Errol nodded.

"I must contact him. Efflewhist the Librarian charged me to do so. I came to Ravensroost to apprentice under the Librarian. But I don't think the quiet life of a master of books is in store for me now."

"Why?" Candissa said.

Errol looked at her, and the others, as his blade slowed in its spinning. Errol faintly motioned to it. Cam looked down and watched it. The dark blur resolved into the blade as it at last slowed to a stop. Cam knew the direction it would be pointing before it ceased turning.

He looked up at Errol and the others, exchanging glances.

As one, they understood.

CHAPTER SIXTEEN - ERROL

24 Laborus, Year 197, Eastvale Calendar

Errol led a quick conversation about their suspicions and fears regarding Enthessar and Orrendar. He did not wish to tarry any longer

"So, it's decided We stay together as much as is reasonable, for mutual protection," Errol said. They all nodded in assent.

Let's be candid We're staying together for more than simple protection, Koraymis voiced silently. The lack of any reply told Errol they all agreed with the scholar's sentiment, though Errol could not explain why they were bound together. At least, not yet. He was intent on finding out why they all felt this inexplicable pull. In some ways, he did not like it.

"Errol, what happened with my father and the Captain?" Candissa asked him. He hadn't told them the resolution of that meeting yet.

"They didn't find enough reason to throw me into a cell, nor will they. Whoever tried to slip something to you, lady, likely slew those two poor fellows," he said. "Be that Orrendar or someone else."

"Will they still try to jail you?" Cam asked.

"They may, depending on how influential Lord Allenfar is, or perhaps they'll fabricate some falsehood to incriminate me."

"Or that noble will just kill you," Koraymis offered.

"Yes, of course. Not my preferred outcome, certainly."

"It's late. What now? I suppose you have to return to your estate?" Cam said, looking at Candissa.

"Yes, I most certainly must return. But I have a friend upstairs who will escort me back. Don't be concerned for my safety," she said, smiling a little.

"I really wasn't, to be honest," he replied returning a grin.

Talking is pleasant, but this is faster, more efficient, Koraymis' voice cut into their minds. *Cam and I have rooms here. Where are you staying, Errol? You seem to be most at risk for the moment.*

I have a flat nearby, but they could find that out. Would it be too much of an imposition if I stayed with one of you, for the night?

My room has an extra cot, Cam said. *And we can take the back stairs, so no one will know you're here.*

We need to leave Ravensroost. That will take some planning, I think. Candissa changed the subject.

I don't suppose we know where we're going exactly? Cam asked, his expression sour.

I hesitate to suggest this, but we can always rely on...destiny. That sounds ridiculous, doesn't it? Errol replied, smoothing his unshaven face absentmindedly.

It's as good a term as any for now, Candissa frowned. *I think we have all felt something like that, haven't we? Just tonight, I've learned things about myself of which I was completely unaware. And Errol, you've been looking for some sort of answer since you arrived.*

About that. You'll have to relate your story on how you arrived here, Koraymis said. *At some point.*

We all have a great deal to learn of one another, Errol pointed out. *We are about to embark on a journey that is at best ill-advised and at worst insane.*

Are we to journey west on foot, or on horseback? Cam asked.

My family is wealthy, I can provide mounts, Candissa offered, nodding.

"By horseback it is," Cam muttered softly. He continued, but without voice. *Tomorrow we can start gathering supplies, making preparations. We don't need to rush out of town just yet. Should we choose a day for our departure?*

I need to make more preparations than any of you, I think. Let's put off a firm date until at least tomorrow. I need to see what Enthessar is up to, Candissa pointed out.

We'll have to figure out how much we need to gather for the journey, and decide how long we'll be out there, Koraymis added. Errol was finding himself more and more impressed with the young scholar, the more they became acquainted.

Who said we will turn back? Errol raised an eyebrow.

He's right, we need to plan on a set duration in the unknown wilds. Cam agreed. *If we can't figure out why we are out there to begin with, we head back. Make sense?*

They all nodded in assent.

Then we'll need to make a list of equipment and supplies. I can put something together for each of you to review, Cam offered, being the most experienced of them in the ways of the wilds.

I will provide any funds we need, Candissa said. Cam nodded his thanks.

"Then let us go upstairs, and I will depart, and contact you in the morning. We can all plan on meeting at my house in the afternoon perhaps," Candissa said.

They filed out of the room, heading upstairs by the back way. Once in the upper corridor, they bade their farewells.

Cam's room was one of the larger rooms furnished for those who would stay for weeks or even months. Errol made himself comfortable on the spare cot. His mind was racing more tonight than most nights and he wondered if he could relax enough to sleep.

As he thought to himself, Cam pulled off his boots and turned up the lantern light. He had quill and ink and a few sheets of parchment on his desk. He glanced at Errol. "Will this light bother you?"

"Not at all," Errol replied, working his own boots off. Cam looked at them as he did so.

"You need better boots."

Errol picked up one of his boots, nodding. "Quite right you are, Cam the not-yet-a-ranger."

"It's not my life's ambition to become a ranger, as much as I respect them," Cam said.

"Then what are you?" Errol asked, almost out of impulse. He considered it a particularly rude question, yet he felt compelled to ask. He went on to clarify, "I mean no insult. I am just curious what you would call yourself. Since I've been in Ravensroost, I've found people are far more comfortable if you have a vocation, something they can identify you with."

Cam put his quill down, thinking for a moment. "No insult was taken. I agree, the folk of Woodford are much the same. You choose your profession and that's how you're known. Most there call me a hunter, others, a worker of leather. I'm equally proficient in both."

"Good skills to have," Errol said.

"Those aside, I have read much, owing to my parents and their concern for my education. I can use the quill and ink proficiently, I can work numbers, and I know some Elven and Dwarven," Cam said.

"Very impressive," Errol said, nodding.

"I am not an academic, however. And despite my outward appearance, I've never really considered myself a hunter. I am far more interested in learning about the world around me," Cam said, his eyes becoming a little lost in memories. "When I was younger, I would explore every hollow, copse and creek for miles around our house. Sometimes, without letting my parents know I was exploring. I always carried a little bag with supplies, just in case."

"I hope not that rucksack there. It looks far too heavy for a child," Errol commented.

"No, I was given that by my father, when...he and my mother had to leave. It was his, made by his hand," Cam said, one hand touching it almost reverently.

"They had to leave?"

"Yes, when I was ten," Cam said that much but no more. Sensing the discomfort in his voice and noting his distant expression, Errol pressed him no further. He turned his gaze to the impressive leather pack.

"Fine craftsmanship. I've never seen anything like it."

"Thank you, yes, it is handy," Cam said. "Sometimes I think I would be helpless without it. It holds all that I ever need. Or at least sometimes it seems that."

"All you ever need," Errol repeated, staring at it.

Cam was amused. "What?"

Errol shook his head slowly from his cot. "I'm not sure. It... reminds me of something. And that phrase, all you *ever need.* It may be something I'm trying to remember."

Cam only looked at him curiously. Errol shook his head.

"My apologies, it has to do with the strange story behind my arrival in Ravensroost," Errol said. He then sat up on one elbow long enough to relate the story to Cam Bronwyer. He spoke of his being found in the storm, atop the Wardenstone, by the ranger, the scholar and a younger Candissa. He did not mention the ranger Vink, however. He also described how sometimes he seemed to recognize something – a word or an object, thinking it may relate to his forgotten past.

"A strange tale, truly," Cam said, after it was done. "That dagger you bear is the same one you had that day?"

"Yes, it's long been my good friend," he said, smiling and detaching the sheathed blade from his belt. Drawing the blade from the sheath, he inspected it by the light of the lantern. The symbol gleamed clearly in the yellow light.

"What's that symbol?" the hunter asked.

"I have no idea what it means," Errol said, handing him the dagger. "I know you didn't say anything downstairs, but does it seem at all familiar to you?"

Cam took the blade in hand and examined it closely. He shook his head. "I've read many books and have seen many symbols, but this isn't familiar. Is it a ship cutting through waves?"

"Yes, I think so, but most people wouldn't know that," Errol said. He sat up, suddenly intrigued. "Have you seen a ship like that before?"

Cam handed him the dagger back. His eyes closed as he thought. "No, but I know *of* them. I think from the readings of my mother. It's a tall-masted ship, with three sails, four on some of the masts."

"Yes! But no one in the Kingdom has ever seen one before."

"Why would that be?" Cam asked.

"Because there are no oceans to sail them upon!" Errol said excitedly.

The hunter looked at him with a concentrated gaze. "What is an ocean?"

"*That* is a perfect example of what I go through, half-recalling places, things, even words, that no one knows," Errol said, his speech picking up in pace in his excitement. "An ocean is an immense span of water, bigger than any kingdom or forest or mountain range!"

Cam looked a bit shocked, if not amused. His expression changed, however, as he considered Errol's words. "That sounds almost unbelievable, yet...I'm now quite sure I read about them, though I cannot recall when."

Errol's eyes narrowed. "That is strange in itself. As far as I know, there are no books that mention oceans. I've researched these things. Do you know when the Kingdom was founded?"

"Yes, about two centuries ago," Cam said.

"Correct. Have you ever found a book, or even heard tell of one, that predates the founding of the Kingdom?"

Cam frowned and rubbed his beard. "No, *I* haven't. But I've sometimes wondered about the books my mother read to me."

"So whatever books she had must have come from *before*! We didn't invent writing two hundred years ago! Why are there no written records that go back three hundred years? Or four hundred, or a thousand?"

"I hadn't thought about that," Cam said, dipping his quill in an ink pot "But then again, you may have heard the old adages, the rhymes they tell children. One never asks about the time before."

"It's all part of the mystery. In all the books I've read here in Ravensroost and from speaking to all the learned men and women, there is no record or recollection or reference to long coasts or the saltwater oceans," Errol said, exasperation evident in his tone.

Cam only frowned a little as he continued to write his list and notes. The room grew quiet, save for the scratching of quill on parchment. Errol doubted sleep would come easily.

The scratching ceased, and he looked over to see Cam lost in thought.

"Errol," Cam said after a long pause. "Why would oceans have salt in them?"

"Good night, Cam," Errol said, before rolling onto his side.

CHAPTER SEVENTEEN - CANDISSA

25 Laborus, Year 197, Eastvale Calendar

Candissa left her friends and exited the Bonerest to find Thendarick awaiting her faithfully just outside. It was well into the dark hours of night now. She appreciated his escort, despite feeling quite confident in her skills with the staff.

"Thank you, Rick. If I show up at home without a guard, my father would be upset."

"Think nothing of it, my lady. Never hesitate to call on me at any hour for such a service," the guard said. He seemed almost grateful for the opportunity to assist her. Candissa was quite sure he was smitten with her, as were so many other young men in Ravensroost.

The walk home was uneventful. She bade Thendarick a good evening as he bowed formally to her.

She entered her estate entrance to find a few guests still in the receiving hall downstairs, despite the late hour. She made the conscious choice to enter by the main door, and not the servant's entrance. She also made no effort to hide the white staff she carried. Her appearance had the expected effect, with murmurs and gawking stares elicited from the guests and servants.

As she climbed the stairs, intent on seeking out her father or mother, she gritted her teeth at the sound of a voice.

"My dear Candissa, wherever have you been and *what* are you doing with that silly stick?" Enthessar was making no real effort to conceal his sarcasm and condescension. He stood atop the flight of stairs in his evening attire, a small glass of brandy in one hand.

The sight of him caused her to pause for just a step as her gaze bore into him. In that moment, she saw something she had not before. It was not something she could put into words, nor easily form an image from. It caused her to clutch her staff more tightly, to choose her steps more carefully, to focus her thoughts against an enemy she had never seen or heard or known of, until this moment.

It was as if in him, in that one moment, she had found something that was working against her. Against *them*.

But then it was gone. She thought perhaps it was the late hour, her frayed nerves, or the bizarre events that had unfolded of late.

She marched upwards toward the far side of the steps to avoid him entirely, but he casually strolled in that direction. She said nothing in reply.

"Really, Candissa, why are you in such a mood? Did I misbehave so very much earlier?" he said, adopting a penitent expression, eyes wide. "Please forgive me if I offended-"

She whirled to confront him, her staff held before her, across her tall frame. He nearly dropped his glass of liqueur. Her mental focus seemed to drop, and she could not contain the outpouring of words that followed.

"You offend me at every turn and with every word! You offend my friends with insults and my house with your mere presence!" she bit off her words harshly. "You would do well to never again address me, for I am beyond suffering fools such as you!"

He was agape at her outburst, eyes wide. His hand trembled a little, his brandy quivering in the glass. She was certain it was from rage and not fear.

"My lady, you would do well to offer a sincere apology to me this instant," he said quietly, even menacingly.

"Or *what*, my lord? Will you follow the example of your cousin Lanthred with *me* after you're done with Errol?" she said, her cutting words a clear challenge.

His face reddened at her clear inference. She guessed he was quite upset at her knowing what he thought was a secret passed between father and son. People were gathering at the foot of the stairs to observe the confrontation, whispering in shock. An odd silence settled on the hall.

"Candissa, come here now," her father's quiet, steady voice sounded from behind her. "I think it best if you go to your room. At once."

She brought the staff up straight, setting it before her. A loud *thunk* sounded off the marble floor as she did so. Enthessar jumped a little at the impact of the staff striking the tile.

Candissa stood tall, shoulders back. She realized now that she was just a little taller than the noble son of House Allenfar. She let the tiniest smirk form on her lips before she turned her back on him and walked to her father.

Passing him, she said quietly, "I am sorry, Father."

"We will talk soon, daughter," he said, his voice understanding but still solemn.

As she walked to her chambers, she could hear her father doing the right thing, trying to apologize on her behalf. She had caused enough trouble for one night. Perhaps far too much.

Lendra was waiting for her at her chamber door. "Candissa, we were all so worried!"

"It is late, I suppose," she replied, feeling that she may have to fight back tears soon.

Lendra looked at her with a curious expression, perhaps concern, or perhaps acquiescence. She opened the door for Candissa and followed her in.

"Would you like me to prepare a bath for you, my dear?"

Candissa stood there in the middle of her chambers, holding her staff in her right hand, her grip on it light but sure. She felt taller than she had ever been before. Looking around, she realized the room had somehow shrunk a little. It was filled with all the trifles and trinkets of her childhood, of her life as a proper and courteous young noble lady. All soft and colorful and scented with flowers and delicate oils. It belonged to someone she wasn't sure she knew any longer.

"Candissa?" Lendra repeated softly, reaching out to touch her shoulder.

"Is my mother abed yet?"

"Yes, she waited a while after you left earlier, but withdrew to her chambers not long ago. Would you like me to have Aldrys wake her?"

An amusing thought fluttered through her mind, of how cross her mother's lady-in-waiting would be if she had to awaken her mistress once she had put her to bed. Candissa shook her head.

"I will speak to her in the morning."

"A bath then? Or just to bed?" Lendra asked.

"I...I'm not sure I can sleep right now, perhaps a soothing bath, yes," she said.

Candissa leaned her staff against the wall, near her bed stand. Letting it go was difficult. She breathed deeply. Sitting on her bed, she unlaced her short boots of whitened leather.

From her bathing chamber, Lendra called back to her. "I was hoping you would want a bath. I've kept the water heated, so it will be poured in just a moment. I'll get your soaps."

Candissa took off her evening cape, followed by her surcoat, kirtle, chemise and hose. All white or light gray. As she piled them on her dressing chair, she looked at them. They were all clean. Despite the day's activities, they looked as if she had taken them out of her drawers just now.

Candissa recalled the washerwoman of the house, Marrid, complaining more than once about the time spent in washing her clothing. She would say, "Why waste good soap to clean somethin' that's clean when it comes to me!"

Turning, she regarded herself in the tall, silvered mirror framed in dark oak. She shook her hair and it tumbled about as if freshly washed. It was ever that way. The only fussing she ever had with her long, honey-blonde locks was how to arrange them for some event or reception.

Her body was long and lithe, but something didn't seem quite right to her eyes. She turned a little, looking at her back. She gasped.

Lendra came back into the room. "Oh my, look at you naked as the day you were born!" she said brightly. "And I was there, young lady!"

"Lendra, what's wrong with my back?"

"Whatever do you mean?"

"See there, when I turn, those lines and bulges, is that normal?" Candissa said, her eyes flicked down at her thighs. "And my legs…"

"My dear child, those are muscles! Are you so surprised, with all that training, and all this growing you've been on about? It can't be helped! Don't you worry, you can't see them under a proper lady's clothing. A good thing too. Your limbs are not the slender branches you'd expect to find on a young lady."

Lendra saw the expression of concern in Candissa's eyes.

"Don't you worry yourself, girl! Muscles are just as becoming as not, and no one can see them in any case," she assured her charge, as she turned the levers on the pipes over the bath. The warmed water slowed and stopped.

"All right, I'm sure you're right. Still, I hadn't noticed them before, not like this. It's just…curious," Candissa said. She flexed her arms and shoulders, shocked at how defined they were. "That isn't very ladylike, is it?"

"Come along, it matters not. Into the bath, my dear," Lendra ignored her concerns. "I'll fix some tea to help you sleep."

Easing into the copper tub, Candissa managed to forget the day for a while. She relaxed, letting the floral scents of the steaming water wash over her senses. She used a healer's meditation to calm her mind, Mother Meshana's favorite. She would need to speak with Meshana tomorrow. She was sorry to discontinue her training.

She thought about clothing. Nothing she owned was appropriate for travel. She wondered what suggestions, if any, Cam would make regarding her apparel. She wondered if he was making a list for each of them, or the group as a whole.

She laughed quietly, chiding herself. She put the thoughts out of her mind. No troubles, no Enthessar, no speaking without voice, no Aevaru. She breathed deeply, meditating, slipping into a light slumber.

Zarlenna...Zarlenna, wake up. The insistent nagging voice was almost unwelcome.

Opening her eyes, Zarlenna regarded the young novitiate, a girl of not even fourteen, with auburn hair verging on red. She wore the acolyte smock of gray.

Mirova, why must you vex me so? Is it yet first light?

Beg your pardon, honored lady, but you told me to awaken you at this hour on fourthday, that we might study the stars, the girl pointed out. Her innocence made the fact she was correct even more annoying.

Of course, well done, honored pupil, she replied, visibly putting the girl at ease. Her chamber was lit by one dim brightstone, set to blue. Rising, Zarlenna ran her fingers through her long hair. Walking past the waiting student, she enjoyed the cool night breeze across her naked body. In the bathing chamber, she stood over the grate, holding her hair in one hand and calling the water.

The shower was just above the temperature of the room as it washed down over her entire body, save her face and hair. The coolness helped awaken her senses. It stopped and a moment later she concentrated briefly. The water ran off her body and she was dry. The brightstone warmed to orange, then yellow.

She dressed herself in the usual leg bindings and tunic. Mirova already had her training surcoat at hand, and Zarlenna slipped her arms into it. Taking it in hand, she wrapped the waist bindings across and around.

She slapped her belly hard when she was done, clenching her abdominal muscles. She was awake enough. Just one glance in the mirror, in case something was terribly frightful. She grinned at the thought. Aevaru were many things, but never frightful to look upon.

At her dressing bureau, the mirror was brightly silvered. She touched a small gem on the pewter frame, and light effused the air around her.

Her face was fair with only faint lines to indicate her age and seniority. Her eyes, radiant sky blue in color, regarded her face and the long, ash brown hair surrounding it.

But something was wrong. She frowned, looking deeper into the glass. Mirova must have noticed the change in her countenance.

My lady, what is the matter?

Zarlenna looked into the mirror, at her face. Leaning toward the surface a little, she looked past the mirror, to another. Her eyes locked onto the eyes on the other side. Sky blue eyes framed by blond hair.

Who are you? Her voice was demanding, enthralling, undeniable.

Answer me, girl! Zarlenna shouted, the face in the mirror wincing with the force of her words.

Candissa...my name is Candissa! the other cried aloud. Zarlenna's eyes went wide and she almost stumbled backwards.

Flailing wildly, Candissa splashed water all over Lendra, who shrieked in response.

"Candissa! You were dreaming! Calm yourself, girl!" she exclaimed.

Candissa gasped, wide-eyed, and pushed herself up out of the water. Breathing heavily, she looked around, dripping wet.

"It was so...real!" she breathed. Candissa couldn't shake the feeling of having been in that strange chamber, as though she was inside the mind of that Aevaru.

"Sit down in the tub before you slip and break a bone, silly girl!"

She complied, sitting slowly, her hands shaking a little.

"How long was I asleep?" she said, her breathing rapid but slowing.

"But a few minutes, just long enough for me to fetch the tea. It must have been an unpleasant dream, my dear. What ever was it about? You called out your own name before you awoke."

"You heard me? I mean, I said that aloud?"

"Yes, you shouted your name and then 'my name is Candissa', and you seemed quite alarmed," Lendra said, as she brushed the young woman's long hair. She would work soap and oil into it next.

"I've never had a dream like that before," she murmured. "Who is that woman you once talked about, she could interpret dreams?"

Lendra frowned. "That would be Old Ulma, the street seer, as they are called. I don't put much faith in her, Deesa. Her tellings and so-called prophecies are usually just lies wrapped in clever guesses!"

"Still, I need to speak to someone," Candissa said, then she remembered. "Well, I suppose mother may have something to say about it."

"Why ever would you think that? She's no dream speaker."

"But she is…" she let her words trail off, unwilling to finish her sentence.

"She is what, my dear?"

"Never mind," Candissa shook her head as Lendra applied the oil. "I should really try to sleep."

"I'm delighted to hear you say that! Now, let's rinse off this lovely hair and get you dried off," Lendra said. She used a large ewer to pour bathwater over Candissa's head. Candissa took a body-sized cotton towel from Lendra as she stood.

Candissa stepped out of the tub, dripping wet. Looking at herself in the mirror for a moment, she glanced away, fearful of repeating her discomfiting dream. She remembered feeling the water droplets falling all over her body as that mysterious shower had rained down from the ceiling.

Closing her eyes, Candissa concentrated. She imagined her skin, like smooth marble or the feathers of a bird, the water sheeting off, running onto the tiled floor of the bathing chamber.

Opening her eyes, she felt her belly, her arms. Dry. Water was pooling at her feet. Hanging the towel on a rod, she went to her bed, where Lendra waited to help her into her gown.

"I'll put it on, Lendra. Just douse the lamps and I'll tuck myself in," Candissa said, her voice a little distant. Her governess looked at her with some concern.

"Well, all right, if you insist. Just be *sure* to go to sleep!"

"I will," she nodded. "Oh, Lendra, we need to talk tomorrow morning about my clothing."

"Of course, are you planning on something special? Is there an event you'll be attending?" she asked brightly, always enjoying the prospect of dressing her lady up in something new.

"No. Well, yes I suppose. Special, certainly."

"Are you going to keep me in suspense? I must know, in the case there is anything that requires preparation!" Lendra said, her eyes merry with anticipation.

Candissa drew a deep breath and looked squarely at Lendra.

"I will be traveling with my friends into the wilderness, west over the hills," she told her governess, who went deathly still. "And we will likely be gone a very long time."

"My...my lady…" was all the maid said, her voice quivering in fear.

"It's all right, Lendra, have strength. I will need it. But I must have appropriate clothing for walking and riding distances and making camp. We will talk more of it tomorrow," she said, smiling a little, trying to ease some of the dread that was so clear on the old woman's face.

Lendra only nodded briskly, hiding her face from Candissa. She was likely in tears. Dousing the lamps, the room went almost entirely dark. In the entryway, she left quickly, dousing the last of the lamps. Lendra should have put up more of a fuss. Candissa wondered why she hadn't.

Light filtered through the glazing and shutters of her bed chamber, as both moons were in prominence tonight. It was a feeble light, providing almost no illumination within.

Sitting on the edge of her bed, she set aside her sleeping gown. Taking her staff in hand, she stood and moved to the more open area of her chamber, where the ceiling was highest.

She began drills with her staff, lunging, whirling, chopping and stabbing the air, as she went through the paces learned from her instructors. The silence was punctuated by her short, sharp breaths, controlled and even. Despite the lack of appreciable light, she could see the features of her room with remarkable clarity.

After more than half an hour she put her staff down, leaning it in a corner. She slipped under a sheet to sleep, leaving her gown on the floor.

As she drifted into a well-earned slumber, she put away the thoughts and memories of the troubled day. Her last thought before sleep took her was of imagining what lay ahead of them all, within and beyond the Misthallow Hills.

CHAPTER EIGHTEEN - CAM

25 Laborus, Year 197, Eastvale Calendar

When Cam awoke, he was surprised to find Errol already gone. He was also a little concerned that Errol's departure had not awakened him. However, given his friend's ability to move almost silently, it was not unexpected.

It would be a busy day, determining who would need what, and how much could be carried within reason. He looked forward to seeing what sort of mounts House Demarrae could provide.

His door opened as he pulled his boots on. Errol popped his head in, looking distressingly kempt and bright-eyed.

"Break your fast downstairs with us? Sausages and blue pots!" was all he said before quickly closing the door. Cam did enjoy blue potatoes, if cooked properly. From what he had heard - and smelled - Evan's skills in the kitchen were to be admired.

After dressing, he stood and washed his face over the wash basin, followed by a vigorous brushing of his teeth.

Locking the door behind him, he was downstairs in a moment, his nose pleased by the assault of savory aromas. His stomach voiced its concern at being empty. Koraymis looked up from a small book he had been reading at the table as Errol loaded a plate with victuals, offering it to Cam as he took a seat.

"Too kind of you," Cam nodded to Errol. "I'm starved."

"What are the orders for the day?" Errol asked him, before putting a forkful of sausage covered in gravy in his mouth.

"We need to speak to Candissa. We'll need to agree on a day to depart.

Perhaps in three or four days? I don't suppose you know where we could find a map?"

Errol nodded his head. Swallowing, he spoke. "Deesa has some of the best maps in Ravensroost. But if not her, then Master Penston."

Koraymis looked up, a steaming cup of bitterblack in one hand. "I can talk to him about that, as I need to meet him regardless of our plans."

Errol nodded. "Makes sense."

"I wish to meet this scholar as well. I want to learn as much about whatever lies to the west as we can. Including rumors, wild tales, myths, anything."

"I think Evan may be as useful as Penston in that regard," Errol pointed a sausage-laden fork at the tavernmaster, who noticed the gesture while pouring a cup of steaming tea for a morning patron. He raised an eyebrow in suspicion.

"Then I'll speak to him as well. Any word on your *friends so-called* from the east?"

"I've had a couple contacts in town keeping an eye on them. They don't appear to be making any hostile moves yet," Errol said. "But I don't know about this Orrendar fellow. I think he's in the Demarrae estate now, though he claimed to be at the rented flat. Candissa will be able to tell me more about them, I'm hoping. Until we know what's happening, keep an eye out in all directions. I have a strange feeling about this entire situation."

"Really? I cannot imagine why," Koraymis chimed in, his voice dripping with sarcasm.

Errol laughed at the scholar's observation.

"I need to visit the shops first, to get an idea of what's available here in town," Cam said, then he looked at Errol. "Can you tell me where I should go?"

"All the shops you'll need are on the three east-west avenues that run through the center of town. They all run through the main market square," Errol explained.

"I have this list so far, why don't you two review it quickly," Cam suggested, laying out a sheet of parchment with neat lines of writing in two columns.

Koraymis picked it up, nodding. "You have a fine hand, sir."

"My mother is responsible for that. Lessons in handwriting and numbers had to be completed before I could get a seat at the dinner table," Cam said, smirking. "Where are you off to first, Kor?"

"I'll call on Master Penston, if Errol could direct me to his shop. What about you, Errol?"

"Well, as we are going our separate ways, I need to settle accounts with my landlady. After that, I'll visit House Ythanford and come up with some reason their new factor is fleeing town," Errol said.

"I wouldn't say we are fleeing," Cam said, frowning at the choice of words.

"Given what happened at House Demarrae, I have to imagine they would assume I'm fleeing," Errol said, rolling his eyes momentarily. "I do wonder at the wisdom of going about town on our tasks, when we agreed to stay together if at all possible."

"Do you fear an attack so soon?" Koraymis said.

"I cannot guess at their motives or timetable," Errol said, shrugging. "I think it unlikely they would attack, especially in open daylight and on the streets. Just be about your errands quickly, don't let your guard down, and see if we can use that…" Errol let his words trail off as he gestured with his hands at his temple, pointing to the others.

You mean this? Koraymis said silently, grinning.

"Yes, that's what I mean," Errol said, looking sour suddenly. *We should experiment and see how far away we can use this. We have no real idea, do we?*

Koraymis shook his head.

"Let's meet back here in three hours," Cam said, looking to the clock on the wall across the common room. "It's four rising, so let's be back here at seven rising. Is that reasonable?"

The other two looked at the prodigious timepiece mounted over the archway.

"That's a remarkable clock," Koraymis said. He turned back and nodded. "Seven rising."

"Fair enough," Errol said.

Koraymis handed the list to Errol. "Seems well thought out, Cam."

Errol glanced at the list and handed it directly to Cam, smiling. "I trust you entirely, my friend."

"All right. But you need to let me know about anything you'll want for yourself. I don't know what we're facing out there."

"Whatever we may encounter, we shall triumph over it!" Errol said, finishing the last bite of his meal and standing. "I will see you both soon. If I'm killed on my errands, remember me fondly."

He winked and left.

"Be careful, Kor," Cam said, preparing to leave now himself, having wolfed down his breakfast and morning ale quickly.

"I'll be fine," the scholar said, smiling. He was more casual in his pace of eating. Cam slung his pack more firmly over his shoulder and around his chest and tightened the strap.

"I will let the tavernmaster know what we are doing, in case Candissa inquires," Koraymis told him.

"That's an excellent thought, thanks," the hunter said. The scholar simply nodded and returned to his reading and morning meal.

Cam left the Bonerest, thinking about Koraymis. He was grateful to count him as a friend.

Walking into the crisp early-morning air, his breath hung in front of him. He stared out of the open western gate. It was clear enough that he could see the first of the gentle rolls of the Misthallow Hills, touched by the morning's frost.

He would first determine who had what goods to offer and how much everything would cost. From Errol's account of House Demarrae, Cam was certain Candissa would be able to make the purchases. He just had to contact her regarding the details of the transactions, once they were known. With any luck he would see her on his errands.

Following Errol's directions, he was soon on a long avenue with a fair number of shingles protruding out over the cobblestone streets. The streets were beginning to fill with passers-by: hawkers, farmers, young wives or mothers in search of the day's fare, and a number of people who didn't fit into any readily identifiable category.

He visited a butcher and a linen and canvas goods shop first, writing down some items on his list. The merchants were courteous enough with his inquiries.

The next sign lifted his spirits. It was a leather worker. While he was not intending to set up shop in Ravensroost, he was excited to meet someone in the trade. Entering the shop, he was immediately inspired. The heady smells of cured leather, faint hints of tanning, and even a note of the odd dye filled his nostrils.

The shop was laden with leather goods, from small hand purses for ladies to saddles and saddle bags. There were even some pieces of leather armor, stiffened and reinforced.

"Can I help you?"

Cam turned to see someone in a leather jerkin with the stains on his fingers indicative of someone in the trade. His hair was red and unkempt.

"Are you the master here?" Cam asked, smiling. "My name is Cam, I'm a student of the leather working trades."

"The name's Delmin, glad to meet a fellow crafter," the fellow said, extending his hand. Cam shook it.

Something went wrong. Delmin's eyes, a moment ago appearing almost friendly, darkened instantly. He withdrew his hand, a scowl forming on his mouth.

"I'm sorry, did I say something to offend you?" Cam asked, realizing something was amiss.

The leather master turned back toward his workbench in the back of the shop.

"No," was all he said.

Not sure what to make the turn of the man's mood, Cam cleared his throat and began looking at the variety of products and works hanging on pegs and lying on shelves. There were a few nice backpacks and belt pouches he took note of.

He found a finely-crafted jacket made with a stitching technique unfamiliar to Cam. He examined it, then turned to ask Delmin about his craft, but saw the man's eyes regarding him from the back of the shop. They seemed darker still. A coldness seeped into the air around Cam.

He shook off the strange feeling, concentrating on the task at hand.

"Delmin, the backpacks, how much-"

"They're not for sale," Delmin cut him off. He stood slowly, clutching a thick-handed bevel with which he had been tooling a thick piece of leather.

"I don't understand. Why are they in your shop if not for sale?" Cam asked, sensing the impending conflict.

"You won't find anything here you want," Delmin said, a bit louder. "Leave my shop."

Cam regarded the man for a moment, bracing his feet in case he needed to lunge suddenly. It would be difficult for the man to reach Cam, given the assortment of hanging leather items and tables displaying wares crammed into the small shop. The hunter relaxed his posture. He had been in plenty of fist fights and had drawn blood in a few armed contests.

In that moment, Cam sensed something other than just a man who didn't like him. There was a hidden malevolence behind his eyes. It was almost imperceptible. Yet, Cam knew it was there. He didn't understand what to make of it. Puzzled, he stood his ground, not turning from the man.

"Leave my shop!" the man yelled. Someone came into the shop behind Cam. The hunter smiled at the red-faced Delmin, bowing in an almost ridiculous fashion. Then he turned and departed. The townsman who had just entered appeared shocked, stepping aside quickly as Cam walked by.

Shaking his head once he was back on the street, he resolved to continue his errands. He found success at the next two shops, noting goods and prices. The next shop that caught his eye was a stable. While Candissa had offered to provide mounts through the generosity of her house, Cam thought it prudent to check out the local offerings, and to shop for gear she may not have on hand. He was also curious about how much a riding horse cost.

The stable had a broad yard to one side. The smell of dung and hay grew stronger with each step. Nearing the entrance to the stable, he saw two dogs in the yard. One sat curled comfortably on some straw on one end of the yard, dozing and ignoring passers-by. The other was chained to the opposing end of the yard and seemed quiet as well.

As soon as Cam began making for the stable entrance, the far dog raised its heavy head. The hound was a bull mastiff of some sort, not an unusual dog for townsfolk. Cam imagined it was trained to help manage the horses and to provide some protection from common thieves.

It stared at Cam with flinty, black eyes. He heard a deep, sonorous growl.

"Hey, boy," Cam said, in an attempt to calm the beast.

The huge dog leapt up and charged, the heavy chain rattling as it played out. Cam reached back instinctively for the short sword he kept strapped to his back. He leapt backwards as the massive hound crossed the ten yards in a heartbeat.

He didn't need to draw the blade, seeing the chain run out and snap tight. The dog, barking viciously, was thrown on his side. Recovering, he continued to snarl and snap at Cam, who stood warily just a few yards from the dog.

A stablehand rushed out as a few passers-by paused to observe the snarling beast's reaction to Cam. The boy shouted at the dog and ran over to grab the chain. At the same time, an older man appeared, walking quickly over to put himself between the slavering dog and Cam.

"What happened here? Did you provoke him?" the man asked Cam, his eyes accusing.

"Not at all, good sir, I was merely walking toward your stable to make inquiries."

"That's right sir, I watched him come up, didn't do nothin' to Bick," the stable boy added. "He jus' jumped up and charged. Never seen 'im do such a thing!"

The dog continued to bark at Cam during their conversation, resisting the boy's attempts to pull him back. The stable owner turned and roared at the dog, "Back, you stupid cur! Lay!"

The older man's rebuke had the desired effect. The great hound seemed to jump in shock. He quivered, looking at his master with a wounded gaze. His barks became a whimper and he trotted to the far corner of the yard, the chain trailing behind him. He curled up and looked with sad eyes at the men standing by the stable door. Cam noted there appeared to be no trace of malice in his gaze now.

"I'm sorry, I have no idea why he did that, sir. Please forgive him," the man said to Cam. "Please come in."

"No need to apologize. Animals can be thrown off by something we cannot sense," Cam said. "He seems all right now."

"No matter, he shouldn't have done that. Let me make it up to you. Perhaps there's something inside that catches your eye. Quidmar is my name, sir."

The stabler was kind to Cam as he showed him into the shop attached to the stables. Aside from a fair selection of horses for various purposes, he had saddles, riding equipment, and a few supplies for longer journeys. Quidmar had an easy disposition and seemed genuine and open.

Cam mentioned that he intended to head west, evoking a low whistle from Quidmar. "That's been tried before. If you don't mind my sayin', Master Cam, such journeys usually end badly."

"Yes, I've been made aware it's not an advisable undertaking. My friends and I have our reasons," he said.

The horse master looked at Cam with an appraising eye. "Well then, just be sure to watch yourself out there."

Cam laughed. "We may not know what perils we will face, but we'll be ready."

"Will you?" another voice joined the conversation. It was the boy who had come out first, to restrain the hound. Cam heard Quidmar call him Till.

Cam looked at the lad with an amused expression. "What do you mean?"

"Till, mind your business," Quidmar admonished the boy at once.

"I mean, do you have any idea what you're facing?" The boy's face had taken on a stony countenance.

"No, we don't, Till. But we will deal with whatever we must face," Cam said, a firm resolve in his voice.

"Do not go west!" Till muttered, his eyes growing dark.

"Till! Go clean the stalls. Now!" his employer shouted at the suddenly menacing boy.

"Why?" Cam demanded, turning to face the boy directly. He was seeing something now. "Tell me why."

The stabler appeared torn between defusing the situation and dragging the boy off. "Sir, don't let this stupid boy bother you. His mother warned me he was prone to fits-"

"You can't save the fifth!" Till hissed at Cam, his eyes going wide. "You will only *kill her*!"

The fifth, Cam thought, his mind suddenly alight with thoughts and images. They *must find the fifth.* He grabbed the boy's collar with powerful hands.

"Tell me *why*!" Cam demanded. Quidmar grasped the boy's shoulders.

"Please, sir, he's ill. Don't let his foolish words concern you!" the horse master said, clearly trying to calm the confrontation.

"You will kill her, you will kill her!" the boy repeated, almost shrieking, his eyes bulging in their sockets. Without thinking, Cam struck him full across the face with his open hand, sparing nothing. The boy flew onto the floor in a tumbled heap.

Quidmar stared at the boy, agape, and looked back at Cam. The boy stirred. He sat up slowly, rubbing his face. Half of it was turning a bright red from the impact.

"What...sir?" he mumbled, his eyes confused as he stared up at Cam and Quidmar. "I'm sorry, did I fall?"

Cam opened his mouth, then shut it as quickly. "Yes, Till, you did. Are you all right?"

"Yes, sir. I'm terrible sorry," he said, standing unsteadily, rubbing his face. "I musta hit my face hard."

Cam looked at Quidmar. "See to the boy. I'll be in touch with you about the saddles and gear. Say nothing more, please."

"I understand completely, sir," Quidmar said, taking the boy by the elbow. "Come, Till, let's get you cleaned up. You can have an ale."

"I like ale," he heard the boy mumble, still rubbing his swelling cheek.

Cam departed the stable, thinking about what had happened. While it didn't make sense outright, he was beginning to see something, a pattern.

Outside, he gathered his thoughts. He had visited several shops but needed to visit more. Yet, he felt compelled to speak to his friends. He would have his chance when they convened at House Demarrae later. A growl caught his ear.

Sitting in the shadowed corner of the stable yard was the hound, Bick. He sat, unmoving, just staring at Cam. His eyes seemed to glow with a red, seething malevolence. He did not charge. Cam realized he felt something else in that gaze. Patience.

It would wait for them.

CHAPTER NINETEEN - KORAYMIS

25 Laborus, Year 197, Eastvale Calendar

Koraymis finished his breakfast as Beshanu cleared the table. Errol had already paid for their meals. That did not sit well with Koraymis. He did not like being obliged to anyone, even if he could call that person a friend.

Which brought up many questions in his mind. Why was he doing this? Were these people really his friends or was he doing this because he felt compelled to do so? What was behind their ability to speak with one another without the benefit of voice? Why was he going west? Why, why, why? It was all a bit maddening.

He breathed deeply, calming his mind, using one of the several techniques Master Telmik had taught him. He needed to find the scholar, Penston, as the Librarian had directed him to. He would, despite his inclination to avoid strangers. He resisted that part of him that wished only to hide away someplace quiet and continue his studies with the book Telmik had given him. He knew there was so much more to learn from it.

Already knowing where the scholar's office was, he bundled his dark robes about him, and headed out into the cool morning air. The sun provided some relief from the chill.

Moving through the morning press of merchants, farmers, townsfolk and market-goers, Koraymis generally avoided looking directly at other people. Sometimes when he saw their eyes, he felt as if he could see their fortunes or predict what would happen to them. He had dismissed it as his wild imagination until one of his predictions came to pass.

It was something he discovered about the same time he started changing, not long before Telmik found him.

He tried not to think too much about that time of his life. It was a troubling and difficult period and nearly led to his death, at the hands of fearful and ignorant folk.

He couldn't avoid looking up occasionally, due to the increasing crowd. As he glanced ahead, he could not help but notice some passers-by staring at him. He felt their gazes acutely. Some were kind, sincere, open. Others were not. He suspected his imagination was creating these perceptions.

He chose to walk to the scholar's office via a less-trafficked street, one that Errol suggested to avoid the busier market district. It was a narrow street that ran behind some shops. Alleys and gaps between establishments were common in this town, so he would just cut across to the main avenue when need be.

There were far fewer people along this way, behind the shops, where few shingles hung. He passed a wine shop, with tuns stacked four high. A drunken man in a wine-stained smock sat on a rotted chair, smoking a pipe, a mug of wine in hand. As Koraymis passed, he glared at the scholar as if he had committed some offense.

A few shops down, a fellow looking to be a merchant of some sort approached him as he made his way along the narrow back street, a bundle under one arm. He regarded Koraymis for a moment as they walked toward one another, then suddenly smiled. It seemed to catch Koraymis off guard.

Just as they passed one another, the man grabbed Koraymis' arm, pulling him suddenly to one side. Something wet and foul splashed onto the ground two steps from the scholar.

The stranger looked up and shouted, "Ilgrae, are you blind?"

Above them, an older woman was holding the chamberpot she had just emptied. She simply sneered, staring at Koraymis for a long moment before disappearing into her first-floor flat. The scholar surmised she had taken aim at him with the contents of the pot.

"I have no idea why she did that, friend," the man said to Koraymis, releasing his hold on his arm. "She's usually a very likable and pleasant woman."

"Strange indeed, I've never seen her and I'm new to the town. My name is Koraymis. I owe you my thanks."

"It was nothing. At worst, you would have needed a change of clothes," the man said, then offered his hand. "My name is Anselm. Glad to make your acquaintance, Koraymis. I'm a cartwright. My shop is at the other end of the street. Don't hesitate to call on me in you need anything."

Koraymis found the man's congeniality and openness almost disturbing. As Anselm clapped his shoulder and passed by him, apparently on a hurried errand, Koraymis had only a moment to reply.

"My thanks, Anselm. I will remember your kindness."

"Think nothing of it!" the cartwright called as he strode quickly away.

"I'm your man!"

Koraymis looked back at the receding figure of Anselm. He was dumbfounded. His right hand itched. Scratching it absently, his fingers brushed the heavy ring on his middle finger.

Some are allies, others are enemies. Sides are being chosen by all, though they know not. Koraymis almost stumbled as he began walking forward once more. He was certain it was Telmik's voice.

"Master?" he muttered, still touching the ring.

You will each know those who have chosen. Some will stand with you, others will oppose you. Some will try to kill you. You know what you must do with them.

"Master," he whispered. "Am I doing what I must? I need your counsel."

No answer came. Despite repeated attempts to use the ring to reestablish contact, Koraymis could not reach Telmik - or whoever the voice was.

Shrugging, he moved on. He was soon behind a papermaker's shop, as indicated by a barrel filled with ruined and rotted paper. He turned a corner down a short alleyway and was on the main avenue. The door to the scholar's flat bore a shingle, hanging on a brass arm. It was a depiction of a stack of books next to a quill in an inkwell. Below the iconograph was a smaller sign on a few links, bearing the title "Master Penston Virtrass, Scholar".

Entering through the door, he climbed a precipitous set of steps to the first floor. Knocking firmly, he received a quick response.

"Enter!" came the voice.

Opening the door, Koraymis found himself in a tidy and somewhat confined office. Penston was just rising from behind his desk as Koraymis entered. The desk was a few steps from his front parlor, where he received guests and patrons. The ceiling was low, dark beams crossing it. The room was warm, with a small fire burning in a stove nearby. Two windows, partially shuttered to let in the day's light, illuminated the many narrow shelves and small tables bearing books, scrolls, tomes, and sheafs of paper. The smell was familiar and comforting to Koraymis, as his most pleasurable hours had been spent in a library.

Penston was of middling height, not young but not old. He had deep brown hair cut short and parted down the middle as many scholars favored in the Kingdom. He was not wearing his traditional scholar's cap, which sat on a small table nearby. His eyes were warm and bright, despite being a distinctly dark green in color. His face was narrower than most, with no beard or moustache. His skin was pale, likely from a life spent with books. But Koraymis suspected he was the sort of person whose skin would darken easily if exposed to several days of sunlight.

"Hello, I'm Master Penston, how can I help you?" His voice was warm and open. Perhaps he was an ally, thinking about the warning issued by the mysterious voice. His eyes glanced at the pin attached to Koraymis' tunic. "Ah, a fellow scholar, I see."

"Sir, yes. Well, not quite," Koraymis began. "I have studied in the library in Woodford."

"Did you study under Master Tentrovis?"

"Yes, I did. He awarded me this pin, but I did not complete my first tests yet," Koraymis said. "I just want to be clear on that point."

"Well, if he saw fit to award you the pin, I have no doubt you are more than qualified," Penston said, motioning to a cushioned chair. "Please, have a seat."

"I appreciate it. I was sent here at the recommendation of Master Tentrovis, to secure a position at the library," Koraymis began, feeling almost nervous, as if he was sitting before an academic board of review. He remembered the scroll in his pocket and drew it out. "Here is a letter of introduction and recommendation from Master Tentrovis."

Penston took the scroll, broke the official seal of wax and unrolled it. He quickly perused the contents, his eyebrows rising. "Impressive. Very impressive. But it is addressed to the Librarian Efflewhist."

"Yes, sir, it is. Perhaps you know the situation of Master Efflewhist?" Koraymis said, phrasing his question carefully.

Penston sighed heavily, looking down at the floor. "Yes, I'm well aware. Did he...know why you there?"

"Yes, it was a good day, to quote him," Koraymis said. "But he denied my formal request to apprentice under him at the Library."

"If you're looking for a position here…" Penston began. But Koraymis cut him off.

"Not at all. The good master Efflewhist bade me come here, to see you. But not in any capacity as a scholar or potential employer," Koraymis said. He wasn't sure how the next part would proceed. He continued. "He told me to see you, as you would have things I would need. I know you might dismiss this as merely symptoms of his...condition, but I believe he was earnest in this request."

The senior scholar appeared curious. He put the scroll down. "I am happy to help you any way that I can, especially as you are a fellow scholar and so highly recommended," Penston said. Koraymis found his dark green eyes to be disarming. His first reaction was to be entirely honest with the man. He had never been an especially trusting young man, and events so far in Ravensroost only reinforced that attitude. "I confess I'm not sure how I can help you, however.

"I would require a degree of confidence regarding my inquiries, as my friends and I would not want others in town to know our intentions."

"I understand," Penston replied at once. "You are a colleague and you can be assured of my utmost discretion. Now, what is this all about?"

Koraymis took a deep breath. "My friends and I will be heading west, over the Misthallow Hills."

If the scholar was shocked, he hid his feelings well. Koraymis detected only a genuine response in Penston's voice and demeanor. He relaxed his probing, suspecting the man would likely take exception to someone using magic against his replies.

"I see. And do you suppose Master Efflewhist thinks I can help you in this endeavor? Are you seeking a map, or counsel of what may lie westward?"

"Perhaps that is what the Librarian meant. Any advice would be very helpful. However, as I understand, Lady Candissa - she's part of our group - has an accurate map of the region," Koraymis said, trusting the man enough to tell him this much. "So perhaps just any accounts, legends, whispers, whatever you may have regarding what lies west."

The senior scholar stood now, considering the request. "Let me see, I have several works that have a few accounts of journeys over the hills. You should understand, however, they are scant."

"I would expect that. I know the very notion of traveling over the hills is something one does not speak of, let alone write about," Koraymis shrugged.

"Oh, if you find the right works, you can find a few accounts," Penston said, smiling as his fingers danced over a high shelf of cracked bindings. "So, Candissa is finally going west?"

"Finally? Has she expressed interest previously?"

"Since she was a little girl, even before Errol arrived," he said, tapping on a book he had just pulled down, examining the cover. "This one should have something."

"You know Errol?"

"Yes, since his arrival in Ravensroost. They have both expressed interest in what lies beyond the hills. Not many people do. Well, really, almost no one does. Those that do so publicly can sometimes catch the attention of the authorities," he said.

"Would you suggest we be discreet in that matter?"

"Oh, absolutely. Indiscriminate talk of breaking with such a convention would certainly reach the ears of the town guard, or worse, the authorities to the east."

At once, Koraymis was concerned for his friends. He was particularly concerned about Cam as he was so open and forthright in his manner of speech. Perhaps Penston saw the concern in his eyes.

"Not to worry, it won't lead to arrest. At worst, you would be known to the captain of the guard as a 'concern'. That's what he calls those he doesn't trust entirely," the scholar said with a smirk. He placed four tomes before

Koraymis, one particularly old, none of them especially large. Koraymis picked up the oldest one.

"One does not often see something this aged."

"No, it's one of the oldest in my collection, bound more than two centuries ago. You're free to read it as long as you're in Ravensroost."

"Master Penston, if you don't mind my asking, how did you know Errol was one of my group interested in going west?" Koraymis asked.

The older scholar smirked briefly. "Do you really think what happened at House Demarrae wouldn't be talked about from one end of Ravensroost to the other? And before dawn, at that."

"Ah," the younger man said, nodding. That made sense. He looked at the book in his hands, opening the cracked, heavy cover of corroded leather with care.

Koraymis read the faded title page: *Drogantha's Tales 'Tween Wood and Mountain*. Handling the pages carefully, he turned several over, scanning the text.

"Are these tales based on facts or more myths?"

"I would think more on fact, although he was the first bookbinder in the city of Eastvale. There were a lot of fanciful legends in those days," Penston said. "It was compiled during the formative years of the Kingdom. There were more monsters ranging down from the mountains and more Elves in the river valleys. And I suspect the first king appreciated some prudent embellishment on the part of the tellers of tales."

"Remarkable. A book from the beginning of time itself," Koraymis said, carefully closing the cracked tome, smiling just a little. He glanced over and saw a wry grin on Penston's face in reply.

"You know there's more out there, I can see that. Not only places far more ancient than anything you have seen. There is knowledge as well."

"I have always suspected our little kingdom is an isolated pocket in a vast world," Koraymis replied.

"Errol feels the same way. Is that why you and your friends are heading west?"

Koraymis sat up, peering out a small, colorfully glazed window an arm's length away. It faced west. He thought about how to answer that question.

"I apologize if my question is unwelcome," the scholar said quietly. "Think nothing of it."

"No, no need for an apology. It is not unwelcome. It's a question I should be able to answer without hesitation. For the moment, however, I am not entirely certain."

"No matter. You are welcome to borrow these books, all of them," Penston offered. "If you're staying at the Bonerest, just leave them in the care of Evan. Should you need to depart suddenly, they will find their way back to me."

"You are very generous in your offer, sir," Koraymis said, his eyes studying the scholar. "I don't want to seem suspicious, but you have only just met me, yet you are so trusting."

"Not a great deal truly *happens* here, Koraymis. If I can help you, and in doing so, be a part of something beyond the ordinary, then I am pleased to do so."

Koraymis wasn't sure if he could trust his instincts. He felt nothing untoward about Penston, no doubts. That made him question his feelings. His left hand turned the ring on his right hand idly as he assessed him.

He felt feelings, perhaps words, swirling in his mind. He knew it was from the ring. A few words formed from the whispering: *He can be trusted.* That was enough to dispel any doubts. He nodded to the scholar and smiled as best as he could. "Then I thank you, sir."

"Good. You are most welcome. Now, I have a favor to ask of you. You could say it has to do with our profession," Penston said.

"What would that be?" Koraymis said, mildly intrigued.

"As you are traveling, do you think it would be possible for you to take notes or perchance make sketches regarding where you are traveling? It would be for the benefit of future mapmakers and would greatly aid us here in the Kingdom."

"I had not thought about that, but my answer is yes. I would be happy to do so," he answered. "I cannot know how much time I will have, or what I will find, or even how long we will be out there. But I will do my best."

"Excellent! Let me put together a small bundle for you. It is a carrying case for scholars who are on the road. It contains quills, paper, ink, all neatly arranged. The case will safeguard the contents against rain," Penston said, getting up. He quickly produced a stiff leather case and began adding some smaller sheets of parchment to it.

"This seems all too kind. I must insist on paying you for this, on behalf of myself and my friends," Koraymis said, his voice clearly insistent. "While I intend to return, I have no idea when."

"Yes, of course, I must have coin to buy my morning bitterblack brews. Those are expensive beans," the senior scholar said, smiling.

He finished assembling the carrying case and handed it to Koraymis. "When do you intend to depart town?"

"I am not sure. We are each of us working on preparing for the journey and will be meeting again today I believe."

"I will think on your travels and see if I can find any other works that would be of benefit to you. If you read those tomes there, you'll have as good an understanding as I can offer, of what lies to the west. The collected rumor and myths, even the preposterous ones, are in the thinner work there, by Grevanderson," Penston said. "I doubt that work will be of any practical use, but it will be entertaining reading."

"If time permits, may I visit you again? I may have questions on some of this."

"Of course," he nodded in reply.

Koraymis felt the need to find the others at this point. He collected the books and carrying case. He had brought an empty sling bag and was glad for it now. He was especially happy about the charge Master Penston had laid before him. Map-making had always been an area of interest to Koraymis, even when he was a young boy. Cartography was one of the disciplines he chose to study at the school, despite it's not being a required subject.

He moved to the entrance, offering his hand to Master Penston.

"Thank you for everything, I'm sure we'll see each other before long."

"I look forward to it," the scholar said, clasping this hand. "Please convey my regards to Errol, Lady Candissa, and Master Bronwyer."

"Of course," Koraymis said, nodding. He was soon down the steps and on the busy avenue. He was about to head off to find his friends when he paused. Turning, he looked up the stairs that led to Penston's chambers.

His ring felt warm.

Remember. The word was almost spoken within his mind. Koraymis suddenly knew he would not see Penston again for a very long time.

After half an hour, Koraymis had covered two bustling streets, his eyes having wandered over hundreds of faces, trying to spot Cam amid the growing throng of market-goers and hawkers. Clearly, searching crowds for familiar faces was not a skill he could count among his own. Then he recalled House Ythanford, the minor noble for whom Errol worked. He would see if Errol was there, or perhaps on his way back.

He detested being among so many people. He still felt the strange sensation of their eyes. He sought out a passing town guardsman who happily provided directions to House Ythanford.

Making his way toward the district where the wealthier families lived, foot traffic began to diminish. Koraymis hoped this would allow him a better chance of spotting Errol – or more likely – being spotted by him.

His right hand involuntarily closed into a fist, the ring burning. Clutching his right fist with his left hand, he sensed – no, he knew – something had just happened. Something involving magic.

Errol! Somehow, he knew Errol was in danger. Someone was trying to kill him. Almost by instinct, he closed his eyes and reached out to Cam and Candissa, calling them, warning them.

CHAPTER TWENTY - ERROL

25 Laborus, Year 197, Eastvale Calendar

Errol had spent more time than he wished in settling his accounts with his landlady, Meregrith. But in the end, she had agreed to store his belongings, and for that he was grateful. Being practical, he left instructions they be turned over to Taldrephus, should he fail to return from his journey. He told her little of his intentions. She was a kind woman but enjoyed spreading gossip.

After bidding her goodbye, he was on his way to House Ythanford. He took the back alleys, preferring to avoid the main streets. He was still unsure of the intentions of the visiting noble and his family and preferred to keep out of sight as much as possible. The town of Ravensroost was accommodating in this respect. There were plenty of back alleys, and most were not stacked a full story high with trash, refuse, broken barrels or worse. Such was the case with many larger cities.

He stopped in his tracks, behind a candlemaker's shop. Sighing deeply, Errol buried the observation he had just made. Having never visited the back alleys of any large city, it was yet another errant recollection that didn't make sense.

He realized he was not alone. Standing in a remarkably narrow gap between two buildings was Bursley. The slight fellow tried looking nonchalant but only came off as ridiculous.

"Burz, what are you up to?" Errol said in a low voice.

"I am up to precisely nothing, Errol!" the shorter man almost swaggered out into the narrow street, as if to emphasize his reply. "More interestingly, what are *you* up to?"

"Heading to Lord Ythanford's. Care to join me? I'm sure his guards would be happy to have a long talk with you."

"I don't think there would be much talking involved! You just go on and talk to your fancy lords and ladies," Bursley said, weaving wildly down the alleyway. "Leave us common folk to do all the real work."

"That *real work* is why they don't like you at House Ythanford, Burz!" Errol laughed as he continued on his way.

Lord Ythanford's estate was located toward the center of town, where he had to wend his way behind taller buildings. The shadowy alleys were a place to be wary for most people, but for Errol they were a comfort. He was never fearful of the shadows. He felt comfortable hidden in a dark recess, out of sight. It gave him a feeling of being more in control than when exposed in full sunlight or in a chamber lit by a bright lamp.

He was near the middle of one of the longer alleys in Ravensroost, the nearest exit to a street more than a hundred paces away.

"Ho there!" Errol stopped quickly at the sound. It was a town guard, likely suspicious of a figure darting down a dim alley, especially so close to House Ythanford. He recognized the figure even at a fair distance down the way.

"Bardmore, it's Errol!" he called to the man, waving. Bardmore was an alright fellow, just a bit dim and easily duped. He suspected the guard harbored a resentment for Errol, likely due to his looks. Bardmore was a roundly plain fellow.

"Good, I was hoping I'd find you!" the guard replied, returning the wave and walking quickly toward him. Another guard joined him, rounding a corner several paces behind. It was Tevins, a guard who was barely worthy to wear the colors. Errol thought the Captain had kicked the man out by now, given Tevins' propensity for drink, slapping women and failing to follow orders.

Errol knew at once things were not going well. His right hand strayed down toward his blade instinctively.

"Bardmore, whatever is the matter?" he asked, feigning concern. The sweaty guard finally reached him, panting quietly.

"It's...fine, just wait a minute. We need to ask you some questions," he said, putting his hands on his knees for a moment.

Errol suppressed a grin. He could run circles around the two of them easily. But the last thing he – or his friends – needed now was trouble with the town guard. Tevins arrived momentarily, not bothering to address Errol. The poor excuse for a guard just grinned at him stupidly, licking his thick lips.

"Feel free to ask any questions you may have. You should know, however, I have an appointment with Lord Ythanford. He will not appreciate the delay," Errol said.

"Oh, don't you worry about that. I think your precious Lord Ythanford will understand why you were *delayed*!" Tevins laughed harshly, putting a sinister emphasis on the last word. Bardmore cuffed him on the back of the head, glaring at him angrily.

"We'll be waiting for the Lieutenant now, if you don't mind," he said to Errol. "He'll be here quick like."

"Lieutenant..." Errol asked, letting the question trail off.

"Oh, of course. Lieutenant Skelmark," Bardmore said, turning about and peering down the alleyway. A few figures suddenly appeared, silhouetted by the brightly-lit street beyond. "Oh, here he is now."

The lieutenant was a junior officer to the town guard, recently appointed and due to his family connections. He had no love for Errol and had made a point of letting him know that in the past. He was accompanied by two more guards, and a third figure, in somewhat finer dress.

"Lord Enthessar, a delight to see you again so soon," Errol smiled easily at the young noble. The man had a darkly menacing smile on his darkly handsome face.

"I don't think you'll have the same opinion in a few minutes, murderer!" Enthessar barked. The guards formed a semicircle around Errol, at a goodly distance.

"Oh, do tell, exactly what do you mean by that?" Errol drawled, rolling his eyes. It had the desired effect on Enthessar.

"Lieutenant, the vial?" he said to the officer, who quickly produced a small glass vial. "This vial, containing a drop of the poison that killed those poor men, was found on your body. Or *will* be."

At once, all five guards had their short swords drawn, pointing at Errol.

"It seems when I confronted you with the evidence, you attacked. Pity. Five against one, you didn't have a chance. Stupid little fool!" Enthessar said, his smile broader now. It annoyed Errol the man was so handsome, even as he threatened mortal injury.

"Hehe, yeah, silly fool!" Tevins parroted, almost drooling in anticipation.

Errol quickly assessed his situation. They were in an intersection of alleys, but he had backed up to a recess between two shops. The shadows were deeper here, and a wall of stacked of wooden crates provided some cover in more than one point nearby. He knew there was no door or escape route in the recess.

The soldiers prevented an easy escape to the right, left, or forward. They wielded only the short blades, but no crossbows or short bows. He couldn't tell what Enthessar may have been armed with, under his cloak. He was not sure how to extract himself from this predicament; he did not like the odds.

"All right, lads, make quick work of him! We can't wait any longer!" Lieutenant Skelmark ordered them, glancing down one alley. "Other guards may be along any moment."

"Are you going to beg and plead like a dog, Errol?" Enthessar taunted him, safely behind the guards.

Errol smiled broadly at the noble, flashing his line of smooth, white teeth. He drew his blade, letting them see it briefly. Then he stepped back into the shadowed recess of the alley, quite suddenly obscured by the darkness.

Holding his blade carefully, Errol realized there was no way out, without confronting his attackers. Yet, swathed in shadow, he studied the alleyway behind the soldiers, tall crates and shadows behind them. Just a step away.

"Get out of there, idiot, there's no door there, no escape! You can't hide from us!" the lieutenant shouted, clearly annoyed. "Tevins, is he cowering next to those crates?"

"C'mon Errol, pretty boy, time to…" the guard stepped forward into the shadows, his eyes adjusting. "Oy! Sir! He's gone!"

"What do you mean, you fool-" Lieutenant Skelmark's words were cut off as a boot connected with his head. The officer went sprawling, bowling over Enthessar in the process. Both men tumbled onto the ground, as Errol landed another forceful blow with his boot onto the back of one of the guards.

He stepped back three paces gracefully, and traced a theatrical bow as the others turned, dumbfounded to stare at him. Errol had slipped behind them all without being seen, having struck Skelmark from the shadows. Enthessar was sputtering as he pushed Lieutenant Skelmark off him.

"Gentlemen, I would love to play with you all day, but there are matters that require my attention," Errol said quite loudly.

"Get him, you pathetic idiots!" Enthessar yelled, struggling to rise. He drew a rapier as he did so. "You struck a noble of a first house, wretch! You die for that!"

"Not to contradict, my lord, but it was I who struck the good lieutenant. It was *he* who struck you," Errol pointed out, stepping further back along the wall of the alleyway, amid crates and barrels. He carefully gauged his steps now, keenly aware of the position of all six individuals before him. His blade was never too far from his hand.

The lieutenant shook his head as he slowly rose. "You attacked an officer of the guard, Errol. That was a mistake."

"You are complicit in conspiring to falsely accuse and attack an innocent citizen. You will be stripped of your commission and thrown into your own jail," Errol declared. "If you are fortunate."

The other guards held their swords before them nervously, just behind their commanding officer. Enthessar meanwhile grew steadily more red-faced.

"Attack him, Lieutenant, that's an order!" the arrogant noble growled.

"What do you mean *if I'm fortunate*?"

"If you persist in this attempt to kill me, I will have no choice. *Please* Lieutenant, don't put me in that position," Errol said, his words both a warning and a challenge. Errol tried his best not to grin.

"Just kill him, Skelmark, I'm not paying you to stand there like an impotent oaf!" Enthessar muttered. "He cannot kill every one of you, and he dare not kill me!"

"But who then offers their life in sacrifice, gentlemen?" Errol said, almost casually, as he produced his menacing blade. In the shadows, it almost seemed to gleam, diverting their gazes. "Who offers their blood for this cowardly noble?"

The hesitation was palpable between all of them.

Almost to Errol's surprise, it was Tevins.

His face was twisted into a snarl, his eyes two dark, malevolent orbs. He shocked them all by lunging with a preternatural agility. He jumped as he did so, swinging his sword down in a remarkable display. Errol appreciated the man's technique, watching it arc downward slowly, his senses heightened. He thought it almost amusing that finally, in this last moment together, the man had impressed him.

It was not difficult to counter the motion and the attack, side stepping Tevins easily, half-turning his own body to bring his blade up against the falling weight of Tevins's scrawny body. Errol gripped the guard's sword arm by the wrist as his blade parted the leather armor easily, sliding between his ribs smoothly. Errol could sense it slicing through the hapless man's lungs, severing something fibrous. A fragment of memory flashed in Errol's mind at that instant - a chart hanging on a wall, displaying the anatomy of Humans.

The impact drove the breath from the man, a red spray spattering as he crumpled onto the ground at Errol's feet. Tevins's blade clattered noisily as it slipped from his lifeless grip. Errol drew the blade out easily as the man slumped.

The other guards were slack-jawed and wide-eyed. Briefly, Errol wondered why he didn't feel something more. He had just killed a man. He put the thought away quickly.

"All right. Now there's five of you, including this noble who led Tevins to his death," Errol said. Enthessar took a step forward. Errol anticipated and reacted to the move. His blade was pointed directly at the noble. Oddly, Errol thought for a brief instant, it had no blood on it. "Do not tempt me, Enthessar. A noble of a first house dies just as easily as a gap-toothed drunkard guardsman."

He saw the fear now in Enthessar's eyes, mixing with the outrage. The lieutenant was another matter. His eyes were not unlike Tevins's in that last moment, suddenly malevolent and dark.

"Skelmark, don't," Errol said softly.

"You don't understand!" Skelmark growled, biting off the words. "You must die!"

The officer stepped forward, past Enthessar, brandishing his longsword. There was no finesse in his approach, no strategy. Errol knew the man for a competent swordsman, so this approach made no sense whatsoever.

"Skelmark, you can't beat me. Don't do this!" Errol shouted, attempting to maneuver around the officer. But he was tall and fast. He roared and brought the long blade around. Errol easily dodged the first blow, but he knew it wouldn't last. He did not want to be forced in the direction of Enthessar and be forced to strike a blow against the noble.

Skelmark raised the sword again and brought it down, to be countered by Errol. He did not relent in his attacks. The blows were coming faster and more precisely. Enthessar was moving around the pair, trying to get into an advantageous position. Another guard was moving forward, just behind the lieutenant.

From down on the alleyways, a voice sounded loudly.

"Skelmark, stand down!"

The lieutenant paid it no heed. Again, and again, he lunged, stabbed, and swung the blade, trying to find his mark. Errol was waging his own internal battle. A quiet, almost dormant aspect with his mind knew precisely what to do to end this. He fought to control this urge, not to give into it, not to give up on letting the officer live.

It would not do. Others were pressing in and soon he would be unable to counter every blow. Something was pushing Skelmark and so this aspect of Errol pushed him. With little effort, he reversed his position to the attacking soldier in an instant, Errol's blade sinking deep into Skelmark's back, drawing across forcefully, slicing through the thick leather of his armor. He parted his spine just below his shoulder blades. The lieutenant collapsed.

Other town guardsmen were now rushing forward, led by Lieutenant Thendarick. Bursley was beside him, pointing. "That's the lot of 'em sir, they all attacked Errol with no good reason!"

"Lieutenant, this miscreant just slew an officer and a guard. He must be arrested and hanged!" Enthessar shouted in a theatrical fashion. Errol hid a grin as he watched the performance.

Other guards were behind Thendarick and the alleyway was suddenly buzzing with noise and confusion. The guards who had assaulted Errol looked to one another with uncertainty.

"Just ask these good men, they will tell you. We were simply asking Errol a question when he went mad and started killing!" the young noble claimed.

Thendarick looked at the three wide-eyed guardsmen. "Well, men, is that what happened?" Other guards began surrounding the scene, inspecting the fallen bodies of Tevins and Skelmark. Errol stood back a step or two, still holding his knife, but making no motions. He looked to the three men who a short time ago were intent on seeing him dead. He raised an eyebrow and grinned at them.

"No! It was him that paid the lieutenant and then he ordered us to help kill him!" To Errol's surprise, it was Bardmore who broke, seeming to come out of his reverie. The others quickly followed suit, as Enthessar grew quietly enraged.

"Lieutenant, I will *not* be spoken of in that fashion! I am a visiting Eastern noble and will be accorded the respect due me!"

"Sir, we just have to get everyone's statements. I'm sure it will all bear you out well enough," Thendarick said with remarkable diplomacy.

"Don't be too sure of that, Lieutenant," Errol said with a maddening grin. The noble glared at him with undisguised rage.

Shopkeepers and workers were beginning to pop out of the back doors of various shops and establishments that backed up onto the alleyway. The guards began telling them to stand back or return to their shops.

Errol stood patiently by as Thendarick took quick accounts from everyone, including a ridiculously embellished recounting of events from Enthessar. Coming back to Errol after a few minutes, he sighed as he spoke.

"I'm afraid I'll need you to come down to the hall with me, we need to put this matter before a magistrate, since there were deaths involved," Thendarick said, almost apologetically.

"I understand, Thendarick. I am perfectly willing to cooperate," Errol assured him.

"And at that point we will make sure to throw this murderer in jail, to await his *inevitable execution!*" Enthessar added, much to Thendarick's annoyance.

"Noble sir, I *myself* saw Skelmark assaulting Errol for no good reason whatsoever, nothing can change that account," Thendarick said, almost growling.

"Oh, now who is more reliable in their account, a common soldier or a member of a noble and *wealthy* family?" Enthessar said, a sneer on his lips. He looked over at Errol. "Do you always let those suspected of murder walk about armed, ready to strike again?"

In an exasperated voice, Thendarick nodded. "Fine, yes. You are correct, noble sir. Let me attend to these litters first."

The lieutenant oversaw the quick assembly of two litters for the bodies. Bardmore walked sheepishly over to Errol, his head down. "Sir, I just wanted to say, I'm terrible sorry about what happened. I don't know what came over me."

Errol was impressed by the man's attitude. He seemed truly repentant. "It's not a problem, Bardmore. I don't think you were entirely in control of the situation."

"All right. We should move along. Bardmore, collect his dagger and bring it here if you please," Thendarick called. He was carrying one end of the litter bearing the slain lieutenant.

Nodding, Bardmore looked to Errol, who smiled as he handed over his long dagger. It was entirely clean of any trace of blood. "Take that to your commanding officer."

Two other guards took up the rear, several paces behind Errol, as the whole group began moving slowly down the alleyway. They took the shortest route toward the town hall. It was there the garrison was housed and where the courts of law operated. It was also adjacent to the gaol and gallows, two places Errol sincerely hoped he would not have to visit any time soon.

He watched as Bardmore presented the dagger to Thendarick, who slipped it into his own belt.

"Without your little knife I suspect you're not much of a match," Enthessar purred from a few paces beside him. He walked slowly along with the rest of them.

"You won't try to kill me now, will you? There won't be any question about your guilt then, or the honor of your noble house. Then again, you don't seem too concerned about the honor of your house," Errol said, hoping it sounded as challenging and insulting as he intended it to be.

"That's what no one in this pathetic little border village understands," Enthessar said, smiling broadly and throwing his cloak over one shoulder. "I can do whatever I please!"

He drew forth his rapier, within easy striking distance of Errol. Errol smiled as the nobleman lunged and slashed at him with the finely crafted weapon. In a flash, Errol had his hand up, deflecting the blow easily with *his blade.*

Enthessar stared at it, the expression of shock and bewilderment hanging there for a long moment. Then he roared and moved to strike again.

Errol could honestly say the man had a good form. It was clear his training had been extensive and likely cost his father a great deal. Likewise, his rapier was of a fine quality. But Enthessar failed to realize they were at the intersection of the alleyways, where one narrow street stretched out directly behind him. And he failed to hear or see the figures approaching fast down that alleyway.

The young noble did not, however, fail to see the open expression of delight on Errol's face a moment before the head of a sturdy, white staff struck Enthessar hard on the side of his head with a resounding thump.

CHAPTER TWENTY-ONE - CANDISSA

25 Laborus, Year 197, Eastvale Calendar

Candissa woke early. She felt it was not by choice. It was as though a voice inside her awakened and she just followed suit. She thought of the strange, bizarre dream she had as she napped briefly during her bath the preceding night. But it wasn't that. It was more an awareness that she *had* to get up.

Standing and stretching, she was almost shocked when she noticed her own reflection in the dim gray blue light filtering in from the pre-dawn sky through her shutters and curtains. She was naked but looked taller than she recalled. She no longer felt a girl, a simple nobleman's daughter. That was all gone.

She had ended yesterday with training and now she felt the urgency to continue. So she did. Grasping the staff, she began a set of drills that were both familiar and entirely unfamiliar to her. She ignored that and pressed on.

The exercises helped heighten her senses and get her blood moving. She felt more limber, more able, more alive when she had the staff in her hands. As the minutes passed, her motions became more precise, more forceful, more dynamic. She knew her actions must have been causing some noise below her room.

Stopping and breathing deeply but evenly, she wondered if Lieutenant Thendarick would have been impressed if he could see her. Glancing at the mirror, she almost laughed, thinking to herself. *Well, aside from that.*

A quiet knocking at her door was followed by a hushed, "It's Lendra."

"Come in, Lendra," Candissa said, standing at ease with the tall staff of white at an angle. The governess slipped in and quietly shut the door. Glancing at her charge, she shook her head and muttered something low under her breath. She set about lighting the lamps and opening the curtains and shutters to let in more light. Fortunately, the windows gave no access for others to see into the room. Candissa smirked at her casual attitude in this; she really did not care if anyone *could* see inside.

"I'm sorry, I'll dress," Candissa said, grinning.

"No, wait, child. I need to take a measure or two while you are yet unclothed," Lendra said, much to Candissa's surprise.

"Whatever for?"

"You will see soon enough. Now, stand with arms out, and be still!"

Candissa knew better than to disobey when Lendra was in such a mood. She leaned the tall staff against her bed frame. Lendra held a length of measuring ribbon in her hands and went about making note of certain dimensions about her waist and thighs and legs.

"Goodness, girl, you are growing. I think you'll be taller than your grandmother," she said in a low voice.

"Did you know her, Lendra?" Candissa asked suddenly, realizing what the answer must be.

"Of course, I did, child. I am most honored to have known her ladyship."

"I want to learn more about her," she said, almost wistfully. "I think we are much closer than even my mother realizes."

Lendra looked at her with an odd expression. "Why on earth would you say that now, girl?"

"Do you think I'm wrong?"

"No, not at all! But why would you think to say such a thing?" Lendra looked at her with her shrewd eyes, a rare expression not often seen by Candissa.

"I'm not sure. I think the best way to describe it, and it sounds a little crazy, is that it feels there are more people inside me, than just me. It's just a feeling," Candissa said, having never voiced this to anyone before. "It does sound strange! That's it then, I'm crazy, aren't I?"

"No, child, you're not *crazy*. Far from it," Lendra said, measuring her forearm now. "It actually sounds like something your dear grandmother might have said. Though I didn't have the privilege of serving Lady Galissa when she was a young woman like yourself. I knew her when she was a proper older lady of nobility. Though she never wanted to be noble, I suspect. Rather like you!"

"Yes, I suppose so," Candissa said, looking out the window.

"Goodness, young lady! You've been growing more than muscle since your last fitting." Lendra exclaimed, trying to reach around Candissa's chest to measure her bust, while still maintaining some degree of propriety.

Candissa frowned. "I have no control over that!"

The older woman just shook her head and jotted down a few notes on a scrap of parchment using a writing stick.

"Are you going to tell me what this is all about?" Candissa asked with mock anger in her voice, after another minute of measuring.

"Just you never mind, girl! Now, go ahead and get dressed for breakfast," Lendra ordered her. "And after that, I know your mother will want to sit with you awhile."

"Is she...well this morning?" Candissa asked, concerned about the shocking revelations of last evening and what effect they may have had on her mother.

Lendra went about and laid out a proper dress for taking her morning meal in. She also gathered up a few things. She looked at Candissa. "She's stronger than you can imagine, my dear."

"That's...strange," she replied, pulling on her smock over her apparently rapidly-growing breasts. "She's always seemed so delicate."

Lendra laughed at that, heading to Candissa's chamber door.

"What's so funny?"

"Child, what you just said. Delicate! Your mother is anything but that."

"Why do you say?"

The older governess stopped at her door, regarding the tall, young woman standing there. "Candissa, she is the child of an Aevaru, and the mother of an Aevaru. She is strength embodied."

Lendra closed the door behind her, leaving the open-mouthed young woman standing there. She frowned, gritting her teeth.

"I am the only one in my life who does not know what I am!" she nearly shouted to no one.

Breakfast was served in the second hall, and she sat near the head of the table, next to her father. Her sisters all sat further down the table in their appropriate seats. Her father simply nodded and smiled at her as she sat.

Breakfast consisted of wedges of fruit, heavy cream on cooked grains, warm brown breads, butter, honey, and poached eggs of wild birds. Brenissa sat next to Candissa and eyed her older sister with an almost open contempt. As she began eating, her father still silent, Brenissa couldn't restrain herself.

"We all heard about that ridiculous show you put on last night in front of dear Lord Enthessar!" she exclaimed. "I am so embarrassed that my eldest sister would so dishonor our house!"

Candissa's gaze was withering. Her father cleared his throat after swallowing a mouthful of eggs and bread. "Brenny, you should really hold your tongue until you understand what's happened."

"I know what has happened! Candissa has ruined any hope our house has of allying with a noble house of the east. This will affect all of us," she cried, motioning to her younger sisters, Nalliath and Elena. Nalliath sat in shocked silence, wide eyed, a bit of fruit on her chin. Elena was looking at Brenissa with an expression of exasperation.

"Nalliath, pass the cream, please," Candissa said, blatantly ignoring her sister's angry outburst.

"Is that all you care about now, eating?" Brenissa nearly stood up as Candissa poured the cream over her cooked grains.

"I need to eat, I need the energy it provides," was all her eldest sister said in reply.

"Do you not care for our fortunes? Our futures?" Brenissa cried, nearly in tears at her Candissa's apparent ambivalence toward their situation.

Candissa looked to her father. "Father, I hope you know that whatever I do, I would never intend any discredit or dishonor on our family or your name."

"There is no shame in what you have done, or whatever you must do, my daughter," her father said, patting her hand.

"Would either of you care to explain why no one in answering me? Do either of you care that my world is falling down around me?" Brenissa almost screamed, pounding the table with her fists. She stood with that, and stormed out of the dining hall, sobbing quietly to herself.

Candissa looked at her as she fled. Even as she ate another spoonful of grain and cream, she was worried. Nalliath wasn't sure what to do apparently, so she followed Candissa's example and continued eating, as did Elena.

"Should I speak to her, Father?"

"I don't know what either of us can say to her at this point, Deesa," he said, shaking his head. "I knew a day would come, such as this, and it would be very difficult for all of us."

"Father, can you explain what's going on?" Elena asked. "It seems like something is going to happen, something that will affect all of us."

Her words caught Candissa's attention, in the manner she phrased them.

"What do you mean, *all of us*?" she asked her younger sister. "Do you mean our family?"

Elena hesitated. "I thought I did at first, but I'm not sure now...I feel as if it could affect more than just us."

"Why would you think Candissa's behavior would affect anyone outside of our house?" her father asked.

"I... I really don't know, Father. It's just something I feel," Elena said, seeming to struggle with her answer.

Candissa looked back to her father, concern written in her expression. "I must speak to mother. Perhaps this affects more than just me?"

Lord Demarrae looked at his daughters, one by one. He nodded slowly. "I suspect it will. She is waiting for you."

Candissa stood. As she passed Elena, her youngest sister at just thirteen, she put a firm hand on her shoulder, looking at Nalliath as well. "Be strong, both of you."

She moved quickly through the household. She ignored the eyes of some servants who regarded her with wariness, curiosity or pity. There were various versions of events being whispered among the staff, regarding what had happened over the past day. Taking the steps two at a time in a decidedly unladylike fashion, she was soon before her mother's chambers. Aldrys, her lady-in-waiting, looked at Candissa with open concern.

"She's in the old library, awaiting you," was all she said before returning to her duties.

The old library wasn't really their family's old library. Her father had come to Ravensroost when Candissa was only just born, so this estate had not long been in her family's keeping. It had belonged to another family of some nobility, who had withered away apparently, leaving no heirs. As the house was available for lease when her father's baking shops began prospering, he took it.

The library was not often used, reserved for her parents alone, not unlike her father's study. Her father was never known to spend much time in the small round chamber, with shelves lining two levels.

Entering, Candissa found the room to be charming in the light of the morning. There was a domed window high overhead that let in the sunlight at various angles during the day, though it was only striking the uppermost shelves now. There was a tenuous walkway of worked iron, accessed from below by a winding staircase of similar design.

She studied the walls in the morning light. She had been in this room before, but not often, and usually in the evening, by lamplight. For the first time in her life, she realized the walls of this small tower were made of the same material as the central portion of the Bonerest, as well as some parts of the town's walls. The floor was not, being comprised of masterfully inlaid pavers of fine stone. They were of subtle color and variation, mortared together seamlessly and polished to a dull gleam.

Save for the center of the room. A simple circle of red stone lay at the center, with an almost coarse surface. It was entirely out of place, next to the polished pavers. It was perhaps ten feet across, most of it covered by a finely stitched round rug, embroidered with symbols around the edge.

The shelves throughout the tower were not nearly full, particularly the upper ones. But some shelves below were well-stocked with various tomes and books, including some scrolls bound by ribbons or contained in old, cracked leather cases. Her mother sat in one of a few chairs in the room. It was the most comfortable of them, with embroidered cushions, and sat on the edge of the round circle at the center of the chamber.

She was reading a tall book, bound in a dark blue cloth, with pages yellowed with age. As Candissa entered and quietly closed the door behind her, she did not look up at her. Stepping closer, Candissa saw the book was written in the finely wrought runes of the Elves.

"Good morning, mother," she said.

"You read Elven fairly well, don't you my dear?"

"Yes, Master Calurevar schooled me when I was younger, and sometimes Master Evan helps me with my speech," she said.

"You will need to take some of these books, though I do not wish to burden you on your journey," her mother said, motioning to two stacks of books on a nearby table. "I don't know how long you may be gone or how much occasion you may have to read. You would be well served to study them. I believe they will be of use. My mother suggested I have some books ready for you to take, when it was time."

"She knew I was to go on a journey?" Candissa asked, suddenly excited at the prospect of learning more of her grandmother.

"Oh, yes, she knew full well. She had thought - hoped, I think - that *she* was to go on your journey. But alas, it was not to be."

"Why not?"

"Sit child," her mother said, nodding to a smaller chair across from her, as she put down the blue book. "As she put it to me late in her life, on one of the many occasions we spoke of what your life may entail, she said 'the pieces were not in play'."

"What do you think that meant?"

"She didn't have all the knowledge she needed to really understand what was to happen, and why it didn't happen in her time. But she did have some insights, as is the case with Aevaru."

Candissa desperately wanted to press her mother on that point, that term, to find out all she knew of Aevaru. Her mother saw the expression on her daughter's face and held up a hand, then continued.

"She told me she was awaiting the arrival of certain friends, more than friends, whom she had never met. As it happens, they never arrived. It was not the time, or so she concluded."

Candissa naturally thought of her new friends, as well as Errol. Her mother nodded.

"Yes, Errol is one of them, I'm certain. As are these two new friends of yours, Cam Bronwyer and Koraymis Sleeth, I believe they're named?"

Candissa nodded.

"And the last of them?"

"What do you mean?"

"My mother was certain of few things, but on this point, she had no doubt. She could not embark on her - *your* - journey until she had four allies at her side. You must find the fifth and last member of your group."

Candissa nodded slowly, looking at her hands in her lap. "We have actually spoken of that need."

"Really?" Her mother seemed mildly astonished. "Then events must be moving forward quickly."

"What events?"

She handed Candissa the tall, narrow blue-bound book. "She left an account that would help you understand, at least as far as she could understand events and signs. She spoke of a purpose, a reason to journey west. It could be called a destiny of sorts, I suppose. Though she was loath to use that term."

"I'm not sure what a destiny would entail, but if we are involved in such a thing - even if it exists - it would explain some things of late."

Her mother laughed merrily. Candissa could not get over the appearance of her mother over the past day. It was as though she had been transformed from a doting, almost silly noble mother into something else entirely. "You speak with my mother's voice, Candissa. It makes me feel...younger I suppose is the word I'm looking for. Foolish, isn't it?"

Candissa shook her head. "Not at all. Everything is changing," she said, looking around the room, thinking. "Something else was bothering me last night, mother. I meant to ask you but there was too much going on."

"Yes, my dear?"

"You said my grandmother was more than three hundred years old when she finally died," Candissa said, her eyebrows knitting together. "That would place her here well before the Kingdom was established, before written history."

"Yes, she was," her mother nodded, smiling. Her eyes seemed to mist over. "She spoke of that time often, when I was very young, of the wild adventures. Apparently, though she never revealed any details, she had a hand in the formation of the first Kingdom. She was friends with the first King, Marvachus. I believe some of those accounts are in the books here, and her journal."

"That's incredible," Candissa breathed. She looked at the stacks of books. "What else should I know? What can you tell me, or is it found in these books?"

Her mother took a deep breath. "Some of what you need to know is here, yes. Other books here may have helpful lore for your journey. For myself, I can only hope what wisdom I've imparted so far in your life will prove sufficient. Your training at the temple is equally vital, your healing powers will only grow. You may find them surpassing what you think you know, for that is the way of Aevaru."

"I am planning on seeing Mother Meshana today, to talk of my training."

"She is expecting you, I have no doubt. Your arts will be important on your journey west, and beyond."

"Does she know? About me, I mean?"

"We did not reveal anything about your heritage, but I have long suspected she knows something is special about you," her mother said. Her brows knitted, and she put a knuckle to her lips. "If only there was more time."

"We will be meeting here today. I think we'll be leaving soon, likely within a few days. Do you think we're being hasty?"

"Oh, no, not at all," her mother turned back to her, eyebrows raised. "Too much has happened. This matter of Lord Enthessar is part of it, you see. Some people here, in the Kingdom, will try to prevent you from taking even the first step on this journey west."

"Truly? Are we in danger?"

"You may well be. I fear Enthessar is one of those intent on stopping you. He may not even know it. But it led him to this confrontation with your friend, and now he means to kill Errol. Or so I suspect."

"As do I. What is to be done? What should I do now? Please, give me counsel!" Candissa said, imploring her mother.

Her mother took both her hands in hers and bent close to Candissa. "You are far wiser than you give yourself credit for. I cannot say what is to be done next. That is for you to decide."

Candissa stood. A resolve began to coalesce in her mind. She had to decide.

"But know this, my daughter, we - our family, our house - is yours, and at your disposal. Whatever we can do or provide, it is yours for the asking."

"But mother, what of my sisters? At breakfast this morning, Nalliath was beside herself," Candissa said, recalling her sister's frustration, some of it quite justified. "But Elena, well, she seemed rather different."

"I will speak to them," her mother said, standing now herself. "They will also endure changes, for they are not like other foolish noble daughters, though I seem to have raised them as such."

"I would not call any of us foolish, mother," Candissa said, grinning as she chided her mother.

"Perhaps not, but as I told you last night, I am Seludecian, as are your sisters. It means they will live longer lives than anyone they know. And, depending on what happens, their lives could be...different from anything they could imagine."

"I should visit the temple now," Candissa said, despite the urge she felt to stay at her mother's side and learn as much as she could.

Her mother nodded firmly. "Yes, go. But you must return here soon, Lendra is working on traveling clothes. They must be fitted appropriately. There's no telling how soon you will have to leave."

"That's why she was taking measurements. All right, to the temple, then back here. Hopefully my friends will be coming here soon. If they don't then I *must* find them."

"I'll have these books put into traveling bags, including this one of your grandmother's. You can use one of the rear halls to ready yourselves. We are preparing other supplies and needs for your journey," her mother said. "Give my kindest regards to the good Mother."

Candissa nodded, turning to exit the old library. Then she looked at her mother, standing tall and proud, more alive than she ever knew her to be. Candissa almost lunged at her as she embraced her fiercely. She returned the embrace with an unexpected strength.

"I love you, mother," Candissa whispered, her cheeks wet suddenly.

Then she was off. Nearing her chambers, she sighed loudly to herself, annoyed that she had to bow to the custom of appropriate dress. She ducked into her room and tore through her wardrobe, settling on a passable day dress. Donning it hastily, she did little to properly prepare herself. She must have appeared a fright, and she hoped Lendra would not see her prior to her leaving the house.

Looking in the mirror, she was at least thankful her hair didn't need attention. Then again, it never really needed any special effort. Smoothing the creases in the dress as she stood there, she frowned. She looked fine.

Almost without thinking about it, she found the staff in her hand as she left her chambers. Taking the back stairwell, she was on the streets of Ravensroost quickly. The temple of Arushana was several streets away from their manor house. She crossed the distance easily, with long, loping strides. The streets were filling quickly. Though it was a crisp, cold early winter morning, the bright sun and clear sky called everyone to markets.

The temple was one of several in Ravensroost. Most were devoted to one of the commonly worshipped deities. Chief among them, or nearly so, was Arushana. She was called The Eternal Lady of the Shield and the Word. Her priests and priestesses were devoted to the martial disciplines of sword and shield and the study of written works. Lesser known by most was the faithful's unending quest for knowledge and lore.

There were also noted healers among her ranks. It was said when the Kingdom was founded more than two centuries ago, the chief priest in the company of the first king was the leader of Arushana's following. Candissa was a devoted disciple to the teachings of the church. She had benefited greatly from the works available within the study chambers of the temple.

But she had never felt the true calling of a priestess, to make it her one vocation. She could heal, she knew that. She never suffered a cut or bruise or scrape that she didn't mend or cure almost at once. She had even healed a few serious cuts that she had inflicted on poor Thendarick, during her first days of training with an axe.

As she entered the tall doors of the church, one of the acolytes nodded to her respectfully. Candissa had a flash of insight. In the many years she had been instructed under the kind and patient tutelage of Mother Meshana, the chief cleric in the matters of healing and education, she had never been asked to choose a branch of the church.

By the age of twelve, any disciple, boy or girl, would be asked to choose a path - one of study and reflection, one of the healing arts, or one emphasizing the practice and skill in arms.

But this question, this choice, had never been asked of Candissa. She sometimes felt a resentment from the other students and she now realized that was likely why. She had thought perhaps it was because of her noble status that she was receiving special attention and being excused from making a choice.

With all she had learned over the past day, perhaps there were other reasons entirely.

She found Mother Meshana in a quiet reflecting chamber, sitting on the edge of a still pool of blessed water. Students and masters alike came here to calm their spirit, relax their minds, or to seek guidance.

She was an older woman, with almost stringy gray hair, gathered in simple braids this morning. She turned as Candissa approached and smiled.

"Good morning to you, Mother Meshana," Candissa said warmly. She saw tears in her mentor's eyes. "What is it?" She sat down quickly on the edge of the small pool. Meshana put a hand to the young woman's cheek.

"You're leaving us soon, it saddens me," she said. "But you are ready. I'm certain."

"Mother said you knew. Perhaps you always knew."

"I've always known you were unlike anyone the church has ever seen," Meshana said, dropping her hand to touch the surface of the pool. Her green eyes followed the expanding ripples. "At least, anyone in this age."

"This age?" Candissa asked, curious at the term she used.

"We have so little lore to offer you, child, works that go back only two centuries or so, as you well know."

"Of course. That was the beginning of the Kingdom."

"But there's more, so much more, before our little Kingdom came to be. Surely you have realized that by now."

"Yes, I have. But why do we know nothing of the times past? The past ages, is that what you call them?"

"Yes, there have been many. No one knows how many. So little is really known about what lies beyond our borders," Meshana said. "What you are doing is remarkable. You're embarking on what was once called a great adventure!"

"I thought those were tales told to children," Candissa smiled.

"Yes, they are. That is the point. We are taught they are just foolish, childish things, not to be considered by a grown man or woman. We have all been taught certain rules about the world, from a young age."

"*Everyone knows*," Candissa murmured, recalling the recurring response to a child's question. "You don't think about what may lie beyond the mountains or the woods, and most certainly not the hills!"

"But you are not here to talk of fables and facts," Meshana said, her knees cracking as she rose slowly. "You are here to ask me if there is any more training I can give you, any advice, anything for your journey."

"Yes, Mother. It's clear I must go, and I have no idea where my friends and I will be going, and not even a vague idea of *why* we must go. I am more interested in the *why*."

Mother Meshana walked out of the reflection chamber and led Candissa toward her private chamber, off the main temple sanctuary.

"I truly wish I could impart such wisdom, child, to tell you some secret lore that would serve to guide you," she said, shaking her head slowly as she sat in a chair, before a long table laden with sheaves of papers, books, and bound scrolls. "But alas. Such truly ancient lore is denied us."

"Denied?"

"Perhaps," she said, rummaging around her papers and curios. She found what she sought, a simple iron key. "Here it is. Follow me now."

She led Candissa down a corridor toward the supply rooms of the temple, then down a narrow stairwell into the cellars. Candissa had never been here before, thinking it reserved to servants and workers, for storing and fetching goods.

Meshana led her deep under the main sanctuary, to a dusty, poorly lit corridor. Cobwebs, or spiderwebs - she could not be sure which - brushed her face in the darkness.

"Curse my old bones for forgetting a lantern, we can't go on without light," she muttered, turning around.

The word rolled around Candissa's head, *light*. She stood there in the dark passage, Mother Meshana waiting for her to turn about and go back toward the stairwell. "Child? Move along, I can barely see you and that grand walking stick of yours in this light."

Light. It was more than just a thought, or a memory. *Light. Light!*

"Oh," Candissa said, as if she had just realized the simplicity of it. "Light."

With that word, the staff glowed, as if lit by bright sunlight. From where it touched the floor of the passage, light flowed up and down the corridor, a radiance flooding the entire length of it.

Meshana drew in a breath of wonder. She looked back at Candissa, and her staff. "Truly, you are meant to find the answers."

"I... I've never done that before," Candissa said.

"Child, I suspect it is the first of many...such events. Come." She moved down the now well-illuminated corridor to an unremarkable and locked door. The key she had found upstairs unlocked it, and she had to push hard to force the scraping, squeaking door open.

"This temple is one of the oldest structures in Ravensroost, and I suspect one of the oldest in all the Kingdom," she said, entering the dark chamber slowly. "There's a lamp here in the middle I think."

Entering behind her, Candissa tried again. Touching the staff to the floor, she thought and then said "Light." Sure enough, her word achieved the same result. The chamber's floor was quickly bathed in a light whose source was not apparent.

The chamber was large and square, perhaps fifty feet long and wide. There were a few odd boxes stored here, along with a table bearing a lamp. Along two walls were barren shelves.

Meshana turned to Candissa, smiling in a somewhat patronizing manner. "A word of wise counsel. You may want to be careful about the wanton use of magic, child."

"Of course. Forgive me, Mother." Candissa had learned throughout her training that people, for the most part, do not like to see magic displayed, and most did not trust it.

Meshana waved away the younger woman's apology.

"Now, look at these shelves against this wall," she said, leading Candissa over to one wall. The shelves were built from a heavy, dark, almost black wood. She realized suddenly they were built of ebony, that strange black wood that Errol pointed out in the surface of the wooden bar, back in the Bonerest.

"This temple was first claimed by the faithful of Arushana during the founding days of the village of Ravensroost, more than a hundred years ago. Those of Arushana did not build this place. They found it much as you see it, though it was just a ruin. This building predates the founding of the town and the Kingdom of Eastvale. The room before you was found only recently, and it has remained untouched since its discovery."

"But the door looks like any other in line with others in the corridor," Candissa pointed out.

"Yes, but if you examined the entryway, you'd see the evidence of a false wall. You see, there was just a storage closet there, for as long as anyone could recall. A worker tried shutting the door after stuffing the closet too full. He pushed through the wall unintentionally. That was just four years ago."

"Curious," Candissa breathed, looking around at the huge chamber. It was quite tall, the ceiling being more than three yards above the floor. The shelves that lined the full length of two walls appeared to be bookcases with four shelves, being about twelve feet long or a little more. She counted four of them on each wall. Examining them more closely now, she found them in poor condition.

"You didn't do much to clean up it appears. Didn't you ever want to use these for something?"

"That's the mystery, child, look at each shelf, what do you see?" Meshana said, her eyes glinting with a bit of excitement.

Candissa looked closer, but the light her staff had called was not enough to illuminate the shelves. Meshana brought the lamp over, having lit it. "Here, look more closely."

Holding it up, she found nothing remarkable. Just a thick layer of dust on each shelf. She touched it. It wasn't just a heavy layer, it was more than an inch thick toward the back of the shelves. And it was all perfectly even in its distribution.

She rubbed her fingers together. It didn't feel like dust. She smelled it carefully.

"Well?" Meshana pressed her.

"Is this...ground paper?"

The elder healer snapped her bony fingers. "You see? There! It's the same on each shelf, on both walls. It varies only a bit in the color and consistency, but it's all the same."

"What does it mean?" Candissa asked, not seeing the connection yet.

"These shelves were untouched since well before the founding of the Kingdom. The faith of Arushana puts a high value on learning, on the written word, on *books*."

Candissa's eyes went wide. "These...were books?"

"That is exactly what we suspect! Something long ago reduced these all to dust somehow. This is the crushed remains of what they once were. Thousands of books!"

"Why would anyone want to destroy so much knowledge?"

"We have not a clue on that question, but it has occupied our minds since we made this discovery and arrived at our conclusions," Meshana said, looking down the long, empty shelves. "But I truly hope your journey can shed some light on what happened."

"So much lore…" Candissa sighed. Tears came to her eyes suddenly and she had no idea why. "So... much lost!" She closed her eyes tight, and panic gripped her. She took a step forward, eyes snapping open.

"Child, what is wrong?" Meshana said, seeing the young woman suddenly distraught.

She blinked back her tears. "I'm sorry, I don't know why I did that, I...it was nothing. I thought I was somewhere else for a moment. It's just so overwhelming, imagining all the knowledge lost."

The old woman patted her arm. "It's nothing you can change, I'm afraid. I just wanted to show you this, so you'd understand that there was once so much more. I only hope that out there you may find some knowledge or perhaps even books, from the lost past."

As she conducted Candissa back upstairs, Candissa noticed the light in the corridor fading gently. They were soon in one of the temple storerooms, where they kept their ritual items and robes.

"Here, before you leave, I want you to have these. We, the masters of the temple, collected them from our stores, for your journey," she told Candissa, as she retrieved a box from a table in the back of the chamber. She presented it to her.

"How many people in Ravensroost knew I was to journey west before I found this out?" she asked Meshana, exasperation clear in her voice. She didn't really expect an answer and received only a slight shrug in reply.

"Only a very few, and only those close to you. We all knew that one day you would make a journey. We thought it would be a simple journey of self-discovery, something small. Clearly it will be something more," Meshana said. For a moment, the older woman's eyes misted over. She avoided looking at Candissa.

Candissa opened the box. It was an exceptionally well-constructed wooden box, requiring the metal latch to be pushed from two sides to open it. Within, there were several small glass vials. Each vial was heavy, with a heavy base and a cork cap sealed with wax.

"What are they?" she asked, picking one up.

"You'll find a simple runic symbol on the bottom of each. They are simple salves and elixirs, balms and curatives against wounds, diseases and such. They are potent, so be sparing."

Candissa realized it was a remarkable gift for a novitiate such as herself.

"I don't know how to thank you for this. These may save our lives," Candissa felt the emotion rising in her voice. "How can I repay the temple for such gifts?"

"By doing whatever it is you were born to do, child," Meshana said. "Come, we must say our goodbyes for now, though I hope you can come by again before you and your friends must depart."

"I certainly hope our departing won't be so hasty," Candissa said. "You must have a room full of acolytes awaiting you."

They returned to her own study, where Meshana donned her instructional robes. She had some momentary difficulty with one of the sleeves, and Candissa helped her. Her old hand suddenly grasped Candissa's.

"I cannot bear keeping anything from you, child," she suddenly said, tears in her reddened eyes.

"What is the matter?" Candissa said, sinking with her to sit on a bench.

"We, myself and the other elders of the church, have recently been praying for guidance regarding you," she began. "We knew you would be making this journey. Some of us saw things, warnings perhaps, small auguries. The other elders thought it unwise to say anything, unless we were all of one mind on the matter. But I feel I must."

"You can tell me anything, I'm not afraid," Candissa assured her.

"I know, my child, you are possessed of courage beyond your knowing. But know this," she said, her kind eyes becoming almost unnerving in their intensity. "There is a... spirit perhaps, no, more an awareness, that is here."

"What do you mean?"

"It works against you, my child, you and your friends I fear," Meshana said, her voice low, almost as if to avoid being overheard. "It is affecting people, in varying degrees. Those people you will find opposed to you. I wanted you to know this, before you left."

Candissa wasn't sure what to make of her warning, dire as it seemed. She just hugged the elder healer suddenly, a fierce hug given in return. Meshana whispered in Candissa's ear, "Sides are being chosen."

Sitting back once more, Candissa considered all her words, especially the last. She nodded solemnly, finding no words to speak in reply. Meshana smiled, stood again and smoothed her robes.

"My mother sends her warmest regards. I'm sure you'll see her, no matter where I may be," Candissa said as she stood.

"Of course. Now, off with you, I just wiped my eyes. I don't want to face my students with fresh tears!"

Meshana shooed Candissa out of her study and she was soon outside the main doors of the temple. The morning was getting on, and she felt the need to find her friends. Yet she had promised her mother she would return after the temple.

Wasting no time, she strode quickly home. She didn't know if she was simply noticing more people staring, or that more people were staring at her now than before. It was a bit windy as the sun climbed this morning, and her hair was not done up in any fashion. Perhaps that was catching their attention. But she couldn't deny her feelings about who was watching her and why, given the new warning Mother Meshana had relayed.

She was back at House Demarrae within a few minutes. There was no word of any of her friends having arrived. She was concerned, but chided herself. Her concern was likely misplaced. They had tasks to go about, and they hadn't set a time to meet. She would go out and find them eventually.

She found Lendra and another servant girl, a seamstress named Ilmera, were awaiting her in her chambers.

"How long will this take? I would like to find my friends," Candissa asked.

"This sort of thing shouldn't be rushed, my dear," Lendra said, immediately helping Candissa out of her morning clothing, with Ilmera assisting. She was standing before them both, stark naked, in short order. Lendra sorted through the stack of clothing articles laid out on the bed. Ilmera seemed a bit ill at ease at the sight of the much taller and strikingly beautiful young woman.

Candissa wondered if she should exercise more discretion, never having felt the need for modesty. She understood the need for propriety, but in her own home she never felt uncomfortable if she was seen wearing less than was suitable for a young lady of her station.

"Now, on with this first," Lendra said, handing Candissa something she had never seen before. "It's an undergarment, sort of a loincloth but I think it's called a *bracca* or something like that."

Candissa looked at it dubiously. It seemed too small. Shrugging, she slipped on the white linen bracca and immediately liked it. It was unlike any undergarment she had ever known a young woman, low or noble, to wear, as it fit her so closely.

That was followed by a close-fitting smock, more of an under shirt of white linen. Looking at herself in the mirror, she was almost shocked into feeling modesty. "Where did you get these? Did you come up with them yourself?"

"By the gods, no, girl! These were made following the patterns and clothing left by your grandmother," she said.

"She wore such things?" Candissa breathed.

"Apparently, it was vital to allow her to move and such. I suppose if you carry that staff about with you, you can't be hampered with wearing a skirt or shift."

Next came white leggings, equally surprising in that no noble woman would be expected to wear them. They all fit perfectly. Then came a most peculiar coat. With short sleeves and a short collar, it wrapped about her torso and waist, fastening with a sort of buckle she had never seen before. Fortunately, it was low enough that it formed a sort of skirt, over her thighs. Still, her knees were in evidence, which would be sure to raise some eyebrows, despite the leggings.

"Now, I can only hope these fit, we can't alter them in any way," Lendra said, producing from beside the bed a pair of tall white leather boots, adorned with many buckles and straps. They appeared to be in nearly immaculate condition.

"Were these...my grandmother's?" she asked, eyes wide.

"Yes. I know, they're in exceptional condition," Lendra said, shaking her head. "Better than any leather should be. I can't imagine how old they are."

Candissa sat and began working on the boots. "How old do you think?"

Lendra looked at her assistant. "Mera, go fetch me my tea. I think it's in the upstairs kitchen."

The girl nodded, looking a little wide-eyed as she left. Candissa suspected the girl knew she was simply being dismissed momentarily. Lendra leaned in closer to Candissa after the door shut.

"More than two hundred years, my lady."

That seemed impossible, as far as Candissa understood leather. She was not well-read on the subject of leather working. Still, she knew her father's boots, forty years old at most, were already showing cracks along the edging.

After that came a broad girdle, or belt, as Candissa wasn't sure what to call it. Fashioned from the same white leather, it felt almost sculpted to her waist, curving down at the middle, buckling with another curious metal device. The girdle bore small pouches on either side, and loops for holding she knew not what.

"What are these buckles? I've never seen them before."

"Your grandmother never mentioned, to my recollection, but it must come from a lost craft," she said. With Ilmera's help, she quickly measured and apprised the fit to this point, finding it to her satisfaction. "How does it feel so far, Deesa?"

"Marvelous," Candissa said, turning to look at herself in the tall mirror. She turned and twisted at the waist. "As if it were tailored to me."

"Hold your hands out," Lendra said. Doing so, her governess held out a pair of leather bracers. They slipped over her hands easily and were fastened and tightened with some small, cleverly fashioned hooks. They were, as with all the other items, white. "Here's the gloves that go with them, they feel like white doeskin, see if they fit."

Candissa slipped on the finely made, and remarkably supple, leather gloves. Perfect. She smelled one. It could have been newly purchased.

"I don't understand, surely these are new."

Lendra simply shook her head, picking up one more item. The girl, Ilmera, returned with Lendra's tea, putting it down as she assisted the governess.

It was a cape, of slightly darker material, more of a light gray canvas, yet not canvas. Stepping behind Candissa, she and Ilmera draped it over her back, then attached it to loops of leather sewn into her coat. She then found small straps that attached the coat to her girdle. That secured the cloak firmly.

Candissa turned, letting it whirl gently around her ankles. It had a leather hem, and she thought she could make out small inscriptions on the white leather. There was a hood attached to the cape that hung behind her. Jumping up and down a bit, she felt it all sort of settle into place, the cloak snugly wrapping around her shoulders as it hung, and her wrap-coat tightening a little under the pull of its weight.

Examining herself in the mirror, she raised one eyebrow.

"Oh my," Lendra said. Even the girl Ilmera was wide-eyed. The entire ensemble was quite impressive in appearance, and fit Candissa as though she were born to it. "I confess, my lady, I was expecting to make quite a few alterations after we fitted you, but very few are needed! Still, perhaps the sleeves could be brought up a touch, and the leggings seem a bit loose."

"This is amazing. My grandmother wore something like this?"

"Almost exactly. Did you see her portrait?"

"Of course," Candissa said quietly, recalling the aged painting. It was the same clothing she wore now. "Do you know, did she wear this just for travel?"

"I don't know, but I don't think so. I think this...ensemble of clothing was important to her," Lendra said, thinking back, her eyes distant. "It meant something."

Candissa picked up her staff from where it was leaning. "Step back," she said simply, and the two others moved instantly.

"Girl! What are you doing?" Lendra said in alarm, pushing the smaller Ilmera toward the door.

Candissa gripped the staff in both hands and executed a few maneuvers that were part of her drills, swinging the staff around in a wide circle, bringing her leg up and around in a sweeping and kicking motion, and lunging, legs wide.

Her two attendants were thoroughly shocked by her actions, but it felt perfect.

"It doesn't interfere at all!" Candissa cried. "It feels made for this. I wonder if she fought in this?"

"You'll think of doing no such thing, young lady!" Lendra nearly shrieked.

Candissa flashed her a wicked grin.

Her grin faded.

"Koraymis?" she said aloud.

"Who is Koraymis? That friend of yours?" Lendra asked.

Candissa's eyes went wide, gripping her staff hard now.

Errol is in danger!

"I must go!" she said, her voice commanding.

"In this? My lady, you cannot! This is meant for your travels, not running about town!" Lendra protested. "I still have to make several alterations!"

"Lendra! I must find my friends, one of them is in trouble," she said calmly, moving past the older woman decisively, pushing her by the shoulder gently. "Let my father know there is trouble."

Bounding down the corridor and gliding down the steps quickly, she felt the cloak billowing behind her. The servants and staff nearly jumped back, one of them dropping a tray, at the sight of her.

Outside, she ran, yelling to the gate guards. "Open!" They scrambled to open the gates in time as she ran through. Somehow, she had a sense of where she had to go. The morning townsfolk and market patrons, coming or going, openly gawked at her as she passed, all white with her cloak undulating like a gray banner behind her. Not two corners later, she nearly ran into one of the town guards, running in her direction. She recognized him as one of the guards always in the squad led by Thendarick.

"Lady Candissa! Oh good!" he exclaimed. "Lieutenant Thendarick sent me to fetch you." He suddenly realized she was wearing something quite revealing, and his eyes went a bit wide as he tried not to look up and down her form.

"There's trouble, isn't there?"

"Yes, m'lady, he said to tell you he thinks your friend may be in danger."

"Errol, yes, I thought so. You know where they are?" she asked with some impatience.

"Yes," he said, still gawking at her.

"Then lead on, boy!" she shouted, holding the staff at the ready, to run. She almost laughed at herself as the young guard turned and nearly ran as he led her toward the center of town. She had no right to call him boy, as he was likely a few years her senior. She was of low noble birth, however, and he wouldn't take offense.

As they moved toward the center of Ravensroost, and more markets and shops, the traffic became more troublesome. Their progress was stymied more than once, as much by the traffic as by people stopping and staring opening at her.

"Move aside!" she found herself shouting, and to her delight, the townsfolk jumped nimbly aside at her command. After a few more shouted warnings, the guard led them into a long alleyway.

Candissa could sense it was just up ahead. She could feel Errol. But somehow, the sense of danger had subsided. Still, she knew she had to join him quickly.

"I think the lieutenant is up here," the guard said breathily.

They approached an intersection. There were at least a dozen guards there, walking slowly down another alleyway, with no real commotion apparently. But as they slowed their pace, to Candissa's amazement, there was Lord Enthessar, walking next to Errol, his back to her.

He drew his rapier with a remarkable quickness and attacked Errol. Her friend easily deflected his blow with his blade, looking at ease in doing so.

Without thinking she lunged forward, moving rapidly, smoothly, staff whirling.

Enthessar moved on Errol in another attempt to slash him with his rapier. Out of the corner of her eye she saw Errol grinning broadly as she brought the stout staff around, striking Enthessar's head. She did so following the training Thendarick had given her, careful to avoid striking the temple, which could have easily killed him.

He went down in an undignified heap.

"Hello, Candissa!" Errol said loudly, sheathing his dagger. "Oh, and here comes Koraymis and Cam!"

CHAPTER TWENTY-TWO - CAM

25 Laborus, Year 197, Eastvale Calendar

Cam and Koraymis slowed their pace as they assessed the scene. A guard was already kneeling beside the fallen Enthessar, examining him. "He'll be fine, just got a hard knock," the man reported to his superior.

Cam murmured to Koraymis, "And here I thought they would need our help."

Koraymis just shrugged.

"Candissa! You may have just saved your friend's life," Thendarick said, as he bent over the unconscious nobleman.

"No, I saved Enthessar's," she said, trying not to grin. Cam noted the smirk on Errol's lips.

The lieutenant looked at Cam and Koraymis. "Your friends, I see. Why are you here?"

Cam thought a moment before answering. He was not yet accustomed to this strange new connection he had with his three friends. It was only a few minutes ago when he had heard Koraymis' call and began making his way hurriedly toward where he knew not.

Fortunately, he had intercepted the scholar as he was rushing this way. The black-robed young man was unerring in his route here, somehow.

"We -" Cam began, but to his surprise, Errol interrupted.

"I had agreed to meet them nearby. They simply happened by at a fortuitous moment."

"And they likely saw me running along with the good guardsman here, and hurried to catch up," Candissa added. She looked at the fellow. "I'm sorry, I don't even know your name."

"Oh! Beg your pardon, my lady. Sergeant Romellor, at your service!" the guard answered, clearly grateful to have the attention of the beautiful young noblewoman.

"Lady, could I beseech you to examine Enthessar," Thendarick said, somewhat apologetically. "I know you don't feel too kindly toward the man, but you are a skilled healer, or so I'm told."

She smiled. "Of course." She put a hand to the man's head. He was bleeding a bit from where she had struck him. A guard was preparing a bandage to wrap about his head. She took it and applied it to him, touching his hair.

Cam saw her eyes close briefly. She dabbed at his hair, wiping away the blood. No more was forthcoming.

"He'll be just fine. May be out for a short while. Perhaps another litter?" she suggested, looking at the two others. Her eyes widened as she stood.

"Errol…" was all she said.

"They attacked him without provocation," Thendarick said. "These others will give testimony. They were sent to kill him apparently."

"By Enthessar?" Cam asked.

Candissa nodded. "Of course."

"You'll be taking Errol to make a statement I suppose?" Cam asked the officer.

"Yes, I must," he said, then turned to Errol. "After I disarm him for a *second* time."

Errol looked at him with feigned innocence. "Oh, yes, here you are." He drew out and handed over his blade, hilt first.

"Second time?" Koraymis queried.

Errol shook his head at the young scholar.

"Would it be acceptable if we accompanied you to the hall?" Candissa asked. "He is our friend and frankly I'm concerned he could be attacked again. We don't know the extent of House Allenfar's associations in Ravensroost."

"I would appreciate you joining us, my lady. You are part of this now, as you thumped him with your staff. You'll need to make a statement as well. As for the noble House Allenfar, they are wearing out their welcome in my opinion," Thendarick ventured. "Let's move."

Cam joined the others as a dozen or more guards, carrying the three litters, escorted Errol, moving quickly down one street then another. They were soon nearing a tall building at the center of Ravensroost. Cam had overheard it being called the town hall, council hall, or center hall. Woodford had something like it, though larger. It housed the courts, magistrates, town records, officials and administrative offices. This one was adjacent to the town gaol and across the street from the garrison barracks.

As they moved, Cam noticed all eyes were on them along the busy street. The sight of two slain bodies and a third wounded caused a steady stream of gasps, cries, mutterings and exclamations. It was only heightened by the accompanying quartet of curious figures. Errol was apparently well known, but the Cam and Koraymis added to the intrigue.

More guards joined their party, to keep back curious onlookers.

Candissa clearly caused more than her share of astonished remarks that even Cam could hear in passing. He hadn't said anything, but her garb was a little off from what he had seen her wear previously. It looked remarkably practical but was nonetheless scandalous.

As they marched through the streets, buyers and sellers alike scrambled as Thendarick shouted at them to move aside. Cam walked as close to his friends as he could manage. With the noise of their marching and the dull roar of the crowds, their conversation was sufficiently masked from anyone overhearing them.

"Errol, you slew those two?" Cam asked.

"I didn't have much of a choice."

"Have you killed before?" Candissa asked Errol. "I mean, other than when you arrived. You seem just too at ease about it."

"You know I don't recall that...incident at the Wardenstone. Apart from that, no, I've killed no one in Ravensroost before today," came Errol's carefully-worded answer.

"You've killed before," Koraymis interjected. "Not in Ravensroost, well before you were here."

The other three looked to their black-haired friend.

"How would you know that?" Cam asked him.

"I just know. With certainty."

"This is not going to go well for us, I'm afraid," Errol said.

"We need to get out of this town, sooner than later," Cam added. "I have a feeling there are people who will try to stop us."

"He's right," Koraymis said. "Sides are being chosen."

Candissa looked shocked at the scholar's words. "How...it doesn't matter. Yes, sides are being chosen. We must be careful in dealing with anyone until we know if they are with us."

"Well, we do know a few, I think," Errol said. "Enthessar for one, and we should assume most of his family."

"That fellow from his retinue, Orrendar," Cam added. "I'm sure Kor is right about him."

"I believe we can all expect to find that some people will be openly hostile towards us, for no reason," Koraymis said. "I encountered some of that today."

"As did I," Cam said. "Half the shopkeepers almost threw me out on sight while the others took me in as an old friend, though we'd never met."

As for allies, I think we can count on Evan, Penston, and Thendarick, Koraymis

Mother Meshana, at my temple, certainly, Candissa added. They silently discussed a few other people in town they had encountered, who were likely to have chosen for or against them, before Candissa spoke again.

"Errol," she said. "What will happen at the council hall? With you?"

"Depends on how hard they press the case against Enthessar. He was seen attacking me, by a dozen guards. But he is a noble from the east, so I'm not sure how much sway that will have with the magistrate."

"If the magistrate sides with him?"

"Then, I may find myself awaiting a trial. But they would have to ignore, push back, or turn every one of those guards, including Thendarick," Errol said.

"Thendarick is with us, of that I'm certain," Candissa said. Cam couldn't resist asking her a question at that point.

"Candissa, I don't want to offend you, but you seem a bit different this morning. I don't know if it is the new outfit or your bearing. But there is a definite change."

"For the better, I hope?" she said in reply, smiling.

"My mother was wise in bringing up her son," Cam replied, holding up his hands defensively. "If I say better, then you could take it as if I thought you somehow less yesterday. That is not the case."

Candissa smirked at that.

"Well put," Koraymis said, grinning, clearly appreciative of Cam's cleverness.

Candissa looked at Cam, pursing her lips. Then she spoke using their silent voices.

To answer your question, yes, there is a change. But it is best to save that for a later discussion.

They were soon heading straight for the three-storied council hall. Errol looked back at his friends.

"I don't know how long this will take. The balance of the day could be lost."

"Not if I have any influence here," Candissa said. "Or my family. We have more to do before we leave, and I don't want to waste an entire day on this."

They filed into the hall, where Thendarick split the group. The bodies were taken to a separate room for examination. Enthessar was taken to a separate chamber to recover, attended by a guard. Cam noted that the officer made sure to take his rapier and dagger into his keeping.

Errol and the guards went into a larger chamber, to stand on a platform along one side. Cam, Koraymis and Candissa all filed onto long benches, where observers sat. A court officer spoke to Thendarick for a bit before running off again.

"Have you seen one of these proceedings before, my lady?" Cam asked

Candissa.

"No, this is the first time I've been in one of these chambers. Will this take long?"

"The magistrate has a full schedule of minor cases, but he's been informed of the situation. He's reassigning some cases and will hurry through the others. We may be here for an hour or more before we see him."

Candissa seemed to consider her thoughts for a moment. "Thendarick, if I give you a note, could you have someone take it to my father?"

"I would be pleased to take it myself," the young officer replied smiling. Cam realized the two must have known each other for some time.

He trained me in various weapons, came Candissa's reply to his thought.

"Now, I just need a quill and pap-" Candissa began, as Koraymis deftly produced both quill and paper from within his cloak.

Candissa smiled, nodding, and quickly wrote down a message.

Letting him know what's happened? Errol said, looking at them from across the chamber.

Yes, but also asking his assistance for our journey, getting things about, preparing quarters in case we need to stay at my estate, Candissa replied.

The note was quickly finished and handed off to Thendarick.

And now we wait for the magistrate? Koraymis asked, though he knew the answer.

Yes. Given the families involved, I think the wait will be shorter than usual, Candissa said.

Cam was relieved it was not too long of a wait. After a half hour, Thendarick had returned. Less than an hour later, a pair of officials entered the chamber, lighting some lamps and placing some tools of the court before the magistrate's seat. After a few minutes, the magistrate entered.

He was easily marked by the black mantle worn about his shoulders, as strode in and took his high seat. He adjusted his robes as he viewed the room. He reviewed the documents before him, and spoke quietly with one of his junior assistants, before turning to face the court.

After the court was called to order, people were called to make statements. It went smoothly at first, with Thendarick offering his sworn testimony regarding the slain Lieutenant Skelmark and his henchmen. He had seen them gather and head off. Some of the guards in the barracks had overheard their plans. It was clear they were intent on finding Errol and were to meet Lord Enthessar beforehand. Knowing there was trouble afoot, he took it upon himself to gather a squad and pursue Skelmark.

His guardsmen testified likewise, supporting and corroborating. Then came the testimony from three of the guards who were swayed by Skelmark to accompany him on the dubious mission. Their accounts of the attacks on Errol were convincing enough, as was their contrition at being pulled into the plot. The hearing looked to be going well, in Cam's opinion.

Until the elder Lord Allenfar burst into the proceeding, accompanied by several other people.

"There's the murderous swine! Your honor, that man," Allenfar shouted pointing at Errol with a waggling, fat finger, "slew two men in House Demarrae yesterday and this very day viciously attacked my son!"

The magistrate stood up swiftly. "Who are these people?" A court officer signaled to him and then stepped over to explain. As he did so, Allenfar and a handful of his court milled about the side of the room. The elder lord glared at Cam and his friends, clearly not sure what their connection was.

"Lord Allenfar!" the magistrate boomed, startling the eastern noble. "You are most assuredly misinformed."

"What do you mean? Do you deny that criminal attacked my son?"

"There is no need to deny it, as we know precisely who attacked your son. We also know your son attacked without provocation. It was someone else who struck your son before he could kill Master Blackmar!"

"One of your guards, I suppose?" Allenfar pointed at Thendarick. "Do you know the penalty for striking an eastern noble, you buffoon?"

Cam was almost shocked as Candissa laughed, a musical, rolling laugh. Lord Allenfar turned to her suddenly, apparently as shocked.

"What do you find so amusing about this, Lady Candissa?" Allenfar spat. "And why is a supposedly noble daughter doing at a common judicial proceeding?"

"Because, my *lord*, whatever the penalty may be, it would go against me. *I* was the one who knocked your lout of a son senseless. And you owe me your thanks!"

"How...dare you!" Allenfar quivered. "Your honor, arrest this pathetic excuse for a nobleman's daughter this *very instant*!"

Cam, Koraymis and Thendarick rose to their feet instantly, having taken offense at the insult hurled at their friend.

"You really shouldn't insult her, my Lord," Errol said, chuckling, from his seat.

"Order! All of you! Lord Allenfar, I will *not* be ordered in my own chambers by anyone, particularly a visiting noble whose son led an assault on a citizen of Ravensroost!" the magistrate replied in his remarkably loud voice. "You will remove yourself from my chambers or I will instruct my guards to forcibly remove you. Now!"

Cam watched as Lord Allenfar's face drained of color. His hands shook visibly as he muttered to one of his courtiers.

"Very well, *your honor*, but know this," he said as he and his people slowly exited the chamber. "Your mantle was bestowed upon you by a high justiciar. I have close friends among the justiciars of Eastvale. I will see your mantle ripped off your shoulders and laugh as you sit in your *own gaol*!"

"Sergeant, remove these miscreants!" the magistrate bellowed.

As soon as the rooms were cleared of the members of House Allenfar, the proceeding continued. The magistrate calmed down and reviewed his notes, taking additional testimony regarding the events of the morning. It took nearly an hour to complete the questioning.

It became clear to Cam that he was only interested in the assaults on Errol and the two who were slain. They did not even discuss Candissa's striking down of Enthessar.

At the end of the testimony, the magistrate spent several minutes consulting a large book his assistant had brought in. After taking nearly a full page of notes and conferring with a court officer, he turned his attention at last to Errol.

"Errol Blackmar, it is found by this court that there are no grounds on which to bring charges against you. Your actions are found to be in self-defense. Additionally, there are no charges to be brought against you regarding the attack on Lord Enthessar." With the last statement, his eyes moved to Candissa. "The court does find sufficient cause to bring charges against Lord Enthessar, and hereby instructs the town guard to take Lord Enthessar into custody at this time, or at the soonest opportunity after his recovery."

With that, he struck a roundel of wood with his gavel, signaling the close of the hearing. Before Errol could join his friends, Cam noticed a court officer rush in to speak to the magistrate, a frantic look on his face.

"What do you mean he's gone? You fool!" the magistrate exclaimed.

They filed out of the chamber to find a knot of guards in uproar. After a short but frenetic discussion, several of them bolted out of the hall while Thendarick approached Errol and his friends.

"It seems the Allenfar lot slipped gold into the hands of the right guard and managed to spirit away Enthessar even before he woke up. Oh, Errol, here, before I forget."

He handed Errol his blade, which he had taken earlier in the alley. "You'll have to tell me someday how you did that little trick back there."

Errol only grinned in reply to the comment.

"Are you taking steps to apprehend him?" Candissa asked Thendarick.

"Yes, we shouldn't have any trouble in that," the young officer said.

"I think you may," Errol countered. "They've had too long to take action. I won't be surprised if their entire entourage is already heading out the eastern gates."

Thendarick grimaced, then nodded, heading out.

"No matter the outcome of all this, we must prepare," Cam said. "We should make our way back to your estate so we can talk. If that is permitted, of course."

"I would insist on it, actually," Candissa said firmly.

"My lady, I am loath to further involve your good family in whatever these events may lead to," Errol protested.

"That is no longer a concern for me. These events take precedence over such trivial matters as society and decorum," Candissa replied. "We all have a journey to prepare for. The first step will be finding our fifth."

"Our fifth?" Cam asked. Then he recalled their meeting at the Bonerest.

The fifth member of our group, Koraymis chimed in, his words echoing in all their minds, his lips unmoving.

"Let's head to my family's estate," Candissa said quietly, more for the benefit of those around them. She continued, without speaking.

I've come into knowledge that without a doubt, our group must consist of five. That is why we felt the fifth one missing when we first met, she explained.

Will you tell us more of what you learned and why you're so confident? Cam asked her.

Yes, but another time. For now, we should make our way to my estate and share our plans about leaving. This seems to be a much faster method of conversing than speech, don't you think, Koraymis?

Yes, without a doubt. The words and ideas flow much faster this way than by speaking, Koraymis agreed.

Then, let's talk about what we have, what's to be purchased, and what we each need to do.

With that, Cam led the discussion, being more familiar with traversing wilderness than perhaps all of them together. It was not a long walk to House Demarrae. In that relatively short span of time, he felt as though they had shared a conversation that would otherwise have taken at least three hours.

At the end of it, they had a clear plan on how they would acquire or purchase what they still needed, and how they would be leaving the town. Cam still hadn't fully adjusted to their being able to converse in this fashion. He knew it was beyond uncommon, and certainly something to do with magic. Despite this, it did not feel unusual. He knew they were involved in something far beyond what his father used to call *the mundane world.*

They were at the small gatehouse of House Demarrae when Lieutenant Thendarick intercepted them, with a small contingent of guardsmen.

"You were entirely correct, Errol," he said, clearly out of breath. "They've already left the town, every last one of them. A scout caught up with them, but they claim they have no knowledge of Enthessar's whereabouts. We haven't the right to search their wagons once they're on the highway east."

"Then our only concern is if they left anyone here with instructions to work some evil upon us," Candissa said. "Thank you, Lieutenant Thendarick."

He nodded. "I will stay in touch with your house, to ensure all is well. Keep a runner at hand in case you need to send a message to me."

They watched him depart.

A good man, Errol commented. *I'm glad he's on our side.*

"Agreed," Cam said aloud. "Let us inspect these horses of yours, my lady. Koraymis and I will collect our belongings from the Bonerest soon."

Candissa led them through the gate, ensuring the house guards understood they were each to be accorded respect and free passage into and out of the grounds. She led them to a large hall, though smaller than the main hall. It was in the back of the house, which was to her liking.

It was there she set to assembling their provisions and equipment. She directed a servant to show Errol and Cam the mounts from which they could choose. Koraymis had indicated he would take whichever mount would be the easiest for an inexperienced rider.

At the stables, Cam was not unimpressed with the mounts it had to offer. Still, they would each have to try their mount out before embarking on a long journey.

"Have you ridden much before, Errol?" he asked his friend as he inspected the horses.

"I had one occasion to ride a horse since I've been in *Ravensroost*."

That gave Cam pause. Errol's reply was clearly not all he had to say on the matter. "Go on."

Errol grinned. "I'll take whichever horse remains. While I've only rode once for any length of time since my arrival, but I know I've been trained extensively on horses."

Cam shrugged. "You are a mystery."

"To myself, most of all," Errol muttered low in reply.

They soon chose four mounts.

"Should we take a fifth?" Cam asked Errol.

Errol thought on that, pulling his dagger out to trim a thumbnail. "That is a good idea, my friend. Assuming House Demarrae can part with another."

Heading back toward the servant's entrance, Cam looked at Errol's impressive blade as he resheathed it.

"Errol, what did Thendarick mean by 'that little trick'? It was something to do with your dagger."

Errol didn't reply for a moment. Then he looked at Cam. "I've been wondering about that myself."

"Come again?"

"One of those mysteries," he said in a low voice. Cam wasn't going to pursue the matter until Errol stopped. They were just a short walk from the entrance. "Will you entertain a notion of mine for a moment?"

Cam nodded, facing him. Errol drew forth and handed him his dagger, hilt first.

"Inspect it, look at the markings, it's unique," he told Cam. Doing so, Cam found it to be a unique blade indeed. He was no expert in metals or weapon making, but it seemed to defy his experience.

"Impressive. Keen edge, too," Cam remarked, noting it easily peeled off a callus from his thumb. He handed it back to Errol, but Errol refused.

"Take it back to the stable. Hide it."

Cam raised an eyebrow. "Why am I doing this?"

"Just...entertain my silly notion," Errol smiled easily at him.

"Fine," Cam said, chuckling. It took him all of thirty seconds to walk back to the stable and find a spot high over one of the stalls where he could secret the blade. Doing so, he returned to Errol.

"Done. What do we do now?"

Errol looked at him with some sort of concentrated gaze. "I'm not entirely sure. Could you see your way to striking me?"

"What?" Cam exclaimed.

"Hit me, or at least look like you will," Errol said.

Cam was dumbfounded. Still, he agreed, nodding. He pulled on the buckle securing his pack, so it wouldn't throw him off. "All right. Stand to, knave!"

He did his best to put on a good show of making a fist. He turned, ready to throw his considerable weight into the blow. Being much bigger than Errol, he knew he could inflict a serious blow unless the faster man dodged him, which he fully expected would happen.

Lunging forward, Cam threw his right arm outward to strike Errol. As expected, his far nimbler opponent stepped back as he attacked, forcing Cam to overextend. Errol dropped down and swung a leg outward, felling the larger man.

Standing over him suddenly, Errol quipped, "Think twice before getting up." In his right hand was his blade.

Cam was in shock. It appeared to be the black blade. Getting to his feet, he took it as Errol offered it. Turning it over, he couldn't deny it.

"No, you have two. You're taking me for a fool, as you did Thendarick."

"Let's return to the stable," Errol offered.

Nodding, Cam went to the stable, Errol following. Cam held the dagger in his hand. Reaching up onto the beam where he had hidden the dagger, he found nothing.

He stared blankly at Errol. Handing the dagger back to Errol, he hauled himself up far enough to inspect the entire length of the beam. There was nothing there.

"I don't understand," was all Cam managed.

"A better idea," Errol said. "Take it. Mark it with the soot from that lamp." He pointed to a lamp mounted on a post just outside the door of the stable. Errol then proceeded to walk to the servant's door, not looking at Cam.

Cam took up the challenge, taking a finger and gathering a smudge of the black residue. He made a line on the blade, but to be certain, he also took a bit of dried dung and worked it into the grip. He then found a nearby saddle and lodged the blade firmly into a space between the saddle and the blanket beneath.

Returning to Errol, who was leaning casually against a tree near the servant's entrance, he nodded firmly. "Let's see you pull off your little trick again. Do I need to threaten you?"

"No. It's easier now that I've had some practice," Errol said, grinning broadly.

"What do you mean?"

Errol just glanced upward, at a low branch of the small tree. Cam followed his gaze. The blade was stuck into the branch.

"No," was all Cam said. Reaching up, he pulled the dagger free. The dung was there, as was the mark he made with the soot. He handed it back to Errol, after wiping the grip on his pants.

"Dung? That was not necessary," Errol grinned, resheathing the blade.

"So, you can use some sort of magic to retrieve your dagger?"

Errol shrugged. "It appears so. Come, Candissa may be wondering where we are. We all need to get back to the Bonerest, as well, to get our belongings."

"We can bring yours along," Cam offered.

"I'd rather go with you. Candissa will be safe here without us."

Back in the hall, they found Candissa and Koraymis going through the items she had ordered for them so far. Errol was mildly surprised to find Taldrephus standing with them.

"Hallo, sir," he said, nodding to Errol.

"You worked up the nerve to have a guard contact the good Lady?" Errol teased him.

"Yes, I managed. I'm happy to purchase whatever you need. There's still time today, I can make several of the shops," he said, holding a list he had been making.

"Good. It saves us all some grief, I assure you," Errol patted the shoulder of his tall friend.

"Candissa, can you spare a fifth horse for our journey?" Cam asked. "We are planning on finding a fifth rider, after all."

Candissa looked back at Cam thoughtfully. "That is an excellent idea. Of course."

"We should head to the Bonerest while we still have daylight," Koraymis suggested. "Then we can meet back here and assemble everything."

"And you're all welcome to rooms here," Candissa said.

"You're certain Lord Demarrae is in approval of all this?" Errol asked her. "I don't want to be awakened at some early morning hour and thrown out of the estate."

"Yes, he's more than approving. Have no concern there," she assured them. "And my mother as well, if not more so."

"Then we should away to the Bonerest," Cam advised.

It was nearly evening by the time they reached the tavern. Shops and markets were closing as people returned to their homes or made their way to taverns. Cam noticed with some amusement that without Candissa, there were far fewer eyes on the trio. Still, he felt some gazing at them, unsure of what feelings lay behind their eyes.

At the Bonerest, they went straight to the long bar, where Evan seemed to be awaiting them.

"Gentlemen," the courteous half-Elven tavernmaster nodded. "Errol, your satchel is here." He nodded to a place just behind the bar.

"We will be leaving the Bonerest. Did Taldrephus mention this to you?" Cam said.

"Of course, the rooms are yours until morning, should you forget anything," Evan said. "And let me know if you need any assistance. And just drop the key off here, when you're finished."

"We shouldn't be too long," Cam said to Errol. "Why don't you wait here, and we'll be down shortly."

"I'll enjoy one more glass of fine Elven wine," Errol nodded, smiling.

Cam followed Koraymis up the narrow stairs. An oil lamp lit the likewise narrow hallway. The scholar moved ahead to his room around the corner, as Cam retrieved the small key from his belt. Unlocking the door, he entered the darkened room. The only light was a dim blue light of evening, issuing from behind the shuttered window. He turned and shut the door.

He didn't know if it was his instincts honed from years of hunting, or just an intuition brought on by the events of the last few days. He pivoted on one heel an instant before the blade struck him. Instead piercing his side, which would have likely killed him, it deflected harmlessly off his pack, with its thick, nearly impenetrable layers of leather.

Spinning, he tried to grasp his attacker's arm, but the man spun out of the way. He glimpsed the blade again, ducked out of the way, and brought his knee up forcefully, making some sort of contact. He pushed his attacker away with one arm, while trying to draw his own weapon with the other. But the man was remarkably fast, and clearly trained in close quarters combat.

For one dark moment, the fleeting thought occurred to Cam - that he may not survive this attack. It may have caused him to hesitate, he wasn't sure. His pause may have provided an opening for his attacker. Something solid and small struck his head hard.

Falling backwards, lights bursting in front of his eyes, he could only vaguely see his opponent move in for a final stroke, as Cam toppled, disoriented and defenseless. The attacker's blade was bright in the dim light, somehow.

The door burst open. Light filled the small chamber. His attacker reacted with remarkable quickness, bringing his blade to bear on this new foe.

Even though Cam's eyes were not clearly focused, as he tried to regain his senses, he saw his attacker by the light of the open door. It was Orrendar. His face was a mask of terror, his eyes suddenly wide, his pupils tiny, mouth agape. In that moment his blade froze in his grip, and he shook.

The figure in the door grasped Orrendar's face with one hand, flame erupting from the palm and fingers. The flames seared Orrendar's face, the tendrils of fire intensely bright in the dim light of the chamber. His scream was muffled as his face was scorched, his hands dropping the weapon, grasping the arm of the figure. Orrendar's foe moved into the room as Orrendar fell back, another flame-wreathed hand grasping Orrendar's burning head. Both hands gripped the dying man as he tried to scream, tried to pull free from the lethal grip. Smoke and vapors filled the air, and Cam blinked hard against the sting of the foul stench.

The robed figure looming over the fallen Orrendar did not relent, even as his victim kicked and clawed at his arms. The man struggled for another breath, then went limp.

A moment before Cam lost consciousness, the robed figure turned to look at him. His skin was reddish, with small horns of black on his temples, brow, and jaw. His hands were black, smoking claws.

The eyes though, Cam knew.

"Koraymis…" he whispered before slipping into darkness.

CHAPTER TWENTY-THREE - KORAYMIS

25 Laborus, Year 197, Eastvale Calendar

Koraymis had only just entered his room when he thought he heard something. He was ready to dismiss it as the wind or the building shifting. Then he felt Cam. He was in distress. *He was being attacked.*

He did not think. He simply bolted out of his room and around the corner. Cam's door was shut but he knew there was someone else in there, someone of dark intent, a murderer. Later, Koraymis would remember the tingling sensation of his ring as he shouldered the door open forcefully.

It happened all too fast to recall clearly. He reacted out of pure instinct. The man, Orrendar, a deadly purpose in his eyes, clutching a dagger, looked at him as the door flew open.

Let go the guise, the voice was there in his head, in that instant. He didn't so much remember and use the magic Telmik had imparted. It rather snapped outward from his mind and his hands, a compelling force of thought he shot at Orrendar as though a crossbow bolt had left his fingertips. It was that thought, forced upon the hapless assassin, that caused the man to freeze. He saw what Koraymis was, and it terrified Orrendar to his core. Koraymis felt the terror. In that instant, he *liked the taste of his victim's terror.*

That moment of sheer panic allowed Koraymis the time he needed to step forward and clamp his hand on the man's face, letting the flames burst forth. Covering Orrendar's mouth, he hoped it would muffle his screams. Using his left hand to grasp the back of Orrendar's head, he let the scorching fire blacken Orrendar's skin and sear his skull. He felt the heat penetrate instantly, and he wondered at that moment - in a sort of detached fashion, as he would later recall - how long it would take to cook the man's brain inside his skull.

He flailed for a moment, trying in vain to pull Koraymis' hand away. Then he was dead. Koraymis let him down onto the floor, vapors and smoke wreathed about both their heads. Orrendar's eyes were ashen pits, his mouth open wide, yellow smoke curling out of it. His head was nothing but a blackened, flaking orb. Koraymis looked at the other figure in the room.

"Koraymis…"

The sound of Cam's voice, as the hunter slipped into unconsciousness, snapped Koraymis out of his black reverie.

He can see me! Koraymis thought. He heard the bounding steps of Errol on the stairwell.

Turning, he held his black, clawed hands close to his horned visage, and closed his eyes. Concentrating, he felt the ring do something, help him somehow. His fingers returned to normal, or what others considered normal.

He felt the change taking place, as he used to feel when it was not something that happened easily. Turning, Errol was standing in the door. He looked at Koraymis, the slain form of Orrendar, and the unconscious hunter.

Errol quickly closed the door behind him. "Open the window, we need to get the smoke out."

Koraymis did so, and the air began clearing immediately. The room was much better lit now, but that only revealed the extent of what he had done to Orrendar.

"It was smart to cover his mouth, I don't think anyone heard his scream," Errol said, as he stepped over the dead man to examine Cam. "He's coming around, good. Did Cam see you?"

Errol's question came as a shock to Koraymis. Looking down at the ruined, scorched face, Koraymis sat suddenly on the bed.

"I... didn't want to kill him," he said, but knew that wasn't enough. Or was it too much?

"Of course not. You haven't killed before, have you?"

Koraymis shook his head slowly, still looking at the agonized ruin that was the dead man's face.

"Looks like Cam just took a knock to the head," Errol said, as he shifted the considerable bulk of the hunter to a sitting position. Cam groaned a little, his head wobbling. "It doesn't matter if he saw you, you cannot keep it from us now."

"Keep what?" Koraymis asked, his voice unsteady. His stomach felt badly all at once.

Errol looked at him. "Now, just breathe deeply, don't look at him, look out the window. If you must throw up, do it out the window."

Koraymis thought he may just do that. He had killed a man. He remembered the voice, from earlier today, *you know what you must do to them.*

Cam hissed quietly, sitting up now, rubbing his head. He looked at his hand, finding a dab of blood on it. "What did he hit me with?"

"A sap of some sort," Errol said, picking up the leather-bound weight and pocketing it.

Cam looked up at Koraymis, who looked pale in the light of day. He didn't want to meet Cam's gaze.

"Thank you, Kor," was all Cam said.

Koraymis looked out the window again. "What are we to do now?"

"I'm not even sure he can be identified by anyone in Ravensroost," Errol said, studying the blackened, ruined flesh of the dead man's face. "But for now, that doesn't matter. I will need Evan's help in getting this body out of here. Unless either of you gentlemen have a brilliant idea."

Koraymis had none to offer, having trouble enough simply trying to deal with what he had done.

"He could have been drunk and fell face first into a fireplace, knocked himself cold," Cam suggested. "If we could get him downstairs later. Or, if Master Evan is willing, he could tell that story to the town guard."

"No, that sounds a bit far-fetched. Cam, how soon will we be departing?"

Cam scratched his short beard. "If we push it, we could leave as soon as later tomorrow, but I can't say for certain. I was hoping for a couple days at least to prepare."

"So," Errol said, rubbing his hands together, thinking. "We need to do something with this body for the night, and the longer term. We have to convince Evan to help us."

"I killed him," Koraymis said suddenly, panic suddenly blooming in his stomach. "If they find out, I'll be a wanted man." He looked at Cam and Errol with fearful eyes.

"If they can tie you to this man. But can they? Orrendar is from the east, you are new to town. But there's nothing to connect the two of you. In truth, *I* would be a far more likely suspect in his death."

Koraymis didn't know what to say in reply. Errol was right. There wasn't really any way to tie him to Orrendar's death. His silence answered Errol.

"Good. If you don't let on that you're a sorcerer, you're in no danger," Errol said.

Koraymis was dumbfounded. He realized Errol must have seen him. "So, you're not..."

Errol laughed. "Worried that you're not exactly what most people would call human? No, not at all."

"I, for one, am grateful. Your...powers saved my life," Cam said, as he took a blanket Errol handed him and began wrapping the body in it.

Errol lifted Orrendar's body by the shoulders, so Cam could slide the blanket under. "Tell me Kor, does that change in your appearance happen every time you use your power, or just when you kill someone?"

Koraymis felt better once he could not see the dead man's face. "How would I know? I've never killed anyone. But I've never lost control like that."

"Then you will need to watch for that," Errol said in a matter-of-fact tone.

Koraymis was somewhat stunned his new friends were taking this development with such ease.

A knock at the door caused them to all freeze.

"It's Evan," came the quiet voice.

They all stood. Errol shrugged, and opened the door, silently adding, *He's with us.*

Evan nodded as he saw Errol. His nose visibly wrinkled as he no doubt smelled the fleeting traces of burned flesh. He regarded the body wrapped partially in a blanket.

"It's been a long while since someone was killed in my tavern," he said. Koraymis thought the older man's eyes looked sad but resolved somehow.

"My friend, we need your help," Errol said.

"I figured as much. Beshanu heard the commotion, but I didn't know it was as bad as this," the tavernmaster said, rubbing his chin. "Let me see the face."

Cam bent to lift the blanket, but Koraymis' hand stayed him. Cam looked at the sorcerer.

"I'll show him," was all Koraymis said. He bent and lifted off the blanket slowly, revealing the ruin of blistered, charred and twisted flesh that was Orrendar's face.

Evan sighed deeply. He looked squarely at Koraymis. Then he saw the knife on the bed. "That's his blade I suppose? He was attacking you, Cam?"

The hunter nodded.

"His folk have left the town, he had no relations here, no ties I'm aware of. If Lady Candissa can lend her family's aid, we could spirit the body away," Evan said. "When do you plan on leaving?"

"The sooner the better, but likely a day or two," Errol answered. Evan nodded.

"Let's get this downstairs. There's a cellar I never use. It can stay there until I get rid of it."

With that, they wrapped the body and picked it up. Koraymis felt badly that it was Errol and Cam doing the lifting, while Evan cleared their path. But they were stronger than he was; Koraymis doubted he could lift even half the weight of the body.

"Are you well enough to do this, Cam?" Errol asked. "You were knocked pretty good."

"I'll be fine," Cam said, almost growling.

Evan directed them to the cellar. It was small but near the stairwell. It was filled with old barrels of coal and other seldom-used commodities. They laid the body down, and Evan directed them to cover it in some older sheets of canvas that were half covered in mold. "I'll have Beshanu stack more old linen on it, until we move it again."

"Let's get back upstairs and get our things, quickly," Errol advised. The three of them left the small room, but Koraymis remained for a moment.

He regarded the lumpish pile of old blankets and linen which was the body of Orrendar. He didn't know how to feel. His stomach was still upset.

"Were you evil?" Koraymis asked the body of Orrendar, ignoring the irrationality of it. "Will you be missed by someone?"

He thought of his own mother and wondered if Orrendar's mother was still alive. If she was, how would she feel, despite his murderous intent, when she learned of his death? What would his own mother have thought, if she had seen Koraymis wield such awful power? Perhaps it was a good thing she was gone. She would likely have thought her son an evil and vile creature. His father would have been far angrier at him, or so Koraymis imagined.

He felt tears threatening. He blinked them back.

You had to kill him. He was an enemy. He chose. He died for his choice.

Koraymis didn't question the voice, as he felt the warmth of the ring on his right hand.

"I'll be forced to kill again, won't I?" Koryamis murmured.

The voice did not reply. There was no need. He knew the answer.

Errol appeared in the small door frame. "Come upstairs, we need to depart."

Koraymis nodded and left. Evan pulled the door shut, the harsh sound grating in Koraymis' ears. He would not forget that noise. The door shutting on the first man he killed.

Upstairs, they were expeditious in their gathering and packing. Within just a few minutes, they had all they needed.

"We are in your debt, my friend," Errol said, clasping the tavernmaster by the forearm.

"It is nothing. Drop by before you leave, whatever the hour. I'll have food for your journey." With that, Evan nodded, returning quickly to the common room.

Errol led the way out, carefully surveying the yard and narrow alley behind the Bonerest before motioning for the other two to join him. They were on the street momentarily.

Their quick pace returned them to House Demarrae within a short while, though Koraymis thought it overlong. He saw gazes of suspicion and condemnation in anyone's eye he happened to meet.

They entered the small hall, located in the rear of the house, where Candissa was waiting. She was sitting and reviewing a list of goods she had prepared. She looked up. Her expression was solemn and knowing.

"What happened?"

"Orrendar is dead," Errol said as he tossed his satchel on a table and began to extract his belongings.

"Orrendar nearly killed me," Cam added. "And would have, if Kor hadn't stopped him."

She looked at them all, nodding. "I thought as much. I nearly took a horse to the Bonerest, but it was over so quickly," she said. Then she looked at Koraymis. "You did what you had to, Kor."

The scholar just looked down then began sorting out which items he would take.

He didn't see Candissa standing and moving over to him. She suddenly took his hands in hers. He looked up, into her eyes. They were like sky-blue rings. They were kind eyes.

"You are a good man," she said, with absolute sincerity in her voice. She then moved a hand to the side of his head, gently pressing against it. He felt his anxiety, his dread, fade. Even the knot of pain in his stomach dissipated after a moment. He blinked, smiling a little at Candissa. She returned the smile with a warmth that seemed to fill him up. He was almost sad when she returned to her preparations.

"He's made of iron, he'll be fine," Errol quipped. "In my experience, when someone kills for the first time, they are usually sicking up by now."

"What experience is that exactly?" Candissa replied, smiling a little as she knew it was more a jest than a question.

"If I could tell you, I would," was all Errol said in reply. Koraymis wondered how Errol could be so easy with having no memory of his early life. "Ah, lest I forget, Master Evan needs your help, Candissa. Rather, that of your house. Regarding moving the body."

She thought on that for a moment. "I'll speak to my father. He'll have someone talk to Evan."

"Will your father have qualms about being party to disposing of a body?"

"He knows that the events surrounding all of this are serious. I will explain it to him. He will understand."

"Excuse me, but why did Orrendar want to kill Cam?" Koraymis said. The question had been nagging at him since they had left the Bonerest.

The four looked at one another for a moment. Candissa spoke.

"I think he is part of something he may not understand. Something is trying to stop us, and that meant killing us, at least to Orrendar. If he had killed Cam, he may have intended to move on to you," she said. "Though I'm really guessing at this point. It's just what I suspect."

"He likely thought Cam a more difficult opponent, so he wanted to take care of him first," Errol added.

Koraymis wasn't very satisfied with their suggestions. He sighed and continued in his preparations. It was not easy to pick and choose what to take, but he was gradually determining what must be taken and what need not be.

While there was more to be done, after a few hours, Koraymis was done with his preparations for the day. His eyes were once more drawn to Cam's pack. He had noticed earlier that Cam had laid out several items on a table near his pack, and they were now packed. Yet, the pack didn't appear to be at capacity, or even particularly laden. It was puzzling.

He knew Cam's pack was magical. He could see a glimmer of enchantment about it whenever he tried to look for it. Koraymis was not very knowledgeable about the various enchantments that could be placed on objects, so he could discern nothing more about Cam's pack. Hopefully his girdle tome contained some passages regarding this matter.

And there were other magical objects nearby. Candissa's staff was remarkable. It radiated what seemed an extraordinarily powerful magic. Errol's blade was nearly as powerful, at least by the degree of magical radiance. What caught his senses was how distinctly different the magic of the blade was from her staff. They were each unique, possessing what Telmik amusingly referred to as 'flavors'.

Koraymis frowned. All of the packing was well and good, yet they had no idea where they were going. He could accept being thrown into this unlikely band of new friends, given the strange course his life had been taking of late. What bothered him most at this point was their lack of direction. His concerns were felt by his companions.

We go to find the fifth person of our group, came Candissa's voice. *That is our first objective. I believe we will find enough clues on the way to lead us there.*

And with today's events, it's clear we have little choice but to leave. There would be too many questions if we stayed, Errol added.

"I suppose you're right," Koraymis sighed.

"I've dealt with wilderness in her every season and in her many moods," Cam said. "I can't say exactly what's out there, but together we should be able to face most anything."

"I only wish we knew more."

"We have some books to study. They may impart some little wisdom on these matters. And, we will learn more as we go," Candissa said, trying to reassure him. She looked around at the long table. "We've done enough for now, I think. Come, let us feast. We need to get as much sleep as we may over the next night or two, before we depart."

Errol was inspecting the various traveling cloaks Candissa had produced from her family's storerooms. As winter was coming on, they would all need to dress against the cold. Koraymis saw a few that were black.

That was good. If they were venturing into the unknown west, looking for someone they knew nothing of, with no clear idea of where to look, he could at least be wearing black.

CHAPTER TWENTY-FOUR - THE OTHER

It breathed.

It had forgotten what it was to breathe. It didn't know how long it had slept; it only vaguely remembered its task, given by the wizard. A wizard? Perhaps a powerful priest, but it didn't recall the difference. No matter. It had been given the task. The task was now its purpose.

It had power, but the power slumbered. It didn't remember how to use the power.

No eyes! It needed eyes. It needed eyes – and hands – to work its will in the world. It had some few in its grasp now, though it could not see them, and they did not know they were being affected. Feelings, just feelings, emotions. Fear and rage, mostly. It knew those feelings well.

It had never felt fear, *true* fear, until *she* had touched it.

It had no body yet, not a true form. But it would. Pieces were slithering, shifting, forming. The energy just above it was unimaginable. It would have to use that energy, tap into it, if it could find a way. It no longer feared *her*. But there were others.

They moved now. It would have to stop them, to turn them, to direct others to defeat them. Kill them. But how? It had not the body. Yet, it breathed. It must have a body, it thought. In the pit. At the bottom, in the crevasses. There were spaces. It had found them, oozed into them.

Now it breathed. Others would come, it would tell them. They would help it, follow its orders. *They* must be stopped. It had been trying, but only in its sleep. It had been sleeping.

What had awakened it? Death. Yes, it was the death. One of its followers, firmly in its grasp, had been killed. It didn't understand how, but with the Human's death (He was Human! But what *was* Human?), it had grown in awareness. The death seemed to have granted it some of the slain man's knowledge and living essence.

It was pleased by that. Perhaps, even if its followers were slain, and could no longer work its will in the world, their death would aid it somehow. It would have to think about that.

It had time to think. There was only emptiness here, a blankness it could not penetrate. It did not know where it came from, why it was here. It only remembered its purpose, its task. And *her*.

It hated her. But she was gone. It thought about that; she must have been dead for so long now. She did not matter. It would focus its rage on *them* now. But how? It did not know. Did it have much time? It did not even feel the passing of a day. (A day? When the great burning orb crossed the sky. It *hated* that orb!) It needed eyes. And hands. And then it would work its will in the world.

Things slithered toward it, it would grow.

But *they* moved! They moved toward another. If they found the one nearest to it, they would grow in strength. It would have to reach out and try to stop them. It focused on this.

Where would they move? What was their path? It did not know. Then, in a flash, an image came to its nascent mind, and suddenly it knew.

The tower! *They must not reach the tower!*

CHAPTER TWENTY-FIVE - ERROL

27 Laborus, Year 197, Eastvale Calendar

It had been a very busy two days at House Demarrae. Errol was ready for a full night's sleep before they departed in the morning. After one of the cook's bountiful meals to break their fast, of course.

Since the attack on Cam two days ago, both Candissa and Errol had carefully and quietly put their contacts in town to the task of listening, making discreet inquiries, and observing. But there was no evidence of additional agents of House Allenfar in Ravensroost, following their hasty departure. It would be a week at least before their caravan of wagons and carriages reached the Eastern district the Allenfars called home. Errol and his friends would be well away from Ravensroost long before that.

Candissa's family had been remarkably accommodating. They had each chosen their preferred mount, though it took a few attempts to find one suited to Koraymis. He had settled on a roan, black of course, with a particularly ill temper. The beast was strangely calm with Koraymis. Cam had worked with the young scholar on his riding techniques, as he had the least experience on horseback. For himself, Errol had chosen a dark brown bay, with black mane, tail and legs. His name was Teago, and he got along with Errol very nicely.

Over the last two days, Candissa and Koraymis had spent the bulk of their time reading, although he and Cam had perused one or two of the books Koraymis had borrowed from the scholar Penston. Some of it was interesting reading, accounts of what people encountered in the mist-shrouded hills - or *thought* they encountered. Errol felt a great deal of the accounts were exaggerated or embellished.

Koraymis had contacted Master Penston, through Taldrephus. The scholar had told Koraymis to keep the books until his party returned from their journeys. Penston seemed to think they were better used by Koraymis and his friends rather than collecting dust on his shelf. Koryamis had also charged Errol's man to obtain from Master Penston a book on cartography, which Penston refused payment for.

Between the provisions Evan had given them, and the food and drink supplied by House Demarrae, they were well stocked for more than a month of travel, if not closer to six weeks. Cam assured them he would be able to hunt and trap game to supplement their meals. He also imagined there would be some opportunity for foraging berries, nuts, or even fruits from the woodlands.

Cam had also taken time to school Candissa and Koraymis is the fundamentals of setting up a camp - erecting a tent and how to start a fire. He even showed them both how to hold a bow and knock an arrow. Candissa seemed to be a natural. Koraymis, however, was more a danger to others with a bow in his hands.

They had all changed out their footgear and clothing for more suitable garb. Cam pointed out they would have to be prepared for almost any sort of weather, including heavy rains or snow. After all of it, at the end of today, Errol felt they were as ready as may be.

The four of them had avoided venturing out into town. They had all shared their respective tales of how some people were inclined to be their fast friends, allies without even knowing them, while others were very ill-disposed, even at the mere sight of any of them.

Candissa had told them all earlier in the day how her parents had been forced to dismiss four of the staff. They had been vocal in their feelings about Candissa and her friends, to the point of being a potential threat. That alone made their decision to leave the next day all the easier.

Errol had sensed as much. He hadn't put it into words, or discussed it outright with his companions, but he sensed something amiss. It was like a rising tide of darkness, emanating from those in Ravensroost who were - for reasons he did not understand - against them. They had made their choice.

It did not make getting to sleep any easier this night. He managed to still his thoughts by midnight, slipping finally into sleep.

Errol gasped, waking with a start.

He sat up, wondering for a moment if he was in dream. But he was still in the guest bedchamber, on the second level of House Demarrae. Looking at the shuttered window, he knew it was perhaps three hours before dawn. Something in his dreams had disturbed him, though he could not recall what. He rarely remember his dreams.

Perhaps that was why he was always awakened by his dreams. Tonight was no different. He recalled only vague shapes. There was something tall, white, jagged. Perhaps a dead tree?

Penston had suggested once that his absence of dreams was part of his memory being blocked. He seemed convinced Errol could regain his memory but offered no ideas how that could be accomplished.

Sitting up, he ran his hand through his hair. His memory, like his dreams, were there, lurking somewhere in his wretched mind. He doubted sleep would be possible now. Sighing deeply, he stood, stretching, and commenced a series of movements designed to maintain flexibility and build strength.

It felt good to use his muscles, feel the blood pumping. The exercises were soothing to him, letting him forget his situation, the insanity that had gripped him and his friends. Out of all his friends, perhaps he had the most to gain from such an unlikely endeavor. What better way to find out who he was then to embark on a journey such as this? Surely there were clues out there that could lead him to unlocking the mystery of his origin.

He wore only a pair of silk trousers. The maid servant had laid out a nightshirt, but he never liked those. As he went through his exercises, he vaguely recalled training naked. There were dozens in the room. He closed his eyes. He could smell the sweat of many bodies as they all moved in unison. He heard their quiet grunts and breathing, sharp intakes of breath as their limbs whirled and stretched. All to the harsh commands of a trainer.

He lost it. Slamming a fist on the floor, he gritted his teeth. So often, he thought he would have a breakthrough, an epiphany. But no. It ever eluded him.

He sat. His clothing was in a neat pile on a table across the room. Although there was only dim moonlight filtering in between the slats of the shutters, he could see clearly in the darkness. Certainly, eyes adjusted to dark conditions. Yet, he knew this was unusual.

Errol could make out the shape of his dagger in its sheath. It was the biggest part of the mystery. He stood, walked over, pulled it free of the sheath. It gleamed in the dim light.

Swinging open the glazed window frame, he felt the cold night air wash over his body, enjoying the sensation. The shutter opened outward. He inspected the ground below. His room overlooked a small yard that was used by the servants and delivery boys. Stacks of crates and disused barrels lined the wall some forty feet from where he stood. He listened, sensed the night air.

No one was about. All were asleep. He grasped the dagger by its blade and flipped it downward with practiced ease. He could hear the solid thunk as it seated in an old barrel.

Closing the shutters and the glazed window, he sat, his back to the door. He imagined an enemy behind it, a hired killer, sent to slit his throat in his sleep. Errol could feel his heart rate increase, his muscles tense. He shifted his legs, so he was in a crouch, ready to lunge. His hands were just brushing the floorboards of the chamber as he waited.

In his mind, he imagined the killer unlocking the door and ever so slowly opening it. Errol sprang into action, whirling, ready to attack the assailant before he had any idea his efforts were for naught.

The dagger was in Errol's grip as he whirled, no longer lodged in a barrel in the yard below. He released it, his arm snapping forward. The blade bit deep into the door with a satisfying thunk.

His mind reeled. *The tower!* An image burned in front of his eyes. A tall white tower cracked and broken at the top, on a desolate rise amid a wilderness of low scrub.

It faded. He was standing, as if ready for an attack. His breath had quickened, his heart pounding in his chest. He retrieved his dagger from the door. He heard heavy footfalls outside, in the corridor, recognizing the cadence of Cam's stride.

He opened the door before Cam had the chance to knock. Cam looked surprised for an instant, then that expression faded. Errol tipped his head to one side, inviting him in.

"It woke you as well?" Cam asked. He looked at the blade in Errol's hand.

"I was already awake," Errol said. "Did you see the tower?"

Cam nodded. "I expect Kor and Candissa are awake now."

"It's too early. We should have slept more," Errol grumbled.

"Perhaps it's a better thing, to get an earlier start. And maybe now we have a destination."

"The tower?"

"Why not? It could be where we must go. Do you think your scholar friend may have some inkling of what it may be?"

"I can certainly inquire before we depart," Errol said. "You won't try to sleep then?"

Cam shook his head. "No chance." He stepped over to a table and turned a knob on an oil lamp. A spark lit the wick, and light slowly filled the room as he adjusted the level.

"Hmm, that's odd," Errol said, stepping over to the table, peering at the lamp.

"What? The striking stone?"

"It's called a wickstone. Is this common?"

"No. Some old lamps have this feature, there's a small wheel of flint or something like it, and you just turn it-"

"I know how it works. I've seen them before," Errol said, frowning.

"Before you came to Ravensroost, you mean," Cam said, understanding.

Errol nodded. Then he looked at the partially open door. "If the others are up, why aren't they here?"

Cam narrowed his eyes. He walked out into the corridor, and Errol followed him. Almost without realizing it, he had his dagger in his hand, having no sheath or other means to conceal it.

Candissa's and Koraymis' bedchambers were lit, but unoccupied. Heading downstairs, being careful not to wake anyone. Errol and Cam joined Koraymis and Candissa in the smaller hall. They were poring over her extensive patchwork map, unrolled on a long table.

"We were wondering if you would be joining us," she commented.

Cam let out a low whistle. "It's an impressive map, when you have the entire thing assembled."

"I've created it from many sources, as you can see."

"What of the tower? I assume you both saw it," Cam said.

Both nodded.

"Then we are all in agreement this is our destination?" Errol said.

Candissa turned to look at him, assessing his demeanor. "Do you think it may not be?"

"I just want to be sensible in how we approach this. Why did we all see this vision? Is it a marker for where we must go, or a warning? We have no way of knowing."

She looked down, thoughtful. "You are correct, we really don't *know*. But I *feel* it is our destination. I cannot say more than that."

Errol was not satisfied with her answer, but he conceded. It likely was. Still, he felt something behind it.

As if in answer to his qualms, Koraymis spoke. "I agree, Candissa. But I suspect it was not intended for us to see."

"What do you mean?"

"I sensed something behind it, when the image woke me. A presence," he replied to her. His voice took on a darker note when he spoke again. "A malice."

She furrowed her brows. "You must have an awareness I lack. Did you sense anything more than that?"

"Nothing I can put into words, just a sense there was something dark, distant, lurking in shadow. I'm sorry I can't be more specific."

Errol focused on Koraymis's words. Something struck a nerve in him.

"Why did we see the image then?" he asked Koraymis.

The young scholar frowned, looking down at the map. Errol saw him fidgeting with his heavy, dark ring. "I suspect it is growing in power, and it made some sort of connection about the tower, and us. And…"

"And?" Errol said, pressing Koraymis. Koraymis' dark eyes met Errol's deep blue.

"We weren't the only ones in town who just awoke."

Errol grimaced. "That's it then. We leave as soon as is feasible. There will be...problems, if we delay."

"What sort of problems?" Cam asked.

"Those who would stop us," he replied. "They are likely already moving."

"Wait," Cam said, raising a hand. "I don't understand why…" His words seemed to fade as his expression turned pensive. He glanced toward one of the long, dark windows. A noise caused all of them to look sharply toward the entrance to the hall. But it was nothing.

"He's right. We all feel it," Candissa whispered.

Koraymis nodded. "We must away."

Candissa thought for only a moment. "We must ready our mounts and leave as soon as we may, dawn or no."

Her declaration left no doubt or hesitation. They each sprang into action, returning to their chambers to dress and gather what they needed. Errol took a moment to awaken a house messenger, giving him a task.

They soon met again in the small hall, where cloaks were donned and packs collected. Given they were going into an uncertain situation, Errol armed himself with his extra daggers, one in each boot, and a few secured in hidden sheaths under his cloak and belt. They each carried their saddlebags to the stable. By now, servants had been awakened by the ruckus caused by their impending departure. Stable boys were readying their mounts.

The four of them worked together to secure their bags and packs to the horses. The yard was lit by several bright torches. With the sudden activity, the house was in a mild uproar, lights appearing in many windows.

Candissa's white-gray mare, Torren, was holding perfectly still as they secured the saddle and bags. Cam's horse, a tall chestnut stallion with a reddish-brown coat and flaxen mane and tail and named Rufus, was only a bit skittish at the sudden activity. Koraymis' mount, William, was not faring so well. The sorcerer had to stay with the mount nearly the entire time anyone was working to secure straps and saddlebags, to prevent the horse from rearing up or bolting. Errol's mount, Teago, had to be calmed, but quickly settled down as they prepared to leave. The fifth horse, a lighter-colored dun, with an almost flaxen-colored coat and black points, legs, mane and tail, was acquiescent as servants laded her down with supplies. Errol didn't know her name.

Candissa's parents and sisters appeared in the yard as they were finishing loading the saddlebags. Errol was surprised to see them in such a ready state; the girls appeared to have made up their hair and all were dressed in their morning attire. He realized they must have been up for some time.

Her three sisters had eyes reddened by tears, but her mother and father appeared more resolute, their expressions almost stoic as they approached their eldest daughter.

Candissa stood before her parents, and nodded slowly, a sign of familial respect. "I can never thank you enough for all you've done for me, both of you," she said.

Errol could hear the emotion in her voice as she struggled to control it.

"And we are sorry we do not have more time to prepare you," her father said. "We should have shared so much more with you."

"You had no idea. None of us did," his daughter said.

"I want to tell you so much more, everything I can remember, but alas..." her mother's words trailed off. They embraced. Errol could see Candissa shaking a little as they hugged one another fiercely before stepping back.

"I do not intend to be gone forever. I just don't know when we may be back," Candissa said, her voice a little hoarse now.

"Keep reading your grandmother's journal on your way. Girls, bid your sister farewell," the older woman said, stepping aside. Brenissa was first, being the eldest.

"I'm sorry I could never be the sister you deserve," she said, releasing her older sister after a long pause. "Mother told us some things about...our family. I cannot imagine what you're going through."

"There is nothing to be sorry for, Brenny," Candissa said.

Nalliath followed, saying little but openly weeping. Errol thought she seemed a strange girl, almost mute. As they embraced, Errol saw her whisper something in Candissa's ear, but he couldn't make out what she had said. Candissa looked at her with a puzzled look, but Nalliath simply shook her head, murmuring something while trying to smile a little.

Elena was last, and Errol could see the bond of friendship between the oldest and youngest daughters of House Demarrae. Candissa had mentioned this in past conversations with him.

"I will await your return," Elena said.

"I hope it will be soon," Candissa said. She turned to Lord Demarrae. "Father, there will likely be trouble once we depart. I don't know what will come of that...matter at the Bonerest. There is no telling if others will take issue with us leaving."

"We will work through any such problems, my dear," her father nodded. He opened his arms and Candissa went to him, almost falling into them. "I will miss you, even if you are gone for a short time."

"And I you, Father."

He kissed her on the cheek, nodding. "All right. You should finish up here and be off."

Quence, the house steward, murmured something to Lord Demarrae. He raised his eyebrows and looked to Errol. "You have a guest?"

"Yes, forgive me my lord, I needed to send for Taldrephus," Errol said, bowing slightly. He saw the tall young man standing in the servants' entrance.

As the others tended their packs and saddlebags, he spoke to his friend.

"Here's a list of matters that will need your attention," he said, passing a folded piece of parchment to Taldrephus. "You know who you can trust. I spoke to Krebbick, so you have access to my vault. I plan on returning."

"Of course, sir, I'll do my best with these," Taldrephus said, tucking the note in a vest pocket. "Best of fortune, Errol."

They nodded, clasping hands, before Taldrephus disappeared into House Demarrae.

Errol needed only a minute to secure his belongings.

He inspected the others, but Cam was already on that task and he trusted the hunter more than his own experience in this. He saw Cam had to work with Koraymis more than the others in tightening the straps sufficiently.

"Are we ready?" Cam asked his three friends. Errol nodded in the affirmative, as did Koraymis and Candissa.

"I'm sending a detachment of guards to escort you to the western gate," her father said, motioning to three guards. They quickly mounted and took up a position ahead of them, at the smaller side gate of the estate.

"That's kind of you, Father, but hardly necessary,' Candissa said, as she adjusted a stirrup.

"Still, it would make your father happy."

"You will need them," Nalliath suddenly blurted, startling everyone. She spoke almost too loudly. Candissa's sister stepped forward, her almost skinny form seeming suddenly taller. Errol thought her expression not just distant but possibly a bit out of touch.

"What do you mean, daughter?" Lord Demarrae said, furrowing his brow.

"They are moving now. You must go!" she said, eyes wide open, staring at Candissa and her three companions. "They will find you before you reach the gate, hurry!"

"Nalli, whatever do you mean?" Candissa asked, confused as to why her otherwise unremarkable younger sister would make such a wild claim.

She's right! Came Koraymis' voice, in Errol's mind. He glanced at his dark-eyed friend. His hands were together. The sorcerer sensed something. Errol felt it, too.

"Mount, now!" he said in a low voice. In moments, the four were ready. Candissa could only look upon her family as she followed the three mounted guardsmen as they led the way out of the compound.

Cam took a position just a bit ahead of Koraymis and Candissa, with Errol centered between the two, but behind by a half-length. In the dark of the pre-dawn streets, Errol could feel his senses heighten. He could almost imagine he had eyes in the back of his head, he was so keenly aware of his surroundings.

"Mind your flanks, men," Cam said quietly to the guards. He must have sensed something as well.

Candissa, has your sister ever exhibited foretelling? Koraymis asked.

No, never. This is new. You believe her then?

Of course. I can sense it now myself. She has a gift. Is your entire family gifted?

Errol didn't like this distracting conversation.

Let us speak of this later. We could be in danger. Eyes and ears, Errol cut in. That ended the exchange.

They cantered in silence toward the main avenue.

Not twenty yards from the intersection, the sudden clatter of hooves moving quickly in the darkness put them all on alert. The guards drew swords, and they each stopped, turning.

Out of the alleyway just north of the main avenue came Thendarick, not quite at a gallop but clearly hurried.

"Lady Candissa! Thank the gods, come this way, don't take the main way!"

"Why?" Cam cut in.

"There's trouble at the garrison house. Some of the guards have deserted and are coming this way," the young officer said. In the dim light of a distant streetlamp, Errol saw he was not in his armor, but just his nightclothes.

"They mean to arrest us?" Candissa asked. Errol could not stop the quiet laugh that erupted from his throat.

"They mean to kill us!"

Thendarick looked at Errol sharply, but nodded. "Follow me, move as quietly as you can."

With no further argument or discussion, Thendarick led them on their way. Errol motioned to the guards to take up positions on their flanks and one in the rear.

They moved as quietly as eight mounted figures could, clopping softly along the cobbled alleys. Thendarick led them more northward, finding dirt paths behind some lesser shops even further north of the main way. Errol was sorry there were only two gates to choose from.

"Are they armed with bow?" Errol asked the officer.

"They had little time to prepare, there may be one or two with shortbows but no more," the lieutenant said.

"Are they led by an officer?" Candissa asked.

"A sergeant Scralleck I heard."

"Why would they do this? Was there any word?"

"No. It seems they are gripped by some form of madness. Most of them come from one squad. There was a guard in that squad who tried to stop them," Thendarick said, slowing as they turned a corner. "He's dead now. The lot of them will be swinging at the end of a rope by nightfall."

"Unless they intercept us first," Errol said. His hand itched to wield his blade. As he peered down alleys they passed, he could feel his eyes adjusting, almost supernaturally. He could perceive shapes and objects hidden by shadow and the predawn darkness. He suspected he could even fight in those conditions, without the benefit of direct light. While he hoped it would not come to that, he couldn't deny relishing the prospect of engaging in combat.

"How many are there?" Cam asked quietly.

"We believe nine but there could be ten or eleven."

"Are no other town guardsmen coming to our aid?"

"They know there's trouble brewing. A detachment will be sent to the western gate soon," Thendarick said. "I wanted to get you there safely."

Errol saw Candissa move closer to him.

"I don't know how to thank you, Thendarick," she said, smiling at the young man. "Not just for this, but for all the training you've given me over the years."

Even in the darkness, Errol was sure he could see the man blushing "I only hope you don't have to put it to use, my lady. And there's no reason for thanking me. It was my privilege."

"There's the gate," Cam said in a low voice, back to the others. They all looked ahead, past the dim shadows of streetlights as alleys intersected the narrow alleyway. Some distance ahead, the paved square before the gate was relatively well-lit. Even from this range, they could see the gates were closed, as they always were at this hour.

"Good, let us move quickly but carefully," Thendarick advised.

They followed his lead, any thought of conversation dismissed.

Trouble, came Koraymis' voice.

Certain? Candissa asked.

The scholar only nodded in the darkness as they pressed on.

Ahead of them, the light illuminating the gate square faded by steps, dimming once, twice, then vanishing almost entirely

"Well, *sard*," Errol muttered.

"The streetlamps," Thendarick whispered, signaling them to slow and halt. "Someone's doused them."

"We should move ahead but then dismount and deal with them. I don't want to risk the horses being wounded," Errol warned.

"That seems reasonable. We'll have to face them one way or another," Thendarick replied. He turned in his saddle. "Are you all ready for this?"

They all nodded, with Koraymis adding, shrugging, "Not much of a choice in it."

Errol watched as Cam strung bow quickly and expertly. He had an arrow nocked, after slinging his quiver over his shoulder. Candissa followed suit by freeing her staff from its harness and now gripped it in one hand as they advanced. He didn't see Koraymis doing anything in preparation. The young scholar's breathing was quickened, however.

"We could make for the garrison and wait there. The deserters will not return there. We would track them down and apprehend them. You would be free to move on," Thendarick suggested.

Errol shook his head. "That's no good. We endanger ourselves the longer we stay. The more people who know of our intent, the more attackers will appear out of the shadows."

"He's right, we must make our stand and depart as quickly as we may," Cam said, nodding.

"The guard on the gate is either with them, or dead," the officer said. "We must make for the gate and open it."

"We should dismount just ahead, after that intersection. I can make my way to the gate without being seen," Errol said. He wasn't sure how, but he knew he could. There was ample shadow and darkness.

They neared the point to dismount.

"Someone's there, around that last corner," Koraymis said quietly but firmly.

As if in answer, there was a sound of some sort. Errol knew it was a boot slipping in the gravel where Koryamis had indicated.

"He's warning his fellows, we've been marked!" Errol said in a low but audible voice.

"New plan, we charge for the gate, draw them out!" Cam said, gripping his reins in one hand, his bow in the other.

"Agreed, move!" Thendarick commanded the house guards behind them.

Errol cursed silently that only Cam had a bow, but they would have to make do.

The alley filled with the thunder of eight charging mounts, as the young officer led the way, followed closely by Cam. One of guards flanked Candissa, with the others moving to the fore and rear. Not the best arrangement, Errol noted, but there was nothing to be done for it.

The group burst onto the darkened square. The light of the two moons provided enough light for reaching the gate, while providing ample shadows for attackers. Errol realized the conditions were almost perfect for his purposes.

As they charged, all attempts at stealth abandoned, he made a rapid assessment of their situation.

The gate was closed, the wide doors bolted as they were every night. The square, which was more of a semicircle, had six streets leading onto it.

They charged from one, and Errol saw one or two figures at each corner, save the last one on their right. The Bonerest was one of the buildings on the square with attackers on either side. Like the other establishments bordering the square, it was closed,

He hoped their charge had caught their attackers off guard.

An arrow hissed by, only a few yards away. He slowed his mount enough to scan the area. He found one of them.

"Cam, archer, there!" Errol shouted, pointing. The figure was crouched atop the roof of merchant's shop.

He heard Koraymis shout in pain. An arrow protruded from his leg, below the knee. His charge faltered. Thendarick was at the gate, dismounting in a leap, along with one of the house guards. Cam had heeded Errol, already on the ground, bow drawn. He was trying to draw a bead on the archer. Candissa was turned now, having heard Koraymis' cry.

Figures ran from the nearest streets, rushing them. Errol grinned, grasping a spare dagger in his left hand, his blade in his right. He slid off his mount as it halted in the darkness, confused by the shouts and movements in the shadows.

He dashed for the corner through which they had charged, drawing the attention of at least two of the assailants. An arrow missed him wide. He was pleased to draw the archer's fire.

Before he reached the corner, he feinted a tumble. The ruse succeeded, as the closest attacker shouted in glee as he raised his shortsword, moving quickly on his prey. Errol's crouched legs were concealed by his long cloak.

Quicker than the hapless swordsman could react, Errol sprang forward, slashing deep across the man's gut. In the same motion, he pivoted, turning and lunged forward at the other attacker, deflecting his sword arm with one hand while plunging his blade through the man's heart with the other.

As the second man fell, he glanced upwards to see the archer clutching an arrow embedded deep in his shoulder. A third man was already moving toward Errol.

Without thinking, he twisted and stepped forward, launching his dagger with a forceful and exacting precision. The blade flashed through the air to embed in the man's left eye. The man screamed, clutching the grip as he fell to his knees. He was dead before he struck the ground.

Turning, Errol raced toward the gate, where more than half a dozen assailants were nearly upon his friends. Cam had taken one of the attackers with an arrow, but was now forced to draw his sword, as melee ensued. Koraymis was on the ground, clutching his leg, but leaning against a wall. Candissa stood in front of him, her staff at the ready as attackers rushed forward.

Thendarick had unbarred the gate with the aid of another guard, but there was no time to remount and head out.

One of Candissa's house guards screamed, clutching an arrow buried in his gut. Errol quickly spotted the other archer, cursing loudly. He was high atop a roof across the square. Two more figures charged from the street that ran along one side of the Bonerest tavern.

Errol resolved himself to running across the square, despite the risk, to find a means to reach that rooftop. To his shock, the fletched end of an arrow sprouted from the archer's neck.

Evan Devenuar stood outside the main door to the Bonerest, a tall bow in his hands. He was nocking another arrow.

Errol grinned. His blade was already back in his grip.

Making for the gate now, he was nearly blinded by a flash of light as Candissa struck an onrushing attacker. Her staff glowed brighter than ten streetlamps, surrounding her with light. It swung down hard to strike another man who was engaging Cam.

Errol saw there were more coming from the far side. He saw the shadows formed by the heavy pillars of the gate, near the rushing attackers, from where he was.

He had to help his friends. In the darkness, he closed his eyes for a moment, moving, stepping. The cold stone of the wall was suddenly at his back. The attackers were rushing toward the gate, mere steps from Errol. It took him only an instant to reorient himself.

Lunging out, both weapons drawn, he took two of them at once in their chests, before whirling around to kick another. Still spinning, he flung his dagger into the face of another attacker, who fell back onto the ground, unmoving.

Two were suddenly on him, swords flashing.

"Now you die!" one of them shouted with such a ridiculous flourish it nearly made Errol laugh. With the one dagger, he blocked the blow, dropping, tumbling to one side to spoil the other's attack, then leapt upward, his blade once more in his hand.

Both blades found the first man's ribs, while one of Evan's long arrow shafts was buried in the back of the other man. He dropped to his knees, trying to reach behind and grab the arrow. Errol took a step to one side and his blade flashed in the shadows. A crimson arc splashed across the wall indecorously.

A man screamed in agony. One of the attacking guards had been unfortunate enough to step within reach of Koraymis. The sorcerer grasped the man's throat, both hands wreathed in flame. The man dropped his weapon, letting loose a horrifying gurgle as smoke filled the air.

Candissa had just felled another with her staff with Cam's assistance. The last attacker fell under Thendarick's blade.

Sooner than he thought it could be, it was over. A bell began ringing in the distance.

Candissa was at Koraymis' side, as he slumped against the wall, the arrow still protruding from his left calf. His face was twisted in pain, sweat gleaming on his face.

"I must pull the arrow out, Kor. It will hurt," she said with no trace of doubt.

"Quickly!" Koraymis growled. Errol was certain his eyes were glowing red.

Candissa was quick and sure, pulling the arrow out cleanly. She clapped a palm against his leg and closed her eyes, murmuring words. Koraymis' eyes went wide at whatever sensation her healing was causing. She was done as quickly, standing already.

"We need to wrap that," she said.

"We don't have time," Cam said, pointing. Townsfolk were gathering at the edge of the square, with a few inspecting the fallen bodies near the Bonerest. One of them pointed at Candissa, shouting something ugly. Someone next to him balled up a fist and struck the shouting man hard in the face.

Evan was running over to them, longbow still in hand, an arrow nocked. "You should go, my friends. There is trouble brewing. I will attend to the fallen guard, Candissa."

Candissa looked at the dead guard, her eyes suddenly stricken. She looked to Evan.

"I can't thank you enough for helping us!" she said. "I can only hope we can repay the debt we owe you."

"You will have that chance. You will return someday, I know."

"How do you know that?" she asked.

"You are not alone. I have waited for you, for many long years, though I did not know it was you for whom I was waiting," he said, his expression utterly solemn. "My part is not done for now. Fare thee well on your journey. I will keep my watch."

"Mount up, we need to go, now!" Errol said. "Kor, do you need help getting in your saddle?"

Koraymis shook his head, as he managed to pull himself up into his saddle. Cam was already securing his weapons and tying the fifth horse's lead rope to his pommel. Candissa slung her staff over her back, once more securing it with leather loops. The flood of illumination from Candissa's staff was beginning to diminish.

"I will explain all," the young officer assured them all. "It's best if you make haste. We don't know what will happen if the crowd grows in size."

Errol glanced back at the more than two dozen townsfolk. There were at least two fights taking place, which served well to distract them. There could be more attackers among them, he imagined.

"Errol, we will meet again. Sooner than you may think, I believe," Evan said, extending a hand as Errol was the last past the gates. Errol clasped the offered hand.

"May fortune favor you," Errol said.

"May your path lead you home," Evan responded with the traditional reply. Errol found it to be especially fitting in his circumstance.

An arrow suddenly thunked into one of the slowly-swinging gates.

"Go!" Thendarick shouted, pushing hard to open the gates fully, while trying to see who had fired the arrow. Errol slapped the rump of Koraymis' mount, spurring it on through the gate. The four riders were through momentarily.

Thendarick was already swinging the gates shut. "Fare you all well!" he called after them, before shutting the gates with a low, heavy thump. Errol heard the reassuring sound as the heavy bar secured the gate. Shouting could be heard as more fighting ensued.

Cam set the pace for the moment at a trot, to put some ground between them and the gate. It was still dark but behind them, a blue haze painted the sky over the awakening town of Ravensroost.

"Stop here, I need to bandage Koraymis," Candissa called, as they were suddenly at the edge of the Wardenstone.

Errol had almost forgotten about it. As Candissa jumped off her mount to inspect the sorcerer's leg, Cam watched for trouble at the gate. For the moment, it remained shut. Candissa quickly produced a strip of linen and pulled up Koraymis' legging to access the wound. It was much improved after Candissa's ministrations but still needed tending.

"That's good enough," Candissa declared, moving quickly to remount.

"Good, let us ride. We need not be here when the curious finally open those gates. We don't know if more attackers will be riding out after us," Cam warned.

Errol sighed as he looked back once more at the town wall, and the Wardenstone. It was the only world he could remember. Turning back around to face forward, he knew without a doubt that the answers to what came before his time here lay in the hills or beyond.

With that, the four riders guided their mounts into the first of the low rises that would become the Misthallow Hills. They did not speak as they rode together. They only looked at the veiled horizon, not knowing what it would bring.

There were no words exchanged, spoken or otherwise. Yet Errol knew what his three friends were thinking as they rode into the unknown.

West.

CHAPTER TWENTY-SIX - PRAESEOS

No bearing of day nor month nor year

He awoke. The waking did not startle him. He was of an even-handed nature. Yet, he was puzzled.

It was dark, but he was not afraid of the dark. He attempted to pierce the darkness with his sight, but it was a fruitless effort. He knew he was facing a few degrees north of true west, though that helped him not. Raising his arms, he reached forward to see if he could feel anything.

Ah, a door. A latch. Good.

He pulled down on the latch, and the door yielded.

Light flooded the tiny chamber which had been his home for an unknown span of time. His eyes took a moment to adjust.

"Is this the dawn or the light of the setting sun?" Praeseos spoke aloud. He had a habit of speaking to himself at all hours of the day, whether alone or in the company of others. Given the angle of the light and the direction, he supposed it was late afternoon, though it was only a guess.

The area before him was in a frightful state of disarray. A long table and several chairs were overturned, some broken. Glass was shattered throughout the narrow, curved chamber. In some respects, the chamber was more a corridor, being only slightly wider than the broad door in which he stood.

Dust and debris were gathered in corners. A lone, tall window set high in the arcing wall before him let the light in, a long, narrow beam cutting through the air to illuminate the wall above the door in which he stood. Stepping into the chamber, he tested his legs and arms. They seemed well enough.

"Hallo!" His voice was strong, and this pleased him. There was no reply. This made him sad.

The window was broken, thick shards of glazing lying on the stone floor beneath. Praeseos stepped forward and picked a piece up. The glazing was tinted and well made. He knew it was so as he had some knowledge of how glass was crafted. Outside, through the shattered remains of the window, he saw the blue sky.

"The sky is a welcome sight," he spoke. "But why is this fine window so smash'd?"

He examined the broken table before him. The leg was stout maple, carved, with feet of formed metal. Looking closer, he recognized the pale amber metal alloy for what it was commonly known as - white gold. He knew the proper name, however - electrum.

"Yet, why would such a precious alloy be put to such base use?" he wondered aloud. He laughed briefly, realizing his pun. "Base, indeed."

He gripped the leg of maple. It was finely carven, a work of some master wood carver. Yet, it was desiccated, somehow sapped of a vital component, diminishing its inherent robustness.

He gripped it with some strength and was not surprised to see the wood wither under his grip, cracking and splintering. Dust fell to the floor, along with a few small bits of broken, dried wood.

"What ill hath befallen this place, that wood turns to dust in my hand?"

Ahead of him, he saw the chamber had another door, set in the narrow wall. Praeseos looked to his right and left. Shelves mounted upon the wall were barren. In one corner, to his consternation, he found a pile of dried bones.

Picking up one of the bones, a long length, he adjudged it to be the thigh bone of a Human or Elf. It was dried, fragile. Clearly, it was cursed by the passage of many long years, as was the table.

"Do not judge me for handling your bones, friend. I mean no disrespect," he said, addressing the remains of the long-dead individual. "I only seek to answer the questions wracking my poor mind." He placed the bone where it had lain.

He looked to the door, then the window, thinking.

"What infernal curse is upon my head? Beyond my name, I know not one thing!" His voice rang out loudly.

Turning about, he found he had been standing within a closet of some sort, formed of well-crafted metal, looking for all the world like a vault built into the wall. He was not pleased with his situation.

"My name is Praeseos, yet, whence do I hail? What is my home? How did I come to be here?" he muttered.

He felt anger growing within his plated chest. Stepping over to the far door, he tried the handle. It would not yield. Not yet, at least. The door was made of wood, and that was something he counted in his favor. Like the table, the wood appeared to have seen the prime of its days.

"A mere portal of wood shall not block my path, this I know!"

Clenching one plated fist, he drew his arm back. With one titanic stroke, he drove his fist into the door, near the latching mechanism. The wood cracked and splintered under the force. He ignored the minor pain it inflicted. Drawing his fist back again, he drove a second and final stroke through the door, shattering the wood around the metal latching assembly.

The door swung open slightly as the handle and latch fell away along with shards of ruined wood.

Pushing the door wide, Praeseos found himself in a longer hall of some sort, but still with a wall that curved along in a gentle arc, as did the last chamber.

"What is this? The walls follow not a line of geometric order but turns, ever turns!" he said in a low voice. "What is the meaning?"

The hall was much longer than the room behind him, and only a little wider. A few steps forward revealed a ramp at the far end, leading downward. That much was a blessing, for it could lead downward, and with luck, to a better understanding of where he was. But like the other, this chamber had furnishings sundered and worn by the wrath of time. The floor was covered in no small amount of dust and dirt, soil and leaves. The southwestward-facing windows, numbering three, were tall and broken, and welcomed in beams of golden sunlight. They were set low enough in the wall that they afford him a view outward. Peering out, he found he was a good distance off the ground below, which consisted of dried yellow grasses on a sloping hilltop.

The realization came to him in a flash. "I am in a tower!"

He made for the ramp, excited at his discovery. The rampway curved around the wall of the tower, a few small windows set high in the wall.

In the level below, the ramp gave way to a wide corridor that followed the outer wall, curving. He found more windows, smaller and lower to the floor.

Along the inner wall of this level, he found two stout wooden doors and a narrow corridor after them, turning toward the center of the tower. Beyond the corridor was the rampway down to yet another level. Torn momentarily between simply moving downward or investigating the place, he chose the latter.

Opening the first door, he found what he surmised was once a spacious sleeping chamber. There was a large bed with nearly rotted sheets, a broken table, and windows looking out across the desolate rolling reaches of grass. A small privy was built into the chamber, and a pair of shelves had naught but dust. Peering out the windows, he realized this was not a wide tower, with a diameter of perhaps twenty paces.

The second door was locked and appeared to be exceedingly well-built. He chose to return to this door at a later point and turned down the corridor instead.

It was a short hallway, with one door immediately on his right. It opened onto a small chamber with only a scattering of old linens, sheets and blankets and the like. They were strewn about along with a collection of other seemingly random objects. Broken shelves told him the chamber was perhaps once a storeroom.

The corridor led a short way to what Praeseos knew was the center of the tower. It was a round chamber, with two doors, and a broad column that ran from floor to ceiling. It appeared to be a support column, clad in smooth stone. "Curious, indeed, that this smallish tower requires such a broad central spire," he murmured, before trying one door. It was a well-made door, with an intricate latching mechanism, requiring two hands. Yet, he was familiar with it, and after a moment, he opened the door. It was another sleeping chamber, nicely appointed, with furnishings in better repair. The windows were intact and there was no evidence anyone or anything had visited the chamber in untold years. Still, he found it strange the shelves bore only dust.

Quitting the chamber, he tried the other door. This room was yet another bedchamber, showing signs of intrusion and deterioration, as he had seen in other chambers. None of the rooms had shown any signs of recent occupation.

Returning to the locked door, he tried it again. It was stuck fast. He twisted the handle with what he considered sufficient force to operate such a mechanism, yet it only barely budged. Choosing not to destroy the door, he instead used both of his metal-clad hands to grip the stout iron handle.

Bearing down with his most of his weight, the handle yielded after a long effort. It was not an easy task. He knew it would have taken the strength of ten Humans to do this. "Whatever lies within must be of great value, with such a portal to guard against intrusion," Praeseos said.

The door opened wide and Praeseos froze, not understanding at first glance what lay before him.

"By the fires of the forge..." he breathed.

The room was small, even more so than the storage chamber. It lacked any window, illuminated only by the light from the corridor and by the ghostly green radiance emanating from the most unexpected sight.

A woman, seemingly frozen in place, unmoving, as still as a statue. She was shrouded in a green light, encapsulating her in an orb of glowing energy. Praeseos knew at once it was magic of some sort. But the spell-wreathed woman was no wizard. He could discern nothing more of what it meant.

The woman did not appear dead or slain, but rather, appeared to be in perfect condition. She had red hair and amber eyes, with skin not quite weathered but tanned. She seemed young, yet not a youth. Dressed in leathers of some strange design, she was standing almost as if she were about to take a step.

Praeseos was tempted to reach out and try to take a hand that seemed to be rising as if to hail him or greet a friend. But he knew better. With magic, best to leave it be, unless you have a wizard at your side.

Studying the young woman, Praeseos judged her a warrior of some sort. Her build, along with the clothing and equipment she bore, spoke of a life of physical activity, if not martial training. The middle of her leather tunic, bedecked with straps and metal attachments, featured a large, round medallion, made of a light gray metal. The disc bore an insignia that seemed familiar to Praeseos.

Stepping only a bit further into the room, he studied the insignia, and the woman, frozen in place by magic. Though Praeseos was certain the stylized art embellishing the medallion had a special significance, he could not recall what it was. He shook his heavy head slowly, frustration mounting within.

"Though I rack my mind, it yields naught. Enough!" Praeseos cried, his voice deep and resounding. "Why am I tormented by memory like so much blank parchment?"

The woman had a kind expression, not one frozen in a moment of terror or aggression. Praeseos imagined she appeared even grateful, somehow. Her eyes were warm in her countenance. Her hair was a bit ragged and loose, bound loosely behind, and looked like so much coiled copper wire, as what one would find in a Tamnati workshop. Tucked in her leather belt were a pair of heavy riding gloves, of exceptionally fine craftsmanship. The leather tunic, upon closer inspection, was something like leather armor, yet clearly had more functionality.

Heavy straps of leather were attached to steel loops or hooks, with at least one attached to her leggings, also made of heavy leather. Praeseos found himself mesmerized by the curious design of what the woman wore.

"Ha! I may well have known precisely the maker of this curiosity," he muttered. "As I am robbed of my memory, there is no settling the matter!"

Stepping back from the figure, he saw no other identifying marks or signs that stirred his recollections. There was nothing in the room save the young woman in her ensorcelled confinement. His frustration unabated, he left the place, closing the door partially.

"Mayhap I will find others in this place, and there find an answer or two."

Descending the curving ramp, Praeseos found small windows lining the way, some unbroken but choked with a dusty film. Others were breached enough to afford a view of the ground below. He saw he had at least twenty yards to descend before reaching the dried grassy expanse.

The next level within the tower offered a much wider view of the plains outside. Entirely half of this level was a single room, with a rampway leading up and down, and a long window with a metal frame. Only a few fragments of glazing remained attached to the frame. Tiny pieces were scattered along the broad sill but little else of it within. As the window was more than five paces wide, Praeseos could survey the entire southern horizon. No matter what remained of his memory, he was fully aware of at least some of his faculties. This included an unerring sense of direction, for which he was grateful.

The rest of the half-round chamber had only bits of broken wood, what looked to be the remains of a fire pit long abandoned, and a long, curving bookshelf on the wall near the downward ramp. There were two more smaller chambers in the northern half of the level, with both doors open. He could not discern the prior purpose of one, but the other once served as a kitchen of sorts.

Inspecting the shelves next to the wide window, Praeseos found them to be lined with a thick, dried layer of dusty debris. Moving back to the window, he leaned out far enough to look over the edge of the outer sill.

Below, he saw the curving wall of the round tower as it sloped outward almost imperceptibly. At the ground, the tower was ringed with broken stone fragments of varying sizes, piled unevenly. There was more than stone in the weed-choked piles, but he could not determine what from his present vantage point.

Small trees grew from the debris at points, and the near-barren branches of brown, dried leaves still clinging at points, told Praeseos it was autumn. Looking up, he surveyed the gently rolling grasslands, dotted by only a few patches of low trees. Wind blew steadily across the plains, creating an almost mesmerizing effect, not unlike the undulating waves upon the ocean.

Beyond the grasses southward, he saw nothing but the darkening sky. To the east, he thought he could see hills rising, but he could not be sure. If so, they were many miles away. To the west by north, the lowering sun picked out a range of mountains likely fifty miles away.

"Mayhap another window will grant the northern aspect," Praeseos spoke to the horizon, wishing it could answer him. Like all his kind, he held the gift of speech in highest regard. As such, he exercised his speech often. He knew it was simply the way of his people.

Descending once more, he found the next lower level full of signs of previous occupation. There were three small rooms off the main, all with smashed shelves and furnishings, some clearly having been used in fires. Animal bones were strewn in a pile, and judging by the color of the blood, they were not so old, perhaps only months.

Inspecting the considerable piles of debris, using his foot to brush to and fro, he found no immediate clues that would provide any information to him about where he was or how he might have arrived here. He did find evidence this place was once home to a number of people. Torn bits of clothing, cracked leather boots, writing tools, broken ink pots, personal items and the like, were all scattered within the broken furnishings, dust and leaves.

Given the number of bookshelves and the evidence of writing, Praeseos was surprised at finding not a single book or piece of parchment had survived whatever catastrophe had befallen the place. This made him sad, as any reference to a place or a date would give him some measure of solace.

"I must not think upon my ruined mind," he said, shaking his head. "It will drive me to the edge of my sanity if I do."

Resolving to continue his exploration of the tower, Praeseos headed down what he judged was the last set of curving rampways. This one stretched a greater distance, as the lowest and final level had a much higher ceiling.

That was when he heard the noise below. It made him stop his descent.

It was an animal-like grunting, quick and sharp noises, but punctuated with other sounds. Not the sounds of animals, by Praeseos' judgment. Focusing on the sound, a recollection seemed to rise from the depths of his desolate memory. Drawing in breath, he used his sense of smell. *Yes,* he thought silently to himself to avoid drawing attention by speech, *I know this scent.* It was an unpleasant smell, rife with musty, earthy rot, old skins and molded hides, poorly tanned leather, dirt, feces and bile.

His hand instinctively went to one of his weapons, this one resembled a slightly curved broadsword. He was pleased it was still in its sheath, over his right shoulder. Sliding it out quietly, he gripped the long haft firmly, feeling it seat securely in his palm and forearm, his fingers molding tightly to the indentations. Quiet clicking noises told him it was secured resolutely to his hand.

Inspecting the weapon, the blade appeared as keen as the day he...the memory of whatever that day had eluded him.

Stepping downward more slowly now, he crouched as he moved, intent on seeing them before they spied him. As he descended, masking nearly every noise of his steps, the lowest and largest chamber in the tower came into view. It was lit by the open entrance, a tall, narrow archway. One cracked door clung to its hinges, while the other lay on the floor near the central column. Arches rose from the central column to join with the ceiling, providing support. One of them gave him cover as he descended the ramp.

For the time being, his attention was focused on the three creatures squatting near the center of the chamber. They hunched over a pile of dried sticks, atop the remains of an old fire pit. They were striking flint, attempting to coax enough spark to ignite the dried grass piled on the sticks.

They wore crude hides and scavenged leather, bound by crude cords. Their feet were unshod, but the skin of their soles were thick. They were brutish and strong, as evidenced by the knotted muscles of their shoulders and neck. Their skin was a grayish-green, with a mottling of pale and brown spots. Their brown and black hair grew in stiff clumps. With a thick brow ridge and a jutting jaw sprouting oversized teeth better for tearing meat than chewing food, they were truly beast-like in their appearance.

While they resembled Humans in only a vague way, they were in no way kin to Human or Elf or Dwarve. They were called many things, Praeseos was sure of that. But the only name for them he could recall was the most common, he believed. *Chom.*

While Praeseos could not remember much, he knew without a doubt these were dangerous, often deadly if they had advantage in numbers. Their aggression was unrelenting. While not as senseless as animals, they were inclined to follow their instincts and could not be reasoned with on a reliable basis. He expected their meeting would end badly.

His right foot crushed a stone as he stepped downward. The noise drew their attention instantly. Standing as one, the three creatures looked up the ramp, their mouths momentarily agape. Small, dark eyes stared, as their pointed ears pressed back against their heads.

He knew they possessed the power of language, despite their animalistic tendencies and appearance. Praeseos realized he knew their language, as he knew so many other languages.

"*Ayak shogo un!*" He spoke their language with a harsh tone. *We need not fight.*

The three Chom looked at one another furtively. One stood a little taller, his dark, sunken eyes gleaming green in the fading light of day.

"Are you with the others?" he demanded, gripping a club now that had been attached to his broad belt of crude leather.

"I am alone," Praeseos replied in their tongue, carefully taking another step down. The three brutish creatures did not fail to notice this, as they brandished their weapons.

"No! Are you *with them*?" the first one shouted now.

For a moment, Praeseos noted to himself their dialect seemed strange, unfamiliar yet discernible. It mattered little, but such things rarely escaped his notice.

"I do not know who *they* are. I am with no others," he replied. He would have been more nuanced in his words, but their language offered few options in conveying subtleties.

"Lies!" one of them spat, hefting his spiked club in his powerful grip.

"I seek only words with you," Praeseos chose to make at least one attempt at reason. He was only a few steps from the floor of the chamber now.

The first one answered, his face twisted into an animal snarl, baring sharp teeth. "Words are for prey! We drink the blood of prey!"

With that, the three brutes charged Praeseos, despite his higher footing and much greater size. He did not wish to engage in combat. But they left him no choice.

As the lead Chom leapt for him, swinging a club studded with iron spikes driven through, Praeseos jumped down as he easily dodged the vicious weapon. Using the momentum of his leap, he brought his right arm down and across, his bladed weapon parting the Chom's head from his hulking shoulders. Blood flew forth in a long gout as his body toppled.

Spinning, he raised his left arm to ward off the blow of a lesser club. The wood cracked as his armor easily absorbed the impact, though the spikes did manage to pierce his outer armor. He drove his blade through the Chom's ribs, the tip protruding out his back, under a shoulder blade.

The third Chom had a fire-sharpened spear instead of a club. The creature drove it hard into Praeseos' side, and the tip managed to find a gap between the bands of metal that comprised his rib armor. It was a minor wound and did not affect him for the time being. The Chom drew it back and attempted another strike. Praeseos reoriented himself, wrenching his weapon free of the second Chom. The spear missed badly as it attempted to skewer Praeseos in the neck.

Praeseos blocked a second stabbing attack with such force it knocked the spear from the creature's grip. The sharp stick clattered on the floor well away from the melee.

The Chom looked at Praeseos, expecting instant death. To Praeseos' surprise, the creature did not lunge for his weapon in an effort that would have simply led to a killing blow. Its eyes darted to Praeseos' side, where a dark, brownish liquid oozed out of the spear wound, into the seams between metal plate. It was thicker than blood.

"What are you?" the Chom uttered, its tiny eyes so wide as to almost show the whites.

"Your people call us iron spirits."

The Chom licked its lips in desperation. The fear in its eyes was evident as it glanced around the room, perhaps looking for some sort of advantage.

"Others call us the Forgewrought, or Saarici," Praeseos said, almost pleased to educate the creature, or at least delay the inevitable. He did not lower his guard. The creature's eyes stopped darting around and looked up at his.

"You...have not chosen?"

This question perplexed Praeseos. "What do you mean *chosen*?"

"You must choose," it said, rising, its eyes suddenly menacing. Fear was replaced by dark rage. "We chose! You chose too I think!"

It lunged for the spear. As the Chom whirled back around, spear in hand, Praeseos buried his blade deep into the creature's gut. It dropped the weapon, making a gurgling noise as it slumped, dead. Its blood pooled on the floor with the blood of his two companions, mixing with ash, dirt, leaves and debris.

He looked at the dead creatures, shaking his head slowly. He always regretted taking life, regardless of the circumstances. "I hope you find peace," he murmured.

He cleaned the bladed weapon extending from his right hand with an aged linen pulled from the debris. When it was clean enough, he replaced it on his back. He pressed a hand against his side. The damage was minor. He would attend to it later. On the northern side of this lowest chamber, where the long rampway descended from above, there were two doors. Both were open, and he inspected them to insure there were no other Chom here. They were both unoccupied and strewn with debris like the large entry chamber.

Looking at the corpses, he knew he could simply leave them lying on the floor to rot. But that did not sit well with him. It would be entirely uncivilized to depart the tower without burying the dead in some manner. Perhaps the piles of debris without would offer an easy means of interring them.

Praeseos stepped outside. The wind was chill and getting colder. Breathing in, he sensed autumn in the air. He judged it to be sometime early in the month called Tempestus. Taking several long strides, he turned to assess the place. The sky was clear, though clouds loomed far to the south. Looking north, he was greeted by the sight of a massive range of mountains, perhaps thirty miles distant. They dominated the northern horizon, stretching off to the northeast, tapering gradually and fading into the twilight.

Examining the tower, it was white as ivory. The light of the setting sun colored it gold. He now understood the heaping of debris all around the base. The top of the tower was shorn off, jagged teeth of white bared to the sky. The torn top of the tower was well over fifty yards above the grassy plain. Praeseos could see more than just the white stone of the tower wall. There were also broken timbers and what must have been twisted beams of metal. Along the length of the rise there were a few windows, varied in size. There was an especially large one facing west. It seemed to be shuttered somehow.

He set about circumnavigating the tower base. The debris was lumped more on one side, but there was no shortage of loose rubble and stone. It would be simple to inhume them amid the detritus.

He found an area to the west of the tower with more smaller pieces of debris and dirt that had accumulated over the years. It was difficult to say how old the ruined tower was. There was significant growth and decay of plants and trees. More than a century of it, by his estimate.

Finding a length of straight metal more than two yards long, he commenced to turn a sufficient area of earth and stone. It did not take him long. He knew Forgewrought were especially suited to this sort of labor. In short order he was done, and he returned to the lowest chamber of the tower.

He carried the Chom out one at a time, placing them with appropriate respect into the excavation. He even found the head of the leader and included it in the grave. Using the metal beam, he shoveled loose earth back over the corpses, but it was insufficient. Surveying the tower's base again, Praeseos chose more than two dozen stones, carried one or two at a time, to place upon the entombed creatures. They were heavy stones and not easily moved.

When he was done, he saw the light of the sun fading rapidly. The tower had lost its golden luster, replaced by the indigo glow of the twilight sky.

Praeseos stood over his work and took a deep breath.

"I know not what your customs are, nor do I know what brought you here," he said in a voice that would be normally reserved for addressing a large group. He did not think it appropriate to murmur such words. "I am not worthy to judge you on the balance of your life, having seen only the ragged end of it. But I know all life has worth, and I can only hope you will find your way in whatever may come after."

"They will find their way," a harsh, deep voice called out from just around the curve of the tower. Praeseos was rightly startled.

He stepped back, arming himself in a lightning-quick motion.

A hulking creature stood there, having had approached from the eastern side of the tower, concealing its approach in the growth along the base. The creature was taller than Praeseos, which was remarkable in itself. Wrapped in no end of furs and skins, it held a ten-foot tall staff of gnarled oak.

Cords strung with bones, polished stones, feathers and rune-carved totems hung across a broad chest. An immense club was affixed to a belt of wide, dark leather. The hand that gripped the staff was as gnarled as the wood, and sported long, claw-like nails. Atop its head was a cap fashioned from various pieces of fur, antlers and claws. The face of the creature was unlike the Chom that Praeseos had just interred, but it was still monstrous. In the visage, unlike the Chom, Praeseos saw something more refined. Its nose was more of a snout, and the mouth sported sharp teeth. Unlike the Chom, this creature was entirely covered in short hair or fur. The fur was a mottled dark color, with patches of gray.

The head was set upon a long neck, much longer than any Chom, and below the ragged patchwork of furs and skins, Praeseos saw broad feet that were clawed and jointed like those of an animal. They were better suited for loping than walking, he imagined.

The eyes caught Praeseos's attention. The eyes were large, appearing thoughtful and brooding as they assessed him. The Forgewrought did not sense any hostility in the creature.

It raised a free hand, palm up. It was a hand larger than Praeseos', clawed, and bore more than one ring.

"Peace, Forgewrought. I will not attack you as did my lesser kith," it said.

"You speak my tongue," Praeseos said.

"Aye, but it is an old tongue, which I have not heard spoken in a very long time," the creature said. "I was going to ask you why you were speaking it. But who I thought was a man in armor I find is a spirit of iron. I bid you welcome. I am Sevok, a shaman of Moon Howlers clan."

Replacing his weapon, Praeseos bowed slightly. "I am Praeseos. I have no lineage to mention. I mean no disrespect." He ever strove to respond with courtesy when courtesy was offered.

Sevok was already waving his hand. "I would expect none. You are Forgewrought and you have no memory of your past, like all your kin."

"You have seen others as me?" Praeseos said, suddenly excited.

"Yes, but that was more than forty years ago. Those I met were old beyond my imagining and had no recollection of their former lives."

"You are Ur'chom, are you not?"

"Yes, indeed. You know the old words. Humans call my kind dog giants, or sometimes trolls. Both are entirely incorrect."

"What brings you here, Sevok?"

"At first, a calling. The setting sun told me to come here," it said, looking toward the horizon. "Now I suspect it was to meet you."

"Why?"

"Destiny does not always give us complete answers," Sevok chuckled, a low sound, almost a growl. The Ur'chom looked at the fresh graves. "I appreciate the honor you accorded them, though they were here to kill you."

"You believe they were?"

"Yes, as surely as I am not. Others will come here. I know not if you are to remain here or if you will now depart. But in making my way for this tower, I heard tell of some of my folk, and the lesser Chom. They are falling under the influence of a spell or some evil beyond my understanding."

"I know nothing of this, for I awoke but a short time ago."

"Awoke? I do not understand."

"Nor do I. I have no memory, as you said. I awoke perhaps an hour before sunset and found myself in this tower. Then I encountered the Chom. I tried to reason with them, but you see the result," he said, looking at the stones and earth.

"You may not be as fortunate in the days to come. I know the might of the Forgewrought is legendary, but many of my kind seek to kill you, and journey here even now. At least, that is what I read in the signs," Sevok said, grimacing as he studied the tower.

"Why would anyone wish to kill me?"

"I know not. But I have heard tales of voices that whisper to their minds. Dark, malevolent voices. They speak of someone in the tower they must kill, to please some nameless master."

"I do not know why anyone would wish ill upon me. Is that all you can recall from your travels?"

"There is little more than that. A person trapped by magic some said, waiting to be freed," the Ur'chom mused, scratching a short, bristled beard. "They seek to slay this person before he can be awoken. They failed in this. For you are awake."

"Did these whispers mention simply a person? Or did they indicate a Human? I am Forgewrought, and those distinctions are often ignored by other races."

Sevok's head shook. "My kind rarely care about other races in their speaking, it only whispered of a person, with no distinction of race or gender."

Praeseos frowned. "What if they were not seeking to kill me?"

"Who then?"

"I can show you," the Forgewrought offered. "Come."

He led the lumbering shaman into the tower, up the winding stairs. On the fourth level, he revealed the chamber that contained the young woman, frozen behind the curtain of green enchantment.

Sevok had a difficult time squeezing into the chamber. The Ur'chom's nine-foot tall frame, half as wide, took some effort to get through the door sized to Human proportions.

"Incredible. This must be who they seek!"

"You're certain?"

"Yes. I was called by the setting sun. In a vision, I saw that medallion. It bears the mark of a griffon, I remember that now."

Praeseos remembered now. *Griffon*, that was the insignia.

"I know this sign..." he whispered. The massive Ur'chom turned.

"What do you remember?"

"Griffons, I remember...something...immense, so large, filling the sky..." he murmured, torn between wracking his mind and letting it ease forth. It was to no avail, as the memory flickered and faded.

"Truly these are times of change, if Forgewrought begin recalling the past," Sevok said, shaking its huge head. "I only wish I knew what to do with this one."

"What do you mean?"

"If we quit this tower and abandon her, they will likely find and kill her, despite whatever enchantment this is."

"The door was held fast. It took all of my strength to open it," Praeseos murmured. "I am responsible for exposing her to the malice of those who seek her death."

"Perhaps we should try to awaken her, that she could flee?"

"I am loath to try this enchantment. I remember little, but my common sense is still intact. Magic unknown is something to be avoided."

"Like most Forgewrought, you are wise," the shaman said. "Still, perhaps I will try this green shell that encases her. Stand back."

Shaking his metal head, Praeseos stepped out of the chamber entirely, that Sevok could back against the door. Taking the gnarled staff, Sevok extended it, so just the end touched the greenish glow.

It sparked brightly, not unlike heated metal being struck on an anvil.

"Ah, perhaps not then," Sevok said, withdrawing the staff and examining the smoldering tip.

"Mayhap our helpless friend is not so helpless," Praeseos suggested.

"Perhaps. But still, if enough Chom come, they could defeat it, even if some die trying," the Ur'chom said, turning to look at Praeseos. "They are that senseless, I am certain."

"Then what is to be done of it? I am not inclined to abandon a stranger to what could be certain death, when it was my errant actions that led to her vulnerability."

"I suspect others from the mountains to the east will be here within days, though I cannot be certain."

"Then I must secure this place against intrusion, on the chance they will be here sooner than not. The doors looked mighty in their design. Perhaps I can effect repairs."

"Have you explored the tower levels above?"

"Nothing beyond where I awoke. I can show you that."

Praeseos led him up to where stood the tomb of iron. "This was where I found myself."

"Curious, there are no steps leading upwards from this level," the shaman commented, looking around. "There is more here on this floor, I have no doubt. I saw windows above as well. Perhaps..."

Sevok pushed Praeseos aside politely and shouldered his way into the iron sarcophagus. Striking the back with his staff, it sounded hollow.

"Ha! As I suspected," Sevok said, grinning in a fashion that was almost unnerving, even to the Forgewrought. "Do not be alarmed, I am using some of my magic."

With that, Sevok spoke quiet, dark syllables, in a tongue Praeseos was surprised to find he could not recognize. An orb of light suddenly blossomed into being just near the tip of the tall staff. It seemed to float near the staff, as if tethered by an invisible cord.

It served to illuminate the dark, metal interior of the vault. Waving a free hand about the confined space, Sevok seemed satisfied. "There, I sense it. A trigger. Here, you get in here, and push. It may be that simple."

Unable to offer any alternative to further exploration of the tower, Praeseos waited for the Ur'chom to shuffle back out, then entered. He placed both hands against the back of the metal enclosure. Pushing hard, he immediately felt a click. A passage was revealed as rear of the vault slid back and to the side with a gentle grinding noise.

"Well done!" Sevok said. "Let us explore the rest of this place."

"I suppose we must," Praeseos said, a cautious person by nature.

The opening was easy for him to pass through, while Sevok had to stoop. It led to a curving set of steps, on up to the next level. Praeseos was immediately gladdened at what greeted them there.

"A forge and shop!" Sevok said, surprised. "And in perfect order. Clearly no one has been able to access the tower beyond where you slept."

Praeseos inspected it cursorily. He nodded. "Furnace, coals, tools, materials, even molds and anvils. Truly a complete forging facility."

"Are you skilled with the use of such things?" the shaman asked. Praeseos nearly laughed but resisted. That would be most discourteous.

"Yes, like most of my people, I am. More importantly, I now have the means to effect complete repairs to the doors below."

Looking at some of the finer tools neatly aligned along a shelf, Praeseos also realized he would be able to mend his wounds fully, once he had the time.

"Of course," Sevok said, looking around. "It seems the shop fills this level. Save for the ramp upwards. Let us press onward"

Praeseos motioned for him to lead the way. The glowing orb provided the light they needed, given the windows yielded almost no illumination at this point. Above, they found something beyond his expectations. No mere level in the tower was this chamber. Praeseos estimated the chamber was at least fifty feet in height, though he was not certain. The only light was the dim blue illumination offered by the small windows dotting the walls of the tower. Shadows obscured the ceiling.

From the stone floor to the shadowed heights, the room was filled entirely with a mass of machinery. He marveled at the long and turning pipes of every description, cables strung like webs, gears, massive tanks, tall crystal and metal tubes, strange controls consisting of dials and handles, narrow, and winding metal steps leading to platforms, catwalks and ledges.

"Forgewrought, I have never seen such wonders," Sevok breathed. "I've seen a Dwarven workshop on a few occasions and even a tinkerfolk lair once. But nothing like this!"

"It is remarkable," Praeseos agreed. "What is its purpose, though?"

He moved to a spiraling rise of steps, far too narrow and confining for the girth and height of the Ur'chom. It led to a central area where several catwalks intersected. Examining the immense tanks, cables, lever arms and gears in the dim shadows, Praeseos could discern no purpose.

He found himself standing before what was certainly some sort of a control panel. It stirred memories he could not clearly recall. "So dark," he commented, trying to adjust his crystalline eyes. But there was little light with which to discern the machineworks before him.

"I can send my light to you, would that help?" Sevok called from below.

"Please, yes, I would much appreciate it."

A moment later, Praeseos observed the floating orb of light slowly rising. It was soon at his side, providing much needed illumination.

"Many thanks," he called down to the shaman.

"What do you see?"

Praeseos surveyed the angled metal panel before him. It contained knobs of crystal and metal, small round jewel-like orbs embedded into the surface, levers of bright metal topped by brightly enabled grips. Some were small, others large, and some moved in just two directions while a few could be moved into various positions according to the slotted paths cut into the panel.

It all seemed familiar somehow yet strange to him.

Pull the lever on the right.

Praeseos frowned, leaning over the edge of the platform, to look at the Ur'chom. "Did you just say something?"

"No, nothing. Did you hear something?"

Praeseos looked around. "I am not sure."

Pull the lever on the right, wait for the red...

"Now I am certain, I am hearing a voice. I fear it may be a sign of my mind slipping," he said loudly, that Sevok would hear.

"No, my friend, perhaps that voice is for you what the voice of the setting sun was for me!"

"Destiny?"

"You cannot know unless you listen to it. What does it say?"

"To do something here, before me. But I know not what it could lead to. Will it lead to weal or woe?" Praeseos was truly unsure if he should follow the voice.

Pull the lever on the right, wait for the red glow, move the second lever leftward to the second setting...

"Wait, something is odd..." Praeseos said, concentrating on the voice. "It's not so much a voice as a message. It keeps repeating."

"I think you are meant to follow it, clearly whatever left you here left that message," the shaman called up.

"Truly?" Praeseos was intrigued at the possibility.

"You either listen or we continue on our way," Sevok said. Looking around the shaman shrugged massive, fur-clad shoulders. "I do not see a further way upwards, so we would return below, if that is your wish."

He thought for a long moment on the matter. That was it, truly. Either follow the instructions the voice was repeating or climb down and set about repairing the doors. He tapped his chin with his forefinger, making a sharp clicking noise.

He listened.

He pulled the large lever on the right, downward. It was not easy, as it had likely been in that position for untold years. As he forced it down, it clicked loudly. Through his feet, Praeseos felt a faint shuddering vibration.

"What is that?" Sevok's question echoed his own. Looking around, he spied movement. A massive gear was turning slowly through the jumble of pipes, cables and lever arms.

A deep gurgling noise could be heard echoing through the cavernous chamber. It faded away. Silence.

"Is that all?" Sevok called. Praeseos knew it wasn't. The instructions continued to sound quietly in his head.

A great booming noise rocked the platform, as a massive assembly of tanks, pipes, gearworks and he knew not what else shook. An orange light suddenly issued out of numerous small round windows on a tall, vertical tank. Gears turned slowly, throughout the chamber, as cables groaned and tightened.

Dust and bits of debris scattered about, falling from perches obscured by shadow, having likely lain there for untold years, only now disturbed by whatever was happening.

He glanced down at the panel before him. A glassy orb suddenly was alight, glowing with a bright crimson light. Following the message, he found the second lever and moved it into the position indicated. An amber light appeared on the other side of the panel. He pulled another lever down, as it clicked loudly. Then a dial had to be turned twice around until another light appeared.

Finally, he pulled the last lever, locking it into a certain position. By now, the entire chamber was humming with the turning of massive gears, pipes rattling, cables singing, huge levers cranking slowly.

"What is happening?" Sevok called out over the din which was increasing by the moment. The shaman gripped a nearby rail.

"I know not!" Praeseos called down. "But know this: I have done what the voice instructed, and it has ceased plaguing my mind!"

"Then it is done," the shaman shouted. "I think we should quit this place!"

"Yes, I would agree," Praeseos said, making for the narrow winding metal stairs.

A screeching cacophony filled the chamber, accompanied by a violent shuddering. Praeseos had to grasp the railing to keep his footing, while the Ur'chom shouted in pain, covering tufted ears.

Looking across the chamber, they both saw immense metal panels slide sideways. Praeseos realized they were the huge doors in the side of tower. They were moving in a metal track as they slowly parted. The fading blue of twilight filled the chamber.

Above them, a huge assembly of crystal and metal, supported on massive arms driven by gears and cable, moved pendulously to one side. It turned, lowered, and moved towards the opening doors. A resounding clunking noise marked it reaching some sort of final position.

Light bloomed along a series of pipes and tanks, seeming to trace a path from the lowest, largest metal tank upwards to the assembly of crystal and metal gears above them. The noise was growing, forcing the shaman back toward the ramp. Sevok was yelling something, but Praeseos could not discern his voice amid the cacophonous roar of the gearworks and other strange devices.

The sliding doors at last stopped, and with it the shuddering diminished. The noises retreated almost to a point where they ceased. But Praeseos could feel the hum, the waiting potential of *something*.

"Is it done?" Sevok shouted, yelling too loudly.

Praeseos looked up at the assembly, which was growing brighter by the second. The crystalline components were not just crystals, but enormous *lenses*.

A shrill keening noise filled the air as a thick, almost liquid column of light pierced the darkness of the chamber. As a Forgewrought, Praeseos recalled he had a set of eyelids that protected him from unduly harsh radiance, such as this. They snapped over his eyes instantly; to anyone looking at him, his eyes would now look like dark, lusterless orbs.

The radiance flooded the chamber. Through his darkened sight he could perceive every detail of the gearworks and assemblies. Poor Sevok had turned and huddled down, to avoid being blinded. Praeseos hoped the shaman's vision was not permanently affected.

Climbing down the spiral stairs, he helped the shaman up, proceeding directly for the ramp downward. Once they reached it, Praeseos' eyes reverted to normal, that he could see again in less brilliant conditions.

"Are you all right, Sevok? Is your vision affected?"

"No, I just need a moment," the Ur'chom replied, relying on the steadying assistance of the Forgewrought in climbing downward. "I will recover shortly."

Praeseos could still feel the vibration of the machines above. He made for the ground level. By the time they reached the blood-stained floor, dark save for the light cast by the glowing orb still trailing behind the shaman, he had recovered sufficiently to guide his own steps.

"Let us move outside," Praeseos said, leading the way. He moved quickly, eager to see what he may. His suspicions were quickly confirmed.

It was nearly night without. Stars twinkled over the entire sky, save due west, where an indigo veil still colored the horizon. The vista was stunning, yet it was not the fading light of the receded day that drew the gaze of them both.

It was the beam of white light, piercing and brilliant, like an endless shaft, stretching from the tower to an unseen point beyond the distant range of mountains to the west.

"What is it?" Sevok whispered.

Praeseos thought on the question. He sighed. "I must make haste and repair the doors."

"Why?"

"I know not what it means, or what it may be. But above all else, it is a beacon. I fear what it might attract, or whom," the Forgewrought said in a low voice.

"Then let us set to it."

"My friend, you should probably flee this place. Those you spoke of will likely double their pace. This is may be visible from any of those mountains north and east."

"I was called here, Praeseos. Here I will stay to aid you," the Ur'chom said, already walking back toward the entrance, the tall staff steadying the shaman's somewhat unstable gait.

"I would be beside myself if you suffer for staying," he said, still unhappy with the Ur'chom's decision. "I have not the faintest idea where this will lead, or how it will end."

Sevok stopped and turned. "Must you know the answer? Besides, I have a good idea of where it will lead us."

"And that is?"

The shaman pointed one bent, clawed finger along the direction of the piercing white beam that cut through the darkening horizon.

"West!"

CHAPTER TWENTY-SEVEN - CANDISSA

27 Laborus, Year 197, Eastvale Calendar

They were riding into the mist before the sun rose.

Candissa wondered what it would be like, to cross the threshold, into the hills. She was looking for a distinct marker, or perhaps a point where it was clear they were in the hills. But, like the others, she kept glancing back, to see if a contingent of attackers had forced their way past Thendarick, or escaped Ravensroost via another gate.

Don't slow, Kor, came Errol's voice, in their minds. *If your leg is causing you pain, we can stop soon so Candissa can look at it. Until then, we need to keep our pace.*

It's not that, I'm just having trouble convincing William to keep up, was Koraymis' reply.

Candissa almost grinned at hearing the name Koraymis had given the black horse. She had not asked him why he chose such a banal name for a mount. Her own gray-white mare was named Torren. Candissa had chosen the name many years ago, when they first purchased the white horse. She could only guess why she gave the yearling such a name.

Remember, he needs to know you're in control, he's a willful beast, Cam joined in. *I'm still unsure why you insisted on this one.*

There was no more discussion on the sorcerer's mount. As the morning arose, they found themselves wreathed in a relentless mist. The ground was still flat, hard-packed soil covered in short tufts of sturdy grass and dotted occasionally by stunted bushes. Their visibility was no more than fifty yards. Apart from the sound of hoofbeats on the hard ground, it was eerily quiet.

"Are we sure we're heading due west?" Koraymis asked aloud at one point.

Candissa realized the mist had a damping effect on sounds, which contributed to the preternatural quiet of the surroundings.

"I trust my senses enough," Cam said. "We shan't circle back, if that's what you fear."

"Not at all, I only asked as I would be hopelessly lost in this mist," the sorcerer replied.

Should we be speaking so loudly? Errol's asked silently.

"The mist will mask our voices," Cam said. "If we are pursued, it will be our tracks they will follow. I'm hoping we'll run into a rill or something with flowing water to throw them off, if we are indeed being pursued."

The conversation ended as they kept a steady pace, Cam in the lead. Candissa and Koraymis rode abreast, with Errol in the rear to help Koraymis' mount maintain his gait.

Candissa guessed it was an hour past dawn when Koraymis finally relented.

"Can we stop a moment?"

She sensed he was in pain. They all slowed and stopped. Their mounts were not yet winded. Cam's picked at a clump of grass as Candissa wordlessly slid from her saddle.

She moved to Koraymis. Seeing the protest in his expression, she raised a hand in warning. He relented. She placed an open palm over the wounded area. Concentrating long enough to feel the flow of energy, a technique she had learned long ago at the temple, she probed the wound. In their hasty flight from Ravensroost, she had only a moment to effect a curative on the laceration. The worst of it was healed; he had stopped bleeding.

But there was a deeper wound that needed tending. Breathing deeply, Candissa called on a mending discipline, one meant to restore wounds unseen. She had had only used it once, but the magic flowed easily from her fingers into his leg. There was more now, however. A depth of understanding she had not previously glimpsed. In her mind's eye, she could see the underlying layers of muscle and sinew, how they were torn and ragged. She directed the healing energies to the specific wounds, allowing ligaments to rejoin, and sinew knit.

It didn't take her very long. When she was done, she sat back, breathing. She felt a surge of exhaustion, slight but discernible. It faded quickly.

"That felt...strange," Koraymis said, wide eyes blinking. "But much better now."

She stood and nodded. Errol had dismounted while she had been tending the wound. He stood away from the horses and riders, peering east into the mists, listening. His body seemed tensed, as he stood, almost leaning, one foot resting on a small stone.

She did not move, not wishing to make any noise that may interfere with his perception. She heard only the breathing of the horses, and a vague, distant whisper as the mists rolled across the land.

Cam spoke. "Do you hear-"

Speak with your mind, Koraymis cut him off.

Of course, Cam said silently, his expression self-deprecating.

Errol relaxed, shaking his head.

"Nothing," he said. "But there's no reason to slow our pace. And quite right you are, Kor, my hearing isn't affected by the pathing."

Candissa paused before she mounted. "Pathing?"

Errol looked at her. "Yes, that's what you call…" His eyes went wide. A grin slowly crept across his face.

"What is it?" she asked him.

"I remember...I *remember!*" Errol breathed. "It's called *telepathy*, the way we speak with our minds."

"That word sounds familiar to me," Koraymis said. "I think I read it in some dusty tome my master had in his collection. But that was a long time ago."

"Those who use telepathy were said to *path* with one another," Errol said, his eyes still bright.

Candissa could not help but smile at his expression. "You seem almost giddy, Errol."

"Well, it's more than that," he said, as he swung up onto his horse once more. "I don't just recall that word. I can see the room where I first learned about it, the wood grain of the floor, the feel of the table under my hands, even the teacher."

Candissa hauled herself up onto her white mare now. She smiled. "Perhaps part of all this will be you recalling more, as time goes by."

"Perhaps it's because we're moving west," Koraymis offered.

Perhaps we should stop guessing and move along, Cam suggested, grinning. *We need to put many more miles between us and Ravensroost.*

Agreed, Errol pathed.

"Cam," Candissa spoke. "When will we be in the Misthallow Hills? Properly, I mean."

Cam grinned. "We're in them now. You may not have noticed, but we're on an incline."

Candissa looked around. "These are the hills?"

He nodded. "Soon enough we'll be riding up and down the slopes. But the ground changed. We're in the Misthallows now."

She felt disappointed somehow. It didn't seem any different.

Koraymis and Errol looked in various directions, peering intently, almost as if expecting something dreadful to lunge out of the quiet fog.

Let's move, Cam pathed.

True to Cam's words, in less than an hour they were riding up a gradual slope, to a ridge. They paused briefly to examine their surroundings from the higher vantage point. Their visibility was still very limited.

"Nothing too mysterious yet," Cam remarked, smirking.

"Some accounts of explorers claimed they walked into the hills for two or three days, and still managed to return," Candissa said. "But they always had some terrible tale."

Likely as not those were just tales, Koraymis pathed.

"We'll see!" Errol said, evoking a frown from the sorcerer.

They continued at a relatively brisk pace throughout the morning. While the sun was rising, and the mist brightened around them, they saw not a single ray of sunlight. It was midday when they stopped to eat and drink.

"Just rations, no fire," Cam commented. Errol listened carefully as they ate in silence. Cam watered the horses and let them eat some of the tough knots of grass that dotted the hills.

After Errol was satisfied there were no pursuers nearby, they continued their journey. Candissa lost track of number of low ridges and valleys they traversed over the day, but it was around a dozen.

The light was diminishing, the mists now a dull iron gray around them.

"We should stop for a quick supper soon," Cam suggested. The others nodded, while Errol's gaze was transfixed ahead of them.

"There's something ahead," Errol said, his voice quiet. They all pulled up and stopped. Candissa could hear the wind blowing harder, but it was still barely audible. She saw nothing ahead of them.

Where? Cam pathed.

A hundred yards, just south of west. It's tall, was Errol's reply.

They advanced very cautiously, Cam and Errol leading. It was not long before Candissa could see it - some sort of spire, rising out of the mist.

Could it be the tower? Koraymis asked, excitement clear in his pathing.

No, was all Errol replied.

Soon, they saw what it was - a rise of stone, narrow, square, reaching perhaps forty feet into the dim air. It was perhaps half as wide at the base. They silently approached and rounded it. Broken stone walls extended from two sides of it, while a small set of steps were built into one side.

"It was a fortification of some sort, I would guess," Errol said. "See how the walls extend south and west."

"Are those steps safe?" Cam pointed at the two flights of narrow steps.

Errol approached and dismounted. "Let's find out. They look to lead to the top."

"Be careful!" Candissa hissed, glancing around. Errol threw her an annoyed gaze.

Nearing it now, she examined the stonework. While it was broken, the masonry was in excellent condition. The stone was dark and damp. "This looks almost as if it was only recently fallen," she commented.

Cam nodded. "Yes, the weather hasn't aged the stone much if at all."

Errol mounted the steps easily and was shortly atop the structure. He called down to them.

"An excellent view if not the damned mists," he said.

"Nothing else up there?" Koraymis asked.

"No," Errol said as he climbed back down. "It would make an excellent place to camp for the night, but we couldn't get the horses up there."

"And I won't leave them alone," Cam said. "We should press on and camp when it's darker still."

Candissa had to agree. They wanted to get as far as possible, especially on the first day of their flight.

It was a few hours later, and the sun had gone down when they were all surprised by the sudden turn of weather. Within the span of what seemed like a few minutes, the mists retreated, then vanished, revealing the rolling hills in every direction. There was a faint smudge along the horizon, but visibility was clear otherwise.

The sky began to show stars, and one of the two moons rose behind them, the other soon to follow. A faint wind could be felt picking up. It was cold.

"This is strange, isn't it?" Koraymis said.

"Not necessarily, I've seen mist fade that quickly before," Cam said. "It'll be a cold night. We should set up camp soon."

"I say we press on by star and moonlight," Errol countered. "If we *are* being chased, they'll have this same advantage."

I suppose he's right, Koraymis chimed in.

Then let's keep moving, Candissa pathed.

They moved at a slower pace, keeping quiet as darkness descended on the hills around them. The two moons provided ample light well after sunset. It was near midnight, or so she guessed, when they came upon a low wall running north-south in one of the valleys between ridgelines.

It was a few feet tall, stretching several hundred yards.

"This is a good spot, low, hidden, a bit of cover," Cam said. His voice betrayed his exhaustion. After dismounting, Cam and Errol set to erecting the two tents.

Candissa looked at the two tents standing in the moonlight and considered their sleeping arrangements.

"Do you wish to have a tent to yourself?" Errol asked.

"No, I appreciate the offer, but I don't like the idea of forcing the three of you into one tent. Who do I sleep next to?"

"Entirely the lady's prerogative," Errol replied with a mock bow of formality.

Cam chuckled as he tightened knots on the tent lines. She considered the three young men before her. Cam was a somewhat large sort of fellow, tall and broad. Errol just grinned at her, while the sorcerer looked at her with somewhat wide eyes before averting them from her gaze.

"Kor," she said, enjoying how he seemed to slump a little at her selection. Errol clapped his hands over his heart, pretending agony.

"I am undone!"

Candissa rolled her eyes at his mockery.

"Not that I'm offended, Candissa, but I'm curious. Why me?" Koraymis asked.

"Cam is too big. Errol is, well, Errol," she said. Then she looked at Koraymis who returned an expectant stare. "You're the warmest. There's a cold wind blowing."

"The warmest?" Cam said, raising an eyebrow. He looked at Koraymis. "If you say so. All right, in you all go. We need sleep."

"What if something approaches during the night?" Koraymis asked.

"If the horses don't alert me, I'm a very light sleeper," Cam said. "I sincerely doubt much could creep up on us unawares."

"I don't imagine any of us will sleep much regardless," Errol said, echoing Candissa's thoughts. "I'll be up after a few hours in any case, if you wanted to get some solid sleep."

"We'll talk then, I'm sure," Cam said, as he secured the first tie on Candissa's tent flap. She nodded to Cam and crawled into the tent first, pushing her belongings over to one side, so there was more room for her tent mate.

Having laid out her blanket and bedroll, she found it to be more comfortable than expected. Koraymis followed her in and then secured the remaining tent flap ties. The tent was of a superior quality, given the resources of her family. It was of a sturdy canvas and would hold well against most weather.

Settling down on her side of the tent, she was amused at how Koraymis fidgeted and adjusted his bedroll, in an apparent attempt to minimize any chance of bodily contact. This despite them both being fully clothed in their riding gear.

After a full minute of suffering his restlessness she had to speak.

"Still yourself, Kor, just relax. We are sharing a tent for warmth. I hope you're not trying to be gallant or something like that."

"No, I - well, perhaps you're right," Kor said. He seemed to relax a little after that.

"Are you tired enough to sleep?"

"I don't think so, but we should try. Riding tomorrow will be difficult if we aren't rested."

"Yes, we should try. I think I can, if I set my mind to it."

After a short pause, Kor turned to her.

"Candissa, what did you mean I'm the warmest?"

"Simply that. You exude more warmth than Cam or Errol."

"How do you know that?"

She studied his face. Even in this near darkness, she could tell. It was difficult to put into words.

"I'm not sure how to explain it. Some things I just know, or I can just see them. I can *see* that you're warmer than the others," she explained as best as she could. "Does that sound strange?"

"No, not at all!" he said emphatically. "I thought maybe it was because I was...I am different, you know."

"Kor, we, and I mean all four of us, need to start being more honest and direct with each other," Candissa said, leaning on one elbow now. "I don't expect it to happen all at once, but if you need to ask me anything, don't hesitate. And please understand if I seem to be asking you personal questions. It's only because I want to understand more about you."

"It's all right. I agree with you. It's just that I've always been...guarded with who I am, what I am. What I can do."

She could feel the unease in his voice and manners. She wanted to help him, to let him relax his guard. Not because she wanted to extract information from him, but to make him feel better. She put a hand on his shoulder in the darkness.

He looked at her. "What are you doing?"

She drew the hand away. "I'm sorry, I was just touching your shoulder."

"No," Koraymis said with an unusual pointedness in his voice. "You were working magic upon me."

"What?" Candissa said, truly surprised. "No, it was just a touch-"

"I can sense magic, Candissa," Kor said. "In objects, places, people. Just now there was a flow of magic from you into me. It made me feel more peaceful. Did you not intend to do that?"

"I suppose I did intend for you to feel more peaceful, to lend you comfort. But that was simply my thought. I did not know I was doing so with magic. Are you certain?"

"Absolutely," Kor nodded. "I have seen and felt a great deal of magic of late. That gray block back there, the Wardenstone as some call it? It's highly magical."

"I always suspected," Candissa breathed, recalling her vision that fateful day so long ago when Errol first appeared. She was not in the least surprised by the revelation.

"Your staff is intensely magical, as is Errol's blade. And Cam's backpack."

"His *backpack*?"

"Yes, I cannot explain why. Only he could do that. If he even knows. Your outfit as well. There is a faint aura of magic about all of it," the sorcerer said. She wondered if all sorcerers had this gift. He knew he was right about what she wore. As it was altered from what her grandmother had worn, it was doubtless infused with magic from when she had made it or worn it.

"What about you? Do you bear any magic?"

He held up his right hand, indicating the heavy ring on his middle finger.

"What does it do? I know little of true magic. There is almost nothing written of it, that I had access to," Candissa said. "And the wizard in town is always guarded with his lore."

"That is likely because he knows so little of magic himself. My master told me magic is somehow diminished and distant from everyone. I don't know why we all seem to be surrounded by it. As for this," he explained, holding up his ring. "I think it's more of a focus for me, to help me use my magic more easily and more proficiently."

"Is that all it does?"

"No. It also gives me insight into things, sometimes it even tells me things indirectly. But sometimes it's almost as if I can speak to my master, and I imagine I hear his voice through it."

"He is somehow bound to it?" She hoped her questions were not too prying.

"I think so. It was a gift from him," Kor said. He suddenly stared at Candissa with a sort of blank stare. Then he grinned.

"What?"

"I am to commend you," he said, still grinning.

"What do you mean by that?"

"I would never reveal all this to just anyone who asked. You were using your magic again," Kor said. Then he glanced at his ring. "Or so I'm told."

Candissa stared at the dark ring. "Are you speaking with your master now?"

"No, it's not like that. It's more a *knowing* that is conveyed to me. It's difficult to explain."

"I'm keeping you from sleep, forgive my questions. And please know I do not mean to use any sort of magic," Candissa said, relenting. "Please, let us both try to get at least a little sleep."

Koraymis nodded, turning over to face away from her.

Resolving to sleep at last, Candissa nestled into the bedroll. She could already feel the warmth being radiated by her friend. Cold would not be something that would prevent sleep.

She was surprised to learn she had been utilizing some sort of innate magic without consciously controlling it. She would have to master that. Perhaps her grandmother's book would provide insight.

Breathing deeply, she used some calming techniques she learned at the Temple. They were always useful in situations such as this. She chuckled silently, commenting to herself that there were no situations quite like this one. She could not deny the doubts and fears she felt about their almost reckless adventure. She set those feelings aside. They would be there tomorrow. For now, she had to sleep.

The wind outside was not too strong, but it was steady. She expected it to be misty, even at night. With the onset of winter, there would be fewer mist-veiled nights, as mist turned to frost. Breathing deeper, Candissa slipped further into a state of rest.

Sleep came quickly with the aid of her meditative method.

As she slipped deeper, she was not surprised to find herself in dream.

Zarlenna sighed. She rubbed her face from the fatigue of two days without rest. *Such were the rigors trainers must endure*, she reminded herself. She stared down at the vast, open area of smooth stone tiles. They were of varying sizes, some brightly hued, others muted pastels. From high above, one could make out the vast symbol they formed, that of the Aevaru. But from the ground, it was impossible to see.

The last of the acolytes had just departed the training arena. Past it, mountains thrust upwards into the sky, wreathed in snow. As she turned, her long robe of silvery white rustled in the brisk wind. She looked up at the brightly enameled towers that rose behind the training area. At least a dozen spires rose upwards, no two the same height.

Atop one of them was a flat disc, so far away as to look small, but Zarlenna knew it was a hundred paces wide. Lying on the edge of the disc was a dragon, lounging almost lazily. She was a silvery-gold in color, her scales reflecting brightly in the sun.

Zarlenna reached out with her mind and greeted her. The dragon's head rose slightly and regarded her from the lofty perch. She felt the response in her mind.

A bright day and clear sky to you, Zarlenna. The dragon's voice was warm and intense. *Is there someone there with you?*

Zarlenna looked to one side then the other, replying in the negative. Then she realized.

You just forced me to lie to a Dragon, Candissa, Zarlenna said.

Candissa was dreaming, but it was more than a dream. She had suspected that previously. Now she knew.

I am sorry, I cannot control this.

Understandable, this sort of communication is not easily managed. You'll learn, I'm sure, Zarlenna said. Candissa couldn't see her exactly, but she knew she was not speaking aloud, only with her mind. She wasn't certain, but it felt as if they were in the same body.

That is exactly the case, Candissa, came the Aevaru's reply. Clearly Candissa's thoughts leaked through to her awareness.

I am lost. Who are you? I know your name is Zarlenna and you are an Aevaru. I know nothing more. Candissa hoped she didn't sound desperate.

Then we know as much about one another, for I know you are Aevaru and your name is Candissa. But I must ask you, why do you contact me like this?

I do not mean to. I am in dream, yet here I am, Candissa said.

Ah, that explains more, sleep is often the catalyst for powers or awareness untapped. Can you tell me where you are? What realm? Zarlenna's question made no sense to her.

I cannot. I am from the Kingdom of Eastvale.

All right. In which realm does this small kingdom reside?

No, you don't understand. That is all I know. The Kingdom of Eastvale is surrounded by mountains, forests and hills to the west. We know nothing else of the world. Candissa hoped she didn't sound crazed.

Zarlenna seemed to ponder her words.

That is curious. You are a hidden kingdom, indeed. I have not heard of Eastvale, and I know a great deal of the world.

No disrespect is intended, I assure you, Candissa said.

Of course, my child. I sense you are a novitiate Aevaru, is that true?

Candissa wasn't sure how to reply. *I think that is as good a term as any. I only just recently learned I was Aevaru. There are no others I know of.*

Are you saying you've had no formal training as Aevaru?

That is correct. There are none but me, to my knowledge.

This is a mystery, Candissa. I've determined you are not a fabrication of my mind, and that you are real. I sense you are not lying. But beyond that, I am perplexed.

As am I, Zarlenna.

Tell me about where you come from. What is the last city you visited?

I hail from a small town called Ravensroost. Our kingdom's capital is called Eastvale. There are a few cities more, but none as large as Eastvale. I suspect the cities you are accustomed to are much greater than even our capital.

Zarlenna walked back toward the cluster of colorful spires. They were nestled in a vast fortified compound of some sort. Candissa could sense she was thinking, but her thoughts were masked. She stopped, holding up a pointed finger.

You are asleep, yes?

That's right.

Then it is night where you are.

Yes, close to midnight, I think. But it's daylight there! Candissa was suddenly intrigued. She didn't know what to make of it, but it recalled something she had read long ago.

You must be on the other side of the planet, Zarlenna said.

I'm sorry, planet? I'm not familiar with that term.

That seemed to throw off the Aevaru. *That is telling in itself. It is common knowledge that we live on a world that is a great sphere, called a planet. As it turns, the sun rises and sets at different times depending on where you are.*

Candissa now recalled an old account of theories on astronomy that mentioned something like that, how the sun does not actually rise, but that the world was an orb that spun. *Of course, that makes perfect sense!*

Zarlenna grinned. *So, if it's close to high day here, and its past midnight there, you must be nearly on the opposite side. Let me think.*

Candissa now harbored a real hope her friend could tell her more about the world, where they were and what else could be found.

Have you heard of the Gruthik Mountains? It's the largest range on that side of the world. Or perhaps the Traejari, or the Prull mountains?

I'm sorry, none of those are names I've read. We have so little history to read here.

So, you're isolated in a hidden valley kingdom, cut off from the world, with no knowledge of what lies outside your realm, Zarlenna said, clearly annoyed.

I wish I could tell you more.

As do I, Candissa. I am more concerned that you are an untrained Aevaru with no guidance. If you are what you say you are, and I have no reason to doubt you, then I would prefer to instruct you on what it means to be an Aevaru, rather than comparing notes on geography.

Candissa was thrilled at the prospect. *Yes, please, Zarlenna, anything would be welcome. My friends and I are on a journey into the wilderness with no clear idea of what we're doing out here, or where to go.*

What compelled you to leave the safety of your kingdom?

Events, something driving us, like a shared destiny, it's difficult to explain, Candissa said. She felt strange now, thinking perhaps their link was growing more tenuous.

No, I understand that perfectly. I feel that same call of destiny, many of us do. There are great events moving about the world. If you want to know where to go, what to do, I have this advice. As Aevaru, look for signs. You will find you are keenly aware of them, and where to look for signs and portents. Heed those feelings, those impulses.

Is it as simple as that, look for signs?

Yes, Zarlenna replied, with an affirmative nod. *I'm afraid we must discontinue our conversation. I must attend to other training. Having you in my mind like this would surely interfere with my work.*

I understand. I felt our time was near an end. While I cannot control this yet, I hope to speak with you again soon, Candissa paused a moment. *But I have a question.*

Yes?

Is that truly a dragon atop that high platform?

Zarlenna laughed lightly. *Yes, it is. You have never seen one?*

To my knowledge, they are but myth. No one in the kingdom believes they exist!

That is strange. I will think on this more. Let us talk again soon, Candissa of the hidden Kingdom of Eastvale.

Zarlenna nodded to her, though Candissa didn't actually see the nod. She could see who approached Zarlenna, however. A group of students, Aevaru clad in simple robes. The lead student was the one she had seen in her first vision, Mirova.

Her nearly-red hair shone brightly in the warm sunlight, her deep green eyes bright and large. She had her hair done back in a tie of some sort, revealing slightly pointed ears, not unlike Cam or Evan. She was half-Elven.

As Candissa's vision of the scene faded, she could hear Zarlenna's voice trailing off. "*Mirova, I hope you and your group are well rested. Today, we begin the study of combinative castings…*"

CHAPTER TWENTY-EIGHT - CAM

28 Laborus, Year 197, Eastvale Calendar

The night passed, and morning came without incident. Cam was grateful for that. He had been awake since well before dawn, as had Errol. It was a cold morning, telling him winter's bitter winds would soon be sweeping down from the mountains.

At least, the winds would be visiting the forests and valleys of Woodford and the Kingdom. Here, he had no idea what the season would bring. There could be heavy snows early or driving rains of ice and sleet. While they were well-provisioned, it could prove insufficient if the conditions were worse than anything he'd encountered.

The clear sky had given way to low clouds before dawn. A dreary, cold rain began pelting their tents before Candissa and Koraymis had even stirred.

Cam tended the horses, feeding them a little grain, as he peered at the sky.

"How long will this last?" Errol said as he fetched his oiled cloak from his saddlebag.

"Feels like a steady rain all day, but I can't be sure out here," Cam said. "We should move. There's no telling if we're being followed."

Their first breaking of camp was a hasty and grim affair, as they roused their two friends out of their slumber. Quickly donning their rain cloaks, they set about packing the tents as quick as they could.

Koraymis showed signs of moving slowly as he packed his belongings in the saddlebags of his mount.

"Kor, I need to look at your leg," Candissa said from under the hood of her light gray cloak.

"I'm fine, it's healing," the sorcerer said.

"I wasn't asking you. You *will* hold still," Candissa's voice was low and left no room for debate. Koraymis grimaced as she pulled up his legging. She quickly changed the bandage, inspecting the wound. Cam peered over her shoulder.

"I've seen a lot of wounds. That one looks like it's been healing for more than a week," he murmured. No one commented on it.

"No infection, good," Candissa said. She tucked his legging back into his boot and placed an open hand over the bandaged area.

"Candissa, you don't have to-" Koraymis began, but a stony glare from the healer cut short his protest. She stood.

"There, you'll have no lasting effects from the wound," she said.

Cam made sure they each had cold rations to eat on the ride. They were all quickly mounted as the rain intensified a little.

"Lovely," Errol said, as Cam led the way up and around the low wall, before turning west again. No one else spoke.

It was a miserable day's travel, with the rain pelting them steadily for several hours. There were respites, but only brief. The horses found plenty of standing water to lap up, and grasses, but the riders had to content themselves with more cold rations.

Twice they paused to examine broken shapes of stone. One was an inscrutable pyramid of light stone, perhaps fifteen feet at the square base rising no more than ten to a point. The point was keen, despite however long it had stood there, weathering. Later, they happened upon a row of broken columns of a dark, gritty stone, sheared off seemingly, standing only a few feet out of the ground. Cam suspected there was much more of them buried.

It grew colder as the day progressed and the rain finally relented. By the time they made a decidedly miserable camp near a small clutch of stunted bushes, Cam thought it might start snowing. But a featureless shelf of low clouds moved in, cutting off any hope of moon or stars, but acting as a blanket against the worst of the night's cold.

The steady rain that day precluded finding any dry wood. They made their camp quickly, ate more rations, and fell into an exhausted sleep.

The next morning brought a mist flowing through the hills before dawn. When Cam woke, the muted blackness was turning a dim gray. It was a chill fog, allowing them to see perhaps a hundred yards or so.

He suspected there were no clouds above the fog, though the fog felt heavy.

Errol had arisen earlier, which seemed to be his habit. He had found a few pieces of wood nearby, suitable as logs to sit upon. They were now arranged in a circle and he was sipping from a water flask when Cam joined him in the dim gray light of early morning.

"Should we have a fire?" Cam saw now Errol had found some pieces of kindling good for starting a fire. He had formed a small pile, ringed with small rocks.

"That kindling doesn't look promising, but if you can coax one out, I'd welcome a warm breakfast. Did you sleep much?"

Errol shrugged. "I'm adapting to sleeping on the ground. I've had to do before."

"You don't look too bad for it. I wish I could say the same," Cam commented with a grin. He knew his hair was likely frightening to behold. He found his water, drank a swig, then poured some in his hands. Splashing his face and head, he ran his hands through his hair several times, trying to force it into a more presentable appearance.

Errol went over to one of the horses and retrieved some rations they had packed for breaking fast.

"I would ask you how far you think these hills stretch, but I've seen Candissa's maps."

"I know Kor has some books that may be of use, but even those aren't likely to provide any useful information," Cam said. "I just wish I had some idea of the game out here. Nothing like roast rabbit over an open fire."

Errol was chewing on a piece of jerky. "Don't talk of that. I'll grow sad for lack of it."

"I'm more worried about whatever may be out here that's bigger than a rabbit," Cam said, biting into a reasonably fresh apple.

"Such as?"

"That's just it. Tales claim monsters and huge beasts roam the desolate ruins beyond the hills, waiting to make meals of foolish travelers. If we do run into something large and dangerous, how will we fare?" It was a real concern of his. He was competent with his longbow and broadsword, and he had seen how deadly Errol was with blades. But would Candissa and Kor fare well in a pitched battle? His question must have escaped his own thoughts and was shared with the others.

"Remember the gate, she's not bad with that staff, and he has his tricks," Errol pointed out.

"Yes, but that's not enough. What do you think about training them?"

"As in combat drills, close combat techniques?" Errol said, raising his eyebrows.

"Exactly. We've pushed the horses too hard these first days. We need to ride a reasonable number of hours, and then we'll have time when we stop for the day. No reason not to put it to good use," Cam said.

"I think it's an excellent idea. We can start whipping them into shape tonight, wherever we end up."

"Whipping who into shape?" came Koraymis' weary voice from his tent flap, as it moved aside. The sorcerer looked worse than Cam, which, he was ashamed to think, made him feel a little better.

"You and the young lady. Sword, bow, combat drills, that sort of thing," Errol replied happily.

"Sounds delightful. I don't suppose there's any hot water?"

"No fire. Wood's still too wet."

Cam didn't like the glare Koraymis gave him. "I brought bitterblack, I was really looking forward to a steaming mug."

"It will take at least a half hour, probably more, to get a decent fire going with this cold and damp wood. I do not think it wise to tarry so."

Kor looked at him with a neutral sort of stare now. Without a word, he fetched his pack, found his metal cup, a small pan, a piece of steeping cloth, and his packet of ground bitterblack.

He settled down on one of the logs Errol had provided, pulling his sleeves up past his elbows.

"Kor, I don't mean to be a taskmaster, but I would prefer you not take the time to—" Cam's words faded.

Koraymis reached down with both hands, holding them over the pieces of wet kindling as the hunter spoke. Bright flames erupted from both hands, trailing down his fingers. They were almost too bright in the dim light of the misty dawn. Damp wood hissed angrily as it was heated through. Cam could feel the radiance of the flames dancing off Kor's fingers from a few yards away.

He stopped, clenching his hands into fists as the flames flickered away and died. The wood crackled to life merrily, a small but warm fire burning between Errol and Kor.

"Errol, water please?" the sorcerer said, holding out the pan. Errol smiled and poured some from his flask into the shallow pan.

"Or, you can do that, then," Cam said, not sure how to react to the remarkable display.

It didn't take long for the water to be heated to boiling, and for Kor to steep his precious dark tea. He was sipping it happily when Candissa exited the tent.

Quick glances at her turned to open stares. She saw their gazes and was immediately concerned. She looked down at her outfit. "What's wrong?"

Errol rose and walked over to her tent, peering in.

"What are you doing?" she asked, appearing somewhat vexed.

"Seeing if you brought your governess and a dressing table with you," Errol said.

Cam was amazed at her appearance. The three of them sitting there each had disheveled clothing, hair matted or mussed from sleep, and eyes that were varying shades of red. Yet, there stood Candissa in the dim light of dawn, looking as if she could receive nobility. Her hair was flowing and smooth, as though it had been brushed through for an hour. Her outfit appeared to have been freshly pressed, having almost no wrinkles. Her eyes were bright and her face as beautiful as ever.

"Yes, I know. It's...a family trait, I suppose you could call it," she said. Her eyes brightened at the sight of the fire. "Ah, good, that should help warm things up."

She sat down as the three men continued to stare at her, before at last returning to their simple morning fare. After warming her hands, she broke fast on dried fruit and something her father called rangers bread. She told them it was full of grains and nuts and would suffice as a meal, if need be.

"This isn't bad," Errol commented, as he chewed on the nutty bread.

"It suffices. Still, I would far prefer Lendra's fry cakes," Candissa said, her eyes twinkling as she stared into the small fire. "She makes them with bacon grease and sprinkles them with sugar dust. They are so delicious."

She lowered her gaze. Cam knew she was sad.

"I already miss her," Candissa murmured.

Cam looked at the young woman. She was six years his junior, yet he was happy to have her lead their curious group. He had an immense respect for her, despite having known her for only a short time. This was due, in part at least, to the strange bond they shared, and whatever that entailed.

At that moment, he felt a deep empathy for her. He did not want her to hear or sense his thoughts, for fear she would misconstrue them. He chewed a bite of the rangers bread. Suddenly, he could taste Lendra's fry cakes, the subtle savory quality of the bacon grease, the faint sweetness. They were just cooked, hot off a massive round cooking pan Lendra favored.

Cam looked at his backpack. What was it that Errol had said? *All you ever need*, Cam recalled now. That's what it was. His Everneed.

Without thinking about it, Cam reached into his backpack, his *Everneed.*

His fingers found what he was looking for. He drew forth a small bundle, just large enough to fill his palm. It was wrapped in a white paper, tied with twine. The others clearly sensed something. They had stopped eating and were staring at him.

Cam offered the small bundle to Candissa, reaching out, his hand open.

She looked at the bundle, her eyes curious. Then they widened. He saw her nostrils flaring.

"No, it cannot be…" she whispered. She picked up the bundle as if it were a delicate flower. Pulling on the twine, she unwrapped it. Within, a freshly baked cake was revealed. Everyone could smell the sweet and savory aroma.

She looked at Cam, saying nothing, then took a small bite. Her eyes closed, a single tear running down a cheek.

"It's one of Lendra's cakes," she said. Eyes wet, she looked at Cam again. "How is this possible?"

Cam only shook his head. "I'm not sure. I just...you *needed* it."

She took a larger bite and smiled, crumbs on her lips. "It's warm."

Koraymis only studied Cam with thoughtful eyes, saying nothing. Errol grinned, saying only one word, "Interesting."

Candissa offered the others a sample of her cake, but they declined, letting her enjoy it. She did not ask any more questions on the matter, and Cam was glad for that. He did not understand his backpack, his Everneed, but he suspected there was much more to it than he knew.

Once they had finished their meals, they made sure to feed the horses before striking camp. After packing up, they were ready to depart. Cam hoped to find water for the horses on the way but had brought some along in case it was scarce.

As Cam put out the fire carefully, quickly piling earth over it to minimize any escaping smoke. He examined the pieces of wood Errol had found for their seats. He turned one over with his boot.

"Where did you find these exactly?" he asked Errol.

"Just on that rise there," Errol replied, pointing to the low hillside to the west. "They were half buried in the dirt. Why?"

"They don't feel natural, they're all the same width," Cam said quietly. He shrugged. "But it matters not."

Mounting, he joined the others as they resumed their trek west, climbing the rising ridge before them, still cloaked in the brightening mist of the morning. It was eerily quiet. Cam preferred the sounds of the wilderness and wildlife. This land was strange to his experience.

"Look, there's another length of wood," Kor pointed. Sticking out of the ground near the top of the low hill was a length of broken wood, too straight and cylindrical to be natural.

As they surmounted the hilltop, it led to another hill not too far to the west. The mist prevented them from seeing anything more than the next hill. The wind was steady but mild. Cam still felt an unease at not being able to hear or sense any sort of wildlife. Even in this season, a few bird calls would have been heard by now.

They cantered down the hill to the depression before the next. A few small bushes grew here, a good sign. He studied the area.

"Rain flows here, we should find standing water eventually," he told them.

"What is this?" Errol interjected, suddenly dismounting. He walked over to a clump of tall grasses and pulled forth a heavy wooden object. It seemed vaguely familiar to Cam, reminding him of something he had seen in one of his mother's instruction books.

"What is it?" Kor asked.

"It's called a block and tackle," Errol replied, turning it over and shaking off some sand and dirt. Cam saw now there was a wheel of some sort lodged inside the heavy wooden housing. "But why is it here?"

"What does it do? I have not heard of this," Kor pressed him.

Errol frowned. "This is a big one, it's made for heavy sheets. I'm sure it was on a sea-going vessel, a three-master at least."

"A sea? You mean like the Silvermere Sea?" Kor suggested. Cam was familiar with this body of water, the largest known to anyone in the Kingdom. It was not far from his boyhood home, and its southern shore was in the Elven woods.

Candissa shook her head. "That is a lake, a large one. It is called a sea by some, but a sea is much larger."

"You are aware of seas? Oceans?" Errol asked.

"I cannot say I have *read* of them. I just know they exist," she said.

"How large are these oceans?" Kor asked.

"They can be thousands of miles across, from one shore to another, and as deep as a mountain is high," Errol said. Cam recalled the conversation he and Errol had, days ago.

Koraymis appeared to think of this revelation for a moment, scowling. "They sound awful. We should avoid these *oceans*."

Cam suppressed a grin. "Come on. Keep your ears open, if we're being pursued, they could come up on us unawares in this fog."

Errol dropped the aged wooden object, muttering "Still curious about this."

Over the next rise, one question was answered while a much larger question arose.

Scattered in the next vale, in an area stretching more than fifty yards in every direction, were smashed and broken remains of a vast wooden vessel. Beams were thrown randomly, planks of heavy wood were in abundance, half-buried in the soil or scattered in small fragments and large sections, still held together by huge iron brads. Rotted coils of rope and heaps of crumpled, torn and weathered canvas could be seen here and there.

They all paused, taking in what they saw. Errol moved first, guiding his mount down into the field of debris. He was followed by Cam, then Candissa and Koraymis. They all took different routes, picking their way through, studying the wreckage.

"We aren't that far from town," Koraymis said. "Has no one seen this, and brought word back of it?"

"You have no idea how forbidden the thought is to everyone in Ravensroost," Errol replied. "No one, *no one*, goes into these hills."

"It's true. We are all carefully educated on that point," Candissa added.

"That's the keel," Errol said, pointing at what was clearly the longest piece of wood, perhaps forty yards in length. It curved gradually and was remarkably thick, with other pieces of wood protruding from it at intervals, all broken off save a few which still bore lengths of planking.

"It was immense," Candissa breathed.

"There's a lot of metal here, too," Koraymis said, pointing at some long pieces of bent and twisted metal, some rusted but other lengths untouched by the withering effects of time and rain.

"That mast has to be at least forty yards long and it was just the lower two portions," Errol pointed at a length of wood Cam would have mistaken for a fallen pine, bare of branches. "That means it was a fantastically long ship."

"I don't understand, how could a sailing vessel be here?" Candissa murmured.

"Perhaps a great storm washed it up here," Cam suggested. "And there's a nearby body of water..." His words trailed off as he realized it was a highly unlikely proposition. He would have sensed a nearby lake.

"Odd that so much metal is fastened to the hull," Errol commented. "Perhaps it was a warship."

Koraymis felt a length of twisted metal protruding from the ground. Some eight feet of it was above the soil, and it was more than two fingers thick. He pushed it, letting it bounce up and down.

"This is a strange metal," the sorcerer declared. He dismounted slowly.

"Kor, we cannot tarry," Cam reminded him.

"I know, this won't take long." The dark robed young man examined it closely. "It has holes for rivets. Yes, this one still bears wood fragments."

He pulled down on it forcefully now, letting it bounce back upwards. It did so vigorously.

"Strange…" Kor murmured, touching the metal lightly with his fingertips.

"And that means what?" Errol asked him.

"Well, if I'm correct," Koraymis began, as he grabbed the twisted length with both hands, working it back and forth violently, clearly intent on freeing it from the compacted soil that trapped it. "We will know how it came to be here."

It took just a few twists before the dirt was churned sufficiently. He pulled back with all of his limited might, freeing it from the ground.

"What's this going to prove?" Errol asked. Cam could tell from his voice he was vexed with the delay. He, too, wondered why the sorcerer was playing with the metal fragment.

Koraymis grunted as he twisted it to and fro. It proved to be longer than Cam would have thought. Koraymis fell backwards on the ground as the last of the bent length of metal slid free from the soil.

The fragment, perhaps twelve feet long, slipped not just from the ground but from Koraymis' grasp. It flew upward, twirling end over end, faster and faster. It disappeared into the mist overhead within seconds, silently. A clump of dirt hit the ground, shaken loose from the metal. The others stared slack-jawed at the display, heads craned skyward.

"As I suspected. This was a flying ship," Koraymis pronounced, standing and dusting off his cloak.

"Surely you must be jesting with us," Cam said, finding the idea outlandish.

"No, this wreck is littered with pieces of this metal," Kor said, surveying the area. "But what brought the ship down is not clear. Just the method by which it flew."

The sorcerer climbed back onto his black roan.

Cam shook his head. "Let's keep moving. We cannot take the time to investigate this."

"Pity, I imagine that metal is worth a fair penny," Errol said with a grin.

As they trotted away from the patch of upturned earth, Candissa looked back. "Truly, a flying ship?"

She shook her head, still clearly dumbfounded. Koraymis only grinned, offering no more on the matter.

They rode through the misty hills for perhaps another two hours, as Cam tried to keep their pace brisk.

"We are descending," he said at one point, sensing the almost imperceptible incline of the ground. The mist was still thick here, preventing them from seeing more than a hundred yards.

He raised a hand, calling for them to halt. He strained to listen in the muffling mist. He heard something.

"Errol, can you hear that?"

Leaning in his saddle, Errol looked around slowly. Then he nodded. "A brook. Water."

Sure enough, over another slight rise, they entered an area with higher grass that gave way to a small rill, flowing south to north. The horses drank their fill.

"Should we follow it?" Kor asked.

"West still feels like the right direction," Cam replied. Candissa nodded, and they continued across the shallow stream after the horses were done.

The day brightened, despite the ceaseless mist.

They came upon the first standing column a few hours after midday.

It was a dense, pale stone. The column was more than two feet thick, standing nearly straight upward more than twelve feet. A sickly vine grew along one side of it.

They all slowed and examined it. It bore no identifying marks or carvings, so they pressed on without discussion. The second column was found a minute later, alongside a length of a fallen wall. There were a few flagstones protruding from the soil near it.

"A temple stood here once?" Kor suggested.

"Perhaps a fortress, and these few bits are all that remain," Cam said.

Errol peered down the slight depression between rises in which they now stood. "I don't think so."

He cantered up the rise to the west, the others following behind. From the top of the rise, they could all see a little more than a hundred yards ahead of them.

Broken stone columns, fragments of walls and corners of buildings stretched on as far as the mist allowed them to see.

"A town then, perhaps a large city," Candissa said. Errol nodded.

They all rode quietly down into the remnants of the forgotten city. Hooves clacked on scattered fragments of flagstones, as they wended their way between phantom shops and residences. Cam could only imagine what they could have been, but they could see the foundations of many buildings that no longer stood.

The ruins stretched onward as they picked their way west, until Cam estimated they had covered more than a mile.

"A vast city, without a doubt," he said. Suddenly, out of the mist rose a monolithic structure, dark stone standing against the pale fog. It was perhaps twenty feet tall and just as wide.

"What is this?" Errol breathed, as they guided their mounts around both sides. Cam spotted the doorway cut into the dark stone, facing south. About four feet of the opening extended above the soil. He guessed at least as much was buried. He wondered how the structure came to be buried under more than three feet of earth.

Inside, he could see more soil, and vines. It was open on the top, lacking any roof.

"This stone, it's the same as some of the walls of Ravensroost," Errol said. He felt it with one hand, pressing his palm against it. "And the central tower of the Bonerest. The same stone."

"It must be this sort of stone is of ancient origin," Candissa said.

"Predating our two-hundred-year-old Kingdom," Kor added.

"We must keep moving," Cam said. "And it's getting late. We have only a few hours if we're lucky and this mist holds."

"Perhaps we'll find another tower such as this, to make camp. It would provide us some shelter against whatever may be out here," Errol said.

As if in answer, they heard for the first time a sound emanating from the misty desolation. It was a long, almost mournful, howling. Deeper than a wolf, Cam did not recognize it. They all froze in place and their mounts shifted in their stances, betraying their fear. Cam thought it came from the south.

Another call, even further away, sounded in response. It was shorter, more abrupt.

"Don't ride on stone, we don't need to attract the attention of anything," was all Cam said. The others nodded mutely.

They heard the forlorn call again, but it was further away. Their pace was quickened as they moved through the fallen remains of the city, until they finally gave way to the low, rolling hills once more. The hills here were not as high, with wider gaps between. They crossed another sluggish stream, broad but flat, and easily forded.

Cam slowed and urged his horse to drink, but the beast refused. The other horses did likewise. Kor's nose wrinkled.

"Something is wrong with the water, I can smell it," the scholar said.

Cam smelled nothing, while Errol and Candissa both shrugged. Once they were on the other side of the stream, he dismounted. Touching the water, he put it to his nose. It was faint, but something was wrong with it.

"Don't taste it," Koraymis urged his horse over toward Cam.

"All right. Do you know what's wrong with it? I smell nothing," Cam said, wiping his hand off on his breeches.

"Perhaps *smell* was not the right term. I sense something is wrong with it," Koraymis said, looking to the southwest, in the direction of the stream's source. "Something ill is up there. It's tainted the water."

Cam was learning to trust the instincts of his fellows. He nodded, and they were on their way quickly.

The light was fading quickly after another hour. The mist was relentless but at least it was not worsening. They would have to make camp soon.

He was relieved to happen upon a low broken wall. It was granite, Cam thought, or something close to it. Some of it seemed cracked and crazed in ways he had never seen. He thought either a mighty impact or extreme weathering but could not be certain.

They made camp along the wall, where it was met with a pile of rubble. A few stunted shrubs grew out of the rubble, providing shelter against whatever wind may blow from the west during the night. It was also a defensible site, if they were beset by creatures.

It was not yet full dark when they had chosen where to pitch their tents and tend to the horses. They pitched the tents quickly. Cam made sure to keep the horses tied together, with appropriate slack, and knotted the rope at the trunk of a stunted tree growing from the rubble. He made sure the rope and knots were secure. If they lost their mounts, their journey would be challenging indeed.

Koraymis moved two pieces of broken wall to form an embankment for a fire pit. It would prevent the flames from being seen at a distance.

"A fire should be safe, don't you think?"

Cam nodded, and the sorcerer set to building and lighting the fire. Candissa was happy to get out pans to warm some evening fare. As she was by far the most experienced in preparing food, they welcomed her assistance in this. It was only after she had finished warming the breaded mush and seasoning it with spices in a pan lined with flavored oil that they realized how good she was.

"It comes of growing up in the house of a baker," she smiled at their muted nods as they stuffed their mouths. "I know a great deal about cooking."

They finished their meals quickly and set about banking the fire.

As they sat about the stone-ringed fire, feeling a bit of its warmth, Cam passed a bottle of ale he had packed. Errol was grateful and Kor took a swig. The young lady declined.

"In this mist, we could miss a tower entirely, even as tall as it is," Errol pointed out.

"I was thinking about that," Koraymis voiced his concern.

"Do not worry," Candissa chimed in. "We will look for a sign and it will guide us."

"How do you know that?" Errol said. Cam sometimes thought Errol pushed her a little too much. He still could not figure those two out.

"I am Aevaru. A sign will show us the way," she said with a small smile.

Cam had not heard this word before. "What is an Aevaru?"

Then he noticed Errol. His eyes were dark, his gaze almost poisonous, as he stared unblinking at Candissa.

"Errol, what's the matter?" Cam said, rising from where he was sitting. Candissa now noticed Errol's gaze.

"What is it, Errol?" As she asked, Cam saw she had placed a hand gently on her staff.

Kor took note of the exchange as well, studying Errol closely, not moving.

Cam saw Errol had one hand over the grip of his dagger. But it was still in the sheath.

"Errol?" Candissa said.

Cam had a tin cup of water, poured from his water flask. With a quick flip of his wrist, the water arced through air to splash across Errol's face.

He jumped upwards, yelping in shock and confusion. At once, all four were on their feet. Candissa had her staff in hand, Koraymis held one hand out defensively and Cam had his hand on the hilt of his broadsword.

"Sard! By the six and seven, why did you do that?" Errol demanded of Cam. He wiped his face, his shock replaced by a puzzled expression.

He looked around at his companions, seeing their state of readiness. "Did I not hear something?" He looked around, peering into the dim mist.

"Errol, you weren't answering us," Candissa said. "Frankly, you were frightening me the way you were staring."

"Staring?" His expression betrayed a seeming ignorance of what had just happened.

"She was telling us of how she is an Aevaru, and you seemed to slip into some sort of...state," Koraymis said, trying to explain. "It looked as if you were about to lunge at Candissa."

"I don't recall that, Candissa," Errol said, apparently genuine in his response. "And it is stranger still I would act in such a way."

"Well," Cam said, after a pause. "You seem better now."

"I would hope," Errol said. He turned to Candissa. "What exactly is an Aevaru?"

She slowly sat, as did the others. "It is why I can do what I do," she began. "My grandmother was Aevaru, and my mother tells me that is my lot. I confess I know little of what they are, save that I am the only one I know of."

"Is that why your staff does that little trick with the light?" Errol asked.

She nodded. "I believe other abilities will manifest, but I can't be sure what or when. I'm glad this came up, because I need you all to understand this is new to me, and I won't have all the answers. I'm sure more will come to me as time passes."

"I think that can be said for me as well," Koraymis said. "I am not sure of the extent of my ability as a sorcerer. I know of some things I can do, and I suspect they will grow in power as I learn more. There may be new *tricks,* as Errol calls them, that I will discover along the way."

The others nodded, saying little by way of reply. Cam chose to break the somewhat uncomfortable silence.

"We should settle in for the night. It seems quiet out there. It should be as peaceful as last night."

He would recall those words in the morning. He would remember to never say them again.

CHAPTER TWENTY-NINE - KORAYMIS

2 Procellus, Year 197, Eastvale Calendar

The words came slowly at first, dark and unclear, like the air outside his tent.

But they were persistent, growing slowly in intensity. Koraymis awoke slowly, still groggy. It had been only an hour since they had settled down, Cam and Errol in their tent, he and Candissa in this one.

On the edge of his perception, still half-dreaming, Koraymis had thought perhaps Errol was outside speaking to Cam. But he realized that was not the case, that the voices were not normal.

Then the voice was there, cutting into his mind, startling him almost violently.

Beware! The voices seek to deceive!

It was his ring, speaking to him with a clarity he had not experienced before. He was fully awake now, but did not move. His eyes wide, he listened, sensed. There were mutterings in the dark without, whispers in the muted black of the night mist.

Awaken the Aevaru, she will protect you all!

He needed no more impetus than that.

"Candissa, get up!" His voice was a harsh whisper.

She turned to face him, awake but not yet especially alert.

"What is it?"

"Voices."

He sat up, straining to listen. He could hear them, but they were faint, indistinguishable from hissing wind that blew ceaselessly.

"Who are they?" Candissa was also trying to hear them. He didn't know if she could or not at this point.

"They will try to deceive us. You will protect us?"

"What are you saying?" Her voice was demanding.

"I was just told," he said, holding up his right hand. "The Aevaru will protect us."

She had an almost angry expression, but she gripped her staff and climbed up and out of the tent. Koraymis followed her.

It was the dark of night. Koraymis expected it to be dark. But this was different. The darkness was too close in around them, and it was getting closer.

The blackness was nearly impenetrable, but he could see her face clearly. She concentrated, holding her staff up off the ground. It began to glow.

"Something is out there," she said aloud.

The sorcerer clutched his ring instinctively. He felt it too, more clearly now, more distinct. It wasn't just voices.

"They are angry, almost evil, but not quite," he whispered.

Cam burst out of his tent, bow in hand. "What's happening? What are those voices?"

Koraymis could see a note of terror in his eyes. Errol followed Cam but seemed far less alarmed.

"We don't know, I cannot see them yet," Candissa said. She held the staff with both hands now, seeming to struggle with it. Koraymis sensed her conflict. She was not as experienced as he was in the use of magic, he suspected.

"Candissa, I don't know what you are capable of, but you must let it flow from you," Koraymis counseled her. "Hold the staff, use it as a focus, but let your power flow from inside you."

She will kill you, you know that? A voice seeped into his mind from the darkness beyond their camp. At the same time, he saw Cam nock an arrow, his Elven eyes wide, casting about, looking for he knew not what.

Fear gripped Koraymis's heart as the darkness formed a wind, seeming to swirl around them. Shapes were moving in the slowly turning vortex. Voices, terrifying and sibilant, began making sense to him.

They will use you, then they will cast you aside. They don't trust you! She will kill you for the deformed freak you are!

"No! Lies!" Koraymis shouted. The swirling darkness increased in tempo. Candissa's light, which had grown a moment before, seemed to retreat now. He held his hands up defensively. "I will not listen!"

You know truth when you hear it! You are more intelligent than all of them, they need you for your intellect but when it is time, they will let you perish! Run from them now! Run while you can!

The voices were not from his ring, he knew that. They spoke a truth he had hidden from himself; he could not deny he had those same thoughts.

He could see an opening in the dark mists, the voices beckoning. He could run; they would not give chase.

Candissa's light was almost gone. She didn't even take his advice, stupid girl! She didn't deserve his counsel. His hands flared to a brilliant orange, lighting the swirling darkness before him. He could see faces more clearly now, friends, welcoming him, appreciating him for his talents, his intellect, his power.

An arrow hissed over his shoulder, brushing his cloak. Rage burst forth from within him. "Traitors!" Koraymis bellowed, his voice suddenly deep and menacing.

Whirling, he extended both hands and a gout of yellow flame poured forth, filling the air before him. He roared as it tore through the darkness, trying to find the traitor, the so-called friend, who had tried to kill him! They would all burn!

A brilliant burst of white light filled the air all around him, instantly pushing back the dark, swirling mists. The fires from his hand faded as he closed his eyes tight against the brightness, more brilliant than the midday sun.

"Kor!" a friend's voice shouted. Opening his eyes, he saw Candissa standing just behind him, her brilliant white staff firmly on the ground. Cam was crouched, panting, his bow on the ground next to him. Just past their tents, a long stretch of the wall was blackened and still smoldered. To the other direction, Errol was calming the horses, looking back at Koraymis with concern in his eyes.

The entire area was lit by a clear white light, centered on Candissa. Beyond, he saw the dark vapors fading, vanishing.

"Koraymis?" Candissa's voice was like a balm.

"I'm sorry, Candissa," he said. He looked at her, his eyes not quite right, as he peered out from under a brow sporting small horns. He realized he was still in his changed form. She touched his shoulder, her eyes a cool silver now, and a sense of relief spread through his body. He shuddered a little as he changed back into the Koraymis they knew.

"You heard the voices too?" Cam asked as he stood slowly. He was clearly affected by the experience. "I'm sorry I nearly struck you."

"Did you think me an enemy?"

The hunter nodded. "They told me you would burn us all."

"I was a fool. I should have acted sooner," Candissa said. "Your counsel was wise, Koraymis. I won't doubt it again."

"But you didn't know what we were going through. How could you know what to do?" Kor asked.

"I'm beginning to realize it is my...role, I suppose is as good a word as any, to protect my friends. You said so yourself. A voice spoke to you through the ring, did it not?"

He nodded. "It may have been my master, I cannot be sure. But it was certain you could do exactly what you did."

"How are the horses, Errol?" Cam asked their friend.

"They were terrified when Kor started sprouting flame, but they're fine now."

Koraymis looked around, and realized the stunted grasses were scorched.

"How far did I hurl the flames?"

"It was impressive. If you can call on that in battle, I pity anyone who stands against you," Cam said, inspecting his bow.

"I'm sorry. I put you all in danger," he said, realizing what he could have done. Then he thought about Errol standing in the other direction. "Wait a moment, Errol. Were you over by the horses during that...attack?"

"When you were looking in this direction, I moved to calm them, yes."

"But...then you must have been in the darkness, in the vortex. How did you manage that?"

Errol looked at him with somewhat confused expression. Candissa spoke.

"He did not sense what we did, the voices, the terror," she said.

"Truly? Errol?"

Errol shook his head. "It did not affect me so, no."

"How is that?" Cam asked now. "They were terrifying. If I had plunged into those shadows, I would think myself lost utterly."

"I don't know why," Errol said firmly. "They were creatures of shadow, or spirits perhaps. I'm not sure. They didn't affect me or the horses. But I could do nothing to drive them away."

Candissa was walking around the area now, holding her staff aloft. It was still shining brilliantly. The night air seemed clear, out to where the mists resumed. Koraymis could see it was a dim, white mist, as one would expect. "I think we are safe for now. I do not think they will return."

"And tomorrow?" Cam asked.

"I don't know," she said, sighing. Her shoulders slumped. She looked weary.

"Do you know of wards, Candissa?" Koraymis asked.

She shook her head.

"Tomorrow, I will teach you what I know of them. Perhaps we can figure out how you can create one, to provide some warning and even protection," he said.

She seemed relieved at his words. "Thank you, Kor."

"We all need more sleep," Errol said. "Candissa, if you could douse that light of yours, assuming nothing else is lurking out in those shadows."

"Whatever may be is likely frightened away," Cam said. "Candissa, I can't imagine what would have happened if you didn't do that."

"Perhaps this is one of the reasons people don't survive to tell of their wanderings beyond the hills," Errol said, slipping back into his tent. "I won't sleep for long I suspect."

Candissa sighed and lowered her staff. The light around them began fading immediately. Koraymis held the tent flap open for her. She nodded and climbed back in.

After slipping back in, he didn't bother securing the tent flaps. He thought it prudent to make it easier to exit the tent. Darkness once more surrounded the tent. It was a simple darkness, no whispering threat lurking behind it.

Candissa's breathing was quiet.

"You likely think me a monster," Koraymis said. "I didn't mean for you to see that."

"You are no monster. You cannot frighten me so easily, Koraymis Sleeth," Candissa said. In the darkness, even without looking, he could hear her smile.

The morning was brighter, but colder. They were concerned about being pursued, after surviving the previous night. Koraymis made a good-sized fire, and despite Cam's concerns about attracting attention, Candissa set about warming cakes for breaking their fast.

Before they set out, they took extra time to tend the horses.

The mist was thinner now. They could see farther than yesterday. The hills were covered in short grass and clumps of long grass and shrubs, all looking ill. There were pieces of stone jutting out of the soil, dotting the landscape as far as they could see.

"Ruins of homes? Or was this part of that city we passed through?" Koraymis asked no one in particular.

"Seems we're outside of whatever that city was," Errol guessed. "I suspect these were the homes of more wealthy, landed gentry, who kept estates outside of the city, in these hills."

Cam looked at him with some surprise. "You sound as if you know this place."

Errol laughed. "No, but I seem to have some familiarity with how a city and the surrounds are arranged. Do not ask me why."

"Logic would say it is because you come from a large city, such as this," Koraymis said.

"Perhaps. Without my memory, it matters little," Errol said, perhaps a little annoyed. "Let us finish this fine fare and try to find some water for the horses."

"We'll find water, I can smell it," Cam said.

Koraymis admired Cam's senses. He suspected it was more his Elven heritage than his training in the ways of the wilds. While Cam had not been inducted as a member of the rangers of Ravensroost, he had all the skills they utilized. Or so Koraymis understood.

They were done, packed and ready to ride within half an hour. As they guided their mounts along the long wall and then away, Cam was studying the ground. Koraymis took note.

"What are you looking for, Cam?"

"Tracks. I'm not sure what they are, but animals are in the area. Keep a sharp eye. If it's a hungry predator, we could lose a horse before we can react."

They decided to keep the spare in the middle of their group, against such an attack. The day's travel was pleasingly uneventful. They heard another long, low call, and a few howlings. But all were distant. Cam even spotted a few birds, which pleased him for some reason. They found clean water, and the horses had their fill. Cam topped off their water skins as well.

The ruins diminished over the course of a few hours, until they were riding through trackless wastes of short grass and a few bushes. The afternoon was bright, but the mists persisted. Cam pointed out they could see some faint blue overhead, meaning it was a low mist. The thought of escaping the pervasive mists lifted their spirits.

Night approached, and they caught a fleeting glimpse of what may have been a pack of deer or similar creatures. Cam told them he expected to see herd animals, given the signs. He thought they were either deer or elk. He had also seen droppings not unlike a bear's, he cautioned them. Before sundown, they found the remains of a long-destroyed fortification of some sort. It was just two walls standing at a corner and little else. The foundation told them it had been a strong shelter. The stone, while weathered by untold years, was badly fractured. Some of it crumbled easily, appearing scorched somehow. They could only guess what had brought it down.

With two standing walls, it served well as a campsite, and Cam set about erecting the tents. As Koraymis had promised, he retrieved his book from his pack, and using the light of Candissa's staff, he studied what he could of wards. They discussed it, as it was essentially theory. He could not provide any practical advice to her on the matter. Nonetheless, she appreciated it and assured him she would contemplate on what he had shared. He could only hope it would lead to something tangible for her.

As they had some time before retiring to their tents, Cam and Errol brought up their idea of training. They would train Koraymis in the use of a bow and blade, if he was so inclined. Candissa asked to learn the bow as well but would also work on her techniques with the staff.

Errol pointed out it would help pass the time while the horses rested, allowing everyone to share in their own skills. He pointed out he was a novice with the bow, while Cam wished to learn more of close-in fighting techniques.

"This sort of training has more benefits than simply increasing your proficiency with a weapon," Errol said as they discussed the training. "This will allow us to understand one another better. The more we are able to predict the movements and actions of others, the more cohesive we will be as a fighting force."

"Errol, you keep surprising me with how much you know," Cam said. It was clear to everyone that Errol had a thorough background in military tactics and training.

"I am certainly up for this training," Koraymis said. "But I'm afraid there's little I can offer to any of you."

"That's quite all right, Kor," Cam said, grinning. "I don't think I would wish to know how to cast fire about."

"We could share our lore with Cam and Errol, though," Candissa pointed out. "We both brought some books with us. As we study them, we should let them know what we find out."

Koraymis nodded. He liked the idea. "Agreed."

The evening progressed, first with their meal and then training. It ended with some time for reading. They brought some small lamps for that purpose. Koraymis noted Candissa was once again reading from her blue-bound book, as she had the previous night.

Before they lost all light, he took out a handful of sheets and a booklet, and his drawing implements. He had not forgotten what Penston had charged him with. He had managed to jot down notes and observations on their travels - commenting on the terrain, distance they had traveled, and other pertinent information for map-making purposes. Koraymis was delighted to find the scholar had included in his bundle a few simple but very useful tools - rulers, tools for marking distances, fine parchment, a sighting tripod with a lens, and a compass. While he hadn't the opportunity to begin a proper map, he was collecting information to do so. Once he had clear skies and a good view of the two moons, he would use the tools to begin plotting their position and noting it.

The night passed uneventfully, to everyone's relief. Cam reported he heard what he called normal noises of the night and nothing more. They all slept well and were refreshed for another day of riding. The only complaint Koraymis had this morning was the imposing of a new routine. If time allowed, after their morning meal they would all engage in physical activity designed to improve their bodily strength and flexibility. Errol could not emphasize enough how important this was. Koraymis found it exhausting. Errol assured him it would improve with time and repetition.

They rode for another four days in the thick mist, over low rolling hills.

There was little but coarse grass and scrub, interrupted by a trickling stream twice. There was no rain or snow, though it was still bitter cold at night.

Training continued, and reading continued. Koraymis kept careful notes and even made some simple sightings using the tools Penston had provided. He and Candissa had even begun to share insights and observations about their own unique skills. She would tell him about the healing arts, and he would share concepts and methods he had learned in his arcane training.

The sorcerer did his best in the exercises and training provided by Errol and Cam. He grew more familiar with the broadsword and bow. While his skill with weapons would never amount to much - he knew that full well, and expressed as much on many occasions - what he gained from the training was far more valuable. He was gaining an insight into how they would function as a group in combat, understanding how long it took Cam to knock an arrow, or Errol to change position, or how much room to give Candissa as she employed her whirling staff of bleached wood.

The mist was still pervasive on that night, as they settled in. There was no sign of reaching an end to the obscuring mists, and they were resigned to rising tomorrow to face another day of the dim, gray pall.

Cam and Errol had all but dismissed the possibility of being followed now. Cam had even had luck in snaring a cony, and Candissa had provided them a spiced and succulent dinner. Their tents were pitched next to a jagged stretch of stone that seemed to erupt from the earth. They were not settled on if the stone was natural or the remnant of something made by mortal hands.

It was that night, as they settled down next to the fire, that Koraymis sensed something odd.

The horses were all tethered to column of stone not ten yards from the tents. While Candissa was reading her mysterious blue journal, and Errol and Cam engaged in a game of dice, Koraymis got up to pace the area. He walked over and inspected his mount, William. The night-dark horse was fully awake, and nuzzled Koraymis' hand as he offered it. William stood away from the other four horses. They did not seem to like his company.

The sorcerer had learned about horses on their journey. They slept standing for the most part, but laid down occasionally. At the moment, Candissa's whitish mare, Torren, and Errol's dark bay, Teago, were laying on their side. Cam's reddish chestnut, Rufus, and the tawny fifth horse, were both standing, apparently dozing.

Koraymis couldn't shake the strange feeling that compelled him to stand and walk. He looked around. Errol saw his wandering gaze.

"You know, Kor, your horse doesn't sleep much," Errol comment quietly.

"Really?"

"I've noticed as well," Cam added. "It is strange."

Koraymis turned to the midnight-hued horse, leaning close to his muzzle. "Are you not tired, William?"

The horse only looked at Koraymis. Then he turned his long, black head to one side and the other. He snorted just a little. Koraymis' heart quickened

He smells the shadows...they're coming!

"Candissa! Your staff!" Koraymis all but shouted, striding back to the fire, pushing his cloak over his shoulders to free his hands.

"Sard! Whispering shadows again?" Errol jumped up as Cam rose as quickly, retrieving his bow.

On her feet, staff already glowing white, Candissa shook her head at Cam. "Put the bow down, Cam. Arrows and blades will do nothing against this."

Reluctantly, the hunter dropped his bow. "What are we to do then?"

"Stay by the fire," Koraymis said. He turned to Candissa. "Pace the campsite. Try to put a ward up."

She nodded and struck the staff to the ground. Koraymis had to shade his eyes against the brilliant light. He watched as she walked a tight perimeter around the fire and their tents, murmuring quietly.

Koraymis felt the magic as she wove it, leaving strands of invisible energy in her wake. She tapped the ground intermittently, as the magic grew in intensity. After a minute, she returned to her three friends.

"Is that some sort of fence you just put up?" Cam whispered. Koraymis could see it too, a faintly visible ring of glowing energy.

"Yes, it's a ward of sorts," she said. "I'm hoping it's enough to keep the shadows away, to prevent what happened the other night."

"But you can still do that trick with your staff, yes?" Errol asked, grinning.

"Of course!"

Koraymis and his friends watched as the air seemed to thicken with darkness, just beyond the glow of Candissa's ward. The dark mists swirled, but not nearly as quickly as they had before. Overhead, the ward apparently extended to a dome shape, as the darkness seeped over them completely.

But there was no storm of whispers, no crowding of hissing voices in his ears. Everyone waited, but all Koraymis could hear were faint mutterings, dull and distant.

"The ward is working," Cam said.

"Still, how long will it last?" Errol said.

"You could try using your staff to perhaps convince the mist to leave?" Koraymis suggested.

"I'm afraid if I do that, the ward could collapse. I need to keep my focus on it to maintain it. Still," she murmured. "There's something here…"

She stepped away from the fire, closer to the glowing ward of faint but intricate lines. Koraymis realized they were vaguely blue and white and green in color.

"What are you doing?" Errol said, a hard edge on his words.

"I'll be careful, I need to do something," was all she said.

She neared the boundary, a few feet from the slowly swirling darkness. She lowered her staff, and extended it carefully through the ward, while holding her left hand up, defensively.

"Don't be foolish!" Errol said, taking a step towards her. Koraymis understood his concern. If something happened to her, they could suffer the full effects of whatever the hissing darkness was.

She turned her head for a moment to look at them. Her eyes were glowing silver. "It's all right, it can't hurt me."

Turning back, she bowed her head, her staff now further into the dark mists.

Koraymis could sense something in her, seeping through their bond. Emotions spilled into their minds.

Do you feel that too? Cam pathed. Koraymis only nodded.

Sadness.

Candissa shuddered. He thought at first she was in a trance of some sort, but then it was clear she was sobbing quietly.

"I'm...sorry," she murmured. "I'm so very sorry."

"Candissa," Errol said, stepping closer to her. At first, Koraymis thought he was going to try to pull her back. Instead, he just put a hand on her shoulder.

She shook at his touch. Koraymis felt it as well.

Both of you, come here, Candissa pathed.

Koraymis and Cam joined Errol. The sorcerer put one hand on her other shoulder, while Cam put his hands on Errol's and Koraymis' shoulders.

"Please...know this...I am sorry," Candissa whispered. Koraymis could see tears rolling down her cheeks, her eyes shut tight.

The swirling mists suddenly grew in intensity. The whispering voices could again be heard. Her staff moved in her grip, as the darkness buffeted against it just outside of the wards.

Errol glanced at Koraymis and Cam, concern clear in his expression.

"It's all right…" Candissa sobbed, shaking gently.

The mists rose to a maelstrom around their glowing circle. The whispers grew to a clearly audible cacophony of shouts, screams, guttural cries, weeping, laughing. The buffeting of the dark mists appeared to threaten the ward, as the glowing lines flickered, brighter then dimmer.

The voices were jarring, intense, and profoundly disturbing. Koraymis gritted his teeth, seeing Errol and Cam struggling as well.

Despite the noise and the palpable danger of the mists, just an arm's length away from them, Koraymis could hear Candissa's whispered voice.

"Be at peace…"

Her staff erupted with a blue-white light, a sphere of faint light that moved out quickly in every direction. With that, the noise vanished, the maelstrom disappeared. They were suddenly surrounded by an almost glowing gray mist. Everything was a clear and visible around them as daylight.

Then it faded. Looking up, Koraymis thought he could see vague shapes drifting away, like steam rising from a hot cup of bitterblack. It was dark once more.

Candissa went down on hands and knees, weeping, the ward gone. Her staff glowed faintly.

"Are you all right?" Errol said, crouching to attend her.

She only nodded, rising slowly.

Koraymis looked around. He blinked. There were lights above them. The two moons.

"What...just happened?" Cam said. He turned around and around. The sky was clear as glass, from horizon to horizon.

"The mists...they're gone," Koraymis said, feeling a little silly for stating something so utterly obvious.

Candissa wiped her face. "They were so sad, such sadness, I couldn't imagine."

"Who were *they*?" Koraymis asked.

"I'm not sure, but they all suffered, died, here," Candissa said, motioning in a broad arc all around them. "These hills, or at least I think so."

"When?" Errol asked.

"Long ago, I don't know how long. They were full of bitterness, rage, sadness, desperation," she said, another tear rolling down her face.

"Were they-" Errol began.

Let her be, came Cam's voice.

"I am very tired," she said, moving to her tent. "We'll talk in the morning."

After she retired to her tent, it was not long before Koraymis and the others followed her example.

The following morning was unlike any other they had experienced in the Misthallow Hills.

To the east, the hills appeared to roll onward forever. The morning air was clear, the sun preternaturally bright. They could see bits of ruins dotting the rolling landscape, like tiny bones. There were clouds to the west, but high, harmless tatters, none portending a foul day.

The vistas were so bright and vivid, Koraymis could not help but feel as if his spirits were lifted.

As he stretched, preparing for their morning routines, he noticed Errol perched on the ridge above their campsite, just to the east. He stood atop a broken column, one of many they had been encountering on their journey westward.

You seem concerned. How so, on such a glorious morning? Koraymis pathed.

Cam laughed at that, as he built their morning fire.

"This makes no sense," Errol called down to them from his perch. "The mist is gone."

"It's just an especially clear morning, Errol," Cam said.

"No, it's not that. There's always been a light mist over these hills. Well, perhaps we're at the western edge of them," Errol said, jumping down from the broken stone. "That must be it."

Cam set about preparing breakfast, heating up pan bread with cooking oil.

Candissa was the last to arise. She looked almost tired to Koraymis.

"Are you well this morning?" he asked her.

She nodded, running her fingers briskly through her hair, the morning sun complementing her honey-gold locks. "Yes, but groggy. Last night took a lot out of me."

"Then perhaps Errol could see his way to release you from morning exercises," Cam grinned over the frying pans as he tended them.

Candissa looked at the pans. "What is that you're cooking?"

"Pan bread?" Cam said. Koraymis could see there were two pans, however.

"And the other? Is that meat I smell?" the Aevaru asked, her eyes narrowing.

"Yes," Cam said, almost sheepishly. He tilted the pan. "Sausage."

"Sausage?" Errol blurted. "I don't recall packing any sausage."

Koraymis glanced down at Cam's mysterious backpack. He grinned. "We didn't take any."

The three of them stepped over to the fire, looking down into the larger frying pan. It held four generously-sized casings of meat. The smell of the sizzling grease was aromatic, almost intoxicating.

Candissa looked down at the pack pointedly. "I would like to know just what that pack of yours can do."

Cam only shrugged, declining to look up at her. She left the question at that.

They were soon about enjoying a bountiful breakfast, followed by study and exercises. Candissa joined them in both, despite her weariness from the previous night's efforts.

As they broke camp and readied to once again ride, a tatting of high clouds moved in from the west. The wind was cold, but brisk, and promised no snows of winter.

They rode through the hills easily, spying more large fragments of stone and walls or columns tumbled here and there, poking out of the tough ground. The horse had ample grasses to feed on, and they slaked their thirst from a small rill of fresh water they crossed later in the day. On their midafternoon rest, Koraymis took measurements with his mapping tools, adding to his notes. With the clear skies, there were many markers to sight in the distance.

Before they camped for the evening, it was clear to them all the hills were changing, subsiding. Plant life changed as well, as the hard soil gave way to darker, more yielding earth. As night fell, the sky cleared once again, yielding the canopy of bright stars.

They had found an accommodating gulch between ridges to make camp, allowing a larger fire and providing cover from observers or worse.

"You know, for all the talk, the hills weren't so bad," Errol quipped, sipping from a slender flask he had brought.

"Really? Do you think those dark winds were just folly?" Candissa retorted, raising an eyebrow.

"All right, *aside from that*," Errol acquiesced. "And to be honest, I was jesting with you a bit there. I don't imagine most people would have survived those nights."

"The tales did mention travelers returning without a shred of sanity," Koraymis nodded.

"I'm more interested in this change of weather," Cam said. "I'm sensing something strange. Winter may be put off for a while."

"How so?" Errol asked.

"The winds are more southwesterly today, and carry warmer air, with some hints of life I wouldn't expect," the hunter said. "If it holds, we could be moving toward a gentle winter."

"That would not be unwelcome," Errol said, raising his flask to Cam.

The evening was eventless, although later they all heard a distant sound not unlike a howling of a wild animal. Nothing followed, and they all slipped into a deep and dreamless slumber.

The following day found their path leading them downhill, the rolling hills behind them as the land opened onto a sloping plain. The sight of the open, blue sky and unhindered land was almost a cause for celebration.

While the open sky was welcome, their attention focused on other sights as they moved steadily west.

To the south, a range of mountains filled the horizon, spreading to the southeast until they faded from sight. The mountains were part of a larger mass ahead, to the west. Even at this distance, it was clear the mountain range ahead was far more massive than those surrounding the Kingdom of Eastvale.

While a light mist obscured the distant horizon, Koraymis thought he could make out a line of treetops. Cam suggested it was perhaps a massive forest.

To the north and northwest, the land descended rapidly, a rocky landscape of ravines and washes. From their higher vantage, they could make out the edge of what must be an immense gorge. One of the washes leading down toward the gorge had flowing water, making a faint rushing noise as the water cut into the ground before emptying into the chasm. From their current location, they could only see the edge of the gorge and could not see how far east or west it stretched.

To the distant north, more mountains rose. Clouds were on the far horizon to the north and east. Looking back later in the morning, Koraymis saw nothing of the ominous Misthallow Hills.

It was later, as they approached evening, when their otherwise eventless day was interrupted. The land was not entirely flat here, and as their path west took them over a broad rise, it appeared before them.

Perhaps a half mile away, the ruins began. A ragged, broken wall stretched north and south for more than a quarter mile. The length of it was pitted, collapsed, cracked and breached dozens of times. They could see the top of the mighty wall in a few spots, and it was easily a hundred feet tall.

Beyond the wall lay the ruins of a city. Broken walls, sheared columns and shattered domes littered the remnants of what must have been a magnificent metropolis. Two or three towers rose well above the ruins, while one especially hulking shape stretched even further.

As they rode slowly toward it, Koraymis could see the stone was not just the bleached gray of granite or chalky limestone. There were colors in the stonework, and he could see ghosts of fantastic designs, curves, flying arches, and bold, jutting promontories.

"What was it?" Cam breathed.

"A city?" Candissa suggested.

A temple complex? Koraymis pathed.

"No, it was a fortress," Errol said. He offered nothing more.

"How can you be sure?" Cam asked. "Do you...remember it?"

"In a sense. All I can say is that I'm convinced this was a fortress, or perhaps served as one. We'll find more signs of it within," he said. His eyes narrowed. "But what by six and seven brought down the outer walls? They look immense."

"Perhaps we will find evidence," Cam said, leading them onward, increasing his pace. They cantered across the uneven plain, as the ruins grew larger by the moment. Koraymis noticed a few flagstones in the ground, some half concealed by time and growth.

"Roads," he pointed at them. The others nodded.

As they moved closer to the extraordinary ruins, Errol pointed them toward a gap. "The gate, it was there." As the perimeter of the field of debris and rubble was evenly lined with fallen and shattered stone, it was curious he was able to identify it from this range. Koraymis wondered if more of this sort of thing would help restore Errol's lost memories.

The young sorcerer marveled at the walls on their approach. While ruined and collapsed for the most part, they were easily forty feet thick at the base and made of solid stone.

Heading for the area indicated by Errol, they indeed found the twisted remains of iron bars as thick as a man's thigh. Just inside the perimeter, as they picked their way carefully between immense fragments of shattered stone, they could more easily see the streets and fallen structures within. While sundered and broken, the foundations were clear.

"Should we explore this place?" Candissa asked.

"I'm inclined," Errol said, not surprisingly.

"We'll need to make camp in two or three hours, it would take that long at least to inspect the larger structures," Cam said, surveying the ruins better by standing in his stirrups. "Ho, have a look at this." He suddenly spurred his mount between two partial walls along what was once a narrow street. Rounding a corner, they entered an immense square, weed-choked and strewn with broken columns. Across the way, hundreds of yards Koraymis guessed, was the object of his curiosity.

Standing at the farther end of the ruin was a partially destroyed structure, by far the tallest and perhaps most intact building. They had spied it on their approach, but at this range they could truly appreciate how immense it was. While round, it was too squat to be called a tower, in Koraymis's opinion. It was shorn in twain, with the eastern half of the structure in tatters, a vast pile of rubble about the base. What remained rose more than four hundred feet above the streets and wreckage of whatever this place was. There was a flat roof of some sort above the intact half of the building.

Broken and twisted lengths of wood or metal could be seen protruding from the exposed half of the rise, and even from here they could see the structure held many levels.

"Since we really have no plan, no schedule to keep, I would suggest we camp somewhere here for the night. We can spend the time before in exploration," Errol said.

"Aye, I would have to agree with you. There is much to see," Cam said.

With no reason to hurry on, they all agreed to stay. Moving slowly, they kept together, in the off chance a threat lurked somewhere in the tumbled stones of the razed fortress.

They each had occasion to dismount and inspect something. Candissa studied the pattern of flagstones on the floor of an immense dome, while Cam studied numerous tracks and remains. He also found human bones in spaces and crevasses inaccessible by wild creatures. Some of the tracks he found defied his experience. He pointed out a stretch of oddly roundish prints more than two feet long and almost as wide. It was clearly a four-limbed creature, but more than one made the tracks he found. This, among other tracks, made him wonder what sort of creatures roamed the plains surrounding the ruined fortification.

Errol pointed out the scattered and plentiful swords, shields, breastplates and helmets, clear indications of the nature of the place. Picking up a shirt of corroded mail, he gave a low whistle. "A scrapper would sell his family for all the wealth here in good iron, bronze and copper."

"I am surprised how it is all just lying about," Cam said.

"It means either everyone was slain at once or that no one has ever been able to find this place," Koraymis said. His observation was sobering. The others glanced around, wondering why the fortress, and the entire region, was abandoned.

"This is more than a fortress, Errol," Cam said.

"Yes, I think you are correct," Errol replied. "Fortified, certainly, but more a small city of some sort. There are too many buildings here, and streets."

After more than an hour of exploration, they had found broken wood, shattered tiles, no end of weapons and armor, and even some lumpish bits of gold in loose pieces of debris. Errol pointed out they resembled what was in his pocket when he arrived in Ravensroost.

But no real clues were found to help them on their way. Candissa searched some of the more covered ruins, hoping that she could find some fragments of written pages in places shielded from the weather. She found none.

When they had finally wended their way through the ruins to the half-torn structure, they marveled at the sight. Standing at the base, they saw now it was not a building of stone and tile, but a vast framework of ponderously thick metal beams, over which stone and tiles were attached. There were wooden planks and beams as well, shorn and splintered, just as the gray metal beams were ripped and twisted.

"What a strange way to build something..." Koraymis wondered aloud.

"Yes, but what force could have done this?" Errol said.

Looking up at the sundered face of the edifice, Koraymis could make out at least a dozen levels. Accessing them did not appear an easy task.

"Perhaps there are stairways or ramps within we cannot see," Errol's statement seemed in reply to his unspoken question.

"Should we attempt even entering it? I fear the place is unstable given the destruction it suffered," Candissa cautioned.

"I will. I want to get to the top and survey the land around us," Cam volunteered. "If I find it safe enough, we could even make camp up there. It could provide a degree of safety from anything that may be roaming these plains."

Koraymis agreed silently, given the diverse and numerous tracks the half-Elven hunter had found.

"If you're going, then we all go." Candissa's pronouncement left no room for discussion.

"Do we take the horses as far as we can then?" Koraymis asked.

"Yes. We can hopefully find a safe spot to tie them up," Cam said.

Errol took the lead as they entered the chaotic jumble of the lowest level of the building. He took only a few minutes to lead them to a rising ramp. They were amazed at the artistry of the colorful tiles affixed to the ceilings and walls. There were no words, just vague shapes and colors. The ramp was of an easy grade and the horses navigated it without incident.

Cam noted a few instances of nests or sleeping areas that creatures had used in the past. But nothing about them caused any concern. The next few levels had ramps like the one they first ascended. Everything was littered with varying amounts of rubble and debris. Closer to the shattered end of the build, or nearer the open windows, there was growth. Cam surmised that over the centuries, wind had carried a great deal of dust and dirt to the farthest reaches of the intact edifice. Even far within the darkened corridors, they found fibrous, dark vines creeping along the walls and ceilings.

They found a safe chamber where they left their mounts, tying them up with a generous lead of rope. It was a fine spot to make camp as well, if that proved the sensible thing after further exploration.

With broad windows all shattered and torn, illumination was not an issue as they ascended the building. Succeeding levels were accessed by stairs. By the time they had reached the seventh level, by Koraymis' reckoning, there were few signs, if any, of animals save the nests of small birds. They could only guess at the purpose of the various chambers through which they passed. Any furnishings seemed ruined beyond recognition. In the corners and crevices, they found a great deal of ash, dirt and dust.

At one level, Candissa glanced through an open portal, seeing an intact chamber lined with shelves. She dashed into the room without warning, to Errol's consternation.

"Damned be," she muttered. Koraymis was mildly shocked, having never heard the fair young lady utter a curse. "Dust."

She ran a hand along a shelf, wiping off a heavy accumulation of dust from the shelf.

"So?" Cam said.

"These were books once."

"Why do you say that? If they had burned, it would be ash, and the shelves would be gone. And even a thousand years wouldn't render the cover of books to dust," Errol said.

"And yet, they were turned to dust," she sighed.

Koraymis' finger itched. He touched his ring.

It was a spell, he said to them, silently. He was certain.

A spell? Errol managed to convey his sheer incredulity even through their mind speech.

"Yes," Koraymis said, speaking now to reaffirm his statement. "I know this."

He saw Candissa staring at his ring, as he touched it with this left hand.

"Is there any way to undo it?" she asked, in a tone that almost sounded hopeful.

Koraymis knew she was asking him to somehow use his connection with the ring to pose the question.

It doesn't work that way, he replied silently, not intending to do so.

Cam and Errol both looked at him with questions in their mind, but let it pass. Cam led them up another stairway, then another. They were nearing the end of their ascent.

At last, they found a final set of steps leading upward, with daylight lighting their way. Koraymis was fatigued from the effort, but carried on, seeing none of his fellows flagging, even Candissa.

A strong wind blew against them as they ascended the last set of steps onto the roof. They squinted as their eyes adjusted to the clear, open skies overhead. The sun was behind a cloud, but the air was clear and offered an astonishing view.

They exited the steps onto the top of the ruined structure. The roof extended a hundred yards to the west and east. The roof turned to a cracked and splintered morass as it stretched to the east, but it appeared sound where they stood. Turning, they surveyed the land surrounding the ruined city.

The crevasse to the north was staggeringly massive. It stretched to the eastern horizon, where it met the hills. It seemed to terminate some miles to the west, but they were not sure. Beyond, there was a rising landscape, more hills, and specks which Cam identified as more ruins. Beyond that, a massive range of mountains.

To the west, it was clear that beyond this stretch of plains lay a vast forest of trees taller than any of them had ever seen. Beyond the forest lay more mountains, majestic and blue. These mountains stretched south gradually and then eastward, diminishing in stature as they trailed away. To the south, the land became more uneven, fading into mist and cloud cover.

The wind was fierce and chilling. Koraymis estimated they were nearly five hundred feet over the streets and ruins of the sprawling destruction. His cloak whipped in the wind and he gathered it about him.

"Well, I do not think we will be camping here!" Errol called over the noise of the wind.

"No, but where we left the horses will suffice!" Candissa called in return.

Why are you two yelling? Koraymis chided them, smirking. Cam laughed aloud.

He's right, as usual, the hunter added.

The sun is close to setting, Candissa pathed, looking west. *We should find a place below. There are plenty of open windows to survey the land. We can find one without so much wind to hamper a fire...*

We'll need wood for the fire, Koraymis said.

There's broken furnishings below, Errol reminded them. His attention was drawn elsewhere suddenly. *What's this about?*

They had not explored the rooftop extensively. It bore some half-broken walls stretching at length. Cam followed Errol's gaze and moved behind one of the lengths of low, broken walls. He raised his eyebrows in surprise.

All of you look at this, was all he pathed. Joining him, Koraymis and the others saw what had taken him by surprise. In a partially sheltered corner, formed by an intersecting wall, a vast pile of branches and dried vegetation was piled. It was an enormous heap of tightly packed branches, sticks, dried vines and shrubs, along with a few odd bits and pieces.

And feathers.

Koraymis picked one up. It was a long plume, rich brown in color, almost shimmering in the low rays of the sun, as it peeked out from behind the clouds.

"What makes a nest four feet thick and fifteen feet wide?" Cam called out, astonishment clear in his face.

Errol stepped up onto the considerable heap of sticks and debris, inspecting the central depression. It was there the feathers were concentrated. He plucked at a few things.

"Pieces of leather, linen, and what's this? Ribbon?" Errol said, holding aloft a yard-long piece of colored fabric.

"Whatever it may be, perhaps we should leave the area before it returns?" Candissa suggested.

"No fear of that. The nest is recent, but quit," Cam said.

I don't follow, Candissa said.

Animals that nest use the nest only for broods. Clearly, the young have flown. We don't know when their breeding season is, but as winter is upon us, I'm sure they won't return for many weeks to come.

Well, do you have any idea what 'they' are? Koraymis asked.

"Griffons," Errol replied loudly, before Cam could phrase an answer. He held up a fragment of shell in his hands, then climbed back out to show it to his companions.

Koraymis was astonished. The fragment, barely curved, was thicker than his little finger and larger than his hand. It was weathered, but only months old. The outer side bore a distinct color and pattern. The curvature told him the egg must have been immense.

"I've read of mythical creatures called griffons," Candissa said, as they were standing in a close circle. "They are supposed to be legend, at best."

"I've read of them as well, but I had always supposed they were real," Koraymis said, handing the fragment to Cam. "Just something no one has ever seen in living memory."

"They are real enough, I've read of them, and I've spoken to those in the far west of the Kingdom who claim to have seen them in the mountains there."

"Fascinating," Candissa said. Then she looked at Errol. "But how do you know this belongs to a griffon?"

"I recognize the markings, and the feathers," Errol said, producing a feather he had plucked from the nest. It was longer than his forearm.

"Are they especially fearsome creatures?" Koraymis asked. He had read little of them, knowing only they were large. They were supposed to be a combination of a bird and another creature.

"Yes, fearsome is a good word for what they can do," Errol chuckled. "If tearing a man limb from limb or ripping his guts out in a single swipe qualifies as fearsome."

They all scanned the horizon in various directions at that point.

"The roof doesn't look safe toward the north, we should head back downstairs," Candissa said. With no arguments, Errol led the way back. Returning to the level below where they had left their mounts, they found a chamber with high ceilings and a window facing west that provided an excellent view of the plains. They were soon putting down bedrolls and gathering pieces of broken wood for a fire.

"I should really do some hunting tomorrow," Cam said, as he surveyed their packaged rations. "I would greatly enjoy some sizzling game over a fire right now."

"Did you see signs of game down there?" Candissa asked as she laid out plates and pans. She enjoyed overseeing the meals, even though Errol and Cam had both volunteered more than once.

"Where there's tracks, there's predator and prey. They're out there," Cam said. "Perhaps we can take some time tomorrow for a hunt."

"Ever west, my friends," Candissa chimed in as she mixed some water in with flour and other ingredients. "We must look for a sign. A hunt could slow that down."

"Deesa, be reasonable," Errol interjected. "We need to survive, and we have no idea when this *sign* will appear!"

"Of course. I will always point out why we are here. We must consider this against every action we take."

"Naturally," Cam said, raising his hands. "There's no need to deviate from our path. I won't take long tomorrow to figure what game might be found."

They ate a nicely spiced mush bread prepared by Candissa, along with dried meat and fruits. While they had water aplenty, they also enjoyed a little brandy provided by Errol.

Given they were perhaps forty yards over the streets of the ruined fortress, and reaching them would entail navigating several ramps, they decided a watch was unnecessary.

Despite this, sleep did not come easily to Koraymis. He stayed up for a long while, listening to the quiet snoring of Cam and Candissa's deep breathing, as he read his book by the light of his small lantern. After more than an hour of studying the mystic runes, absorbing knowledge and making connections he hadn't before, he decided to stand and stretch.

The others were asleep, so he tiptoed carefully down the length of their room. The horses were sleeping in an adjoining chamber. He checked on them. Seeing they were fine, he moved to the one window in their room.

Peering out, the night sky was blazing with stars, a glorious carpet comprised of thousands of points of light. Beneath, he could make out the features of the land nicely, given the two moons were out.

He slowly peered across the shadowed landscape, letting the icy wind blow against his face.

For a moment, he wondered if that point of light was campfire.

There was a light!

He clutched the edge of the window frame, carefully so as not to cut his hands on the fragments of glazing still protruding from the wooden casement. Sure enough, there, amid the desolate plain stretching westward, there was a single mote of light.

It was orange and winked vaguely. He knew it was a fire, likely the size of a campfire. The thought that someone else was out there was alarming, almost shocking. He would have to tell the others. But waking them now was pointless. Whatever the light was, it lay more than a mile or two off.

In an instant, Errol was next to Koraymis, at his left elbow. How he had come from the far end of the room to Koraymis' right without alerting the sorcerer was puzzling.

"What is it?" Errol asked, his eyes peering outside.

"Look, there," Koraymis said, pointing fiercely at the point amid the sweeping plain. "A campfire."

Errol peered, leaning a little himself. "So it is."

"Should we be concerned?"

Errol smirked at his comment. "I'm always concerned. But one fire does not alarm me."

"What does it mean?' Koraymis said, peering out into the darkness.

"It means we're not alone out here. You can take comfort in that or be more the wary for it."

"We should at least tell the others in the morning," Koraymis said. Errol nodded before returning quietly to his bedroll.

Koraymis remained at the window, peering into the darkness, studying the point of light. It twinkled for a while, before slowing fading away.

CHAPTER THIRTY - ENTHESSAR

8 Procellus, Year 197, Eastvale Calendar

Enthessar surveyed the long rows of vines, running the length of the road that bordered his family's estate on the north. He remembered running along the paths during high summer, dodging the servants working the prized grapes. He often chased his cousins here, the sons of lesser nobles.

He always beat them in contests involving racing or any athletic activity. Enthessar had always excelled in physical disciplines. On the few occasions when a cousin would manage to beat him back to the estate grounds, or best him in throwing balls, Enthessar would punish the victor.

He usually pushed them down and kicked them. But he recalled one instance when his cousin Kelbrin bested him in a foot race. The taller, lankier youth was leaning idly against a low stone wall, grinning at Enthessar as he puffed past him, well after Kelbrin had arrived. Enthessar was only twelve, but he was strong and sturdy for his age.

He pretended to congratulate his cousin, slapping him on the back. Kelbrin never had a chance as Enthessar pushed him with both hands over the low stone wall, down into the stone-lined enclosure outside of a stable. Kelbrin broke both legs in the fall and took a day to awaken.

Enthessar claimed the boy was showing off, walking along the wall, and fell by his own misstep. No one doubted the noble's son. The wounded lad's memory was addled from the knock, so he could not contest the account. Kelbrin never ran another race again, as their healer could not mend his bones soon enough to prevent permanent damage.

Enthessar sat atop his powerful stallion as he surveyed the harvested vines in their long, tangled rows. He grinned at the memory, his dark eyes twinkling. His grin faded as he scratched his hair, feeling the lump that was still there.

His eyes darkened, and a scowl replaced the grin.

It had taken his family's entourage a full week to return to the estate in the east. Enthessar had awoken late in the day of their departure. He had been enraged. It took his father and all of his officers to restrain him. He would have taken a horse straight back to Ravensroost to kill Errol, and perhaps even Candissa, if they hadn't.

It was wise. He was glad for their intervention. It had given him time to calm himself, to think on the situation, and to steel his resolve for what must come next.

He heard his man, Lancarm, approach on horseback. Turning, the older man's expression told him he had news. Lancarm had served his father all his life as a guardsman and senior advisor. He had been given to the training of young Enthessar, and the two of them bonded over the years. Lancarm was as ruthless as need be, and he helped to bring that quality out in his young charge. Now, he was all but Enthessar's second, having transferred his loyalty from father to son.

"Lancarm, what is the word?"

"Your father received a message from his contacts in Ravensroost. Orrendar's body was found. In a ditch."

"So much for any more leads on Errol and the dear Lady Candissa," Enthessar said, frowning. "Death by blade I would assume?"

"No, that's the odd part," the veteran soldier said, guiding his mount closer. "He was burned to death..."

Enthessar looked at his advisor, incredulous. "Burned? Was it an attempt to hide his identity?"

"No, our man inspected the corpse closely. There were no signs of a dagger or cuts, no sign of any weapons used against him. Just his face and head were badly charred," Lancarm said, his face growing a bit worried at the recounting. "What's more is our man claims, and this is just his account, so I don't know if he's a bit raving or -"

"Out with it! What did he report?" Enthessar said, annoyed by the delay.

"He claimed the burn on his face was in the shape of...a hand."

Enthessar considered the words. He was about to laugh and dismiss the claim. But he felt something, a feeling, an urge, something that had been growing over the past weeks. *A voice.*

"What do you think of that, sir?" Lancarm asked after a long pause of silence.

"I think we are dealing with more than just common miscreants," he replied. "Did you bring what I asked?"

"Yes, sir," the man said, retrieving a scroll tube from his vest. "Anstrym finished it early this morning."

Enthessar opened the tube and examined the neatly penned message within. "A fair approximation of Orrendar's hand, don't you think?"

"Yes, sir, it is. There were samples, so no one can contest it."

"Good. You know what will happen. You're having no qualms about it, are you?" He looked at Lancarm with a piercing, direct gaze.

"No sir, I am with you," he replied, betraying no reluctance or hesitation.

"Good, good. Go to Telbridge, you know who to gather under my banner. Return to the estate in two days," Enthessar directed him.

Lancarm saluted him, smiling. Enthessar knew he could trust him.

It was late, the sun nearly fled. He returned to the estate and joined his family for their evening meal. His mother did little save prattle on about some perceived slight by another noblewoman, as her daughters voiced their opinions on the matter.

His father just rolled his eyes, sharing a secret smile with his son. The meal was typically sumptuous, and the steak was especially rare, which Enthessar appreciated. Appropriate for the evening, he thought silently, as he bit into a particularly bloody piece.

"My son, we need to talk after dinner, in my study," his father said, between courses. Enthessar nodded dutifully. The course came that included his father's traditional brandy.

Not long after, his father suffered a coughing fit, irritating his wife. His face turned an alarming shade of red before a servant brought sufficient water to quell the fit.

Enthessar noted with satisfaction the looks of concern in the faces of the servants and steward. After the dinner, he was helped to his study by the steward. He was annoyed at the attention but relented. Enthessar made sure to exchange a worried look with the steward, nodding.

Before the wide, roaring fire in his study, he sat with his father.

"Enthessar, I've received word from Ravensroost. It appears our man Orrendar was slain, or at least died by some means."

"That's terrible! Did he have family here?" Enthessar said, feigning concern.

"No, I suppose that's a blessing. But we have no more leads on the whereabouts of this Errol or Lady Candissa. They departed with two others, it was reported."

"I see. Then there's not much to be for it, is there?"

His father shook his head. "I know you wanted to bring them to justice, but they headed west over the hills apparently. Raving mad, they must be."

"Did the town send any force to pursue?"

"West? That would be the height of foolishness. There's nothing save wild beasts, monsters, and ruins without end past those hills," his father said. "If they are not killed outright or die of starvation, they'll drag themselves back within weeks. We have people there to alert us, fear not."

"Very well, of course. Does anyone else know of Orrendar's fate?"

"Just Lancarm, no reason to worry anyone about it at this point, eh?"

"Certainly not, Father," Enthessar said. "Shall we have a game of chess?"

His father was happy at that, and they spent another hour in his study talking idly and playing their game. When it came time to withdraw for the night, Enthessar called for the steward, who attended to his lord father.

Once he was alone, he found the message from their man in Ravensroost. He read through it to ensure he didn't miss anything pertinent. After that, he crushed it in his hand and threw it into the fire, watching it flame brightly then fade into glowing ash. Drawing forth the false message Lancarm had delivered, he placed it among his father's papers, on his desk.

He was in his chambers shortly. On his way, he snapped his fingers at one of the servant girls, one among several he enjoyed. She nodded, a small smile on her lips. She appeared at his door a quarter hour later. After an hour of tumbling about his bed with her, he sent her off without a word. She seemed insulted at his silence, but he did not care. He couldn't let her think he had any feelings for her.

It didn't matter, he enjoyed it regardless. Once a suitable amount of time had passed and he was sure the entire estate was well abed, he retrieved something from his desk. Stepping over to a tall mirror, he smiled at his form, bathed in the moonlight. Pushing on a hidden panel along a decorated seam on his wall, he heard a faint click. The hidden panel swung silently inward.

As a boy in the sprawling estate of Allenfar, Enthessar had discovered many hidden doors and passages. They were no longer used, save by servants engaged in criminal actions. The house guard had caught a few in the past, attempting to steal silver or other valuables. Their hanging corpses dissuaded any further attempts and the secret passages became a forbidden thing.

He had been secretive enough in his explorations that no one knew how much he knew of the network of passages. It was pitch black within, but he knew them by touch. His only hesitation was stepping on a dead rat. Their alchemist, Gebber, sometimes put out dishes of poisoned bread to help reduce the population. Enthessar would forgive Gebber if he happened to step on one. The old man was a little touched, given his long years of exposure to poisons, but he had been particularly helpful to Enthessar.

In the dark he made the necessary turns, and he was soon at another hidden panel. Opening it carefully, he slipped into the bedchamber silently. Having tested the door earlier in the week, he knew it would not creak.

His father snored quietly in his immense bed. Drawing forth the tiny vial he had stolen away from Gebber's shop, he deftly waited for an inhalation by his father, and poured the few drops into his mouth. Not a bit of the liquid missed the mark.

Lord Allenfar coughed briefly as he slept. His snoring trailed off. Enthessar watched his expression closely, unsure of what may happen. His father gasped, his eyes opened.

He looked around wildly. One hand went to his chest. He suddenly saw his son.

"Enth..." he managed. His son put a finger to his father's quivering lips.

"No talking now, father, all is well," he said, smiling down at the old man. "This had to be done. You see, you are not up to the task."

"My...heart..." he said through a wheezing cough. It wasn't too loud. He tried to rise, but Enthessar had a small pillow at hand. He placed it over his father's mouth and nose, applying enough pressure to stifle any noises his father would make.

"Yes, your heart. It's weak, Father, and it will fail you now. It's amazing how a bit of poison will look as though your poor old heart gave out tonight. But this was just the final nudge. It was necessary to feed you poison in your brandy for the past few days."

His father's eyes were wide now, his hands grasping at the pillow uselessly, his voice audible but faint. He was no match for his son's strength.

"Father, they must be stopped. And the message sent by Orrendar will seal the resolve of our House. The message I wrote, of course," Enthessar said, feeling what little vigor remained in his father rise. The old man was trying to say something, or shout for help, but Enthessar did not care.

"You can't hear the voice, can you? You see, I am the one chosen to lead the way. They must be stopped."

His father tried to claw at his son's face, but his attempts were weakening, his strength fading. He convulsed, one hand going to his chest, his eyes glazing over. Enthessar released his hold slowly, as his father jerked a bit. He lifted the pillow off his mouth, hearing the final breath escape his mouth.

Lord Allenfar's eyes stared sightlessly upwards. Enthessar ensured he had passed and closed his dead eyes. "Can't have you frighten the steward in the morning, can we?"

Pocketing the vial, he returned to the hidden door. Entering the lightless passage once more, he secured the panel behind him. It was completely black.

"It is done," Enthessar murmured to himself in the dark.

Good. Gather your forces, pursue them into the hills.

"Yes, I will," Enthessar said, knowing it was not truly a reply. He did not know what or who the voice in his mind was, but it was the guiding force in his life now.

He lost his orientation for a moment, lost in the dark.

A gift... came the voice. Enthessar blinked, and suddenly, the utter darkness was lifted. He could see the passage now. It was a strange, a colorless light, dim, dark shades of gray. Yet it was enough that he could see. He smiled.

"Thank you, my..." he paused, unsure for a moment. Then he knew. "Master."

It felt right. Whatever was guiding him, directing him, it was that. His master.

He delighted at his ability to see in the darkness. He was certain this would serve him well in his tasks to come.

Back in his bed, he was tempted to seek out another servant girl. He felt like celebrating. Tomorrow he would be made the next Lord of House Allenfar. Unlike his father, he was intent on taking the title of Baron. It as a politically risky thing, but he would deal with that later.

Lancarm would return soon with a brace of followers, all solidly *with* him. Then, they would ride west. They would hunt down Errol, and Candissa, and their two friends. He would see them all dead. If not twisting in the wind, then sliding off the end of his sword point. Yes, he decided another hard rutting with a servant girl was called for.

He crept out of his room and found his way to another favorite. She answered the door wordlessly, accustomed to his late-night demands. Back in his bed chambers, he was not gentle, satisfying himself repeatedly, leaving bruises on her face in the process. She crept out of his room an hour before dawn. He would have little sleep, but that would make his display of grief and sorrow all the more convincing.

He arose shortly after dawn, to dress in suitable morning clothes. Leaving his chambers, he was soon greeted with the wailing of a servant girl. The steward came to him then, his eyes stricken, and Enthessar began his own dramatic performance. His heart-rending sobs could be heard throughout the manse.

Inside, however, he was laughing.

CHAPTER THIRTY-ONE - ERROL

10 Procellus, Year 197, Eastvale Calendar

Errol was confident Koraymis had no idea he had used his "little trick" as the scholar stood at the window, moving from one shadow to another. Errol was by nature a light sleeper. He had dozed lightly as the others settled into deeper sleep. But he never lost track of Koraymis, and his restlessness. When Kor had moved to the window, Errol slipped out of his doze into a comfortable rest.

When the scholar had become suddenly alarmed, it awoke him fully. He sat up slowly, seeing Koraymis was entirely drawn to something, peering at it intently. Errol crouched in the darkness of the chamber, swathed in soft shadow, only the starlight illuminating the room.

He saw the far end of the room, where Kor stood. It was in near-complete shadow. Errol just concentrated a bit. He imagined Koraymis was looking at an enemy, a threat.

With that, he simply *stepped* into the shadow, across the room, about forty feet from where he had been crouching. It was that simple. He hadn't done so before with such intent. The prior times he had done this were situations of extreme stress. In both cases, his life – or the lives of his friends – were under imminent threat.

This was anything but. He did need to imagine there was a threat, however. Perhaps the next time he wouldn't need to do even that.

After seeing the distant campfire, and being unable to do anything about it, he returned to his sleep. He was fortunate in that he managed to get some sleep. He wondered when the night would come when he would enjoy a truly deep and full sleep.

As the dawn broke, he awoke surprisingly refreshed. Over their simple breakfast fare, Koraymis revealed what he had seen. There was little to be done about it. They would simply have to keep an eye out for others on the path ahead.

Given the account of the fire on the plain, Cam chose not to hunt for game this morning. He would prefer to head out and perhaps try elsewhere later.

Heading back down the ramps after breaking camp, they found the day to be clearer than the day before. Riding slowly out of the ruins, they navigated through the rubble to a breach they had spotted from above. In less than an hour, they were following a fading road of steadily subsuming flagstones westward, the towering city of ruins behind them.

The immense crevasse to the north tracked a little south now. They angled their path a bit south to avoid the sloping ground adjacent to it. After a few hours of easy riding, they stopped for a midday meal. As they sat on the ground and chewed their dried meat and bread, washed down with water and a few sips of light mead, the horses grew suddenly skittish.

They sat in an open plain of stunted grass and a few twisted trees. Occasional stones pocked the landscape. The horses seemed to be concerned about something to the south.

Cam stood and peered intently at the ragged horizon. They could not see far from their current position, given the uneven terrain. He cocked his head and listened, turning his keen Elven ears to the task.

"What is it?" Candissa asked.

"Judging by their reaction, a predator, perhaps wolves," Cam said. "I cannot smell them myself. But we should get moving, now."

No one argued. They were on horseback within a minute. Riding more quickly now, as Cam felt pushing the horses was prudent, they tracked dead west as they kept the crevasse on their right and the unknown open plains of the south to their left.

Even so, Errol could sense the growing trepidation of their mounts.

All at once, Cam shouted. "Follow me!" He broke into a full gallop, saying no more and giving his friends no chance to waver, as they each drove their mounts onward as fast as they could run.

Despite this, Errol risked a glance backwards.

A pack of more than a dozen creatures hurtled towards them, running low and fast. They were dark against the dull brown ground. He couldn't make out what they were at their pace. Yet the momentary glance told him it was unlikely the horses could outrun them for long.

It was clear Cam was trying to outrun the hunters, seeing if the horses could manage a pace sufficient to tire the predators. It did not seem to be working.

Errol looked ahead, seeing that Cam was driving them toward rocky rise perched near the edge of the crevasse. It was conceivable that they could make a stand on the rise.

We ride around that rock, hopefully we can bring the horses up onto it. From there, we should be able to mount a suitable defense, Cam's voice was clear and forceful in their minds, despite the noise and tumult of their frantic pace.

Errol cursed silently that they hadn't had more time to train together. They had only covered basics so far, and he really had no idea how his fellows would react with close-quarters melee.

They reached the rocky rise quickly, riding around the far side. They dismounted, as there was no easy way to ride up onto the top of the rocky rise.

"Bring them up, I'll start loosing arrows!" Cam shouted, grabbing his bow and quiver and leaping atop the rocks in a few easy bounds. Errol joined him as Candissa and Koraymis led the horses onto the tumble of black stone.

The creatures were racing toward the rocks, snarling viciously. Cam was already pulling back an arrow. Releasing, he found one of the creatures, sending it into a howling tumble. Nocking another arrow, he buried an arrow into the eye of a second beast.

What are these creatures? Cam's voice betrayed his shock at the appearance of the animals. Errol could see them easily now. They were something like wolves, but far stranger.

Closer inspection would reveal the rear legs had the hooves of a deer, though more claw-like while the front legs bore clawed feet resembling a wolf's. They were taller than any wolf, their legs longer. Their coat was a mottled light brown, uniquely adapted to the rough grass and dun vegetation of these plains. They bore long snouts filled with sharp teeth, but the most off-putting feature were the horns.

Not quite antlers, they appeared to be a set of horns that branched out two or three times. They were low and back-swept unlike the antlers of a buck.

The bony ornamentation did not concern Errol; the savage bite the teeth could inflict was his chief concern.

Nearly upon them, the creatures broke up, half of them rushing to leap upon the rocks and attack Errol and Cam, while others ran to the west, apparently to attack the mounts.

Errol drew his blade, readying to hurl it. He drew an extra dagger in his other hand. As Cam nocked a third arrow, he glanced toward Errol.

Doesn't seem sufficient, was Cam's only comment.

Don't concern yourself with me, Errol pathed in reply, grinning.

The lead beast was close enough, as he rushed up the tumble of dark stone. Errol hurled his dagger with force. It found its mark between the shoulder and neck of the wolfish creature. Cam released his arrow, downing another of the strange predators. He dropped his bow in favor of his broadsword, as they were nearly upon them both.

Get behind me, Cam pathed, his voice somehow loud in their minds. Errol understood why Cam said that, thinking him unarmed. But in a blink, his blade was back in his right hand.

With a forceful flick of his wrist, he sent it into the open mouth of an on-rushing beast. It collapsed messily on the rocks below his feet, blood gushing from its open maw.

He moved backwards with Cam to where Candissa and Kor had brought the mounts. They would have to make their stand in front of them. The horses were too valuable to risk losing. Candissa was swinging her staff in a broad arc, cutting off the advance of the creatures that had rounded the rocks. Errol knew that would not last long.

"Behind us, Kor!" Cam shouted. Errol disagreed but didn't voice his concern. He suspected Koraymis could hold his own, perhaps even against these strange beasts.

Errol was not pleased. Despite hurling his dagger once more and wounding another creature, and Cam warding off another with a swing of his broadsword, it did not bode well in his mind. A part of him whispered in the recesses of his mind. He could escape, if things went badly. He knew this. He resisted, silencing the whispers.

Candissa's staff struck the head of a beast, sending it yelping and tumbling. She was whirling it faster than Errol knew she could. Kor was closest to the horses, who were near panic, by the sounds of their whinnying. The rocky rise was too close to the gorge. If the mounts were driven to terror, they could plunge off the edge.

His blade back in his grip, he slashed outward at the over-large head of one of the creatures. He didn't feel panic. He did feel a gnawing concern things would not turn out well.

The remaining beasts lunged almost as one. A beast nearly felled him, as he drove a dagger into its throat and his blade into its chest. It slumped as life fled its body. Cam managed to drive his broadsword into one of them, frantically trying to avoid the leap of the next.

Behind him, he heard a cry from Candissa as one of the creatures bit her arm. He couldn't see it happen, but knew it was so. A horse shrieked in terror. One of the beasts managed to clamp their jaws around one of Cam's legs, below the knee.

Two things happened at that point, but Errol could not tell which happened first. Candissa did something as a brilliant white light burst outward from behind him. Bright as a second sun, it washed over him and struck the beasts. The lot of them rolled backwards, as if pummeled by a wave of force, tumbling, snarling.

Save for three of them Errol could see. Those suffered a far worse fate.

Gouts of flame lashed forth, bright orange with a searing intensity that threatened to singe Errol's hair. The gouts engulfed the creatures in a torrent of blazing fire. They howled in mortal agony, flailing about on the rocks as they suffered an excruciating death.

Errol slung his blade at one of the tumbling creatures, smiling as he saw the hilt buried in the beast's ribs. Turning, he saw Koraymis. Errol had seen him like this before: his skin red and scaly, horns sprouting from his forehead and temples, his hands black-tipped claws.

Twin gouts of painfully bright flame rushed out from his hands, setting two more of the creatures ablaze as they tumbled downward. Another was alight, but not mortally so. Errol watched as that one howled in mindless panic and went hurtling off the edge of the crevasse. He only heard it's fading howls, not the impact below.

There were two creatures that survived the onslaught of light and flame. They were already well away, racing as fast as they could for the safety of the plains to the south.

Cam was sitting, attending to his calf with a strip of bandage. His leg was bleeding badly. Candissa's left arm was bloodied and she leaned her staff in the crook of her right. Cam's horse, Rufus, was wounded, but alive.

Despite being untouched, Errol realized Koraymis was not unaffected. His appearance had returned to normal. Errol thought to himself he really didn't know what *normal* was for the sorcerer.

The dark-haired sorcerer lowered his hands, the cuffs of his cloak smoldering from the intensity of the flames that had so recently burst forth. His eyes appeared almost blank. He fell to his hands and knees, then collapsed.

"Kor!" Candissa cried, stepping quickly to his side, crouching. Cam looked at Errol.

"Are you wounded?"

Errol shook his head. He saw Cam quickly apply another length of bandage around his leg, tying it tightly to stanch the flow of blood.

Looking east and west, Errol's keen vision revealed their rest would be short.

"We need to ride. There are more of them on the rise!" he shouted, pointing. They could make out dozens of forms suddenly appearing along a long rise more than a quarter mile away.

"Kor is not fit to ride!" Candissa declared. "We'll have to make our stand here!"

Errol wracked his brain for a solution, an option, a trick he could pull out of his hat. Nothing was forthcoming.

"This could go badly for us," Cam said, tying the last knot on his leg bandage.

"I'm...I'm fine," Koraymis managed to say, his eyes still shut. He was nearly unconscious from the effort he had put forth. Candissa had both hands on his head, studying him.

"You would think the bodies of their pack would keep them at bay," Errol said, trying to evince hope. There were at least ten fallen creatures scattered about the rocky stand, four of them smoldering.

"If they have strength in numbers, they - wait, what's that?" Cam said, suddenly drawn to the west.

"They're coming!" Candissa shouted, pointing at the ravening beasts as they suddenly broke as one, rushing down a slope. There were more than two dozen.

Cam and Errol were looking west now. Errol felt it. A quaking, like thunder hidden beyond the horizon.

To the west, the sere grasslands were hidden by gentle rolls. Errol thought there was a mist lying along the ground, then he realized what it was. Dust.

Candissa turned now, as she helped Koraymis to his feet, at his insistence. She peered west with them, to see what it was.

Massive shapes moved in the wind-driven dust. They rushed eastward. Their passing along the dry ground was creating the billowing dust, which preceded them. Advancing quickly, their strides appeared slow, as they were enormous, towering. Errol could see them now, each of them supported by four legs as thick as tree trunks.

Vast grayish-brown creatures, with immense ears, two long white protrusions sprouted from their mouths, while their nose was stranger still. Errol could not name them, though somehow, they seemed familiar.

They rushed quickly toward the rocky rise.

"Sard," Errol stated in a tired voice.

"We are undone," Cam said with a note of finality in his voice.

"No..." Candissa whispered. "We are saved."

Errol did not understand. The enormous creatures appeared to be charging at a breakneck pace directly for them. There were more than he at first realized. The lead one let loose a bellow louder than anything he had ever heard from an animal. A long, grayish appendage rose as it bellowed, revealing the long, fearsome-looking white horns jutting forward out of its mouth. Something was rising in his memory now.

Looking east, he saw the charging wolf beasts suddenly slow. They were barking and snarling viciously. The towering creatures appeared to be turning toward them.

"I don't understand!" Cam shouted.

"They are with us!" Candissa cried, almost exultant.

The massive creatures thundered close now, turning to confront the charging horned beasts from the grasslands. The ground quaked, feeling almost unstable as the creatures thundered past them. He could not tell how many of the massive animals rushed by, as the dust was obscuring their numbers.

The lead animal was taller than the rest of the herd by a Dwarve's height. He charged forward, swinging his head threateningly side-to-side. The wolf beasts snarled and halted their charge. Before the massive creature could reach them, they turned and fled.

Their vision was obscured as the vast cloud of dust rolled over the rocky rise, brought along with the pack of towering creatures. As it cleared, they saw the lead animal slowly approach them.

Koraymis slowly stood, aided by Candissa. They all stared in mute astonishment as the grand, almost regal, creature walked slowly up to them. It stood at least twenty feet tall, from its stump-like feet to the top of its massive head. Its long, leathery nose swayed as it approached.

"Should we be afraid?" Cam asked.

"Of course not," Candissa replied, smiling.

"What...are they?" Koraymis asked. The dust was almost entirely gone now, and they all saw the extent of the thunderous herd. There stood before them at least thirty of the remarkable animals.

Something tugged at Errol's memory. He sighed, closing his eyes. He did not try to pull the memory forth. He only thought of the grass, and the open sky. Candissa must have sensed something in him.

"Errol, what is it?" she asked.

He opened his eyes and smiled at her.

"Elephant."

"What?" she asked. Errol pointed at the towering creatures.

"They are called elephants. I remember," Errol said, a hint of satisfaction in his voice.

"I haven't read of these," she said.

"Nor have I," Cam echoed.

"They are mighty creatures of the plains, intelligent and wise," Errol went on. "The long thing there is called a trunk, and those two teeth sticking out are called tusks. They are a source of ivory, a fine white material prized for carving and decoration."

The immense male, now only ten feet from the group, turned its titanic head sharply at Errol as he spoke. His eyes, huge and discerning, took on a slightly menacing appearance.

Errol held up his hands in mock defensiveness, smiling. "But decent folk do not harvest ivory from the noble 'phants unless they offer it. There are other sources of the stuff."

That seemed to satisfy the elephant.

"Wait, he can understand you?" Cam said, wincing as he struggled to stand.

"Yes, they are as wise as any of us. They cannot speak our language, but they can understand the meaning behind what people say. At least, that seems to be what I recall."

"And they are with us you say, Deesa?" Koraymis asked, his voice a bit reedy after his exertion.

"Yes," she said, stepping closer. She raised a hand, a gentle smile on her face. The elephant bowed his head slowly and let her place her hand on his rough skin. "He's majestic."

She closed her eyes. *I can sense his thoughts!* she told her companions.

Without warning, a deep, resonant voice sounded in Errol's mind. It was the lead elephant.

Aevaru! That was the only word they heard, as the elephant pulled back in shock.

"It's all right!" Candissa said, clearly disappointed at breaking the contact.

At once, the entire group of towering creatures slowly backed away. To Errol's astonishment, almost as one, they each bent their forelegs, tucking one under, and bowing their heads in what was unmistakably a reverent respect.

"Clearly, yes, they are with us," Errol said quietly.

With that, the leader elephant stood, and the herd followed suit. He slowly moved away, turning to look at the group as he did so. The elephants didn't move in one direction, however. They appeared to fan out in various directions.

"What are they doing?" Koraymis asked.

"He's sending them out to patrol the area," Candissa said. "We should move as soon as we can. I think they will watch the lands for more of those..."

"Hornwolves!" Errol made Cam start with his outburst. "Sorry about that, I just remembered their name."

"That's good. You may be regaining your lost memories," Cam said, wincing as he eased himself down to attend to his bandage.

"Cam, I'm terribly sorry," Candissa said, suddenly realizing she had not yet seen to his wounds.

Errol watched in fascination as the elephants moved off in groups of four or five, spreading out in a pattern. The lead male was more to the west, with a few of some slightly larger males. He imagined they were his lieutenants.

Candissa used her healing skills, and the abilities she learned at the temple in Ravensroost, to mend Cam's leg and her arm as well. She also attended to the wounded mount.

"Cam, you probably didn't notice," Candissa said, her hands over the upper foreleg of Cam's chestnut horse. "Rufus here actually put himself in harm's way to defend the other horses. The wo- hornwolves tried getting around him and he cut them off. He was very brave."

"Is that brave or just lacking wit?" Errol said, grinning.

Candissa threw a mock-angry gaze at him. She was done tending the horse quickly.

Finally, she saw to Koraymis again. She aided him directly, but it had little effect on his state of exhaustion. She then took the time to teach him something about her meditative techniques, and how he could utilize the same techniques. The sorcerer had spent a tremendous amount of energy in his fiery attacks. He was drained physically and mentally, apparently. With Candissa's aid, he was ready to ride within a half hour.

They rode as quickly as Koraymis could manage. Candissa stayed by his side as they rode, with Cam in the lead and Errol trailing. There was little conversation. The sky was clear and bright, with a wind that seemed a little warmer as the sun began setting.

After a few hours, they spotted a stony rise, flat and almost featureless. Closer inspection revealed it to be the foundation of a tower, ruined like all they had seen previously. They decided to make camp here, as it offered an excellent view of the surrounding plains. It was a hundred yards south of the gorge.

As they chose a camp site tucked against a small broken wall atop the stone circle, the wind began tapering off. They could hear distant howls. They set about preparing their evening repast.

"Are those hornwolves?" Koraymis asked, feeling a little more himself after drinking a sip of wine.

"I think so," Errol said, scanning the horizon. The rolling, uneven landscape made for a poor range of vision, despite the slight rise. "I hope the elephants are giving chase."

"They will safeguard our passage as long as we are in their territory," Candissa said. She placed dried leaves and straw on a pile of twigs and branches. Koraymis was sitting nearby and raised a hand to assist in lighting the fire. She batted it away, having already retrieved a striking stone.

"You seem sure of that," Errol observed.

"I am. I had more contact with the Baron than I could share."

"*Baron?*" Cam blurted, as Errol laughed.

"The leader elephant. It's the closest word he could relate, I suppose," Candissa said, trying to force back a grin.

"No," Errol said. "That's his title. It sounds right. They have a hierarchy not unlike Humans."

"So, the elephants are with us, but the hornwolves are against," Koraymis said, as he stood carefully. He braced himself against the low, broken wall. "Can we expect more of this? Animals hunting us, defending us?"

"I suspect so," Candissa answered. "At least we need to assume that, until we understand more about what is happening."

"And how exactly are we going to do that?" Errol posed.

"Look for signs, seek lore, hopefully we can find others out here that can help us figure out what our next step is."

"And until then, we must rely on the munificence of animals?" Errol was feeling uncomfortable with their lack of guidance. He was beginning to realize how important a plan was.

"Yes, we must rely on whatever we may," Candissa said. "I have no doubt we shall have a sign. It will guide us."

He did not appreciate her reliance on something so intangible, almost fanciful. He knew he was letting his feelings slip past his typically jocular behavior.

"And you have no idea what this sign would be, what it would look like?"

Candissa took a deep breath, drawing herself up. Errol had no intention to argue with her, he just wanted to make sure she was absolutely sure about this, particularly since her friends would follow her. Whatever she was prepared to say in response to Errol's gentle challenge was cut off.

"Perhaps it looks like that?" Koraymis said, pointing north.

The others turned, looking across the huge chasm, to the lands beyond. The fading light of twilight hid whatever was on the other side of the gorge, and they could not make out much of the gently sloping land, nor the mountains in the distant north, though their highest peaks were still glowing with tips of orange.

The fleeting light of the setting sun was not the focus of the sorcerer's question.

A perfectly straight line of white light stretched from somewhere to the northeast, drawn against the twilight sky and dark mountains, westward, until it vanished in the mists of the retiring day.

Koraymis did not appear surprised at the sight. Cam opened his mouth but did not speak. Candissa looked at it, her eyes alight. Then she turned and smiled just a little at Errol, raising one eyebrow.

His expression of wonder at the sight of a brilliant, razor-thin trace of light turned to a frown. He grunted.

"The match is yours," he said, grinning and bowing in a slightly absurd fashion to Candissa. She held her chin up and turned back to study the sight. The sign.

"How far away is that?" Kor asked.

"There's no good way to gauge," Cam said, as he studied it. "We have to find a way around or across this gorge. If we can do that, I can lead us to the eastern end of whatever that is."

"Tomorrow," Errol said. "Kor needs his rest."

"We all do," Candissa nodded. "After we eat."

"No training tonight?" Koraymis said with an exaggerated weakness.

Candissa only glowered at him.

After they had seen to the horses, made their camp and eaten, sleep came quickly to the others. Errol stayed up, studying the stars at first, then peering into the darkness of the plains to the south and west. There was no wind blowing. It was unnaturally quiet.

As he studied the plains, an elephant appeared from the low mist hugging the hills. He slowly approached their camp, turning an eye toward them. Errol raised one hand to him, seeing it was a bull. The creature stopped, staring at Errol for a long moment. He raised his trunk in reply, then turned and moved along, no doubt following a patrol route of some sort.

Errol returned to the camp, sitting. He leaned against the ancient stone of the ruin, staring at the unmoving, unchanging line of light, traced along the horizon. He wondered what awaited them there, at the eastern terminus.

It seemed even more brilliant. He sighed deeply. He would never admit to his friends the degree of trepidation he felt. While they were all going into an unknown future together, the others at least had a past they could rely on, call on. He did not.

As he at last slipped into sleep, he dreamt. Dreams were rare for Errol, and fleeting. This one was different. When he awoke the next morning, he would realize it was not a long dream. But it was vivid. Faint images of the white tower, the top of it cracked and uneven.

Within, he saw someone. A young woman, dressed in more leather than even Cam typically wore. Her leather coat was tight-fitting, attached to leather leggings of some strange sort, all decorated with metal loops and buckles. She had red hair, and a curious, almost expectant expression on her face, and sharp, amber eyes. A distant voice whispered to him, across a vast gulf, barely perceptible.

You will kill her.

CHAPTER THIRTY-TWO - CANDISSA

11 Procellus, Year 197, Eastvale Calendar

The morning brought a renewed sense of urgency. They, at last, had a goal, even if it was just to reach the near end of whatever the mysterious light was.

Candissa felt good about it. She wondered if it was, in fact, a sign they needed to follow. Her searching seemed to support the decision. She meditated every morning, and after this morning, she felt no hesitation or reluctance.

Reading her grandmother's journal every morning, as time permitted, was also reaffirming in this. Candissa was determined to read Galissa's journal front to back, so she was still working on the first passages. The form of Elven was strange, but she learned better with each reading how to interpret certain phrases. She even found that some words that were at first mystifying to her, became clear to her understanding later. She often asked Cam about a word or turn of phrase that was unfamiliar to her. He often had insights that helped her.

The first part of the journal was written when Galissa was just twenty-two. It began with her reflections on the nature of the world, of life, magic, and even philosophy. There were references to training with weapons, drawing maps, and her yearning to explore the world beyond the confines of her home and community. Candissa found the young Lady Galissa was truly a kindred soul. Among her grandmother's reflections was a surety in visions and signs, a trust she placed in them. That aided Candissa in her decisions. She packed away the journal for the morning.

She suddenly remembered a dream she had, just before waking. A young woman, with red hair, and curious amber-colored eyes. She had the distinct feeling she was in the broken tower of white.

Clearly, her thoughts intruded into the awareness of her friends.

The dream? Koraymis said as he was finishing his meal. *The red-haired woman?*

"You saw her too?" Cam said aloud.

Apparently we all did, Errol added.

"She must be the fifth!" Candissa said, excited at the prospect of having seen him.

Seems logical, if the term logic can be applied to any of this, Koraymis said with a half grin. *I wonder if the shared dream is part of the link we have, or if it's something else.*

It's the first time we experienced the same dream, so I suppose it's more about this damnable destiny we seem tied to, came Cam's response. *Remember when we met at the table in the Bonerest.*

Candissa nodded. She clearly recalled the feeling that something - someone - was missing.

Breaking camp shortly after dawn, they were on their way before the sun rose over the mist to the east. Her mood was further improved when they spotted the elephants making their way slowly westward.

"How far do you think this gorge will last? We haven't a hope of crossing it," Koraymis pointed out. Their path had taken them closer to the edge of the yawning gulf. It appeared almost bottomless.

"It's narrowing, I would be surprised if it stretched more than another five miles," Cam said.

Riding next to Candissa, Errol appeared to be inspecting her, almost uncharacteristically. She frowned.

"What is it, Errol?"

"Your arm, you were wounded."

"Yes, I tended to it," she said. She did not like to talk too much about her healing powers. They knew she had the ability to heal, but she never spoke of how far she might be able to stretch her abilities. She was quite honestly unsure of the extent.

"But, your sleeve. That strange outfit you wear," he said, pointing to her arm where the wound had been. "It's untouched. There's no blood. More importantly, it's not torn."

She wasn't sure how to answer his question. "I...it was mended," was all she offered. He frowned.

"That seems a silly answer," he said.

"Must you pry, Errol?" Koraymis interrupted. His tone was entirely out of character. He was typically almost timid, and rarely spoke up. "We, each of us, have our secrets."

"Do we?" Errol said. Candissa felt her patience tested, but only a little.

He was likely just having a little fun at their expense.

"Especially you," the sorcerer said.

Errol laughed. "Do tell."

"You have your blade, I have my flames, and Candissa has her own unique abilities."

"That includes her clothing mending on their own?"

"Yes," Kor said, and nothing more.

Errol raised his eyebrows. Candissa sighed loudly. "It matters little. Yes, apparently my outfit, it's called a *leralet*, is enchanted in some ways. That includes mending tears and never needing cleaning."

"Hmm, fair enough. But what of our peerless hunter?"

Koraymis looked at Cam, who did not turn as they rode onward steadily. "His secrets are his own. If he wishes to divulge them, he will."

"Ever the voice of reason," Errol nodded to the black-cloaked scholar. He turned back to the hunter. "But we know it has something to do with that pack. What do you call it again? I think you told me once, didn't you?"

"Perhaps. I call...no, it is called the Everneed, if you must know," Cam said. "Do you have more prying questions for me?"

Errol held up his hands defensively, grinning.

"Don't let him bother you, Cam," Candissa called ahead, though she knew the roguish needling would not affect the hunter.

"He doesn't bother me," Cam said, turning his head to speak back to them.

"Does anything bother you?" Errol returned.

"Bridge."

Errol frowned. "Bridges bother you?"

"No," Cam said, bringing his mount to an abrupt halt, pointing ahead. "Bridge!"

They all stopped and peered ahead. The morning sun had risen above the mists far behind them, and the landscape ahead was bathed in morning light. Stretching across the immense chasm, perhaps five miles away, was the largest bridge Candissa could imagine. For a fleeting moment, it reminded her of something she had seen in a vision with Zarlenna.

It seemed to take them all a moment to grasp the size of it. The stone from which it was worked was a light gray, and from this vantage point seemed to grow from the chasm walls. There was nothing graceful or delicate about this structure.

"I once crossed a bridge over the Silverush River in my youth," Cam said. "That was more than a hundred yards long. Gondrim said it was the largest bridge in the Kingdom."

"This is a fair sight more than a hundred paces," Errol grinned.

"Who could have built such a thing?" Koraymis mused.

"Dwarves," Cam said.

Errol nodded. "No doubt. Dwarven craftsmanship."

Koraymis narrowed his eyes at them. "You two seem to know a lot of things that I do not."

Candissa laughed lightly. She could tell the sorcerer was saying that with a note of sarcasm, yet there was truth to it. She knew Koraymis prided himself on his intellect. Aside from their own individual areas of knowledge, she was certain his mind was the sharpest among them.

"We have our way across," she said. "Lead on, Cam."

They stepped up their pace, having a tangible destination in sight. They stopped at one of the streams leading down into the gorge, to water the horses, after less than an hour of riding.

"That bridge is larger than I had estimated," Cam said, peering at it carefully. They had moved at least two miles closer to it, yet it had grown in size but little.

"Another five miles at least, indeed," Errol said.

Candissa was surprised as well. She couldn't imagine what it would take to construct such a thing.

As they crossed several gulleys, their path took them ever closer to the edge of the chasm. It was clearly deepening and widening as they neared the bridge. At one point, the rocky edge appeared stable enough to approach. Errol did so without any prompting. As he walked his horse toward the edge, Candissa grew alarmed.

"Errol! Step carefully, we cannot know if the cliff edge is unstable!"

"You worry when you shouldn't," he smirked.

Within a few yards of the edge, he dismounted. They heard him whistle.

"Could be a half mile down now," he said. Looking up, he surveyed the bridge once more. "The base of that bridge is formed into the rock wall almost flawlessly."

Candissa could see what he was referring to. The Dwarven builders of old had skills she could not imagine.

"Let's keep moving. We don't know how long we'll have the protection of the lords of the savannah," Candissa said. She was not surprised when they all looked at her.

"Lords of the savannah?" Koraymis said, raising a dubious eyebrow. "What exactly is a savannah?"

"I'm not sure, I think it's a great expanse of grassland. But it is the name they have for their people," she said, trying to sound like a gentle teacher. "I respect that, and I suggest you do the same. Their wisdom may be far greater than that of Humans."

Cam chuckled, muttering to himself, "Elephants are people. Amazing."

Candissa led the way, not waiting for Errol to rejoin them. The others hurried to catch up with her. As they continued along the edge of the chasm, the bridge finally began growing larger, closer. The bases of the bridge were massive arcs of stone, rising from both sides. It was incredible to behold. The length of the span was likewise a remarkable feat of engineering, being probably more than two hundred feet thick.

They had to round a sharp rise of rock and a small copse of old fir trees, before finding their way to the entrance of the span. Candissa was not surprised to find a fairly intact roadway leading south, away from the bridge.

"It makes sense a major highway would cross here. Why else invest so much time and effort in building it?"

"How far does it stretch?" Koraymis asked.

Cam stood in his saddle. "More than half a mile, less than three quarters. Hopefully that debris won't hinder our crossing."

Errol rejoined them, coming up next to Cam. "That is a massive pile, whatever it is," he said, looking ahead at whatever lay ahead on the bridge.

Candissa peered straight down the length of the bridge once they had moved onto the ancient, weed-choked highway. Indeed, there was something huge and uneven blocking the way close to the midpoint.

Errol led the way now, easing his mount forward. The surface of the bridge was finely worked tiles, still intact after unknown centuries. No weeds or roots grew between the seams, though there was growth in the piles of dirt that had accumulated along the edges.

They kept to the center of the bridge, as the walls on either side had breaches along the entire span. Candissa marveled at the design. It was more than a hundred yards across. The wind picked up as they entered the sprawling, immensely wide chasm. She looked east and west. It looked as if a mythic god had carved out a ragged gash in the earth. It curved out of sight to the east and trailed off to the west, where it seemed to lessen in depth and width. She could not clearly see the bottom of it, as it was hidden in shadow.

They were soon at the debris that dominated the middle of the span. To their collective relief, there was space on either side to allow passage by horseback. When they were close to the obstruction, they stopped in their path, speechless.

Before them lay a heap nearly a hundred yards across and as tall as a three-story building. It consisted - for the most part - of twisted metal beams and smashed or splintered lengths of wood. It lay in a field of debris comprised of dirt, vines, growth, and fragments of every manner of material. Glass, stone, metal, and wood could all be seen as they approached.

The larger ruin of metal girders and torn wood was fascinating. Most of the metal was not rusted, indicating it was not iron. From her readings, Candissa knew there were few metals that resisted the onslaught of weather. While the destruction was almost complete, it still seemed to hint at the former structure. Curves and lines could be discerned here and there.

"What was this?" Cam asked. Candissa noted that he asked Errol, more or less directly.

Errol narrowed his eyes. He paused longer than she would have expected.

"I cannot...recall," he said, exasperated. "It distresses me greatly, for it seems to be at the edge of my memory."

"No matter. We can pass by on the right," Cam said, pressing his mount forward.

They passed silently by the chaos of riven ruin. Candissa could pick out fragments of metal both dull and bright, seemingly untarnished by the ages, and large fragments of crystal and glazing. There were also vaguely familiar shapes, perhaps the frames of seats or tables; she could not be certain. She blinked as she studied the jumble. The sky was clear and bright, the wind biting and swift.

If we had the time, I would very much like to explore this debris, came Koraymis' voice. Candissa noted he was usually the first to use their unique form of conversation.

But we must press on. We have no idea if we will even be able to see that light when evening comes, Cam pathed. They had lost sight of the piercing line of light with dawn, to no one's surprise. Cam had a good fix on it, and no one doubted his sense of direction.

At least let me pause a while to take measurements and notes, for my mapping, Koraymis pathed.

With no objections, the sorcerer climbed down from William and found a clear spot on the low wall that bounded the bridge at this point. The others stayed on their mounts as the scholar quickly made use of the mapping tools, scribbling notes and figures in a small book.

After several minutes, he closed the notebook. "Just about done. Now I'd just like to make a sketch or two," he said, drawing forth another, larger notebook.

"Kor, really, can't we just move along?" Errol said, rolling his eyes a little.

Candissa cast a chiding glance in his direction. She noticed in the sunlight his beard was quite long now, more gold than brown.

"Kor?" Cam's voice caught her attention. He was staring at Koraymis. She looked and saw his gaze was transfixed on the massive heap of debris. His hands were in an all-too-familiar pose: his left thumb and forefinger turning the heavy ring on his middle right finger.

What is it? she pathed, urgency clear in her unspoken voice.

"We should move along now," was all Koraymis said, as he quickly packed his things and mounted William.

The others glanced about, looking or warning signs or threats. Like

Candissa, they saw none and sensed the same. Moving their horses at a brisk pace, she studied the sorcerer.

Can you share anything with us? she pathed.

Only that there is something there...something that slumbers. For now, Koraymis answered.

Something dangerous? Errol asked.

I don't know. I only know that we needed to move along, the sorcerer pathed. He said nothing more on that matter.

It wasn't long before they reached the other end of the massive bridge. Errol slowed unexpectedly. The others followed suit. Candissa could tell he was lost in thought. He turned, looking back at the ruined mass of metal and wood.

"Tamnati..." he breathed.

"What?"

He looked at her. "That wreck. It was a Tamnati ship. I just remembered."

With no further explanation, he turned Teago and moved onto the remnants of the highway north of the great bridge.

Across the chasm, the land rose slightly but inexorably to the east. Cam set them on a path leading north by northeast. He told them it may be two days ride before they reached the source of the light. They could only hope it was still visible at sundown.

They were more than a few miles north of the bridge before Candissa realized something. She stopped, concerned.

"What is it?" Koraymis asked her.

"The elephants, they cannot protect us here...their range is south of the chasm," she said, feeling a distinct sadness. She wasn't sure, but it almost felt as if they were reaching out to her to say their farewells.

"Perhaps we will pass into their range again," Cam suggested, lifting her spirits a little.

There was nothing to do about it. They moved on, through climbing plains of short grass and stunted, woody bushes. It had clearly rained here recently, as there was still water gathered in small depressions and the plant life was wet.

Along their path, they spied many small rises of stone. They chose to camp at in a small, round tower of stone, broken but remarkably smooth in its composition. It bore three perfectly circular windows facing three sides, with an entrance on the west. Inside, they found a curious runic inscription on the walls, just over the windows and door. None of them could decipher it.

They made their camp, ate a simple meal, and enjoyed a warm fire, as they had excellent cover. Candissa was pleased to see Koraymis was strong enough to produce a robust flame capable of igniting the damp kindling.

As the sun lowered in the west, the sky still clear, they were all relieved to see the line of light reappear to the north. After their supper, she inspected both Cam and Koraymis, to ensure their wounds were fully healed. Before the sun set, Cam circumnavigated the entire area. He found there were almost no tracks or signs of animals, benign or hostile.

Training commenced the following morning, and while she was intrigued with the techniques behind swordplay, she was more engaged in training with the bow. They broke camp and headed toward the source of the light, which faded from their sight with dawn's light.

Cam found few signs of animal tracks or droppings in the vast plains they traversed that day. He told them it was no surprise, given the short grass. It was sparse and dry, clearly a poor source of food. He noted that meant few herd animals, meaning fewer predators. She was glad for that.

Three days passed uneventfully. They found low spots in the otherwise featureless plains, in which to make their camps. Candissa was heartened by the sight of the unnaturally straight line of light in the distance. It grew brighter with each evening.

Morning brought clouds and a steady wind. The land became dotted with ruins, stony extrusions rising from the ground. They realized there was once a city here, sprawling but with almost nothing left to show for its grandeur.

At one point, they passed through what Candissa imagined was the center of the long-dead city. There were tall, broken obelisks of some dark, unnatural stone, and the broken shell of a dome. Cam led them onward, true to his mark.

That evening, they happened upon a small rise with a patch of twisted trees atop it. Cam deemed it a fine spot to camp, so they did. From their vantage point, the beam of white light was clear along the northern horizon.

She awoke once during the night. Curious calls sounded from the west, distant and mournful. She wondered what sort of creatures could make such a sound. She was certain it was not the elephants.

Morning was colder, though there was no threat of winter. The terrain was increasingly uneven, dotted with ruins, and gradually rising. The ruins diminished but did not disappear. Koraymis suggested this was a much larger complex of cities and towns.

Their route was not as easy today. Cam had to lead them into a lower region of the sprawling plains, as the direct route was blocked by a ridge they had no chance of climbing. At one point, he even doubled-back to see if he could find a better way. But it was for naught. By the end of day, the half-Elven hunter was in a foul mood.

The terrain had redirected them, tacking at least a day onto their travel to whatever their destination was. As well, they were now in a low valley, dotted with rocky ruins and strange shards of stone, some thirty or forty feet in height. With the quickly setting sun, they had to settle for camping against a curious cubic rise of dark stone.

The wind was stronger tonight. It chilled them to the bone. By pitching their tents to the leeward against the stone rise, they avoided the worst of it.

"Keep an eye and ear out, tonight," Cam warned them all as they ate their simple fare. "There are tracks here, not recent by any measure. Not sure what they may be."

"Will we have more training in the morning?" Koraymis asked.

"It would still be a prudent thing," Errol replied. "We have no idea what we're going to face when we reach the source of that light."

Cam suddenly stood, gathering some items from his horse's pack. "I saw some saplings not far from here, across the valley. I want to see if I can set a snare or two. Perhaps we can have some fresh game for breakfast."

"I don't like the idea of you going off on your own," Candissa said.

"Worry not, Mother Deesa, I'll be due west, not more than two hundred yards," Cam said. "And I don't need anyone tagging along, stinking up the area."

With that, he left the camp. Candissa was dissatisfied with the situation. Errol grinned.

"He can take care of himself. There's still light enough."

"I think I'll do some reading," Koraymis said, getting out his small lantern and setting up a reading area along a long piece of fallen stone.

"I will survey the area from atop this stone," Errol said, assessing the cube of dark stone. It was almost twenty feet high and just as wide. The surface was remarkably smooth.

"How do you propose scaling it?" Candissa asked.

Errol simply frowned at her disapprovingly. He retrieved a long coil of rope from his pack and proceeded to tie one end to an immovable jutting of stone that rose from the ground just to one side of the monolith. Candissa realized what he was doing and felt a little foolish for not seeing it sooner.

"Oh. Of course."

He flung the coil up and over the stone, winking at her in the process. She watched him disappear around the other side. The rope went taught and Errol appeared atop the stone.

"Anything interesting up there?"

He crouched, one hand on the surface of the cubic stone. "Yes. There's a strange indentation in the center of this, square. But..."

"What?" Candissa called up, after several seconds. He seemed lost in thought.

"This stone is the same as the central tower of the Bonerest tavern, and some parts of Ravensroost walls."

"I thought it was," Koraymis said idly, eyes still fixed on his book. "It must be a common building material for the old structures."

Errol leaned over the edge of the monolith, above the sorcerer. "Do share your insights with us next time, perhaps."

Koraymis only grinned. "I would have eventually."

"Do you see anything else around the valley?" Candissa asked.

Errol turned in a careful circle, scanning the surroundings. He shook his head.

"Small ruins, no animals, just a hunter *so-called* building a trap," he reported. He dropped back down deftly. "I may as well share the scholar's lamplight and read something myself."

"Help yourself to the books in my saddlebag," Candissa said, nodding.

She had settled down to meditate and read from a study book she had received from the Temple of Arushana. After a minute, Errol was at her side, a small book on history in hand. It was getting darker by the minute, and she considered finding a seat closer to the sorcerer.

Errol tapped her on the shoulder. She looked up. He just nodded toward Koraymis. The scholar was seated cross-legged, his back against the dark mass of the monolith. His lamp sat in front of him, illuminating his book.

In the deepening dark of twilight, they could both see glowing runes in the surface of the stone, just above Koraymis. There were several of them glowing a faint amber, just a few hands above the sorcerer, stretching across perhaps four feet of the dark stone surface. They appeared to fade at both ends.

Candissa was about to say something, but Errol stopped her.

"Kor, could you move that lantern a bit in this direction?" Errol asked him idly, picking a stone to sit on near the long, fallen stone that served as a table.

"Surely," Kor replied. He sat up, leaning forward as he repositioned the lamp. Candissa and Errol both saw the glowing runes fade. When he sat back against the stone surface, they began to glow again.

Without looking up, he spoke. "Would either of you care to tell me why you're staring at me so?"

"Don't move, and look up and over your shoulder," Errol said.

Koraymis did so and was clearly surprised at the sight of the glowing sigils. Shifting his body as he turned, he watched the runes fade as he lost contact with the stone.

Without prompting from Errol or herself, he turned around fully, sitting back from it, and reached out. Touching the surface, they saw the runes commence glowing again.

Do you sense anything? Candissa's asked him.

Faint magic, very faint, Koraymis replied. He stood now and ran his hand along the surface. Wherever he touched it, the line of glowing runes, several inches tall could be seen. Candissa and Errol both approached him and watched as he walked along the entire face of one side of the cube.

She could not decipher the runes. They were captivating.

"Should we copy these? Could they be significant?" She wondered aloud more than asked.

Errol touched one of the faces. Runes sprang to life under his touch.

"What?" was all he managed to say.

"What are you all do-" Cam said, then stopped, seeing the glowing runes. "And those are?"

"Candissa, touch," Errol nodded to the other end of the face he had his palm against. She understood. Sure enough, her touch produced the glowing runes. Now they saw the stretch of glowing runes under all their hands had lengthened.

Candissa had a strange thought, but it made sense. "Cam, touch another side of the stone."

He frowned as he stared at the strange display but nodded. To no one's surprise, the effect each of them had in touching the surface increased. They moved around the perimeter of the monolith, seeing how each of them produced a line of glowing runes more than ten feet long.

The magic just increased in strength. What does this mean? Koraymis asked.

I haven't any idea, Candissa replied.

This could be a beacon in the darkness, we should stop, Errol pointed out.

"Of course. You're right on that point," Cam spoke. He released his touch, and the others followed him. They watched as the last of the glowing runes faded.

They all stood there in the darkening evening, thinking on the strange event.

"We need to settle down," Errol broke the silence. "Might I suggest not leaning against the stone."

They all nodded and went about their evenings, reading for the most part.

Sleep came fitfully for Candissa, for the glowing runes still nagged at her mind. The glowing turns and lines formed half-dreams, insistent but indecipherable.

Morning brought misty weather, though it was the familiar sort of mist. They enjoyed a small meal of roast cony, snared by one of Cam's traps.

The meat was delicious and buoyed their spirits. They broke camp and were on their way before too long, as Cam was insistent on making good time today.

By midday, the mist had burned away as they continued their trek north and east. By evening, when they could once more see the line of white, Cam revised his estimates. It was much further north than he had guessed.

Five days followed of cold winds, hard ground, and scarce water. The terrain was strangely unpredictable, leading them on countless switchbacks, reverses and dead ends. Cam had surrendered his frustration to resignation. There was no sense to this land, so he led them forward to the best of his ability.

It was on the seventh day after they had crossed the great bridge, that brought a brighter morning, and winds that were a little warmer. Candissa could not shake the feeling that something was underway, that some event was to soon occur.

It was then no surprise at all to her, around midday, as they made their way up a small rise of sere, yellow grass, that something came into their view. They each stopped on the last ridge, forming a line, to peer in wonder and relief at the sight, though it was miles away.

A tall, broken tower of white.

CHAPTER THIRTY-THREE - PRAESEOS

20 Procellus, Year 197, Eastvale Calendar

They had worked almost ceaselessly for seven days. Praeseos was impressed with how much they had accomplished. While he was not at all certain their efforts were entirely necessary, simply having the task set before him was both invigorating and calming.

He knew the Forgewrought were a people of tasks. He - and by extension, they - were never satisfied idling away any portion of a day. With Sevok declaring they would be visited by those who would attempt to break into the tower, perhaps even with the intent of slaying whoever was trapped within the curious bubble of magic, Praeseos dedicated himself to repairing and securing the tower.

The main door was fully repaired and had additional reinforcing bars attached to it. He had drawn on his own skills to craft and fasten the reinforcements. He had fired the forge on the level above and brought it to life. The tools and equipment were all familiar to him. Yet, he was utterly unable to draw forth the memories of how he knew them, where he had learned what he knew, even what he was, truly.

Still, the activities, the purpose, had been a salve on his wounded soul. He had found all the material he needed for his work within the wreckage strewn about the perimeter of the tower. He had set himself to the task of repairing the doors, clearing the debris, and fortifying the lower windows. He had even found spare panes of glass in storage vaults on the fourth level and replaced broken panes in the windows on the third level and higher.

He was not alone in his efforts. Sevok had aided him a great deal. While the Ur'chom lacked the technical skills the Forgewrought possessed, the shaman's brute strength was more than sufficient in hauling heavy loads and objects as needed. More importantly, the shaman provided guidance and counsel.

As Praeseos had lost his memories, he relied on the monstrous philosopher to tell him what he could about the world and to provide insight into what he should be doing. That included how best to defend the tower against the likely onslaught of Chom.

Aside from their motionless friend on the third level, the tower had proven fascinating in what it revealed upon further investigation. The beam of white energy was still active, having been their nearly-silent companion for these many days.

The machinery and gearworks that surrounded the device from which the beam emanated hummed along quietly, with only a few occasions when it made a noise that concerned them. Those incidents were few and lasted for only a brief duration.

Sevok had no idea what the beam meant and offered no speculations. Instead, the shaman was concerned with assisting Praeseos in any way possible, and in keeping a sharp eye out for any trouble. Being Ur'chom, Sevok had a remarkable sense of smell. Still, with the wind blowing from the west, it did them little good in warning against imminent threats from the east. The Forgewrought was more impressed with Sevok's shamanistic abilities and senses. The shaman had related to Praeseos how the shamans of the Ur'chom, regardless of clan – had a close relationship with the elements, nature, the weather, and with each other.

More than once, Praeseos found Sevok engaged in a quiet ritual, clutching the gnarled staff, murmuring in a speech he did not recognize. Sevok later told Praeseos it was method of reaching out to other shamans in the region. On their fourth day at the tower, Sevok laid out a small ring of stones, scribing sigils on them, then sat in the middle in a ritual trance for most of the day.

The following morning, the shaman told Praeseos the ritual allowed a deeper sharing of information.

"Does this afford you the opportunity to speak with them?" Praeseos asked.

"No, it is not like speech. It is more an awareness of the other's well-being, of where they may be, and whatever information about *their* location they could provide," Sevok said. "There is more to it, but it is not important."

"Did you find any of your ilk in the region?"

"Yes, I believe so, to the east, as I expected. They may be heading this way. Yes, I am quite certain they are. They have chosen and will stand with us," Sevok said. "But I fear it may be a dangerous journey. For others, Chom and Ur'chom alike, who are against us, are in that same region."

Praeseos pressed the shaman for more details, but Sevok could provide little more.

As the day matured, he turned his efforts to reinforcing the interior doors of the place. Sevok had chosen to spend the day foraging for roots, from which a hearty stew could be made. The Ur'chom had returned early that day with some small, slain mammal which the shaman had proceeded to skin and dress.

Praeseos found the entire affair slightly disquieting. Being a Forgewrought, he had no desire to eat flesh of any sort. Fortunately, Praeseos did not feel the need to eat yet, and he also knew it was an infrequent urge. The Ur'chom had restored a kitchen they had uncovered on the second level, where the stew was being prepared. Sevok had been gone for a few hours, but it was of no concern to the Forgewrought. The Ur'chom was at home in the dry plains of grass and ruins.

When he heard the distinct sound of the massive doors on the ground level being slammed and barred, he knew the day had taken a sudden turn.

"Praeseos!" Sevok bellowed from below.

He knew better than to call to him for any form of clarification. Praeseos set his tools down and ran for the ramp. He found the towering Ur'chom hurriedly attempting to move a long table in front of the door.

"What, pray tell, are you doing?"

"Figures on horseback approach! We must make ready!" Sevok replied, clearly out of breath from running.

"The table will do nothing. If they breach this door, there is naught to stop them," the Forgewrought said evenly. "How many are there?"

"Four, maybe five, but they could just be the van."

"Do Chom use horses?" Praeseos asked. He knew the answer.

Sevok halted, thinking. "I suppose not. No, none I can think of."

"Let us survey these riders from a window above," Praeseos suggested. He motioned up the ramp.

Above, the Forgewrought had fashioned a number of reinforced shuttered windows. Opening one of these, the two of them peered outward to the south, whence Sevok had indicated they approached. Praeseos found it odd they were not coming from the east.

Sure enough, he saw four mounted figures approaching. They seemed in no particular hurry. Something didn't seem right. Adjusting his vision, he viewed the group more clearly.

"Why are they leading a riderless horse?"

"Perhaps...it carries supplies?" Sevok suggested.

"It bears only a saddle, nothing more," Praeseos said.

"Hmm, they aren't Chom, and they don't appear to be hostile," the Ur'chom admitted.

They watched the riders slow in their approach as they studied the tower, moving around toward the eastern face, where the entrance was visible. Praeseos adjusted his vision again.

"One of them appears to be a white-clad female, and they are all Human, I believe," he reported.

"This is very odd. I have never heard of Humans, alone or in a group, riding into the wastes so very far from home."

"I suspect they are not our enemies. Let us go forth and see why they are here."

"Be careful! We cannot know what to expect."

"Of course," the Forgewrought assured the Ur'chom.

Sevok followed him down below and stood well back as he lifted the two bars from the door. Praeseos swung the doors wide open, stepping out into the bright light of day, though the sun was lowering in the west. He strode around the tower slightly and walked toward the riders, advancing perhaps twenty paces before stopping.

At once, the four riders saw him, as they were not even a hundred yards from the entrance. They stopped in their movement as one, regarding him.

He did the same, simply looking at them, watching for one sign or another of intent. They did not appear to be speaking to one another, though there were a few nods.

After a minute or so, the woman in white broke from the group and approached him. She bore a long staff of white across her back. Even her horse was a bright whitish-gray.

She walked her mount to within ten yards of the Forgewrought, where she appeared to study him intensely. With a half-smile, she spoke to him. It took him just a moment to recognize the language she spoke. It was a curious dialect of the Imperium Common, also called Kanthric.

"If that is a suit of armor, sir, it is like nothing I have ever seen before," she said.

Praeseos realized her misapprehension. But courtesy took precedent in this situation. He bowed in a traditional manner, befitting a young woman of unclear lineage or nobility.

"My lady, greetings to thee. I am Praeseos, of the Forgewrought," he said in a voice not too loud, but hopefully enough to carry to her companions. "I would be humbled with the honor of your acquaintance."

She seemed almost shocked but maintained her composure.

"I am Candissa of House Demarrae, of Ravensroost," she replied courteously, nodding to him. "It is an honor to meet you, Master Praeseos."

She dismounted and walked toward him. Her fellows approached from behind her, and he gained a better view of them.

One, he was not sure he could trust. His countenance was almost menacing by the manner he looked at the Forgewrought, despite the easy smile on a handsome face framed in dark gold hair. The middle one was all in black, with jet black hair and eyes that spoke of his heritage. Praeseos knew the man was of Konuran descent. The third man was a Thiravani, as those of mixed Human and Elven blood preferred to be called. He had a bow slung over his chest. Perhaps he was a warden or tracker. For some reason, the Forgewrought felt he could easily trust this one.

The lady approached. She cocked her head, staring at his face.

"I do not intend any disrespect sir, but I would like to see your face. Could you remove your helmet?"

"My lady, this *armor* is to me as your skin is to you. The metal visage before you is my face. I pray it does not offend," Praeseos bowed his head as he spoke. While his memory was void in respect to particulars, he felt more than recalled that some people were frightened of the Forgewrought, if they had never encountered one.

Her eyes went a little wide. "Not at all, sir, it is just that...I have never seen one such as yourself."

Her three friends had dismounted and were approaching.

"Candissa, the door," the one on the left said in a low, warning voice. His hand had moved to the hilt of a blade. Likewise, the Thiravani had freed his bow, with a hand reaching for his quiver.

Praeseos turned to see the figure of Sevok standing in the portal. All the newcomers could see was a hulking form covered in ragged furs, with clawed feet and hands, as the shaman moved carefully forward.

"My friends, there is no need for concern. Sevok is a friend and ally," Praeseos spoke loudly.

"A friendly Ur'chom? I have not heard of such a thing before," the Thiravani called.

"You hail from the Human kingdom to the east, do you not?" Sevok bellowed so all could hear. The fierce voice appeared to unnerve the black-cloaked one.

"Aye...and you speak our tongue?" the white-clad woman replied.

Sevok strode out of the portal now, standing fully more than eight feet in height, clutching the gnarled staff, furs, leather, beads, and feathers draped about a hulking form.

"Then you perhaps encountered my ill-tempered cousins from the foothills there. That clan has known nothing but the arrows of Humans and the axes of the mountain Dwarves. I am not of that line."

"I see that," the tracker said. "No insult was intended."

"And I suppose you are here because of that!" Sevok shouted, turning and pointing with the twisted staff at the brilliant column of energy leading into the large recess in the middle of the western face of the tower.

"Yes, in part, we are," Candissa said. "Did it draw you here as well?"

Praeseos raised a hand. "My lady, perhaps introductions before we relate particulars?"

They appeared to agree silently.

"Of course. Gentlemen, if you don't mind," she motioned back to her companions. "This is Errol Blackmar. Next to him is Koraymis Sleeth, a scholar. The bearded one is Cam Bronwyer, of Woodford. He is a hunter."

"I am Sevok, shaman of the Moon Howler clan," Sevok boomed. "I am a mystic of sorts, or so I believed most of my life. Until not many days ago, I was not sure. Now, I am certain."

"Why is that?" Candissa asked.

"I saw this tower in visions. Those visions brought me here. I met Praeseos shortly after he had awakened."

"Awakened?" the one named Errol spoke abruptly.

"Yes, I was in some sort of sleep, a magical stasis I suspect. For how long, I know not," Praeseos explained. "Unfortunately, I can offer little more than that by way of my story. For when I woke, my memory was robbed."

"Truly?" the one named Errol exclaimed. He was smiling. The Forgewrought did not know what to make of that.

The black-cloaked one named Koraymis looked at his friends pointedly but did not speak. Candissa turned to look at them. To Praeseos, it almost appeared they were speaking to one another, but they did not speak.

"You are using the *hashi'haklo*, the speech of the night!" Sevok exclaimed. As one, they all regarded the towering Ur'chom.

"Whatever do you mean, Sevok?" Praeseos asked him.

"I am a mystic and seer. I can sense such things. They speak with their minds. This I am sure of."

"You are perceptive," Koraymis called back to the fearsome mystic. Errol looked at the sorcerer sharply. Koraymis turned to his friend. "It doesn't matter. It's clear they have chosen."

"What did you say?" Praeseos asked, quite sure of what he heard but feeling it required repeating.

"He said chosen, Praeseos," Sevok said, walking with an unsteady gait up to stand next to the Forgewrought. "Just as those *Chom* said. They chose against us, and you slew them for it. These people are friends, for we are all on the same side."

"Side of *what?*" Errol said, his tone seeming almost challenging.

"We know not, my friend. It seems there is some sort of conflict, and we are - all of us - on the same side of it."

"And these Chom you slew, they were clearly on the other?" Candissa asked.

"Yes. I found them in the base of the tower when I awoke. They attacked me. I had little choice but to defend myself."

"How many were there?" Cam asked.

"Three."

"You defeated three Chom alone? They are fierce warriors. That is...remarkable," Cam said, looking at the Forgewrought with perhaps a little more respect.

"There are more coming here," Sevok said. "We have been preparing for them."

"Why do you think more are coming?" Errol said.

"I know of a madness of sorts, gripping some of my clan. They are being driven to gather and will find their way to this tower."

"You are certain of this?" Candissa asked.

"Without a doubt," Sevok replied.

"Then why are you here? Why not quit the place if you suspect danger?" Errol said.

"We cannot. I am honor-bound to stay and defend it, and Sevok has chosen to join me," Praeseos said.

"Why?" Errol pressed him. "It is just a ruined tower with a..." he motioned to the brilliant white beam. "Light!"

"It is not the tower nor the strange light," Praeseos said. "It is the one within I must defend."

"The *one*?" Candissa said, stepping closer to the Forgewrought. "Who is that?"

"We know not, but during my exploration of the place, I broke open the chamber which would have protected her. Now, we fear the Chom will attempt to kill her."

"Is she helpless? Why is she not out here now?" Cam asked.

"It is difficult to explain. It is best I show you," Praeseos said.

"Wait. She doesn't happen to have red hair, does she?" Errol asked, half-grinning.

As a Forgewrought, Praeseos knew he had a limited range of facial expressions, in respect to Humans. It was therefore unlikely they would realize from his expression that he was entirely dumbstruck by the question. He stopped and turned to Errol.

"How did you know this?"

CHAPTER THIRTY-FOUR - ENTHESSAR

12 Procellus, Year 197, Eastvale Calendar

Enthessar was quite pleased. He had been installed as the new Baron of Allenfar. He had displayed the expected mourning of a wounded son, bereft of a father he loved deeply. His histrionics increased by a factor when the message sent by the slain Orrendar was revealed.

His situation improved when he took advantage of wild rumors that sprang out of the collective gossip of his subjects. While Enthessar contended his father died of a weakened heart, others claimed it was a poison, and that the malefactors from Ravensroost were responsible.

He couldn't have thought of a better solution to whipping the people into a frenzy, when he confirmed the suspicions that their much-beloved Lord of Allenfar had been murdered by the wicked and cowardly criminals from the unruly border town.

Enthessar's call to bring the murderous lot to justice was met with exuberance bordering on bloodlust. He played the part of a restrained and wise young Lord. He insisted only a few join him, for it would be an arduous journey and he would not risk those he loved on such an endeavor.

Lancarm returned within a day, with several men. Enthessar reviewed them, pleased to find them all stout warriors, courageous and skilled, and dark of heart. They were with him, he had no doubt of that. A few more had been called to his side over the course of putting the murdered lord to rest and being instated as Baron.

He could see it in their eyes. They knew they were meant to serve under his banner, though they had no idea they in fact served a nameless master. That was for the better. If Enthessar suspected one of them had a link such as his, it could be a threat to his position, and he would kill the man on the spot.

They departed well before dawn of the following day, having selected good horses and gathered provisions for a long journey. It was cold and clear as they rode through the darkness. Enthessar enjoyed the night with his newly-acquired ability to see unerringly in shadow and darkness.

It was nearly midnight, when the group came to a fork in the road. They were all bitter cold from the ride, despite the pace. By the light of the moons, they saw the signposts - the route veering southward to Woodford and onward from there to Ravensroost, while the other fork kept them on a northerly route. He paused, letting his men drink. Enthessar was sorry to miss the opportunity to visit Ravensroost once more. He entertained dark fantasies of slaying Candissa's family. Perhaps another time.

Lancarm leaned in his saddle towards his lord. "Sir, we're heading to Woodford?"

"No, we are not. Our road lies along the northern highway," Enthessar declared. "We'll be heading into the hills from Feldan's Post."

There were grunts of surprise, but nods and shrugs otherwise. They were not there to question him, only to follow. They found a small village shortly after the fork; the innkeeper was alarmed to be woken so late, but seeing Enthessar's demeanor and accepting his claim of nobility, he gladly gave up his common room and his own bedchamber.

In the morning, they continued their hard pace, switching horses in another town. Enthessar knew his dark master was working his will along their route. The horses were ready and waiting for them, handed over by men with grim and smiling faces, without asking for coin or favor in return.

This allowed them all to push their mounts to their limits, and beyond, in the days to follow. One night, two of their horses died as they reached the town of Trillmere. As in the preceding villages, horses were waiting for them.

The last leg of their journey through the Kingdom ended one day at the village of Feldan's Post, a small mining village just off the foothills of the Starfall Mountains. It was peopled by hard men and women, accustomed to dealing with the occasional raid by Chom as well as the hard life imposed by mining and smelting.

A haggard old woman, tall of frame, with steel-gray hair met them at a stable attached to the village's sole tavern. "Well met, m'lord," she said, nodding. Her eyes were black as pitch. Enthessar liked her at once.

"Well met, my lady," he said with a sardonic grin and flourishing half-bow after dismounting. The old woman laughed uproariously at his greeting.

"Your mounts are ready, my boys will move your gear. There's food and drink inside," she said, chuckling and wiping one eye. "Will ye be staying the evening or departing at once?"

"We'll leave as soon as the horses are loaded," Enthessar said. She just nodded and went back inside the rough-built tavern, shouting at three younger lads who immediately set to unloading and loads their mounts. She didn't bother introducing herself, which Enthessar appreciated.

After they'd taken their fill of food and drink, Enthessar and his men mounted the fresh horses, near the gate of the village.

"We can't ride so hard from here, men. These mounts will need to get us all the way to the tower," Enthessar said.

"How long will it take us, m'lord?" one of the men spoke, a bearded dark-haired fellow with missing teeth. Enthessar looked at him sharply. "Beggin' yer pardon, m'lord, I don't mean to talk out of turn. I just want to get to killin!"

This elicited a few short laughs and growls of assent from the men. Enthessar wasn't offended by the man's question, though he wouldn't let the man knew that.

"At least a week, through the Misthallows," he said. He noticed his men glancing at one another. They wouldn't dare speak of any misgivings. "And we'll be meeting up with reinforcements on the way."

"My lord?" Lancarm spoke, knowing he would be speaking for most of the men there.

"You will see, when the time comes," was all Enthessar said in reply.

"Will the mists slow our pace?" one of the men asked. Enthessar was growing tired of questions, and he decided to make a minor example of the man. But before he could see who had spoken, the old woman from the tavern interrupted.

"There ain't no more mists!" her voice was shrill, harsh. She came hobbling out to them, a jug in one bony hand. Brown liquid ran down one side of her hairy chin.

"What do you mean?" Enthessar said. This didn't sound right to him.

"Up and vanished, poof!" she said, snapping her fingers. "Six nights ago I think, maybe it was seven. We woke up and it was gone, clear as far as the eye could see. And the mists always hug the hills here." She pointed out of the gate with a bony finger.

Enthessar didn't know what to make of this turn of events. He chose to make the best of it.

"Well, it seems our trip will be unimpeded by the mists after all," he grinned, looking at his men. Their expressions brightened visibly. They had all grown up with tales of the horrors that lurked within the Misthallow Hills. Enthessar spoke in a low voice now. "I call it a good omen for our travels!"

His men were once more at ease, as they crowded through the narrow gate of Feldan's Post. The old woman caught his attention with her curious glare. She would not look away from him. That vexed him, so he turned his mount and approached her, as she put the cracked jug to her withered lips and drank.

"What is it?" he said in a harsh whisper.

"You think it a good omen, and maybe it is for you crossin' the hills. But it was no doin' of the master," she said. Enthessar started, shocked to hear someone else mention that which only he had been privy to. He turned to ensure his men were well away from them.

"Explain," was all he said.

"It was *her*," the woman said, wiping her lips. "With her white staff and all. You be careful with that one."

"How do you know?" Enthessar growled through clenched teeth. He was near to running the old hag through.

"Old Ytha has a little sight, m'lord, an' the dark master improved it," she said. "I felt it, near to saw her in my mind. She can't live, that one, she'll be too much trouble."

"Worry not, old mother," Enthessar said, righting himself in his saddle. "She will be dealt with."

The old woman gave him a hard stare. She nodded once. "My lord."

Enthessar turned and joined his men. Their moods were lifted at the prospect of clear skies as they rode toward the hills, and he let them have their relief. But in his mind, Enthessar resented the absence of the mist.

It was a reminder of Candissa's power.

The following two days were cold, but clear. They found water for the horses and had sufficient provisions. Despite the lack of mist, when darkness fell about them, his men seemed to huddle close to the fires, still untrusting of the hills. Enthessar dismissed it as old tales not easily forgotten, or simple stupidity. But he didn't need their brains, just their swords.

They thought he could not hear them, but his hearing seemed to have improved along with his sight. They murmured of creatures that likely still roamed the hills, ancient horrors, or slain men from ages past.

Enthessar smirked at their fears. He could remember whispers in his mind just before sleeping and just as he awoke, telling him things. Among them was the assurance that the curses that wandered the land would not touch them. He also remembered something about others joining them and to look for allies where one would expect enemies.

One of the men at an adjacent campfire stood suddenly, shouting. "What is that?"

Enthessar was not worried, but he stood, slowly drawing a weapon. He heard something in the darkness. A flapping noise.

"Bats?" Lancarm said, his eyes darting, wide.

"No, I think not," Enthessar said. He sensed something familiar.

He nearly jumped as Lancarm shouted in alarm at the sight of the small creature that dropped onto the ground between them. Lancarm had his shortsword out, but Enthessar raised his hand to stay his friend's blow.

"Do not fear. This is not an enemy," Enthessar said, looking down at his new ally.

The thing stood no taller than Enthessar's boot. Its skin was gray and mottled, rough like leather, and covered in moles or growths, he could not be sure. Its head was overly large for its tiny frame. Wiry legs sported long clawed feet, and its arms ended in small, nimble hands, with tiny claws as well. Tiny horns jutted from its spine, shoulders, elbows, knees and jaw.

Its mouth was full of razor-sharp teeth, under a pointed nose and large, glassy eyes, black and unreadable. Its ears were pressed back against its head. From its back sprouted two bat-like wings that were now folding up neatly.

It whipped a short tail about as it glanced up at Lancarm and Enthessar. It appeared to be grinning as its hands writhed pointlessly.

Enthessar smiled down upon it. "Hello, friend."

"You know this creature?" Lancarm whispered, still a good distance from his master.

"I've never seen it before this moment," Enthessar said in a quiet voice. "Yet I feel I know it, yes."

Its black eyes studied Enthessar's face. "It says I must serve you, it does, it says so…"

"It speaks?" Lancarm said, his mouth hanging open as he eased his sword back into his scabbard. Others were moving around to examine the bizarre creature, keeping a careful distance.

"What is your name?" Enthessar asked the small thing, with an almost kind tone.

"Nikkrilik! My name is Nikkrilik, so it says, that who made me so long ago!" it said in a voice sibilant and raspy.

"Sir, I don't know if this thing can be trusted," Lancarm said.

"I assure you, it is an ally," Enthessar said. "All right Nikk, then you shall serve me."

The creature called Nikk jumped a little, rubbing its hands together. "Nikkrilik is happy! What can Nikkrilik do for the master now?"

"For now, you can scout the area, far and wide. If you find something that looks dangerous, come back and tell me. Do you understand?"

The thing nodded its head vigorously. With a surprisingly powerful leap, it was gone, launched into the dark sky. They heard the flapping of its leathery wings fade quickly, its silhouette dark against the stars for only a moment.

Lancarm only shook his head, grinning a little at Enthessar's broad smile.

A day later, they were out of the hills, moving steadily over open plains. There were occasional ruins, but they did not tarry to inspect them. Nikkrilik reported nothing of interest in any of them, and no sign of any forces other than their own. While the bizarre creature was useful for scouting, he was not overly reliable, disappearing for many hours at a time for no reason.

One evening, his men grew worried, seeing shapes moving in the darkness just beyond the edge of their campfire. His winged scout was not in the area, so Enthessar investigated, walking away from the fire, despite the calls and pleas of his men.

His vision allowed him to see well into the dark of the night. A pack of fearsome wolf-like creatures lounged in the shadows beyond, watching him idly. Their eyes glinted of malice. He smiled at them and returned to his camp.

He assured his men the beasts they sensed were their allies.

The following day, close to high sun, they could all see the pack moving along with them, but at a good distance. They proved their worth the next day.

Enthessar never saw clearly what it was. But something immense rose from the earth along a ridge to the north. Apparently covered in moss or dirt, it made a strange roaring sound and began lumbering towards them. Its motion was almost serpentine, undulating in a strange fashion, unlike any natural beast. It kicked up a tremendous amount of dirt and debris as it rumbled toward them, obscuring its features. Enthessar guessed it was at least thirty feet long and half as tall, or so it seemed. It was dark, but he could make out no other features, save for a pair of bright blue points of light, piercing the debris. They could have been eyes, but Enthessar was not about to stand there to find out.

The wolf creatures moved quickly to attack it, as Enthessar ordered his men to move at a gallop away from the area. They lost sight of the fray as the ground was rising and falling in this region. Enthessar did catch sight of more than one wolf creature being flung high into the air.

However, the massive creature was not seen again.

It was two mornings later they found the Chom.

As they crested a ridge dotted with crumbled ruins, they were suddenly upon the camp of perhaps a dozen of the monstrous creatures. They were fearsome, inhuman, and larger than any Human.

Enthessar knew at once they were with him. He had heard tales of the Chom that lived in the mountains far to the north but had never seen one. They were as ugly as the tales told. Armed with crude spears and clubs, a few of them bore badly nicked axes.

His men shouted, grasping weapons. He calmed them quickly.

Leading them down into the camp of the Chom, he looked around at each of them, exuding a confidence he could not have imagined a few weeks ago.

"Do any of you speak the Human tongue?"

They looked at each other with their dark, animal eyes. One of them stepped toward Enthessar, causing his horse to whinny nervously.

"Speak Human do," was all it said.

"Good. I lead you all, yes?"

The Chom nodded, his eyes telling Enthessar of the comprehension behind them.

"Where go?"

Enthessar smiled. "To the tower, to kill everything there!"

The Chom related the words to his kin and they bellowed their approval. Enthessar had to tell the Chom to stay behind the horses a goodly distance. Once that was understood, they were again underway, his force doubled, if not tripled, in strength.

That night, when they camped, he heard the dark whispers before he slept. With the recent additions to his company, plans were reshaping. He called Lancarm aside, out of earshot of his men.

"Lan, I've been thinking about our plan when we reach the tower," Enthessar said.

"Sir?"

"I believe there is a new plan in order. We must make certain preparations. Not everyone needs to know of these plans, however. But I will share with you the most important of our objectives."

"Beyond capturing or killing the four of them?"

Enthessar smiled. "Yes. We must make sure to kill the fifth."

In the darkness, Lancarm raised his eyebrows. The two spoke at length, forming thoughts into a plan. When Enthessar was satisfied, he sent Lancarm to tell a few others of their intent.

He laid back down on his bedroll as the camp quieted down. The voice returned to his mind.

Well done. Tomorrow, you will reach the tower. Kill them all.

The words came easier these days, especially in the dark. They were not words as Enthessar would speak them, rather it was his mind translating the feelings he was receiving from his master. In fact, the dark murmurings he heard within his mind were unsettling, if not disturbing. But he could interpret them, and his mind gave them a voice of sorts.

"I would like to keep the woman, my master," Enthessar whispered.

No. You must kill her at the first opportunity. The power I have invested in you is not to be squandered on your lusts. There is work to be done.

In the dark, Enthessar grimaced. "Yes, my master."

Rolling onto his side, he wondered if this dark master could read his every thought. As he breathed deeply, he felt the disappointment fester in his heart. He wanted Candissa. He would have her.

Enthessar braced himself for a rebuke from his master. But none came. He smiled one of his wide, handsome smiles that melted the hearts of noble daughters. Perhaps the master could not see and know all. Perhaps he would have his way with Candissa. For a moment, he felt hesitation, wondering how powerful his master was, truly. But he dismissed any doubt quickly.

For there was work to be done.

CHAPTER THIRTY-FIVE – THE TOWER

20 Procellus, Year 197, Eastvale Calendar

Cam

Cam stood beside his three friends as they crowded the small chamber. He understood why Praeseos needed to show them.

"It is her, truly," Candissa murmured.

"You have seen her in vision then?" Sevok asked from outside the chamber, the shaman's gruff voice almost a snarl.

Can we trust these two? Koraymis asked silently. *How do we know the Ur'chom is entirely with us? And what of this gearworks man? I've never read of such a creature.*

He's called Forgewrought. His – folk, I suppose you would call them – seem familiar to me, Errol added. *I have no qualms about being forthright with them.*

Nor I, as they were called to be part of this as we were, Candissa said. *I understand your hesitance, Kor, but I trust them.*

Cam nodded his agreement to Koraymis, as he sensed a silent acquiescence from the sorcerer in their momentary exchange.

"Yes, we have," Candissa continued. "We believe she is the fifth member of our...group."

Cam studied the red-haired young woman trapped in the magical orb. She was probably Cam's age, perhaps a bit younger. Her amber eyes were strange. He had never seen such a color.

"Have you tried touching her through that green energy?" Cam asked.

"Yes. Anything that touches it is forced back and there is a discharge of deadly power," Praeseos said.

"Here, let me show you," Sevok said, shouldering into the room, forcing the Humans to press against the walls. "I touched the orb just yesterday."

"Sevok? After that first incident? That was unwise in the extreme," Praeseos chided the Ur'chom.

"Bah, I did not wish to worry you. Here," the towering shaman extended the twisted, wooden staff. As it touched the perimeter of the translucent sphere, sparks erupted, forcing it back. "And watch now."

Reaching out with one clawed hand, Sevok touched the green energy. With a sizzling crackle and a puff of smoke, the Ur'chom's hand flew backwards. Sevok bared impressive fangs, snarling.

"It is painful. Enough to keep anyone away," the Ur'chom said.

"Why would you do that?" Praeseos asked.

"Because I needed to sense the magic."

"What did you find?" Koraymis asked, his expression expectant. He knew something, Cam guessed.

"That beneath the magic protecting her is something else," the shaman said, slowly moving out of the chamber.

Koraymis looked at the red-haired woman. "Death."

From outside the chamber, Sevok swiveled a shaggy head around to the sorcerer, pointed ears snapping upwards. "You sense it as well?"

Koraymis nodded. "If we breach the magic, it will kill her."

Cam grimaced. Candissa studied the leather-clad young woman, her eyes intent. "Can we even breach the magic?"

"My visions have been limited on this," Sevok said, sharp-nailed hands twisting a long braid of leather hanging from one shoulder. It bore beads of crystal, bone, and other materials. Cam suspected it was somehow special to the mystic. "I know only the Chom *will* be able to kill her. So, I think brute force can break through."

"By doing so, they will kill her, one way or another," Cam sighed.

"Your visions yield nothing else on this?" Candissa asked Sevok. The shaggy head of the Ur'chom shook, ears dropping back.

"Candissa, can you sense anything?" Errol asked.

"I've been trying, but nothing yet."

Cam froze for a moment and knew Candissa and Errol were likewise rapt. The three of them instantly sensed something occurring with Koraymis.

The sorcerer stood against a wall, his right hand in the palm of his left. His eyes were closed. He was somehow communicating. No…*communing* was a better word, Cam thought to himself. But with who or what?

"What's happening in there?" Sevok said abruptly. Errol held up a hand.

Candissa stepped closer to Koraymis. "What is it, Kor?" she whispered.

The sorcerer's eyes snapped open. He was staring at Errol.

"Your blade," was all he said.

"What of it?" Errol asked.

Koraymis visibly relaxed as he let his hands drop to his sides. "You can break the confining spell and release the death magic, without killing her."

"Why me?" Errol asked.

The sorcerer looked down at the sheathed blade at Errol's belt. "It is made of something special."

"It can act as a conduit?" Sevok asked from outside.

"Precisely."

"Oh, bah! Not a good alternative!" Sevok barked.

"What does that mean?" Candissa asked.

Koraymis took a deep breath. "His blade, if pushed in slowly, will pierce the protective magic, and then trigger the killing magic. But the effects of the spell will go *outward*, not inward."

Errol laughed aloud. "That is a fine thing, indeed! I need only give my life. Is what you're saying?"

Sevok had managed to bend down enough to poke the oversized head into the chamber. Koraymis looked at the Ur'chom.

"Tell him," the shaman said.

"No, you won't be harmed, Errol."

"I don't understand."

"The spell will be triggered by your blade, but you will be safe. The protective magic will surround you. The death magic will not affect the wielder. It will affect the person closest to the wielder," Koraymis explained.

"You're certain of this?" Candissa asked. Errol was glad she raised the question. He didn't like putting his trust in lore acquired through unseen agents. "Absolutely certain?"

"Yes, without a doubt," the sorcerer replied.

Cam understood why Koraymis had been slow to explain the situation as he understood it.

Candissa looked at him with a long, thoughtful gaze.

"We should learn more about this *death magic*. Surely, there must be a way to release the magic without the need of a..."

"Sacrifice?" Errol said. Candissa seemed reluctant to say the truth of it.

"Yes, but what sort of sacrifice is required to release it? I have no knowledge of these matters," she said, clearly irritated.

"I have studied something of this," Koraymis said. "Correct me if you have information to the contrary, Sevok."

"You would know more than I, sorcerer," the Ur'chom's head shook, beaded braids rattling.

"The death magic, assuming it is just that, can be satisfied only by taking a victim that knows what death is. Only then is the exchange made - a life against the death," Koraymis said, as if reading from a book. He suddenly looked at the Ur'chom. "How did you know I was a sorcerer?"

The shaman only snorted in amusement. "I have a nose. We can smell that sort of thing."

"A victim that can know death," Errol repeated. "I am not sure what that means."

Candissa frowned, her expression almost angry. "It means the victim must understand that it can die. They must be aware! In short, no tricks, no one unconscious, no animal sacrifices. It has to be someone alive and aware, so they can understand what is happening when the death magic takes them from this world, to the next."

"Silence! Please, all of you," the voice of the Forgewrought suddenly boomed. Cam couldn't imagine any normal Human speaking with such a loud voice.

All heads turned to Praeseos. His head was inclined at a curious angle. He suddenly stepped over to a window.

"You should move your horses inside, to the chamber under the ramp. It should be able to house them all."

"Why?" Cam said.

"I can hear the approaching howls of Chom. They will surely butcher the beasts."

At once, the group quit the fifth, trapped in the green orb of magic. They bounded down to the ground level quickly. As Cam and Kor, aided by the Forgewrought, herded the horses through the broad doors and into a smaller chamber, Errol and Candissa scanned the horizon.

They could see nothing at this point. A cold wind blew, but the haze overhead was bright.

"They would be coming from the east I am guessing?" Candissa asked. "I hear nothing but the wind."

"Our metal friend must have impressive hearing," Cam remarked, as he and the others joined them outside.

"Wait, there," Candissa said, pointing. Just over a rise some hundreds of yards distant, they could see figures running. There were more than a dozen of them, and they were quickly followed by perhaps a dozen figures on horseback.

Errol squinted his eyes against the bright haze of the day. He laughed. "This is a surprise!"

"It's Enthessar, isn't it?" Candissa said, her voice almost weary.

"How did you know?"

"I suspected he would not let my besting him go unanswered. It was clear he had chosen, after he attacked Errol," she said. "I just didn't know he would sink to allying himself with such beasts as Chom."

"Some may have bows. We had best get inside. Hopefully Praeseos' defenses will hold."

Returning to the tower, they told the others. Praeseos quickly secured the main doors and led them up two levels.

"We can view their approach better from this vantage," he said. Indeed, the windows he had repaired offered Cam an excellent view.

"Fifteen Chom at least. Humans number at least nine plus Enthessar," he reported. "Some of the Chom have spears. We'll need to watch for those. How long can your doors hold below?"

"Against such a horde of Chom, if they use pieces of debris as battering rams, I fear it will not hold long. Perhaps a quarter-hour. And that is a favorable estimate."

"Even if the doors are broken quickly, they have at least three choke points to contend with," Errol pointed out.

"They'll be here in just a few minutes," Cam said. He turned to the Forgewrought. "Are there weapons available against a siege?"

"None, I'm afraid. The tower has not even a single murder hole to take advantage of," Praeseos said. Cam thought his voice sounded a little forlorn.

"What of windows facing east. We could break one or two and perhaps fire upon them as they approach?"

Praeseos shook his head. "They are poor windows for such a purpose, small and set high. This tower was not designed to repel such an attack, I suspect."

"We need to assess our situation. Sevok, you are an Ur'chom, so I know you can hold your own in a fight, to say the least," Errol said. The shaman snorted, nodding briskly.

"Yes, we are fierce opponents in combat. But do not think my magic will aid us in battle. As a mystic, my magic is not of that nature," Sevok said.

Errol nodded. He turned to Praeseos.

"I will serve well in battle, though I cannot hold off nor single-handedly defeat so many Chom," the Forgewrought declared.

"A question, Praeseos. Do you have a weapon, or do you just use your fists?" Cam asked him.

In response to the question, the Forgewrought stood straight, reaching behind his head with both arms. Cam saw his limbs were bending at almost impossible angles, but he reminded himself this was not simply a man in a suit of armor. He watched from behind as Praeseos' hands appeared to slide into metal apertures that opened above where shoulder blades should have been.

In one quick motion, he drew both hands back. Attached to each were weapons, one being sword-like in appearance while the other resembled an axe. Where they met his grip, the hafts of the weapons seemed to merge with his hands. His fingers were lost in the curves and depressions on the handles, with overlapping plates securing them.

Cam realized it would be nigh on impossible to wrest the weapons from the Forgewrought's grasp.

"You have satisfied my curiosity," he said, grinning. As the others spoke of preparations for the impending battle, Cam took a moment to sling his quiver of arrows over his shoulder and tighten his pack. He knew he would be using both bow and blade today.

Almost as an afterthought, while he still had his pack out, he checked the tiny pocket inside. He felt the paper there, pulled it out.

It had changed. His heart seemed to freeze as he read, *Remember, the Everneed can provide many things, but it cannot change the fate of what must be.*

Errol

Errol needed a plan. They didn't have long to make one.

"Those ramps will be difficult to negotiate. For them, but also for us," he said, rubbing his scruffy beard. "They will break down the doors, so we need to have a plan of defense."

"Defense won't take the day," Koraymis pointed out. "They are here to kill us. We must kill them."

"Perhaps we can inflict enough harm to drive them off," Candissa suggested.

Errol snorted. "Don't be ridiculous. Kor is right. We need to end their lives. They won't relent until they take ours."

"You don't know that for certain!" Candissa said louder than necessary. Errol thought he saw a challenge in her eyes. He had to be careful, as he saw a hint of the familiar silvery gleam. He knew what she was capable of.

"We *know* they are driven to kill us. If you can break that hold on them, so be it. But until you can demonstrate that capability..." Errol drew his blade lightning-quick, making a drawing motion across his throat.

"If they are drawn into this against their own nature, it is wrong of us to condemn them so. We are not compelled to go into this battle with the intention to destroy them to the last. We harm only those we *must!*" Her words were wise, but too generous in Errol's opinion.

"I suspect I *must* harm any who cross my path today, my dear," Errol quipped, grinning with an intentional malice.

Candissa's eyes seemed to grow a little darker in their aspect, despite the silvery glow.

Koraymis stepped between them, raising two hands. "They are nearly upon us. This is pointless."

Cam turned back to the nearest window, having been distracted by the confrontation while preparing his weapons. "He's right, they're faster than I thought. They're going around the other side of the tower."

"I suspected they might," Praeseos said. "There are piles of rubble from which they may extract a battering ram. Likely they will select a stout beam of lumber, as there are many stacked there."

"All right, I'm no battlefield commander," Errol began. "But I do have training in this sort of thing."

He looked at each of them in turn, then settled his gaze on Koraymis. The sorcerer already had a pained expression.

"Kor," Errol said. "Once they breach the main door, you could-"

"Please, no, Errol," Koraymis said, holding his hands up. "Keep me in reserve. I-"

"Don't want to kill?" Errol said, taking no effort to hide the hard edge in his voice. "You already stated they are here to kill us. You are the best weapon we have."

"I don't want to, Errol. I will if I must, but please, *please*! Don't make me start the battle," Koraymis said, his voice pleading.

"Errol, don't force him!" Candissa said, her voice harsh.

Errol looked at Candissa, then Koraymis. He gritted his teeth, sighing.

"Very well. Praeseos and I can attack them first, on the ground level, working our way up the ramp as need be. Cam, you should be waiting on the first level with your bow as they reach the top of the ramp. Sevok and Candissa can be ready at the next ramp, to support us to that point. We'll use the tables and chairs as obstacles to slow their ascent and to provide cover, on levels one and two."

"And what of me?" Koraymis asked, raising his eyebrows.

"You just be ready on three if things go badly. But if things go badly..."

Koraymis was already nodding vigorously. "Yes, I know. I won't hesitate."

They discussed a few more details as they readied themselves. A minute later, a great booming could be heard on the front doors. They held, for the moment. Errol waited in the shadows by the ramp, while Praeseos was at the base. Cam readied to fire what arrows he may once they breached the doors. He had his extra arrows on hand, as Sevok had warned them a single arrow would rarely bring down a Chom.

Errol felt his heart quicken, but his breath remained steady. He knew he was tempered for combat, trained for it. He was unsure of the others.

We will persevere, came Candissa's voice, in response to Errol's uncertainty.

I wish I had your confidence, Koraymis replied.

Then you shall, Candissa said. Her statement puzzled Errol.

While Errol was below and entirely out of sight of the Aevaru, he suddenly felt her concentrating. Though he could not see her, he knew she was gripping her staff, lost in a form of meditation.

All at once, Errol was filled with a warmth, a suffusing energy that both lent him resolve and subdued his anxieties. It was invigorating, and he could not help but grin.

How did you do that? Cam asked, echoing Errol's question.

I cannot say. I just…did, she replied.

The booming continued but was joined by howls of rage. Errol wondered if perhaps her power was having a contrary effect on their enemies.

The efforts to break down the door seemed to falter, becoming less organized. Yet they were having an effect. The stone was cracking around the hinge plates and even Praeseos's additional reinforcing bars were bending.

There was a pause in the booming. Errol sensed they were gathering their might for a more concerted effort. *Ware the door!* he warned his friends silently.

A moment later, the doors shook violently, cracks appearing all around. Praeseos armed himself instantly, standing ready at the ramp. Errol breathed slowly, his blade held lightly in his right hand, his left hand holding a long dagger. He had other daggers ready for throwing, if needed.

The doors exploded inward, fragments of thick wood and broken metal scattering ahead of the surging mass of Chom. Four of the creatures burst into the room. Errol knew at once there were too many, but he could perhaps slow them.

He flung his blade forcefully into the ribs of one, causing it to stumble. It was not a killing blow, but it would slow the Chom. He glanced around the room as his blade returned to his palm a heartbeat later.

Another of Cam's arrows found its mark. The wounded Chom slowed their advance. A hurled spear clattered off a wall. Another pushed through and rushed Praeseos, who was more than ready.

Praeseos's bladed arms swung and struck rapidly and accurately, slicing and biting deep into his opponent. While Cam's arrows and Errol's blade strikes had limited effect on the Chom, it was clearly not the case with Praeseos' blows. Cam put an arrow into the one Errol had struck twice, and it was likely out of the fight. Errol did not depend on it, however, as he was not familiar with how resilient the Chom were.

Errol's blade flew again and lodged deep in the chest of an enemy, as another shouldered around the wounded Chom. Errol chose to make a tactical retreat to avoid being rushed. He was able to move up the ramp past Praeseos as the Forgewrought struck again, lopping an arm off the nearest creature.

Praeseos backed up carefully along the ramp, allowing Errol to get in behind. Cam managed another shot before retreating. The fallen and dead slowed the advance of the other Chom, as did the arrows protruding from their own bodies.

Praeseos had been struck numerous times, and his arms bore evidence of the blows. Errol wondered if the Forgewrought even bled, having seen no evidence of blood as yet. They regrouped at the top of the ramp, out of sight of the chamber below.

Another Chom appeared quickly, much to his undoing. A moment later, he was rolling back down the ramp, lacking a hand and an arrow protruding from his left eye.

Errol knew there was room here on the first level if the Chom managed to get up the ramp. They could not defend the open space, but a long table was overturned by the next ramp, making it an ideal chokepoint to defend. This would allow them to retreat up the ramp to level two, if the Chom surged through in force.

"Why the delay? What are they up to?" Cam asked tersely.

"Chom are not prone to cleverness. I suspect their Human masters are directing them!" Sevok said, clutching his staff, ready to strike if need be.

Praeseos risked a glance down and around the ramp. A huge spear clattered against the wall where his head had been a moment before.

"Shields. They advance with a shield wall," the Forgewrought reported.

"Ready another retreat!" Errol shouted, positioning himself favorably.

Let me help! Koraymis said to his friends, from the third level.

"Not yet, Kor!" Errol called out. The Chom advanced up the ramp now, having cleared the bodies of their fallen kin. They bore a mix of metal and wooden shields of uneven size and shape. It was a crude, but effective, shield wall.

Cam continued firing arrows, finding gaps between the shields. An arrow struck the calf of a Chom, which only howled and continued advancing. Errol struck another in its thigh, causing it to drop a shield. Praeseos took the lead Chom to task, ramming their shields with mighty blows from his sword and axe. The mass of Chom slowed, but Praeseos's efforts were unsuccessful in breaking them. Their advance continued, nearly to the top of the ramp.

"Sard! Retreat!" Errol shouted. Once they were beyond the edge of the ramp, the Chom could rush the level. "Praeseos, withdraw to the next ramp!"

The Forgewrought was swinging his beweaponed limbs with fierce determination and deadly skill. He felled another Chom as blows from the others continued to rain down upon his armored body. It was clearly taking a toll. Dark fluid now ran from several seams along his chest and midriff. Praeseos made his way around the overturned table and onto the ramp curving upwards to the next level. As they retreated up the second ramp, Errol and Cam continued providing cover fire, killing at least two more Chom. The grip of Errol's blade was slick with the blood of the fallen, returning each time to his hand with more of the viscous, dark-crimson stuff.

A crossbow bolt glanced over the top of Errol's left ear. The proximity of the bolt filled him with an instant and dark anger. The axe of a Chom managed to strike close enough to rend one of his boots, as he worked his way upwards. Another bolt struck Cam, who shouted in pain.

Sevok suddenly appeared, pulling the wounded Forgewrought back and taking his place. The shaman's nine-foot frame filled the ramp and the Ur'chom roared as the gnarled staff came arcing downward. The Chom seemed to hesitate, as they were natural subordinates to Ur'chom and were likewise loath to attack their betters. It gave Errol, Cam and Praeseos time to regroup as the towering shaman managed to knock down two Chom, at the cost of taking one or two blows from club and ax. With another strike of the staff and a surprisingly deft kick by the Ur'chom, the Chom fell back messily, regrouping below, their snarls of rage filling the tower.

"We can hold them here. They cannot breach the next level nearly as easily!" Cam shouted through his pain. He pulled the bolt free of his hip, wincing as he did.

At the top of the ramp on the second level, as Sevok joined them, Errol assessed their situation.

Praeseos was wounded, dark fluid seeping from his torso. Despite that, Errol sensed his resolve and knew he was still a force. Sevok was wounded but not too seriously. Cam could fire his arrows, although Errol did not realize he had so many to fire. They had yet to call on Kor's fire magic.

They held the higher ground, and the curve of the ramp was such that the Chom would suffer severe losses if they tried to storm it. The open half of level two had no real cover of any sort, save the entrance to what was once a kitchen. Praeseos was moving quickly to pile what remained of the broken furnishings in front of the ramp down to one.

Sevok snarled, glancing down through the broad window of the second level, repaired and reglazed by Praeseos. "I have always loved to watch the sun set. I fear I have seen my last!"

Errol darted over to the window. At least six or seven more Chom were loping toward the entrance below.

"What is it?" Candissa shouted from the ramp leading up to the third level.

"Reinforcements, more Chom. At least a half-dozen," Errol said, biting his words off. "I suspect this will embolden them."

Then, almost as if in answer to his fears, the Chom surged upwards. Roaring, they fell under the continuous onslaught of arrow, blade and axe. Still, their numbers pushed Sevok and Praeseos back. Errol and Cam provided support, killing more of the Chom. The dead impeded the Chom's advance and they were able to hold the top of the ramp.

As the Chom reinforcements arrived below, Errol did not wish to dwell not the outcome of the battle. But something troubled him. Something did not make sense in their surge. It was too costly, despite their gains.

Something was wrong. A dread filled Errol, bleeding into the awareness of his friends.

Where are Enthessar's men? Errol asked the question silently, realizing he had seen only one of them, far behind the press of Chom.

Errol jerked as he felt a searing pain in his gut. It wasn't anything that touched him; it was Koraymis.

From above came Candissa's desperate plea, ringing in their minds.

His men are here! Koraymis is wounded!

Candissa

For an instant, Candissa was dumbfounded. An arrow had struck Koraymis, lodged just above his belt. His face twisted in agony as he collapsed. She shouted to her friends, through her mind, and turned to face whatever was coming around the curving corridor behind them.

She sensed Cam already racing up the ramp, nearly beside her now. Raising her staff, she commanded light, and it shone brightly. She could see four or five Humans advancing towards them.

Koraymis! Hold fast, I'll get to you soon! Candissa shouted silently, bracing herself. She sensed the intense pain Koraymis was feeling but could not afford the time to aid him.

They are nearly to the door! Her mind blasted within theirs. Their enemies were closer to the chamber than any of them. One of the Humans fired a crossbow, striking Cam, but he managed to return fire, an arrow finding the man's shoulder.

One of Enthessar's men rushed her. Using a technique she learned from Thendarick, Candissa brought her staff around, parrying his blow. As she reversed her staff, she felt something flow from her core, through her hands, into the staff. A bright flash of white light erupted from the end of the staff as she connected the Human's head. He collapsed, unconscious.

There were too many foes before her. She heard Cam shout in pain as an arrow found his leg. His arrows could not keep the Humans at bay down the corridor, and if she moved forward, they would surely overwhelm her.

Raising her staff, she saw it blaze with an unearthly white brilliance. Power flowed from her core into the staff, building, surging. Words formed in her mind and she shouted them. She did not know the tongue, yet it felt as though she were born to it. The words, like a solemn and purposeful music, formed the power into action, channeling the energy threatening to explode in her hands.

White, radiant force burst down the corridor, erupting from her staff. The wave burst forth just as the lead attacker lunged towards her, swinging downward with an ax, intent on killing her. The weapon bit into her thigh even as the man tumbled wildly down the passage, having taken the brunt of Candissa's magic. She did not react to the pain, still feeling the surge of energy as it careened down the passage, felling several more Humans. One of the attackers was thrown into the small chamber she was so intent on guarding.

As the radiance diminished, she staggered, leaning heavily on her staff, realizing how much of herself went into the blast.

Errol

Errol rushed past Candissa, jumping over her fallen attacker. One of Enthessar's followers was already in the chamber containing the ensorcelled young woman. The attacker laid just inside the room, having been stunned momentarily by the radiant burst.

Another attacker, just past the door, was staggering to his feet, holding a sword loosely.

In the opposite direction, the Chom, having sacrificed many of their fellows already, were gaining an advantage on the wounded Ur'chom and Forgewrought as they pressed up the ramp. Koraymis was on his hands and knees, clearly in pain. Cam turned to fire on the advancing Chom, trying to give the sorcerer time to recover and escape.

Glancing back down the rampway, Errol saw the number of Chom swelling, bolstered by fresh reinforcements. Praeseos was nearly surrounded and badly wounded, numerous wounds oozing dark fluid. With a howling bellow, Sevok plunged into the surging Chom, the gnarled staff whirling overhead. The bellow halted the Chom's advance long enough to allow the Forgewrought to retreat. Errol saw two Chom fall under the shaman's attacks before losing sight of the Ur'chom entirely.

Errol saw the swordsman outside the door raise his weapon, intent on attacking Candissa. A voice bellowed from behind the man. He readied his blade in an instant.

"Do not kill her! She is mine!"

Errol knew the voice. Enthessar. He was close. Errol remained out of sight, just inside the small room.

The man at his feet stirred. Errol looked down at him, a plan forming rapidly in his mind. He kicked the man in the head, ensuring he would remain unconscious.

Koraymis! Attack! Errol shouted as loudly in their minds as he could manage. He could not see the kneeling sorcerer, but knew he was just steps away, and in pain.

Outside the room, Cam and Candissa were engaging Enthessar's men, Cam swinging his shortsword while Candissa pressed her advantage with her staff. Enthessar was not at the fore of the action yet, and his men could not attack her. Errol saw another of the attackers fall unconscious, struck by her staff.

Despite this, their situation was dire. There were far too many Chom pressing upwards, driven by the Humans behind them, and several more of

Enthessar's company in the corridor to the right. Errol could hear the raucous laughter of Enthessar as his men pressed forward against Cam, Candissa and the still-kneeling Koraymis

"My dear Lady Candissa! I am so happy we meet once more!" Enthessar shouted exultantly, his voice rich and cruel. "I look forward to the pleasures your body will give me, before I watch you die beneath me!"

Errol could sense the desperation of his friends, and the pain felt by Koraymis. He tried to reach out to the sorcerer. He closed his eyes, and he felt as if he were slipping into something he did not understand. For that brief instant, he spoke to Koraymis through the darkness of their predicament.

Kor! Rise!

Koryamis

Koraymis had felt the projectile pierce his abdomen. It was an arrow; the jagged head lodged inside his gut. The pain and shock knocked him to his hands and knees. He gritted his teeth, tears coming unbidden to his eyes as he shut them hard against the agony.

This was not to be. He would not die here, in a forgotten ruin.

Pull the arrow out, Koraymis... It was not his friends speaking to him. His right hand was tingling, and he knew it was blazing hot, though heat could not touch him. It was the distant voice he sometimes heard through the ring.

Reach into the wound and pull it out now! Your power will sear the wound!

He obeyed. With his right hand he forced his fingers into the bleeding wound. At his touch, the arrowhead grew red hot instantly and he tore it out. The heat did not affect him, but tearing it out did. He bit back a scream.

They need you. The ramp. Stand and turn.

He shook his head, not understanding, still blinded by pain.

Then it was Errol's voice in his head, bidding him to act. It hurt so much! In desperation, he clutched his wound with his right hand. Flames erupted from his palm as claws sprouted from his fingers. The fire was a salve to his wound. He was filled with a rage, the pain receding.

Errol's voice again. This time, it was more intense, somehow closer, darker.

Kor! Rise!

Koraymis rose, pressing himself against the wall, smearing blood on the stone. Before him, Cam and Candissa were locked in desperate combat. To his right, Praeseos was fighting the onslaught of Chom, his beweaponed limbs whirling, dark blood splashing both walls of the passage. It was clear he would not last much longer. Koraymis saw a few Humans down the rampway, but there was no sign of Sevok.

In answer, the distant voice sounded in his mind.

Sevok is dying. Nothing can stop this.

For the second time in his life, Koraymis felt his heart turn to black stone.

"Stand aside!" Koraymis roared, his voice monstrous and deep. The Forgewrought nearly fell to one side in shock at the sound of the sorcerer's bellow.

Koraymis stepped forward, both hands engulfed in flame, blackened claws extending from his fingertips, smoke rising from his robes. He felt the transformation, as horns sprouted from his temples, flame dancing over his head as he threw the hood back. A pair of Chom were there, clubs swinging, now hoping to take advantage of their foe's sudden withdrawal. They saw the rage-wreathed face of their attacker too late.

Twin geysers of flame erupted from Koraymis' hands. The flames were bright orange and searing hot, as they roared down the ramp with the force of a dam breaking. The howls of the Chom and Humans were lost in the thunderous conflagration that followed them downward, as it filled the level below, killing all in its path.

The mortal screams of Chom and Humans resounded through the corridors of the broken tower, as they burned to death in searing agony, the raging streams of fire lasting for only a long breath.

Koraymis' head snapped up – he knew what had to be done. Errol's plan was suddenly clear to him – and he had provided the opening.

Errol! Kill him!

Errol

The blast of searing heat struck Errol like a physical blow. It was what he was waiting for.

Enthessar tumbled into the room, momentarily panicked by the conflagration. His sword clattered on the floor.

Errol brought the pommel of his blade down on Enthessar's head with sufficient force to stun him momentarily – he hoped – but not enough to render him unconscious. The young noble collapsed, a shout escaping his lips.

Grasping him by his armor, Errol hauled the taller and heavier man to his feet, and in one smooth, practiced motion, he twisted and pinned the noble's arms behind him. Enthessar shouted in pain, his voice almost unseemly in its high pitch. Errol slammed his foe forcefully against the glowing green orb, face-first.

Enthessar howled in pain and shock as sparks and smoke erupted from the green orb, searing his face and chest, singing his hair and cloak. The noble turned his face sideways, a scream coming through clenched teeth, as his skin began to blister. Errol's blade pressed against his throat.

Enthessar's eyes fluttered open and looked into Errol's, less than a hand's width from his own.

"Don't move, Enthessar," Errol whispered in a hoarse voice. He had him pinned forcefully against the magical barrier, his long blade nearly touching the scintillating green aura.

Outside the chamber, the corridor filled with the light and noise of the inferno that had been wrought by the sorcerer. Cam and Candissa were still engaging Enthessar's men. Errol paid it no heed. Then he heard Koryamis' voice, *Errol, kill him!*

Errol, no! Candissa knew in an instant what Errol was doing. They all did. But her plea would not turn him from this course.

Enthessar blinked, suddenly realizing his predicament. His eyes went wide, seeing his own death before him. "Master! Help me!" he shouted.

Errol pressed the blade just to the side of Enthessar's throat, cutting his skin but not with the intent to kill. He grinned wickedly at Enthessar and the malignant evil behind his eyes. Turning to his task, he saw the tip was close to the magic, green tendrils of light glancing along the point of the blade. He pushed it into the shell of magic slowly and deliberately. It felt like he was pushing his blade into dense wood, and it stuck fast. Green energy seeped along the blade as Errol felt a curious tingling all over his body.

A movement caught his attention, to one side. One of Enthessar's men was struggling to his feet.

"Lancarm! Aid me!" Enthessar shouted. With a strength Errol did not expect, the noble wrested himself free of Errol's hold. He could not move the blade. In one motion, Enthessar grasped the outstretched arm of his lieutenant and yanked him toward Errol.

Errol's blade pierced the green barrier. Enthessar pushed Lancarm against the magical orb, sparks flying. Lancarm seemed to be held fast to the magic orb now. "My Lord!" the man cried. Errol tried to move but he, too, was held fast by the green magic. Enthessar fell as he released his grip on Lancarm, leaving him to his fate.

A keening noise came from the green barrier. Errol saw Lancarm's eyes for a moment, as they went wide, realizing his doom.

A flash of green light suffused the entire level, followed by a keening shriek that became a horrible wail. A darkness, violet and black, tore from the point where Errol's blade had pierced the magic.

A voice resounded in Errol's head, and he knew everyone there could hear it as well. It was a voice sounding in their minds from far, far away.

NO! NO! NO!

A dark veil of shadowy magic found Lancarm and wrapped about him, like an inky cloak. He howled in horror as he fell. Errol was released from the aura as well, stumbling backwards. Lancarm turned to Enthessar, one hand reaching out toward the noble, who kicked backwards on the floor, trying to distance himself from his henchman. Lancarm's skin and nails turned black and began to rot as they watched.

"Help meeee..." he pleaded miserably as death stole over him slowly and agonizingly.

His shriveling, dying eyes tried to find his lord's, but it was too late. Lancarm collapsed in a desiccated heap of dried, blackened flesh and bones, tumbling loosely within his clothing. Yet the horrible display did not draw Enthessar's eyes. He stared past Errol, at something on the floor.

Errol backed up, blade firmly in hand, and turned.

The green magic was gone, the magical orb of energy dissipated. The young woman was on her knees, one hand on the floor, as she breathed, steadying herself.

She looked up, her amber eyes meeting Errol's deep-violet eyes. They locked for a moment.

Errol didn't close his eyes, but he felt himself suddenly removed. He seemed to be in a room, perhaps it was round, he wasn't sure. Cam was there. As were Koraymis and Candissa. Across from him stood the young woman with red hair and amber eyes. They each wore simple, unblemished clothing.

They all stared at one another in mute wonder, and in that instant, removed from time, Errol knew it was not a dream, or a vision, or an illusion. They were there. Each of them saw and felt exactly what he was feeling and seeing at this moment.

Candissa stared thoughtfully at the center of what appeared to be a circular table, around which they all stood. She broke their awed silence as she looked up at them.

"The five are one..." she murmured.

The young woman's eyes fluttered, and she collapsed, unconscious. Errol's eyes snapped to Enthessar. The noble was already on his feet, scrambling for the door.

A long, mournful wailing could be heard, but it was not a sound. It was in his mind, and in the mind of his friends. Errol realized Enthessar could hear it as well.

Errol tried to lunge forward but Enthessar was quick. Quicker than he would have thought possible. The green magic he had been subjected to had slowed his reaction. Enthessar was back in the corridor before Errol could reach him.

A brilliant torrent of energy filled the corridor, and Errol knew it was Candissa, having found enough strength for another burst of radiance. Her attackers, along with Enthessar, were hurled backwards along the passage.

Errol was likewise thrown back by the impact of her power.

Candissa staggered into the room, her eyes ablaze. She saw Errol, then the young woman on the floor.

"She's all right, Deesa," Errol assured her. "Did you see Enthessar?"

A putrid stench filled the air, evidence of Kor's handiwork. Candissa said nothing, her eyes still bright, shining silver orbs. Her staff glowed brightly in her hand. He thought she was leaning on it more than usual. Then he saw the blood on her leg.

In the corridor, smoke was overcoming Cam. He almost fell into the room, bleeding badly from several wounds. He clutched his thigh, blood seeping between his fingers. Candissa crouched to inspect the wound, ignoring her own.

Errol tried to see through the billowing smoke, but it was useless.

The seven-foot-tall form of Praeseos appeared in the door, through the smoke. He was unfazed. "Do you need my help?"

"Can you see Enthessar? Where did he go?" Errol said, coughing.

"I will investigate," he said before disappearing into the smoke. Errol and Candissa had to stay low, as smoke filled the chamber. But it was being directed out of the room by ventilation shafts they had not noticed before. It was clearing slowly.

The Forgewrought reappeared from the billowing smoke in the corridor. "Enthessar escaped. He used grappling lines they had affixed to a broken window. That is how they entered behind us. I could hear the hoofbeats of his horse riding east."

They all heard a noise further down the corridor, a muffled scream.

"Where is Koraymis?" Candissa asked, her eyes flashing brightly silver again.

"Two of the Humans who survived your attack surrendered, and are bound," Praeseos said. He seemed to hesitate. "But two others…did not."

Koraymis appeared in the doorway, black claws wreathed in guttering flames. His head was hooded, but they could all see his glowing red eyes in the shadows.

"They chose. They are dead," the sorcerer said, his voice dark, inhuman. As he stood there, smoke swirled around his head, but he seemed unaffected.

"Where is Sevok?" Praeseos asked, his head quickly surveying the chamber.

"Sevok is below," Koraymis answered him, his voice flat and devoid of emotion. "There is nothing we can do."

"No…" Candissa said, her eyes wide. She looked at Cam.

Praeseos was already shouldering his way past Koraymis.

"Go!" Cam said, gesturing for her to join Errol, as he headed for the door.

As he brushed past Koraymis, Errol could feel the heat radiating from the sorcerer.

The sorcerer grasped Errol's arm, turning two fearsome red eyes upon Errol's face. The eyes were terrifying so close, and somehow *familiar.*

"*This* is why I chose not to start the battle!"

Errol felt a lump of fear rise in his throat. His arm was burning hot from Koraymis' hold. The sorcerer released it, and Errol almost stumbled away.

He followed the wounded Forgewrought down the ramp, keeping low to avoid as much as the acrid smoke as possible. Candissa limped along behind him.

Praeseos

Praeseos lurched down the rampway, his footfalls uneven thuds as he descended. The wounds to his left leg were considerable, impairing his ability to move any faster.

Though his face could not betray it, he felt a certain dread, as he stepped over and around the charred and smoking corpses. They were almost all Chom, with one or two smaller bodies. Those were the few Humans Enthessar had sent with the main force of Chom, likely to effect his deception.

It had worked. The onslaught of Chom had distracted them enough to allow Enthessar to scale the tower and flank them.

Tendrils of smoke rose from the mouths and eye sockets of most of the corpses.

On the level below, the bodies of Chom were heaped in a grim mass, dominating the center of the half-circle room. It was the killing ground where Sevok had made a last, fatal stand. Praeseos spied the tip of the Ur'chom's long, gnarled staff protruding from beneath the charred pile.

Despite his wounds, the Forgewrought grasped the corpses and flung them aside, ignoring the grisly remnants clinging to his hands.

By the time he had removed the bodies covering Sevok, Errol and Candissa had joined him. Her leg wound was still untended, and she limped badly as she approached. Cam was moving even slower, as he made his way down the rampway.

The Ur'chom had made a valiant effort. Praeseos knew the shaman's sacrifice had been for him; the Chom would have easily swarmed over the Forgewrought, otherwise.

Sevok had wounds beyond counting, and more they could not see. The head of a spear protruded up through the shaman's midriff, wet with blood. Another spear was buried deep in the Ur'chom's ribs. Praeseos was surprised to see the shaman was barely touched by the torrent of fire Koraymis had sent down the ramp, while the surrounding attackers were all terribly burned.

Praeseos reached behind his friend's immense head, lifting it a little. He sensed a sliver of life in the shaman.

"My friend…Sevok, we are here," the Forgewrought said.

Sevok's face was slashed badly, a deep cut running across one eye and along the snout. Teeth along one side were laid bare, the Ur'chom's lips reduced to ragged flesh.

The one good eye opened enough to look at Praeseos.

"He's alive!" Praeseos almost shouted. He looked up at Candissa. The silver in her eyes was but a glimmer at the moment. "Can you heal him, Lady?"

Candissa looked over the ruined body of the Ur'chom, her eyes stopping on the spears protruding from and through the shaman. Praeseos could not fail to see the emotions playing across her strained features. A cut over her eye bled, a single tear of blood running down her fair cheek. He knew her answer.

"I don't know," Candissa said, kneeling painfully next to the Ur'chom. "I will do what I can."

Sevok raised one bloodied hand, missing two clawed fingers, and spoke in a thick rasp. "No…"

"Sevok, let her try," Praeseos said, almost pleading.

The shaman looked up at the Forgewrought, fixing the one eye on Praeseos's. "No. She knows she cannot. Her magic is not…powerful enough. I am dying. I wanted to journey west. But I cannot. You must…go, my friend."

Errol looked up at Cam as he joined the circle of companions crouching around the dying Ur'chom. "Cam, is there nothing you can do? Anything you may…have with you?"

Praeseos saw Errol glance and nod at the pack slung over the Thiravani's shoulder. Cam only shook his head slowly. Turning back to look at the shaman, Praeseos felt the sliver of life fading.

"We can help you, Sevok. You can stay here and heal, you-"

"No!" Sevok's voice was hoarse but unyielding. A bloody froth ran out of torn lips.

The shaman reached over and grasped the gnarled staff.

"Take my staff, Praeseos. Promise me you will keep it…" the Ur'chom's voice weakened.

"Yes, Sevok. I so swear," Praeseos replied, almost whispering.

"Another…will find you…give the staff…"

"Another? What do you mean, Sevok?"

"Take the staff…I will…be with you…"

Sevok's final words trailed away as the claws slipped from the staff. Praeseos wrapped his metal-sheathed fingers around the twisted length of oak. Candissa rested one hand on the shaman's bloodied head. Sevok's final breath eased forth.

"I'm so sorry, Praeseos," she said, weeping. "He was too far gone."

Praeseos stared down at his dead friend. The pain of his wounds faded as an ache took shape in his chest.

Holding the staff, Praeseos heard the beads of crystal and bone making a tinkling sound.

"What is that?" Candissa said, looking up, tears still streaming from her eyes.

"A breeze. From below I think," Errol said.

"That smell…it's like fresh bread," the Aevaru murmured.

"I smell wood, freshly sanded, and spices," Errol said, his eyes suddenly far away.

Praeseos breathed in through his nostrils, sensing the strange breeze carefully. He smelled the clean, sharp minerals of a deep cavern, and the nuanced scent of warm oil.

"It is Sevok's spirit," Praeseos murmured, looking at the staff in his hands. "It slips into the world beyond."

Errol frowned. He seemed about to say something but chose not to.

"He's right," Candissa said quietly. Her tears still flowed, but Praeseos knew they were not tears of sorrow. "Sevok is going home."

The Forgewrought saw Errol's expression darken, his fists clenching.

"I'm sorry, Praeseos. I should not have let him venture so far into the fray," Errol said, looking at the slain Ur'chom. "Sevok is dead because my tactics failed."

"That is not true, my friend," Praeseos said. "Sevok knew the price that would be paid, and was willing to do so, in order to save us all."

"There's nothing you could have done differently, Errol," Candissa said, wiping her eyes. "Don't put that on yourself."

Errol only shook his head, turning and stepping aside. Praeseos knew Errol wanted to be alone in his thoughts.

Praeseos stood slowly, holding the staff. He was full of sorrow at losing his only true friend. His leg buckled, but the staff bore his weight as he leaned heavily on it.

"Let me help you," Candissa murmured, standing and wincing, as she touched the Forgewrought's forearm.

"You are bleeding, Lady. See to your own wounds, and those of the others," he said, his voice solemn. He looked at the Aevaru. "I think Koraymis needs you most of all."

Candissa appeared to think for a moment. Her eyes widened a little. Praeseos saw a silver gleam as she concentrated. Placing her hand over her wounded thigh, she whispered inaudibly. Even his own superior hearing could not discern the words, though he knew they were syllables of magic.

Standing now herself, she made for the ramp. Her limp was negligible.

Errol followed her.

Praeseos crouched down slowly. He carefully removed the leather strap from around Sevok. He fastened it across his back and shoulder, before attaching the staff with a leather loop.

The Forgewrought closed Sevok's eye carefully, then briefly touched the bloody head of the shaman. Standing with difficulty, Praeseos clasped his lowered face with both hands and stood silently. Praeseos remembered so very little of his past. But this, he knew, was the way of his folk. He was mourning. After a moment of reverence, he spoke.

"Sevok, you are my friend and I will miss you."

CHAPTER THIRTY-SIX – CANDISSA

20 Procellus, Year 197, Eastvale Calendar

Koraymis, his robes black untouched by flame, stood at the top of the ramp. His face was a mask of rage and horns, his blackened, clawed hands still wreathed in small flames, looming over the charred corpses of the Chom. The stench was almost overpowering.

Candissa rushed forward to him. She raised one hand to his red, scaled face, blood-red eyes regarding her silvered pupils. The sorcerer winced and withdrew a step at her gesture.

Errol helped Cam up the ramp, followed by Praeseos.

"It is all to right, my friend," she said, her voice soothing. She laid her hand on his face. His skin was hot, almost searing, with a rough, almost stony texture. She let a tiny sliver of power pass from her touch into him.

Before them all, Koraymis returned. The horns, claws, scales and flames vanished in two heartbeats. The scholar they all knew stood before them. He clutched his belly, stumbling, before leaning against a wall.

"I'm sorry," was all he said, his eyes stricken. His knees buckled, but Errol caught him gently, keeping him on his feet.

Candissa knelt along with him, reaching out. Her eyes gleamed silver. Koraymis saw this and held up a hand. "I will be fine. The wound is minor now. You have spent too much. See to the others first."

She sensed he was not deceiving her; his wounds were not severe. She looked around. Praeseos struggled as he climbed the ramp to join them, Sevok's staff visible behind the Forgewrought, strapped to his back.

Candissa turned and strode into the chamber where their new friend lay unconscious. They all followed, even Koraymis, though slowly.

Within, they found her knelt over the unconscious young woman. Candissa put a hand on her head. She looked up at Praeseos.

"Is there someplace away from all this we can take her? I suspect she'll be asleep for some time."

"Yes, I can carry her. There's a bed in the adjoining chamber."

Praeseos went to pick up the unconscious woman, but his leg failed him. The Forgewrought made a noise Candissa knew was due to his pain. Dark brown fluid ran freely down his wounded leg, pooling at his foot. He put one large hand on the ground firmly, simply to steady his immense frame.

"Praeseos, wait," she said, looking around at her friends.

Koraymis eased against the wall, still holding his injured abdomen. Cam was nursing three wounds that clearly needed tending. Errol had more than one cut he was trying to ignore. Candissa's own leg wound was not fully healed, and she had other cuts, including the one over her eye.

Standing tall, she grasped her staff. The words and actions were reflexive, having only read of this technique. Closing her eyes, she extended one hand and raised the staff just off the floor. Phrases issued from her lips, in a strange, ancient language. Power welled up within her. She felt it suffusing the very air.

She brought the staff down soundly but gently. A faint, white aura radiated outward, with a thumping sound almost outside the range of their hearing, as it passed through all of them.

Candissa's effort fatigued her, but she also felt renewed. She looked around at her friends.

Errol was tentatively probing his side and shoulder, an expression of incredulity on his face.

Koraymis stood, cautiously checking his abdomen, where the arrow had struck. Cam likewise felt each of his wounds and smiled to Errol. The towering Forgewrought looked at Candissa as he slowly stood fully straight.

"My lady, I thank you for the gift of your healing," Praeseos uttered. "My wounds were extensive, and now feel but minor. Your powers are remarkable."

Candissa breathed deeply. She nodded and smiled. "It is...quite all right, my friends. But I fear I will be able to do nothing more until I sleep."

"I will take this one to the chamber," the Forgewrought said, returning to his task of carrying the unconscious fifth. They followed him to the largely empty chamber that Praeseos suspected once served as quarters. The bed was not the most comfortable, but it sufficed.

"How long before she awakens?" Errol asked Candissa.

"I cannot say for certain but some hours at least, perhaps much longer," she said. "We must keep watch over her. In the meantime, we should secure the tower."

"Should we pursue Enthessar?" Cam asked.

"No," Errol said. "He'll have too much of a lead."

"And we are unfit to mount such an effort," Praeseos said.

"And he's going in the wrong direction," Koraymis said in a quiet voice.

"Why do you say that?" the Forgewrought asked.

Errol looked at the sorcerer, and then Candissa, and then Cam. They did not even need to speak silently. They each knew.

Candissa stepped over to the westward-facing window. The beam of white was unchanged.

"I thought we would…sense something by now. That we would somehow know we had done what we must do," she said.

"Sevok said we must journey west, that I must take the staff with us," Praeseos said. "I intend to honor that request."

"We have many bodies to bury. We can't leave them to rot," Cam muttered.

"And we have two prisoners," Koraymis added.

"And we must bury Sevok. I would not quit the place without doing so," the Forgewrought said. Candissa smiled a little at this. She knew Praeseos had a good heart under his plated chest.

"I really didn't know what to expect," Errol said, his expression uncharacteristically uncertain. "But when we freed her, I too, thought perhaps our journey would be over."

Candissa looked at each of them, before turning to look back out the window, to the western horizon. Her eyes clouded.

"It is only beginning."

CHAPTER THIRTY-SEVEN - ENTHESSAR

20 Procellus, Year 197, Eastvale Calendar

Enthessar was exhausted to his core. His mount was frothing at the mouth. He had ridden harder than he should have been able. He was broken, wounded, lost.

He could not clearly recall how he had left the tower. He must have grabbed one of the grappling lines and slid down without thinking about it. Looking at his hands, they were blistered and cut.

He had made it to his horse before his enemies could give chase.

But where? Where was he going?

His horse shook and halted, making a wretched noise, before collapsing. Enthessar barely avoided being crushed by the mass of the beast as he all but fell on the cold, hard ground. He had no provisions to speak of, no gear, not even a bedroll. His men were all slain, along with the Chom. Even Nikk had deserted him.

He had failed.

Enthessar shook as he sobbed silently, scraping his blistered face on the coarse grass.

"Master...I am sorry," he said quietly to himself. He had felt his master flee in that corridor in the tower. When that last one had awoken and looked at Errol, his master's presence had simply vanished, after that terrible howling.

Now, Enthessar was lost. He wept. He was nothing.

I am here, faithful servant. The voice turned his sorrowful weeping to tears of joy.

"Master!" Enthessar shouted exultantly in the deepening twilight air, standing suddenly.

Be still, my servant. There is much to be done, and I am giving you the authority in these matters. Be strong but be watchful. I will send more servants to you.

He was thrilled. His weakness was replaced with a resolve.

"Master, yes. What will you have me do now?"

Continue east. You will go home. But there will be others who will find you first. Wait for them here and I will tell you more.

"Master, I have never heard you so clearly before," Enthessar said. Truly, the prior messages from his master were at best his own interpretations of vague feelings.

Truly. It is because the Five are now together. As they grow in power, so do I. So, do we.

"Yes, Master. I will wait."

So, Enthessar made what camp he could, and he found fortune was once more his. There was wood nearby for a fire, and after searching the saddlebags of his fallen mount, he found a skin of water and a few dried rations.

As the small fire he built grew, he did not worry about what may be wandering the ruins. His Master was watching over him. Not long before he fell asleep, he was joined by a monstrously huge animal. It was a wolf, but with antlers. It padded quietly up to him, to nuzzle his hand. Enthessar smiled, feeling the hate within the creature.

It lay down near the fire and looked at his new master. Enthessar understood and lay down against the warm flank of the beast.

Enthessar awoke a few hours prior to dawn. He was cold, but the creature had kept him warm through the night. The fire was now just embers. He sat up to stir them, to coax more heat from them, perhaps flame.

In the shower of sparks, he saw a pair of red eyes sitting across from him. He was not shocked, not even a little fearful.

It was an Ur'chom, towering huge, hairy, with long fangs, clawed hands. It had a vicious-looking greatsword across its lap as it sat on a stone. It appeared to be waiting patiently.

Enthessar regarded him. "Why are you here?"

The Ur'chom looked back at him, raising its head a little. It spoke with a deep, grinding voice.

"To serve."

Enthessar smiled.

CHAPTER THIRTY-EIGHT - TYENIA

She awoke slowly. Her eyes adjusted to the bright light of the sun.

Blinking, she sat up on her elbows. She was in a lumpy bed, of middling size, in an unfamiliar bedchamber. There were windows, and one was a partially open window, letting in a chill breeze.

Across from her bed sat a young woman. She was dozing as she leaned against the wall, on a small, padded bench. She was clad all in white, with a long, white staff in the crook of her arm. A word danced about in her foggy head, but she couldn't grasp it. Still, she knew young woman in white was a good person. She smiled at the sight of her.

The stranger opened her eyes. She was even more beautiful awake.

"Hello, lady," she said in a hoarse, almost croaking voice. She coughed. *How long had she slept?* She began thinking. She tried to recall why she was here, where she had come from, what had happened.

Confusion filled her mind. The young woman in white must have sensed it. She stood quickly and came to her side, putting a hand on her shoulder.

"You are fine, be still. You likely have many questions," she said, her voice oddly reassuring. She spoke with a strange accent and cadence. "What is your name?"

It was a fair question. Introductions were important.

"My name is..." she struggled for a moment. "Tyenia. Tyenia Alexandoru."

"Hello, Tyenia. My name is Candissa Demarrae," the young woman said. "Are you hungry?"

Tyenia licked her lips, still trying to find her bearings. "Perhaps a little, yes."

"I trust you are not in any pain. You did not appear to be injured when we found you."

"Found me? How did you find me?"

"You were trapped in a sort of magical orb of energy," she said. Her words made little sense to Tyenia. "We freed you yesterday. You slept all day and night. It's morning now."

"I... I don't understand," she said, trying to remember something, anything.

"Why don't we go down and have something to eat and drink. Do you remember anything about yesterday at all?" Candissa asked with a peculiar expression, almost expectant. Tyenia looked into her eyes.

"Silver..." she whispered.

"What?"

"Your eyes were silver...yesterday." Tyenia remembered that now. There were four others, including her. A dark robed sorcerer, a blade-wielder, and a Thiravani ranger of some sort.

The five are one. The words sounded in her mind and for a moment she remembered a brief dream.

Candissa smiled. "Yes, they were."

"They are a very nice blue now, like the sky. Please do not be offended," she corrected herself, loath to imply an offense. Candissa only laughed lightly as she helped her stand. Her legs were strangely weak.

"Slowly, Tyenia. You will meet the others. We will tell you all we know. Perhaps you can share what you may."

She shook her head. "I fear that may be little. And please, call me Tye. My friends call me Tye."

"Very well, Tye," Candissa said, her smile filling Tyenia with an almost affirming sensation.

Below, she found a table prepared with food. There, she met the unlikely group, which included a Forgewrought.

As she ate and drank slowly, introductions were made. They shared their stories, how they had come together, and how they were driven to come here to this tower. After her meal, they walked her about the tower, showing her the various levels. Some of the rampways were still badly scorched from the battle they described, prior to Tyenia's waking. But they were still being cleaned, according to Praeseos, who seemed almost apologetic for their condition.

That pleased Tyenia. The Forgewrought were notoriously polite.

They escorted her out of the tower, where there was a great deal of freshly overturned earth, forming many mounds. The Forgewrought told her they had buried the dead there.

They also showed her the inexplicable beam of white energy the tower was emitting.

Somehow, for some reason, she figured into it all. She could not begin to fathom how or why. That was due to her memory. Like the bladesman named Errol and the Forgewrought, Tyenia's memory was gone.

After much discussion, which had to be slowed and repeated many times owing to their outlandish accents, she could tell them only a few facts that she could recall presently.

She knew Candissa was Aevaru and Praeseos was of the Forgewrought. She knew what Chom were, and Ur'chom. But she did not know where she was, how she had arrived, what she was doing here, or why they found her trapped. Nor could she guess how long she had been in the ensorcelled slumber.

"Much seems familiar to me, but I cannot tell you why. I feel as if I have buried knowledge, but few facts that I can recall," Tyenia said.

"That is precisely how I felt years ago when I appeared outside of Ravensroost," Errol said, nodding. They all gathered inside the tower, at the long table. Their discussions turned to many questions and answers, over the course of hours. Once more, Tyenia lamented her inability to remember any details of her past.

"However, now that I am trying to remember anything, there is one fact I seem to recall," Tyenia said to them after a long exchange. "It is not because of what you've told me, I'm quite certain. It is something from...before."

"What is that?" Koraymis asked.

"That beam is more than a sign. It's more than a clue. I know that now," Tyenia said, suddenly excited.

"What is it then?" Candissa asked.

"A point on a compass that we must follow. It will take us to the place I need go, that *we* need go," she said. She was glad to have remembered this, though she couldn't explain why she knew it. "That must sound very strange, coming from someone you only just met."

Errol grinned crookedly. "After what we've been through, it doesn't sound so strange, Tye."

Candissa smiled at Errol's words.

"Do you have any idea of where we are going, when we do head west?" Tyenia asked Candissa.

She shook her head slowly. "We have not a single idea."

Cam shook his head in mild disbelief while Koraymis only smirked.

"Then I would suggest we leave as soon as may be, so that we can find this place," Tyenia said, smiling and gesturing with her hands for emphasis.

They looked at one another for a moment, exchanging expressions of confusion, amusement and wonder. Koraymis was the first to laugh and was followed by Cam and then Errol. Candissa was next, her laughing almost musical. At last, and to Tyenia's surprise, the Forgewrought began to laugh, an odd, deep noise, joining them in the hardest laughter any of them had heard or felt in a very long time.

Tyenia Alexandoru laughed as well, delighted at their reaction to her suggestion. The laughter finally died down, as they wiped eyes and drank. Despite her predicament, the strange surroundings, and having no idea what the future would bring, she felt glad.

"Oh," she said, a thought occurring to her. "Did you happen to bring an extra horse?"

THE END

ABOUT THE AUTHOR

West in Ruin is Eric Lockwood's first novel. He is a life-long fan of epic fantasy and science fiction, and he plans on writing many more in this series. Eric lives with his wife, and two cats that do not get along with one another. Their home is currently in southeastern Michigan, and not in Kinsale, Ireland. He hopes this will change one day.